From stage actor and ibuster
bestselling author, Judy l

Her first forays into a cribes
as her 'entertainment se e and
Araluen, three novels set e and
film respectively, each be

Next came her 'city set': *Kal*, a fiercely passionate novel about
men and mining set in Kalgoorlie; *Beneath the Southern Cross*, a
mammoth achievement chronicling the story of Sydney since first
European settlement; and *Territory*, a tale of love, family and
retribution set in Darwin.

Territory, together with Judy's next novel, *Pacific*, a dual story
set principally in Vanuatu, placed her firmly in Australia's top-ten
bestseller list. Her following works, *Heritage*, set in the Snowies
during the 1950s; *Floodtide*, based in her home state of Western
Australia; and *Maralinga*, set in South Australia during the British
atomic weapons tests, have consolidated her position as one of the
country's leading fiction writers.

Judy Nunn's fame as a novelist is spreading rapidly. Her books
are now published throughout Europe in English, German, French,
Dutch and Czech.

Judy lives with her husband, actor-author Bruce Venables, on
the Central Coast of New South Wales.

www.judynunn.com

JUDY NUNN

Tiger Men

WILLIAM HEINEMANN

A William Heinemann book
Published by Random House Australia Pty Ltd
Level 3, 100 Pacific Highway, North Sydney NSW 2060
www.randomhouse.com.au

First published by William Heinemann in 2011

Addresses for companies within the Random House Group can be found at
www.randomhouse.com.au/offices.

National Library of Australia
Cataloguing-in-Publication Entry

Nunn, Judy.
Tiger men/Judy Nunn.

ISBN 978 1 86471 218 6 (pbk.)

A823.3

Cover design by Design by Committee
Inside cover by Blue Cork
Internal design by Midland Typesetters, Australia
Tasmanian tiger illustration by Shane Nagel
Maps by Darian Causby/Highway 51 Design Works
Typeset in 12/14.5 Sabon by Midland Typesetters, Australia
Printed in Australia by Griffin Press, an accredited ISO AS/NZS 14001:2004
Environmental Management System printer

10 9 8 7 6 5 4 3 2 1

The paper this book is printed on is certified against the
Forest Stewardship Council® Standards. Griffin Press holds
FSC chain of custody certification SGS-COC-005088. FSC
promotes environmentally responsible, socially beneficial
and economically viable management of the world's forests

FSC
www.fsc.org
MIX
Paper from
responsible sources
FSC® C009448

In loving memory of Molly Venables
(1917–2010)

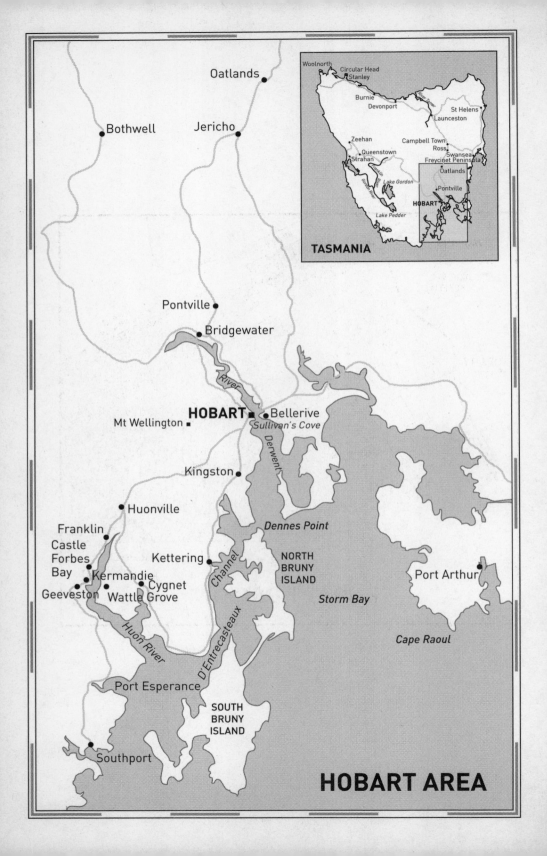

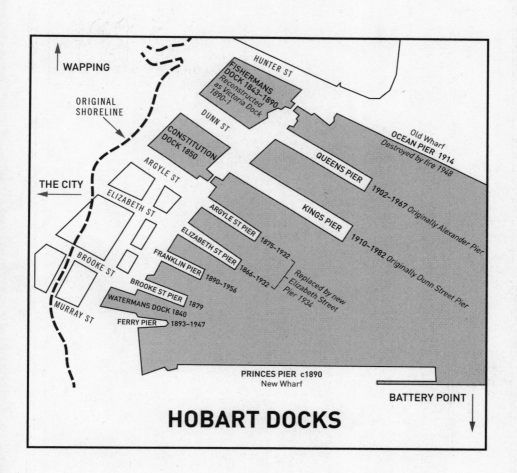

WAPPING

HUNTER ST

ORIGINAL
SHORELINE

FISHERMANS
DOCK 1843-1890
Reconstructed
as Victoria Dock
1890-1

DUNN ST

CONSTITUTION
DOCK 1850

THE CITY

ARGYLE ST

ELIZABETH ST

BROOKE ST

MURRAY ST

ARGYLE ST PIER 1875-1932

ELIZABETH ST PIER 1866-1932

FRANKLIN PIER 1890-1956

BROOKE ST PIER 1879

WATERMANS DOCK 1840

FERRY PIER 1893-1947

QUEENS PIER

KINGS PIER

Old Wharf
OCEAN PIER 1914
Destroyed by fire 1948

1902-1967 Originally Alexander Pier

1910-1982 Originally Dunn Street Pier

Replaced by new
Elizabeth Street
Pier 1934

PRINCES PIER c1890
New Wharf

BATTERY POINT

HOBART DOCKS

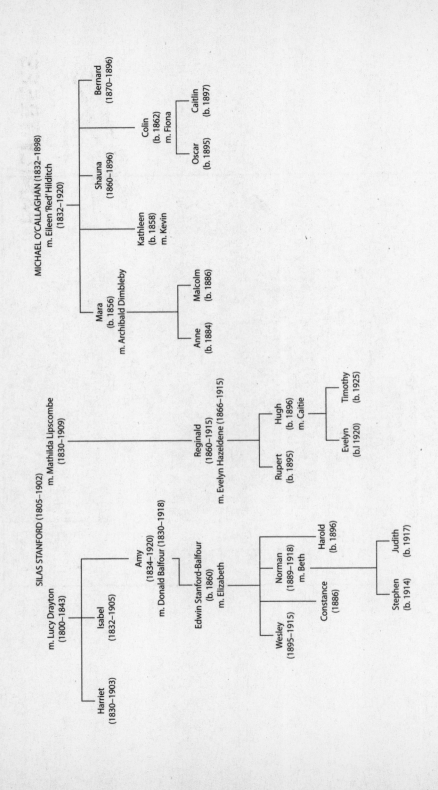

MICHAEL O'CALLAGHAN (1832–1898)
m. Eileen 'Red' Hilditch
(1832–1920)

Mara
(b. 1856)
m. Archibald Dimbleby

Anne
(b. 1884)

Malcolm
(b. 1886)

Kathleen
(b. 1858)
m. Kevin

Shauna
(1860–1896)

Colin
(b. 1862)
m. Fiona

Oscar
(b. 1895)

Caitlin
(b. 1897)

Bernard
(1870–1896)

SILAS STANFORD (1805–1902)
m. Mathilda Lipscombe
(1830–1909)

Reginald
(1860–1915)
m. Evelyn Hazeldene (1866–1915)

Rupert
(b. 1895)

Hugh
(b. 1896)
m. Caitie

Evelyn
(b.l 1920)

Timothy
(b. 1925)

m. Lucy Drayton
(1800–1843)

Harriet
(1830–1903)

Isabel
(1832–1905)

Amy
(1834–1920)
m. Donald Balfour (1830–1918)

Edwin Stanford-Balfour
(b. 1860)
m. Elizabeth

Wesley
(1895–1915)

Norman
(1889–1918)
m. Beth

Harold
(b. 1896)

Constance
(1886)

Stephen
(b. 1914)

Judith
(b. 1917)

FAMILY TREES

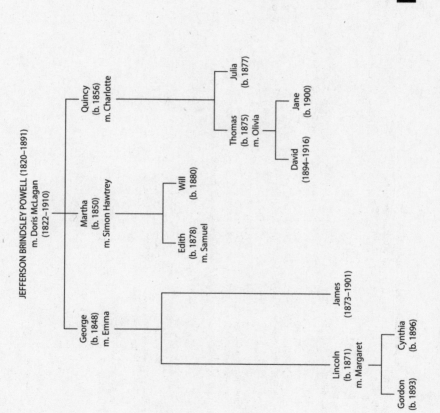

JEFFERSON BRINDSLEY POWELL (1820–1891)
m. Doris McLagan
(1822–1910)

George
(b. 1848)
m. Emma

Martha
(b. 1850)
m. Simon Hawtrey

Quincy
(b. 1856)
m. Charlotte

James
(1873–1901)

Lincoln
(b. 1871)
m. Margaret

Edith
(b. 1878)
m. Samuel

Will
(b. 1880)

Julia
(b. 1877)

Thomas
(b. 1875)
m. Olivia

Gordon
(b. 1893)

Cynthia
(b. 1896)

David
(1894–1916)

Jane
(b. 1900)

'Only remember that two-legged tigers . . . are much more dangerous than those who walk on four.'

Alexandre Dumas, pére, 1802–1870

PROLOGUE

The animal approaches the river with stealth: not for fear of predators, but in order to avoid alerting possible prey. It is early dusk and others may be slaking their thirst – a kangaroo perhaps, or a wallaby, or wombat. She hopes for a large kill (she has three hungry cubs to feed) but if necessary smaller prey will suffice. Her keen ears are alert to the slightest rustle among the grasses and foliage as this might signal a potoroo or a possum.

She is a nocturnal hunter and has come down from the woodlands to the valley, leaving her offspring in the safety of their rocky lair on the hillside. The cubs have been out of her pouch for some time, but they are not yet old enough to join her on the hunt. When they are she will teach them her skills.

The early evening air is crisp and clear with the chill bite of autumn. All is breathlessly still and, upon the glass-like river surface, the mirror-images of willows and ferns meet to create a magically perfect twin world.

There is no prey in sight, so the animal lowers her head and drinks, oblivious to the destruction she wreaks as ever-widening ripples spread in all directions. Then, her thirst assuaged, she slinks off into the undergrowth, barely visible, the black stripes of her tawny back melding with the shadows of fern fronds. The riverbank has not provided easy prey and she is on a more purposeful hunt now, her ears and eyes attuned to the slightest sound or movement.

Unlike some hunters, she relies more on sound and sight than she does on her sense of smell; and unlike others she relies on stamina rather than speed. She will run down beasts much faster than she, simply by chasing them into a state of exhaustion. She is strong.

She has travelled barely five minutes, covering considerable ground at an easy trot, but keeping low in the grasses, her sharp, black eyes searching the bushes and thickets for any sign of movement. Then she hears a sound. It is the low snuffle of a horse, and she instantly halts. This is not a sound she associates with prey, but rather with predator. She remains motionless, little more than the faintest ripple amongst the broad sea of grasslands.

The horse snorts again, nervously this time: it has caught her scent. She can see it now. Its form silhouetted in the soft half-light, it is tethered to a tree in the thicket up ahead. She has no fear of horses, but where there are horses, there are men, and she greatly fears men. She is right to do so, for man is her one true predator. She keeps away from his settlements, but more and more he encroaches upon her territory and more and more she is forced to retreat. Her world is changing.

The horse tosses its head. Aware of her presence, it is restless.

Her muscles tense, and she makes to flee. The predator cannot be far off. But before she can move, a shot rings out.

The man steps from the thicket where he has been watching the slight tell-tale movement in the grasses – he too is an experienced hunter. He approaches the corpse and rolls it over with his foot. A fine specimen, he thinks, in excellent condition. On top of the tiger bounty, there'd be money for the hide. What a stroke of luck. He'd only come out to set his traps.

BOOK ONE

CHAPTER ONE

HOBART TOWN, 1853

Van Diemen's Land was a place of profound contradiction. The sheer beauty of the island could stir a man's soul, yet the savagery of life on its shores could rob him of all faith. This alarming paradox continued to disturb Silas Stanford, even after ten long years in the colony. He did not doubt that many a poor creature had lost sight of God in the midst of this glorious wilderness where His hand was so evident. Fifty years on, the history of Van Diemen's Land remained, to Silas, a shocking condemnation.

The British had decided, in 1803, to extend their occupation of the Australian continent to include Van Diemen's Land, roughly 150 miles off the south-east coast, and they had done so purely in order to prevent the French laying claim to it. A penal colony had quickly been established for the provision of labour, and a thriving new port had been created at Sullivan's Cove, a picturesque bay on the west bank of the River Derwent. Convict settlers had been transported from Norfolk Island and Port Jackson to people the township and develop the land, and a new society had been born in the wilderness.

Over the ensuing decades, the busy port of Hobart Town, nestled at the base of mighty Mount Wellington, became home to rough, tough men: to jailers and convicts,

and sealers and whalers, and to those seeking refuge from
the law. Van Diemen's Land, it seemed, was designed for
the lawless. Whether they arrived in chains, or whether
they simply walked off ships in a bid to escape justice,
the island appeared a magnet to the wicked. Here was
no haven for the weak or the squeamish; here only the
toughest survived. Escaped convicts and bandits roamed
the countryside, while settlers, men who considered themselves civilised, embarked upon the systematic eradication
of those whose lands they'd invaded.

The eradication of the natives proved swift and efficient.
The last of the surviving Aboriginal population was event-
ually rounded up and transported to the islands of Bass
Strait, where they continued to die in the process of being
Christianised and civilised.

The Aborigine of Van Diemen's Land was not the
only species to be brutally annihilated. While eliminating
human competition on land, the invaders embarked upon
a bloodbath at sea. The indiscriminate slaughter of seals
and southern right whales soon put an end to the local
sealing industry and, not long afterwards, to shore-based
whaling. Undeterred, however, the merchants simply built
bigger and stronger ocean-going vessels fit to meet the
demands of pelagic whaling, and turned their attention
to the highly productive sperm whaling grounds farther
afield. In the interests of profit, all was fair game. Besides,
the fine timbers of the island had made logging highly
profitable and had introduced a burgeoning ship-building
industry. There were limitless opportunities on offer in
Van Diemen's Land for those who knew how to avail
themselves of its riches.

The plunder of land and sea had reaped rewards for
many who were perhaps undeserving, but as free settlers
started to arrive in numbers, wealth became the result of
hard work and ingenuity. Among such men were those
determined to lead the way in moral enlightenment.

Philanthropy abounded. Rich benefactors built churches and funded schools, not only for their sons, but also for the poor. Worship and education was to replace licentiousness and ignorance. An influential lobby group of respectable colonists and clergy formed the Anti-Transportation League in a bid to call a halt to the convict system. Appeals were made directly to the British Government and to Queen Victoria herself. No longer should the island serve as a penal settlement and dumping ground for the dregs of humanity, they argued. Van Diemen's Land must become a free and civilised society modelled along the lines of Britain, with a stratified class structure ruled by the powerful elite.

There was no man more dedicated to the cause of freedom and reformation than the successful wool grower and merchant, Silas Stanford. But Silas differed from many of his fellow benefactors in the way that he sought neither self-aggrandisement nor power. He considered it his bounden duty to care for those less fortunate. And of even greater importance, he considered it his mission to help lead the way out of a brutal past into a bright new future. He needed no reward for his efforts, at least not in this world.

Silas cut an impressive but austere figure as he marched solemnly down Collins Street in his signal black frock coat and top hat, his greying beard as neat in its trim as his well-tailored suit. He might have been leading a procession of mourners, or so his youngest daughter was wont to tell him.

'Why must you always wear black, Father?' she would tease. 'Why not a pair of check trousers, or perhaps a grey waistcoat? Both are fashionable, and black is so very funereal.'

'Black is dignified and respectful, Amy,' he would reply. 'One must avoid any show of ostentation, particularly when one is calling upon those less fortunate than one's self.'

But Amy never let him have the last word. She knew
only too well that her father chose his sombre form of
dress for pure personal preference. 'The poor rather like
a little colour,' she said good-humouredly. 'I always wear a
bright scarf or carry a silk kerchief myself. Such items are
greatly admired. So much so I must admit that I often find
myself giving them away.'

'You are of age, my dear, and it is your prerogative to
dress as you wish – within the bounds of respectability of
course ...' Silas knew that he sounded stuffy. He couldn't
help himself, it was his nature, but the twinkle in his eyes
betrayed him as he added, '... just as it is my prerogative
to dress in funereal fashion.'

'So it is, and so you must.' Amy laughed and kissed his
cheek. It didn't stop her playful nagging, however, just as
it didn't stop his enjoyment of the game, for Silas adored
the youngest of his three daughters.

Nineteen-year-old Amy had always been her father's
favourite, even as a child, although Silas would never have
admitted the fact to a living soul. And now that his older
daughters, Harriet and Isabel, had left home, Amy was more
precious to him than ever. He dreaded the day when she too
would fly the nest, abandoning him to a solitary widower's
existence. But he was resigned to the inevitability of such a
fate. Unlike a number of his contemporaries who had lost
their wives, he was not one to keep a daughter standing by
as a servant to nurse him into old age. Besides, Amy did not
want for suitors; it would be only a matter of time before
one would claim her heart. She was not as striking as her
sisters, it was true, but she was pleasing in appearance, and
her feisty streak of independence, which aroused in Silas
a strange combination of pride and concern, was found
attractive by many. Then of course there was the prospect
of her substantial inheritance. In a place such as Hobart
Town where scoundrels and opportunists abounded, a
young woman like Amy Stanford, with or without physical

attributes, was considered a worthy prize. Silas trusted implicitly in his daughter's strength of character and sound common-sense, but he was nonetheless on the constant look-out for any who might seek to take advantage.

Upon reaching the intersection of Campbell Street, Silas halted and looked down towards Macquarie Street and the hustle and bustle of the harbour, where the cries of the hawkers could clearly be heard ringing out from Fisherman's Dock. On any given day, there were vessels of all descriptions sitting at the docks, or resting at anchor, or working the harbour waters: whalers and merchant ships, fishing boats and barges. They might be the powerful ocean-going barques and ketches and clippers and schooners, all with masts towering above the highest of the nearby stone warehouses, or they might be the smaller boats and ferries that plied the river trade. Hobart Town revolved around the hub of its harbour, and the dockside was under constant development to increase its capacity. The newly created Constitution Dock was completed only three years previously.

Silas continued to gaze down at the harbour, oblivious to the traps and the drays and the pedestrians passing by as he watched the road gang of convict labourers. Work never ceased on the foreshore, and the next stage of dockland reclamation was well under way. The men toiled in silence like mindless beasts, paying no heed whatsoever to the brutal barks of their overseers. They were plainly accustomed to being cursed like dogs. Silas, as always, found the sight and the sound offensive. Little wonder, he thought, that spirits have been broken and souls lost here, for European settlement has brought to this paradise everything that is base in mankind.

Well, all that is about to change, he told himself with a surge of satisfaction. Oh yes indeed. Changes were most definitely afoot in Van Diemen's Land, and not a moment too soon!

He crossed the road and walked on down Lower Collins Street and, by the time he reached the junction of Sun Street, he found that he was holding his breath. He always avoided inhaling deeply when he visited the suburb of Wapping, but today, in the heat of early December and with a strong southerly breeze, the stench from the Hobart Town Rivulet was particularly disgusting. More so than ever to Silas, because he had recently returned from his property in the southern midlands, where the air was pure and the river waters pristine.

He turned left into the narrow lane where Polly Jordan lived and, unable to hold his breath any longer, reluctantly exhaled to breathe in the stench of rotting animal parts and sewage and all the other forms of putrid matter that was washed down the rivulet from the abattoirs and households and mills upstream, only to end in Wapping.

The surface of the narrow laneway, which for much of the year was a soggy, muddy mess, particularly when the rivulet flooded as it often did, had dried in the summer sun, and several scruffy little girls were playing hopscotch in the dust. Silas scowled. They should have been at school. Women leant against the doorways of conjoined tin shanties and squalid wooden huts, gossiping and enjoying the pleasant weather, seemingly mindless of the fearful stench. In deference to their feelings, Silas resisted the urge to hold a kerchief to his nose. Instead, he tipped the brim of his hat as he passed by. They waved. ''Allo Mr Stanford,' one of them called. The women of Wapping knew Silas Stanford, just as Silas Stanford knew them.

To Silas, Wapping epitomised the shameful dichotomy that was Hobart Town. Here, where the rivulet wound its way into the Derwent, the muddy streets and the network of poverty-ridden back alleys and lanes were little more than a cesspit, while barely a half a mile to the west were the grand homes of the prosperous and powerful. Silas, in his mission to help redress the balance in whatever way he

could, was today making one of his many routine house
calls on behalf of the Hobart Town Businessmen's Philanthropic Society. A whaler by the name of Albert Jordan had
died accidentally six weeks before and had been buried at
sea. The society was providing his pregnant widow with
a monthly rental allowance and weekly supplies of fresh
rations for her children.

Polly Jordan's poky tin shack was at the far end of the
lane, and its front door opened directly onto the street,
where two boys were squatting in the dirt playing marbles.
Upon his approach, Silas recognised the older boy.

'Charlie Jordan,' he said sternly, 'you should be in
school.'

'Oh. Hullo, Mr Stanford.' Nine-year-old Charlie scrambled respectfully to his feet. His mother's instructions had
been well drummed into him for the past month.

'I want you nice and proper, whenever anyone comes
from the society, Charlie,' Polly had ordered, 'your best
behaviour, mind. They're good people, that lot, and
they deserve our respect.' Her son had correctly read the
warning to mean: *We need that lot, Charlie. Don't go
messing things up.*

It had been Silas himself who had founded the Businessmen's Philanthropic Society five years previously, but most
people had lost sight of the fact. Bigger names than his had
attached themselves to the cause, many for the purposes
of self-promotion, which did not in the least bother Silas.
So long as they offered money along with their names, he
was perfectly happy for them to reap whatever benefit they
wished.

Respectful though Charlie's manner was, the boy didn't
appear too dismayed at being caught playing truant.

'I haven't been able to go to school, Mr Stanford. I've
had the grippe something awful this past week.' He gave
a pathetic cough to emphasise the fact, then before any
further discussion could take place he charged for the open

front door. 'I'll tell Ma you're here,' he called as he disappeared, and the shriek of 'Ma! Mr Stanford's here!' echoed back out into the lane.

Silas looked down at the urchin still squatting in the dust. 'You should be in school too,' he said.

The urchin grinned back with a cheeky arrogance. His dad was a fish-hawker and his mum was a washerwoman: they didn't need handouts from the HTBPS do-gooders.

'Hullo, Mr Stanford.' Polly Jordan was at the front door in an instant. 'How nice to see you; do come in.' She smiled a welcome that was meant to be winsome, but her once-pretty face was weathered well beyond her twenty-nine years, and two missing front teeth did nothing to help, although they gave her a girlish lisp, which was strangely coquettish.

'Good afternoon, Mrs Jordan. Thank you.'

She stood to one side and he edged his way past, trying not to make contact, but she was so hugely with child it was difficult to avoid her altogether as he clutched his top hat to his chest. She seemed to have grown to twice the size in the month since he'd last seen her. He wished she would take more pains to cover her condition; the cotton dress, which was designed to hang loosely, clung to her distended belly in a most distracting fashion. He wondered whether he might suggest Amy bring a smock with her when she next visited the household, although perhaps that would be insensitive.

'Sit down, Mr Stanford, do.' Polly indicated the mothy armchair, which had clearly been her husband's and which dominated the tiny room, then she plonked herself heavily onto the small hardback chair that sat beside the rickety table where upturned packing cases formed the remainder of the family's seating arrangements. A little girl of around four was perched on one, solemnly watching the proceedings, and an eighteen-month-old infant lay sleeping in a cradle, also assembled from the wood of packing cases.

There was no sign of Charlie, who'd ducked out the back door into the rear of the neighbouring house, and was currently making his way through to the front lane to resume his game of marbles.

'Go outside and play, Sal,' Polly said. 'Mr Stanford and me want to have a chat.' The child stood. 'And shut the door after you, there's a love.'

The little girl crossed the room silently, her eyes never leaving Silas. She peered back at him as she closed the door. When she'd gone, Polly, in an automatic gesture reached out a hand and rocked the cradle.

'Do sit, Mr Stanford, please do,' she insisted.

But Silas remained hesitant. 'Perhaps under the circumstances you might be more comfortable ...?' He indicated the armchair.

Polly gave a guffaw of laughter as if he'd made a fine joke. 'Oh Lord no, Mr Stanford. God bless you, I'd never get up, not with this barrel of lard.' She embraced her giant belly with both hands in a gesture Silas found extraordinarily vulgar, then returned to rocking the cradle.

'Very well.' He sat. As Polly Jordan was not in the least concerned by her appearance, he ignored his own self-consciousness and spoke with a greater severity than he normally would to a woman in her delicate condition. 'I am most displeased to see that Charlie is not at school,' he said, resting his top hat on his knees.

'Yes, poor boy, he's had the grippe something awful.'

'I have checked the attendance records, Mrs Jordan.' Silas periodically ran a check on the school attendance of those youngsters whose families were receiving benefits from the society. After all, if the society was paying rent and supplying fresh rations, there was no justification for young children to be put out to work when they should be receiving an education. 'I believe Charlie has not been to school for the whole of this week –'

'Miss Amy made exactly the same comment late

yesterday afternoon when she dropped by with the delivery man, Mr Stanford.' Polly dived in before the lecture could begin. 'And I made exactly the same reply to her as I now make to you. Charlie will be back at school first thing Monday morning, I promise. Today being Friday, I thought I'd start with a fresh week – give him time to get over his cough and all.'

Polly wondered briefly whether young Amy Stanford might have snitched to her father about Charlie. The girl was Charlie's teacher after all, and had queried his absence. But no, she decided, Miss Amy was no tittle-tattle. Besides, Silas Stanford was as cunning as a rat – he didn't need his daughter to sniff out truancy. It's just my luck, isn't it, she cursed, that the old bastard should choose this week of all weeks to run a check on the records.

Polly Jordan refused to think ill of Amy. She liked Amy Stanford. All the women of Wapping did. That one really cares, they said. Not like the other wowsers and do-gooders and toffs. That one has a heart.

Amy taught at the makeshift charity school the society had established in a nearby warehouse to provide education for the poor. She was a favourite with the children, just as she was a favourite with their mothers when she arrived with the drayman who delivered fresh produce and supplies on behalf of the society. Taking part in the deliveries had been Amy's own idea. 'It will be the perfect way to make contact with the people of Wapping, Father,' she'd said when Silas had voiced his misgivings. 'I'll get to know the families of my pupils, I'll gain the trust of their parents.' She'd been most insistent. She'd also been right.

'My goodness, Mr Stanford, she's a breath of fresh air, your daughter, and that's a fact. It's always such a treat to see her. And just look what she give me.' Polly picked up a silk scarf that sat folded on the table and shaking it free she displayed it with pride. 'Look at that for colour, now.

You'd never use it, mind, would you? Silk like that's just for show.'

The scarf was bright pink. Silas recognised it.

'I admired the colour was all I did,' Polly continued, 'and then suddenly there she is giving it me. Oh she's a generous girl, your daughter. I'm keeping it for best, mind.' She stroked the scarf, then refolded it with care and placed it reverently back on the table. 'Only special occasions for silk like this.' Special occasions, my arse, she thought. She'd sell the piece at the first opportunity, but it didn't prevent her appreciating the gift. She enjoyed the touch and the brief ownership of such a pretty thing, but she would enjoy the money it would fetch even more. Miss Amy was a saint, she was.

'I can't offer you a cup of tea I'm afraid, Mr Stanford, I'm fresh out at the moment.' It was a lie, but Polly knew tea was the only offer the man would accept, and she had no wish to encourage conversation. She was feeling a little nervy, to tell the truth. Silas Stanford couldn't possibly know that Charlie had worked several days at Bob Bates's smithy shop around the corner when Bob's own boy had been taken sick. But if she were to be asked questions outright, and then if it were to be later discovered that she'd lied, she might risk losing her widow's monthly rental allowance.

She heaved herself up from her chair. 'I did make some lovely lemonade last night though, with the sugar that come yesterday and some of those nice fat lemons that was with the fruit Miss Amy brought –'

'No thank you, Mrs Jordan.' Silas hastily rose. 'I can't stay long, I'm afraid. I have other calls to make.' Under no circumstances did Silas drink Wapping water unless it was in the form of tea, and even then he always made sure it was scalding hot and that he could actually see the steam rising from the kettle. Wapping's water supply came from the Hobart Town Rivulet, and God only knew what sort of disease he might invite should he accept Polly Jordan's lemonade.

Silas was wise to practise caution. Upstream, where the rivulet ran cleanly down from the mountain, people imbibed its waters with impunity, but here in Wapping, disease had been known to reach epidemic proportions. Deaths from dysentery, cholera and even typhus were not uncommon.

He reached a hand into the inner breast pocket of his frock coat and took out a small cloth purse, which he placed on the table.

'There we are, Mrs Jordan: on behalf of the society, your monthly widow's rental allowance at two shillings per week. Eight shillings in all.'

'Oh Mr Stanford ...' Polly's lisp intensified. 'It's so good of you, it truly is. I don't know how to thank –'

'There is just one way you can thank the society, Mrs Jordan,' Silas interrupted, 'and that is to keep your children in school for as long as is humanly possible.' Which will mean only until they were twelve, he thought. After that, they'd head off for the hop- and apple-picking seasons, which was the way so many of the poor subsisted. But at least, by then, they would have received the elementary education that would serve them throughout life. 'I cannot stress enough the importance of learning to read and write. Nor can I stress enough the importance of acquiring basic arithmetical skills. It is imperative we safeguard the future of our children, Mrs Jordan, for they are the future of this colony.'

'Oh indeed, Mr Stanford, indeed! My Charlie'll be back at school on Monday, I swear. Why, little Will's there right now, learning his sums. He's clever, that boy. I'm dead proud of him, I am.'

With four children and another on the way, Polly Jordan couldn't wait for every one of them to be twelve years old and out picking fruit and hops. She loved each child with a

passion, she always had. She'd loved the two she'd lost as
well. But she was tired. It was time someone looked after
her for a change. Dear Mother of God, she'd earned the
right, hadn't she?

The interview over, Polly waddled thankfully the several
steps to the door, Silas accompanying her.

'I'm delighted to hear that Will is doing so well,'
he said.

Outside in the lane, as the front door opened, Charlie
nudged his mate, and they gathered up their marbles
and scuttled out of sight. Best to avoid a lecture, the boy
thought.

'I shall see you again in one month,' Silas said, putting
on his top hat.

'That you will, Mr Stanford, and without this, eh?'

She flashed her toothless grin and clutched her giant
belly, and Silas felt himself flush with embarrassment. But
to his credit, he did not look away.

'I wish you luck with your confinement, Mrs Jordan.
May God watch over you and see you safely through your
ordeal.'

'Thank you, Mr Stanford.' Polly wasn't sure why, in
that instant, she felt a desire to communicate with this
stern man. Perhaps she was making a personal plea,
fearing that the society would no longer support her once
the baby was born, or perhaps she felt genuine sympathy
for Silas Stanford because of what she'd learnt from his
daughter.

'It's hard bringing up youngsters on your own, isn't
it, sir?'

'Yes, I'm sure it is.' The question was no doubt
rhetorical, but she was looking at him as if they shared a
secret, and Silas felt uncomfortable.

'Just as it's hard losing your loved one to the sea. You'd
know that too, wouldn't you, sir?'

There was no misunderstanding her now. The starkness

of her words and the meaningful look in her eyes clearly stated that they had a common tragedy.

Silas was rendered momentarily speechless. This is my daughter's doing, he thought. It had to be. How else could Polly Jordan know of their personal family history? He was bewildered. Why would Amy share such an intimacy? It was tantamount to betrayal. Why would she do such a thing?

'I appreciate the difficulty of your circumstances, Mrs Jordan,' he said stiffly, 'and I give you my personal assurance that the society will continue to supply your widow's allowance until you are able to return to work. In the meantime, I wish you good day.'

He tipped the brim of his hat, and walked off down the stinking lane without looking back.

Polly watched him for a moment or so. A hard man, she thought, a hard man with no heart. How a bastard like that had managed to sire the likes of Amy Stanford was beyond her. She left the front door open to let in a little breeze, and went back inside. Baby Jake was crying.

Ah well, she thought as she sat and lifted the child from its cradle, at least I'll have another month or so before the society cuts me adrift. She jiggled the infant on her knees and baby Jake stopped crying immediately, reaching out to play with her hair. What the hell; she'd scored well with her widow's allowance. She was thankful for that, particularly as it was quite possible she wasn't a widow at all. She put the child on the floor and smiled as he crawled, then stood, then staggered about the room like a tiny drunken sailor.

Polly wasn't at all sure that her husband had died at sea. In her opinion, Albert Jordan was too canny to cop it in an accident. He'd more than likely run off because she'd got pregnant again. 'You keep popping them out like this, Poll, how am I expected to feed them?' he'd say. Mostly in a good-natured fashion, she had to admit – he was fond of his children. But she'd sensed the prospect of this next one might have pushed him too far, particularly so soon after the last. Well, it was hardly her fault the babies kept coming, was it? He had to keep poking her, didn't he? The bastard never stopped. What did he expect? God, but she missed him. She missed him and hated him at the same time.

Polly Jordan's overwhelming grief at the news of her husband's death had been quickly replaced by anger. Whether or not he'd died, as his crew mates aboard the whaler had reported, was immaterial. A careless death, or a callous abandonment, either way she'd been left pregnant with the prospect of bringing up five children on her own. The only mitigating factor in Albert Jordan's favour, should he have abandoned her, was that he had rigged his own death in order for her to receive assistance. For that, Polly was grateful.

She stood and, hefting baby Jake onto one hip, grabbed the bag of fresh fruit that had arrived yesterday. She'd pop next door and share it with Meg Henderson who had six youngsters and a drunken husband who beat her. There's always someone worse off than yourself, Polly thought.

Silas walked down Campbell Street towards the harbour. He would look at the ships, he decided, while the wind off the water cleared his head of the foul rivulet odour.

As he passed the City of London Arms, two men staggered drunkenly out onto the street and a brawl ensued, others joining them, mugs of rum and ale in hand, to urge them on. It is early afternoon, Silas thought vaguely. Why were men drinking in the early afternoon? But then why men chose to lose their senses in drink at all remained a mystery to Silas. He ignored them and walked on.

Upon reaching the harbour, he looked across to Hunter Street and Old Wharf. Beyond the impressive stone facades of warehouses and businesses lay the further network of

Wapping's lanes and alleys and rows that were bordered to the east by the rivulet's outlet. Housing principally fishermen and labourers, here too life was hard and uncompromising, and here too were the pubs and brothels where drunkenness and lasciviousness were a daily ritual.

Although he believed in the aims of the temperance movement and the banning of spiritous liquor, Silas, unlike many others, did not stand in judgement of men and their drunkenness. Nor, surprisingly, did he stand in judgement of women who sold their bodies. Most of the poor wretches had come from a convict past: they had endured the unspeakable. What right had any man to judge those whose spirits had been broken? The lunatic asylums, of which there were a number in Van Diemen's Land, were overflowing with pitiable creatures who had been pushed to the brink of madness and beyond. Silas did indeed pray for their souls, but it was his aim to offer help of a more practical nature, help that would lead the colony into a future where such torment had no place.

He slowed his walk to a dawdle and, ignoring the raucous cries of the fish hawkers, looked out at the mighty ships resting on the water. He was so deep in thought, though, that the beauty of the ships was lost on him. His mind turned to the previous day's meeting of the Legislative Council when delegates had arrived from Launceston for final discussions on the drafting of the new constitution. It had been a meeting of great significance, and the principle reason he had returned from his property near Pontville. Since Westminster Parliament had passed the Australian Constitutions Act of 1850, granting the right of legislative power to all six colonies, Van Diemen's Land had grown closer with each successive year to becoming a self-governing colony of the British Empire. It will not be long now, Silas thought as he stared blankly at the harbour. These were momentous times. Momentous times indeed ...

He lifted his gaze out across the river and was distracted by a particularly fine-looking ship in the distance. Under full sail and with the wind behind her, the clipper was making her way up the Derwent in spectacular fashion. He halted to admire the vessel and, as he did so, he realised that his mind hadn't really been on the meeting of the Legislative Council at all. It hadn't even been on the new constitution and the prospect of self-government. He'd been trying to distract himself, he realised. He'd been trying to distract himself from the moment he'd left Polly Jordan's house.

'It's hard bringing up youngsters on your own, isn't it, sir?' He couldn't get her words out of his mind. 'Just as it's hard losing your loved one to the sea. You'd know that too, wouldn't you, sir?' Yes, he thought, oh yes, indeed I would. Why, he wondered, had Amy chosen to confide in Polly Jordan of all people? He had no idea what could have possessed his daughter to do such a thing, but whatever the reason, it had brought back the past.

CHAPTER TWO

'He's a fine lad, is young Silas, Lucy,' Bernard Drayton had declared. 'You'll need a husband to run the business one day when I'm gone, and you'll find none more worthy, I'll warrant.'

Silas had not heard this declaration from the mouth of his future father-in-law, but rather from the mouth of his future wife, whose impression of her brashly likeable Yorkshire father had been both amusing and accurate. Lucy was a skilled mimic.

'Why, young Silas Stanford knows the wool and cotton trade better than I do myself.' She stabbed the air emphatically with a pointed forefinger as Bernard Drayton was wont to do, then laughed and dropped the act. 'Father seemed to believe I needed convincing. Little does he know it was *I* who proposed to *you*.' She hadn't actually proposed to him at all, but in suggesting he take the initiative, she might just as well have done so. 'Don't be shy, Silas,' she'd said. 'If there is something you wish to ask me, I can assure you, the answer will be in the affirmative.'

Silas's reluctance to declare his intentions had not been due to shyness. He was quite confident that he would make an excellent husband and he had very much wanted to propose to Lucinda Drayton for the past six months.

But he was aware that his intentions might have appeared suspect, if not to Lucy herself, then most certainly to her father. In the four years since he'd started out as a raw, young accountant with Drayton's Wool and Cotton Company, he'd worked his way up through the ranks to become assistant manager at the age of twenty-three. Bernard Drayton had not only taught him the business, but had offered him every conceivable opportunity for advancement. Surely, after such generosity, if he were to propose marriage to the man's daughter he would appear the most shameful opportunist.

'So we have your father's blessing,' he said. 'I am so very glad, my dear.' He was more than glad: he was profoundly relieved. There would be snide mutters from some that he'd married the boss's daughter in order to inherit the business, but let them say what they wished. They were wrong. He loved Lucy. At least he was reasonably sure he did. He couldn't be altogether positive, as he'd never been in love before, but he certainly loved being in her company. Lucy was everything he was not. She was funny and uninhibited, and the way she spoke her mind openly was even a little outrageous. There were times when Silas wasn't entirely sure what to make of Lucy, apart from the fact that she quite simply delighted him.

'Oh yes, we have Father's blessing all right,' she replied airily, 'he's so keen to be rid of me he can't wait for you to make a formal request. The poor dear's been sure I was destined for life as an old maid. In fact he's probably been grooming you for the role of husband all along.'

Silas laughed. 'You're being wicked now,' he said.

Lucy *was* being wicked. She liked to make him laugh. Silas was an attractive, intelligent man whose conversation she enjoyed, but he was so terribly, terribly serious. Making him laugh was a challenge that gave her inestimable pleasure. Her banter, however, was closer to the truth than she realised.

Bernard Drayton, a widower for the past five years, was certainly not keen to be rid of his only daughter, whom he dearly loved. However he did worry greatly that at twenty-eight she remained unmarried. For a woman to lead a ful-filled life she needed a husband and children, and Bernard had, for some time now, viewed Silas Stanford as a potential son-in-law. The five-year age discrepancy he considered irrelevant for there was no youthful fecklessness about Silas. Indeed the lad seemed a good decade older than his years, a fact which only added to his credentials in Bernard's eyes.

But most important of all to Bernard Drayton was Silas Stanford's apparent failure to register the fact that Lucy was plain. Lucy had never appeared to register the fact herself, which to Bernard remained both a mystery and a blessing, particularly when suitors with an eye to the main chance treated her as if she were a thing of rare beauty. Frankly she was not. She was by no means ugly, but she had inherited the square-jawed, snub-nosed Drayton features, characteristics that in Bernard's opinion were overcome by her vibrant personality. This only made the sycophancy of suitors with ulterior motives all the more irksome. He'd come to realise, however, that he had no cause to worry, for Lucy never succumbed to their flattery, failing even to recognise it as such. She merely found the young men shallow and uninteresting.

And now here was Silas Stanford, a somewhat humour-less and strangely middle-aged young man who loved Lucy for who she was, just as she did him. Bernard wished the couple well with all his heart. He would pray for their hap-piness although he had a feeling his efforts would not be necessary. They seemed an oddly apposite choice.

Bernard Drayton proved an astute observer. Throughout the years of their marriage, rarely was there a cross word between Silas and Lucy. She bore him three daughters in rapid succession, but seemed unable to conceive a son, for which she felt guilty. Silas assured her she mustn't.

'Oh dear,' she said, when Amy was born. 'Another girl. I am so sorry.'

'I am not,' he said. 'I am the happiest man in the world.'

The two elder girls took after their father. Chisel-boned with fine features, Harriet and Isabel were considered handsome children. The baby of the family took after her mother in every single way. Little wonder that Silas delighted in Amy.

Bernard Drayton died in 1842, just one month shy of his seventieth birthday. He left his share of the business to his son-in-law, for by the time of his death the two had become partners. Drayton & Stanford Wool and Cotton had steadfastly grown into an impressive company with distribution throughout Great Britain.

Not long after his father-in-law's death, Silas decided to extend the business, his express purpose being the provision of top quality imported stock for the company's ever-expanding UK market.

'I intend to purchase a sheep property in Australia,' he informed his wife over supper one Friday evening, after she'd tucked the girls into bed and kissed them good night. He had given the matter considerable thought, he told her. He had discussed it with his colleagues that very afternoon, and they were all in agreement. There was no finer quality wool anywhere in the world than that of the pure-bred Australian Merino.

'Superior even to Irish wool,' Silas said.

Lucy made no comment as she poured the tea.

'I hope to establish the business within three years,' he continued, 'after which I shall return to England, leaving a manager in charge.'

'So you intend to run off to the colonies,' she coolly re-marked, passing him his cup, 'and for a whole three years.'

Silas paused. Her comment had surely been made in jest. There were still times when he couldn't tell whether or not Lucy was being flippant. 'I wouldn't exactly be "running off", my dear,' he said with a smile, 'and many a colonial business venture takes a great deal longer than three years, I can assure you.'

'Very well.' The way she put down the teapot was a definite statement. Lucy was most certainly not jesting. 'I shall come with you.'

'Don't be ridiculous, Lucy.' How thoroughly silly, he thought. 'There are the girls to consider.'

'The girls shall come too.'

Silas was shocked as he registered she was in deadly earnest. 'But they're children,' he protested. 'They're too young.'

'They're healthy and they're strong. That's all that matters.'

'Australia is halfway around the world.'

'Exactly. It will be a wonderful adventure for them.'

'You can't really be serious, Lucy, surely you can't.'

'I most certainly can.'

The conversation had gone on well into the night. He'd tried over and over to talk sense to her, but she'd refused to listen.

'If you are to disappear to the colonies for years, Silas,' she said, 'then we are coming with you, it is as simple as that. We are a family.'

Try as he might, he couldn't budge her.

Then, the following morning as the family sat down to breakfast, she made the announcement. 'Girls, we are going to Australia. Isn't that exciting?' Her daughters were understandably bewildered, but it hadn't taken Lucy long to drum enthusiasm into them.

Silas found the prospect exciting too, he had to admit, and his attempts to dissuade his wife from her plan of action grew feebler as the months passed. He had never travelled farther from home than Ireland, and then only for a month or so at a time – he had not relished being separated from his family by such a fearsome distance and for so long a period. Lucy's spirit of adventure, further-more, was infectious. What he had perceived to be merely a business decision, a bold one admittedly, but a business decision nonetheless, now took on new meaning. They were embarking upon a voyage of discovery. They were pioneers, and a whole new world awaited them.

'What thrilling times we live in, Silas,' Lucy said shortly before their departure early the following year. 'Who knows what lies ahead for us in Australia? Who can possibly guess what our future holds? The mystery of it all is so very enthralling, don't you agree?'

Silas had certainly agreed. It was impossible not to agree with one as spirited and passionate as his wife. But no one could possibly have guessed Lucy's future: that the strength of her body would not match the strength of her spirit.

'Peritonitis, I'm afraid,' the ship's surgeon had said when he'd been called to their cabin where she lay writhing in agony. 'Her appendix has burst.' He'd been sympathetic, but they were so very far from land he clearly didn't hold much hope. 'There must have been considerable inflam-mation prior to the rupture. I take it she's been experienc-ing pain for some time?'

She had. Silas had seen her in pain. She'd borne it bravely, believing she was suffering the usual abdominal cramps. He'd had no reason to suspect there was anything seriously amiss – neither of them had. These were just women's problems, she'd told him, aggravated by seasickness.

She'd known at the end though. In a lucid moment, drifting somewhere between the pain and the laudanum, she had known she was dying.

'Forgive me, Silas,' she'd said. 'Please forgive me, my love.'

They'd buried her at sea, in the middle of the vast South Atlantic Ocean, halfway between Rio de Janeiro and Cape Town.

The girls had stood beside him during the burial service. Harriet, just turned thirteen, Isabel, eleven and Amy, nine, had stared uncomprehendingly as their mother's body was committed to the depths of the ocean.

Two months later, Silas had arrived in Van Diemen's Land, a widower with three young daughters.

He'd gone about his business, doing what needed to be done and doing it with his customary efficiency. He bought a house in Hobart Town, hired a housekeeper and a governess for the children, and purchased prime sheep land in the southern midlands. Everything appeared to be going according to plan, but it wasn't. Lucy's death had changed the course of their lives. In his loneliness, Silas agonised over why God had chosen to take his wife from him. Her death must surely have had some Divine purpose. As the months became a year, and then one year became two, that purpose, he decided, was the salvation of Van Diemen's Land. It was not God's intention that he set up a business and return to England to enjoy the spoils. His destiny lay here. Without giving the matter a second thought, he wrote to his lawyers and arranged for the sale of Drayton & Stanford. This was where he belonged. This was where he was needed. Silas Stanford had become a driven man.

Staring out over the Derwent, Silas no longer saw the schooner racing for the harbour and he no longer heard the cries of the hawkers. He saw nothing but Lucy's face, and heard nothing but her voice.

'*What thrilling times we live in, Silas. Who knows what lies ahead for us in Australia? Who can possibly guess what our future holds?*'

Who indeed? he thought. Lucy's words remained as clear as they had been ten years before, but it had taken Polly Jordan to bring them to mind. He turned his back to the water and walked up Macquarie Street in the direction of home.

*

'I saw Polly Jordan today,' he said.

They were seated in the downstairs front drawing room. Clara had just arrived with the afternoon tea, a ritual impeccably timed to coincide with Amy's return from school. When Silas was away in the country, Amy would take her tea alone, setting herself up with her books and papers at the desk by the windows, which looked out over the small front garden to Macquarie Street.

The two-storey sandstone house was starkly Georgian in design. Functional and lacking any ornate feature, it was comfortable enough, with adequate servants' quarters out the back, but compared to the lavish homes of other successful businessmen it was an exceedingly modest dwelling. Silas, as always, avoided any form of ostentation.

'Given her delicate condition, she seemed well enough,' he added, doing his best to sound casual. Unsure how to broach the subject, he feared his voice might give him away.

'Yes, I saw her myself yesterday, and I agree. She didn't appear to be suffering any undue physical discomfort. ' Amy clearly sensed no tension. 'Thank you, Clara. I'll pour.'

'Very good, Miss Amy. I baked a lemon cake this afternoon.' Friday was always Clara's baking day. 'Shall I bring in a slice or two?'

Clara Goodall served as both cook and housekeeper, while her equally efficient husband, Albert, carried out all the duties required of a general manservant. The two had come to Silas as 'ticket-of-leavers', convicts who through good behaviour had been granted a ticket permitting them to accept employment on the condition they regularly reported to the authorities. Within a year of their service, and upon Silas's personal recommendation, the Goodalls' sentences had been commuted and both had been granted conditional pardons. Fiercely loyal and devoted to their master, they had been in Silas's employ for eight years now, and were the only servants he retained these days.

'How could I possibly resist your lemon cake, Clara?' Amy said with a smile. 'What about you, Father?'

'No, thank you. Not for me.'

Clara nodded and as she left Amy busied herself with the tea.

Silas waited until the housekeeper had closed the door behind her.

'You know, don't you, Amy, that I have always respected your desire to make contact with the parents of your pupils in order to gain their trust.' There was an element of peevishness in his tone as he fought to avoid the issue uppermost in his mind. He had never before had a disagreement with his daughter, and did not relish the prospect now, but he could not ignore what he saw as a betrayal of trust. 'It is why I have never queried you regarding absenteeism, although frankly I believe you should have told me about Charlie Jordan.'

'You knew of his absence?'

'Yes. I checked the attendance records.'

Amy stopped pouring the tea and looked up, concerned. 'Polly didn't think I told you, did she?'

Silas found the familiar reference grating, and his daughter's misguided sense of priority annoyed him intensely.

'I would have no idea what Mrs Jordan thought, Amy. It is not my duty to enter into personal discussion with the society's beneficiaries.'

'Oh.' For the first time Amy registered her father's disapproval. She could hardly fail to do so. Silas Stanford spoke sternly to many people and often, but rarely did he adopt such a tone with her.

'If you wish to pursue a personal relationship with the woman,' he continued, 'that is entirely your affair, although why you would bother giving her a silk scarf is beyond me. You surely cannot believe that she values the gift.'

'Yes, I believe she does.'

'She will sell it.'

'Of course she will.'

Silas was taken aback by the light of rebellion in his daughter's eyes.

'And whatever money she gets for it will go to her children. That certainly doesn't mean to say that she does not value the gift.'

Conversation ceased abruptly as the door opened and Clara arrived with the cake.

'There we are, Miss Amy,' she said, setting down the plate.

'Thank you, Clara.'

The housekeeper withdrew, once again closing the door behind her, and the cake, like the tea, sat untouched before them.

'What is it, Father?' Amy asked gently. 'You don't mind at all about the scarf. I know you don't. Tell me what's wrong. Please.'

'I consider it a betrayal to your mother's memory that you should discuss her death with a virtual stranger.' The words sprang out with the alarming force of a slap to the face. 'I am appalled that you saw fit to talk intimately to Polly Jordan of our personal family history.'

Amy resisted the temptation to retaliate with equal force, though she found the accusation grossly unjust.

'I did not talk intimately of our personal family history,' she said calmly. 'I merely told Polly Jordan that my mother had died at sea.'

Silas gave a snort of derision. 'And you do not regard such a disclosure as intimate?'

'No, I do not. I regard it as an offer of sympathy and understanding to a woman who is suffering grief.' Sensing his further annoyance, Amy carried on hurriedly before he could interject. 'Polly cried as she spoke to me of her husband, Father. She loved him dearly, and I wanted to share with her the fact that I too had experienced the loss of a loved one at sea. I hoped it might be of some comfort –'

'And what if Polly's beloved husband did *not* die at sea?' Silas's interruption was as jarring as he intended it to be. 'What if the man abandoned his expectant wife in order to escape the responsibility of yet another child?' He paused, allowing the impact of such a suggestion to hit home, and was gratified by his daughter's look of utter bewilderment. Good, I've shocked her out of her complacency, he thought, and the knowledge softened him a little. 'Do you honestly think that such a possibility has not occurred to Polly Jordan, my dear? It would be the first thing to cross her mind, I can assure you.'

'In which case, she has my sympathy tenfold, for desertion would cause her even greater distress.'

The scenario her father had presented had indeed taken Amy by surprise, but Silas had misinterpreted the true cause for her bewilderment.

'But if Polly was abandoned,' she continued, 'why then did the society accept her as a beneficiary? Proof of widowhood is required, is it not?'

'Of course it is. I personally interviewed members of the whaler's crew who witnessed both the accident and the burial.' Silas regretted having lashed out in so vulgar a fashion; he rarely lost his temper. 'I was merely stating a hypothetical possibility,' he said stiffly. 'A possibility that I'm sure would have occurred to Polly Jordan, even in her grief.' He stared distractedly at the cup of tea Amy had poured him. It would be tepid by now.

'What of the captain? What of the ship's log?'

'Eh?'

'Burials at sea must be recorded. Was the log checked?'

'Possibly. I can't be sure. Shall we call Clara for fresh cups?'

'My goodness, Father.' Her tone was one of disbelief. It couldn't be possible, she thought. 'You didn't lie, did you?'

'I most certainly did not.' Silas was horrified that his

daughter could suggest such a thing. 'I received eye-witness accounts. I took men at their word, and why should I not?'

Yes, Amy thought, just as the members of the Hobart Town Businessmen's Philanthropic Society would accept the word of their founder. If Silas Stanford recommended Polly Jordan as a beneficiary, they would of course assume the records had been verified. Had her father chosen not to delve too deeply into the circumstances in the belief that Polly Jordan, an expectant mother with four children, qualified for support regardless of the rules? It appeared quite possible.

Amy felt a wave of affection as she studied him, his attention now focused studiously on the teapot, signalling an end to their conversation. She thought how tired he looked, tired and vulnerable and suddenly older than his forty-eight years, and she wondered if she were in any way responsible. He was such an intensely private man. Had she indeed betrayed his trust?

'I am sorry, Father,' she said. 'I am deeply sorry that I offended you in speaking about Mother to Polly Jordan. I promise I shall never again –'

'Oh, but my dear, you must.' Silas reached across the table and took her hand in both of his, though he was not physically demonstrative as a rule. 'You must speak of your mother whenever, and to whomever, you wish,' he said. 'I do not hold sole ownership of her memory.' He was overcome with guilt as he realised how selfish he'd been. 'The apology is mine, Amy. Please forgive me, I beg you.'

'Of course I forgive you,' his daughter replied brightly, and she kissed the hands that held hers. Like her mother before her, Amy was never one to shy away from physical expression.

She jumped to her feet. 'I shall tell Clara to make a fresh pot,' she said as she picked up the tea tray. 'You need your tea: you look weary, Father.'

I am weary, he thought as he watched her sail off to the kitchen. Revisiting the past had been strangely tiring.

Several minutes later, upon her return, she insisted he eat some lemon cake while they waited for the tea. And then she further insisted upon hearing all the news from the latest meeting of the Legislative Council, news which she accused him of having been keeping to himself.

'Come along now, Father, I shall swear an oath of silence if you wish, but do share some secrets with me. Do you really believe London will agree to the renaming of the colony?'

'They will have to agree when we achieve self-government, my dear, and that is only a matter of time. The new constitution will be passed within the next several months I'm sure, and once it has been given Royal Assent by Queen Victoria, the Privy Council will have no option but to approve our decision.'

Silas was aware of his daughter's ploy. Amy was fuelling his passion, just as Lucy had done whenever she'd sensed his despondence, and just like Lucy she was succeeding. Amy's spirit and good humour were a daily reminder to Silas of the wife he had lost, but he found no pain in the fact, only pleasure, for he had long ago accepted Lucy's death as a message from God.

'Imagine, Amy! No longer will we be Van Diemen's Land. The dark days will soon be behind us.'

'But surely now with the end of transportation, the dark days are already behind us, Father. Why, just the other day an article in the *Courier* said something about "an end to the shameful stain upon our history", which I must say I found very dramatic. The journalist called the Jubilee Festival Dinner "a triumph for the Anti-Transportation League and a testament to its members' belief in a free land for our children". Or words to that effect. I can't quite recall – I may be misquoting a little. In any event, I wholeheartedly agree with him.'

Following the docking of the last convict vessel on 26 May of that year, Van Diemen's Land had indeed given itself up to endless celebration. Hobart Town and Launceston had conducted lavish festivities, the Jubilee Festival of Hobart Town culminating in a giant outdoor banquet for the children of the colony. A massive marquee had been rigged among the trees, rows of cloth-covered trestle tables placed end to end, and huge platters of food laid out for the hundreds upon hundreds of children who had gathered for the feast and for the fireworks that followed.

'How proud you must be, Father, after your years of striving, to finally see an end to our days as a penal settlement.'

'I am proud, it is true,' he admitted, 'to have played my small part in the proceedings.'

Silas was being overly humble. He had played a large part, and the battle had at times been hard. He had made powerful enemies in the group of wealthy landowners and merchants who, having prospered under the assignment system, had banded together in a bid to retain convict transportation and the ready availability of cheap labour it provided. But they lost, Silas thought with a sense of triumph. Times had changed. Those days were over. And every minute of the fight had been worth it.

'You are right, my dear, I am proud of our achievements. Although we may well be witness to further inhumanities before the day is done,' he added, his face clouding slightly as he recalled the road gang he'd watched at work on the docks. 'I fear the government will continue to employ convict labour on its public works until the current prisoners have served their sentences. In the interests of future integration, I would have preferred to see a greater concentration upon the acquisition of trade skills for high-risk prisoners, and the general issue of tickets-of-leave to all those convicts considered low-risk. I'm afraid I was outvoted on these issues, however. The majority of my colleagues considered my suggested course of action premature and impracticable. They accused me of being unrealistic.'

Amy was not particularly surprised. There was much that was unrealistic about her father. Silas Stanford was so driven in his quest that he sometimes failed to see the real world at all, and that included the real world of his family.

'Education,' he announced, changing the subject with surprisingly dramatic flair. 'Education is the way of the future, Amy. The education of a new generation to lead a new free colony.'

She could certainly not disagree with him there.

The tea arrived and for the next half-hour they talked about the plans for the Hobart Town Ragged School Association, or rather Silas did. He was joining forces with the philanthropist Henry Hopkins in the creation of a new welfare scheme modelled upon the English ragged school system.

As he spoke, Amy was heartened to see the change in him. No longer did he look tired and old. In his excitement for the future, he was rejuvenated. It is a pity, she thought, that so few can see the man for who he really is, including, sadly, his two older daughters.

Amy remembered how marooned they'd felt, she and her sisters, upon losing the woman who'd been the very anchor of their existence. She recalled how, in the wake of their mother's death, Harriet and Isabel had so craved their father's affection that they'd competed with each other to see who could best garner his interest. But Silas Stanford had appeared barely to notice his children, leaving them in the sole care of the governess he'd employed, and Amy had often wondered how it was that she had not shared her sisters' desperation. Had she been more resilient simply because she was younger? Or had she perhaps sensed her father's love? He'd displayed no favouritism, and her sisters had never appeared to suspect any, but she'd always known Silas loved her. Unfortunately, neither Harriet nor Isabel had experienced a similar confidence and, as the years had passed, their father's perceived indifference had had radical repercussions.

Harriet Stanford had embraced the Church with fervour, perhaps in a bid for her father's approval or perhaps as a replacement for the love he'd failed to give her, but she'd certainly succeeded in gaining his attention when, as a twenty-year-old, she'd left to join the Sisterhood of the Holy Communion, an Anglican order of nuns in Sydney. Silas had been immensely proud of his eldest daughter.

Isabel Stanford had given up trying to please her father at the age of fifteen, and at nineteen had married Percival Buxton, a young captain in the British army whom she'd met just six months previously at a gala fundraising function held by the Hobart Town Businessmen's Philanthropic Society. The couple had moved to Launceston where Nigel was stationed, and they planned shortly to return to England upon the completion of his two-year commission, all of which suited Isabel perfectly. Silas had been bewildered by the speed of events, but happy that his daughter had apparently found her ideal match.

'No child in the colony, no matter from how impoverished a family, will be denied an education.' He was now at his pontificating best.

Amy nodded encouragingly, although she wasn't paying attention to his actual words. This is the only father Harriet and Isabel knew, she thought, a father whose compassion for his fellow man had added to their sense of deprivation. But it shouldn't have, for he had always loved them, and still did in his own mysterious way. Silas Stanford's tragedy in life was his inability to show his personal feelings. He did today though, didn't he? Amy thought. Today Silas Stanford, albeit unwittingly, had revealed a glimpse of his innermost self. She hadn't known he still ached with the pain of his wife's death. None of them had known.

'And you, my dear, will be a part of it all,' Silas announced with pride. 'When the ragged school system is established, we will be in need of teachers, and you shall be one of our first.'

'I would consider that a great honour, Father, a great honour indeed.' She picked up the teapot and started pouring herself a second cup. 'Now finish your tea and let me make you a fresh one.'

'Oh dear, I've been ranting, haven't I?'

'No more than usual. Now finish your tea please, I wish to propose a toast.' She smiled as he obediently drained his cup.

'So what is the toast?' he asked, watching her pour.

'To the forthcoming success of the Hobart Town Ragged School Association, of course,' she replied.

'But of course.'

She passed him his fresh cup and they made their toast. Then Amy proposed a second.

'And even more importantly,' she said, 'let us drink to Tasmania.'

'Oh my goodness me, yes.' Silas considered the imminent renaming of the colony after its Dutch discoverer, Abel Tasman, to be of the most profound and symbolic significance. Van Diemen's Land was to be newly baptised. The sins of the past were to be washed away. 'To Tasmania,' he said, raising his teacup, 'a new name for a new land and a new people.'

'To Tasmania,' Amy said and they clinked cups. But changing the name won't really change the people, she thought as she sipped her tea. Van Diemen's Land was a wild place that attracted a certain kind. It always had, and quite possibly always would.

As if to prove her right, it was at that very moment that Mick O'Callaghan caught his first sight of Hobart Town.

CHAPTER THREE

After rounding Cape Raoul with a blustering southerly at her stern, the *Maid of Canton* had fairly raced up Storm Bay. She was a clipper built for speed and few vessels could match her. A former opium runner, the *Maid*, as she was affectionately known, served a more respectable master these days, working the British trade routes for a wealthy merchant company.

Past Cape Direction and on up the Derwent the *Maid* had sped, her skipper eager to make dock before afternoon became dusk.

Then off the port bow, beyond the endless masts of ships at anchor, the hustle and bustle that was Hobart Town suddenly came into view.

To Mick O'Callaghan it was a magic sight.

'There she is, Mick.' Seamus gave him a nudge. 'You've made it, you lucky young bastard.'

'I certainly have,' Mick responded with a grin, 'and most obliged I am for your help, Seamus.' I've made it all right, he thought. And as far as luck went, Seamus didn't know the half of it. Arriving in Hobart Town was perhaps not remarkable, but arriving as a free man was little short of a miracle. He should have been one of those poor bastards dragging their chains off a transport ship.

'Happy to have been of service,' Seamus replied. And he

was. Despite an eight-year age discrepancy, he'd been close
to young Mick in the old Dublin days, even closer than
Mick's older brothers. Mick being the youngest of his family,
and a late arrival at that, had had five siblings quite a deal
older than he was and they'd tended to ignore him. The lad
had always been a bit of a tearaway, and it hadn't surprised
Seamus to hear, via his own family, the rumour that Mick
had got mixed up with the Young Irelanders movement
and had left Belfast in something of a hurry, although
no-one knew why. Seamus had thought little on the subject,
however. He was not one to pass judgement, and there was
nothing he could have done anyway, for by then he was
a seasoned merchant sailor and the sea was his home. On
those occasions when he wasn't aboard ship or holed up in
a foreign port, he stayed at a seamen's hostel in Liverpool;
apart from the odd family letter he'd lost all contact with
Ireland. The coincidence of his having literally bumped into
twenty-one-year-old Mick at the Liverpool docks where the
lad was seeking work as a deckhand had seemed to Seamus
the intervention of destiny. He'd been only too happy to
lend a hand, and he hadn't asked questions when Mick had
said he wanted to sign up for a one-way voyage only. 'I need
to get as far away from Ireland as possible and stay there,'
Mick had said, and that was enough for Seamus. If young
Mick Kelly now wanted to call himself Mick O'Callaghan
that was nobody's business but his own, and whatever
intrigue the lad had got himself entangled in was of little
interest anyway. Seamus kept well out of politics himself.

'How about America?' he'd suggested. 'There's a ship
leaving tomorrow and I'm good friends with the first
mate.'

'Too many Irish in America,' Mick had said. 'I was
thinking more of Australia.'

'And you don't reckon on finding Irish there?' Seamus
had wryly queried.

'Not the same sort of Irish.'

'Ah yes, you do have a point, I agree.'

Young Mick's choice of Australia had appeared to Seamus another portent of destiny's hand in the scheme of things, for his own ship the *Maid* was due to sail for Van Diemen's Land in only weeks.

'You're in luck,' he'd said. 'The *Maid of Canton* departs within the month. I'm first mate, and you're welcome on board.'

'Seamus, you're a godsend, you truly are,' Mick had said and he'd hugged his old mate with fervour.

But neither luck nor destiny had played any part in the fortuitous reunion of Mick Kelly, now O'Callaghan, and his childhood friend. Mick had known exactly where he would bump into Seamus, just as he had known that Seamus was first mate aboard the *Maid*, which was shortly to set sail for Van Diemen's Land. The naiveté of his friend in accepting the coincidence of their meeting had not been in the least surprising, for even as a ten-year-old Mick had recognised how easily he could manipulate Seamus. But then Mick Kelly had discovered at ten that he could manipulate most people.

'He has the gift of the blarney, that one,' his father would boast. 'He could charm the wings off a butterfly and the butterfly would walk away flightless and happy. The boy has the true gift, there's no doubt about it.' Patrick Kelly was a dreamer with a romantic love of his tribe, which his youngest son grew to find pointless and rather foolish. Being able to talk your way into people's affections was one thing, but knowing how to use your power once you got there – that was something else altogether.

As the crew went about their work in preparation for docking, Mick wondered how Seamus might react if he knew the facts. Good, honest Seamus had believed he'd been rescuing an innocent lad from political thugs. And indeed he had, Mick thought. Sweet Jesus, those crazy bastards had been hounding him for years. They'd

followed him from Belfast to London; it would have been
only a matter of time before they'd traced him to Liverpool. But Seamus hadn't known the catastrophic conse-
quences of this innocent lad's involvement with the Young
Irelanders. No-one knew, and no-one was ever likely to
find out, for the movement had long since disbanded. The
problem now lay in distancing himself from its several
fierce supporters who remained bent on revenge.

There were other facts of which Seamus had been
ignorant, and it was to Mick's advantage to ensure he
continued so. Seamus had had no idea he'd been aiding
a criminal. The knowledge of that would surely have
worried him more than anything, Mick thought, for
Seamus although a simple rough seaman was fiercely law-
abiding.

Mick O'Callaghan thanked God for both Seamus and
his own good fortune. Given the thieving he'd done in
London he'd been lucky not to land in gaol – there'd been
several close encounters with the law. But he'd not been
deterred. Fuelled by the excitement of danger he'd kept on
taking chances. Why he'd even pulled off a couple of jobs
in Liverpool during the last several weeks before they'd set
sail. He wondered what Seamus would say to that. Poor
Seamus would no doubt be appalled. Not that it mattered.
They wouldn't be seeing each other again. Seamus had
served his purpose.

The skipper brought the *Maid* in under virtually no sail,
with just the skilful use of wind and tide; as the clipper
pulled alongside the dock, the crew worked with smooth
precision, the bosun's commands barely necessary.

Mick and a crew mate secured the main bow line, and
the Irishman rejoiced in his escape. He'd been a doomed
man, there was nothing surer. If the Young Irelanders
hadn't got him, then the British constabulary would have.
He revelled in a sudden sense of liberty. The sights and
the sounds and the very smell of Hobart Town all spelt

freedom to him. Once again he gave thanks and, if he'd not been busy with the bow line, he might even have crossed himself, a superstitious gesture only for he'd long ago relinquished the faith. There'd be no more lawless- ness, he decided. He'd arrived here a free man when, but for the grace of God, he should have been in chains. I've done with thieving, he told himself, and he made a solemn vow. To what or to whom was vague. Mick swore his allusions to God were merely 'habit', but for a professed non-believer he seemed to refer to Him rather a lot.

Several hours later, as he wandered the dockside's dark streets, canvas kit bag slung over one shoulder, the lights of each and every alehouse and tavern seemed to signal a personal welcome. Mick O'Callaghan was exploring his new surrounds and his new freedom and he was savouring every minute.

Upon leaving the ship, he'd felt duty-bound to have a quick drink with Seamus and they'd shared an ale at the Sailor's Return on Old Wharf. The Sailor's Return was the crew's favoured pub when the *Maid* was in port, and Seamus had obviously presumed he and Mick would progress from there to a night on the town. Mick had quickly put paid to the idea.

'Why do you think I scrubbed myself up?' he'd said, stroking his now beardless chin. 'It's a woman I'm after, and the sooner the better.'

Seamus had burst out laughing. He understood the impatience of youth, but he found Mick's vanity highly amusing. With the exception of a flamboyant moustache, the lad's face was as smooth as a billiard ball, and the glossy black curls of his hair gleamed from brushing. His moleskin breeches were neatly tucked into knee-high boots that had seen a good polish; he wore an open-neck shirt that looked brand new; and a bright red kerchief, also apparently new, was tied at his throat.

'You going courting, are you, Mick?' Seamus had queried, and his own remark had brought about another guffaw. No doubt he too would end up with a woman after a night on the drink, but he was hardly going to dress for the occasion. Whores took note of a man's purse, not his appearance. Looking Mick up and down, he'd winked and given him a hearty nudge in the ribs. 'You've dressed up special, eh? I'm sure your efforts will be deeply appreci-ated,' and he'd laughed again.

Mick hadn't allowed Seamus's humour to grate, although he'd considered it further evidence that the time for their parting had come. Instead, he'd flashed one of his roguish grins, the likes of which had caused many a female heart to flutter.

'All women like to be courted, Seamus,' he'd said. Then he'd drained his glass, stood and offered his hand. 'Farewell, my friend, I shall be forever in your debt.'

'Hardly farewell,' Seamus had countered good-naturedly, amused by what he saw as Mick's youthful flair for the melodramatic. 'The *Maid*'s in port for a week. We'll surely be seeing each other.'

'Yes indeed, we surely will.'

We won't, Mick had thought as he'd left the pub. He would avoid the Sailor's Return and the crew of the *Maid*, and most particularly Seamus. When starting a new life, one needed to adopt new friends.

Now, having walked away from the docks and into the narrow streets of Wapping, he heard something that made his heart leap. From a nearby pub came the sound of a fiddle belting out a wild Irish reel. It was a sound that, for some time, had sent him in the opposite direction. In London and Liverpool, he'd kept well clear of the haunts of the Irish. But this was Van Diemen's Land, he told himself. He had no need to fear his countrymen here. Turning the corner he strode boldly through the front doors of the Hunter's Rest.

Mick felt at home the moment he entered the pub. The golden glow of its lamp-light was warm and inviting, and he was greeted by the sound of Irish voices and the music of his homeland.

As he looked, a bold girl picked up her skirts and started dancing to the fiddle. Men made space for her in the centre of the room, pulling aside wooden benches, clapping along as the fiddler quickened the pace, cheering as her bosom bounced and her bare legs flashed. The other women present, a good half dozen or so, were even more vocal than the men. 'Show 'em your stuff, Maevy,' one bawdy wench yelled, 'give 'em a good look,' and as the dancer's skirts reached crotch level a huge cheer went up.

Mick was intoxicated by the atmosphere. In the closeness of the pub, the smell of human sweat mingled with the odour of the whale oil that fuelled the lamps and he found the mixture heady and erotic.

The dance came to an end and one of the men claimed the girl. He was a big man, strongly built and clearly known to many of the drinkers, and no-one disputed his claim. The girl laughed as she clutched at the coins he fed between her breasts and, after a brief negotiation with the beefy man who stood guard at the door near the bar, the pair disappeared up the narrow stairway to the rooms overhead.

Mick bought himself a mug of ale, careful not to reveal his stash as he paid the barman. Along with the wages he'd collected from the *Maid*, he was carrying quite a sizeable amount of cash from his Liverpool jobs and some smart new clothes he'd purchased before sailing. Seamus's presumption that he'd 'dressed up special' had been incorrect. Mick always dressed stylishly. He considered clothes and grooming of the utmost importance. But in a place like this, it was not wise to be conspicuous about the valuables one carried, and he kept his kitbag tucked firmly under his arm.

'Hello, handsome. Fancy a bit of fun?' The wench who'd yelled out to the dancer had sidled up to him and was resting her breasts invitingly on the bar. They spilled from her low-cut bodice, full and milky-white and obviously her calling card.

'You're very enticing, my lovely,' he said, his eyes and his smile telling her she was. 'The fact is, though, I've just arrived and I'm drinking in the atmosphere.' Enticing as the woman's breasts were, she had to be at least thirty and he felt not the remotest desire for her, but Mick was never rude to a woman. 'Perhaps a little later – that is if you're available. I imagine they're queuing up.' With breasts like that they probably are, he thought, and with a few ales under his belt, he might well want her, but for now he just wished to drink in the night. Having a woman was not his major priority anyway. He'd been lying to Seamus simply to rid himself of the man's company.

'The name's Peg,' she said. By God, but I'd give this one a poke for nothing, she thought. He was as handsome as the devil himself. 'You only have to ask; they all know me here.'

'Peg,' he said. 'I'll remember it, and I'll surely be asking.'

Peg reluctantly turned her attention to the foul-breathed man who was kneading her right buttock with one hand and jangling coins in the pocket of his breeches with the other.

The fiddler played another tune. He was joined by a man with a tin whistle and the music became even more infectious as women twirled enticingly, selling their wares, inviting men to join them in the dance. Some of the younger men willingly did, while others more intent upon drinking shooed them away like flies.

Mick, although he was not standing in the forefront of the crowd, was singled out by several of the women, but he demurred with a smile for each, gesturing to his half-finished ale. He was not in the mood to dance. He finished his drink, dumped his mug on the bar and made his way out to the lane at the rear of the pub to relieve himself.

As he stepped outside he was vaguely aware of a couple in the gloom up ahead. They appeared to be copulating against the sandstone wall of the pub, but he took no notice as he undid his breeches and started to urinate in the gutter. Then he heard the woman's protestations. She obviously had no wish to call the attention of others to her plight for the pitch of her voice was low, but her tone was nonetheless urgent.

'I said no,' she hissed. 'Get away, you bastard. Leave me be.'

Mick peered into the darkness. He could make out their shapes about twenty paces away, and he could see now that the woman was putting up a fight.

The man, a huge brute of a fellow, had her pinned against the wall. He'd hoisted her skirts up around her waist and was fumbling with his trousers. Within seconds he'd freed himself and, lifting her bodily off the ground, he spread her thighs with his hips, thrusting for his mark.

'I don't want your filthy cock,' the woman snarled through clenched teeth, fighting with all her might to push him away. 'Keep it to yourself, pig.' She was young and feisty, but her struggle was ineffectual, and the man simply grunted with satisfaction as his thrusts hit home.

Then she stopped trying to free herself. Instead, she raked the claws of her fingers down his face, her nails tearing the flesh of his temples and his eyelids and his cheeks before losing themselves in the mass of his beard.

Her attack was successful. The man roared in rage and as he broke his hold on her she staggered free.

Upstairs, a shutter was opened and someone peered down from the lamp-lit room to the laneway below, but the man was undeterred by the presence of an onlooker. The woman had angered him now. He grabbed at her, slamming her against the wall.

'Slag,' he roared, 'cunt,' and he smashed his fist into her face.

The woman's knees buckled. All fight had left her. The man hoisted her skirts up once again and was about to take her, when Mick stepped out of the shadows.

'You shouldn't hit a woman like that,' he said. He didn't know why he was interfering; as a rule he avoided trouble whenever possible.

The man peered through the gloom, puzzled more than anything. 'What's it to you, Irishman? Mind your own fucking business.' And he redirected his attention to the woman.

'She doesn't want you, my friend,' Mick said. 'Let her be.'

The man released the woman, who slowly slid down the wall, to remain in a huddled heap, semi-conscious, broken-nosed and minus several front teeth. 'Let her be?' he queried threateningly as he turned to face Mick. He was not one accustomed to taking orders, and certainly not from a man half his size. 'Who says?'

'I believe I do.' Mick put down his kitbag. Oh God in heaven, he thought, why am I behaving so foolishly? What sort of trouble had he landed himself in now?

Upstairs, Ma Tebbutt brought the oil lamp to the window in order to get a better view of the proceedings. Weight for weight it's certainly no contest, she thought as she looked down at the bulk of the brutish oaf and the slim figure of the young man. But then, the young man looked fit, and he had twenty years on the other. He'd be more agile. If he could land a few punches and avoid getting hit, he might just stand a chance. Ma was a Londoner, born within the sound of Bow Bells, and she admired a man who could use his fists. As a betting woman she was interested in the outcome. She might even put her money on the lad, she decided, he looked like a cocky young devil. Then she saw the oaf's hand dive behind his back to the sheath that hung from his belt. Different odds altogether, she thought as the knife flashed silver in the lamp-light.

She paddled her way to the door – the combination of age, weight and arthritis rendering movement awkward these days – and, popping her head out into the hall, gave an order to one of the girls who'd just come upstairs.

'Tell Len he's to bust up a fight in the back lane,' she said. 'He'll need Billy with him and tell him to take a pistol. Evie's copped a bashing and the bloke's got a knife.'

Then she returned to the window to watch. A good fight was one thing, but she would not have murder on her turf. Not if she could help it anyway.

Mick was grateful for the spill of light from the overhead window. He could see the knife quite clearly now. It had taken him by surprise, he had to admit, and he wondered if he would have acted with such gallantry if he'd noticed the man was carrying a blade. Bit late to ponder the fact though, he thought as he circled warily, dodging each time the man lunged at him.

Mick dodged the lunges with ease, second-guessing the man, catching him off balance, changing direction, then circling again, waiting for the next lunge. This is where my strength lies, he told himself, in the man's clumsiness, for strong though the man no doubt was, he did not use his weight well. Mick decided he would use it for him and, biding his time, he continued to lead the dance.

Mick O'Callaghan was an accomplished fighter when cornered. He preferred to avoid physical conflict if possible, but when necessity dictated he was a canny opponent. His use of tactics and quick wit had bested many a formidable adversary.

The man was becoming angered beyond endurance: his laboured breathing was now mingled with snarls of frustration. All he needed was one stick of the knife. One stick and then I'll gut the little prick from top to toe, he told himself. One stick and he'd disembowel the bastard. He'd pull the guts from his belly before his very eyes and feed them into his fucking mouth. With a bellow of murderous intent he charged.

Mick feinted and the man barrelled past, missing him by only inches, as had been Mick's intention. The fury of his aggressor was essential to his plan.

The man staggered and recovered himself, then turned to charge again, during which time Mick backed off, creating more space between them. He started to circle in the opposite direction. Now, he thought, now's the moment. Both the positioning and the distance were perfect. He just needed the man to get a good run at him.

Tantalised by his near miss, the man didn't pause for breath but charged once again, hurtling towards Mick like an enraged bull. When he was nearly upon him, Mick stepped to one side and, grasping a fistful of the man's hair with one hand and the back of his belt with the other, he whirled him off course, altering the trajectory of his charge and heading him straight towards the sandstone wall of the pub. The sheer force of the man's weight did the rest. He hit the rock-face head first and crumpled to the ground unconscious. The fight had lasted exactly two minutes.

There was a round of applause from the upstairs window.

Mick looked up. He couldn't quite make out who it was, but he was distracted as the back door of the pub opened and two men appeared, one of them bearing a pistol.

'You're too late, Len,' a Cockney voice called from above, 'the lad won without landing a single punch.' Ma Tebbutt leant her considerable bulk out of the window and gave Mick another round of applause. 'Come on up here, boy. Show him the way, Len, and you Billy,' she gestured to the other man, 'you see to Evie. She copped a blow that'd down a mule.'

Mick did as he was told. Shouldering his kitbag, he accompanied Len, a beefy, taciturn Englishman, back into the pub and up the narrow staircase, which led directly to Ma Tebbutt's quarters.

She ushered him in, eyeing him up and down, apparently liking what she saw. 'Thanks, Len,' she said.

The Englishman closed the door and disappeared without having uttered a single word.

'You handle yourself well, lad.' Ma carefully lowered her body into her favourite armchair, which sat beside the table in the centre of the room.

'Thank you, ma'am.' Mick nodded amiably and looked about at his surrounds.

He was in a cosy sitting room that smelt of whale oil and pipe tobacco, which was not surprising as a clay pipe and tobacco pouch rested in a bowl next to the oil lamp on the table. There was a door to one side, which he presumed led to a bedroom, for the woman was clearly infirm and unlikely to travel up and down the steep staircase with ease. He further presumed, and correctly so, that the other rooms leading off from the passage outside were reserved for the girls and their clients.

As if in verification, there was the sudden clump of boots on the landing, followed shortly by a girlish giggle and the slam of a door further down the hall.

'What's your name?'

He quickly returned his attention to the woman who was studying him intently. He hoped he hadn't appeared rude, but it was a habit of his to vet any new location, just in case he should need to beat a hasty retreat.

'Michael Patrick O'Callaghan, ma'am,' he said respectfully. 'They call me Mick.'

Ma nodded and introduced herself. 'Margaret May Tebbutt,' she said with a welcoming salute of her arthritic right hand. It so galled Ma that she could no longer shake hands with the strength of a man as she once had that these days she refused to shake hands at all. 'They call me Ma.'

'Pleased to meet you, ma'am.' Mick returned a salute of his own.

'Ma,' she corrected him.

'Ma,' he said with a smile.

Handsome bugger, she thought. 'What do you do for a crust?'

'Nothing yet. I just arrived in town.'

Ma did not ask 'from where'. A person's background was never queried in Wapping. But she couldn't help making the wry observation that if the lad was fresh from the penal settlement at Port Arthur, then he'd certainly managed to outfit himself well. Mine not to question how or why though, she told herself.

'If you're after a spot of work, I could put some your way. Enough to tide you over until you get yourself settled. Not much money, mind, just expenses, but board and lodging, what do you say?' As always, Ma got straight to the point.

'I say yes.' Mick grinned, unable to believe his good fortune. 'I say yes, indeed.'

'I rather thought you might,' she replied drily. 'The luck of the Irish, eh? You lot with your gift of the gab, you always land on your feet.'

He wiped the grin from his face – it seemed he was being chastised – but Ma was quick to reassure him otherwise.

'No cause for alarm, son: I cater to the Paddies. Big drinkers, big womanisers – they're my favourite clientele. Half my girls are Irish too. Fancy a tot of rum?'

Mick nodded. Ma Tebbutt's disability was physical only; her mind moved with extraordinary agility.

'The dresser over there, bring us the bottle and a couple of mugs, there's a good lad.'

He dutifully fetched the earthenware bottle, pulled out its stopper and placed it on the table before her together with two pewter mugs.

'Grab a seat.' She indicated the hardback chair in the corner by the desk, which was littered with paperwork.

He pulled the chair over to the table and sat.

'I'm grateful to you for looking after Evie like you did,' Ma said, pouring them both a liberal measure of rum. 'Not many would have come to her rescue.'

'Oh that's not so, Ma,' he protested modestly. 'Any gentleman would have done likewise, I'm sure.'

She gave a pig-like snort of derision, which Mick sensed was personally directed at him rather than the inanity of his remark. He would need to take a different tack, he realised, if he were to find favour with Ma Tebbutt, charm was obviously not enough.

'To be honest with you,' he admitted, 'if I'd known the fellow had a knife I wouldn't have called him up at all. That poor lass would be down there now, raped and beaten to a pulp, I fear.'

He was rewarded with a cackle of delight, which pleased him. He knew how to play Ma Tebbutt now. She enjoyed a dose of the downright truth, and he'd be more than happy to oblige – within reason, of course.

'Cheers,' she said and raising her mug she drank.

Following her example, Mick took a healthy draught and the effect was instantaneous. He nearly gagged as the rough rum seared his throat and the fumes brought tears to his eyes. As his preference was ale, he rarely drank hard liquor.

'I could do with a chappie like you around here,' Ma said, the rum having no apparent effect upon her at all, 'a chappie who has his wits about him. Since Sid's gone, some of the men take advantage of my girls.' She downed the remainder of her liquor and poured herself another, Mick wordlessly waving aside the bottle she offered as he regained his breath.

'Len looks after the clients and Billy handles the bar,' Ma continued, 'and between them they can break up a fight if need be, but they can't stop one from starting, if you get my drift.' Another hefty swig of rum found its way down her throat – fresh company being a rarity, Ma was enjoying herself. 'Just between you and me,' she said confidentially, 'Len and Billy aren't all that bright. They can't sense trouble and deal with it the way Sid used to do. I need someone with wits and diplomacy. Someone who can pick the troublemakers, and steer the girls clear of the bastards before things get out of hand, because frankly some of the girls aren't all that bright either. Think you can handle that, Mick?'

Having recovered himself, Mick looked her straight in the eye. 'I know I can.'

'Good lad.'

They toasted each other and Mick downed the remainder of his rum with comparative ease. After weathering the initial assault, the second time around was much easier to take. He accepted Ma's offer of another tot, but rested the mug on the table while he took a bit of a breather.

'I'll only need you nights; the days are no trouble,' she said. Digging a wad of tobacco from the pouch she started tamping it into her clay pipe. 'But that'll give you time to sort yourself out, won't it? Get the lay of the land as it were, being newly arrived in town. Like I said, there'll be no money to speak of, but I'll sling you the odd bob now and then, and board and lodging'll be thrown in. Do we have a deal?'

'We most certainly do.' Mick was about to offer his hand, but Ma gave another salute and, realising it was the way she did things, he once again returned the gesture.

'It'll be good to have someone about the place with a bit of a brain,' Ma said, clenching the stem of her pipe between her teeth and lighting a taper from the flame of the oil lamp. 'God, but I've missed Sid.' She applied the flame to the tobacco and sucked away furiously, her face disappearing behind a thick, grey cloud. 'Sid was a smart bugger, sharp as a tack.'

'Sid was your husband, I take it?''

Ma was so obviously in the mood for a chat that Mick had no qualms about asking the question, and indeed Ma displayed no hesitation in answering.

'That's right,' she said, 'the best husband a woman could ask for and that's a fact. He died two years ago, more's the pity. Things have never been the same since.'

Ma felt one of her maudlin turns coming on, as was quite often the case when she thought of Sid, although in reality she was mourning the loss of her old life rather than the loss of her old comrade in arms. Everything had gone wrong from the moment Sid had died. She'd turned sixty that very same week. The girls had thrown her a birthday party to cheer her up and, drunk as a lord, she'd fallen down the stairs fracturing bones she'd never known she had. That had been the beginning of the end. She'd healed after a fashion, but arthritis had set in and, unable to leave her upstairs rooms, her weight had ballooned, compounding the problem immeasurably. These days she put everything down to the loss of Sid.

'He was a good man, my Sid,' she said, gazing nostalgically into her pewter mug as if it were a magic crystal ball that could transport her to the past.

'Was he a Londoner too?' Mick asked. 'Did you come out here together?'

Ma's eyes snapped up, sharp and shrewd and beady-blue. Was the boy playing games? Was he mocking her? No-one in Wapping would dare make such an enquiry. But when her eyes met his, she saw only innocence there.

'You really *are* new in town, aren't you?'

'I am indeed,' Mick replied. 'I arrived as a deckhand on the *Maid of Canton*; she docked just this afternoon.'

'Ah.' Content with his answer, Ma poured herself another tot of rum. The lad was sharp, there was no doubt about that – he couldn't have fought like he had without being canny as all hell – but he was new to the place and naive. He'd learn soon enough.

'Yes, me and Sid took passage from London ten years ago.' Sucking away at her pipe, she settled comfortably back in her chair. 'We'd heard about the prospects that lay awaiting enterprising folk here in Van Diemen's Land and we set out to start a new life for ourselves. We had such dreams, we did,' her smile was beatific, 'and they all come true, as you well can see. We bought up our very own pub, just the way we'd planned ...'

Ma's story was a tissue of lies. She'd been in Van Diemen's Land for nearly forty years, the first seven of which had been spent at Port Arthur. Sid, a Yorkshireman who'd been transported in 1810, had served a fourteen-year term and the two had met in Hobart Town shortly after his release. They'd never wed, but they'd hired themselves out as a respectable married couple, accepting employment as housekeeper and overseer on a wealthy cattle property to the north. For fifteen long years, they'd pooled every penny of their hard-earned cash, and when they'd finally returned to Hobart Town they'd purchased the Hunter's Rest, a rundown alehouse with cheap upstairs rooms, which they'd converted into a successful pub and brothel.

'This pub meant everything to Sid and me,' Ma said, puffing on her pipe and peering affectionately through the pall of smoke at the stone walls that surrounded her. 'This was where we'd planned to live out the twilight of our days. The Hunter's Rest meant the very world to us, it did.'

The latter part of her story at least was true. She and Sid may have fought like cat and dog, hating each other more often than not, but the Hunter's Rest had been their mutual salvation. The pub was the unbreakable bond they'd shared, for it represented their freedom.

'And now he's gone,' she said. 'Dead and gone, and nothing's the same.' She shook off her mood with a businesslike shrug. 'Ah well, that's life, isn't it? People come and people go, and you've got to get on with things, don't you? You can't just sit around and wait for it to be your turn.' She skolled her rum and set the mug down on the table with an air of finality. 'Not when you've got a pub to run.'

Ma no longer felt maudlin. She'd enjoyed telling her story. It had been some time since she'd had a stranger to tell it to. Everyone in Wapping had a story, which everyone else in Wapping pretended to believe: it was an understanding shared amongst neighbours. Some of the stories might even have been true, but no-one would ever know, because no-one would ever question them.

'I got paperwork to do,' she said, heaving herself up from the armchair. Mick jumped to his feet, aware he was being dismissed. 'You head off downstairs,' she instructed, 'and tell Len he's to set you up in the little room out the back –'

He tried to thank her, but Ma paid him no heed.

'Bring the chair over here,' she said as she lumbered her way to the desk in the corner.

He did as he was told, placing the chair for her, but she waved away any further attempt at assistance.

'And introduce yourself to Freddie in the kitchen.' She sat, glancing down at the clock on the desk. 'You've missed out on the pub dinner, the stew finishes at nine, but he'll find you something to tide you over.'

'I'm grateful to you, Ma. I'll be forever in your debt. What is there I can possibly say –?'

'Nothing.' She cut him off and glared up at him. 'If all you can come up with is your Irish shite, then say nothing at all.'

'It may well be Irish, but it isn't shite, I can assure you.' Mick stood his ground, deciding to call her bluff. She was starved for company and she liked him, he could tell. Surely she didn't expect him to behave like a lackey. In any event, he had no wish to be bullied, even for free board and lodging. 'It's the way I talk, Ma, so you'd better get used to it.'

Cheeky young bugger, she thought, but she didn't say anything. She waited for him to go on.

'You have welcomed me, a perfect stranger, into your home,' he said with a dignity that dared her to make fun of him, 'and I thank you from the very bottom of my heart.' He took her hand in his, and Ma didn't withdraw it as she would normally have done: she was too intrigued. 'May God bless and protect you always.' He bent and kissed her hand, then gently released it and stepped back. 'There now, I've said my piece. Thank you for hearing me out.'

Ma searched his eyes for the faintest sign of mischief, but she could find none. He appeared deadly serious. Was he playing a game or wasn't he? It was impossible to tell.

'Get yourself downstairs,' she said, 'and come back and see me tomorrow.'

'Right you are then.' He picked up his kitbag.

'Not before noon. I don't receive visitors until after noon. We'll have another chat then, and in the early evening I'll come downstairs and introduce you to the girls.'

Mick nodded and strode to the door, unaware of the honour being bestowed upon him – Ma's excursions downstairs were rare.

'Oh and Mick.' He halted, turning back as she called. 'Welcome to the Hunter's Rest. You're going to fit in real well here, I can tell.'

'I know I am, Ma.' He grinned as he slung the kitbag over his shoulder. 'I know I am.'

AN EXTRACT FROM 'A TIGER'S TALE',
A WORK IN PROGRESS BY HENRY FOTHERGILL

CIRCULAR HEAD, FAR NORTH-WEST TASMANIA, 1836

The horse stomped its front hoof and snorted nervously.

'Easy, old girl.' Jim leant forwards in the saddle and patted the mare's neck. He knew why the horse was nervous. There was a tiger in the vicinity. Or at least that's what people had taken to calling the animal, probably because of the stripes across its back and hind quarters. Jim thought it more like a dog.

Jim Daly was a boundary rider for the Van Diemen's Land Company, a man whose job it was to wander the company holdings checking and repairing the fences and shepherding stock when necessary. He'd been riding all day from Woolnorth, the company's far western sheep run, and now from up on the ridge, he could see way below the main company settlement at Circular Head on the rugged and remote north-west coast.

The mare snorted again, and again he calmed her. He never failed to be surprised by the reaction of European animals to the so-called tiger. It made them skittish and Jim couldn't for the life of him understand why. In all the years he'd been in the colony he'd never once seen a tiger display aggression, and yet his company overseers were

obsessed with killing the damn things. In fact the
company had a bounty on the animals of ten shillings per head. Why that was he would never know
and he'd made little attempt to find out. Jim was
not an inquisitive man by nature; he'd learnt as
a child to keep his nose out of other people's
business.

He looked down at the settlement of Circular
Head. Situated on a promontory about five miles
long and a mile wide, it extended finger-like in
a northerly direction into Bass Strait. From where
he sat on his horse it looked idyllic, but Jim
knew that in reality it was quite the opposite.
It was a festering wound of decaying huts and
shelters full of angry, unhappy men and women.
People who'd been promised an Eden by the damned
company, he thought, and who were now left to rot
in squalid, unsanitary conditions ruing the day
they'd ever signed their indenture papers.

Nothing, in Jim's opinion, had gone right from
day one. Apart from several hundred acres near the
settlement, the area chosen by the company was
rugged wilderness and dense forest that proved a
nightmare to clear for farming purposes. The wild
westerly winds known as the roaring forties seemed
almost constant and during the winter months
could destroy the soul. And then there was the
company's appalling disregard for the welfare of
the local native tribes. That had been the most
soul-destroying of all. Rather than come to the
aid of the Parpeloihener and Pennemukeer, the Van
Diemen's Land Company had ignored their plight.
They had turned a blind eye to the atrocious
behaviour of the sealers, men barely human, who
inhabited the local islands, kidnapping and raping
black women and, on one particularly gruesome day
in 1828, massacring thirty of the local black men
and throwing their bodies off a cliff.

Jim shook his head. The injustice of it all was
beyond imagining. He was about to nudge the mare

in the ribs when his eye caught a movement in the ferns to his left.

Tiger pups, he thought. It had to be tiger pups: she would have dropped them in her flight. Jim knew that female tigers carried their young in a pouch beneath their body, like kangaroos and wallabies, and that when they detected danger or felt threatened, they ejected their young and ran, hoping to lure the threat away.

He dismounted and walked the thirty-odd feet to the low-lying fern scrub where he discovered three pups, a male and two females. He picked them up one at a time, quickly dashed their brains out against a large rock and placed them in his saddle bag. Thirty shillings bounty was not a sum to be sneezed at and he was not about to pass up the chance of adding so considerably to his savings.

He closed the bag, hauled himself into the saddle and nudged his mare in the ribs. With a bit of luck, he thought as the horse made its way down the hillside, I'll be home before dark and a tot of rum would be a fine thing after the long journey back from the Woolnorth Run.

CHAPTER FOUR

In the months that followed, Mick O'Callaghan not only fitted in well, he became so much a part of the place that Ma Tebbutt wondered how she'd ever functioned without him. So did the girls: they quickly succumbed to the charm of their protector and it wasn't long before they were competing for his attention. Mick found himself with a veritable harem at his beck and call, should he have wished to take advantage of the fact.

Ma was aware of the situation. Upon the girls' regular visits to her quarters when she would chat to each, sort out any disputes, and one by one inspect them for any sign of disease, Mick O'Callaghan was invariably the topic of conversation. She finally decided it necessary to issue a warning. Not only to the girls.

'No sampling of the goods during working hours, Mick,' she said. 'If my girls want to give you a free poke, they can do it in their spare time. What they get up to then's none of my concern, but they're here to make money and I've a business to run.'

'You've no cause to fear, Ma. I've not been with one of your girls yet, either in or out of working hours, and I'm not about to avail myself of any offers. I've no intention of mixing business with pleasure.'

Mick was telling no lie, though his practise of self-control had not proved difficult for he'd hardly been celibate. He'd sated his lust any number of times in the little room out the back with pretty Molly Bates, the smithy's daughter who lived several blocks away in Sun Street.

Sensing the truth, Ma gave a satisfied nod. Her next comment, however, took him completely by surprise. 'You could do Evie a favour and give her a bit of a jig though. Make her feel good about herself, you know what I mean?'

'Eh?' He wasn't sure if he'd heard right. Ma wanted him to bed Evie? Why?

'The girl worships the very ground you walk on, Mick.'

The statement bore an element of exaggeration, for young Evie couldn't actually recall the night of her assault beyond the moment she'd scratched her attacker's face. She did, however, see Mick as something of a hero, a view based purely on hearsay, for Ma had circulated the story of the fight, embellishing the action with heroic detail in order that her girls should feel safe under the protection of one as deceptive in appearance as the handsome young Irishman.

'Brawn is no match for brains,' she'd said to them collectively on the evening she'd come downstairs to introduce Mick. 'Mick here will look after you like he did Evie: that's his job. But if you're smart and pay heed to him, he'll steer you clear of the troublemakers and you won't find yourself in the predicament Evie did. That way you'll get to keep your front teeth,' she'd added meaningfully, 'do you follow me?' The girls most certainly had, and they'd nodded obediently.

'It's a matter of pride, Mick,' Ma now said, sensing his bewilderment. 'Evie was the most popular girl I had, the youngest and the prettiest, and now she's stuck in the kitchen.' His confusion still evident, she went on patiently to explain. 'It's her teeth, you see. Teeth are one of the main

things that'll put a whore out of business – all the other stuff
can be hid behind paint and rouge.' Ma surreptitiously ran
her tongue over her own teeth. Yellow as they were they
were still there for the most part and she was proud of the
fact. 'The loss of teeth's a sign of age,' she said, 'and that's
a hard cop when you're nineteen like Evie.'

Ma poured herself her first tot of rum for the day. It was
late afternoon and Mick always called upstairs for a chat
before the evening trade picked up.

'She's a hard worker, Evie, which is why I've kept her
on as a full-time domestic, but that's quite a step down the
ladder for one who's been as popular as she was.' Ma took
a swig of rum before repeating her proposition. 'So what
if, out of all the girls, Evie was the one to find favour with
you – just for one night, mind – you being her hero and all.
Well for starters, it might keep the others off your back,
mightn't it? And it'd give Evie "face", like the Chinee say.
She'd be able to hold her head high with the girls. She
could go back to the kitchen and bugger the lot of them.
What do you say?'

'I say you're not as tough as you pretend you are, Ma.'

A number of things suddenly made sense to Mick. He'd
noticed several women about the place, women scarred
or minus teeth, and he now realised they were whores
no longer able to ply their trade. They didn't live on the
premises, but Ma provided them with part-time employment as laundrywomen, kitchen helpers and cleaners,
alongside her own girls who were expected to lend a hand
with menial tasks during the day.

'In fact, it's my guess you've a real soft heart underneath,' he said.

'Keep your Irish shite to yourself,' Ma replied not
unpleasantly. 'Will you look after Evie or won't you?'

'In or out of working hours?'

'Whenever there are most eyes upon you I'd say. Working
hours, but a slow night when there's little custom.'

'What's wrong with tonight then? Tuesday's never busy.'

'I'll look forward to hearing the gossip,' she said with a smile. 'The girls won't be able to resist.'

Ma was right. The gossip reached her ears within less than twenty-four hours. Peg and Maeve couldn't wait to spread the news. They paid her a visit shortly after midday.

'Evie? Really?' Ma raised a quizzical eyebrow. 'My, my, how surprising.'

'He was feeling sorry for her,' Peg said, not spitefully but put out nonetheless: she'd had her sights set on the Irishman. 'Well we all feel sorry for Evie,' she hastily added, 'poor thing. Mick took pity on her, he did.'

'That's not the way it looked to me.' Maeve was quick to disagree. 'He couldn't keep his hands off her. Lusting after her something fierce, he was, Ma.' She gave a saucy wink. 'Peg's just jealous is all.'

'I am not, Maevy. You take that back. You take that back right now. I am not jealous, not one bit, I'm not!'

Maeve laughed. Peg's fierce protestation spoke for itself. 'And it didn't sound like pity the way Evie told it neither,' she said. 'They had a right good time together, Ma. That's what she told me.'

'And you can't begrudge her a good time, given what she's been through.'

Ma intervened before Maeve could twist the knife any further. Maeve and Peg liked to egg each other on. Two of her top girls, they'd been at the Hunter's Rest longer than the others and, both Irish, they were close friends but fiercely competitive. Despite their advancing years, for they were now thirty, they were popular with the men, Maeve's provocative dancing and Peg's voluminous breasts keeping them in regular demand.

But neither had come anywhere near Evie for prettiness, Ma thought with a tinge of regret. Evie had been pretty and gutsy and fun, and it was a bleeding shame she was washed up so young.

Ma would never have openly acknowledged the fact, but she'd always had a soft spot for Evie. Evie was a fellow Londoner and she reminded Ma just a little of herself as a girl.

'Oh, we don't begrudge Evie, Ma.' Worried that Ma's sudden pensiveness might signal disapproval, Maeve was quick to protest. 'We don't begrudge her at all,' she said and Peg nodded in vigorous agreement. 'We're really sorry about what happened to Evie.'

'I know you are, love, I know. You're a good girl, Maeve. You too, Peg,' she added (Ma never displayed favouritism). 'Now off you run, and leave me to my paper-work.' Like dutiful children they kissed her on the cheek and departed. They *are* good women at heart, Ma thought. Despite the competition Evie's youth and prettiness had presented, neither Maeve nor Peg took any pleasure in the girl's predicament.

The bedding of Evie changed a number of things, Mick discovered.

Although he and Ma never spoke of the subject again, he sensed a subtle shift in their relationship. An unspoken bond of something approaching fondness seemed to have developed between them. Far more noticeable though, was the change in the girls. Overnight, they appeared to accept the fact that he was unavailable. Even Peg stopped vying for his attention. Ma was right, Mick thought. Bedding Evie had been the way to keep the others off his back. And as for Evie herself, far from posing the problem he'd thought she might, Evie's response from the outset had been remarkably healthy.

'Why'd you pick me?' she'd asked afterwards as they'd lain, bodies entwined, on his narrow cot. 'Why'd you pick me over the other girls?' She'd been extraordinarily forthright. Bold even. 'It was because you felt sorry for me, wasn't it?' Confronting though her manner was, she'd shielded her mouth with her hand as she'd queried him, and Mick had found the gesture strangely affecting.

'No,' he'd said, 'it wasn't because I felt sorry for you at all. It was because you're the only one I'm allowed to sleep with.' His reply had taken her by surprise. 'Ma told me I'm not allowed to sample the goods.'

Evie had let out an involuntary hoot of laughter, forgetting for a moment to shield her mouth, then, registering her exposure, quickly returning her hand. 'I'm no longer the goods all right,' she'd replied without rancour, 'blimey, I'm out of the race altogether.'

'Oh, I wouldn't be too sure about that, my lovely.' He'd run his hand over the perfect twin curves of her breasts. 'You're a fine runner-up.'

She'd laughed again and, rolling on her side, she'd ducked her head into his shoulder to avert his gaze as her fingers reached for him. 'Well, if you're ever after damaged goods, Mick, you know where to come.'

'I do indeed,' he'd said.

As a result of that night, a relationship had developed between Mick and Evie: a relationship not of lovers, but of friends. Perhaps even something akin to siblings, for Mick felt protective of Evie, tough though she was, and Evie looked up to him as she would a big brother. She delighted in the knowledge that she was his favourite among the girls, even though she was relegated to the kitchen. And she was not offended when, as time passed, he didn't take her up on her offer. She hadn't really expected him to. Men didn't pay for toothless whores, so why should Mick choose to bed a girl who had no front teeth, even for free?

The reason Mick didn't take Evie up on her offer was not because of her lack of front teeth. Nor was it because of any compunction he might have on moral grounds given his brotherly feelings for her. It wasn't even because of pretty Molly Bates, the smithy's daughter, who regularly hung around the pub in the hope of an invitation to the little back room. Molly, too, was for the most part ignored. Mick's life had undergone a radical change, and it had all started with Eileen.

Mick met Eileen on a bleak and wintry August afternoon. It was a Saturday and he'd popped out to buy a treat for Ma from the little baker's shop in Bathurst Street. He would purchase a bag of scones, freshly baked and piping hot from the oven, and she would eat them while they were still warm with great dollops of butter, and swigs of rum on the side. After eight months at the pub, Mick was attune to Ma's every whim. Indeed, his place in her affections was by now so well established he even referred to her as his 'special girl', a term she dismissed as 'Irish shite', but which she clearly enjoyed. Sometimes he catered to her fancies simply to keep on side with her, but at other times he genuinely wished to please. Today, the latter was the case, for Ma's chest was unsettled by the dank winter conditions and she was suffering from a severe bout of bronchitis.

He walked up Campbell Street. Ahead reared the forbidding sandstone walls of the gaol, home to public hangings in the past, and to the vilest of acts man could perpetrate upon his fellows. God alone knew what still went on behind those walls, Mick thought. He never once passed the place without giving thanks. The very sight of it is enough to keep a man on the straight and narrow, he told himself. There but for the grace of God ...

He'd come out hatless and, as he turned into Bathurst Street, he pulled the collar of his heavy woollen coat up around his ears. An icy wind seemed to sweep down directly from the mountain, which loomed in the distance, its peak shrouded in mist. There'll be a right blizzard blowing up there, he thought, and he stood for a moment gazing up at Mount Wellington. Up there, a man wouldn't stand a chance: he'd be lost to the elements, dead as a maggot and no-one would know. It's easy to feel safe down here in the busy, self-important heart of Hobart Town, he thought, but the mountain makes a mockery of us all. It just stood there laughing at the whole of mankind, a timeless reminder of the fragility of human existence.

Mick actually found the danger of Van Diemen's Land thrilling. It was rather like being on the run from the law. You never knew what fresh threat lay around the corner.

He ducked his head from the biting wind that was making his eyes water, and digging his hands deep into his coat pockets, for he'd also come out minus gloves, he crossed Argyle Street and headed straight for the baker's shop.

He was just several paces away when the door opened and he collided with a woman on her way out.

'Oh, I do beg your pardon,' he said automatically. Given to gentlemanly behaviour in the company of women, Mick would have doffed his hat had he had one and then, eager for the warmth of the shop, he'd have excused himself and edged his way past. On this occasion, however, he didn't. He remained exactly where he was, for this was a woman who demanded attention. She was tall. In her buttoned boots she stood only an inch or so shorter than he and, despite her heavy bell-shaped skirt and matching velvet pelisse, he could tell at a glance that she had a fine figure, for the pelisse, while forming a full cloak at the back, was stylishly cut in at the front to reveal a slim waist. Her features were fine and her milk-white skin flawless, but it was her eyes that most captured his attention. Her eyes were animal-like, green or hazel, it was impossible to tell. And beneath the fashionable poke bonnet was a glimpse of hair as red and vibrant as a fox's brush. This is a woman of style and breeding no doubt, Mick thought, but this is also a wild one.

With no hat to doff, he placed a hand to his breast and gave a quick formal bow. 'So clumsy of me,' he said. 'Do please accept my sincerest apology.'

She appeared amused. 'Your sincerest apology is accepted. But it's just as well I didn't drop my scones now, isn't it?' she said, holding up the bag she was carrying. 'I'd never have forgiven you for that.'

Her voice was pleasing in timbre, but to Mick it was not the voice of a gentlewoman. She was clearly from Dublin; and although the lilt of her accent might have seemed well bred to some, as indeed might his own for he'd worked hard on eradicating the rough edges, he was sure he could detect a remaining hint of the backstreets. He curbed the desire to laugh in triumph, for if such was the case, he was surely on a winner.

'You're a long way from home,' he said with the cheekiest of grins.

'As are you,' she replied coolly, and she stepped to one side about to make her way past him.

Her bearing was so haughty and her attitude so dismissive that Mick wondered whether perhaps he may have been wrong, but he refused to be deterred. He held up his hand and automatically she halted.

'But surely ...' he said, his face registering a show of the deepest concern '... surely you're not travelling unaccompanied.' He looked about at the passing traffic. He could see no carriage or trap waiting by the curbside: although his concern may have been feigned, he was genuinely surprised that a young woman so attired, albeit from a background possibly similar to his own, should be walking the streets without a companion.

'I am indeed.' Her tone patently said *and what of that?*

She was young, around twenty he guessed. As the hands that extended from the draped sleeves of the pelisse were naturally clad in gloves he was unable to see her ring finger, but she seemed far too free-spirited to be married.

'Do you not consider walking alone a little risky, Miss ...?'

The blatant question hung awkwardly in the air as she stared back at him, refusing to offer any name in response. Then, 'Not at all,' she said briskly, 'I very much enjoy an invigorating walk without the interference of conversation from another.'

'I promise then that I'll not utter a word, if you will allow me the honour of escorting you safely to wherever it is you are bound.' His hand on his chest, he gave another formal bow. 'Michael Patrick O'Callaghan at your service.'

The corners of her mouth curled into a smile that could have been one of either amusement or mockery as her animal eyes flickered over him, taking in every aspect of his appearance. Mick sensed she liked what she saw in the man, but not what she saw in the cut of his cloth, and he cursed himself for having come out so poorly attired. His woollen coat was of good quality, but it was not the latest fashion. And as for being hatless and gloveless – well, that was unforgiveable if one wished to make an impression. But then of course he hadn't known in popping out for Ma's scones that he would be called upon to make an impression.

'Thank you for your concern, Mr O'Callaghan,' she said, 'but I am in no need of an escort.'

'I'm afraid I beg to differ there. In fact I must insist –'

'No, Mr O'Callaghan, *I* must insist.' Her steady, fox-like gaze now signalled a clear warning, although her tone remained pleasant enough. 'I must insist that you allow me the pleasure of my own company. I thank you once again for your offer, and I bid you good day.'

With that, she sailed off down the street, leaving Mick to once again curse his ill luck. She'd found him attractive, he was sure, and had he been wearing his new waisted coat with satin-faced lapels and quilted lining, and his top hat and gloves, he would undoubtedly have passed scrutiny.

Oh well, he thought, shrugging off his disappointment as he entered the baker's shop, Hobart Town isn't exactly London – I'm bound to bump into her again. In fact, he was surprised he hadn't encountered her before – she was hardly one to go unnoticed. Perhaps she was a new arrival. He would conduct some enquiries, he decided, and maybe orchestrate an accidental encounter when he would be better prepared to make a favourable impression.

Upon ordering his dozen scones, he was told by the baker, a dour Scot, that he'd have to wait if he wanted them fresh from the oven.

'The lass who just left, she bought the last lot. I've another batch baking, but they'll be a good half-hour.'

'Who is she, do you know? Where does she come from?'

'What's that?'

'The young woman who just left, who is she?'

'No idea.' The man's reply actually said, *Are you daft, man? Do you think I'd tell you if I did?*

Mick realised he'd been foolish to ask. 'I'll be back in half an hour,' he said.

He took a shortcut through the laneways to the corner of Campbell and Liverpool where he sat quietly at the bar of the Union Hotel, nursing a tankard of ale. His encounter with the girl had set him thinking. The life he'd been leading of late had been enjoyable but costly and his stash was running low. He'd known that he would soon need to refurbish the coffers, but until now he'd given little thought to the problem of how he should actually go about it. He'd vowed not to return to a life of crime, but the alternative option held little attraction. With no skills to offer a prospective employer, the only jobs he could seek would be menial, the prospect of which he found thoroughly irksome. Which way was he to turn? He could no longer rely upon gambling to see him through: he'd had an unlucky run with the cards lately.

For the past several months, Mick O'Callaghan had been leading a lifestyle well beyond the means of a resident from the dockside suburb of Wapping. On his one night off a week, which Ma was happy to vary so long as it wasn't a Friday or Saturday when the pub was at its busiest, he was invariably to be found at the card tables of Farrington's Exclusive Gentlemen's Club in Molle Street, on the western, more salubrious side of town. Many an afternoon too would see a visit to his tailor or hatter or boot maker, each of whom presumed they were catering to a member of the gentry, or if they didn't they certainly made a good pretence that they did, which Mick loved almost as much as he loved mingling with the gentry at his club.

Farrington's was one of a number of gentlemen's clubs in Hobart Town, but it was certainly not 'exclusive' as it purported to be. Credentials were not required, and among its patrons there were possibly many poseurs like Mick. However, as questions were never asked by the fashionably attired men gathered to drink and smoke cigars and wager heavily at the card tables, the presumption was they were all gentlemen of sorts.

Mick had become quite a popular figure at Farrington's, with his quick wit and personable nature, but just the previous week he'd varied his routine, forgoing the club to attend a performance at the Royal Victoria Theatre. Established by the well-known entrepreneur and founder of the Cascade Brewery, Peter Degraves, the Royal Victoria Theatre was the cultural pride and joy of Hobart Town, and Mick had viewed his outing as a further opportunity to observe and learn while he mingled with the upper classes. Having never been to a real theatre before, he had naturally presumed that, unlike the bawdy burlesque halls back home, such a venue would be the exclusive domain of the gentry as was the case in the west end of London. He'd arrived top-hatted and suitably attired prepared to socialise with the best of them, and he'd bought his ticket for a whole two shillings. There'd been four-shilling and even six-shilling tickets on sale for seats in the upstairs gallery and the boxes, but that had seemed an altogether ridiculous amount to fork out just to see a play!

I certainly learnt a lesson that night, he thought as he gazed out the window of the Union Hotel at the people scurrying by, fleeing the cold. He remembered how he'd stood among the riffraff in the pit – rough men swilling from tankards and spitting gobs of phlegm, sailors and tarts virtually rutting before his eyes – and how he'd stared up at the gentry in their boxes, the ladies all flounces and feathers, the men in tailored suits of the finest weave. Never had there been a clearer demarcation of commoners and privileged, he'd thought. He'd been bewildered that commoners should see fit to pay a whole two shillings for such an experience though. He couldn't even remember the play himself. It was presumably funny, judging by the hoots from the surrounding buffoons, but he couldn't be sure for he'd left barely ten minutes after it had started. He couldn't wait to get out of the place before someone spat on his brand new satin-lapelled coat with quilted lining.

Mick took a sip of his barely touched ale. He would go back to the theatre one day. Perhaps, if he found the experience enjoyable, he may even become a regular theatre-goer. But never again would he stand in the pit with the hoi polloi. He would sit in a box like the gentleman God intended him to be. The only problem with such a plan of course, was money.

It was time to return to the baker's shop. He stood, leaving his tankard nearly full on the bar: he hadn't wanted a drink anyway. Money had been on his mind quite a bit since that night in the theatre, he realised, but it had taken the girl with the fox eyes to make him aware of the necessity for action, and the sooner the better. Although what particular action he should take remained at this stage a mystery.

After collecting the scones, he hurried back to the Hunter's Rest as fast as he could, intending to deliver them still piping hot to Ma. He'd had the baker wrap them in several extra sheets of brown paper.

Bounding up the stairs three at a time, he gave his special knock on her door – two sharp taps, a pause, and then another two sharp taps.

'Come in, Mick,' she called in a loud bronchial croak that was followed by a hacking cough delivered with gusto. Ma never suffered in silence.

'Prepare yourself, Ma!' He made a showy entrance, taking care at the same time to close the door firmly behind him, as was the rule. For discretionary purposes when clients passed by, and also as a mark of respect for Ma herself, the door to her quarters remained closed at all times. 'A special treat for my special girl,' he said crossing to where she sat in her customary armchair beside the table, the corner desk chair pulled up beside it, presumably awaiting his arrival. She wore a thick woollen shawl, despite the fact that the room was warm and close, a fire crackling in the small grate beneath the mantelpiece.

'Hot scones,' he announced and, producing the paper-wrapped bundle with a flourish, he was about to place it ceremoniously in front of her when he noticed the plate on the table. It bore two lone scones, an abundance of crumbs, and beside it sat a half-finished bowl of butter.

'You're a bit late, I'm afraid,' Ma said.

It was only then Mick saw the girl from the bakery. She'd been standing motionless by the window, staring down at the lane below, and now she turned. She no longer wore the poke bonnet, which dangled abandoned over the arm of a chair, and her flaming red hair hung in careless disarray to her shoulders. She'd divested herself also of the velvet pelisse, and had even removed her gloves, which Mick found most unusual, for he'd noted that ladies kept their gloves on at all times. The blouse she wore was high-necked, long-sleeved and demure in style, but the way it displayed her shape, tucking neatly in at the waist as it did, only seemed to accentuate the promise of what lay beneath the voluminous skirt. It's as if she's half naked, Mick thought. He was fascinated not only by the woman's magnificence, but by the sheer impropriety of her state of undress. Fascinating too was her audacity, for she showed not a hint of embarrassment, but stood coolly observing him with her fox-like eyes.

Ma registered the direction of his gaze. 'Oh, you haven't met Red, have you, Mick?' she said. Then she called over her shoulder to the window, 'Red this is –'

'Michael Patrick O'Callaghan,' the woman said. 'Yes, Ma, we've met.' She crossed to join them, her hand extended in the most forthright manner. 'Good to see you again, Mr O'Callaghan.'

They shook like men, and Mick was aware of the silky softness of her skin. A gentleman would rarely get the chance to shake hands with a gloveless lady, he knew. But then this was no lady. He'd been right.

'Mick,' he said. 'Mick'll do just fine.'

'Eileen Hilditch.' She looked down at Ma and the two shared a smile, 'but as you're a friend of Ma's you can call me Red.'

'Thank you, I'm honoured.' Mick wondered briefly what Red's connection with Ma could be. She was not the gentlewoman her appearance had first suggested, certainly, but she wasn't a working girl. Eileen Hilditch was way out of Ma's class.

'Sorry I bested you with the scones,' she said. 'I wasn't to know.'

'Of course you weren't.'

'That's funny, that is.' Ma gave a cackle of laughter. 'Red hasn't been to see me for the best part of a year, but on the very day she chooses, you both turn up with scones. I think that's real funny.' She gave another cackle that quickly turned into a cough, which went on for some time, after which she produced a hefty gob of material that she unashamedly hawked into a cloth on the table.

Mick and Eileen said nothing throughout the performance, but stood boldly surveying each other, neither prepared to be the first to look away.

Ma finally drew breath and, glancing up, her shrewd eyes darted from one to the other.

'Put your clothes on, Red,' she said, 'you'll catch your death in that blouse.'

Red obeyed in an instant. Crossing wordlessly to the chair by the window, she took up the velvet pelisse and eased it over her shoulders, gently feeding her right arm, then her left, through the drapes of its sleeves, playing out every step with slow grace. She fastened the cloak's collar and did up each of its front buttons with meticulous care, and her eyes remained on Mick all the while. Then picking up her right glove, she started teasing her fingers into it, delicately, sensuously.

'I must be going now anyway,' she said, her words addressed to Ma, but her eyes still on Mick.

He stared back, mesmerised. It's like watching a woman strip in reverse, he thought. Every action was extraordinarily provocative. Had she been this seductive taking *off* her outer garments? he wondered.

Red had *not* been seductive in divesting herself of her outer garments, but she had indeed stripped with a purpose. In fact she'd put on quite a show for Ma as the old lady had scoffed back her scones.

'So what do you think, Ma? Am I the goods or am I not?' she'd said and she'd twirled about the room, pulling off her gloves and caressing her garments with her bare fingers. 'Feel that for velvet.' She'd hoisted her skirt up over Ma's lap, heedless of the crumbs which nestled there. 'And how's that for petticoats, now?' she'd said ruffling the many layers of ruched cotton beneath.

'That's fine fabric all right,' Ma had said, stroking the velvet reverently with the back of her hand, careful not to touch it with her buttery fingers, 'that's fine fabric indeed.'

'And the bonnet, Ma, just look at the bonnet.' Releasing the ribbon at her throat, Red had pulled off the bonnet. Her hair tumbled to her shoulders, for the bonnet was all that had been holding it in place – she never cared much for combs and pins. 'Take a peek at the lace in that brim.'

'Easy girl, easy,' Ma had scolded as the bonnet was plonked on her lap. 'A thing like this should be treated with care,' and she'd wiped her hands with the cloth on the table before touching the fine ruffled lace.

But Red wasn't listening. Hauling off her cloak, she'd thrown it around Ma's shoulders. 'And try that for warmth,' she'd said, 'that'll beat your old shawl any day.'

'My old shawl will do me just fine, thank you, Eileen,' Ma had said, her tone now one of distinct reprimand, and she'd taken the pelisse from her shoulders, folding it carefully. She never addressed Red as Eileen unless they were alone, and then only when she had a point to make, which she now did. 'You show some respect for fine clothes like these, girl,' she'd said, 'they're worth a tidy sum, and you never know when a tidy sum might come in right handy. Now you put them over there on the chair by the window before they get covered in butter.'

'Oh for heaven's sake, Ma.' Red's shrug had been dismissive, 'I can get clothes like these whenever I want –'

'There'll come a day when you won't be able to say that, Eileen,' Ma had said ominously. 'The good times don't last forever. Now put your fine clothes on that chair.'

Red had done as she was told, albeit a little sulkily, but she'd quickly perked up when Ma had poured them both a rum and they'd settled down to talk.

'Right,' Ma had said, starting on her fourth scone. 'How's it all going at Trafalgar? You tell me everything you've been up to, Red.' And Red had.

Both gloves were now in place, and Mick continued to watch spellbound as Red raised her arms and slowly drew her mane of hair back from her face. It was an action so uninhibited he felt he was peeping through a keyhole observing a lady at her toilette.

Then in one swift movement she deftly twisted her tresses into a knot at the back of her head and turned to Ma. 'I won't leave it so long between visits next time, Ma,' she said. The sensual act for his benefit was obviously over. 'I can't promise when I'll be back though.' Pinioning her hair with one hand, she picked up her bonnet with the other. 'I don't get out the way I used to these days.'

'So I've gathered,' Ma replied drily, and Mick could only wonder at her meaning.

Having anchored her hair with the bonnet, Red tended to the ribbon and, within only seconds (despite the impediment of gloves) a perfect bow rested at the left side of her throat. 'It's been grand meeting you, Mick,' she said with a smile, 'particularly grand, you being a fellow countryman and all.'

She offered her hand and they shook.

'Yes,' Mick said, 'it's been grand indeed.' He was lost in admiration. With not a hair out of place she was once again the impeccably attired young lady he'd bumped into at the baker's shop.

'I'll see you when I can, Ma.' Red kissed Ma on the cheek and, with a wave to them both, she was gone.

'My, my, but she's a flirt, that one.' Ma stared affectionately at the closed door before turning to flash him a yellow-toothed grin. 'She had you going there, didn't she, Mick? You fancied her something rotten and don't you try denying it.'

'Oh I certainly did, Ma, I'll not deny it for a moment.'

'Mind you,' Ma said in all fairness, for Mick's honesty won her over every time, 'Red took a bit of a fancy to you too, I could sense it.'

'Did she really, Ma?' Of course she did, Mick thought. God in heaven, a blind man could have sensed it. 'Do you think so indeed?'

'Oh yes, she wouldn't have flirted with you like she did if she hadn't found you fanciable. She wouldn't have wasted her energy.'

'So you think I'm in with a chance, do you Ma?'

His smile was roguishly confident and his question light-hearted, but Ma recognised the underlying seriousness of his intent, and the answer that came back at Mick was totally unexpected.

'Not for one minute. You don't stand a chance in hell.' Knowing her brutal response had come as something of a surprise, Ma patted the chair beside her. She'd wanted to have a personal chat with him for some time, but she'd been wondering how to broach the subject. Red now seemed to have provided the perfect opening. 'Sit down, lad,' she said. 'Come on, sit down and have a drink with me.'

He sat and she poured him a tot of rum in the mug Red had used then topped up her own.

'You won't score a win with that one, Mick,' she said, 'you won't even score a place. You need money for a woman like Red. She's way out of your price range.'

Mick didn't like being talked down to by the likes of Ma Tebbutt. 'There are other ways to win women, Ma,' he scoffed. 'I've not needed money to find favour in the past, and I'm not about to start paying for the privilege now.'

Ma, in turn, did not like being scorned. Oh, she thought, so I've punctured his ego – poor young buck's pride is wounded – well, too fucking bad. 'I'm telling you here and now, boy, if you don't have the money, you won't make it with that one, so don't bother bleedin' well trying.' She knocked back her rum in one hit. Damn his hide, she'd only been offering a word of advice.

Realising that his pride had got the better of him and

that the old woman actually did know what she was talking about, Mick tried to make amends.

'Will you tell me why then, Ma?' He appealed to her with all the boyish earnestness he knew charmed her, but with a genuine desire for the answer 'Will you tell me why, if Red had no interest in me, why on God's earth she flirted with me in such a way?'

'She was having a bit of fun, that's all.' Ma's tone was still short: she wasn't about to be mollified that easily. 'There's business and there's fun. You're no good for business, so she flirted with you for fun. But Red doesn't fuck for fun, I can tell you that here and now.'

Mick was taken aback. 'So she's a whore then?' He didn't know why, but the notion came as a mild shock. He'd gathered that Red was no gentlewoman, but he'd thought perhaps she was a wealthy man's mistress or ... Or what? he wondered. Upon reflection, he realised he hadn't actually thought what Red might be at all: he'd been far too intrigued by the woman herself.

'Course she is.' Ma's attitude softened. Sharp as young Mick was, he could be downright naive at times. 'Not your run-of-the-mill whore though. Our Red's for select use only. She works at Trafalgar.'

Of course, Mick thought. That explained everything. Trafalgar would be right up Red's alley.

'Trafalgar' was an impressive two-storey stone townhouse in Barrack Street. Built as a personal residence for a rich English merchant who had since returned to Britain, it had been purchased by a fast-thinking entrepreneur who had retained the name of the building but not its residential status. Now a haven for the wealthy, Trafalgar was a gentlemen's club where the term 'exclusive' had genuine meaning. Catering to the rich and powerful, the club boasted a fine bill of fare, a plush lounge and bar, and the requisite green-felt gaming room. Indeed, Trafalgar offered everything an elite gentlemen's club was expected to offer, and something else besides. The exotic hostesses who entertained the members as they dined and drank were known for their beauty and also for the fact they could be bought. Should a club member wish, he could, for a substantial price, be provided with further entertainment upstairs in one of the well-appointed apartments, and he could do so without fear of damage to his reputation, for at Trafalgar 'exclusive' was another term for discreet.

'I take it you've *heard* of Trafalgar.' Ma's remark was heavily laced with irony, but Mick didn't pick up on it.

'Yes, I've heard the place mentioned.' Of course he had. Several of the men at Farrington's spoke of little else. They'd been trying to inveigle him into joining them for some time, but he was not interested in the offerings of a high-class bordello, and the club as a facility was beyond his means.

'I thought you might,' Ma said, 'given the circles you move in.'

This time he registered an innuendo, although its meaning escaped him.

'I see a lot from up here, Mick.' Ma gestured to the window that looked down over the laneway. 'I see you leaving all decked out in your finery. And what I don't see the girls report to me anyway. I see and hear everything. Nothing escapes me. I know what you're about, lad.'

'Oh, is that so? And what is it I'm about?' There had been no accusation in Ma's words, but Mick felt a surge of anger. How dare they spy on him? How dare they talk about him behind his back? 'I like fine clothes, is that a crime? I've never hidden the fact. And what exactly is wrong with fine clothes, may I ask?'

'Nothing, nothing at all; no-one's saying there is. The girls love seeing you in your fancy clobber. They think you look downright handsome and they can't wait to tell me. Don't get yourself wound up over nothing, Mick.' She picked up his mug and held it out as a peace offering.

'Here, have a swig of rum and calm down; no offence was intended.'

Mick knew he'd overreacted, and he felt rather stupid. The girls always gave him whistles and cat-calls when they saw him dressed up – of course they would talk about him to Ma. He accepted the mug and sipped his rum.

'There's a good lad.' Ma poured herself another. 'It's not the clothes, Mick, it's what they signify.' She paused long enough to take a swig. 'I'm going to give you a word of advice, whether you like it or not, but I'd appreciate you listening because it's well meant.'

Mick nodded, attentive but wary: he was not seeking advice.

'I don't know where you get the money for your fancy clobber –' He was about to protest, but she would have no interruption. 'Hear me out. I don't know and I don't care. I'm not accusing you of any wrongdoing. Not yet anyway. But you lust for the good life, and that can be dangerous. You're going to have to choose a path soon, lad, and I wouldn't like to see you choose the wrong one.'

He quelled another surge of irritation. She was telling him everything he already knew, and what business was it of hers anyway?

'I have connections, you know. If you'd like, I could point you in the right direction.'

'And exactly what direction would that be, Ma?' Labouring for a pittance on the wharves, Mick wondered, or sweating it out day and night in a factory, or working in the stinking blood and guts of a tannery? Those would be Ma's connections.

She ignored his obvious cynicism. 'There's a man by the name of Powell,' she said, 'Jefferson Brindsley Powell. American he is, and a right gent too. He come out here as a political prisoner – a *political* prisoner, mind.' Ma clearly deemed this fact to be of huge significance. 'As a youngster he got caught up in the colonial wars,' she went on to explain. 'He joined the French-Canadians in their fight for liberation from British rule. Called themselves the Patriot Movement they did, and a whole mob of them was rounded up and shipped down here in 1840. Close to a hundred there were in all, Canadians and their American sympathisers like young Jefferson. I remember the talk that went on at the time. None of us thought it was right. It didn't seem fair to be sentenced to life for something you believed in. It didn't seem fair at all.'

Ma had contradicted herself yet again, but as always Mick didn't point out the time discrepancy. Whether she'd forgotten her original story that she and Sid had taken passage from England ten years previously, or whether she simply couldn't be bothered keeping track of the details, was immaterial anyway. He'd long since discovered her story was pure fiction, as were the stories he'd heard from so many others.

Although he was in no mood for the advice Ma was plainly eager to give, Mick found he was interested in spite of himself. Ma never spoke of a convict's background. No-one in Wapping did. Yet it appeared a political prisoner was a different matter altogether. At least it would seem so to Ma, for she was determined to tell him all about Jefferson Brindsley Powell.

'Jefferson was granted a ticket of leave in '44 and that's when me and Sid met up with him. He was only a lad in his twenties, not much older than you, but he was having trouble fitting in and getting a job. In those days, people never quite knew how to handle political prisoners, least they didn't around these parts.' Ma lowered her voice conspiratorially as if, through the pub's impregnable stone walls, neighbours might be listening. 'They still don't, to tell you the truth. Political prisoners aren't the same as convicts, you know what I mean? A lot of locals feel uncomfortable around those who have a political background. They've done nothing criminal, see?'

It was a further giveaway that intrigued Mick, the virtual admission that Wapping was inhabited principally by ex-convicts. Ma's really opening up today, he thought.

'Anyway, Sid and me took a shine to young Jefferson,' Ma went on. 'And why wouldn't we, I ask you. A right young gent he was, and by all accounts still is, although I haven't seen him for some time. We set him on his feet, we did. Sid talked old Hamish McLagan into giving the lad a job as a waterman with the McLagan Road Transport Company's ferry-boat service.'

Ma leant happily back in her armchair, mug clasped to ample bosom. 'My Sid did the right thing by the lad there,' she said with pride, 'for the McLagans was the making of young Jefferson Powell. It wasn't long before they took him into their home – he became practically one of the family, he did. Only a year or so later he was granted a full pardon and he could have gone back to America if he'd wanted to. But he didn't. By then he'd decided his true home was here. Right here in Hobart Town.' Her tale concluded, she downed a triumphant swig of rum.

'What are you're getting at, Ma?' Sensing advice imminent Mick's interest had waned. 'You think this Jefferson Powell could offer me a job, that's it, isn't it?'

'Yes, that's it exactly.'

'As a waterman on a ferry boat?' He did little to disguise the sneer in his voice.

'What's so bad about that?' she demanded. 'You've got to start somewhere and you have the wherewithal: you're an experienced sailor. What else have you got to offer?' She could see that her reasoning, sound though it may have been, was making no impression. 'I'm telling you, Mick, if you want an honest job with the prospect of advancement, you need look no further than Jefferson Powell.' She plonked her mug on the table and leant in with fierce intent. 'He's going up in the world Jefferson is, and you want to know why?'

'Why?' He didn't even bother feigning interest. She'd tell him anyway.

'Because he married the old man's daughter, that's why. And Hamish died last year. McLagan left everything to Jefferson Powell, lock stock and bleedin' barrel.'

'Well, well, well.' Mick smiled. Now that really *was* a matter of interest. 'How very clever of Jefferson Powell.'

'I've heard tell he's expanding the business,' Ma said, glad that she'd finally made an impact, 'and a bright young man like you could move up the ranks real fast. That is if you had a mind to make something of yourself.'

Mick wondered why Ma was showing such concern for his future.

'You don't have to be born to the gentry here, Mick,' she continued. 'A man can be accepted if he works hard and proves himself. Half the toffs in Van Diemen's Land aren't gentry anyway: they're pretenders when all's said and done. And they know it, what's more. You've just got to play the game is all.'

'Why are you doing this, Ma?'

'Eh?' She was caught out.

'Why the sudden interest in my well-being?'

The question was a little confronting, and Ma wondered why herself. She'd developed a soft spot for the lad, it was true, but she knew it went deeper than that. Perhaps young Mick O'Callaghan had become the son she'd never had. Perhaps he was making up for those much regretted self-induced abortions forty years before, when she'd been on the game. Or perhaps he was the boy she and Sid might have produced if by then she hadn't deprived her body of the ability. She had her girls around her, it was true, all of whom were like daughters, but she'd like to have had a lad of her own.

'Just an old woman's motherly advice, son,' she said with a touch of humour. That was as close to the truth as she was prepared to go.

Mick grinned. 'There you are now, you see? I always said you've a real soft heart underneath.'

Ma ignored the charm; it was commitment she was seeking. 'So if I have Len line things up, you'll see Jefferson then?'

'Sure, I'll see him.' What do I have to lose? Mick thought, and it'll keep the old girl happy. 'But there's someone else I'd rather see first.'

'Oh?'

'Where would I find Red when she's not at Trafalgar?'

He can't be serious, Ma thought. Hadn't he heard a word she'd said? 'You don't want to set your sights on a girl like Red, Mick.'

He laughed. 'I'm hardly setting my sights on her, Ma. I just want to meet up with her is all.'

'You'll be after more than a chat, I'll warrant,' she replied drily. 'And you say you don't pay? She'll knock you back quick as look at you.'

He gave a careless shrug. 'Maybe, maybe not,' he said, 'we'll see.'

Right, Ma thought, if he won't listen to me then let him learn it the hard way. 'Try the ten o'clock mass at St Joseph's tomorrow,' she said. 'Red's a good Catholic girl, at least she pretends to be. She goes to church every Sunday.'

'Thanks, Ma, much obliged.' He drained his mug and stood. 'And thanks too for the rum,' he said.

'Shall I see if Len can get Jefferson Powell lined up for next week?' Ma remained persistent to the end.

'Why not?'

Mick had half expected, given Ma's warning, that Red might knock him back on business grounds. His ego had convinced him that she found him as exciting as he did her – why else would she have flirted with him so out-rageously – but he was prepared to accept a rejection. Red was a working girl after all. He was totally unprepared, however, for the response he received.

She hadn't noticed him in church; there'd been no reason why she should, for he'd sat up the back. And dressed in his charcoal grey suit and silk waistcoat as he was, with his top hat resting on his knees, he'd no doubt blended in with the other gentlemen present. He hadn't taken part in the holy communion – that might be pushing his luck, given that he and God had parted ways – but he'd watched her receiving the sacraments and thought how serenely beautiful she looked. Her dress was less showy than the preceding day's, her skirt not as full and of cotton not velvet, her bonnet bordering on austere without frills and lace, the pelisse replaced by a simple paisley shawl. She seemed so demure, he thought, a lady through and through.

He ducked outside towards the end of mass and waited in Macquarie Street, watching as the congregation left the church. She'd been in no hurry to get home it seemed, for she'd lagged behind, dawdling with the stragglers, and she might even have passed him by had he not stepped in front of her.

'Hello,' he said, waiting for her to make some comment upon his fine clothes and his shining top hat. He looked devilishly handsome and he knew it.

But she made no comment at all. Her expression was unreadable as she stepped around him and walked on.

Undaunted, he kept pace with her. 'I noticed you in church,' he said, 'and as you appear once again to be unaccompanied, I thought I might offer my services as your escort.'

'You know where Trafalgar is then, do you? I'm headed there.' Her eyes remained trained directly ahead.

Although a little nonplussed Mick didn't miss a beat. 'Yes, I know where Trafalgar is.'

'I take it Ma told you. Just like she told you I'd be in church.'

'Ma told me a lot of things,' he said with a smile, deeming it wise to keep the exchange light-hearted.

'Like what?' She halted abruptly and turned to him.

'Well ...' He hesitated. She didn't seem on the attack, but her manner was so direct he was a little unsure what to say.

'Did she tell you that I can only be had for money, and that if you don't have any then you won't stand a chance?'

'That's exactly what she said.' Mick did away with the niceties. If Red wanted to get straight to the point, then that's the way they'd play it.

'But you thought that in your case I'd make an exception, didn't you, Mick?'

Her fox eyes flickered over him the way they had outside the baker's shop, appraising him, taking in every detail, and Mick's heart started to pound. She liked what she saw: he could feel it.

'I only know that we shared something,' he said. 'Something happened between us, Red, you must have felt it yourself.'

'Well, I've decided I *will* make an exception in your case,' she said, and he held his breath, hardly daring to believe his good luck. 'You'll be the exception who won't stand a chance no matter how much money you have.'

The words came as such a surprise that he stood for a moment trying to work them out, wondering whether perhaps he'd got them in the wrong order, whether perhaps he'd heard incorrectly. But with a cold and calculated intent to wound, Red drove her message home even harder.

'My favours are bought by gentlemen, Mr O'Callaghan, and no matter how finely you dress you'll never be a gentleman.' She gathered her paisley shawl tightly around her shoulders, warding off the bite of winter. 'Face it, Mick,' she said, 'you're as common as muck,' and she left him standing there in the broad, dusty avenue of Macquarie Street.

CHAPTER FIVE

On first meeting, Jefferson Brindsley Powell appeared everything Ma had promised. He also appeared everything Mick had expected.

'You'll learn from Jefferson, Mick,' Ma had said when he'd popped in to see her before setting off for the McLagan house, which was a twenty-minute walk away in Battery Point. She'd insisted upon vetting his appearance, warning him that Jefferson Powell was not one to be impressed by 'fancy clobber'. 'He's a man of true values is Jefferson,' she'd said after giving her approval to the moleskin trousers, boots and woollen jacket. She'd felt dubious about the signal red kerchief knotted at Mick's throat, but she'd wisely said nothing: Mick wasn't Mick without a touch of flamboyance. 'A gentleman through and through, he is. You can tell just by being in his company. If you want to move up in the world, Mick, as I know you do, you can learn a lot from a classy gent like Jefferson Powell.'

Ma's lecture, surprisingly enough, had not grated with Mick, for indeed he intended to learn a great deal from Jefferson Powell. Driven by his humiliating encounter outside the church with Red, he was now determined to better himself. He would not do so in order to prove his worth to Eileen 'Red' Hilditch, whom he had chosen to despise.

What would a whore from the backstreets of Dublin know of the gentry anyway, apart from the tricks she'd learnt between the sheets? He would make his mark for his own sake. He would become a gentleman with the best of them, and Jefferson Powell, obviously a smart operator with an eye to the main chance, would provide the wherewithal.

The McLagan house in Napoleon Street, which Jefferson had inherited just the previous year upon the old man's death, was attractive and roomy with wide wooden verandahs and a pretty front garden where the winter-bare fronds of birch trees drooped gracefully over green grass and flowerbeds. Although not opulent, the overall effect was one of space and comfort, luxuries unknown to the residents of Wapping. Not bad, Mick thought as he tapped lightly with the brass door knocker, not bad at all for a convict who'd spent four years in Port Arthur, albeit as a *political* prisoner.

'Mr O'Callaghan, welcome, I'm Jefferson Powell.'

To Mick's surprise, the door was opened by none other than the man himself. To his further surprise, the man himself was dressed in a flannel shirt, breeches and leather jerkin. By all appearances he could have been a labourer.

'How do you do, Mr Powell?'

Mick accepted the hand on offer and the two shook.

'Come on in, please do.' Powell's accent was distinctly American, but his voice was well modulated and pleasing to the ear. It's a voice that has the ring of a gentleman, Mick thought.

'Thank you, sir.' He responded with just the right air of deference to a prospective employer and one ten years or so his senior before stepping into a pleasingly light and airy front sitting room with windows that looked out over the garden and down the hill to the broad expanse of river beyond. There was no-one else in sight, but from another part of the house, he could hear the sound of children's voices.

'Let's go through to my office, shall we?'

Powell led the way to a door at the far end of the sitting room and Mick followed. He was impressed already. Jefferson Powell was everything he'd been led to believe. In his mid-thirties, sandy-haired and strongly built, he was good looking certainly, but it was his manner that impressed above all, for his manner belied his working man's garb. Powell bore the easy grace and confidence of one secure in his standing in society. Ma was right, Mick thought, the man has class.

He was ushered into a masculine room that smelt of wood and leather. Finely carved model boats of all size and description lined the surrounding shelves and an imposing desk made of local pine was strewn with plans and designs which at even a glance Mick could see were of vessels.

'Take a seat, Mr O'Callaghan; please make yourself comfortable.' Jefferson left the door slightly ajar and circled the desk to sit opposite. 'I've been told you're a close friend of Ma Tebbutt's,' he said.

Mick wasn't sure how he should reply. Certainly, the contact had been made through Ma, but should he admit to a close personal friendship? She did after all run a brothel in Wapping.

'I know Ma, yes,' he said, hedging a little, buying time. 'A good woman ...' Fortunately that was enough.

'A good woman indeed,' Jefferson said in hearty agreement. 'As was her husband, Sid, God rest his soul.'

Mick automatically crossed himself, an instinctive and meaningless gesture, but it did not go unnoticed by Jefferson.

'You knew Sid Tebbutt, did you?'

'Sadly, no, sir. I've been in Van Diemen's Land only eight months now.'

'Ah yes, of course: so I was told. You were a seaman aboard the *Maid of Canton*, I believe.'

'That's right, Mr Powell. I served aboard the *Maid* for

three long years, I'm proud to say: one of the finest vessels in existence.' Mick and Ma had agreed there was no need for Jefferson Powell to know he'd signed up for a one-way voyage only, and as a deckhand. Better he should have served his apprenticeship and be fully qualified, they'd decided.

'Forgive my asking,' Jefferson said, puzzled and with an air of apology for he had no wish to pry, 'but given your calling, what led you to forsake a life at sea?'

Mick could have felt cornered, but he didn't. Suddenly he saw an opportunity, and he grabbed at it. 'I think, perhaps, I may not have had a true calling at all, sir. I think perhaps the sea may have been an escape to me.'

'An escape, in what way?'

'I got myself into a spot of trouble in Ireland, sir. Not of any criminal kind, I can assure you,' he paused thoughtfully before adding, 'although the British might not agree with me there.' Mick's mind was ticking over furiously, recalling Ma's story of Powell's past. The man was an idealist, or at least he had been in his youth. Surely, Mick thought, just a hint of his own past would find favour.

'Like many of my fellow countrymen I am a nationalist, sir,' he said, 'and in joining those who choose to take a stand for their beliefs I placed myself in a rather dangerous position.' Powell's bound to identify with such a story, and it isn't far from the truth anyway, Mick thought. The only variance in his case was that due to his disastrous botch-up it was his own mob that was after him rather than the British. 'I am no fugitive from justice, Mr Powell,' he said, 'but had I remained in Ireland I may well have become so.'

'I understand, Mr O'Callaghan.' Jefferson respected the young man for both his conviction and his candour. 'I understand, indeed. Several of your countrymen were transported here to Van Diemen's Land for the part they played in the uprising of '48. They were members of a movement known as the Young Irelanders.'

The very words sent a frisson of shock through Mick, but he kept his voice steady. 'Yes, that's right. They were a little before my time, the Young Irelanders,' he said. 'The movement disbanded after the uprising I'm told. Are any of them still here, would you know?' he asked casually.

'I believe not. I believe upon receiving their pardons they all went their separate ways.'

Mick could only hope so.

'It is wrong,' Jefferson said, 'that a man should be treated as a criminal when he has done no more than fight against what he perceives as injustice.'

'It is indeed, sir, and I thank the good Lord that I did not have to pay such a price.' Mick felt it wise to change the subject. 'I arrived here a free man, albeit a poor one, and was lucky enough to be taken under Ma Tebbutt's wing, God bless her. She gave me lodgings and a job the very day I stepped ashore. She's helped me a lot, has Ma.'

Jefferson registered the change of topic, although he'd had no intention of pressing young O'Callaghan any further about his past. Much as he would happily discuss his own past in detail, Jefferson Powell respected the unspoken rules of the working classes of Hobart Town.

'Ma has helped many over the years,' he agreed. 'She and Sid both, good people at heart.'

Jefferson well remembered the Hunter's Rest and the little room out the back where he'd stayed rent free for a whole month in exchange for chopping firewood and carting barrels of ale. He remembered the bowls of hot stew Ma had personally doled out for him on those wintry nights when he'd returned from another fruitless day's search, bewildered by people's reticence to employ him. He'd never thought to lie about his political background. What would have been the point anyway? His accent gave him away the moment he opened his mouth. I was so unworldly in those days, he thought. Dear God, it had been a whole two weeks before he'd realised there was a brothel upstairs. When one of the girls had propositioned him he'd gathered she was a prostitute and quickly knocked back her offer for fear of catching the dreaded pox about which his father had warned him, but even then the thought of a brothel upstairs hadn't crossed his mind. Why would it? He'd arrived in Van Diemen's Land a virgin of barely twenty, and four years later when Ma Tebbutt had taken him in, he'd been a virgin still. Jefferson smiled at the memory. How naive he'd been.

He hauled his mind back to the present. 'I owe a great deal to Sid and Ma Tebbutt,' he said. 'In fact I can safely say they altered the course of my destiny, for had Sid Tebbutt not gained me employment with McLagan Transport I would not have met my future wife. And had I not met my future wife, I would have returned to whatever America had in store for me.' He smiled as he added, 'Which could never have compared with the life I now lead.'

Mick was amazed. He didn't know what to make of the situation. The man appeared to be blatantly admitting that he'd married his employer's daughter for personal gain, yet his admission was made with such charm and frankness it was difficult to believe him capable of such an action.

Then, as if on cue, the door was pushed open to reveal a small boy who was prevented from entering the room by the firm grip of the woman standing behind him.

'That's naughty of you, Georgie,' the woman said, with a Glaswegian accent. 'Very, very naughty: I told you to knock.'

'But it was ajar,' the boy argued. 'When the door's not closed I'm allowed to come in, aren't I, Pa?'

'Not when your mother's told you to knock, George – you know that.' Jefferson frowned with mock severity and the boy looked duly chastised.

The two men rose to their feet.

'This is Mr O'Callaghan, my dear,' Jefferson said. 'Mr O'Callaghan, may I introduce my wife, Doris, and my son

George?' He winked at the boy who grinned back. Discipline in the Powell household was obviously Doris's domain.

'Mrs Powell.' Mick nodded deferentially.

'How do you do, Mr O'Callaghan?' She gave a brief nod of acknowledgement in return before addressing the boy. 'You may shake hands, Georgie,' she said, and the boy stepped forward to offer Mick a handshake that was firm and confident. He was a six-year-old replica of his father.

'How do you do, sir?' he said.

'A pleasure to meet you, George.'

'Forgive the interruption, dear,' Doris said to her husband, 'but I wondered whether you gentlemen might like a cup of tea.'

'What an excellent idea, although I think upon our return might be preferable.' He looked a query at Mick. 'I suggest we take a walk down to the river, Mr O'Callaghan. I can show you the lay of the land so to speak and perhaps, if it would suit you, we might have a brief sail?'

Mick was pleased. He was being put to the test. 'That would suit me perfectly, Mr Powell.'

'Very well,' Doris briskly replied. 'I shall have tea ready for ... let us say, eleven o'clock?'

She seems rather bossy, Mick thought.

'We shall be back on the dot of eleven, I promise,' Jefferson said as he crossed to the door.

'Can I come too, Pa?' George asked.

'No, you may not.' It was his mother who answered. 'Your father and Mr O'Callaghan have business to discuss. I'll expect you in one hour, dear. You too, Mr O'Callaghan. I hope you like fruitcake.'

'I do, ma'am, thank you.' He smiled politely before following Jefferson down the hall that led to the rear of the house.

Now that the mystery was solved to his satisfaction, Mick was delighted. Doris was proof positive that his original deduction had been correct. He'd begun to question whether perhaps Jefferson Powell was not an opportunist at all, whether perhaps he really was the true gentleman Ma believed him to be, but the arrival of Doris had dispelled any such doubt. Doris was homely. In fact Doris was more than homely: Doris was decidedly plain. Powell, handsome as he was, could surely have had his pick of beauties, and yet he had chosen Hamish McLagan's dumpy daughter, Doris. As a result, he was now a man of property with a respectable position in society, and he behaved, furthermore, as if he'd been born to it.

Mick was lost in admiration. Powell was not only an opportunist and a smart operator, he was a consummate performer. His only giveaway was Doris herself. No man like Jefferson Brindsley Powell would marry such a woman without an ulterior motive. Perhaps he is an out and out fraud, Mick thought. The name was certainly splendid enough to be an invention. Mick rather regretted now that he'd not gone to a little more trouble with his own name. Michael Patrick O'Callaghan had seemed very grand compared with plain old Mick Kelly, but it didn't come close to Jefferson Brindsley Powell.

He stood watching as Powell donned his work boots and work coat in the back porch.

'Doris won't have muddy boots inside,' Jefferson said.

'Very sensible.' Ah well, Mick supposed, a plain and bossy wife is a small price for an ex-convict to pay in exchange for a life of relative luxury.

They walked around the side of the house, hands in pockets and coat collars pulled up as, though the weather was fine with not a cloud in the sky, the winter breeze was chilly. They crossed through the garden and out the front gate and Jefferson explained the workings of the McLagan Ferry-Boat Service.

'We use small craft,' he told Mick 'Easily manoeuvrable for an oarsman, and just a spritsail and jib when the breeze is right.'

Mick nodded. He'd seen many such vessels plying the Derwent carrying passengers and goods shore to shore, principally between the wharves of Hobart Town and the settlement of Bellerive on the eastern side.

They turned down the track that led to the water.

'The boats work mainly out of Waterman's Dock,' Jefferson said, 'but our business is run from here on the south side of Battery Point where I have a slipway for annual overhauling and general repairs. I keep one craft here permanently for the transportation of people and goods from ship to shore,' he continued. 'A tricky business when there are many large vessels at anchor, particularly in rough weather conditions.' He cast a meaningful look at Mick. 'That job I reserve for my most experienced waterman.'

'And how many craft do you have, Mr Powell?'

'Currently five in all.'

'But you intend to expand.' It was a statement rather than a question.

They'd arrived at the water's edge and as they came to a halt, Jefferson glanced keenly at the young Irishman. 'Why do you say that?'

Powell seemed to be studying him intently and Mick hoped he hadn't appeared presumptuous. 'You said *currently*, sir. You said you *currently* have five craft.'

'Ah, yes, I did indeed.' Satisfied with the answer, the American shifted his focus to the view. 'Just look at that. Magnificent, isn't it?'

'It certainly is.'

There was silence for a moment as they stood on the shaly shoreline and looked out over the vast, ever-widening river as it neared the end of its journey to the mighty Southern Ocean. To their right was the burgeoning conglomeration of shipbuilding yards, so at odds with the majesty of the surrounding landscape. Ugly jetties intruded clumsily upon the river's beauty; launching ramps tumbled into the water like so much discarded firewood; and up on the slipways sat the naked skeletons of half-made vessels, raw and somehow obscene. To the uninitiated it no doubt appeared an unsightly mess, but to a man like Jefferson Powell this hive of industry was exciting, for here was where his future lay. Here he would build the ketches that would ply the D'Entrecasteaux Channel and the Huon River servicing the fruit and timber trade. Jefferson Powell was most certainly expanding his business, but he was not about to tell young Mick O'Callaghan any details yet.

'This way,' he said, abruptly breaking the silence and, turning their backs to the shipyards, the two men set off along the shoreline.

Several minutes later, they rounded the point and Mick saw before them a slipway and a jetty with a vessel approximately fifteen feet in length and four feet abeam moored alongside. A small sandstone cottage sat fifty yards or so from the water's edge. Jefferson led the way towards it.

'Welcome to the headquarters of the McLagan Ferry-Boat Service,' he said with a smile.

As they climbed the two steps leading up to the front porch he took a key from his work coat pocket; when he'd unlocked the door they stepped inside.

Mick looked about. The room, with a low wooden-beamed ceiling, was not large and appeared to serve as both office and store room. To the left sat a desk and chair together with a bookshelf and cabinet, and to the right was an array of boating equipment. Oars and boat-hooks were propped in a corner. Rigging and canvas sails were loosely suspended along one wall to keep them damp free and protected from the ever-present threat of mould, and from hooks in the overhead beam hung ropes and all forms of tackle. Directly ahead was a door that led to the rest of the cottage.

Jefferson too was looking about. 'Strange to think this used to be our bedroom,' he remarked incongruously. Then he laughed, aware of the Irishman's bemused response.

'Doris and I spent many happy years in this cottage,' he said, handing Mick a set of oars and rowlocks. He picked up the rigging and sails and they stepped back outside.

'You lived here?' Mick asked. The information having been freely offered there seemed no harm in asking for clarification, and he was keen to know all he could of Powell's past.

'We did indeed,' Jefferson said as, rigging and oars slung over their shoulders, they set off for the jetty. 'The cottage and this half-acre of land that it stands on was a wedding gift from Doris's father, Hamish. I took over the ferry service, allowing him to concentrate on the McLagan Road Transport Company, so the acquisition of the property was very much to Hamish's advantage.'

'Yes, of course,' Mick said. To *Hamish's* advantage?

'Doris and I spent seven happy years waking up every morning with all this at our doorstep,' Jefferson's sweeping gesture encompassed the whole of the mighty Derwent. 'It enriches the soul, Mr O'Callaghan, I can assure you.' They'd reached the jetty. 'I must admit though,' he added as they walked out towards the boat, 'the cottage became very cramped after our second child, Martha, was born. We're far more comfortable now in the big house.'

How very convenient of the old man to die, Mick thought, astounded once again by Jefferson Powell's unashamed series of admissions.

'It's a fine thing to have such fond memories, sir,' he said.

'It certainly is, Mr O'Callaghan.'

Mick climbed into the vessel and Jefferson handed the oars and the rigging down to him.

'A good stiff breeze,' the American said. 'Are you happy to set out under sail and take up the oars on the way back?'

'Perfectly happy, Mr Powell.'

Jefferson climbed aboard and began tending to the rigging.

'Do you not think, sir,' Mick suggested lightly, 'that as I'm the one being put to the test, it might be a good idea if perhaps I rig the vessel on my own?'

'Why yes.' Jefferson smiled. There was something particularly charming about the young Irishman. 'Yes, that would be an excellent idea.'

Although Mick had not previously rigged a craft of this particular design, he had rigged other small craft, and the spritsail, spar and jib fittings hardly compared to the complex rigs he'd worked with aboard the *Maid*. In only minutes he'd completed the task as Jefferson sat amidships watching approvingly.

Everything was in readiness. All they now needed to do was raise the canvas.

'You take the helm,' Jefferson said.

They worked as a team, swift and efficient, Jefferson releasing the bowline, Mick casting off from the stern. When the solid wooden vessel was adrift, they raised the spritsail.

The heavy canvas cracked, whip-like and angry. Then as the sail caught the wind, Jefferson hauled on the mainsheet, taking in the slack, Mick simultaneously set them on a tight starboard tack, and they were off.

Once safely underway, they raised the jib, picking up even more speed, and for the next twenty minutes Mick took great pleasure in showing off his skills. He'd enjoyed sailing light craft with Seamus when they'd been holed up in Rio de Janeiro and Cape Town, the *Maid* taking on provisions and undergoing repairs; Seamus had been a very thorough teacher. Now, with several large ships at anchor in the bay, he tacked from one to the other, manning both the tiller and the spritsail while Jefferson manned the jib, a task which would normally have been that of the forward hand and junior member of a two-man team.

It wasn't long before Jefferson suggested they turn back. He was more than satisfied with the Irishman's skill as a helmsman, and clouds were now gathering overhead. 'We might be in for some rain,' he said.

In typically perverse fashion, the weather had indeed changed. Hobart Town was renowned for its mercurial weather.

Mick made several tacks on their way back to Battery Point, but they were still quite some distance from the McLagan jetty when Jefferson gave the order to lower the sails.

'We'll row from here,' he said, the 'we' clearly meaning that Mick was to row.

Jefferson Powell sincerely hoped young Michael O'Callaghan would pass this final test: he'd taken a liking to the Irishman. He had his doubts, however. As a yachtsman O'Callaghan was more than competent, but how strong was he as an oarsman? He'd have a stiff south-westerly to contend with and he didn't appear to be carrying much muscle.

Mick turned the vessel into the wind, the canvas flapping wildly, and they lowered the sails.

When the rigging was secured, the men changed positions. Mick settled himself amidships and started to row, while Jefferson sat in the stern, ready to take over when the Irishman's strength gave out, as he suspected it would.

Mick rowed methodically, concentrating on his breathing and the rhythm of his actions as Seamus had taught him. 'Let your lungs do the work, Mick,' he could hear his old friend say, 'your strength lies in your breathing. Match it to the rhythm, Mick. Match your breath to the rhythm and row with your whole body.'

The wind cut across the vessel's bow and in order to stay on course he had to favour his starboard oar, but he didn't once alter his rhythm. He concentrated on the landmarks he'd lined up as sights on the far eastern riverbank and rowed with his whole body as Seamus had taught him.

Small though the boat was, she was sturdy and heavy,

but she was also well-crafted and built for a good oarsman. She ploughed cleanly and steadily through the water like a well-trained horse obeying its master.

On and on Mick rowed. He could feel the blood pumping through his body and he could feel his heart pounding with the effort. But his stroke remained constant. Not once did he break the pattern of his breathing and rhythm as he continued to the chant of Seamus's voice. *Match your breath to the rhythm and row with your whole body. Match your breath to the rhythm and row with your whole body.* He kept his eyes on the opposite bank and his landmarks, but he knew Powell was watching, waiting for him to weaken. He must show no signs of fatigue. On and on he went, following the chant, refusing to alter the pace he had set for his body, and despite the coursing of his blood and the pounding of his heart, he felt he could row forever.

Then, suddenly, they were on the lee side of the point, out of the prevailing wind and in calm water. Mick didn't stop rowing, but he finally allowed himself to break rhythm enough to look over his right shoulder. Up ahead, off the port side and barely two hundred yards away, was the McLagan jetty. He adjusted his course accordingly, altered his pace and, still inhaling and exhaling in time with each stroke, he rowed slowly and steadily towards it. By the time he'd reached the jetty, he'd recovered from his efforts. Or at least, it appeared that he had. As they came alongside and he stood to secure the bowline, he felt distinctly light-headed and even a little giddy but he managed to conceal it.

Jefferson climbed on to the jetty and took the oars and rigging that Mick passed up to him. He was pleased with the outcome of the test. Young O'Callaghan didn't appear to have overexerted himself at all: he was obviously stronger than he looked. Whatever the Irishman lacks in muscle he makes up for in stamina, Jefferson thought.

'Well done, Mr O'Callaghan,' he said as Mick joined him on the jetty, 'well done all round.'

'Thank you, sir.'

'Let's dispense with the "sir" shall we?' Contrary to old Hamish McLagan's practice, Jefferson Powell used first names with his men. Having been a waterman himself, it was his belief that a familiar relationship between employer and employee promoted loyalty and honesty. 'Call me Jefferson,' he said. 'And you're Michael, am I right?'

'Yes. I'm Michael.' Mick decided that he liked being called Michael. At least he did by a man like Jefferson Powell.

'Well, Michael, it appears you have a job.' Jefferson offered his hand and they shook. 'Welcome to Powell River Transport.' The statement was delivered with a certain éclat intended to impress, which it did.

'What happened to the McLagan Ferry-Boat Service?' Mick asked.

'Changes are afoot, my friend,' the American said with a grin. 'You are about to become part of a whole new enterprise.'

The clouds had rolled in and at that very moment, as if to lend extra drama to Jefferson's announcement, it started to rain.

They grabbed the oars and rigging and sprinted for the cottage, beating the cloudburst by seconds.

'It'll blow over quickly in this wind,' Jefferson said as they stood on the porch watching the sheets of rain sweep across the bay.

But Mick wasn't interested in the weather. 'You were telling me about Powell River Transport?' he prompted. By God, but it hadn't taken the man long to commit old McLagan to obscurity. Mick wondered how Doris felt about her father's name being so summarily dropped from the very business he'd created.

'Yes, so I was. Powell River Transport will expand over

the coming years, Michael ...' With his two ketches still currently under construction, Jefferson considered it premature to announce that his principal enterprise would be Powell Channel Transport. '... I'm not at liberty to be specific as yet, but in the months to come I shall be looking for a manager to take over the ferry service.'

'Really, is that so?' Mick's casual expression of interest concealed a growing excitement. Surely Jefferson Powell wasn't hinting that the job could be his?

But Jefferson was hinting at no such thing. He was talking of his own future, not Mick's.

'I intend to employ a ticket-of-leave couple to live here and manage the business,' he said, 'a man with knowledge of the trade and an ability to handle the bookwork, while his wife helps Doris out with the daily chores.' Jefferson laughed. 'Although Doris hardly needs helping out: she likes to work, and she won't even consider a live-in servant at the big house. She has a girl come in twice a week to look after the children while she goes shopping.'

Mick was not remotely concerned about Doris and her domestic arrangements. He was wondering how best he could convince Jefferson that a single man taking over the cottage and the ferry management would be vastly preferable to a couple. But as the American continued, he realised persuasion might not be that simple.

'Van Diemen's Land has been good to me, Michael,' Jefferson said looking out over the rain-swept river, 'and I feel it's my duty to help others. I'd like to give a young ticket-of-leave couple a step-up in life.'

Mick found it wryly perverse that, had he been a convict, he would have stood more of a chance. If I'd only known earlier, he thought, I would have lied, but it's too late now. He wondered briefly whether he might introduce Evie as his ticket-of-leave fiancée, but he dismissed the notion. Too obvious a ploy. And besides, Evie's past was all too apparent: she was not fiancée material. He refused to be daunted, however. An opportunity would present itself given time. He would get around Jefferson Powell one way or another.

They discussed briefly the conditions of employment. The job Jefferson offered was that of ship-to-shore waterman, which as he pointed out was a compliment to Mick's skills. The boats were manned by a team of two, and an apprentice would be employed to serve as his forward hand. The two-man teams worked on an honour system, recording where and how often they dropped passengers or goods in the log books supplied. At the close of each work day, Jefferson collected the takings and checked the log books, and the men were paid at the end of the week, with a bonus for the team that had scored the top takings.

Under Jefferson Powell's management, dishonesty was no longer the problem it had been in old Hamish's day, for the McLagan Ferry-Boat Service had developed a fine reputation. Men were proud to be a McLagan waterman, and a keen sense of competition had developed among the teams to see who could win the weekly bonus and the boast that went with it of being the best at their trade.

As most of the men were illiterate or semi-literate at best, they simply made their marks in the log books. It was a perfectly satisfactory arrangement, but Jefferson was nonetheless delighted to discover that Mick could read and write. He was not altogether surprised though, for there was something stylish about the young Irishman that set him apart from the average working-class man.

'Oh, my father was a stickler for education,' Mick said. '"A man is measured by the books he reads, Michael." That's what he was forever saying to me.' His father had said no such thing. Indeed, it was doubtful whether Patrick Kelly had ever read a book in his life. Recalling the quote from a teacher, Mick now blessed his mother, who had doggedly insisted against her husband's wishes that, as five of their six children were now working, the youngest was to attend school until his fifteenth birthday.

'There was a time when I even considered a career as a teacher,' Mick continued, another outright lie, 'but then I got caught up with the nationalists, and ... well, one thing led to another ...' He tailed off leaving just that hint, just that faint reminder of the youthful idealism with which Jefferson Powell was so bound to identify.

'Of course.' Jefferson tactfully did not pursue the subject. 'Well goodness me, will you just look at that?' he said, gesturing at the sky. 'I said it'd blow over, and it certainly has.'

The clouds had rolled on by as quickly as they'd rolled on in and the sky was once again clear blue.

After locking up the cottage, they made their way back along the foreshore.

'All I need to do now is line you up with a for'ard hand,' the American said.

'I'd be more than happy to do that myself, Jefferson,' Mick offered. 'It would leave you free to concentrate on your other interests. I have many contacts, and I'm sure upon enquiry I'll be able to find an apprentice waterman who would meet with your approval. Perhaps someone seeking ticket-of-leave employment?'

'Excellent, Michael, excellent. I shall leave the recruiting to you then.'

Things are going very nicely, Mick thought. It shouldn't take him too long to convince Jefferson he was indispensable and the perfect choice to take over the ferry service management. For one so clever, the American seemed surprisingly receptive to suggestion.

Upon reaching the house, they entered via the back porch where Jefferson divested himself of his work boots and coat, and Mick rubbed his own boots on the doormat until inspection showed they were completely mud-free.

They'd arrived home nearly an hour later than arranged, but Doris had assumed they'd sheltered from the rain.

'I'm brewing a fresh pot,' she said and she disappeared to the kitchen, leaving them with the children, both of whom were under strict instructions that, as they were in the front sitting room and entertaining a guest, they were to be on their best behaviour.

Jefferson introduced four-year-old Martha.

'Hello,' the little girl said, looking boldly up at Mick.

'Hello,' he replied. How very unfortunate, he thought. The child had inherited her mother's looks. The same broad face, with eyes like currants and a heavy brow that seemed to offer a perennially dour expression. Even the healthy, stocky little body threatened to become squat and dumpy like her mother's. How sad, he thought. 'That's a pretty dress you're wearing, Martha,' he said and he flashed a dazzling smile.

She studied him with grave deliberation. 'You're very handsome,' she said.

He gave a gracious bow in acknowledgement of the compliment. 'Why thank you, ma'am,' he replied, and the little girl smiled.

Who would have believed it possible? Mick thought. The child was not remotely plain when she smiled. She had dimples that lit up her face. The fact that her little currant eyes disappeared into slits only added to a merriment that was utterly contagious. He found it impossible not to grin back. In that single moment, with just one smile, Martha Powell had won Mick O'Callaghan's heart.

Doris returned with the tea tray and the serving ritual began, the two children playing their obviously well-rehearsed parts. George, with great care and without spilling a drop, delivered the cups of tea his mother poured, first to their guest and then to his father, Martha following with the sugar bowl.

'Thank you, Martha,' Mick said, hoping the little girl would smile again, but she was so focused upon her duty she just nodded at the sugar bowl.

'You may offer the cake now, Martha,' Doris said when the tea had been served. She passed the plate with its meticulously arranged slices of fruitcake to her daughter.

Eyes riveted on the dish, hands fiercely gripping either side, Martha made her way over to Mick with resolute and solemn purpose, each step painfully measured.

'Thank you, Martha,' he said when at last she reached him. He took a piece of cake and put it on his side plate, flashing another smile as he did so in the hope that she would reciprocate. But she didn't. Martha's smiles were not an automatic social response and could not be so easily won. She looked up at him with her solemn face.

'My mother made it,' she said.

'Really?'

'Yes.' The beady little eyes didn't leave his.

She's waiting for something, he thought. What?

'It's the best cake in the world,' she said.

She was waiting for him to try it, he realised. He took a bite. He would have lied, but he didn't need to: the cake was delicious. 'You're right,' he said. 'It is. It's the very best cake in the whole wide world.'

And there it was again, that smile. The eyes disappeared, the dimples danced infectiously, and Mick wanted to laugh for the sheer joy of having shared a special moment with a four-year-old.

But sharing the moment cost Martha both her concentration and her grip. The plate wobbled in her hands and pieces of fruit cake slithered about wildly, threatening to drop to the floor.

'Watch out, Martha!' It was George who came to the rescue. He jumped up from the sofa and took the plate from his sister. He had been waiting impatiently for his cake and by now he was thoroughly irritated. 'You're taking all day and you nearly spilled the whole lot,' he said. He presented the dish to his father, who accepted a slice of cake, and then progressed to his mother, who did the same, which meant it was finally his turn. Putting the plate on the tea tray, he picked up three slices and turned away quickly in the hope no-one had noticed. But someone had.

'Georgie took three slices,' Martha said accusingly. She was not normally a tittle-tattle, but she was cross that her brother had taken over her duty as host.

'Yes, he did,' Doris said (George's misdemeanour had not escaped his mother's eagle eye), 'And Georgie is going to put them back.'

The little boy glared at his sister as he put the cake back on the plate, but Martha did not flinch. She returned the glare.

Mick watched the proceedings with interest. Would the children be sent off in disgrace? Doris seemed a most forbidding parent.

But Doris displayed no anger. She spread open a napkin, placed the three slices of cake on it and added a fourth. 'You're to leave us now, children,' she said as she wrapped up the cake. 'If you play in the back garden, don't forget to put your galoshes on: it's been raining.' She entrusted the napkin to her son. 'You're to share this between you. Two pieces each, Georgie,' she warned and the boy nodded. He would obey his mother, and with good humour, for they both knew he'd end up with three pieces of cake anyway. Martha would be able to eat only one slice, and she would quite happily give the second to her brother. The children's spats never lasted long.

At the door, the little girl turned back for a final look at their guest. She was intrigued by the handsome young Irishman.

'Goodbye,' she said. Then, abruptly and without awaiting a reply, she followed in her brother's wake.

'I think you've found a friend,' Doris said.

'I hope so,' Mick replied, 'she's a winner, your daughter.'

Jefferson was pleased the tea ritual was over. He'd been

longing to get down to business. 'Michael is to join Powell River Transport, my dear,' he announced.

'Oh, so you made the grand statement, did you?' Doris said to her husband with dry humour. She turned to Mick and, in the vestige of her smile, he could see the faintest glimpse of a dimple. 'Jefferson's been dying to broadcast the news to the whole world,' she said. 'The change in the company's title is not to be officially announced until next week, but he simply had to tell someone, and it appears you're it, Mr O'Callaghan.'

'I'm honoured,' Mick said. He was also surprised. Doris Powell, nee McLagan, was obviously not in the least concerned about the omission of her father's name. He wondered how Jefferson had managed to accomplish that.

'And who better to make such an announcement to,' Jefferson said, 'than my new ship-to-shore waterman?'

'Congratulations, Mr O'Callaghan.'

'Thank you, Mrs Powell.'

'We're on the verge of a whole new era,' Jefferson continued enthusiastically. 'I was telling Michael about my future plans to employ a ticket-of-leave couple to manage the ferry service and help you with your chores, my dear ...'

'I do not need help, Jefferson,' Doris said mildly but firmly, 'I very much enjoy cooking and gardening, as you well know. Why should I deprive myself of that which I enjoy?'

How intriguing, Mick thought. The wife might well become his ally.

'There are other chores, Doris,' Jefferson waved a hand airily dismissing her argument, 'and just imagine the gift we would be offering a young couple embarking upon a new life.'

Doris was silent: she could hardly contest such an argument.

'It is a gift I owe to others, Michael,' Jefferson said, 'for I was granted such a gift myself. I will be forever grateful to Hamish McLagan for the chance I was offered …' he smiled at his wife '… the chance to carve a new life for myself here in this paradise.'

Doris returned her husband's smile, and this time Mick could see not only the clear indentation of a dimple, perhaps even two, he could see the love in her eyes. Of course, he thought, that's where Jefferson's power lies. A woman like Doris would be putty in the hands of a man like Jefferson Powell.

Grateful to Hamish McLagan, Doris was thinking. Why should her husband be grateful to someone who had taken such brazen advantage of him? Jefferson is speechifying again, she thought fondly. It was the American in him. Good heavens above, wealthy though her father was, he'd been on the brink of selling his three ferry boats when Jefferson had come into their lives. Her husband's management had not only saved the flagging river transport business, it had led to the acquisition of an additional two boats, but had Hamish McLagan ever thanked him for it? Of course not, Doris thought. That had never been her father's way. Instead he'd constantly reminded his son-in-law of the great chance in life that had been bestowed upon him.

'I feel it my bounden duty to take up the mantel of benefactor, Michael,' Jefferson continued earnestly, 'it is the very least I can do in return for my father-in-law's generosity.'

Doris watched her husband with loving exasperation. Jefferson was so naive, she thought. He saw the best in people and always had. She'd never had the heart to disillusion him, and she certainly wasn't about to start now. If she tried, he wouldn't believe her anyway.

She stood. 'More tea, gentlemen?'

Mick jumped to his feet.

'No, please, Mr O'Callaghan, please sit. I do not wish to intrude upon the conversation.'

Mick did as he was told and Doris took the men's

empty cups from them. She returned to her seat and as she poured the tea she remembered the exchange that had taken place when Jefferson had first told her of his plan to expand the business.

'I shall call the new company McLagan and Powell Channel Transport,' he'd proudly announced.

'Why?' she'd asked.

'As a tribute to your father, of course.' He'd looked surprised that she felt the need to ask. 'In honour of his memory and to repay the debt I owe him.'

'You are not indebted to my father, Jefferson,' she'd said. 'The name Powell must stand alone.' He'd been about to disagree, but she'd continued firmly. 'If you have any debt it must belong to the future not the past, my dear.' Then she'd presented the irrefutable argument which she knew would clinch the matter. 'Bear in mind that one day the company will be Powell and Son.'

Having poured the tea, Doris stood. The Irishman again made to rise to his feet, but again she stopped him.

'Please, Mr O'Callaghan, please do not allow me to interrupt the conversation.'

By now the men had moved on to a broader theme, or rather Jefferson had, and it was clear he believed he was speaking to a fellow idealist.

'In principal the debt one owes to an individual is not dissimilar to the debt one owes to one's country,' Jefferson was saying. 'It's a matter of principle and loyalty, Michael, as I'm sure you would agree.'

'I most certainly would, Jefferson.'

A brief hiatus followed while Doris served the tea and then, as she returned to her seat, the men resumed their conversation. But Doris wasn't listening.

It wasn't that I hated Father, she thought as she poured herself a second cup. Far from it: she and Hamish had shared a strong bond. But she'd known him for what he was. Not a bad man, but a hard one who used people to his

own advantage, including his daughter. He'd worked her as
he would a son. Why in the early days of McLagan's Road
Transport Company she'd even driven one of the drays.
And when her mother had died she'd continued to help with
the business while also taking over the running of the household, though by then they could have afforded servants.

Doris remembered with vivid clarity the day Sid Tebbutt
had approached her father regarding the employment of
a young man called Jefferson Powell. She'd eavesdropped
on the conversation, as she always did, and as her father
instructed she always should. They would then confer on
which tack to take, for by then they had become virtual
business partners.

'I know you're not one to judge a man by his background,
Hamish,' Sid Tebbutt had said, 'indeed I respect you as one
who takes a stand against bigotry.' Never having viewed her
father as a man renowned for his principles, she'd found the
approach a little mystifying at the time. 'Well,' the Yorkshireman had continued, 'Jefferson is a strong and capable
young chap unable to find employment because others
are passing judgement upon him. And passing judgement
upon what, I ask you? A blameless past, that's what. The
lad's judged for the very fact he has no criminal conviction.
There's nowt fair about that, as I'm sure you'll agree.'

It hadn't taken her long to realise how very cleverly Sid
Tebbutt was playing her father. The man knew Hamish
McLagan as a canny Scot with an eye for a bargain. He
knew, just as she did, that Hamish McLagan would hire
the American not because of any principles on his part, but
because Jefferson Powell was young and strong and desperate for work, which meant, above all, that he was cheap.

'Aye, send the lad to me,' her father had said magnani-
mously, 'I'm sure we'll be able to find a place for him at
McLagan's.'

That was the start of it all, Doris thought. How she'd
blessed Sid Tebbutt for that day.

She re-directed her attention to the men, guiltily aware that in so ignoring them she was being remiss in her duty as hostess.

'Why my very name is a statement of my own father's ideals,' Jefferson was saying. 'I was named after Thomas Jefferson, the third president of the United States of America, who was so admired by my father and his father before him.'

'Really?' the Irishman said. 'How very interesting.'

Doris smiled to herself. Jefferson was still speechifying. Her inattentiveness had gone entirely unnoticed.

'Thomas Jefferson was a personal hero to my grandfather, who fought in the American War of Independence,' Jefferson said.

'The American War of Independence,' Mick replied. 'I find that fascinating, truly I do. Do you know, Jefferson, such a term is never bandied about in Britain. In Britain the reference is always to the Colonial Wars.'

'As of course it would be,' Jefferson drily remarked. 'The British still have difficulty coming to terms with the fact they were defeated by a rag-tag army of colonists.'

Mick laughed. 'Oh dear me, yes; it would have been a punch on the nose for King and Country all right.'

O'Callaghan is a little too eager to please, Doris thought critically. He seemed likeable enough, and the contact he'd shared with her daughter had been refreshing – Martha was not a child to be easily won – but the young Irishman was ambitious. There's nothing wrong with ambition so long as it goes hand-in-hand with loyalty, she thought. But she would not allow her husband to be taken advantage of. She would keep her eye on Michael O'Callaghan. It would not be difficult to observe him without his knowledge, for he had clearly dismissed her, considering her of little importance. She was not in the least offended. Such a response was quite common.

She looked at the men, Jefferson in eager communication, the young Irishman hanging on his every word, lending agreement wherever possible. I need have no worry about my duties as hostess, she thought wryly, I might as well be invisible. She turned back to gaze out the window, allowing her attention to wander.

Doris Powell was fully aware of Mick O'Callaghan's assessment of both her and her marriage. She had registered his reaction the moment they had met. She had seen such a reaction many times in the past. Why would a man like Jefferson Powell wed a woman like Doris McLagan if it were not for money? That's what they all thought.

Her mind drifted as she gazed out at the garden. If they only knew, she thought.

CHAPTER SIX

Doris McLagan was twenty-two years old when Jefferson Brindsley Powell had come to work for her father.

She'd found the American instantly attractive, as any young woman would, but she'd never admitted the fact, even to herself. Doris did not view men as other women did. She was not seeking a husband and doubted she would ever marry, though not because she was plain. Her plainness, of which she was fully aware, would have presented little obstacle had she wished to marry, for there was a severe shortage of women in the colony, and beauty, although preferable, was not considered mandatory by men seeking healthy wives to bear them strong children. Doris McLagan, had she made herself available, would no doubt have received many offers, and not just from those out to reap the benefits of her father's hard-earned success. But Doris had long since accepted destiny's dictate that her life was to follow a different path.

After the family's arrival in the colony, Doris had worked by her father's side for four long years, serving as the son Hamish McLagan had been denied. When she was twenty, her mother had died unexpectedly and she had come to serve as her father's secretary, companion, cook and housekeeper. It was a position she expected she would continue to fill until the end of Hamish McLagan's days, when she would become his carer and nurse. Such was her unquestionable duty.

A practical young woman, Doris had accepted her lot with equanimity. Indeed, so resigned was she to her future that it was a whole eight months before she finally recognised the first fatal symptoms.

'How about hollyhocks along here?' With his hand, Jefferson traced an imaginary path beside the verandah. 'Such bold and colourful plants, do you not agree?'

The two of them were redesigning the front garden of the house in Napoleon Street, which Hamish McLagan had bought just prior to his wife's death.

For some time now, Jefferson Powell had been ensconced in the rooms at the rear of the house. Designed by the original owner as servants' quarters, the rooms had remained unused by Hamish, who had no wish to squander money on domestic help when the household could manage perfectly well without. Upon Jefferson's arrival, however, Hamish had quickly realised that, in exchange for a rent-free agreement, his new waterman could also serve as gardener and handyman. The arrangement had turned out to be most satisfactory, for the young American had proved not only a hard worker, but highly capable. In fact there seemed little he couldn't do, Hamish had noted with delight. Why, the man was even educated. And furthermore, he was honest. Jefferson could be trusted to collect the other watermen's takings and tally up the books at the end of the work day. Hamish McLagan revelled in the bargain that had come his way. All of these talents were at his beck and call, and for a mere pittance.

It was the garden that was to be Doris's eventual undoing, for it brought her into close contact with the American and forged a bond between them.

On wintry Sundays, after Reverend MacDougall's service at the Presbyterian Church, which Jefferson regularly attended with the McLagans, the two of them would change into their dungarees and work side by side. They hoed and they weeded and they dug flower beds and, as they did, they talked. Or for the most part, Jefferson did. Doris was more than happy to listen. She had never heard anyone talk as freely as Jefferson Brindsley Powell.

He spoke of his family with great love and pride. He had two brothers and two sisters, he told her. 'Free-thinkers, all five of us,' he said. 'We were brought up to develop our own beliefs and to follow our convictions. It's what got me into trouble of course – running off to join the French Canadian rebels in their fight for independence. But Pa didn't try and stop me. "You must do what you think is morally right, son: you must be ruled by your conscience", that's what Pa said. It is the way he believes men should lead their lives.'

He told her he'd been named after Thomas Jefferson, the third president of the United States of America. 'A man of great conviction,' he said with a wry smile, 'so as you can see my parents were making a statement right from the start. Why even my middle name was intended as a statement.' Brindsley, it turned out, was his mother's maiden name.

'Martha Brindsley made her own declaration of independence when she married,' he said. 'My mother was proud of her family heritage. She believes that women should not be forced to sacrifice their identity upon marriage, so she adopted the surname Brindsley-Powell for both herself and her children.' He smiled at the memory. 'She was rather annoyed when at sixteen I dropped the hyphen and kept Brindsley as a middle name only, but by then I was following her example and making my own statement. I found Brindsley-Powell just a little too grand.'

'Your father allowed his wife such licence?' Doris was astounded. She could just imagine Hamish McLagan's reaction should his own wife have suggested so outrageous a notion.

'Oh yes, I'm sure Pa would have expected no less of my mother when they married. He knew her and loved her for exactly what she was. And no doubt still is,' Jefferson added fondly, 'for I cannot see her ever changing. Martha Brindsley-Powell is more than a free-thinker, she's an outright radical. She believes there will come a day when women will be given the democratic right to vote, and she intends to fight for that right. All citizens must have a voice, she says, and until such a day comes we do not have a true democracy.'

'She sounds like a very strong woman, your mother.'

'Oh, yes indeed.'

How I would like to meet such a woman, Doris thought. She had loved and respected her own mother, but she knew well that words such as those could never have passed Barbara McLagan's lips. For as long as Doris could remember, everything she had heard from her parents had related to duty. Freedom of choice and personal views of any nature had rarely come up for discussion in the McLagan household. In fact the more Doris listened to Jefferson the more she realised that very little had come up for discussion in the McLagan household.

'You must miss your family,' she said, recognising as she did how inadequate such a comment must sound.

'I do,' he replied. He didn't appear to find her comment inadequate at all. 'I miss them very much. But I have only a year or so to serve on my ticket-of-leave, and I'm saving every penny. I'll get home one day. I'll see them again.'

He seemed supremely confident, which Doris found rather surprising. Convicts who were granted ticket-of-leave rights were not permitted to return to their homeland upon the completion of their sentence, the reasoning no doubt being they were essential to populate the colony. Besides, she thought, no matter how hard Jefferson saved, the pittance he received from her father was hardly likely to purchase his passage home.

She was determined to assist in whatever way she could, however, and she approached her father that very night regarding a raise in the American's salary. She made no personal plea on Jefferson's behalf – like Sid Tebbutt, Doris knew exactly how to manipulate Hamish McLagan. She merely suggested that, as Jefferson Powell was carrying the workload of two men he should receive, if not double his wages, at least a substantial increase upon his current meagre stipend, or else they might risk losing his services to an employer who recognised his full worth.

'But the man has free board and lodgings, Doris,' Hamish had said, bewildered by his daughter's request, 'why should the company reimburse him any further?'

'I do not intend for the company to reimburse him, father. As most of his extra duties revolve around the house and the garden, he shall be paid from my house-keeping allowance. It will mean some necessary cutbacks in expenditure of course, but I'm sure we can forgo several of our little luxuries, for if we do not I genuinely believe we will lose him to a higher bidder.'

Doris had left no grounds for negotiation. She was willing to forgo the new drawing room curtains and the fine bone china tea service she'd intended to order, she said, and there were other sundry items they could well do without, like the regular deliveries of shortbread and the crate of fine Scotch whisky that arrived twice a year.

Hamish capitulated immediately. They dared not risk the loss of such a valuable employee, he agreed, and he made the magnanimous decision, much as he respected Doris's offer, not to create further hardship for her. The cutbacks in expenditure she had suggested would not be necessary as the raise in the man's salary would be met directly by the company.

Doris congratulated herself on her accomplishment.

Six months later, however, she found herself undone by her own cleverness. She realised, upon reflection, how extraordinarily ignorant she'd been. Of course she should have expected such an outcome. But she had been taken completely by surprise.

'I have an announcement to make,' Jefferson said.

It was a Sunday in November. They were in the front garden, but they were not wearing their dungarees. They were dressed in their best having just returned from church, and they were seated on the wooden garden seat (which Jefferson himself had made) admiring the fruits of their labour. The landscaping had long been completed and an abundance of late spring blossom surrounded them.

'I've been longing to tell you, but I wanted to pick the right time and place, and this is certainly it.' He gazed about with a smile that was positively joyful. 'What a triumph your garden has proved to be, Doris. What an absolute triumph. And when the saplings are grown, they'll complete the picture perfectly. Silver birches are such elegant trees.'

'Longing to tell me what?' she urged with her customary bluntness. She was intrigued by his apparent state of elation and exasperated that he wasn't getting to the point. It was typical of Jefferson.

He turned to face her. 'You will shortly be looking at a time-expired man,' he proudly declared, which left her none the wiser.

'And what exactly does that mean?'

'It means that I visited the offices of the Superintendent of Prisons on Friday,' he announced. 'It means that the Superintendent's Secretary himself has confirmed the fact that my sentence will officially expire in six months' time and that I will once again be a free man.'

'Oh, Jefferson, that's wonderful. That's truly wonderful.' Doris's face lit up with one of her rare smiles, which to Jefferson always seemed like a personal gift, for Doris did not know how to smile falsely. 'I'm happy for you,' she said. 'I'm so very, very happy for you.' She was. At that moment, before her mind absorbed the ramifications of his news, Doris was overjoyed that Jefferson Powell was to be granted the freedom he so rightfully deserved.

'I'll be able to go home, Doris,' he said. 'As a citizen of the United States of America, I will be free to return to my native land.'

It took a moment to sink in. Then she realised. Of course. Jefferson was not shackled by the ticket-of-leave chains that forced British ex-convicts to remain in the colony. He was an American citizen. He was free to leave the moment he had served his sentence.

It was only then that the ramifications hit, and they hit with brutal force. He's leaving, she thought. He's actually leaving! She was happy for him, of course she was. He was to be reunited with his family, why would she *not* be happy for him? But she could not rid herself of an unexpected and devastating sense of loss.

'And it's all because of you,' Jefferson continued, completely unaware of the impact his news had had upon her. 'I know that you persuaded your father to increase my wages, and I'm deeply grateful. I would never have earned enough to buy my passage to America had it not been for you, Doris.'

'Rubbish,' she said briskly. 'You would eventually have come to your senses and found an employer who would pay you your full worth, rather than slaving for the pittance my father gave you.'

He was shocked by her ruthlessness. 'I could never have left your father's employ,' he protested, 'not for as long as I remained in Van Diemen's Land. Why I shall be forever in his debt. Hamish McLagan was the only man prepared to give me a chance.'

'Of course he was: you're quite right.' She stood, calling a halt to the conversation. She could not bring herself to disillusion him, realising as she now did that, for all his liberal upbringing, Jefferson Brindsley Powell was a true innocent at heart. She was two years younger and far less educated than he, but she suddenly felt so much older and wiser.

Jefferson also stood. 'I want to thank you,' he said, taking her hand in both of his. 'I want to thank you, Doris, for all you have done for me.'

'There is no need for thanks,' she replied with a squeeze of her hand. She could have left it at that. But she didn't.

Doris would never know what drove her to act as she then did. She was not a creature of impulse and rarely displayed emotion, but for some strange reason she felt a sudden and intense desire to communicate. She reached up her hand and touched his face, her fingers resting against his cheek with infinite tenderness.

'My dearest friend,' she said, 'for that is what you are, Jefferson. That is what you have become to me. It is *I* who must thank *you*. I will miss you sorely when you leave, but I will be all the richer for having known you.' She gave him the gift of her smile. 'I will value our friendship forever,' she said, and she embraced him.

As she put her arms around him she felt him physically flinch and for a moment she thought he was about to pull away. Then he returned the embrace, but he did so awkwardly, clumsily, and she knew he was embarrassed by the physical contact. They parted quickly, Doris appalled that he had found her action so confronting and possibly even repellent. She felt shockingly self-conscious, and the startled look she met in his eyes made her doubly so, but she was not about to apologise.

'I won't bite,' she said caustically, 'there's no need to be frightened.'

'I'm sorry,' he replied. 'You took me by surprise, that's all.'

'I meant what I said, Jefferson.' She gathered her dignity about her. 'I value your friendship.'

'As I do yours, Doris, as I do yours.' He looked wretched

and guilty. 'Your friendship is so very precious to me,' he assured her desperately, 'please, please believe me. '

'Very well, I will believe you. I am going inside now.'

Over the ensuing weeks they did not speak of the incident, but Jefferson's manner underwent a radical change as he sought fervently to make amends. He was forever doing little things to please her. He would present her with a freshly picked bouquet of flowers, or a jar of her favourite boiled sweets purchased from the confectioners. He is like a forlorn puppy, Doris thought, eager to be forgiven for chewing a favourite slipper or digging a hole in the garden.

'I'm not angry, you know,' she was finally driven to comment. 'You don't need to keep currying favour.'

'I'm glad you're not angry, Doris. I would do anything, anything in the world, rather than anger or offend you in any way.'

Anything in the world? she wondered. Would you stay with me, Jefferson? Would you never return to America, but stay here with me in Van Diemen's Land forever?

'Very well,' she said, 'let's start this Sunday by digging a brand new flower bed just for roses. I have received some fine cuttings from Mrs MacDougall.'

Doris had finally recognised the truth. It had come as a complete revelation. She was in love with Jefferson Powell and had been for a long time, possibly even from the moment they'd first met. The symptoms had always been there, she realised, but she had failed, perhaps deliberately, to acknowledge them as anything other than friendship. She acknowledged them now, and in doing so she found the force of her love frightening. She had not known she was capable of such emotional depths: the sheer joy she felt simply being in his presence; the dismay that engulfed her at the prospect of his leaving. If she were never to see him again her life would be meaningless. If only I could find a way to make him stay, she thought, cursing herself for having been the very instrument of his departure. If she hadn't interfered, he would have remained loyally slaving away for a pittance.

She found the way that very Sunday, as they worked on the new flower bed. It all happened in an instant, in one quick moment of recognition.

There had been a light rainfall during the night and the ground was slippery. The rose bed they had dug was beside the front steps and, while Jefferson added mulch to the soil, Doris fetched the cuttings she'd left on the verandah. She was wearing galoshes: as she came back down the steps, her foot hit the slippery ground and skidded out from under her. She would have fallen backwards and cracked her head against the verandah, had Jefferson not sprung to her rescue.

With one arm, he grabbed her around the back, holding her against him; and to save himself from falling with her, he grasped the verandah upright. For one brief moment, they remained in a precarious embrace while Jefferson fought to retain his balance and, when he had done so, he helped her regain hers. Their bodies were locked together, his arm tightly about her, their mouths close, their breath mingling ... and then the moment was over. He released her and turned quickly away. But not before she'd seen that same startled look in his eyes, not before she'd recognised its meaning. Once again, he'd found their physical contact confronting – and once again he was flustered – but not because she was repellent to him. She had been wrong. His embarrassment sprang from another quarter altogether.

'Thank you for saving me,' she said lightly as he knelt and continued his mulching. 'The act of a true gallant. I'm most impressed.'

'Don't mention it, my pleasure,' he said, his tone equally casual, but he did not look up at her.

Doris knew in that instant she'd found the way, and she

did not question the temerity of her plan. Never in her life had she employed feminine guile – she hadn't even known she'd possessed any. But then never in her life had she been in love. And in love, Doris McLagan was as bold as any woman.

That night she crept brazenly through the house in her nightgown, past the very room where her father was sleeping, to the servants' quarters out the back. Silently, she slipped into the small bedroom that was Jefferson's domain, and just as silently she slipped into his bed.

He was lying on his side, and she curled herself against his back, cupping her body to his, encircling him with her arm. She was naked beneath her nightgown and she could feel the warmth of his flesh through the thin nightshirt he wore.

He stirred in his sleep, aware of her body, aroused even while he slept as if by some erotic dream. Then he turned to her and, in the dark of the room, although she could not see his eyes, Doris knew he had awakened. She heard the sharp intake of his breath. His disbelief was as palpable as his desire.

'Hold me, Jefferson,' she whispered, 'please hold me.'

Doris was a virgin, but she was not altogether ignorant. Her mother, a sensible woman, had informed her of the basics. The experience, she knew, would not be pleasurable. There would be pain, but she had resolved not to cry out and even, if possible, to make a pretence of some form of enjoyment.

What Doris did not know, however, was that Jefferson too was a virgin, and that the long-awaited act of sexual congress, particularly with the woman about whom he had recently been fantasising, would render him completely out of control.

The episode lasted only a minute or so as Jefferson thrust wildly, aware of nothing but the indescribable sensation of being inside a woman, and Doris gritted her teeth with grim forbearance.

When it was over, he sat on the edge of the bed, elbows on his knees, head sunk in his hands, overcome with remorse.

'I'm sorry, Doris,' he said. 'Oh my God, I'm so sorry, I'm so very, very sorry.'

Doris adjusted her nightgown, rose from the bed and lit the oil lamp that sat on the tallboy in the corner.

'You have nothing to apologise for, Jefferson,' she said. 'I seduced you. I behaved disgracefully.' She brought the lamp to the bedside table. 'I think I had best tend to the linen.'

'Oh my God,' he said as he stood and looked down at the blood-stained sheet. 'I'm sorry, I'm so sorry. What a terrible thing I've done.'

She quickly stripped the bed. 'You have not done a terrible thing at all. It is I who have done a terrible thing, and I hope you will not think too badly of me for it.' Now comes the part that requires true courage, Doris thought as she faced him squarely. She mustered all the dignity she had at her command, for there was an element deep within her that was ashamed of what she was doing.

'I have recently come to realise, Jefferson, that I love you. I do not expect this fact to alter your plans in any way, but it is because I love you that I wanted you to be the first, and indeed perhaps the only, man I shall ever know. Forgive me, my dear friend, for taking such advantage.'

Doris wasn't sure which was more difficult, the honest admission of her love, or the lie that she had simply wished to surrender her virginity to him. The sole purpose of her mission was in fact to become pregnant. Jefferson's code of honour, she knew, would never allow him to abandon a woman carrying his child. She only prayed that this quick, sordid coupling had proved successful.

Neither the admission nor the lie appeared to have any effect however. He seemed barely able to hear her. So filled with remorse was he that all he could do was apologise.

'What a shameful thing. I'm so sorry, I'm so sorry,' he kept saying.

Doris could not have known that Jefferson had been riddled with guilt for weeks. He'd been utterly appalled to find himself having impure thoughts about the woman he so admired. His actions tonight were an extension of the unforgiveable. He had been guilty by thought and he was now guilty by deed.

As it eventuated, their brief coupling did not result in a pregnancy, but such an outcome was unnecessary anyway, for Jefferson's code of honour did not require conception. Defilement sufficed. By robbing her of her virginity he had compromised her irreparably and marriage was the only honourable solution.

He made a formal request to Hamish McLagan for the hand of his daughter, but the Scot was initially reluctant.

'You could do better, Doris, surely,' Hamish said to his daughter in private. 'The man has nothing to bring to the union.' Hamish McLagan was decidedly peevish. If he was to lose the services of his daughter to a husband, an event he had not anticipated, it should surely be for the purposes of a business alliance. And dear God, what would happen to him in his old age should Jefferson Powell whisk her off to America? The man would be time-expired within only months. Hamish did not relish the prospect of losing his most valuable employee as it was: he most certainly did not intend losing his daughter into the bargain.

'The man has a great deal to bring to the union, Father, besides which he would expect no dowry.'

Hamish harrumphed. There was at least that, he supposed.

Doris, as always, had the answer to everything. 'Jefferson could take over the ferry service, which as you know has improved immeasurably since his employ. If you were to purchase the property down on the point, he could build a jetty and slipway and run the business from there, developing it into a far more successful enterprise than it currently is, and we could live in the old fisherman's cottage. The benefits would be considerable, Father. You would be gaining a valuable business partner and I would be living nearby, available whenever you need me, and for as long as you need me.'

By God, she's right, Hamish thought. The union was most certainly to his advantage. In fact his daughter had made an ideal choice.

'Well, my dear,' he said expansively, 'if you truly love the man as you say you do, I would not wish to stand in the path of your happiness.'

'I do love him, Father. I love him with all my heart.'

The marriage went ahead with no personal declaration of love on Jefferson's part, but Doris had not expected one. She was only thankful that he had shouldered the responsibility of their marriage as nobly as he had. She had feared he might grow to hate her for entrapping him. Jefferson, however, continued to believe that if there had been any wrongdoing it had been his and his alone, and their friendship remained as strong as ever.

Doris told herself that friendship was a fine basis for marriage. She prayed that love would grow in time and made a personal vow to God that she would be the best possible wife to Jefferson. She would devote herself to his happiness and work hard on his behalf and, above all, if God willed, she would bear him strong children.

Doris's prayers appeared to have been heard for she conceived not long after their marriage and, by the time Jefferson's pardon was granted, she was three months pregnant.

The couple was overjoyed. In a letter to his parents, Jefferson announced the news with great jubilation, adding: *Doris has agreed wholeheartedly that the child is to be named after one of you – William George if it is a boy and Martha Jane if it is a girl. That way you will remain forever a part of her life as you are of mine.*

Jefferson wrote regularly to his parents, as they did him. The letters were eagerly awaited on both sides of the globe, but the exchange could be frustrating for the mail took months to arrive.

'I doubt they even know we're married yet,' he said. 'My last letter is no doubt somewhere in the middle of the Atlantic.' He laughed and added, 'They'll probably get this news when William is taking his first steps.' Jefferson firmly believed his firstborn would be a son and always referred to the baby as William, no doubt in the hope that he would be proved right. Doris went along with the exercise, although she really didn't care whether the baby was a William or a Martha.

The baby *was* a boy as it turned out. But he never took his first breath, let alone his first steps. Baby William was stillborn.

'Strangled itself on the cord, it did,' the midwife told Jefferson. 'Perfectly healthy, tragic thing – happens quite a lot, you know.'

Doris was inconsolable. She withdrew into herself, staring unseeingly at the stone walls of the bedroom, eating nothing, speaking to no-one. She excluded even her husband from her grief, and spoke just four words to Reverend MacDougall when, at Jefferson's request, the priest visited the cottage.

'It is God's punishment,' she said.

Surprisingly enough, it was Hamish McLagan who broke through the barrier.

Like Jefferson, Hamish was fearful for the state of Doris's health. She had now languished for a whole week, taking barely any sustenance. Had his daughter determined to starve herself to death? Hamish McLagan took action the only way he knew how.

'It's time you stopped feeling sorry for yourself, girl,' he said harshly. He'd asked to see his daughter alone, and Jefferson had ushered him into the bedroom.

Doris remained staring at the sandstone wall and the nothingness it represented.

'Your husband is grieving too, you know,' he continued unrelentingly. 'Where's your compassion, woman? The man has lost a son for God's sake. It's your duty to give him another.'

She turned her head, her eyes focusing upon her father. From childhood, his had been the voice of command, and from childhood, duty had been her sole purpose in life.

'You understand me, don't you, girl? You have a duty to your husband.' Having gained her attention, Hamish softened his attack a little. 'You are honour-bound to serve and obey him, Doris, and above all to bear him children: you know that, don't you?'

'Yes, Father, I do.' She hauled herself up in the bed, leaning back against the pillows, her face pale and drawn, dark circles beneath her eyes. 'I understand my duty, and I thank you for reminding me of it. Would you ask Jefferson to come in now please? I wish to talk to him.'

'Good girl. That's my good girl.' Hamish rushed to adjust the pillows in a clumsy effort to make her more comfortable. Then he fetched Jefferson, closing the door quietly behind him when the two were alone together. He was thrilled at the success of his mission. His little girl was back.

Jefferson sat on the edge of the bed. After many a sleepless night, he looked weary himself, but now the breakthrough had been made, he felt an immense sense of relief.

'Your father says you wish to speak to me?' His voice was strained as he tried, unsuccessfully, to sound casual.

'I do. Oh Jefferson, I beg forgiveness for the wrongs I have done you. God has rightly punished me for my wickedness, but in doing so He has caused you the loss of a son. I can only presume He means this to be a further punishment laid at my door, for I feel such guilt at having destroyed your life so completely.'

'The loss of our child is not your fault, Doris,' he said gently, but firmly.

She did not hear him. 'You must go home, Jefferson. You must go home to where you belong.'

'I *am* home.' He was bewildered. 'This is where I belong.'

'No, no, you belong with your family, with your parents and your brothers and sisters.' She shook her head, distressed. 'My father spoke to me of duty, and he was quite right to do so, but he misunderstands where my duty lies. My duty lies in releasing you from your vows. Vows you should never have been forced to make.'

'I made no vows I did not wish to make, Doris, I can assure you of that.'

But Doris had no wish to be so easily forgiven. The gates had been opened and the words poured out. She had seduced him that night, she said, with the deliberate intention of getting pregnant and forcing him to remain with her, thereby depriving him of his homeland and his family.

'I stole from you everything that was yours, Jefferson.' She was starting to weep now. In her weakened state, the purging of her guilt was exhausting her. 'I stole your country and your past and your very heritage.'

'You did not steal my future, Doris.' With his thumb, he wiped away the tears that coursed down her cheek. 'You gave me the gift of a future more wondrous than I could have dreamed possible. I love this country with a passion, and I love my life here, but above all, my darling girl, I love you. I love you more than words can ever express.' She had stopped crying and was staring at him with wide-eyed incredulity. He laughed for the sheer relief of having her back from the dark world that had claimed her. 'Don't you see, my dear, whether you engineered my future by devious means or otherwise, I can only be grateful that you did so.'

'You've never told me you love me.'

'I tell you every day, Doris. I tell you with every look and every deed.' He couldn't help but smile: she was so forlornly childlike. 'However, I will say the words on a regular basis if you would prefer. I'll start now, shall I? I love you. I love you. I –'

'No, no, Jefferson, please,' she said, embarrassed, 'I am aware you love me, of course, it's just that I have presumed your love sprang more from friendship –'

'It does. It always did and it always will.' Jefferson dropped the banter. 'When does friendship become love, Doris? Do you know? I don't. I only know that our friendship has produced a love that reaches beyond all else. My dearest girl, you are everything to me.' He kissed her gently. 'You are my very life.'

Doris gazed into her husband's eyes with newfound purpose.

'I will give you other children, Jefferson, I promise.'

'I know, my dear, I know you will. Once we get you strong again.'

'And I will start with a son. Father says it is my duty.'

'And Father is quite right,' he said with a smile.

One year later, true to her word, Doris bore Jefferson a son. They named the child George Hamish Brindsley Powell in order to keep everyone happy.

'Michael is leaving now, Doris ...'

While Jefferson had been chatting away with Mick O'Callaghan, Doris had remained gazing out at the garden, lost in her memories, oblivious to the men and their conversation.

She looked at the rose bushes that grew from the cuttings they'd first planted, and the wooden garden seat that Jefferson had built, now scarred by the weather but all the more attractive for it, and the silver birches that had lived up to their promise and become elegant trees. The garden is not only a tangible reminder of the past, she thought, the garden reflects the growth of our love ...

'Doris, my dear, Michael is leaving ...'

She was jolted from her reverie by her husband's voice and looked up, startled to discover that both men were now standing.

'You were miles away, weren't you?' Jefferson said.

'Yes, I'm afraid I was,' she replied as she rose to her feet.

'Forgive us for being so remiss, my dear. We got a little carried away in conversation, or rather I did.'

'Not at all. If there is an apology due, it is mine for having become so lost in my own thoughts. Please excuse my inattentiveness, Mr O'Callaghan.'

'To be honest, Mrs Powell, I myself have been so lost in your husband's tales of the past, that any inattentiveness on your part went unnoticed, I assure you.' Mick was quite genuine. He would have pretended avid interest had Jefferson bored him witless, but he had indeed found the man fascinating. 'Why, I had no idea that the infamous George Arthur who was Governor of Van Diemen's Land went on to become Lieutenant Governor of Upper Canada,' he said. 'It is a fact which explains a great deal, I must say.'

Jefferson caught his wife's amused glance. 'No, no, Doris, I have not been telling my life story, I promise you. We were talking of patriotism in general, and Michael simply asked me how it was that the members of the Patriot Movement should have ended up in Van Diemen's Land.'

'I certainly did,' Mick agreed. 'It has been a mystery to me. From the moment I first heard of the French-Canadians and their American sympathisers being sent here, I thought why in God's name?' He had thought no such thing, he was courting favour, but upon reflection, he found the subject extremely interesting. 'Who would think to send them to Van Diemen's Land, I asked myself. And

now I know,' he said with a comical shrug. 'Who else but
the demon governor himself, George Arthur?'

'And what a favour he did me, as it turned out,' Jefferson said, smiling unashamedly at Doris. 'What a very
great favour. Were it not for George Arthur I would never
have discovered this paradise on earth. Nor would I have
discovered the perfect wife ...'

Doris was not a woman who blushed, which was fortunate, for had she been so prone, Jefferson would have
caused many a crimson flush in the early days of their
marriage. His speechifying, his penchant for telling his
life story, and above all his open displays of affection
represented everything that, in Doris's rigid upbringing,
was unacceptable. Now, she loved him for his very lack
of inhibition and for the way he expressed himself with
such freedom. It did not stop her, however, from calling
a halt when she considered he was on the verge of going
too far.

She offered her hand to the young Irishman. 'It has been
a pleasure to meet you, Mr O'Callaghan.'

Mick realised that Doris Powell was putting an end to
the conversation. How extraordinary, he thought, and he
glanced at Jefferson, but Jefferson was smiling benignly,
not in the least offended.

'The pleasure was all mine, Mrs Powell, I assure you,'
he said as they shook. 'Thank you kindly for the tea and
for the delicious cake.'

'I am glad you enjoyed it.'

He proffered a winning smile. 'Martha is quite right
when she says it is the best cake in the world.'

'Martha rarely shares her sentiments so willingly.
You made quite an impression upon my daughter,
Mr O'Callaghan.'

'She's a beguiling child, to be sure.'

Mick wondered what the woman was actually saying.
You made an impression upon my daughter, but not upon

me – was that it? Her tone was pleasant and her manner polite, but for God's sake did she never smile?

The men stepped out onto the front verandah and Mick departed with the promise that he would return in the next day or so with an apprentice waterman.

'I'll find the perfect for'ard hand for us, Jefferson: you need have no doubt of it.'

'I'm sure you will, Michael,' Jefferson said. 'I have great faith in your judgement.'

As Mick walked off down the garden path his mind was on Doris Powell. Was she for or against him? He would need her support in the future if he was to secure the position of ferry service manager and the little stone cottage that went with it. But he had no idea where he stood with her and he was mystified. Plain women were always the easiest to conquer, yet she seemed impervious to charm.

For the life of him, Mick could not fathom Doris Powell.

London, 1840

Pigeons scattered every which way as Sir Albert Broughton strode across Trafalgar Square. He dodged the evening traffic, ducking behind a hansom cab, then skilfully stepped over a pile of steaming horse droppings to reach the pavement and press on through the chill of evening towards his destination, the Voyagers' Club in Pall Mall.

Sir Albert, as a director, had called an extraordinary meeting of the board of the Van Diemen's Land Company and, in anticipation of complaints regarding the necessity of such a meeting, had decided to hold it in an anteroom at his gentlemen's club. This meant he could indulge in a decent supper with his friend Anthony Peters-Tedman, a zoologist and Fellow of the Royal Society, whom he'd invited to attend the meeting to offer information and advice if called upon.

'Good evening to you, Bertie,' Anthony Peters-Tedman called from atop the steps of the Voyagers' Club. 'A chilly night for this early in the season, what?'

'Indeed it is,' Albert replied, removing his glove and shaking his friend by the hand. 'Been waiting long?'

'Barely a minute, old man.'

'Good to hear, good to hear.'

An elderly doorman opened the large oak-and-glass door. 'Good evening to you, Sir Albert.'

'Evening, Sykes.' Albert replied, ushering his friend inside. They handed their coats, hats and gloves to the ancient retainer. 'We'd better hurry along upstairs Tony, I've scheduled the meeting for half-past six.'

'Right you are, Bertie.'

The two men scurried up the several flights of stairs and through the double doors into an anteroom containing eight men seated around a large table.

'Gentlemen.' Albert's stentorian voice caught them all unaware as he knew it would. He was stamping his authority over those present in order to nip any complaints in the bud. 'I won't delay you any further than is necessary, but I can assure you this extraordinary meeting is most definitely called for. So,' he said crisply, 'I shall call it to order, shall I?'

The correct procedures were observed by Albert and the company secretary without interruption and, finally, he sat himself down at the head of the table and introduced his friend.

'My good friend Dr Anthony Peters-Tedman, Fellow of the Royal Society, has seen fit to join us for what should be a brief meeting and shall offer his knowledge on colonial fauna if required.'

'Colonial fauna? What the deuce is this all about, Bertie, if I may be so bold as to ask?'

'You may indeed be so bold, George,' Albert replied with false joviality. George Weekes had recently been appointed to the board by virtue of his father's death the previous year and Albert didn't like him. He thought Weekes an indecisive creature, a pale copy of his father, who once roasted and ate his prized whippet merely because the animal had failed to win a coursing race in Norfolk.

'I have here,' Sir Albert said, waving aloft a
paper, 'a letter from one of our principal representatives in Van Diemen's Land, Arthur Curry,
a man I trust implicitly.' Several mutters of
'hear, hear' echoed around the table. 'He is of
the opinion we increase the bounty payable for the
destruction of those blasted wolves, or whatever
you call them.' Albert looked at Peters-Tedman for
support. 'What do you call them, Tony?'

'Thylacines, Bertie. The Latin name is *Thylacinus
cynocephalus*: it means "dog-headed, pouched" –'

'Yes, yes! I've got it!' Albert interrupted.
'Striped like a tiger! Now I remember. Van Diemen's
tiger.'

'Isn't there already a bounty on those things?'
It was Weekes again. 'My father told me. Correct
me if I'm wrong but I believe it's been in force
for years.'

'Yes, yes,' Albert said impatiently, 'five shillings has been offered for every male hyena,' he
stumbled slightly over the word, 'and seven for
every female, with or without young, since 1830.
It was increased to ten shillings in 1831, and it
needs to be increased again.' He waved the letter
sent to him from the colony as if it contained an
incontrovertible truth.

'Are we – I mean is the *company* legally entitled
to set these bounties?'

'Oh, do hush, Weekes.'

'I mean, what's the colonial government got to
say about all this?'

'We have a Royal Charter to develop two hundred
and fifty thousand acres, Weekes. What we do with
those acres is of no concern to the colonial government.'

'I see. Sorry.'

'Apology accepted. Now, let's get on with it.'
Albert glared about, defying each man at the table
to offer any further disruption. 'Don't want to be
here all night, do we?'

Those present had no intention of interrupting
Sir Albert in full flight. Besides they all had
homes, or better still mistresses, to go to. The
meeting progressed apace and a motion was made and
passed that the bounty be increased. Sir Albert then
called the meeting closed and within minutes found
himself alone with his friend and colleague.

'I thought you handled that superbly, Bertie,'
Peters-Tedman exclaimed. 'No need for me to wade
in at all, eh, what?'

'They're investors, Tony. They know the company
is losing money in Van Diemen's Land. Good Lord,
we've barely turned over ten thousand pounds
in the fifteen-odd years since the company was
founded. And it's all thanks to those bloody what-
ya-ma-call-its –'

'*Thylacinus cynocephalus.*'

'Exactly!'

'They're really that bad, are they?' Peters-
Tedman's scientific interest was now genuinely
aroused.

'According to our supervisors on the company properties along the north-west coast of the colony,
yes,' Albert said as he strode out of the anteroom
and down the stairs. 'The wretched animal is virtually the sole reason for their failure to produce
wool. Vicious predator! Insatiable appetite! I am
informed it is a fierce and determined creature,
and if attacked will fight in the most desperate
manner. Indeed, I've heard one of them was observed
standing at bay, surrounded by a number of dogs,
and bidding them all defiance. Not a single dog
dared venture within reach of the thing.'

'You don't say?' Tony Peters-Tedman said, breathless after trying to keep pace with his friend
down the stairs to the club's foyer. 'I must take
the trouble to study up on this animal.'

'I wouldn't bother.' Albert laughed. 'With the
new bounty imposed I shan't be surprised if there
are none left within a year. Sykes!'

'Yes, Sir Albert?' the doorman answered.

'Supper for two: see to it, will you?'

'As you wish, Sir Albert.' With a flourish of his arm the elderly retainer ushered them into the dining room.

CHAPTER SEVEN

Mick O'Callaghan worked harder than he'd ever worked in his life over the next six months. He'd considered his duties as deckhand aboard the *Maid of Canton* hard work, but they paled in comparison to the lot of a waterman.

There had been times during those six months when Mick had come close to walking away from the job, times when the easy life beckoned and the little voice in his head whispered *Leave the drudgery for those born to it, Mick, you were meant for better things.* At first, his sole motivation had been the lure of the cottage and the job of manager upon which he'd set his sights, but in working hard to prove himself worthy of the position, he'd discovered an even stronger motivation. He was driven to prove his worth to Jefferson Powell, not only as a worker, but as a man.

Jefferson had had a profound effect upon Mick, as he did upon all those who worked for him. Even-tempered and easygoing though he was, the American was tough, and his men respected him for it. His rules were simple. He demanded honesty and hard work, and he got it. No-one cheated Jefferson Powell.

'I'd like to see the man who'd try,' one of the watermen said, a big Welshman from Cardiff.

It had been Mick's very first day on the job, and Jefferson had introduced him and Tim, his young forward hand, to the other teams milling about at Waterman's Dock. It was early morning, but the wharves were already bustling with activity, and Jefferson had left Mick and Tim to get acquainted with the others before the day's business got under way. Men talked more freely and bonded more quickly without the boss around.

'I seen it once,' another waterman said, 'a couple of years back. Father and son team, it was. The dad had been doctoring the log, hadn't he, and Jefferson's waiting for him when he comes in. Dad climbs up onto the dock, and Jefferson says "Can you swim?" Dad says "No," and Jefferson picks him up bodily and hurls him into the harbour. Then he says to the lad: "You better look after your pa: I think he's drowning."'

The men all laughed. They were big men, rough and tough and solidly built. Even the younger forward hands were more thick-set than Mick. He felt puny beside them and was thankful that Jefferson, in introducing him, had said, 'Don't be deceived by size, boys; when it comes to the bonus, Michael will give you a run for your money, you'll see.' Mick had a feeling that without the boss's remark he might have come in for some ribbing.

'What about you, Mick,' the man who'd told the story asked, 'can *you* swim?' Mick had quickly let it be known upon Jefferson's departure that he was a 'Mick' rather than a 'Michael'. 'Michael' was altogether out of place with a bunch like this.

'Not very well,' he said. Then he grinned and admitted, 'Actually, if the truth be known, I can barely stay afloat.'

The man, a hulking brute of a fellow, guffawed. 'Half of us can't, and that's a fact. What a foolish mob of bastards we are.'

They all joined in the joke, sharing it with Mick, who'd clearly become one of them. They were a good-natured lot and, given the boss's approval, Mick O'Callaghan was accepted as a new member of the Powell team.

'Where's the point in cheating anyway,' the Welshman said. 'Jefferson's a fair man. He pays a fair wage, and the bonus is always worth working for.'

The others were plainly in agreement, although Mick later learnt that the comment was something of an understatement. As an employer, Jefferson Powell embraced a philanthropic approach that bred a strong sense of loyalty among his workers. He was a fair man not only to his watermen and the others under his employ, but also to their families. If a man with children could not work because of illness, then Jefferson lent assistance to that man's family until he was well again.

Upon joining the ranks, Mick soon realised that Jefferson's watermen worked for more than the weekly bonus and the proof that they were the top team. They worked for Jefferson's personal approval, and he quickly found himself doing the same.

It was to be four whole months before he and young Tim were able to take out the bonus, however, and during that time Mick's body grew hard and muscular. For the first month or so he relied as much as he could upon sail, avoiding the oars whenever possible. But the more he was forced to row, the stronger he became, until he found he actually enjoyed the physical exertion. He felt powerful as he hauled on the oars with a full boat-load of goods or passengers, the heavy wooden vessel ploughing obediently through the water. Ship to shore and then back again, he could row for hours.

'Well done, Michael,' Jefferson said. 'Good lad, Tim.'

It was a proud day when they took out the bonus ahead of the other four teams. In fact twenty-three-year-old Mick, who had avoided hard work for as long as he could remember, had never felt so proud.

He had not, however, lost sight of his original purpose,

nor had he lost sight of the fact that Jefferson, for all his admirable qualities, and indeed possibly because of them, could be manipulated.

Mick had long since recognised that the American was not the opportunist he'd originally presumed him to be. Jefferson wouldn't know how to take advantage of others, which surely leaves him a little vulnerable to those who have such a talent, Mick thought. Not that he intended to take advantage of Jefferson himself – he admired the man far too much – but he certainly intended to take advantage of the situation. He wanted the top job, and he wanted the cottage. The only obstacle appeared to be Jefferson's determination to employ a ticket-of-leave couple.

Having proved his value as a worker, the next step in Mick's plan was to ingratiate himself on a personal level, which proved a remarkably simple exercise. In skippering the ship-to-shore boat that was housed at Battery Point, he did not work out of Waterman's Dock like the other men, and it was easy to call by the house in Napoleon Street under some pretext or another. When he did he was always made welcome, for Jefferson enjoyed his company, although more often than not the American wasn't there. Jefferson was usually at the shipyards or at the McLagan stables further up the hill, where the horses and drays were housed. His absence suited Mick's purposes to perfection as Doris would invariably ask him in for a cup of tea, and it was Doris whose favour he most wished to court.

'Dour Doris', as he'd mentally nicknamed her, remained a mystery to Mick. He couldn't tell whether she liked him or not. But she certainly liked the relationship he was building with her children, particularly with little Martha.

'She's totally enamoured of you; it's quite extraordinary,' Doris said as Martha dived past her and out onto the front verandah, where she stood beaming her radiant smile up at Mick. He automatically grinned back like an idiot.

'The feeling's mutual,' he replied.

'Jefferson isn't here, I'm afraid. Would you like a cup of tea?'

'I wouldn't wish to impose.'

'It's no imposition, Mr O'Callaghan. The children love to see you.'

The ritual was always the same.

He took off his boots, leaving them on the front verandah, and entered in his stockinged feet, Martha skipping on ahead of him.

Doris was now so accustomed to his visits that she led the way directly through to the kitchen where George was waiting, pretending nonchalance, having heard the Irishman at the front door.

'Hello, George,' Mick said.

'Hello, Michael.'

They shook hands man to man.

For the next fifteen minutes, Mick gave his full attention to the children. He tried desperately not to display favouritism, but his heart was lost every time Martha smiled at him. For some strange reason, the smile appeared quite a lot today. *She seems excited about something*, he thought.

George produced the model ship that he was building out of light pinewood. For a boy of seven, he was clearly gifted. He placed the model upon the kitchen table as he always did in order for Mick to admire its latest progress. George was very serious about his work. He intended to be a shipwright when he grew up.

'I shall not hire ship builders like Pa,' he had proudly announced, 'I shall build my own ships.'

'Excellent work, George,' Mick said as he sat on the bench and closely inspected the model. 'She's coming along a real treat. She's a clipper isn't she? Do you have a name for her yet?'

'No.'

'How about the *Maid of Canton*?' He waited as the boy

deliberated upon the idea, then he added, 'you can call her the *Maid* for short.'

That clinched things for George. 'The *Maid* she is,' he said.

Martha, who had been patiently biding her time, decided that it was her turn. She climbed up on the bench and sat beside Mick.

'Michael,' she said. Her little currant eyes were deadly serious. She had an important announcement to make.

'Yes, Martha?'

'It is my birthday on Sunday.'

'Really? And how old will you be?'

She held up the splayed fingers of her right hand.

'My goodness me, a whole handful of years – that's a mighty age.'

'I will be five,' she corrected him. It was obvious he had misunderstood her so she spelt the facts out as clearly as possible. 'I will be *five years old.*'

'And that's a grand age, to be sure.'

As Doris placed Mick's cup of tea on the table, Martha looked up at her mother with breathless anticipation.

'Now?' she whispered. 'May I ask him now?'

'Yes. You may.'

'Will you come to afternoon tea on Sunday, Michael?' Martha rattled the words out, and in order to prevent any possible refusal, she quickly added the major attraction, 'Mother is making a *very, very big* birthday cake, and there will be candles.'

Mick glanced at Doris.

'She's been dying to ask you,' Doris said. 'Please do come.'

He nodded to Doris, but directed his reply to Martha. 'I would be delighted to come to tea on your birthday, Martha. Thank you very much for inviting me. ' He was rewarded with a sea of dimples.

Mick never lingered over the cup of tea Doris made

him: he knew better than to overstay his welcome. Once the tea was poured, he scoffed it as quickly as etiquette allowed and then left. The principal purpose of his visits was, after all, the contact he had with the children, which he knew delighted their mother. He always had some business pretext for calling should Jefferson be at home, but he no longer bothered to proffer any form of excuse to Doris.

She accompanied him to the front door, instructing the children to remain in the kitchen, which disappointed Martha, who always liked to wave goodbye. But Doris wanted to have a private word with Mick.

'Thank you kindly for the tea, Mrs Powell,' he said as he knelt and put on his boots.

'The pleasure was mine, Mr O'Callaghan,' she said, observing the customary ritual. But when he stood and was about to take his departure, Doris varied the routine.

'As you have so captured my daughter's heart, Mr O'Callaghan,' she said, 'would you mind if I called you Michael?'

'I would be honoured.'

'And you, of course, must call me Doris.' She offered her hand and they shook. 'I look forward to seeing you on Sunday then, Michael. We'll have tea a little earlier than usual – shall we say three o'clock?'

'Three o'clock it is, Doris. See you on Sunday.'

Mick congratulated himself on his success. He was well on the way to conquering dour Doris. In fact things were going splendidly all round. He was making inroads and enjoying himself at the same time. He actually looked forward to Sunday.

Sunday indeed proved a triumph.

The rag doll, a clown with yellow hair, a red nose, and big red smiling lips, which Mick had gone to great pains to purchase, was an unmitigated success. Martha decided, for some mysterious reason known only to herself, to call it Ben.

'Why Ben?' he asked.

'Because Ben is short for Benjamin,' she explained. He didn't enquire any further.

They gorged themselves on the feast Doris had prepared, lit the candles on the cake and, once Martha had blown them out and her mother had cut everyone a slice, they gorged themselves further. Finally, the children went outside to play in the late afternoon summer sun and the adults were left to talk.

They adjourned to the front sitting room where Jefferson poured a Scotch whisky for himself and Mick, and Doris opted for another cup of tea.

'The last of my father-in-law's supply,' he said, referring to the bottle. 'I enjoy a glass now and then.' He didn't really. Jefferson rarely drank hard liquor, even of the finest variety, but today being a special occasion he wished to encourage a sense of camaraderie. The men toasted each other with their cut crystal tumblers – Hamish McLagan had drunk his Scotch out of nothing but the best – and Jefferson sat back, appraising the young Irishman.

'Well, well, Michael,' he said, 'I had no idea you were so very popular with my children.'

Mick inwardly froze. Dear God, he thought, have I overstepped the mark? Did Jefferson find him presumptuous? If so, his plans had gone quite awry.

'The fact that George named his model the *Maid of Canton* was something of a giveaway, I must admit,' Jefferson said with a smile. He was not at all offended, but he was certainly intrigued. And of course Doris has told me of Martha's great fondness for you. But now to see with my own eyes the bond that has been established.' He shook his head admiringly. 'It is obvious you have an extraordinary gift with children.'

Mick breathed a sigh of relief. 'It is the children who offered me the gift of their friendship, Jefferson,' he said.

'I do not know why little Martha chose to adopt me as she did, but I think it was her example that led George to vie for my attention. I do not believe any credit is due to me.' Mick realised all of a sudden that he was actually telling the truth. 'I must say I envy you your family.' He glanced at Doris, who was paying avid attention. He wasn't sure that he envied Jefferson a wife like Doris, but he certainly envied the man his children.

The conversation had provided the perfect opener and Mick embarked upon his planned course of action. 'It is my intention in the near future to start a family of my own, Jefferson,' he said. 'In fact I am currently seeking a wife.'

'An excellent plan,' the American nodded his approval, 'you're strong and fit and of a good age to marry. Don't you agree, Doris?'

'I most certainly do.' Doris sounded surprisingly adamant.

'Yes, I very much wish to settle down,' Mick said, 'and the sooner the better, I must say.'

Having sown the seeds for a future conversation with Jefferson when they were alone, Mick intended going no further, but things suddenly took a turn he could not possibly have anticipated.

'Forgive my asking, Michael,' Doris said in her customary blunt fashion, 'but my husband told me some time ago you are an educated man. Is this so?'

'It is, Doris, yes.'

She turned to Jefferson. 'Perhaps, my dear, you should give some thought to employing Michael as your new ferry service manager.'

Both men stared at her blankly, Jefferson surprised by his wife's suggestion and Mick dumbstruck by his good fortune.

'I take it you would be interested in such a position, Michael?' she queried.

'Well, yes ...' Mick tried not to appear too eager.

'Workers are becoming hard to find in these gold rush days, Jefferson,' Doris said to her husband, who clearly remained sceptical about the idea. 'Labourers and skilled workers both.' She looked interrogatively at Mick. 'You have not been tempted to join the rush for gold yourself, Michael.'

'Not once, no, no.' He shook his head vehemently. It was true. Far too many of his countrymen had become infected by the fever. He'd heard that Bendigo and Ballarat were awash with the Irish. God only knew who he'd bump into on the goldfields of Victoria.

'There you are; you see, dear?' Turning once more to her husband Doris presented the fait accompli. 'In Michael you have loyalty, experience and education. What more could you wish?'

'But as you well know, Doris, I had planned for a couple to take over the cottage,' Jefferson protested, 'a couple to whom I could offer a fine opportunity –'

'A couple *would* be taking over the cottage,' Doris countered. 'Michael is seeking a wife, dear. And what finer opportunity could you offer a young man who plans to settle down and start a family than the very opportunity we ourselves were given?'

They exchanged a fond glance, their eyes reflecting shared memories. How vividly they recalled those early years when Jefferson had first taken over the ferry service and they had lived in the fisherman's cottage.

'I see your reasoning, my dear,' he said. 'It might even be a case of history repeating itself, might it not?'

'I pray it should prove so.' Doris turned to the Irishman and smiled warmly. 'I pray that one day you may be as fortunate as we were, Michael. I truly wish you such happiness.'

Mick was caught out. Her sincerity had an instant and profound impact upon him. Her words and her smile came so directly from the heart that he didn't know what to say.

'Thank you.' He couldn't think of anything else.

'Well, I suppose that's settled then.' Jefferson gave a good-humoured shrug, still somewhat bemused by the swift turn of events.

'Yes it is,' Doris agreed briskly. 'Now all we need to do,' she added, 'is to find Michael a wife.'

'I think, Doris, that is something he can do on his own,' Jefferson said.

Two weeks later Mick shifted into the cottage, and his life changed radically. From Wapping to Battery Point just like that, he thought. And no poky little room out the back either, but a cottage all to himself: by God but he'd moved up a notch in life. He was a man with a title now, the manager of the Powell Ferry-Boat Service, no less. My, that sounded grand.

Along with his improved status and a healthy increase in salary, came an easier physical workload – but more complex duties. Each morning he delivered the log books to the teams at Waterman's Dock, and at the end of each work day he collected them, together with the takings. The other watermen were not resentful of his elevated status, for they were uneducated men who knew the position could never have been theirs. In the early evenings Mick tallied up the amounts and entered them into the ledger, which was to be presented on a monthly basis to Doris, who handled the bookkeeping for all the various Powell enterprises. He paid the weekly wages and was responsible for the upkeep of the boats, slipping them when necessary and doing the general maintenance work. He also recruited new watermen when required and personally trained each new apprentice. Mick's was a position of some authority.

He settled into a comfortable routine, spending more and more time with the Powells, who had adopted him as one of the family. Afternoon tea on Sundays became a ritual. Mick loved his Sundays.

But as the months passed, Sundays with the family started to have a curiously unsettling effect. His lie was becoming a reality. I *do* want a wife, he thought, as he watched Doris pour Jefferson's tea, adding milk and sugar just the way she knew he liked it. Mick no longer saw Doris as dour. He no longer even saw her as plain. He saw her as the perfect wife and mother. I want a woman just like Doris, he thought. He wanted a loyal wife who would love him like Doris loved Jefferson, and he wanted a fine son like George and a ridiculously adorable daughter like Martha. He wanted a family like Jefferson's.

'How I do envy you, Jefferson,' he would say time and again.

'Keep searching, Michael,' the American would reply encouragingly, 'you'll find the right wife. It's only a matter of time.'

But Mick had not been seriously seeking a wife. When he was with the Powells, he longed for the loving family existence they shared, but away from them, restlessness crept in. During his days as a hard-working waterman, his nights had remained much the same, filled with the raucousness of the Hunter's Rest. He'd continued to protect the girls from troublemakers, and there'd been the occasional tryst with pretty Molly Bates in the little back room. The cottage, on the other hand, was a lonely place.

Occasionally he dressed in his finest and visited Farrington's, where he played cards, smoked cigars, drank brandy and discussed politics. The good life still beckoned. And Saturday nights remained as they always had. Saturday nights saw him back at the Hunter's Rest, no longer on duty, but carousing with the gang. Much as Mick enjoyed his newfound status, he missed the old days.

He always popped upstairs to see Ma before joining in the fun at the bar. He'd share a nip of rum with her, and tell her all his news.

'Ah, Mick,' she'd say, 'I miss you sorely, and that's a fact, but the best thing I ever done was point you Jefferson's way. He's the making of you, lad; he's your future, he is.' Ma Tebbutt was as proud of her boy as any mother could be.

Ma was not well these days. Her bronchial condition had become chronic and her visits downstairs, rare as they had been, were now a thing of the past. She remained in the confines of her room, Evie serving as her personal maid, collecting the chamber pot twice daily and delivering the food and the wood for the small fire in winter.

'This is where I'll die,' she'd say, 'right here in this very room, in this very chair, beside this very table.' It was not a complaint, but a simple statement. Ma seemed quite happy about the fact.

Tonight, Mick picked his way through the streets of Wapping with care, cursing the mud and the slime that threatened to ruin his good boots. He'd heard that the rivulet had flooded. Damn it, he thought, I should have worn galoshes.

Following heavy rain, the Hobart Town Rivulet had flooded two days previously, causing chaos as it always did when it spewed out over its banks and into the homes of Wapping. The children, as usual, had loved every minute of it. They'd stood on the bridge watching the torrent charge beneath them, carrying with it the abattoirs' rotting remnants alongside once-prized possessions from people's inundated houses, and they'd splashed about in the streets and lanes that had become giant swimming pools. A flood was fun for the children of Wapping.

Now, two days later, the residential areas around Campbell and Sackville Streets and Lower Collins were still awash with two feet of floodwater. People had either moved up or out. Those in two-storey dwellings had moved upstairs and those in single-storey houses had moved out to stay with friends in nearby streets that were not so devastated. There they would bide their time until the water had subsided. Wapping looked after its own and coping with a rivulet flood was simply a matter of course.

Mick avoided the worst affected streets and arrived at the Hunter's Rest relatively unscathed, although his good boots would need a thorough clean the following morning.

The pub was several blocks from the rivulet and had not received the full deluge of floodwater, but like the whole of Wapping it reeked of damp, and the floors were thick with the mud that had been walked through its doors for the past two days.

None of which helped Ma's chest condition, for the damp and the mud and the mould had all made their way upstairs.

'You could have wiped your boots,' she said accusingly. She was in one of her crotchety moods and it was obvious she was already well into the rum.

'Wiped them on what? There's mud everywhere, Ma, you can't escape it.'

She was about to berate him further, but the breath she took to give voice brought on a coughing fit.

The fit lasted for some time and Mick held the bowl for her while she hawked gobs of phlegm into it. He noticed a little blood there. That surely isn't a good sign, he thought. Finally it was over and she sat back, weakened by her efforts.

'This fucking damp will be the end of me,' she said. 'Pour us another rum, Mick, and fetch a mug for yourself.'

They had a tot each. She'd obviously forgiven him his muddy boots, but she was in a general ill-humour, which didn't make her much fun, and the Irish fiddle downstairs was calling to Mick.

'No thanks, Ma,' he said as she offered him a second tot, 'I'll pop down and say hello to the girls before business picks up.' He stood.

'All right, run off and leave me, see if I care.' She poured herself another rum. 'Make yourself useful while you're down there. Teach that dumb bastard how to do his job. Len told me there was trouble again last night.'

Ma was constantly whinging about the man she'd hired in his stead, a giant of a fellow called Thomas, whom the girls had nicknamed Tiny. Tiny's appearance was a deterrent to the average troublemaker it was true, but he was not very bright. 'All brawn no brains,' she'd say. 'Can't sense when trouble's brewing.'

'Right you are, Ma, right you are,' Mick said, just to keep her happy. 'I'll have a word with Tiny, I promise.'

I won't, he thought as he went downstairs. What would be the point? Besides, he wasn't here to instruct the hired help, he was here to have a good time.

'Hello, Tiny,' he called above the fiddle and the general din of the room, 'how're things going then?'

'Oh, hello Mick,' Tiny called back and he gave his amiable grin. 'Things are good. Going to be a busy night, I'd say.'

He was a nice young man, but Ma was right, he wasn't bright. Mind you, Mick thought, looking around the room, his remark is spot on. The girls were in for a busy night.

The fiddler always got things going and, although it was not yet nine o'clock, the room was lively. Already men were shifting benches and tables to make space as Maeve started her wild Irish dance. Some who were eating their bowls of stew refused to budge, and took no notice of Maeve, or of the girls who were urging her on. But as others stamped their boots to the fiddle, mud splattering on breeches, and as cries of encouragement went up with each fresh exposure of Maeve's bare legs, it promised to be a lusty Saturday night.

Mick popped into the kitchen where Freddie was doling out the last of the stew.

'Do you want some?' Evie asked. 'You're just in time.'

'No thank you, my lovely.'

He kissed her and fondled her breasts as she passed by. With a bowl of stew in each hand she was unable to put up any resistance, not that she would have anyway, and she laughed before disappearing into the main room.

Mick chatted with Freddie for a while then returned to the main room himself, stepping up to the bar and leaning over to talk to Billy, who was busily pouring tankards of ale. Then, his own tankard in hand, he turned to watch the proceedings. He always propped at the bar. On a slightly higher level than the main floor, it offered the best vantage point.

Sheer force of habit found Mick observing the room with a sharp eye. He noted that Len had already positioned himself beside the door to the stairs, although it was a little early for sex to take priority with the customers. As a rule, men liked to drink themselves into a lustful state. Len too clearly believed it was going to be a busy night.

He glanced at Tiny, who was standing beside the main doors, checking out new arrivals, his eyes sweeping the room now and then, but obviously taking in little. Over in the far corner a big man with a massive ginger beard had Peg up against the wall and was all but fucking her. Tiny should be breaking that up, Mick thought. He would certainly have done so himself. 'Excuse me, sir, but would you like to take the lady upstairs?' he would have said very politely; and if the man had refused he'd have shown him the door, with the pistol if necessary. That's what Tiny should be doing. But Mick couldn't be bothered teaching Tiny his job, and he refused to do it for him. Besides, he'd recognised Ginger Beard. The man drank at the pub regularly, and on the occasions he had a woman he invariably chose Peg. She'd get him upstairs before long. Peg could look after herself.

Maeve had set the mood and as the fiddler started up again the girls enticed men to dance with them. Mick's toe was tapping. He was of a mind to dance, but he wouldn't dance with one of the girls – he would leave them for the clients. The kitchen now being closed he was about to fetch Evie when he noticed the man who'd just entered. Every time there was a new arrival his eyes flickered to the main doors, pure habit.

Tiny had given the man no more than a cursory glance, but Mick sensed something disturbing about the newcomer. Unprepossessing in appearance, he was not a big man, nor was he young. He'd be close to fifty, Mick guessed, wiry of build and unkempt, his hair long and his beard scraggy. There were many such men roaming the streets of Hobart Town, lost souls for the most part with minds that wandered. But this one is not lost, Mick thought. Nor was his mind wandering: this one was bent on a purpose.

The man glanced keenly about as he edged through the crowd. He's looking for someone, Mick thought. He didn't appear to be searching among the drinkers though, his eyes were darting from woman to woman. Then, upon spying the couple in the corner, he headed directly for them. It's Peg he's after, Mick thought. This could mean trouble. He glanced over at Tiny, who was still blissfully unaware of any potential problem. Oh well, he told himself, it isn't my place to interfere, and he sipped at his ale watching with interest for what would happen next.

Above the fiddle and the general hubbub, Mick couldn't hear the men's altercation, but he didn't need to. Their dispute was not one that would be solved with words anyway. The newcomer pulled Peg away from the big man and started with her towards the door that led upstairs, but he didn't get more than a pace or so before the big man grabbed Peg's arm and hauled her back to him, protesting angrily. The newcomer, however, remained persistent. The woman was coming upstairs with him.

Scraggy versus Ginger Beard, Mick thought, very interesting. Despite the size and age discrepancy, he'd probably put his money on Scraggy. The man looked tough. There was something feral about him.

Several of the drinkers standing nearby realised a fight was imminent and started backing off to allow the protagonists space.

On the other side of the room, Tiny finally got the message and started edging his way through. But by then Mick had seen the flash of metal. Ginger Beard had a blade. It was going to be a knife fight. And Peg was in the middle.

'Give us the pistol, Billy,' he hissed, and Billy dived his hand under the bar.

Peg screamed as the big man clutched her to him, thrusting the knife at the newcomer, daring him to try and take her. The newcomer, however, was undaunted by the knife. If anything, the appearance of the weapon made him all the more dangerous. He assumed a crouching position and stared the big man directly in the eyes, like an animal about to launch its attack.

A circle quickly formed around the two men, but the fight didn't get any further.

'Let her go,' Mick said as he stepped into the circle, the pistol aimed directly at the big man's head.

Ginger Beard slowly released Peg, who backed off thankfully to join Maeve and the other girls.

'No knives in the bar.' Mick kept his aim steady. 'Give it to Tiny.'

Tiny, who was now standing impotently nearby, stepped forwards and held out his hand.

Ginger Beard looked from the pistol to the giant and back again, but seemed reluctant to relinquish his knife.

'It's simple.' Very patiently Mick spelt out the rules. 'Either leave now with the knife, or if you want to stay give it to Tiny. You can collect it from him later, on your way out.'

Ginger Beard handed the knife to Tiny, and Mick lowered the pistol, although he kept it at the ready.

'Well now,' he said pleasantly, 'if you two gentlemen wish to fight over Peg's favours, I suggest you do so outside.'

Scraggy and Ginger Beard eyed each other off for a second or so. Then Ginger Beard removed his jacket and dumped it on a bench. Scraggy didn't bother removing his. He simply turned and led the way out into the back lane. Ginger Beard followed him and, drinks in hand, the crowd followed Ginger Beard, two of the men fetching lamps to light up the show. This was true Saturday night entertainment.

'Hardly a fair fight though,' someone muttered, and others agreed it was a bit of a disappointment. They would like to have laid bets on the outcome, but most of them knew Dave, the big man. Dave was handy with his fists. Besides, he was heavier and younger than the scrawny newcomer: no point in wasting money.

'Don't you believe it,' Maeve said scornfully, 'your mate Dave doesn't stand a chance against the tiger man, am I not right, Peg?'

Beside her, Peg nodded. 'You are indeed. Dave won't last two minutes, and that's a fact.'

There were one or two others present who knew of the tiger man's reputation and word was quickly passed along. Men started betting one another, the tiger man or Dave.

Mick watched, intrigued. Who is this tiger man? he wondered.

As it turned out Peg was right. Dave didn't last two minutes.

The tiger man was agile, avoiding punches and clinches while landing blows in vulnerable places with lightning speed. There were no rules to the way he fought. Fists or feet – whatever proved effective. After catching Dave off balance and wearing him down, the tiger man closed in to deliver the final blows. A chop to the throat, and the side of his hand connected with the Adam's apple. A further chop to the nose, and there was the crunch of cartilage. A lethal fist to the solar plexus and the big man was on his knees. And, finally, just to make sure, a well-aimed boot to the kidneys.

Dave sprawled face down in the mud. He struggled to rise, making it once again to his knees, but a forceful kick in the ribs found him flat on his back, blinking up through the haze of mud and blood that blurred his vision.

The tiger man placed his boot on Dave's chest, like a hunter posing with his kill. 'Your knife wouldn't have done you much good, my friend,' he said looking down at him, 'I'd have skinned you alive in there.'

It was the first time Mick had heard the man speak. The tiger man was an Irishman, he realised, a northerner – Belfast by the sound of it.

'Perhaps I'll flay you right here and now, what do you say about that?' Reaching beneath his jacket, the tiger man drew his Bowie knife from its sheath. 'I'd need to gut you first of course.' He took his boot from the man's chest and, bending down, he placed the tip of the knife's ten-inch blade between the base of Dave's ribs. 'I'd start around here,' he said and very slowly he traced a line down the stomach, his knife cleaving a path in the mud. 'And I'd end up around here.'

With the knife's tip now resting just above his genitals, Dave continued to blink foggily up at his tormentor.

'But then perhaps not.' The tiger man stood, and his leathery face crinkled into a humourless smile. 'I don't think I'd get much value for your hide.' He turned to the crowd, his eyes searching for Peg. She and Maeve were standing right in the front. 'Come on upstairs now,' he said.

Peg flicked her hair back and puffed her chest out like a pouter pigeon. She was well on the wrong side of thirty and men were still fighting over her: it was something to be proud of, there was no denying it.

The tiger man draped his arm around his prize and

was about to return to the bar when he caught sight of Mick.

'Oh, I forgot. No knives in the bar.' This time the smile was humorous, although it was curiously lopsided, and Mick could see in the eyes that met his the glint of something that might have been just a little unbalanced. 'Perhaps you'd look after this for me, friend,' the tiger man said and he handed the Bowie knife to Mick. 'I'll collect it from you later, on my way out.'

He departed with Peg firmly in tow and the crowd dispersed leaving several of Dave's friends to tend to him.

As he walked back inside with Maeve and the girls, Mick examined the Bowie knife. It was a lethal-looking weapon, but handsome, of the finest steel, coffin-handled and well crafted. This is not a Sheffield Bowie of English manufacture as many are, he thought. This is the real thing, a genuine American 'Arkansas toothpick'. He wondered why the tiger man had entrusted him with such a valuable possession. This knife would be worth a tidy sum.

'Who is he, Maeve?' he asked. 'What's his real name? Why is he the tiger man?'

'He's the tiger man because he hunts tigers,' Maeve said as if Mick was daft for asking. 'I've no idea what his real name is. I don't think anyone around here knows. Peg doesn't, and she's been with him a number of times.'

'How is it that I've never seen him then?'

'He hasn't been near the place for a good two years or more. Used to come in once or twice a year. Never chose anyone else but Peg.' Maeve smiled knowingly. 'The scrawny ones always fancy big breasts – have you noticed that? Anyway, there's been trouble like this before. The tiger man won't wait his turn. If Peg's chatting with someone else, he just drags her off upstairs and woe betide any who stand in his way. Personally, I think he enjoys the fight as much as the fuck. But if the truth be known, Mick,' Maeve gave him a wink – she loved sharing the gossip –

'a man would be wiser to bide his time and wait. A glass of ale and Peg'd be back.' She rolled her eyes heavenwards, indicating the bedrooms. 'The tiger man doesn't muck about up there.'

'Oh is that so?'

'Indeed it is. You just wait and see. He'll be downstairs inside fifteen minutes, and bear in mind that's accounting for the undressing and all. Not that he undresses,' she added with a snort, 'but Peg does. Like I said, he fancies big breasts.'

'Right you are. Thanks, Maeve.'

Maeve's reckoning was only slightly out.

'I'll have my knife back now, thanks.' It was twenty minutes later.

Mick handed over the Bowie knife, and was surprised when the tiger man suggested they pop outside with an ale.

'It's too noisy in here and I'm starved for a chat,' the tiger man said. Then he added with an air of mockery, 'Besides, no knives in the bar.'

Billy poured them their ales and they adjourned to the back lane where they stood in the light that spilled from the open doorway. As they raised their tankards in a silent toast Mick wondered why, of all those present, the tiger man should have singled him out for a chat.

'What's your name?' the tiger man asked, wiping ale from his moustache with the back of his hand.

'Mick. Mick O'Callaghan.' Mick looked the older man boldly in the eye. 'What's yours?'

The tiger man gave a careless shrug. 'Dan will do.' In offering no surname he intended no insult, however, for there was approval in his eyes as he sized up his fellow countryman. 'You did a good job in there, Mick,' he said. 'You're a young man who handles himself well. I like the cut of your jib.'

The nautical reference seemed a bit of a giveaway. 'You're a seaman?' Mick asked.

'Of sorts. In my youth, many, many years ago, I was a sealer. Worked right here from Hobart Town,' he gave another shrug. 'But the seals ran out.'

'So now you're a tiger man.'

'I am that. There's money in thylacines. The Van Diemen's Land Company used to pay a good price, but for the past ten years or so I've found the sheep farmers are offering more than the consortium. These days I collect from both, which proves quite profitable I must say.'

'You're a bounty hunter then?' Mick was fascinated. During his eighteen months in Van Diemen's Land he'd never been outside Hobart Town. He'd heard of the bounty hunters, tough men who lived mostly to the north, but he'd not met one before.

'Indeed I am.' Dan was gratified to see he was making such an impression on his newfound friend. 'I collect bounty on whatever's going. Devils and tigers and feral dogs – you name it – but the tigers fetch the best price. In the old days of course it was the blacks. There was good money in blacks.'

'Blacks?'

Mick was momentarily bewildered, but Dan carried on, oblivious to any confusion on his audience's part. He was very much enjoying the chat.

'Twenty-five years ago now it was, in Governor Arthur's time. I'd have been about your age. Dear God,' he added wryly as he stared out into the night, 'it seems like only yesterday. Back then the government offered a bounty for the capture of Aborigines: five pounds an adult, two pounds a child. Oh, I tell you, Mick, a man could get rich in those days. A black was worth a lot more than a tiger.' He shook his head regretfully. 'But like the seals of course they're gone.'

Mick remembered a conversation he'd had with Jefferson about the shameful annihilation of the Aborigines, and how their dwindling numbers had finally been rounded up and taken to Flinders Island. It hadn't really been a conversation at all, it had been one of Jefferson's tirades. He'd just nodded at the time – he'd been a bit out of his depth. But he wondered now what Jefferson would say if he could hear Dan the tiger man.

'Anyway, enough about me,' Dan said, 'tell me about yourself, Mick. This is what I come into town for,' he urged enthusiastically, 'a woman first and then some hearty conversation. A man gets starved for both out there in the wild.'

'What do you want to know?'

'Nothing too personal,' Dan quickly assured him. 'I wouldn't want to pry, God forbid, only after a bit of a chat. How long have you been working at the pub?'

'I don't work here. I used to once, but not now.'

'Ah.' There was a pause, Dan was a little confused. 'So why'd you break up the fight the way you did?'

'I was just looking after Peg. She's a friend.'

'Really? Had I known that I'd not have entrusted you with my knife.'

'Why *did* you give me the knife?' Mick was curious. 'I didn't ask you for it.'

'I was lining you up for a chat is all; you interest me.' Dan smiled his lop-sided smile. 'There's something about you that reminds me of myself when I was your age.'

Mick wasn't at all sure the remark was a compliment and his dubious reaction was so readable that Dan gave a bark of laughter.

'Oh you're a damn sight better looking, I'll grant you that. But you're out for adventure and a cocky young bastard, just like I was.' He took another swig of his ale and wiped his moustache again. 'So tell me, what are you up to now you've left the pub?'

'I've recently become the manager of the Powell Ferry-Boat Service.' Mick tried to sound casual, but there was no disguising the ring of pride in his voice.

'My, my, a move up in the world, and a big one by the sound of it.'

Unsure whether or not he was being ridiculed, Mick made no reply. He stared defiantly back at the older man.

Dan studied him for a moment or so. 'You're a tiger man too, aren't you Mick?' he said.

'What do you mean?'

'I mean you're out to catch what you can. I mean you're after the main chance.'

'And what if I am?' Mick's tone was belligerent. 'What's wrong with that?'

'Nothing, nothing at all,' Dan said reassuringly. 'This town is full of tiger men. Just look around you. The merchants, the builders, the bankers, the company men: they're all out for what they can get. This is a tiger town, Mick. A place at the bottom of the world where God turns a blind eye to pillage and plunder, and all is fair game. You're living in a tiger town, my friend.'

Mick realised that he was not being ridiculed, but he found the exchange disquieting nonetheless. There was something a bit mad about Dan.

'If you want to move up in this world Mick, and I can tell that you do –' Dan leaned his leathery face close as if sharing a secret '– you'd best follow the path of the tiger man, and you know what that is?'

The question was obviously rhetorical, but Mick found himself resisting the urge to nod.

'You take whatever you can get. And you use whatever you've got to take it.'

The advice, crass though it was, had a familiar ring. How disturbing, Mick thought, to hear my own credo from the mouth of a man like Dan.

'With looks like yours I know what I'd be doing,' Dan said, 'and it sure as hell wouldn't be managing a ferry service.' He polished off his ale. 'Find yourself a wealthy woman, my friend. Don't work for your money. Marry it.'

He laughed and Mick laughed along with him, joining in the joke.

But was it a joke? Dan's words continued to rattle around in Mick's brain. His encounter with the tiger man had left him decidedly unsettled.

CHAPTER EIGHT

Dan the tiger man and the events of Saturday night paled in comparison to the unsettling experiences of the following week.

It all started on Thursday, after a card game at Farrington's.

Mick had had a good win at the card table and he and the Dimbleby brothers had retired to the bar for cognac and cigars. The personal connection he'd recently made with the Dimblebys pleased Mick as Charles and Gerald Dimbleby were a definite step up the social ladder. Dimblebys, Purveyors of Fine Goods, was an exceedingly reputable company.

The brothers Dimbleby had, in their early twenties, been sent to the colony by their wealthy merchant father to open up trade for the family business, Dimbleby Senior's added intention no doubt being to deprive his younger sons of the temptations London offered. Five years on, having successfully established the business, Charles and Gerald were perceived as highly respectable young men of good family, but at heart they remained the ne'er-do-wells they had always been.

Now, as they downed their cognacs, Charles, the elder by just one year, complained that he was famished, and the ever-randy Gerald insisted he needed a woman. The choice was obvious. There was only one venue that would satisfy them both. Trafalgar.

'Supper and a woman, Mick,' Gerald urged. 'What do you say?'

'I don't want a woman,' Mick replied good-naturedly.

'Supper then,' Charles said. 'You don't have to have a woman, old chap, and you must be famished surely – we were at the card table for a whole three hours.'

'And they do a marvellous supper at Trafalgar. Oh, do come, Mick.' Gerald very much enjoyed the young Irishman's company. There was something rakish and dashing about Mick O'Callaghan. But then Gerald had always enjoyed mingling with his social inferiors, and most particularly with those of suspect background. Which is just as well, he thought, when one is stuck in a place like Hobart Town.

'All right,' Mick agreed, 'supper it is.' Why not? he thought. He'd had an excellent win: he could afford it. And if he bumped into Red, he'd ignore her. In fact he rather hoped he would bump into Red. Ignoring her while in the company of the Dimbleby brothers would be something of a statement.

Over a year had passed since Mick's humiliating encounter with Eileen Hilditch outside St Joseph's Church. During that time he'd dwelt upon neither the woman nor the humiliation. He'd rarely seen her in the street, for which he'd been thankful, and on the odd occasion when he had he'd looked the other way, not wishing to be reminded. One time he hadn't been quick enough and she'd caught his eye and given a cheery wave as if they were old friends, as if she had no recollection of the insults she'd heaped upon him that day. He had not returned the wave.

A month or so ago, she'd even left him a message.

'Red said to say hello,' Evie had told him one Saturday night. 'She popped in to see Ma yesterday afternoon and as she was leaving she asked me how you was getting on.'

Mick had been surprised, both by the message and the fact that Ma, with whom he'd just spent the past hour, had made no mention of Red's visit. But then Ma believed Red was not good for him, which probably accounted for the silence.

'She had no idea you wasn't working here any more,' Evie had gone on. 'Ma hadn't told her, goodness knows why. Anyway, very impressed Red was to hear you was in the employ of Jefferson Powell, very impressed indeed.'

He'd made no comment, but he'd felt a smug sense of satisfaction. He'd been unable to resist enquiring, however, about Red's relationship with Ma, which remained mystifying.

'What's the connection, Evie? Did Red work here once?'

'Oh yes. Me and Red started out at the Hunter's Rest around the same time, not long after we got our tickets of leave. Her and me's got much the same background, you know. We was both transported for thieving when we was sixteen, and being as how we was so young we didn't even serve a full year.'

Evie was one of the rare few who admitted to her convict background with complete and utter candour. Mick found it disarming, but he wondered how Eileen Hilditch might react if she could hear her story being so freely bandied about. The thought pleased him.

'Ma took us in and taught us the trade,' Evie went on, 'but there wasn't much Red didn't already know. And Red was clever too: she'd taught herself style by watching the toffs. Red could mimic the best of them,' Evie said admiringly, 'and you'd never tell the difference, that's real clever that is. So when Trafalgar opened up, Ma encouraged her to move on. Ma knows class when she sees it.'

'How very generous of Ma,' he said, although such an altruistic action seemed rather odd to him.

'Oh no, Mick, you got it wrong.' Evie was quick to set him straight. 'Red didn't belong here. Class is the last

thing you want at the Hunter's Rest. Upsets the balance,
you know what I mean? Causes trouble among the girls,
and the men don't much care for it anyway. If you put on
a bit of style around here they think you've got tickets
on yourself. Ma knew that.'

Of course, Mick thought, Ma would.

'Not that she didn't admire Red for it, mind,' Evie
hastily added. 'Red wants to get on in the world and Ma
respects that.'

Now, as he walked up Barrack Street with the Dimbleby
brothers, Mick was gratified by Red's apparently renewed
interest in him. It would make things all the more pleasurable when he ignored her.

From the outside, Trafalgar remained the elegant two-
storey townhouse it had always been, but its interior
was a clear indicator of the purpose this once graceful
private residence now served. The furnishings and carpets
and chandeliers and lamp fittings were neither tasteless
nor vulgar in themselves, but en masse they were just a
little too much, as if each was competing for show. The
statuettes and paintings and tapestries, many depicting the
naked female form, far from being crude were of the finest
quality and well executed, but there were just a few too
many of them. Trafalgar was a rich man's playground, a
bordello for the wealthily decadent, and it looked it.

Mick and the brothers were greeted in the front foyer
by a stylishly handsome middle-aged woman who did
not appear to have been awaiting new arrivals at all, but
rather to have materialised out of nowhere.

'Good evening, gentlemen,' she said.

'Hello, Mrs Bingham,' Gerald replied heartily. He and
Charles were obviously well-acquainted with the woman.

'Welcome to Trafalgar, sir.' She smiled pleasantly at
Mick, acknowledging him as a newcomer.

'We'll be dining, Mrs Bingham,' Charles announced.
'We're famished.'

The brothers hung their top hats on the brass hat rack by the door, Mick quickly following suit. As they placed their canes in the elephant-foot umbrella stand, he reminded himself yet again that he really must acquire a cane.

'Of course,' Mrs Bingham said. 'I shall have a table prepared in the drawing room.' Then she added the seemingly innocent query: 'Will you be dining with company this evening, do you think?'

Gerald dived in before the others could answer. 'Most definitely yes,' he said.

'Very well, your table will be ready in ten minutes. Please do go through to the lounge, gentlemen.' With a gracious wave of her hand she indicated the doors to the left and then sailed off in the opposite direction.

As they proceeded to the lounge, Mick wondered whether Mrs Bingham was the madam, or whether she was just the general hostess. Whatever she was, she looked as though she'd be at home entertaining royalty.

'Even if one requires only supper,' Charles explained to him, 'one is always directed to the lounge first in the expectation that, upon viewing the wares, one will be unable to avoid temptation. And of course if one invites a girl to join one for supper before adjourning upstairs it all adds to the final tally, which suits the management's purpose admirably. Gerald invariably opts for company at supper,' he added, ribbing his brother good-naturedly. 'He says hang the expense, he likes to get in early.'

'I most certainly do,' Gerald said vehemently. 'One wants to have the pick of the crop, doesn't one? Why risk being stranded with the left-overs?'

The lounge was plush and masculine, smelling of leather and the lingering aroma of pipe tobacco and cigars. Invitingly lit, the room appeared vast, but in actuality was not, an effective illusion having been created by a sea of reflections. With the exception of the wall to the right, which was taken up by the bar, the other walls were all

hung with large gilt-framed mirrors, each reflecting the
glow cast by the lamps in their ornate wall brackets. And
along with the lamp-light was reflected Trafalgar's pride
and joy.

Mick gazed about in amazement at the bevy of beauty
that surrounded him. A girl lounging decadently on a
plush leather sofa, a girl seated demurely on a Chippendale
carver, a girl lazily reclining in a rattan armchair ... they
were everywhere, dozens of them, all exquisitely beautiful, all elegantly gowned. Then he noticed the same sofa,
then the same Chippendale carver, then the same rattan
armchair. Then here the same powder-blue taffeta gown,
and there the same raven-haired beauty, and he realised
there were only five or six girls in all. The mirrors magically increased their numbers to give the appearance, upon
initial impact, of a virtual harem.

'Effective isn't it?' Gerald said. 'And several of them
aren't even here. They're probably serving drinks in the
gaming room,' he gestured to the door directly ahead, 'or
having supper in the drawing room.' He checked his fob
watch. 'A little early for upstairs yet, I think.'

They crossed to the bar where, at the far end, two men
were in close conversation, checking the girls over like
cattle, pointing out various assets.

'Good evening, gentlemen.' A burly man in shirtsleeves
and bow tie greeted the brothers. 'Evening, sir, welcome to
Trafalgar,' he said to Mick. It was identical to the greeting
that had been offered by Mrs Bingham, and clearly the
club protocol, with no mention of names or any expectation of introduction. The man's manner, however, was
proprietorial and not at all that of a barman.

Mick had recognised him instantly. Ruby Jack Clanton
was a colourful and well-known figure around Hobart
Town. A former all-England bare-knuckle heavyweight
boxing champion, his pugilistic fame granted him social
access to all circles, his stories being guaranteed to enter-

tain. The giant ruby ring, which he wore on his middle finger and which he swore had been presented to him by an Indian Maharajah, had earned him the title Ruby Jack and, although he appeared a man of independent means, no-one knew exactly where his money came from. Mick now wondered whether perhaps it was Trafalgar.

They ordered ale and, as Ruby Jack poured their drinks and chatted to the Dimblebys, Mick looked around the lounge. Upon catching his eye, each girl responded in her own seductive way, a saucy smile, a sultry challenge, a cheeky wink. They were all tantalising, but there was no sign of Red. He looked at the door that led to the gaming room. Is she in there? he wondered. Even as he did, the door opened and a girl appeared carrying a tray of goblets. But it wasn't Red, and he felt a distinct sense of disappointment.

'Good evening,' the girl said as she placed the tray on the bar, 'I'm Sylvia.' She was fair haired and beautiful and her smile was enticing.

'Hello, Sylvia.' Mick returned the smile.

'After the same again in there, are they?' Ruby Jack asked her.

'Yes, thanks, Rube,' she replied.

The two men at the far end of the bar had taken instant note of the new arrival and, upon registering their interest, Sylvia gave them a pert wave. They gestured for her to join them. She exchanged a glance with Ruby Jack, who nodded, and she left.

'There we are, gentlemen.' Ruby Jack placed Mick's and the brothers' drinks in front of them. He set about tending to the order for the gaming room and signalled one of the other girls to take over from Sylvia, whose duties now clearly lay elsewhere.

'Does Ruby Jack own the place?' Mick asked Charles when they'd seated themselves a little further down the bar, out of earshot.

'I would say he has a share in it, yes,' Charles replied, 'but as to the extent of his investment I've no idea. A consortium owns Trafalgar, and no-one knows who that consortium is –'

'The most respectable citizens in the colony, I'd put money on it,' Gerald chipped in, although his gaze remained fixed on the girls. He'd barely taken his eyes off the raven-haired beauty from the moment they'd arrived.

'That's probably the truth of the matter,' Charles said to Mick, 'but Ruby Jack's the only one prepared to publicly associate himself with Trafalgar. The consortium really should be grateful because he manages the place most efficiently –'

'Oh come along, Charles, do let's make our pick.' Gerald interrupted abruptly; he was becoming impatient. 'It'll get busy soon and I don't want to miss out on Gerda.'

Without waiting for a response from his companions, he raised a hand above his head and clicked his fingers at the raven-haired girl who was lounging on the sofa. She rose, languorous and sultry – for that was Gerda's style – and started towards them.

'All right,' Charles said unperturbed: he was accustomed to his brother's rudeness. 'It's probably a good idea to get in early while we have the choice. Although frankly, Mick,' he confided, 'there isn't a dud to be had here at Trafalgar. I'd recommend Yvette.' He pointed to the fair-haired girl perched demurely on the Chippendale carver. 'She's French and very athletic, quite the contortionist in fact.'

'I'm not interested in a woman,' Mick said. 'Just supper will do.'

Charles was surprised. He'd automatically presumed that once they'd entered the portals of Trafalgar a healthy young man like Mick O'Callaghan would be raring to go. But he nodded good-naturedly.

'Your choice, old chap,' he said. 'I'll take Yvette then.'

He waved at the girl in the powder-blue taffeta. She

rose to join them, and just at that moment, the door to the gaming room opened.

'I've changed my mind,' Mick said. 'I'll take her.'

It was Red.

'Ah.' Charles grinned broadly. 'You've chosen well, the pick of the crop indeed.'

As the Dimbleby brothers were joined by the girls of their choice, Mick rose and crossed to Red, intercepting her on her way to the bar with the three empty tankards she was carrying.

'Well, well,' she said, 'fancy seeing you here.'

He wasn't sure whether he could detect a touch of mockery in her tone, or whether it was simply her genuine surprise at seeing him, but her greeting seemed warm enough and her smile was friendly. He'd forgotten how extraordinarily beautiful she was. Her red hair was not coiffed, but hung free and unadorned, and her simple green satin gown, with clearly no corsetry beneath, exposed her shoulders and bosom to perfection. Unlike the other girls, her complexion was not artificially enhanced. Her cheeks were not rouged and powdered, her lips not reddened with paint. She's like a wild creature, he thought, natural and flawless in its beauty.

'Hello, Eileen,' he said.

She studied him for a moment, as if adding up whether or not he intended an insult. 'It's Red in here,' she said.

'As you wish. Hello, Red.'

'Hello, Mick.'

'Would you care to join me for supper?'

'For supper, really?' The fox eyes held a challenge: an invitation to dine meant far more than supper. 'I had the impression you were the sort who didn't pay for it.'

'Well, there's always a first time, isn't there?'

'There is that.' She smiled gloriously. 'In which case, Mr O'Callaghan, I'd be delighted to join you for supper.'

'A surname,' he said with mock disapproval. 'Shame on you now – where's your sense of propriety? It's Mick in here.'

She was still laughing as they joined the Dimbleby
brothers.

Several minutes later, the group adjourned to the drawing
room, where Mrs Bingham showed them to their table.
A number of men were already dining, although only two
others were accompanied by women. The more common
preference of club members and guests was to dine quietly
together before retiring to the lounge for cognacs and
cigars, and perhaps the choice of a girl for upstairs.

They dined on lamb cutlets and potatoes, a meal which
Mick found inferior to Freddie's stews. The two bottles of
wine that Charles ordered as an accompaniment, however,
and which he informed them were from Bourgogne, were
truly magnificent.

Throughout supper, the brothers ignored the women,
choosing instead to discuss the latest news, which had
arrived via *The Times*, of the ongoing dispute between Lord
Raglan and the Earl of Lucan. Like the rest of the colony,
the brothers avidly followed the reports of the war in the
Crimea, and the disastrous charge of the British Cavalry's
Light Brigade at the Battle of Balaclava just the year before
remained a subject of great controversy. So much so that
of late the war itself appeared to have taken a second seat
to the personal battle between the cavalry commander,
Lieutenant General the Earl of Lucan and his superior, the
Commander of the British Army, Lord Raglan, about who
was responsible for a military disaster of such monumental
proportion as that charge.

'Lucan's being made a scapegoat for the whole disastrous botch-up,' Gerald said heatedly. 'His character is
being assassinated and he's quite right to defend himself in
The Times as he has, and also in the House of Lords might
I add. It's his God-given right.'

Like many caught up in the general public debate, Charles
and Gerald vehemently disagreed upon the subject.

'Rubbish.' Charles was dismissive. 'Lucan misinterpreted

his orders, it was as simple as that. The man should stop trying to squirm his way out of things, and take responsibility for his actions instead of excusing himself through *The Times*.' He looked to Mick for support. 'Don't you agree old chap?'

'I haven't been following the matter much myself,' Mick replied pleasantly. It was true, he hadn't, but he had no wish to be drawn into the discussion in any event. He would rather have conversed with the women and he thought the brothers were rude to exclude them. The women might be whores, but they were women nonetheless, and beautiful ones at that. Mick liked whores, good honest working girls, and he was certainly not accustomed to ignoring beautiful women. One glance at Gerda and Yvette, however, told him they were completely unbothered. They were enjoying their wine and meat and potatoes, and were even feigning interest in the men and what was being said. But they're just waiting to be fucked, Mick thought. That's their job.

'What do you think, Red?' he asked, turning to Eileen.

'I don't think,' she said, smiling at all three men. 'I try very hard not to think. It's not healthy.'

The brothers laughed and continued the conversation on their own. What's the point in seeking a contribution from Mick O'Callaghan anyway? Charles thought. The man is Irish.

Finding himself as ignored as the women, Mick concentrated on his meal and gave up any pretence of interest in the discussion.

Beside him, Red eyed him up and down approvingly. 'You've filled out, Mick,' she said. 'Hard work obviously agrees with you.' She slid her hand under the table and caressed his thigh, feeling the muscularity beneath the fabric of his trousers. He quivered involuntarily, he couldn't help himself. 'You've toughened up,' she murmured, and she smiled as her fingers slowly made their way towards his groin.

A charge of excitement ran through Mick's entire body. The mere touch of her hand had been enough to arouse him. But he had a plan, and he would not be swayed from it. He shifted his leg slightly, signalling her to stop, and picked up the bottle of wine.

'May I tempt you?' he queried.

She laughed lightly. 'Of course you may.' Her hand re-emerged from beneath the table to hold the glass as he poured her wine. 'I'm always easily tempted,' she said, her eyes teasing him.

The moment Gerald had finished eating, his focus changed. Still chewing on a final mouthful of meat, he shoved his plate aside, pushed his chair back from the table and hauled Gerda onto his knee, even though she had not yet finished her own meal. As far as he was concerned supper was over, conversation was over and the night was about to begin. Gerda parted her legs obligingly as he ferreted his hand up under her skirts.

Charles signalled to the waiter that it was time to go upstairs. 'Put the meal on my slate,' he instructed as the man cleared the dishes.

'No, no, Charles,' Mick protested. 'I can't allow that.'

'I insist, old chap. I absolutely insist. As a regular club member, it's my pleasure to welcome a newcomer to Trafalgar.'

Gerald had already jumped to his feet and, with Gerda in tow, was on his way to the door that led to the stairs. Charles now stood, putting his arm around Yvette, who had risen to stand beside him. 'It's your first visit, Mick, you must allow me to treat you to a meal at least.' His eyes flickered to Red and back. 'All other expenses are your own,' he added with a meaningful wink.

'That's very generous of you, Charles.'

Mick watched as the Dimbleby brothers disappeared with their women. Then he turned to Red.

'There won't be any other expenses,' he said.

She was understandably confused. 'What do you mean?'

'I shall take my departure now, that's what I mean.' He made no move to leave, however. He intended to savour the moment.

'I see.' Red looked around the drawing room, which was now quite crowded. 'You wish to humiliate me, is that it?'

'That's it exactly.' He drained the last of his wine.

'And this was your plan from the outset? When you invited me to supper you had no intention of going upstairs?'

'No intention whatsoever. I never pay for it.'

'But you said in the lounge that there's always a first time.'

He shrugged. 'Perhaps I was referring to the supper.'

She was silent, her animal eyes appraising him, her expression unfathomable. What will she do? he wondered. Would she make a scene? Would she slap him and walk off in high dudgeon? Or would she simply sit there and watch as he walked away himself? Whatever she did, she couldn't win. But to his surprise, she smiled.

'Ah, Mick, how very clever of you.' She shook her head admiringly and glanced about once again at the men who were dining. 'To be left here on my own would indeed be humiliating.'

'I had hoped so,' he said, 'which makes us even.'

'There's a more pleasurable way of getting even though, surely.' She leant in to him, her face as intimately close as a lover's. 'What if I gave it to you for nothing?' she whispered. 'You'd be the first, Mick. I've never once offered myself for free. If you were to ask Ma she'd bear me out on that, I swear. You'd be the very first.'

He made no move. She leant even closer, her hair caressing his cheek, her breath warm against his skin, the voice of temptation whispering in his ear.

'No-one's ever had me for nothing, Mick. No-one. Just

imagine it. I'd be giving myself to you. I wouldn't be a whore at all. We'd be like lovers.'

Beneath the table her hand was once again on his thigh and this time, as her fingers edged towards his groin, he did not signal her to stop.

'That'd be the best way of getting even, wouldn't it?' she whispered. 'To be the very first. And you know you want me, Mick.' Her hand was on him now. 'We both know you want me.'

What the hell? Mick thought. Why refuse such an offer? He didn't need to publicly humiliate her. The victory was his anyway.

They went upstairs.

He knew that once they were alone there was the possibility she might drop the seductive performance, give him a quick poke and send him on his way. He was prepared for such an eventuality, but something told him it wouldn't be like that. Something told him that they really would be like lovers, just as she'd said they would. She was giving herself to him after all.

She didn't drop the performance. Quite the opposite. She sat him down in the chair that faced the giant gilt-framed mirror that dominated the room, and slowly, teasingly, she undressed herself, her eyes on him all the while. He watched mesmerised, remembering that day at the Hunter's Rest, upstairs in Ma's room when she'd tantalised him in the same manner while putting on her gloves and her cloak. It was the performance of a true artiste. Finally, when she stood in nothing but a flimsy chemise, she undressed him, just as slowly, just as teasingly, running her fingertips lightly over his body as she did so. Not a word was spoken, not a sound uttered. When he was half-naked she knelt before him and, slithering his trousers down over his buttocks, she freed him, caressing him with the same lightness of touch, sending tremors through his whole being. She was about to take him in her mouth, but by now Mick had had quite enough. He did not intend to lose control.

He stepped out of his trousers and slipped the chemise from her shoulders. It dropped to the floor and she stood before him naked, her body as flawless as he'd known it would be. By now he was rampant with desire.

She was good in bed. Physically she was the most exciting woman he'd ever been with, and he'd been with many. The way she responded to his every movement, the very tightness of her, the undulation of her muscles, all compounded to excite him beyond measure. He told himself that it was hardly surprising: she was an expert at her trade. He'd never been with a high-class whore – naturally he'd never known a woman as adept as Red.

But he could feel himself losing control. Mick was not accustomed to losing control. He was accustomed to pleasuring women. He liked to hear a woman moan and to feel her final quivering moments. Only then would he let himself go.

He stopped, determined to recover himself, and as if obeying an unspoken command, she stopped with him. Both remained frozen; her body was deathly still beneath his. But she was not allowing him to recover himself at all. He could feel, deep inside her, the wave of her energy as the muscles surrounding him urged him on. He was not in control. Red was in control. This was a competition, and Red was winning.

Barely a minute later, he acceded defeat – he could hold back no longer. She met his thrusts with equal force, driving him to his climax, but as the moment approached, she deftly twisted her body to the side, freeing herself from him. She did not desert him, however. She took him in her hands, spilling his fluid over her breasts, and then it was done.

She rose and crossed to the washstand.

He rolled over onto his back, still breathing heavily, and

watched as she poured water from the jug into the basin.
She didn't give herself to me at all, he thought, and we
certainly weren't like lovers. She'd been a whore doing a
job. A very talented whore, admittedly, but a whore nonetheless. He shrugged off a vague feeling of disappointment,
recognising that it had been foolish to think they might
have shared something special. A bit of wishful thinking
there, Mick me lad, he told himself.

He watched her as she washed the semen from her
breasts. She was certainly the most beautiful of all whores,
he thought, and he chastised himself for feeling cheated.
Dear God in heaven, Mick O'Callaghan, you've been
given a gift like that, possibly the most expensive whore
in Hobart Town, and you dare to feel cheated? Wake up
to yourself lad.

She slipped the chemise over her head, rinsed out the
flannel and poured fresh water onto it. Then, returning to
the bed, she sat beside him and proceeded to wash him.
The water was delivered to the room along with clean
linen after the departure of each client: it was all part of
the service.

'You're very good, Red,' he said, looking down at his
cock as she bathed it, gently but efficiently.

'Of course I am. I'm the best.'

'You are that indeed,' he said heartfelt.

'It's a matter of pride. I always give men their money's
worth.'

He grinned. 'Even those who aren't paying,' he said.

'Oh, you're paying, Mick, have no doubt about that.'

'Eh?'

'You didn't think things through, did you?' She stood
and smiled down at him, kindly but patronisingly. 'Did
you really believe I could give you a free fuck? Come
along now, Mick: you've worked in a brothel, you know
the score. Trafalgar might be a fancy place, but it's no
different from the others. The girls don't take the money

or make the negotiations. The girls have no say in things –
they just do the hard work.'

She crossed to the washstand and dumped the flannel in
the basin.

Mick was so taken aback by his own stupidity that he
couldn't feel anger. How very foolish of him. She was
right, he'd been so eager to have her he hadn't thought
things through.

'Clients settle up with Ruby Jack on their way out,'
Red said as she started to get dressed. 'Of course if you're
willing to give it a try, you could walk off without paying
– but I would strongly advise against it. This place is more
than a fancy whorehouse, it's a statement of who you are
around Hobart Town. If a man doesn't settle his debts
at Trafalgar his reputation is ruined – among those who
count anyway.'

He didn't need to hear that from her either. In this town
you didn't welch on your debts, whatever circles you moved
in. If it wasn't your reputation at stake, it was your life.

He stood and pulled on his trousers, annoyed more with
himself than with Red. He was not the victor at all. She'd
won the battle, and purely because of his own stupidity.

'Oh come along now, Mick, don't sulk,' she said play-
fully, 'you had a good fuck when all's said and done. And
if you're short on money, I'm happy to lend you some.'

He paused, his shirt half on half off. What was she up
to now? 'Why would you do that?'

'Because I like you, that's why.'

'You like me?'

'Of course I like you.'

'You've a strange way of showing it. You make a habit
of humiliating those you like, do you?'

'Ah yes, you were out to get even with me,' she said as
if she'd forgotten. 'Do you know I can't recall what it was
I did that was so very humiliating: can you tell me what
you're talking about?'

'That day outside the church, that's what I'm talking about.'

'Oh good heavens above, is that all?' she said dismissively. 'You shouldn't have been there. That was my private time. Private time's very precious to a whore. You had no right to intrude.'

'You said I was as common as muck,' he exploded.

'And so you are to one who knows.' She hauled the green satin dress over her head and started doing up the bodice fasteners, which were conveniently located at the front. 'You can't fool me, Mick,' she said, 'we're two of a kind. You can try as hard as you like and for as long as you like, but you'll never be a gent any more than I will a lady. That's why I like you.' Having fastened the bodice, she re-positioned the shoulders of the dress and lifted her breasts into prominence. 'Now do you need any money to pay Ruby Jack? I'm expensive, I warn you.'

Mick grinned. He no longer felt insulted: he felt elated. 'No thank you, Eileen. I'm flush at the moment.'

'I told you, it's Red in here.'

'And if I was after Eileen, where would I find her?' he asked boldly. 'I'm not allowed to seek her out at church on a Sunday morning, so where would you suggest I look?'

She met the challenge. 'If you're after Eileen you come to Hampden Road on a Sunday afternoon, the white wooden cottage just around the corner from Runnymede Street.' She picked up the hairbrush that sat on the washstand. 'Now hurry up and get dressed or you'll be charged double time,' she said, turning away to look in the mirror as she brushed her hair.

'I thought you lived here at Trafalgar.'

'No. Some of the girls do. In the converted servants' quarters out the back,' she added with contempt. 'So much for the glamorous ladies of the night. Not me. I have a benefactor,' she said with pride. 'He's set me up in my own house for his exclusive use during the afternoon hours when he might wish to visit. The nights of course are for his wife and children.'

'Very impressive.' Mick tucked his shirt into his trousers and sat to put on his boots. 'I don't suppose I'm allowed to know who he is?'

The withering look she gave him in the mirror told him he was a fool for asking. 'He's a devout churchgoer, that's who he is, which is why Sundays are safe. But don't come to the front door. There's a track through the adjoining vacant block that leads to the back door. I'll expect you at two o'clock, and make sure no-one sees you.' She ran a final check over herself in the mirror, took his frock coat from the peg behind the door and helped him into it. 'Now get along with you. I have clients waiting.'

He arrived at the weatherboard cottage on the dot of two. It was a pretty house, situated in an area that was home to master mariners and shipwrights and their families, and to seamen and shipping agents and others who worked in the shipbuilders' yards and on the wharves. Modest and respectable like most of the other houses, it was certainly not an abode one would associate with a prostitute. Which no doubt pleases her churchgoing prick of a benefactor, Mick thought cynically, and of course the back lane offering discreet access would serve the hypocritical bastard's needs to perfection. It was probably the sole reason he'd bought the place.

Mick had thought of nothing but Red for the past two days, and already he was jealous of the faceless, nameless man who held special rights over her. The clients at Trafalgar didn't bother him at all, but the benefactor was an entirely different matter. The benefactor had personal access to Eileen Hilditch.

She was waiting for him. Without a word she whisked him inside and led him straight through to the bedroom, which rather surprised him, although he made no complaint. She was wearing a simple shift, and she undressed quickly and efficiently without any form of tease. Realising she expected him to follow suit, he obliged and before he knew it they were on the bed making love. Except we're not making love, Mick thought, even as he felt his body respond to her every movement. She was working on him like she had at Trafalgar. She was a whore doing a job. He tried to slow down, to take control and give her some enjoyment, but she was clearly not in pursuit of her own pleasure. The experience ended as it had before, only this time when she twisted herself free she took him in her mouth instead of spilling him over her breasts.

Again, while he lay recovering himself, she rose and crossed to the wash basin and jug, which sat on the dresser in the corner. He watched as she poured herself a glass of water. She rinsed her mouth, then filled the basin and washed herself with a flannel. Every action was automatic. Her post-coital routine was obviously as regular here with her benefactor as it was with her clients at Trafalgar.

'Are you going to wash *me* now?' he asked.

'If you'd like,' she said carelessly.

'I wouldn't.' He sat up on the bed.

'The kettle's warm.' She started to get dressed. 'I'll make us some tea.'

'No, don't.'

She seemed surprised. 'You don't want any tea?'

'No, I mean don't get dressed. Not yet. Come and sit with me, Eileen. Let's talk.'

Her look plainly said they could have talked over a cup of tea as she'd intended, but she joined him anyway, and they sat naked side by side, their backs resting against the wall.

Mick would like to have played the scene a little more conventionally. He would like to have lain with her in his arms, her head on his shoulder as if they were lovers, but he knew better than to suggest anything so intimate. There had been no personal pleasure for her in the act, he was sure. He wondered if there ever had been.

'You don't really enjoy sex do you?' He half expected her to take offence at the question, but she didn't.

'I don't mind it.' She shrugged. 'I don't think about it: why should I? I'm a whore. Sex is work.'

'I know whores who enjoy their work.'

'Really?' She raised an eyebrow mockingly. 'And how would you know? I thought you never paid for it.'

'I don't, but that doesn't mean I've never slept with a whore.' He thought of Evie and the other working girls he'd known. 'The whores I've been with seem to enjoy sex.'

'Did it ever occur to you they might be pretending?'

'Of course not,' he replied with a touch of indignation. 'I can tell if a woman's pretending.'

'Can you?' She was genuinely amused. 'Well, well, I am impressed. Can you really now, fancy that.'

'Yes. Yes I can,' he said firmly, although he was aware he sounded more self-defensive than confident. In only seconds she'd managed to thoroughly undermine him.

'Perhaps the whores you've bedded really did enjoy themselves, Mick, you're a pretty dashing fellow when all's said and done.' She winked encouragingly, which only served to make him feel further patronised. 'But as for me, I don't fuck for fun.'

They'd been Ma's words exactly, he remembered. *Red doesn't fuck for fun, Mick.* He could hear Ma's voice now, just as he fancied he could hear her saying, S*ee? I told you so.*

'If a man wants to share something personal,' Red continued matter-of-factly, 'he can look to his wife or his sweetheart. My job is to give good value for money and that's just what I do.'

Mick was starting to wonder whether perhaps he might have missed something. 'So I'm supposed to be paying for today then, am I?' he asked.

'Of course not. You're here at my invitation. You're a friend, not a client.'

'In that case I don't understand.' He gestured at their nakedness and at the bedroom and all it signified. 'If you don't fuck for fun, why this?'

'Because you're a friend who's a man and men like to fuck and I thought we'd get this part of the proceedings over and done with first.'

'Ah.' He remained bewildered. The remark didn't clarify the situation, and it had a distinctly unflattering ring.

She realised that yet again she'd punctured his ego, but she was unbothered. 'Come along now, Mick, admit it,' she said practically, 'you wouldn't be interested in being my friend if a fuck wasn't part of the bargain would you?'

'Well ...' He didn't know what to say. She was very confronting.

'Of course you wouldn't, and why should you? But I'll tell you something for nothing.' She looked him directly in the eye with an honesty that was undeniable. Hard, and at times ruthless as she could be, Red was invariably truthful. 'A whore's life can be lonely. Whores only have other whores for friends. Men use us and women judge us, and that's just the way it is. You're different. You're a rogue, but you don't look down on working women and I like you for that. Besides, as we agreed, we're two of a kind. I'd value your friendship if you cared to offer it.'

He was lost in the green-gold-hazel, whatever-colour-they-were fox eyes and he knew from that moment he was gone. Friendship, he told himself, is a definite start. He could work on the rest. In the meantime, he'd play the game her way.

'Consider me your friend, Eileen,' he said. Then he added with a cocky smile, 'So now the fuck's out of the way, how about that cup of tea?'

In the cosy kitchen, over tea and a lemon sponge cake that she'd bought from the bakery that very morning on her way home from church, they discussed her benefactor. Not in any detail of course – Mick knew better than to seek the man's identity – but he was keen to discover what level of intimacy his arch-rival had achieved.

'What does he think about your clients at Trafalgar? Is he jealous?' he asked casually.

'Not a bit,' she replied, 'he knows they mean nothing.'

Mick could identify with that.

'In fact he feels safe when I'm at Trafalgar. He doesn't like me being out and about during the day though – if he had his way I'd never leave the cottage. I'm a virtual prisoner here throughout the week. He never lets me know when he's going to call, and of course I'm expected to be here when he does. Whores are not supposed to have a life of their own, certainly not whores as well kept as I am.'

So that explains why I've so rarely seen her in the streets, Mick thought. He'd wondered.

'He's terrified that if I'm free to socialise I might meet the man of my dreams and decide to settle down to a life of domestic bliss,' she said caustically.

'That's always possible isn't it?'

'Oh get away with you, Mick.' She gave a derisive snort and helped herself to another slice of cake. 'Can you just imagine me bringing up a parcel of brats on a pauper's pay? I hardly think so. And a rich man wouldn't take me for a wife, I'm damaged goods. No, no, my benefactor has nothing to fear, so long as he keeps providing me with the finer things in life.' She took a huge bite of cake. 'And I make sure he does, believe me,' she said through a mouthful of lemon sponge, 'I never want for the finest. He's generous, I'll give him that.'

'Perhaps he really loves you.'

Red was aware that Mick was fishing for information, but she didn't mind in the least. She hadn't talked so freely with anyone except Ma and she was finding the experience exhilarating.

'Of course he doesn't love me. I'm like a drug to him, that's all. He's addicted. He can't get enough of me and he doesn't want to lose me, so he's willing to pay.'

The way she spoke of her benefactor with contempt rather than gratitude pleased Mick. Only one further question played on his mind.

'Does he call you Eileen?'

'Never. I'm Red to him, always Red. He likes me for the whore that I am. He wouldn't even know that I have another name, and he wouldn't be interested if I told him.'

The serious intent of Mick's query was not lost on her, however. 'No-one except Ma calls me Eileen,' she said, 'and even then only when we're alone. Certainly no man calls me Eileen. I'm Red to everyone but you, Mick.'

That fact put the seal on their friendship.

It was only as he walked home in the early dusk that Mick realised he'd completely forgotten afternoon tea at the Powells. And he further realised that, as Sundays now belonged to Eileen, afternoon tea with the Powells had become a thing of the past. In just several hours, his life had changed irrevocably.

CHAPTER NINE

'So when do we get to meet her?' Doris demanded.
'Well ...' Mick's reply was hesitant. 'It's a little premature ...'

'Now, now Doris, don't hound the poor fellow,' Jefferson interrupted, chiding his wife good-naturedly. 'You heard what he said: they've only just met, and she's shy.'

'But it's such a shame he can only see her on Sundays.' True to form Doris remained persistent. 'You must bring her to afternoon tea, Michael.'

'I hardly think a young courting couple would welcome the company of two rowdy children, my dear.' Jefferson insisted upon having the final say. 'We look forward to meeting your young lady when you feel the time is right, Michael.' He put an affectionate arm around his wife. 'Meanwhile, Doris and I are very happy for you.'

'We most certainly are,' Doris agreed, aware that she may have sounded just a little bit bossy.

Mick had kept his excuse to the Powells as simple and as vague as possible. The young lady he'd met had family commitments, he'd told them, which allowed only Sunday afternoons for their courtship. Jefferson of course had been far too tasteful to enquire after any further detail.

Over the ensuing weeks, there were times when Mick
wondered why he'd chosen to invent a courtship. He
could have been visiting a sick friend on Sundays, or any
number of fabrications that sprang to mind – he was a
very adept liar. Why a courtship, of all things? Could it
have been wishful thinking on his part? Did he perhaps
secretly long to make Eileen Hilditch his wife? He could
not for one minute envisage her living in the fisherman's
cottage, doing his housework and raising his children:
such an outcome was unimaginable. But then he was
finding life without Eileen equally unimaginable as the
days between each Sunday became progressively more
drab and tedious.

Mick was obsessed with Eileen and the challenge she
presented. He told himself that it was simply a case of
ego and that if he could conquer her sexually he'd be able
to get her out of his system. But he wasn't actually sure
he wanted to get her out of his system. He didn't know
whether he loved her or not, but of one thing he was
certain. He wanted her to love him, and he would not rest
until she did.

There were times when he felt he was making definite
progress. She no longer treated him as she would a client,
and on occasions he could sense her relax and enjoy the
sheer sensuality of their coupling. But always, as the final
moment neared, she took control and it became a battle
between them, a battle it seemed he could not win. Until
the afternoon when for some strange reason he suddenly
decided he'd had enough.

She was meeting his every thrust, urging him on to his
climax and, as it approached, he knew any moment she
would twist her body to one side and free herself. This
time things would be different, he decided, and burying
himself deep inside her he grasped her hips and locked her
into position, allowing her no freedom of movement.

'You bastard,' she hissed, feeling herself pinioned

beneath him. She struggled, but to no avail and seconds later he was spent.

'Bastard,' she said. She pushed him off her and rose from the bed. 'Bastard,' she said as she crossed to the dresser. She put the basin on the floor and filled it with water from the jug. 'Bastard,' she said as she squatted over the basin and started washing herself. 'Bastard, bastard, bastard,' she kept saying as she desperately tried to wash him out of her.

He felt guilty watching her frantic ministrations. 'I'm sorry,' he said inadequately.

'You're sorry! Oh well, that's all right then, isn't it? *You're sorry* makes everything better.' She kept washing, trying to force the water up inside her. '*You're sorry* means I don't have to worry about being landed with a bastard child. *You're sorry* means I don't have to have be butchered by some filthy old cow who might kill or maim me in the process. Thanks very much, Mick: I'm glad you're sorry.'

'I'd marry you if you were with child.' As the words sprang out, Mick wondered whether perhaps that's why he'd done what he'd done. He'd thought it had been the need for sexual domination, but perhaps there had been another force driving him. He of all men knew and respected a whore's fears; he would not normally threaten a working girl's existence in such a way.

Eileen was equally suspicious of his motives. 'Is that why you did it?'

'I don't know. I really don't know.' It was possibly the most honest admission Mick O'Callaghan had ever made and something in Eileen recognised that fact.

She stood and pulled on her shift.

'Whores always keep a close check on their monthly cycle,' she said coldly. 'I'm due in three weeks, give or take a few days.' She picked up his clothes and flung them at him. 'Come back in a month, Mick, and I'll tell you whether or not you've ruined my life.'

*

As things turned out he was safe. They both were.

'But don't ever try it again,' she warned him. 'Don't try it for whatever reason, Mick. It wouldn't pay off anyway. I'd never settle with a poor man.'

He hadn't thought of himself as a poor man. He'd thought of himself as a successful man, a man who made a good regular wage and had a job with a title. He was the Manager of the Powell Ferry-Boat Service no less. But that obviously meant nothing to a woman like Red, who was accustomed to the trappings of true wealth.

She'd joke about it at times. 'What a pity you're not rich, Mick,' she'd say as she paraded before him in a new lace-trimmed bonnet or a gown of the latest fashion, which her benefactor had provided in order to keep her happy that particular week. 'If you could offer me all this, I'd be yours. We're a good pair, you and me.'

They *were* a good pair. She made him laugh with her wicked stories about Trafalgar and her clients. She'd act out scenarios, strutting peacock-like before him, puffing away at an imaginary cigar – she was very funny. The references to the men she slept with never bothered him, but mentions of her benefactor could become galling.

'And that shite,' he said gesturing at the pretty new gown with the wide pagoda sleeves that she was twirling at him, 'that shite makes it worth being a prisoner, does it?' Occasionally he bit back. 'I'd take freedom before satin and lace myself.'

'This *shite,*' she archly corrected him, 'is a measure of my value. I'm the best whore in town, and this *shite* is proof of it.'

'Why do you have to keep calling yourself a whore?' he burst out, exasperated. Along with the comments about his so-called poverty, it was another ongoing allusion that annoyed him.

'Because that's what I am.'

'Not with me. You're Eileen with me, for God's sake.

When we're together you're Eileen, you're not Red.'

'Whatever the name, it doesn't stop me being a whore.' She remained unperturbed by his outburst. 'I know exactly who and what I am, Mick. When it comes to a case of identity you're the one with the problem. You really don't know who you are or what you want to be, do you?'

This time she was intentionally goading him, and he could have fought back as he often did – theirs was a volatile relationship. But he didn't bother because he knew she was right. The pride he'd taken in his position with the Powell Ferry-Boat Service was a thing of the past, and he no longer fantasised about a life of respectability and a wife and a family like Jefferson's. She's absolutely right, he thought, I don't know who I am or what I want to be. But he knew what he wanted out of life, of that much he was certain. He wanted Eileen Hilditch, and he wanted her all to himself. And for that he needed money.

'Amy, this is Michael O'Callaghan, the manager of our ferry-boat service.' Doris made the introductions. 'Michael, this is Miss Amy Stanford.'

'How do you do, Mr O'Callaghan?'

'A pleasure to meet you, Miss Stanford.'

He recognised her immediately. Amy Stanford was a well-known and well-loved figure around Wapping. Teacher to underprivileged children, distributer of goods to the poor, she'd been pointed out to him in the street on a number of occasions, as had her father, Silas. Mick had taken little notice of either at the time: they're just do-gooders, he'd thought.

'I'm a great admirer of your father and his good works,' he said. 'The society serves an immensely important purpose.'

There was no specific ulterior motive in Mick's flattery. His behaviour was totally instinctive. He always sought to make a favourable impression upon those of a higher

social status, and his charm automatically came into play
when he was in the company of women.

'Thank you,' Amy replied, although she was a little
puzzled. How could Michael O'Callaghan know of
her father's 'good works'? Silas Stanford, unlike many
prominent businessmen, did not make public his involvement with the Hobart Town Businessmen's Philanthropic
Society.

'I am aware also of your own contribution to the underprivileged, Miss Stanford,' he said. 'I have many friends
among the poor.'

'I see.' Amy wasn't sure she did see actually. Was he iden-
tifying with the poor, or was he a fellow philanthropist? He
seemed humble and grateful on the one hand, and yet on the
other he was well-dressed, well-spoken and seemingly well-
off. Whatever he was, she didn't think she'd ever met a man
quite as charming and quite as good-looking as Michael
O'Callaghan, which made him a little suspect.

Strangely enough, it was Amy's flicker of suspicion that
alerted Mick to the opportunity she represented. Could Amy
Stanford be the answer to my predicament? he suddenly
wondered. Amy Stanford was young, single, not particularly
pretty, and she had a very rich father. His mind started to
whirl with the wildest imaginings. He heard the voice of the
tiger man. *Don't work for your money. Marry it.* He thought
of Jefferson Powell. Jefferson had married above his station,
hadn't he? Dear God, Jefferson had been a convict when he'd
met Doris. Admittedly, the McLagans were not in the league
of the Stanfords, but there was surely no harm in trying.

'Would you care to join us for a cup of tea, Michael?'
Doris asked.

'No, no, Doris, please,' he insisted, 'I have no wish to
intrude upon you ladies in Jefferson's absence. You must
have a great deal to talk about.' Best to establish the first-
name basis of his relationship with the Powells lest Amy
Stanford should mistake him for a lowly employee.

'You would not be intruding, I assure you,' Doris said briskly, 'Miss Stanford and I have concluded our business. Besides which, we do not gossip. Please join us. I'll freshen up the pot and fetch another cup.'

Mick sat and, as Doris left with the teapot, he smiled apologetically at Amy.

'I do beg your pardon, Miss Stanford. I intended no insult.'

Amy smiled. 'She can be rather blunt, can't she? Personally, I enjoy a good gossip now and then.'

Mick surreptitiously placed the ledger on the coffee table beside him. He was thankful it was the last Friday of November. Had he called on any other day, he would have been in his work clothes. He always dressed well when he arrived to present the ledger to Doris, however, as she invariably asked him to stay for afternoon tea.

'Are the children here?' he asked. He rather hoped they were. His relationship with George and Martha would create an excellent impression.

'They were sent out to play while we discussed business,' Amy said. In the pause that followed she felt the need to explain, particularly as he had professed an interest in the society. 'McLagan Road Transport provides a dray free of charge for the society's weekly delivery of provisions to the poor,' she said.

'Ah yes?'

'And they have just agreed to help with the setting up of the Christmas Charity Ball, which is to be held in the grounds of the Hutchins School the week after next.'

'How very generous of them.'

'Yes indeed. The Powells are great supporters of the society.'

'Michael!' It was a child's voice, a very excited child.

Martha launched herself at him while George followed, a little more circumspectly but also eager to see his old friend.

'Hello, Martha.' Mick scooped the little girl up in his arms. He was genuinely delighted to see the children, but he couldn't help thinking how perfect the timing was. 'Hello, George.'

'Hello, Michael.'

He put Martha down, offered his hand to George and they shook man to man as they always did.

'I'm so sorry,' Doris had followed the children into the sitting room, 'but when they heard you were here there was no stopping them.' She placed the teapot and a fresh cup on the tray. 'The tea will be a few minutes brewing,' she said. 'I made a fresh pot.'

'Ben lost an eye,' Martha said solemnly.

'Oh dear, how terrible.' Who was Ben?

'But Mother sewed it back on.'

'Well now, I'm sure he feels a whole lot better.' The clown, of course.

'Would you like to see the *Maid*?' George asked. 'She's finished.'

'May I?' Mick looked a query to Doris.

'Please do.' She smiled warmly. 'They've missed you.'

As the children led him from the room, Martha literally dragging him by the hand, they were followed by the voice of command.

'Don't keep Michael longer than five minutes, children, we don't want his tea to get cold.' Mick was gratified to hear Doris's further comment to Amy Stanford: 'He's so good with the children. They absolutely adore him.'

He left the door to the kitchen wide open in the hope that he might overhear the women's conversation in his absence, but Martha was too busy chattering about Ben's eye, and George wanted him to come into the bedroom to look at the model ship.

'Why don't you bring the *Maid* out here?' he suggested. 'The light's much better in the kitchen. And Martha, you go and fetch Ben. I'd like to have a look at that eye.'

They scampered off, and Mick sat at the kitchen table listening intently.

'It will be a rather strange Christmas with Father away,' Amy was saying. 'We've followed such a routine for years, it will seem odd without him.'

'You're more than welcome to spend Christmas Day with us,' Doris offered, 'although I feel I should warn you, it may be a rather raucous affair. Jefferson intends to invite those of his employees without families to join us.'

Mick thought for one moment that the perfect opportunity was about to present itself. He would be invited to Christmas dinner along with Amy Stanford. But his hopes were instantly dashed.

'How very kind of you,' he heard Amy say, 'but I'm well looked after, I can assure you. I'll be spending Christmas Day with the Lyttletons.' She laughed. 'In fact I'll probably be spending the whole of the next three months with the Lyttletons, they've been given strict orders to look after me while Father's in Sydney –'

'Here's Ben,' the clown was thrust under Mick's nose, 'and that's the eye that came off.' Martha stabbed a finger at the black button that served as the rag doll's left eye. She climbed up on the kitchen bench to join him. 'You can't really tell, can you?'

'No, the surgery has been most successful: you can't tell at all.' Mick strained to hear more of the conversation in the sitting room, but he could gather only snippets as Martha chatted on. The Lyttletons featured again, together with something about St George's. That's handy, he thought. If Amy Stanford worshipped at St George's Anglican Church, then a quick change of denomination on his part could easily find him bumping into her after a Sunday-morning service.

As young George arrived and placed the model on the table with great care, Mick put a finger to his lips and hushed Martha. She obeyed immediately, clamping her mouth tightly shut as if she hardly dared breathe, and silence reigned while Mick set about examining the *Maid*. George stood quietly to one side, bursting with pride at the respect being afforded his work.

The talk in the sitting room was still of St George's Church.

'What a pity,' Doris was saying, 'when that glorious tower was erected, that they neglected to add the porch. It's quite shameful the way such a beautiful building has been left unfinished all these years.'

The completion of the long-awaited church tower eight years previously had indeed been welcomed by all, and for more reasons than one. Situated high on the hill of Battery Point, St George's was known as the Mariners' Church, and its Neo-Classical style tower had been deliberately designed to serve not only as a thing of beauty, but as a mark for shipping.

'Yes, Geoffrey is determined this problem must be addressed,' Amy replied. 'As I said, he and Phyllis are great supporters of St George's. He believes that the church's completion is essential not only for the members of the congregation who worship there, but for the entire community of Battery Point. Being a landmark for sailors, he says it symbolises the area.'

The Lyttletons again, Mick thought. He knew who Geoffrey and Phyllis Lyttleton were. Everyone in Hobart Town did. And Amy Stanford was to be under their wing while her father was away. How very interesting.

'You'll have a fresh cup, won't you?' Doris asked.

'Yes, thank you, that would be lovely. Then I really must be on my way.'

'Children!' Doris's voice rang through to the kitchen loud and clear. 'You've had your five minutes; I'm pouring Michael's tea.'

'Well done, George.' Mick shook hands once again with the boy. 'A work of art, there's no doubt about it, and you've got the rigging just right.' George beamed.

After giving Martha a hug and kissing Ben's eye better, Mick returned to the sitting room.

For the next fifteen minutes discussion centred on the society's forthcoming charity ball. The Hobart Town Brass Band was to perform on the night and, at the request of the society, the bandmaster had also gathered an eight-piece string and woodwind orchestra to perform Viennese waltz and polka music. This year's Christmas Charity Ball was to be the most lavish yet and was already the talk of the town among the elite and the wealthy who would be in attendance.

'A tremendous amount of work is involved,' Amy said. 'A marquee is to be erected and a bandstand and dance floor constructed.' She turned to Mick. 'Mr Powell has kindly agreed to construct the dance floor himself and to transport it in sections to where it will be laid out in the open air,' she said with a grateful glance in Doris's direction. 'No mean feat, which I hope the society's charity ball committee appreciates,' she added drily. Amy had her occasional doubts about the wealthy wives who served on the committee, several of whom she believed were there purely for social purposes.

'I am quite happy to offer my services should Jefferson require assistance.' Mick addressed Doris rather than Amy Stanford, thinking protocol demanded he should. His offer might well be perceived as impertinent. The annual charity ball was strictly for the rich, and even those who volunteered their services were from the upper echelons of society. But Amy laughed.

'Oh good heavens above, Mr O'Callaghan, please do lend assistance. We shall need all the help we can get, I assure you. The committee would be most obliged, I'm sure, and it is my personal opinion that the more able-bodied men we can recruit the better.'

Mick decided he liked Amy Stanford. She doesn't appear in the least bit snobbish, he thought. To the contrary, she seemed very open-hearted and natural. And she was certainly making things easy for him.

'In that case, Miss Stanford, I am yours to command,' he said with a smile.

Ten minutes later they parted company, agreeing to meet mid-morning at the Hutchins School where Mick would assist Jefferson, measuring the grounds and lining up the position of the marquee and the dimensions of the dance floor.

How very convenient, he thought as he walked back down the hill to the cottage. He wouldn't need to bump into her at church all dressed up in his finest. In fact he had the distinct feeling that the more honest he was with young Amy Stanford, the better – within limits of course.

The Hutchins School, established by the Anglican Church in 1846, was a private school for boys boasting the highest quality education. Its intention was to produce the leaders of the future in all fields of endeavour, and it was generally agreed that such a proud and noble purpose should be housed in a proud and noble building. Three years after the school's inauguration, during which time it had functioned at Ingle Hall, a Georgian house in lower Macquarie Street, the Hutchins School moved several blocks up the road and into its brand new, architecturally designed, custom-built schoolhouse.

Mick stood in Macquarie Street and gazed at the massive two-storey stone edifice, which sat well back from the road amidst the splendour of its grounds. So this was where the rich sent their sons to be educated. He must have passed by the Hutchins School hundreds of times, but he'd never really considered its significance – or the vast rift between the rich and the poor that it symbolised. You won't find any Wapping brats here, he thought. The building was handsome certainly, but with its central square tower looming three storeys high and its circular turret reaching even higher it looked more like a castle than a schoolhouse, to his mind.

'Mr O'Callaghan.'

She was beyond the fence and obscured among the activity in the grounds of the schoolhouse: Mick hadn't seen her. She strode purposefully up the drive to the large, open front gate and greeted him. 'Thank you so much for coming along.' She offered her gloved hand and he shook it. 'I'm deeply grateful, I really am.'

'My pleasure, Miss Stanford: glad to be of assistance.'

She was wearing a simple skirt and blouse. The skirt was not plumped out with layers of petticoats as was the fashion of the day, and the bonnet she wore was plain and unadorned. She had dressed practically for a morning's work in the sun, and Mick, who had pondered upon what he should wear, was thankful that he too had opted for practicality.

'Mr Powell is already here,' she said leading the way into the grounds, and he couldn't help noticing as he followed that she had a very neat figure.

Upon seeing Jefferson, Mick was doubly thankful that he'd dressed practically. Jefferson, as usual, could have passed for a peasant; he seemed completely careless of fashion.

'Welcome, Michael,' he said, pumping away at Mick's hand. 'Doris told me you'd offered to help. Good for you.'

Mick returned the handshake a little shamefaced. He hadn't sought permission for time off from his work, and the man was his employer after all.

'I hope you don't mind, Jefferson,' he said, trying to apologise without appearing subservient in Amy's presence – a rather delicate balance. 'I thought perhaps –'

'Good God, man, why should I mind? We're all here for the same purpose, are we not, to raise money for the society and its good works.' Jefferson beamed from Mick to Amy and back again. 'In fact, if you want to call up to the transport yards for an hour or so during the afternoons next week I'd be most obliged. You can give me a hand making up the dance floor. It'll save one of my drivers having to take time off.'

'I'd be more than happy to do so.' Mick was thankful that Jefferson had treated him as an equal, but then Jefferson always did. In fact Jefferson seemed to treat all men as equals.

The American turned to Amy. 'I believe the Hobart Town Ragged School Association is to be one of the major beneficiaries of this year's fundraising ball, Amy, is that correct?' Amy would shortly take up her teaching position with the Ragged School opening in Lower Collins Street early in the New Year, as Jefferson well knew.

'Yes that is correct, Jefferson.' She looked about at the lavish grounds and the massive castle-like structure that dominated them. 'Which makes this particular venue a rather interesting choice, don't you think?' she added, sharing the irony of her comment with both men.

'I do indeed,' Jefferson said with a glance to Mick.

Mick nodded in agreement, thinking what a marvellous leveller charity work was. There seemed no class distinction at all between the three of them, and he wondered if, before the end of the day, he and Amy Stanton might be using one another's first names.

They worked hard for the next hour and a half, Jefferson and Mick pacing out distances between trees and fences and stone walls, taking measurements here and there, Amy jotting down figures and drawing maps in her notebook. They conferred with others: the school's caretaker; the supplier of the marquee, whose assistants were also taking measurements; Mr Truscott, the hard-working bandmaster of the Hobart Town Brass Band; and several lady representatives of the parish committee, who would be supplying the evening's refreshments.

They were nearly done when a trap, drawn by a stylish

bay gelding and bearing an equally stylish middle-aged couple, appeared. The man drove the trap through the open gates and up the driveway, where he reined in the bay. As he alighted he nodded acknowledgement to the school care-taker, who stepped forward and held the animal's bridle.

'Thank you, William,' he said. Then he turned to assist his wife who, parasol held high out of harm's way, accepted her husband's hand and stepped gracefully to the ground. The Lyttletons had arrived.

'Amy, my dear,' Geoffrey called out heartily; he gave her a wave. A handsome man in his fleshy mid-forties, his smooth-shaven chin offered a more youthful appearance than those of his contemporaries who opted for beards tending to grey, and his receding hairline was more than compensated for by a healthy moustache and a fine set of mutton-chops. His wife, straight-backed with a proud and matronly bosom, was of regal bearing and equally striking.

Leaving the trap in William's care, Geoffrey and Phyllis crossed arm-in-arm to where Amy stood, Phyllis warmly greeting the parish ladies as they passed. She was head of the society's charity ball committee and deeply appreciated the input of the parish and its helpers.

'Thought we'd come and lend some moral support,' Geoffrey said as they arrived beside Amy. 'Hello, Jefferson, might have known I'd find you here. She's roped you in too, has she?' He gave Amy a wink.

'She certainly has. I'm to construct the dance floor,' Jefferson said as the two men shook.

'Good for you, old man, the society's much obliged.'

'Good morning, Mrs Lyttleton,' said Jefferson.

'Good morning, Mr Powell.' Phyllis acknowledged the greeting graciously but briefly, her attention more taken by Amy. 'Amy, my dear,' she said, 'it is December, and you are out of doors with no parasol.'

'I have a bonnet, Phyllis,' Amy said with a smile, 'I am well protected from the sun, I assure you.' She ignored the disapproving glance Phyllis cast at her white gloves, which were now looking decidedly soiled. Phyllis was a good woman, but obsessed with appearances and decidedly fussy. 'May I introduce Mr O'Callaghan? He too has kindly offered to lend his assistance,' Amy said, and she turned to Mick. 'Mr O'Callaghan, this is Mr and Mrs Lyttleton.'

'Delighted to meet you, Mr O'Callaghan,' Geoffrey grasped Mick's hand and shook it effusively. 'On behalf of the society I offer my sincerest thanks. The charity ball is a massive undertaking and we deeply appreciate our volunteer helpers.'

'I am happy to serve such a worthy cause, Mr Lyttleton,' Mick said and he nodded respectfully to Phyllis, who rewarded him with the warmest of smiles.

Once again, Mick was struck by the way in which a commitment to charity appeared to eliminate social barriers. Under normal circumstances he would never even get to meet the Lyttletons, let alone be greeted with such enthusiasm. Geoffrey Lyttleton was an extremely wealthy man. A banker and investor known for his good works, he had been one of the founding members of the Hobart Town Businessmen's Philanthropic Society and his contribution to the colony had been inestimable for a good decade or more. The Lyttletons moved in circles that would normally be well and truly closed to the likes of Mick O'Callaghan.

Here was a doorway into society that I'd not contemplated, Mick thought. He must offer his services to charity more often, although he wondered just how binding such a connection would prove. Geoffrey Lyttleton's bonhomie may well be a fleeting thing. Perhaps when volunteer helpers had served their purpose both they and their input were forgotten. He wondered whether this might apply to Amy Stanford. Would her gratitude be fleeting? Would he be discarded from her acquaintance when his services were no longer required?

The Lyttletons did not stay long. They circulated,

thanking those present for their commitment to the cause, and then they climbed back into their trap. Geoffrey took up the reins and as they were about to drive off Phyllis cautioned Amy to beware of the sun and reminded her they would collect her in the carriage for church at half-past nine the following morning.

'I shall be ready. Thank you, Phyllis.' Amy waved goodbye as the trap bowled off down the drive. 'Oh dear,' she murmured, 'I would far rather walk.'

'I beg your pardon?' Mick, who was standing beside her, thought she was talking to him.

'Sorry,' she said lightly, 'just thinking out loud. Phyllis is being overzealous, that's all. I would far rather walk to church than go by carriage. St George's is only twenty minutes from our house and Father and I always walk: we enjoy the constitutional.'

'Oh?' He pretended puzzlement for he was not supposed to know Silas Stanford was away, but he sensed that a God-given opportunity was about to present itself.

'Father is in Sydney,' Amy explained, 'and the Lyttletons have been elected my guardians, so to speak. It is a duty dear Phyllis is taking far too seriously,' she added with a wry moue. 'She still sees me as sixteen, when in fact I shall shortly be twenty-two. I am more than capable of looking after myself.'

Mick found the dismissive way she spoke of Phyllis Lyttleton, who was considered by many to be something akin to colonial royalty, a little outrageous and also highly attractive. He was beginning to realise there was a distinctly non-conformist side to Amy Stanford.

'I would consider it an honour, Miss Stanford,' he said, 'if you would allow me to walk you to church tomorrow morning.'

'Oh good heavens above, I can just imagine what Phyllis would say to that.' Amy openly laughed, relishing the thought. 'Thank you so much for your offer, Mr

O'Callaghan,' she said, 'but with the greatest of regret I'm afraid I must refuse. In the meantime, however, as we have been toiling together under a hot sun for nearly two hours, and as we will be working for the cause over the next fortnight, I do wish you would call me Amy. That is, if I may call you Michael in return?'

'I insist that you do, Amy,' he said and they shared a smile.

She liked him, he could tell, and he certainly liked her. In fact, he found her delightful. She was candid, unpretentious and, when she was animated as she now was, she was really rather pretty. He would very much enjoy getting to know Amy Stanford.

The next day, when he visited the white weatherboard house in Hampden Road, Mick made no mention to Eileen of the week's events. To voice his hopes might be to court disaster. But he could not help fantasising about the possibilities they presented. What if he had the wealth to become Eileen's benefactor? He pictured what it would be like if she belonged to no other man but him. No longer would her beauty be his for just this one afternoon a week. No longer would they need to cram their lovemaking and laughter, and even their battles, into several short hours on a Sunday. She'd be his exclusive property to call upon whenever he wished. He knew that she wanted the same thing herself. She'd said as much only the previous week.

'We're made for each other, Mick,' she'd said, 'what a shame you'll never be rich. If you could set me up properly I could be yours, but there's not much hope of that is there?' She hadn't been teasing and she hadn't been goading, she'd actually appeared regretful. 'Oh well,' she'd shrugged. 'Sundays will just have to do.'

Amy Stanford and a lady from the charity ball committee called in to the transport yards the following Thursday to check on the progress of the dance floor. It was late in the afternoon and at first Mick thought Amy might have orchestrated the visit to coincide with the time he was there – until he realised this was also the time she finished work at the charity school. In any event, he set out to use her visit for the further advancement of his cause.

'Jefferson tells me you will be teaching at the Ragged School next year,' he said.

He'd taken a break from his work and they were standing by the open stable doors looking out over the main yard, a dusty dirty place, particularly in the height of midsummer, smelling of dung and harness leather, but she didn't seem to mind at all. He liked her for that.

'Yes,' she said. 'Conditions at the Ragged School will be basic, but anything would be an improvement upon the present situation, which is quite untenable. The warehouse that currently serves as a schoolroom for the poor is disgraceful. Little wonder attendance is so low.'

'And you think improved conditions will raise the attendance levels?' From his tone he clearly believed otherwise.

'Yes I do,' she said adamantly. 'Given the right teachers and given the policy of the British Ragged School system, which we intend to adopt, I believe we will be able to convince our pupils of the important role education will play in the rest of their lives.'

The way she spoke reminded him of Jefferson: she was clearly an idealist. 'I hope you're right, Amy,' he said. 'I know the people of Wapping – I lived there myself and became very much one of them.' Honesty was undoubtedly the best policy with Amy Stanford, he'd decided. 'They deserve the right to an education.' And of course the only way to attract an idealist was to sound like one.

'They certainly do,' she agreed. 'Education is not exclusively the entitlement of the rich. The Ragged School aims to further the prospects of disadvantaged children so that those among them with the talent and desire might go on to higher levels of scholarship. It is their God-given right to be granted this opportunity.'

Mick supposed that he should admire her passion, but her noble sentiments were starting to grate. Amy Stanford did not come from a disadvantaged background. He felt a sudden and intense desire to challenge her.

'Some children are required to go to work in order to support their families,' he said. 'Opportunity is a luxury they cannot afford.'

'I am fully aware of this,' she replied.

'I was fortunate in being able to remain at school until I was fourteen.' He rather shocked himself saying so: he hadn't intended to be quite *this* honest. 'And the only reason I was able to do so was because my brothers and sisters went to work at the age of twelve,' he declared with an air of defiance.

'Then you are one of the lucky ones, aren't you, Michael? And you've done very well for yourself, I must say. I would be extremely proud to see pupils of mine achieve as you have.'

Dear God, he thought, what a fortunate turn of events. He had not shocked her at all – far from it in fact. He had won her respect. He could see it in her eyes.

Mick's hopes were raised even higher upon the very day of the ball.

It was mid-afternoon and the volunteers had completed their work. The giant marquee was erected and the rows of white-clothed trestle tables set up beneath it. The dance floor was laid out in the open air and the bandstand constructed beside it. All that remained now was the rigging of the lamps that would light up the scene as dusk fell.

'You are coming tonight, aren't you?' Amy asked as she and Mick stood in the shade of the marquee sipping lemonade from tin cups. Throughout the day, the ladies of the parish committee had been offering cool lemonade to the workers, and even damp cloths to wipe perspiring brows as the afternoon had grown progressively hotter.

'No,' he said.

'Why ever not?' she demanded.

'I did not purchase a ticket because I was not invited to do so, and I believe the attendance is by invitation only.'

'Oh.' She was taken aback. 'That is a definite oversight on behalf of the charity ball committee. Those who volunteer their services should automatically be invited, and free of charge I might add. Father always issued such instruction to the ladies of the committee. Were he here now you would most certainly be on the list, have no doubt about that.'

'Ah, well.' He shrugged. He had not expected an invitation. 'It doesn't matter.'

'It matters a great deal.' Amy took umbrage at what she saw as far more than a mere oversight. She was outraged. This confirmed her suspicion that the wealthy wives on the committee considered their duties an extension of their social lives – they were inviting only those they deemed personally acceptable. 'I shall have a word with Phyllis and the committee ladies about this,' she said, tight-lipped, 'and you will come as my guest, Michael. I *insist* that you do.'

'You *insist*?' He raised a cheeky eyebrow at the archness of her tone.

'I *absolutely* insist!'

'Oh well,' he agreed, 'if you *absolutely* insist.'

'I do. And furthermore we will dance every second dance, you and I.'

'That will shock Phyllis and the committee ladies,' he said with a roguish grin.

'I hope so.' She relaxed and the smile she returned him was equally roguish. 'I certainly do hope so.'

In the light cast by the many lamps that were strung about the marquee and among the trees and from the stone walls

of its castle backdrop, the grounds of the Hutchins School
had metamorphosed into a fairyland.

The Hobart Town Brass Band was in fine form,
Mr Truscott leading the musicians in military marches
and quadrilles, while people milled about socialising, the
women resplendent in their full-skirted ballgowns. The
dance music would follow a little later when all the guests
had arrived and the evening was well underway.

Mick entered the marquee and made for the table where
the parish ladies were serving fruit punch, intent upon
fetching Amy a glass. He had left her with Phyllis Lyttleton,
who had greeted him most pleasantly upon his arrival.

'I'm so glad you could come, Mr O'Callaghan,' she'd said.
'Amy has pointed out to me the committee's oversight, for
which I humbly apologise. You are most warmly welcome.'

'Thank you, Mrs Lyttleton.'

'We must circulate, my dear,' Phyllis said, linking her
arm through Amy's, 'there are so very many people who
need to be thanked.'

'Of course,' Amy agreed, 'one must do one's duty.' She
was not about to let Phyllis dictate the rules, however.
Michael O'Callaghan was her guest for the evening and
she intended to make that fact obvious. 'Would you mind
awfully fetching me a glass of fruit punch, Michael,' she
said, 'I'm quite parched.'

Mick was fully aware of the statement being made. 'Of
course,' he replied, 'it would be my pleasure.'

'Thank you so much.' She waved a gloved hand about
airily. 'I'll be mingling somewhere.'

'Have no fear, Amy,' he said with a smile. 'I shall find
you.'

And he'd wandered off to the marquee, aware of
Phyllis's slightly frozen reaction to their easy familiarity
and the bandying about of Christian names.

He made his way through the crowds to the punch table
where one of the ladies from the parish poured him two

glasses and, as he turned to leave, he literally bumped into Jefferson and Doris.

'Hello, Michael.' Doris was delighted to see him. 'So we finally get to meet her, do we?' she said, gesturing at the glasses he was carrying.

'Who?'

'Your young lady.'

'Oh.' He looked caught out and glanced self-consciously at Jefferson. 'I'm afraid not,' he said. 'There has been a parting of the ways, I'm sorry to say.'

'Oh dear.' Doris appeared most concerned. 'That is sad news indeed.'

'Yes. It happened some time ago now. She was very dear to me, and I have had little success in finding a young lady to take her place. I didn't have the nerve to tell you both.' He looked from one to the other, embarrassed. 'I suppose I didn't wish to admit failure. Please do forgive me.'

'Good heavens, man, there's no need to apologise.' Jefferson clapped him sympathetically on the shoulder and cast a glance at his wife that said they should mind their own business. 'I trust you'll join me for a glass of ale a little later in the evening?'

'I'd love to, Jefferson, thank you.' Mick gave a salute with one of the glasses and made his way out into the grounds where the band was now playing 'Pride of the Regiment'.

Upon his arrival, Amy excused herself from Phyllis Lyttleton with the promise that she would continue on her rounds and thank all those who had been of such help to the society. In her father's absence it was her duty, she said.

'Michael will accompany me, won't you, Michael?'

'Delighted,' Mick replied. Offering Amy his arm, he bowed courteously to Phyllis.

'How kind.' Phyllis, powerless to object, was equally courteous in her response, but as the two of them walked away she was left quite nonplussed. How had this come to pass? she wondered.

Mick did not feel in the least out of his depth as he circulated among the guests, Amy introducing him to all and sundry. On the contrary, he felt very much at home. He bowed chivalrously to the ladies and shared a comradely handshake with the men. Here is where I belong, he thought. Amy Stanford was the perfect ticket into society. She knew absolutely everyone including, as it turned out, the governor himself.

Sir Henry Young and his wife, Augusta, were chatting with several other guests, one of whom was Geoffrey Lyttleton. As they approached the group, Mick wasn't sure what sort of reception he might expect from Geoffrey, given Phyllis's rather frosty reaction.

'Good to see you, Mr O'Callaghan.'

Geoffrey Lyttleton however proved most cordial. So cordial indeed that he took over the formalities, introducing Mick not only to Sir Henry and Lady Young, but to the shipping magnate Alexander McGregor and his wife, Harriet, and also the prominent politician Lieutenant William Champ, formerly of the 63rd Regiment and currently Colonial Secretary of Van Diemen's Land. Mick played the scene with his customary panache, although if the truth be known he was just a little in awe of such august company.

'Sir Henry,' Amy said, 'I know my father would wish me to personally thank you for agreeing to speak on the society's behalf. We so appreciate you lending the time.'

'It is the least one can do, Miss Stanford, given the good works the society undertakes.' Sir Henry beamed about at the crowd like an amiable, be-whiskered grandparent proud of his children. 'Excellent turn-up, what? Great pity your father isn't here to share in the triumph. I know the tireless effort he puts into these fundraising events.'

'Yes, he was most disappointed when business called him away to Sydney.'

'I must say, Miss Stanford,' Augusta Young commented, 'how very much we are all looking forward to the special orchestra. The Viennese waltzes are quite glorious.'

'Yes, indeed,' William Champ said, 'very innovative of the society to come up with the idea, an absolute coup in fact.'

'I'm afraid the bandmaster must take all the credit for that,' Amy said with a smile. 'Mr Truscott has worked night and day.'

After a brief conference about the evening's running order, during which it was agreed Geoffrey would introduce Sir Henry following the band's current military bracket, Amy took her leave.

Mick bowed formally to Lady Young and Harriet McGregor, and nodded to each of the men. 'Your excellency,' he said to the Governor.

What exalted circles I'm mingling in, to be sure, he thought as Amy took his arm and they moved off on their rounds.

Surprisingly enough, there were a number of people present whom he knew, or at least recognised. Ruby Jack Clanton was there, regaling a group of men with his wild stories as they stood, glasses of ale in hand, under a conifer. Ruby Jack fitted in anywhere and everywhere it seemed. And there were various nodding acquaintances from Farrington's Gentleman's Club, men of questionable background, probably ex-convicts and possibly with a pedigree no better than his own, but with the money to purchase respectability. It gave a great boost to his confidence. And of course, there were the Dimbleby brothers.

'Well blow me down, Mick, what on earth are *you* doing here?'

The use of his nickname did not bother Mick in the least, but Gerald's tone was a definite insult.

'Hello, Gerald,' he said. 'Hello, Charles.'

'Hello, Mick.' Charles, as usual, was far more polite, covering for his brother's crassness. 'Good evening, Miss Stanford,' he said, tipping his top hat to Amy. 'May I offer my congratulations? The society has done a splendid job. Why, the night is a triumph already and it's only just begun.'

'Thank you, Mr Dimbleby.' Amy addressed Charles, ignoring Gerald altogether. 'And thank you as always for your most generous assistance.' Dimblebys, Purveyors of Fine Goods, had provided not only the tablecloths and napkins, but the cakes and confectionaries, which the ladies of the parish would serve following the savouries.

'Rest assured we are only too happy to oblige at any time the society should wish to call upon us,' Charles said.

'I am well aware of that fact, and we are deeply grateful.' Amy was forced to share her smile with Gerald, who was after all the other half of Dimblebys, but for some unknown reason his rudeness had irritated her intensely. 'Now if you will excuse me, gentlemen, I must inform Mr Truscott that the governor is shortly to make his speech.'

She once again took the arm Mick offered her and, as they left, Gerald turned to Charles with a comically wide-eyed expression, but Charles merely shrugged.

The last fanfare of 'The Marlborough March' rang out, Mr Truscott gave a final flourish of his baton, the band came to a halt and the crowd burst into spontaneous applause.

Geoffrey Lyttleton stepped onto the dance floor. He acknowledged the Hobart Town Brass Band, encouraged another round of applause, and without further ado introduced the governor of Van Diemen's Land, Sir Henry Young.

Sir Henry's speech was succinct. He welcomed all those present and reminded them of the reason they were there. The Hobart Town Businessmen's Philanthropic Society, he said, was a voluntary organisation devoted to providing succour and education for the poor.

'Now, with self-government so closely to hand,' he said, 'we must look more than ever to the well-being of our citizens. We are on the brink of a new age, and it is with the help of organisations like the Philanthropic Society that we will successfully distance ourselves from the past and embrace a future of freedom, prosperity and equality for all. I thank you for your attendance, which is most appreciated, and please do continue to give generously to the cause.'

Geoffrey Lyttleton led the applause that followed, although he didn't really need to. Sir Henry Young was a man well-liked by those who knew him. Then after reminding the crowd of the various donation boxes located in the marquee and about the grounds, Geoffrey thanked all those who had contributed so generously – 'too many to mention individually, I'm afraid' – and declared the official part of the proceedings over.

'Have a wonderful night, everyone! The waltz orchestra will perform shortly, but in the meantime, put on your dancing shoes,' he gestured flamboyantly to the bandstand, 'as we once again welcome Mr Truscott and the Hobart Town Brass Band!' Geoffrey was a born showman.

The band leapt straight into 'Way Down Upon the Swanee River', and within only minutes people were up on the dance floor. The night was now more than under way – it was in full swing.

'Shall we?' Mick asked.

'We shall,' Amy replied.

They danced a sedate two-step to 'Way Down Upon the Swanee River' and 'My Old Kentucky Home' after which the band upped the pace by jumping into 'Oh Susannah' and 'Camptown Races'. The songs of Stephen Foster were firm favourites everywhere, the rhythm of many adapting well to British folk dance, and in colonial outposts around the world highland reels and Irish jigs were performed with gusto to the tunes of America's most popular songwriter.

The Stephen Foster bracket was followed by 'Laird of Strathalbain' and 'Jug o' Corn', after which Amy called a personal halt. By now she was thoroughly exhausted.

She had danced many a highland reel before, and even on occasions an Irish jig, but never the way Mick did, never with such verve and energy. They'd jumped and whirled and twirled until she felt she couldn't dance another step.

'I need a glass of punch,' she panted, and he led her from the dance floor.

'I'm so sorry,' he said apologetically. 'I've overtired you, haven't I?'

'To the contrary, I can't remember ever having so enjoyed myself.' She smiled even as she gasped for breath. 'And as soon as I have recovered, I demand we return for more.'

'Don't move,' he said, 'I'll get you some punch.'

He disappeared into the marquee, and the moment he'd done so, Phyllis Lyttleton materialised from nowhere.

'Amy, my dear,' she said, 'I am a little concerned about the amount of time you are spending with Mr O'Callaghan. Do you not feel –?'

'I have thanked all those who need to be thanked, Phyllis,' Amy said, fanning her flushed face with a gloved hand. 'I have done my duty.'

'Of course you have, my dear. But I am sure there are other young men who may wish to dance with you –'

'Ah yes, but do they dance as well as Mr O'Callaghan?' Amy couldn't help herself: she laughed. She intended no insult to Phyllis, whom she knew meant well, but she felt strangely heady and exhilarated.

'Perhaps not, Amy,' Phyllis said a little sharply, 'and that may well be my point. Appearances must be observed, my dear. When the waltz orchestra commences I would like you to come and sit with Geoffrey and me.'

'Oh no, I couldn't do that,' Amy replied. 'I couldn't possibly do that.'

'Why ever not?'

'Viennese waltzes must be danced to, Phyllis, and I intend to dance to every single one.'

Phyllis reported back to her husband, shocked, but Geoffrey seemed unperturbed.

'Don't fret, my dear,' he said, 'you're being over-protective. The lad's a bit of an upstart, I grant you, but Amy's just having a good time. It's nothing serious.'

An hour later, Mr Truscott's eight-piece string and woodwind orchestra opened their programme with 'Echoes of the Rhine Lorelei' and, as the strains of Johann Strauss the elder flooded the grounds of the Hutchins School, Amy and Mick joined the other dancers to glide effortlessly about the dance floor.

Mick was a naturally gifted dancer. He hadn't needed the lessons his elder sisters had given him. He'd been grateful at the time, but he'd quickly outstripped them in expertise, after which he'd learnt simply by watching whenever and wherever he could. Now, in his element, he could have waltzed and polkaed all night. So could Amy. And they did. As long as the orchestra played, they danced.

Phyllis Lyttleton was not the only person present who took note of Mick O'Callaghan's monopoly over Amy Stanford that night.

Doris Powell said nothing to her husband as she watched the couple. Jefferson did not approve of gossip, and indeed nor did she. But she could not help thinking that young Michael O'Callaghan, having been recently disappointed in love and now seeking a new bride, might be looking a little unrealistically above his station. Doris did not disapprove, nor did she intend to utter a word upon the subject, but she did wonder what Silas Stanford might say upon his return.

The evening concluded with a resounding rendition of 'The Radetzky March', a tribute to the music of Johann Strauss the elder, the success of the ball and the triumph of the night in general.

As Amy and Mick stood on the dance floor clapping to the rhythm along with everyone else, the march signified something far more personal.

'May I call on you?' he asked.

'Yes.' She didn't hesitate. 'You could perhaps start by walking me to church in the morning.' She turned to face him. 'I'm afraid,' she said regretfully, 'that for propriety's sake, Clara would need to accompany us.'

'I look forward to meeting Clara.' He knew the Stanford house in Macquarie Street; most people did. 'What time shall I call?'

'Nine o'clock would be suitable.'

CHAPTER TEN

Not surprisingly, Mick's courtship of Amy Stanford met with the strongest opposition from Phyllis Lyttleton. Within only days, Amy was being firmly lectured, though she refused to listen.

'I have hardly agreed to marry the man, Phyllis,' she said. 'I have simply accepted his friendship.'

'Which is to accept his courtship, my dear – it's one and the same thing, as you very well know. Good heavens above, he accompanied you to church, and then you invited him here,' she looked around the sitting room, aghast at the thought, 'here into your home.'

'For morning tea and in the presence of Clara,' Amy said unperturbed. 'There has been no impropriety. Now please do not worry yourself.'

But Phyllis was unable to stifle her true misgivings, which had nothing at all to do with propriety. 'My dear, he's not good enough for you,' she burst out.

Phyllis should have known better. Such a statement did nothing to further her cause. Indeed it only fuelled Amy's desire to thumb her nose at those who stood in judgement of others.

'I will decide who my friends shall be, Phyllis,' she said pleasantly but firmly.

'Very well, Amy. If you insist upon disregarding my advice,

there is little more I can do or say.' Without waiting for Clara
to fetch her parasol, Phyllis snatched it up from the umbrella
stand. 'But bear in mind your father did entrust you to our
care in his absence. We shall see what Silas has to say about
this upon his return.' And she swept out the front door in a
huff to where her coachman was waiting patiently.

'So you seriously believe Phyllis Lyttleton will try and turn
your father against us?'

The following Sunday, Clara's company did not in the
least inhibit conversation as Amy and Mick sat in the
front drawing room taking morning tea. They simply continued where they'd left off after their walk home from
St George's.

'Oh, most definitely yes. Thank you, Clara,' Amy said
as she accepted the cup of tea the housekeeper passed her.
'Phyllis is a good woman who believes she has my best
interests at heart, but she is very straitlaced and finds my
refusal to accept her counsel tantamount to rebellion.'

'That is a great pity,' Mick said. It might also be a great
worry, he thought. Silas Stanford would surely take note
of anything Phyllis Lyttleton had to say.

'I do not believe so.' Amy was surprisingly dismissive. 'Father is not one for appearances as Phyllis is. He
sees people for who they are, not for where they stand
in society. Despite his old-fashioned manner, Father is a
modern man at heart. Indeed,' she said proudly, 'Father is
a true egalitarian.'

'How fortunate.' During the past week, Mick had developed some views of his own about Silas Stanford, but they
were hardly views he could share with the man's daughter.
'Thank you, Clara.' He smiled at the housekeeper as he
accepted his cup of tea. 'There wouldn't be any of that
marvellous lemon cake left from last week, would there?'

'There would indeed, sir,' Clara said. 'I was just about
to fetch them.'

Clara liked Michael O'Callaghan. So what if he isn't
of the class Phyllis Lyttleton would have preferred, she
thought. Who is? This isn't the Old Country. There was
no blue blood around these parts. Hobart Town society
was comprised of middle-class poseurs and riffraff who'd
made money. Michael O'Callaghan was a good deal
more well-mannered than most and dashingly handsome.
Clara was delighted Miss Amy had found herself such an
exciting beau.

'Cream and jam, sir?' she asked.

'Oh yes please.' Mick flashed another winning smile.
'You certainly know the way to a man's heart, Clara.'

Clara beamed delightedly and left.

Amy laughed. 'You are thoroughly shameless, Michael,'
she said.

'In what way?'

'You have poor Clara completely under your spell.'

'It is the other way around, I assure you. Any man is
under the spell of any woman who can cook like Clara.'

If only I had Phyllis Lyttleton under my spell, Mick
thought as he sipped his tea. He did not at all share Amy's
trust in her father's egalitarianism. Phyllis Lyttleton, to
Mick's mind, presented a serious problem.

An hour later, he left the Stanford house and walked
back up the hill towards Battery Point, retracing the route
he and Amy had taken from St George's Church. But he
did not turn off Hampden Road into De Witt Street. He
continued on in the direction of Eileen's cottage, just as he
had the preceding week.

Eileen had made fun of him when he'd arrived last Sunday
in his best attire.

'Well just look at you, a real toff if ever I saw one,' she'd
said after she'd whisked him in the back door. They'd gone
straight through to the bedroom as usual, and she'd taken
off his top hat and flung it over the bedpost. 'What tricks

are you playing at now, Mick, you naughty lad,' she'd said teasingly as she started to undress him. 'You're up to no good, I'll wager. Who is it you're out to impress?'

He'd joined in the game. 'What a terrible thing, Eileen, to make fun of a man's Sunday best, and when he's come fresh from church at that.' She'd laughed. 'It's true, I swear,' he'd said, although by now her hands were on his trousers and he was becoming distracted. 'I warn you, woman: it is a sin to mock a man when he is in a state of grace.'

Their conversation had proceeded no further at that stage. But afterwards, lolling around unashamedly naked, he'd told her about the charity ball. Normally it was she who imparted the gossip while he watched with delight as she acted out her stories. He was no longer jealous about or even irritated by those that related to her benefactor, of whom she always spoke mockingly, always with scorn. What was the point of being jealous? Her benefactor was no more than a client, just like those at Trafalgar.

The relationship between Mick and Eileen had progressed immeasurably. The sexual act had ceased to be a battle. She no longer brought him to his climax like a whore doing her job: she made love to him like a woman who wanted to please and be pleased, clearly enjoying the sensuality of their union. They took no risks, always parting at the crucial moment, but Mick would keep himself in check for as long as possible in the hope that she might achieve her ultimate pleasure. She never did, and he wondered whether perhaps she was incapable of experiencing sexual release. Perhaps she had practised control for so long that she simply could not let herself go. Whatever the reason, he suspected that their relationship might well be the closest thing to love Eileen Hilditch had ever known. And for once it was not his ego dictating. For once, Mick was quite right.

'I met the governor at the ball,' he'd boasted as they'd

sprawled wantonly on the bed. 'I met Sir Henry Young himself.'

'Really?' She'd pretended to be most impressed.

'Oh yes,' he'd added airily, 'and his wife, and any number of other hugely important people. We talked about the Viennese waltzes.'

'Did you indeed?'

'Well no,' he'd admitted with a grin, 'I didn't talk about them at all. *They* talked about them. *I* danced them. Every single one! Oh I tell you, Eileen, it was the grandest night. It was the grandest night ever.'

'I'm sure it was; it's been the talk of the town for the past fortnight. I've no doubt I'll be hearing about it for the whole of next week.'

'Oh.' Her abruptness jarred, instantly robbing him of all enthusiasm. Of course, he thought, she mingles with the rich and the powerful on a nightly basis at Trafalgar, why should she be impressed by anything I can tell her?

'But I'd much rather hear about it from you, Mick.' She'd meant no harm by her remark and, sitting up on the bed, she smiled kittenishly and traced a playful finger down his chest. 'You tell me everything you've been up to, you wicked, wicked boy,' she'd said.

And he had. She could hurt him and heal him in the blink of an eye and, enthusiasm restored, everything had tumbled out.

He'd told her of his involvement with the Philanthropic Society. 'Charity is the way to break through boundaries, I've discovered,' he'd said excitedly, 'that's how I was invited to the ball.' And he'd told her of his plan to marry money. 'I intend to marry a rich man's daughter, Eileen,' he'd said, carried away in his eagerness to impress, 'and when I do you'll have no need of Trafalgar, nor of any other benefactor but me. I'll buy you a house, I'll set you up –'

She'd interrupted, more amused than anything. 'And do you have any particular young lady in mind, Mick?' she'd asked. 'Now that you've successfully broken into society exactly whose money is it you have in your sights?'

'Silas Stanford's,' he'd announced. 'I intend to marry his daughter, Amy.'

The reaction had been instantaneous. She'd dropped her playful manner. 'You're serious,' she'd said as if she'd only just realised this was no jest.

'Yes. And I believe I have grounds for hope. I know Amy is fond of me – she has agreed I may call upon her. I accompanied her to church today and we had morning tea together.'

'All of which is most promising.' Her eyes had lost their kittenish gleam. They were cat-like and wary and he'd wondered why. 'Take care, Mick,' she'd warned. 'These pillars of society with whom you're mingling are ruthless men. If our relationship were to become known to them, you could endanger us both.'

He'd realised in that instant that she was not referring to her clients at Trafalgar, most of whom would joke about the whores they knew and even compare notes. She was referring to her benefactor. Then the thought had struck him.

'It's Silas Stanford, isn't it?' She'd not deigned to reply, and he'd taken her silence as meaningful. 'Silas Stanford is your benefactor.'

'Well now, that would be the final irony wouldn't it?' she'd said with an enigmatic smile.' She'd laughed and kissed him. 'I wish you well with your endeavours, Mick. I hope you're successful for both our sakes. I'd like you to take care of me.' Then she'd stood, pulling on her shift and he'd known then and there she would never admit the truth to him. 'Just practise caution, that's all I'm saying.'

Throughout the whole of the following week Mick had pondered the subject. The identity of Eileen's benefactor had ceased to be of interest to him once he'd discounted the man as competition for her affection, but now the possibility that it could be Silas Stanford had rekindled a desperate need to know. And the more he thought about it, the more everything fell into place. With the Stanford home in Macquarie Street and the location of Eileen's cottage in Battery Point, how very convenient it would be for Silas Stanford to simply walk up the hill to his mistress's house.

So thoroughly convinced was Mick that he didn't even consider spying upon the cottage. What would be the point? Silas Stanford was in Sydney. He would have to wait until the man's return to discover the truth.

As it turned out, he did not need to wait that long at all.

'If it isn't Casanova.'

This Sunday began as a repeat of the previous one. Eileen made fun of him upon his arrival and in the bedroom she again flung his top hat over the bedpost. 'I shall demand a full report in due course,' she said as she started to undress him, 'but first things first.'

Then afterwards, glowing from their exertions, she opened the conversation with her typical mixture of mockery and affection.

'So come along, Mick, I'm dying to know: how fares the courtship of Miss Stanford? It's been two whole Sundays. Are you engaged to be married yet?'

'I've hit a bit of a snag I'm afraid.'

'Oh dear, poor thing, what's happened? Has she decided you're not good enough after all?'

'No, no, not for a minute, but I fear her so-called "guardians" are going to prove a problem.'

'And who are her so-called guardians?'

'Phyllis and Geoffrey Lyttleton.'

There was no need for explanation. Everyone in Hobart Town knew of the Lyttletons, just as everyone knew of the Stanfords.

'I see,' she said, 'and the Lyttletons are presenting a problem, are they? In what way?'

'Phyllis has taken umbrage at my audacity in courting Amy. She's bound to elicit her husband's support, and between them they'll turn Stanford against me.'

'What a pity,' she said, 'what a terrible pity,' and she left it at that, the subject no longer appearing of any great interest.

But casually as she played the scene, she was not casual enough. He had seen the involuntary flicker in her eyes. Upon the very second he'd uttered the name, Mick had known the truth. Silas Stanford was not Eileen's benefactor. Geoffrey Lyttleton was. And the knowledge opened up a whole new realm of possibility. How extraordinarily fortuitous, he thought.

'Yes, it is a pity,' he said, 'but I do not intend to give up easily. Not with half the battle won.'

'Which particular half would that be?'

'Amy. I do believe she is falling in love with me.'

'Of course she is. What woman wouldn't?' Eileen smiled. 'And are you falling in love with her?' she asked lightly.

'I believe I am a little.' He ran his fingers over her breasts. 'Which would make life very pleasant all round.'

He intended no confrontation. She would make no admission anyway, and he did not wish her to know of the plan already forming in his mind.

Mick wisely decided to seek stronger evidence than the flicker of recognition he'd seen in Eileen's eyes and, after giving some thought to his subject, he caught Geoffrey Lyttleton out with remarkable ease.

There was no need to lie in wait for hours spying on the cottage. The stylish trap Geoffrey drove into town from his stately home in the foothills of Mount Wellington was instantly recognisable. Mick discovered that, as a rule, the horse and vehicle were accommodated at the coach house in

Liverpool Street just a block up the road from the offices of Lyttleton Holdings & Investment. But when Geoffrey visited Battery Point to call upon his shipping agent, or to conduct his ongoing crusade for the completion of St George's Church, or indeed to confer with Jefferson Powell upon some charitable concern for the society, the horse and trap were housed at the stables of McLagan Road Transport.

It was simple to pop into McLagan's intermittently throughout the day and check on the bay gelding and trap. And it was simple, upon discovering them there on the afternoon of the very second day, to set himself up in a secure spot a good distance from Eileen's house and wait, knowing exactly from which direction the man would appear.

How clever of Geoffrey Lyttleton to become so openly involved in the neighbourhood, Mick thought as he watched the familiar figure stride down Hampden Road. Geoffrey had any number of reasons to be in Battery Point, and each was a front, particularly St George's. He didn't even appear furtive as he turned into the track that led to Eileen's back door, and indeed why should he? He could well have been canvassing support amongst the parishioners in his fervent campaign for the completion of the Mariners' Church.

Mick put his plan into action the very next day.

The very next day happened to be Christmas Eve, a fact that proved to his advantage, or so he thought at the time. Upon visiting Geoffrey Lyttleton's offices at ten o'clock, he was told by the clerk at the front desk that Mr Lyttleton would not be coming in until the late afternoon, after which he would work through into the evening hours.

'We close for three full working days over Christmas,' young Frederick said, 'and Mr Lyttleton likes to ensure all is in order. Everyone else gets to leave at four,' he added waspishly on the assumption his complaint was finding a sympathetic ear, 'but I am required to attend the front desk and lock up the premises when he leaves.'

'Thank you,' Mick replied briskly, 'I shall call back later.' How very convenient, he thought, the place will be virtually deserted.

'Of course, sir.' Frederick was suddenly nervous. He'd presumed that, being roughly the same age, the young man was an underling like himself, a fellow overworked clerk on an errand for his employer, but such a confident manner signified he might perhaps be a personal acquaintance of Mr Lyttleton's. 'May I make an appointment for you, Mr ...?' He left the query hanging.

'No, no,' Mick replied airily, 'it's nothing of great importance – just a bit of business for the Philanthropic Society.'

'Ah yes, of course,' Frederick said with a smile that he hoped would ingratiate, 'Mr Lyttleton is untiring in his commitment to the society. I shall tell him you called, Mr ...?'

But Mick simply smiled and gave a wave as he walked off. 'Do, do,' he said and the bell tinkled as he closed the door behind him.

Now, strolling up Harrington Street in the heat of the afternoon, Mick slowed to an amble. It was not yet quite four and he didn't wish to arrive at the offices before the staff had left, or indeed before Geoffrey had arrived.

He halted altogether at the corner of Macquarie Street where a group was gathered outside St Joseph's Church singing Christmas carols. Other passers-by, too, had stopped to listen, many putting a coin in the poor-box proffered by the priest, and Mick added a coin of his own in the hope that a kindly action might lend him good luck for what lay ahead.

'*God rest ye merry gentlemen, let nothing you dismay ...*'

He stayed for a good fifteen minutes enjoying the familiar carols. He recalled Christmases past when as a small child he'd stood up to his knees in snow singing with his older brothers and sisters at the doors of the rich. But here in this dusty street, on this hot afternoon, under this still merciless sun and this cloudless sky, the songs, familiar as they were, had become foreign. They were songs of the north, songs of a different hemisphere, a different climate, a different habitat altogether. Mick looked around at the crowd that had slowly gathered. Had any of them adjusted to this strangeness yet? No, of course they haven't, he thought, as he watched women fanning their faces and men wiping away the sweat that poured from their brows. Would any of them *ever* adjust? It was impossible to imagine that they could. Apart from its obvious religious significance, Christmas was destined to remain an anomaly in this upside-down land.

He walked on, crossing over Collins Street. People were bustling busily about, making last-minute purchases, greeting each other and exchanging season's greetings. There was an air of festive expectancy that Mick found just a little desperate.

Turning right into Liverpool Street, he headed directly for Lyttleton Holdings & Investment, where he bounded up the stone steps and made a bold entrance, closing the door firmly behind him, its bell still tinkling as he crossed to the front desk.

'Good afternoon, sir.' The clerk greeted him. 'I told Mr Lyttleton that a gentleman called on society business, and –'

'Mr O'Callaghan,' Mick said. 'Tell him Mr O'Callaghan is here to see him.'

'Of course, sir.'

The clerk left through the door to the side that led to the offices, re-appearing only seconds later.

'Mr Lyttleton says he will –' But he didn't get any further as Geoffrey Lyttleton himself emerged.

'Mr O'Callaghan, what a pleasant surprise.' Geoffrey smiled a welcome and offered his hand, but Mick could tell by the steely glint in his eyes that he did not consider the surprise pleasant at all.

'Good afternoon, Mr Lyttleton,' he said as they shook, 'I just popped in to discuss some business on behalf of the society.'

'Yes, yes, so Frederick here told me, although as you left no name I couldn't for the life of me think to whom he might be referring.' The cheeky young upstart, Geoffrey thought, *pop in* indeed! How dare he presume such intimacy, and what business could he possibly have to discuss on behalf of the society. But still, he might have been sent by Jefferson Powell. 'Do come in, Mr O'Callaghan.'

Frederick held the door open for them and Mick followed Geoffrey. They crossed through a deserted secretarial office and into an opulent oak-panelled room that was Geoffrey Lyttleton's private realm.

'Take a seat.' After closing the door, Geoffrey indicated a rosewood carver and circled his mahogany desk, which was deliberately and intimidatingly large. He sat in the Queen Anne walnut elbow chair that was his personal throne. 'I presume you're on an errand for Jefferson?' He managed to sound pleasant while making Mick's inferior status thoroughly understood.

Mick had contemplated standing as he conducted his business, but something about Lyttleton's condescension now caused him to change his mind. He sat, refusing to be daunted, and leant back in his chair, languidly crossing his legs.

'No, I'm not on an errand for Jefferson,' he said, 'I'm here with regard to a personal matter.'

'Oh? And what *personal matter* could that possibly be?' Geoffrey dropped any pretence of pleasantness. The cheek of the fellow!

'The personal matter of my relationship with Amy Stanford.'

'Well you've certainly incurred the wrath of my wife

there,' Geoffrey said scathingly. So this is the reason for such outrageous overfamiliarity, he thought. Having wormed his way into Amy's affections, the young scoundrel presumed it gave him some claim to an acquaintanceship with her friends.

'Yes, I have rather upset your wife, haven't I?' Mick agreed. 'Which is why I'm here. I'd like you to call Phyllis off.'

'I beg your pardon?' Geoffrey wasn't quite sure he'd heard correctly. *Call Phyllis off?* What, call her off, like a dog? What on earth did the fellow mean?

'I would like you to instruct your wife ... No, no,' Mick corrected himself, 'I would like you to *order* your wife to cause no interference in my courtship of Amy –'

'Why the deuce would I do that?'

'– and I would like you to tell your wife,' Mick continued, oblivious to Geoffrey's outburst, 'that your reason for issuing such an order is your thorough approval of my suit. In fact, I would be most obliged if you would also make your approval known to Silas Stanford upon his return.'

Geoffrey was flabbergasted. 'What sort of lunatic are you, boy? You do realise, don't you, that you've now thoroughly ruined your chances? I couldn't have cared tuppence whether you married the girl or not: if she's fool enough to give herself to a wastrel that's her business.' He stood. It was time to put an end to this idiocy. 'You can rest assured, Mr O'Callaghan, that as of this very minute I shall join my wife in preventing your union with Miss Stanford.'

Mick also stood. 'No you won't.'

'And why not, pray?'

'Because if you do, your wife, and your son and your daughter and their children, and indeed all of Hobart Town will be informed that you keep a mistress in a house in Battery Point, and that you have done so for the past two years. Where will your fine reputation be then, Geoffrey, when the whole world knows about Red?'

Geoffrey Lyttleton sank back into his chair in a state of shock, his knees literally giving way beneath him, his face ashen: not for one minute had he anticipated this.

Mick was gratified by the reaction. He had been unsure of quite what to expect, but the utter dread he now saw in Geoffrey's eyes told him he'd won. If the news of Red were made public the man would be unveiled for the hypocrite he was and thoroughly ruined, as he very well knew.

Following the initial shock, Geoffrey to his credit recovered very quickly.

'So I presume this will be an ongoing form of blackmail?' he queried icily after a moment's pause. 'I pay you a sum of money here and now, and then over time you keep coming back for more. That's the way scum like you operate, isn't it?'

'Not at all,' Mick replied, and he once again sat. 'I want no more than your assistance in my courtship of Amy Stanford.'

'I see.' Geoffrey nodded. Another pause, and then he continued in a businesslike manner, rather as if he were conducting a board meeting. 'Who else knows about Red?'

'No-one knows but me. I swear it on my mother's life.'

'And how did you find out?'

Mick responded with his carefully prepared answer, aware that he must protect Eileen at all costs. 'I've been following you ever since your wife threatened to ruin my chances,' he said. 'I'd hoped to find out something that might pressure you into calling her off.' He shrugged, 'perhaps a visit to a brothel or some such misdemeanour. Then I saw Red coming out of that house, and I knew I'd got lucky.'

'How do you know Red?'

'I don't. But I've been to Trafalgar on the odd occasion, when I can afford it, after a good run at the card table. I recognised her.'

'I see,' Geoffrey said again. He appeared to accept the

explanation, but his mind was obviously ticking over as he considered a course of action. 'And you expect me to believe you when you say there will be no further demands, and that no-one else knows?'

'Yes, you have my word in both instances ...' Eileen's warning sounded a sudden alarm in Mick's brain. *Take care, Mick. These pillars of society with whom you're mingling are ruthless men.*

'Although there is one precaution I've taken that I feel I must point out,' he continued. 'I have left a sealed envelope with my lawyer, which is to be opened should I meet with any unexpected accident.'

'Have you really?' Geoffrey's smile was singularly unpleasant. This part of the story he did not believe for one minute. What lawyer? he thought scornfully. The little bastard is lying through his teeth. He doesn't have a lawyer – his sort of scum never do.

It was at that moment that Geoffrey Lyttleton's mind turned to the brand new Adams revolver which sat in the desk's top drawer, its chambers fully loaded. How simple it would be, he thought. There was no-one around but young Frederick, and young Frederick was both gullible and obedient. The Irishman was out to rob me from the start, he'd say, and young Frederick would be bound to agree that he'd had no alternative but to shoot the felon.

'In the event of my death under suspicious circumstances,' Mick went on smoothly, 'three letters will be posted.' He was thinking on his feet – there was no envelope, no lawyer and no letters – but he could sense danger in Geoffrey Lyttleton. 'One is addressed to your wife, one to the Hobart Town Businessmen's Philanthropic Society, and one to *The Mercury* newspaper.' He smiled confidently, the way he did when he held a poker hand worth nothing. 'I thought that should just about cover things.'

Across the sea of mahogany they eyed one another like card players, each trying to read the other's mind.

'Well, well,' Geoffrey said finally, 'you have been busy.'
He knew, as they both did, that he dared not call the Irishman's bluff.

'I take it we have reached an agreement?' Mick asked.

'We have.'

'Excellent. Then perhaps you will start by persuading
your good wife that Amy be permitted to accompany me to
the Powells' home for Christmas luncheon tomorrow. She
will of course be suitably chaperoned by Mrs Powell.'

'As you wish.' Geoffrey stood abruptly and without
another word led the way back to the reception area where
Frederick snapped to attention.

'Thank you for your time, Mr Lyttleton,' Mick said,
'and may I take this opportunity to wish you and Mrs
Lyttleton and the family a very merry Christmas?'

'Season's greetings indeed, Mr O'Callaghan.'

'Merry Christmas, Frederick,' Mick said to the clerk.

'Why thank you, sir, and a merry Christmas to you too.'

As the door bell tinkled behind him, Mick told himself
that he really must get a lawyer, and the sooner the better
for safety's sake.

Christmas luncheon at the Powells was just as Doris
had predicted it would be – a raucous affair. Jefferson had
invited those of his employees without families, a good
dozen or so, and mostly young men. Indeed, apart from
Doris, only two other women were expected to be present:
Pauline, the young widow who took bookings at the office
of McLagan Road Transport, and Ada, the girl who came
in twice a week to mind the children while Doris did the
shopping. As it eventuated, however, there was a fourth
woman present – Amy Stanford.

Doris had been most surprised when Mick had dropped
by on Christmas morning to ask if he might bring Amy
with him.

'I'd be delighted, Michael,' she'd said, 'but isn't she

dining with the Lyttletons? She told me nearly a month ago that she was.'

'I think she would rather our company than theirs,' he'd said with a smile, 'and the Lyttletons have no objection.'

How extraordinary, Doris had thought, that the Lyttletons should openly acknowledge young Michael O'Callaghan as an acceptable suitor for their ward. She would have expected Phyllis in particular to object most strongly.

'I would love Amy to be here, Michael,' she'd said warmly. She felt very happy for him.

The day was a huge success. Doris had cooked up a veritable feast. With Ada's help she'd been working for the past several days. There were eighteen people in all and the dining room was crammed, with barely enough space to move, Jefferson having added an extra table, and odd chairs and stools having been brought in from the sitting room. But the very closeness only added to the atmosphere as guests jostled one another, passing along the individual plates of turkey and ham Jefferson carved, and then handing around the bowls of vegetables and gravy boats with gay abandon. They were like one big rowdy family.

'This reminds me of the old days at home,' Mick said to Amy, raising his voice above the general chatter, 'except we didn't get to eat such fancy food.'

Amy laughed. 'It reminds me of nothing I've ever known before,' she said, raising her own voice in return.

Amy was enjoying herself immensely. Given Phyllis's strong antipathy towards Michael, she'd expected to do battle when she'd accepted his invitation at such late notice, but to her utter astonishment, Phyllis had graciously released her from her obligation. Perhaps Phyllis believed the invitation had come from Doris Powell rather than Michael himself, but it was mystifying nonetheless. Now, gazing around at the workmen tucking into their food like healthy young animals, the thought of the horror on Phyllis's face could she see them was both amusing and satisfying.

After demolishing copious bowls of plum pudding and brandy sauce, the men carried the chairs out from the dining room and the party adjourned to the front verandah. Doris served tea for those who wanted it, although most of the men continued to drink ale, Jefferson having ordered in a five-gallon keg from the victualler in Argyle Street.

Upon popular demand, one of the workmen had brought along his concertina. Albert was recognised by his work-mates as the life of every party for there was apparently no popular song he couldn't play. As it turned out, there was no Christmas carol he couldn't play either.

'*The holly and the ivy, when they are both full grown ...*'

The crowd sang along to the concertina, carol after carol. Albert was indefatigable.

'*When the snow lay round about, deep and crisp and even ...*'

'Do you know,' Amy mused to Mick when after the fifth carol Albert took a brief break to consume a glass of ale, 'I have lived here since I was nine years old and it still amuses me that at Christmas and in the height of mid-summer we sing so fervently of everything that is foreign to this land.'

'I was thinking the very same thing just yesterday,' Mick said, 'as I passed by the carol singers outside St Joseph's Church. I do not believe we will ever adjust.'

'Perhaps not in our time,' she agreed. 'We still crave familiarity. But future generations might. They may even *embrace* the difference, who knows? Perhaps the children of our children will invent new songs.'

'Perhaps they will.'

There was a moment's pause and she laughed, self-conscious at having waxed philosophical, or perhaps it was simply the way he was looking at her.

'At least the weather is not as hot here as it is in Sydney,' she said. 'I have accompanied Father on several of his trips in the past and the summers there are quite unbearable. Here at least in the middle of winter we can pretend we are at home, and sometimes there is even snow.' Amy was aware she was chattering on unnecessarily, but she didn't know why.

'Shall we walk down to the water?' he suggested.

'Yes, that would be lovely.' She did not hesitate for a moment.

They stood and he offered her his arm.

Doris watched as the couple walked down the verandah steps. She knew if they were going any distance from the house, she should really offer to accompany them, but Amy had not asked her to, so she decided not to interfere. Besides, she trusted Michael: he would not behave improperly. She watched as the front gate closed behind them and they disappeared out of sight. Dear me, she thought, how Phyllis Lyttleton would disapprove! But then Phyllis Lyttleton was the most awful snob, and what she didn't know couldn't hurt her. Doris picked up the teapot and offered Pauline another cup.

They walked down the hill to the water's edge where there was barely a breath of breeze and not a soul in sight. The shipbuilding yards, normally a hive of industry, were deserted, and all was hushed. Even the mighty Derwent itself appeared lonely, devoid of activity, the boats at anchor sitting still and silent upon its ripple-less water.

'How lovely,' Amy said.

'Let's walk along a little further,' he suggested, 'there's something I want to show you.'

As they made their way along the shoreline, he held her hand in order to steady her. The ground was dry and firm underfoot, but it was stony and she could trip.

Minutes later they rounded the point and came to a halt.

Before them was the slipway and the jetty, and up ahead, sitting on the grassy slope fifty yards from the water's edge, was the small sandstone cottage.

'This is where I live,' he said. He was aware that admitting to such a rudimentary existence was a bold move, but he could sense it was the right one, and he watched her reaction closely.

'Oh Michael,' she breathed, 'how beautiful.'

They were still holding hands; it seemed they'd forgotten to let go. He turned her to him and taking care not to frighten her he very slowly bent his face down to hers and, with the utmost tenderness, he kissed her.

'We should go back now,' he said as they parted. 'We should go back to the others or they may worry.'

'Yes, we must go back.' Amy was amazed at her reaction. She did not feel in the least self-conscious, nor did she feel guilty. She just felt extraordinarily happy.

The dawning of the New Year heralded the birth of a new era.

On the first of January, 1856, Van Diemen's Land became officially known as Tasmania. The island colony had finally been granted Responsible Self-Government with the right to elect its own representative parliament and with a new freedom and a new name came a new sense of pride. Eighteen fifty-six was a year of great importance for the citizens of Tasmania. At long last they could distance themselves from the shameful past of Van Diemen's Land.

There were those among them for whom 1856 was also a year of great personal significance.

For Doris Powell, it was the year she discovered she was pregnant. Despite her prayers, she had failed to conceive for the past five years, and at the age of thirty-three she had thought her child-bearing days were over. Learning that they were not, she and Jefferson were overjoyed.

For Amy Stanford, it was the year she discovered she was in love. She had tried very hard to be practical after the Christmas Day kiss. Michael O'Callaghan is handsome and charming, she told herself, but she must not overreact to one romantic moment. Marriage must be based on a far more solid foundation. But romance had blossomed nonetheless, and not surprisingly taken the place of common-sense.

The year of 1856 was, however, especially significant for Silas Stanford. It was the year when, to the amazement of all who knew him, he arrived back in Hobart Town with a brand new wife.

CHAPTER ELEVEN

Mathilda Lipscombe was twenty-six years old. The only daughter of Colonel Dr Cedric Lipscombe, she had known Silas Stanford since she was sixteen years of age, Silas and her father having become acquainted through their mutual philanthropic interests.

Cedric Lipscombe, fondly referred to as 'the Colonel', was a man renowned for his charitable works. Formerly Surgeon in Charge of the British military hospital in Bombay, he had resigned his commission in 1840 and two years later had accepted an offer from the Colonial Government of New South Wales to work as senior surgeon at the Sydney Hospital. For well over a decade now, the Colonel had offered his services free of charge to those in need, particularly the children of the poor.

Silas and Cedric had met directly through the Sydney Orphan Schools, an organisation with which Silas's eldest daughter, Harriet, had worked a great deal since entering her order. The two men were the most unlikely of friends for they were the total antithesis of each other. Cedric was as loud and showy as Silas was quiet and reserved, but once they each recognised the true philanthropist in the other, their bond had been instant and over the years their friendship had grown unshakeable.

Silas dined with the Lipscombes whenever he was in

Sydney, always staying overnight, as they lived in Kirri-billi on the northern side of the harbour and were reliant upon the private ferry service. He had become very fond of Cedric's wife, Sarah. He had also become very fond of their young daughter Mathilda, as indeed she had of him. But until this recent trip he had not known just *how* fond. In fact he might well never have understood the depth of their mutual affection had it not been pointed out to him by Mathilda's father, of all people.

'Sarah and I were talking about you last night, Silas,' the Colonel had said in his usual bombastic fashion over lunch at the Australian Club in Macquarie Street. Silas had dined at the family home just two nights previously – indeed the very day after his arrival in Sydney – and Cedric had suggested they meet for luncheon on Friday as was their custom when he was in town.

'We both think you should marry again,' he went on. 'Young Amy's bound to fly the nest before long and then you'll be left all on your own.' Cedric had met Amy on the several occasions when she'd accompanied her father to Sydney. 'It's not good for a man to be on his own,' he said tucking vigorously into his roast lamb.

'Yes, I dare say you're right,' Silas admitted, more to keep the peace than anything, 'I probably should give the matter some thought.'

'The obvious choice is right under your nose, old chap, and has been for some time.' Upon registering his friend's bemusement, Cedric gave a characteristically pig-like snort of laughter. 'Mathilda! I'm talking about Mathilda, man! Good God, are you blind? The girl worships the very ground you walk on.'

Silas flushed self-consciously and looked about the club dining room, embarrassed at the thought that others might have heard. 'As a father figure, Cedric, as a father figure,' he said in hushed tones. 'Heavens above, I'm twice her age.'

'You've just turned fifty, she's twenty-six, you need a wife, she needs a husband,' Cedric spelt everything out as if to a child, 'and any fool can see you're inordinately fond of each other. It's the perfect set-up all round. Sarah is in absolute agreement.' He took a swig of red wine. 'Come to the house on Sunday and propose to the girl for God's sake. I shan't utter a word in the meantime, I promise,' he said raising his glass in a salute, 'but I'll wager you won't be disappointed.'

Silas remained silent as he sipped from his water tumbler.

Ten weeks later Silas Stanford and Mathilda Lipscombe were wed. And a week after that, in late February, Silas and his bride left Sydney bound for Hobart Town.

Amy could barely believe the change in her father. The strain and fatigue had gone. He looked ten years younger than he had when he'd left. She was happy for him. She liked Mathilda, whom she'd met several times in Sydney. A strong-minded and capable young woman, Mathilda had trained as a nurse at Sydney Hospital and, following her own father's example, was committed to charitable causes. She will make an excellent wife for a man like my father, Amy thought.

Amy was only four years younger than her father's new wife, but she felt not the slightest twinge of jealousy at the thought that her place in his affections may have been usurped. On the contrary, she blessed the arrival of Mathilda. The timing was perfect. Michael O'Callaghan had proposed.

'He is a man of modest means, Father.'

Silas found his daughter's opening statement somewhat ominous. 'A man of modest means' could well be seeking to improve his circumstances through marriage.

'He lives in a fisherman's cottage at Battery Point,' Amy continued, determined to paint the picture as honestly as possible, 'a cottage which he does not own.'

It is sounding worse by the minute, Silas thought. What on Earth is she thinking?

'He has the cottage as part of his job – he works for Jefferson Powell. He is the manager of Jefferson's ferry-boat service.'

'Ah,' Silas said, 'he works for Jefferson, does he?' Well, this puts a whole new complexion on things, he thought. Jefferson was a good man: he would not employ a rogue.

'Yes.' Amy had known that would impress. 'Michael and the Powells are very close. He is like one of the family to them.' She went on to tell her father about the wonderful relationship Michael had with the Powell children, and about the Christmas Day luncheon at the Powells' and the workmen and the concertina and the carol singing ...

'I'm surprised Phyllis allowed you to attend,' Silas said drily.

'Yes, so was I,' Amy agreed. 'Phyllis was quite against Michael at the start, but she seems to accept him these days. In fact, the Lyttletons have made no objection at all to his courtship, which I must say I find most surprising.'

The Lyttletons' opinion, as Amy had correctly predicted, was of no great consequence to Silas, who considered Phyllis a rather shallow woman and her husband not much better. Geoffrey Lyttleton was one of those who, through his philanthropic works, sought to promote his business and further his personal reputation, a fact which did not in the least bother Silas so long as Lyttleton Holdings & Investment continued to offer its generous support. Indeed, he worked quite happily with Geoffrey, maintaining a friendship of sorts, but Silas did not particularly respect the man. Jefferson Powell was a different matter altogether.

'I look forward to meeting your young man, Amy,' he said.

'I have told him you are a true egalitarian, Father.'

There seemed something very meaningful in the way she made the remark, but Silas didn't quite know what it was. 'As indeed I believe I am, Amy.'

'You will be kind, won't you?'

'Of course I will, my dear.' He was mystified. She surely

did not imagine he would stand in judgement of her suitor simply because he was a poor man. 'Why would you presume for one minute that I would be *un*kind?'

'Kindness is all I ask, Father,' she repeated in the same enigmatic way. She said no more than that, and Silas was once again mystified. He remained mystified until the following day.

'How do you do, sir?'

'Good morning, Mr O'Callaghan.' Silas rose and offered his hand across the desk to the young man Clara ushered into his study. So this is my daughter's suitor, he thought. An unbelievably good-looking Irishman: how very suspect. 'Do sit down, please.'

'Thank you, sir.'

They sat, the desk between them, Mick feeling rather as though he were being interviewed for a position of employment.

'I see a lot has been going on in my absence,' Silas said pleasantly.

'Both here *and* on the mainland,' Mick replied with a smile.

Silas did not return the smile: he did not appreciate the reference to his new wife. 'You are employed by Jefferson Powell, I believe.'

'That is correct, sir.' Mick quickly wiped the smile from his face. He should have known charm was not the way to win Silas Stanford. Humility would far better suit. 'I am a man of modest means –' he started.

'Yes, yes, so I've heard. Tell me all about your position, Mr O'Callaghan. Your duties, your salary, the cottage where you live. I want to hear everything.'

Mick talked for the next fifteen minutes and Silas did not interrupt once.

'A responsible position indeed,' he said finally when the Irishman had concluded. 'Mr Powell has placed his trust in you, I see.'

'He certainly has, sir. Why, Jefferson and Doris have been like family to me.' Mick was unable to resist the first names, which Silas found a little jarringly unnecessary.

'My daughter certainly appears to be in love with you, Mr O'Callaghan.'

'As I am with her, sir, I assure you.' Mick wished like the devil that Stanford would stop calling him Mr O'Callaghan: it was making him most uncomfortable. Surely as a prospective son-in-law he should be addressed as Michael. But then Amy had warned him her father was an austere man. 'It is only his manner, Michael,' she'd said, 'don't be daunted. Stand up to him.'

'I love your daughter very much, Mr Stanford,' he said firmly. 'I wish with all my heart to marry Amy and to prove myself everything she could want in a husband.'

'That is all I need to know, Mr O'Callaghan,' Silas said. So long as it is true, he thought. Why did he have his doubts? It was not right to judge the lad for being handsome and charming, but something didn't seem quite right. Then he recalled his daughter's mystifying remark. '*You will be kind, won't you?*' Did she have her own doubts? Did she not wish her suitor to be tested – was that what she had meant? If such was the case, Silas found he could not oblige.

'I am quite happy for my daughter to marry the manager of a ferry-boat service, Mr O'Callaghan,' he said with care, 'and I am quite happy for her to live in a fisherman's cottage upon the honest wage such a man would make, for I know that Amy would be happy with such a life. If this is the marriage you are offering, then you have my blessing.'

'Thank you, sir.' What is the man getting at? Mick wondered. He seemed to be saying yes and no at the same time.

'However, I will make no outlay upon the marriage. There will be no dowry. No property or large sums of money will change hands, as you may have expected –'

'Oh I assure you, sir, I had not –' Mick was still unsure where it was all leading, but he knew he should object to the inference.

Silas ignored the interruption. 'I would not deprive Amy of her inheritance, certainly,' he continued. 'She will be a wealthy woman upon my death, but that I'm afraid may be a long time coming.' His smile was pleasant and his tone most reasonable. 'As I am sure you will understand, Mr O'Callaghan, having a new wife gives a man new blood,' he said. 'I intend to live until a very ripe old age, and I also intend, God willing, to have a son. Should such an event occur who knows how it might affect Amy's inheritance?' Silas paused, allowing time for an objection.

Things were not going at all as Mick had hoped. What should I do? he wondered. The man is intimating in no uncertain terms that I am a fortune-seeker. Should I protest my innocence, and demand to marry Amy regardless? Silas Stanford was bluffing, surely. He wouldn't allow his daughter to live in a fisherman's cottage. Or would he? Mick was at a loss.

'I have an alternative offer which may be of interest to you.' There was an icy edge to Silas's voice now. The lad had proved himself with his silence. 'An offer which would grant more immediate gratification than a lifetime spent waiting for my death.'

Again Mick said nothing. There was nothing he *could* say. He was utterly exposed and he knew it.

'Cease all pursuit of my daughter, never call upon her again, and I will lodge one thousand pounds in an account in your name with the English, Scottish & Australian Bank. Do you accept?'

Mick stared down at the adornment on the rug at his feet. It was a fine rug with an unusual pattern. 'Yes,' he said after a moment's pause, 'I accept.' He looked up and met the contempt in Silas Stanford's eyes. 'Please believe me, Mr Stanford, I *am* fond of your daughter,' he protested,

'I am deeply, *deeply* fond of Amy.' I am, he thought, I love Amy in my own way, and I would have made her a good husband. 'I swear to you on my mother's grave –'

'Good day, Mr O'Callaghan.'

Amy kept her tears to herself. She would forgive her father one day, she knew it, but for now she blamed Silas for the pain she felt. She had secretly dreaded the thought that he might put temptation Michael's way, for she had just as secretly suspected Michael might succumb.

'I meant be kind to *me*, Father,' she said coldly when he gave her the news. 'Perhaps I did not wish to know he was after my money.'

'I realise that, Amy, but in the long run it is kinder to be cruel, as they say. I could not have the man take such advantage of you.'

'Perhaps I would rather have lived with my delusions,' she said and she left before he could see the tears forming.

That night, as he lay with his young wife asleep in his arms, Silas refused to feel guilty, but his heart ached for his daughter.

Mick did not dwell upon his disappointment. The initial flush of shame he'd experienced quickly vanished and he convinced himself that it was he who had been wronged. What a pity Silas Stanford had misread my potential as a husband, he thought. He would have worked hard to make Amy happy. They would have had a family like the Powells, a fine serious-minded son like George and a dimple-faced daughter like Martha, and he would have been the best of fathers and the most caring of husbands. He and Amy would have had a good life together had Silas Stanford not deprived them of the opportunity.

It was clearly not to be, however, so he set about devising another plan.

The following week was a busy one for Mick. He visited his lawyers and the ES & A Bank, and on the Friday, assured that all was in order, he called into Lyttleton Holdings & Investment.

'Good morning, Frederick,' he said as the bell tinkled behind him.

'Mr O'Callaghan.' Frederick flushed with pleasure at the recognition afforded him and scuttled off to inform Mr Lyttleton that his friend was at the front desk. Two minutes later Mick was ushered into Geoffrey's realm.

'Sit down, Mr O'Callaghan, do.'

As the clerk left, closing the door behind him, Geoffrey gestured to the rosewood carver, but he did not bother rising from his throne behind the desk. He would play the game, certainly, given the power the scoundrel had over him, but playing the game did not require any particular show of respect.

'I've heard your plan did not come to fruition,' he said, trying to sound in some way sympathetic. 'I was supportive of your cause as we agreed, but Mr Stanford was apparently not happy with the match.' Under normal circumstances Geoffrey Lyttleton would have gloated. 'Did you really believe trash like you would be accepted into one of the most respected families in Hobart Town?' he would have crowed. But Geoffrey was far too concerned about his own predicament to revel in Mick's defeat. He was inwardly cursing Silas Stanford. If only the old goat had accepted this handsome young stud as the perfect husband for his plain daughter then everyone would have been happy. God Almighty, now that O'Callaghan's plans had gone awry there'd be no end to the blackmail demands.

'Yes, I was disappointed in Mr Stanford's reaction,' Mick said, 'which means, unfortunately, there is a change in plans.'

'I suspected there might be.' All Geoffrey could think of was the pistol in the top drawer and how he'd so love to blow the bastard's brains out. 'So I'm now to become your alternative source of income I take it?'

'Actually, no,' Mick said. 'There is only one demand I wish to make, after which I shall disappear from your life, I swear. Blackmail is a dirty business and not my game.'

'I'm glad to hear it.' The Irishman was genuine. Geoffrey felt a rush of relief. One lump payment and it appeared he'd be able to put this whole sordid episode behind him. 'And what is your demand?'

'You are to sign the house in Hampden Road over to Red, deeds and all, so she owns it outright. Her name is Eileen Hilditch, by the way.' Mick took an envelope from the inside pocket of his coat. 'Her details are there, along with my name and the safe deposit box number at the ES & A Bank where you will lodge the paperwork, which I will collect next week. After that, I can promise you, you'll never hear from me again.'

Geoffrey Lyttleton's face drained of colour as the realisation struck home. 'You are her lover,' he said.

'That's right.'

'For how long?' Geoffrey was shattered. Why did the possibility not once occur to me? he wondered. He'd been so thoroughly convinced the Irishman had his sights set on Amy, so why should it? How *dare* the scum? Red was his personal property. The men who had her at Trafalgar were nothing – they rented her body for an hour at most. There was one man and one man only who owned the woman herself, and he was that man, not this piece of Irish trash. He was physically sickened by the thought that Red had given herself to O'Callaghan.

'How long have you been her lover?' he demanded. I'll kill the bastard, he thought. I'll kill them both. Better still, he'd have them both killed. He'd have the house burnt down before he'd sign it over to the bitch. She was his and she had betrayed him.

'That is of no consequence,' Mick replied. Lyttleton's

face was murderous and his rage palpable, but Mick had
expected as much. Eileen had told him her benefactor was
fiercely possessive. 'There is another condition, which I'm
sure I barely need mention,' he continued. 'You will never
again call upon Red. As of this moment she will cease to
be a part of your life.'

Mick knew he was treading on dangerous ground, but
he'd come prepared. He took three more envelopes from
his pocket and placed them side by side on the table facing
Geoffrey, the addresses clearly visible.

'Just a little reminder of our arrangement,' he said. 'Inside
each of these envelopes is a letter: as you can see, one to
your wife, one to the society and one to *The Mercury*.
You will note upon reading them that they are written on
carbonated paper, the originals having been lodged with
my lawyers, Hadley & Edgerton. I have included a copy
of my instructions, and you will also note the addition
of Eileen Hilditch's name. Should an untoward accident
befall either Red or myself or indeed both of us, the letters
will be posted, you can rest assured of that. I suggest after
reading them you destroy these copies,' he added drily,
'the fewer around the better, wouldn't you say?'

He stood. 'I think our business is concluded. I shall
expect the deeds to be deposited with the bank at your
earliest convenience next week. I presume that suits?'
He paused briefly for a response, but there was none as
Geoffrey stared up at him in impotent silence. 'Excellent.
Good day to you then.'

He was halfway to the door when he was halted by the
words Geoffrey Lyttleton could not help blurting out.

'Does she love you?'

'Oh yes.' Mick smiled, knowing this would be the
greatest insult of all. 'She loves me all right.' Then he
twisted the knife further with a lie. 'In fact she goes
wild when she's with me, Geoffrey. Red loves me with a
passion you would not believe.' He paused long enough to

relish the reaction and he was not disappointed. Geoffrey Lyttleton's anger had turned to anguish. Mick closed the door behind him and left the man with the images that were destined to torment him forever.

Exactly one week later, in the mid-afternoon when he knew she'd be home, Mick turned the corner from Runnymede Street into Hampden Road and strode boldly up to Eileen's front door. There'll be no skulking down the track to the back door today, he thought as he rapped loudly with the brass knocker.

'Good God, Mick, what are you about?' she whispered when she opened the door to discover him standing there, a bulky envelope clutched to his chest.

'I'm calling upon you, Eileen, that's what I'm about.'

She looked up and down the street. There were several passers-by, none taking any notice of the white weatherboard house, but most importantly there was no familiar figure in sight. There hadn't been for a full week now, and she was mystified. She was also nervous. With the exception of last week, Geoffrey had always visited on a Friday afternoon. There could be a tap at the back door any second, or he could come into view even as they were standing there on the front porch.

'He won't be calling on you any more, Eileen,' Mick said. 'You might as well ask me in.'

She was startled, but said nothing, standing meekly to one side as he entered. It was only when she'd closed the door behind him that she allowed her anxiety to show.

'What have you done, Mick? Dear God in Heaven, what have you done?'

'I've taken care of you just like I said I would,' he announced. 'I've bought you a house. Or rather Geoffrey Lyttleton has.'

She blanched at the mention of the name. 'You've exposed him?' Her voice held an element of panic.

'No, only threatened to, and here is the result.' He opened the bulky envelope and spilt its contents onto the sitting-room table. 'You own this house, Eileen. This property is now yours and yours alone.'

She looked down at the papers and then back to him, her expression a mixture of fear and disbelief.

'There's no need to be afraid,' he assured her. 'Lyttleton will not dare seek retribution. Now get me a cup of tea, there's a good girl, and I'll tell you all that's happened.'

He gathered up the papers and they went into the kitchen where she stoked the stove's fire and, while they waited for the kettle to boil, he told her about the letters that he'd left with his lawyers. Then they sat at the table and examined the deeds to the house, Mick painstakingly reading every word out loud to her, for Eileen could neither read nor write. Throughout her childhood she had worked as a washerwoman with her mother and older sisters and had never been to school.

'It's mine,' she said when he'd finished and the truth had finally sunk in. She looked around at the walls and up at the ceiling and down at the floor. 'This is my house.'

'It certainly is, every stick and stone of it.'

She stood and walked about the kitchen, running her hands over the plastered walls. 'No-one in my family has ever owned a house.'

'No-one in my family has either,' he said. 'You've moved up in the world, girl.'

She turned to him with the sauciest of smiles. 'Well, I suppose as you've given me a house I can't be too angry that you've cost me a rich benefactor now, can I?'

'I have something that might make up for that.' He stood and, taking a folded sheet of paper from the inner pocket of his jacket, he handed it to her.

She unfolded the paper and saw numbers. Eileen understood numbers. 'This is money,' she said. 'This is a lot of money.'

'It's a bank statement,' he explained. 'I have one thousand pounds in an account, Silas Stanford's pay-off for not marrying his daughter. I can buy you things, Eileen.'

She studied him calculatingly with her fox eyes. In black-mailing Geoffrey why had he insisted the house be signed over to her – why had he not demanded the property for himself? And now he was prepared to squander his newfound wealth on her. Why? There could be only one reason of course ... but he'd got it all wrong.

She laughed. 'If you're offering yourself as my new ben-efactor, Mick, don't you think it's rather silly to give me my own house? I'd be far more in your power if you'd kept the place for yourself. A tenant always fears eviction.'

It was beyond Eileen's comprehension that he might have acquired the house for her because he loved her, but then Mick himself hadn't realised that either. He'd thought that he'd simply been out to impress her and that he'd acted upon the impulse of the moment. He suddenly knew better.

'I'm not offering myself as your benefactor,' he said.

'Oh really?' Her eyes told him she didn't believe him.

'No. I'm offering myself as your husband.'

The words took them both by surprise. Mick hadn't planned to propose, but it was true he had been thinking about marriage quite a bit lately. He'd been thinking of Doris and Jefferson and their children, and he'd been thinking of the companionship and the family he might have had if he'd married Amy, and now it struck him that he wanted all these things, but he wanted them all with Eileen.

'Marry me, Eileen,' he said eagerly. 'Stop working at Trafalgar and marry me. We'll live here in this house – you love this house – and we'll have a family. I have money now, I'll look after you –'

'Oh for Heaven's sake, Mick.' She tried to sound flippant, 'One thousand pounds won't last forever.' She was desperately trying to buy time. This wasn't the life she'd planned. But then what was? And how long before her beauty faded and men no longer wanted her – what then? Besides, she liked Mick. She liked Mick more than any man she'd ever known, with the possible exception of her father, who'd so gently initiated her into the world of sex at the age of ten. She would have done anything to please her father, but he'd let her down badly when her mother had kicked her out of the house at fifteen for leading him on. He'd said not one word in her defence.

'We'll worry about money when the thousand's gone,' Mick urged, sensing her weaken. 'For now, we're on easy street. Say yes, Eileen.' He flashed his most endearing grin. 'Come along, girl, you know you want to.'

As she looked at him she thought what a peacock of a man he was, a handsome rogue from the wrong side of the tracks, a male version of herself. We're meant for each other, she thought, and when all was said and done, he *is* my best friend. No, she told herself wryly, he's my *only* friend.

'You don't really want a cup of tea, do you?' she said. On the wood stove the kettle was boiling away furiously. She took it off the plate. 'Let's go to bed.'

Their coupling was sensual, as it always was, the sharing of mutual pleasure, but as Mick approached his climax things took a different turn. This time she did not pull away, nor did she allow him to withdraw. She held him inside her. He tried desperately to slow down, hoping even in his final moments that she might achieve her ultimate release, but she sought only his fulfilment not her own.

He held her close afterwards, moved by the fact that she had so placed her trust in him. Her response had hardly been the grand passion he'd lied about to Geoffrey Lyttleton, but Mick recognised it as a definite answer to his proposal. More than an answer, it was as much a declaration of love as Eileen 'Red' Hilditch was capable of making.

*

Ma Tebbutt was dying. She'd been dying for some time and had accepted the fact with great equanimity. For several months now, barely able to walk, she had insisted upon being helped from her bed into her sitting room and placed in her armchair. The exercise was a painful one, but she refused all persuasion to remain in the comfort of her bed.

'You never know which day you're going to die,' she said. 'It's best to be prepared.'

In the final weeks, sensing the end was close, she had embraced religion, or at least she'd made the pretence of doing so. The local parish priest whom she'd ignored for years visited on a daily basis to say prayers and offer comfort. However she admitted to Mick, who popped in to see her several afternoons a week, that her conversion was more a safety measure than anything.

'Best to cover all bets, isn't it?' she said as they shared a tot of rum. 'Just in case there really is a Heaven and Hell. At least I don't have to confess all my sins like your mob. Better to keep some things to yourself, I say.'

'The good you've done would outweigh the bad, Ma,' he assured her, 'I'd bet my last shilling on that.'

Ma had also called in her lawyer. Always meticulous when it came to business, she had set her affairs in order well before her demise, although she told no-one of her plans until the very end. When she finally did unveil them it was not unsurprisingly to Mick, and only two days before her death.

'I'll be gone in the next day or so,' she said.

They were sitting companionably at the table sipping their rum, Ma's ashtray and clay pipe before her, although only as a reminder. She had not smoked for a long time now: the coughing fits her beloved pipe brought on were unbearable. It was April, and outside people were rugged up against the bite of a bitterly cold autumn day, but the little fire in the grate kept Ma's room warm and cosy.

'Get away with you, Ma,' Mick scoffed, 'you've been saying you're going for months now. We'll get a good year out of you yet.' When she was in one of her maudlin moods, he usually managed to jolly her out of it.

'No, no, my time's up, I can feel it. But there's a promise I need you to make to me before I go.'

'And what's that?' Realising this was no maudlin mood, he dropped the banter. 'I'll do whatever you wish, you have my word.'

'I'm leaving you the pub, Mick.' Her eyes met his and in their rheumy depths the shrewdness of old burnt as fiercely as ever. 'You'll find out from my lawyers as soon as I'm gone that the Hunter's Rest is yours. You'll also find out that there are certain conditions laid in place, but as these conditions will be difficult to meet and as I won't be around to see you observe them, I want you to give me your word here and now.'

She spoke haltingly, her breathing shallow and laboured like the wheezing pant of an old dog. Mick nodded, and waited for her continue. For once he was at a loss for words.

'You've been like a son to me, Mick, just like the girls have been my daughters. You're not to sell the pub straight off. I want you to promise me that, a solemn oath, mind. A new owner could close the brothel, and I won't have my girls put out into the street –'

'I'd never sell the Hunter's Rest!' Mick interrupted vehemently, wounded that she could even consider he would do such a thing. 'I'd never sell it, Ma, I swear, *never*!'

'Never's a foolish word, boy.' Ma's retort was scornful, but she quickly checked her emotions and returned to her measured shallow breathing as exertion of any kind brought on the coughing. 'You can't halt progress, Mick. Hobart Town's changing by the minute. God Almighty, just look at the docks. The waterfront's unrecognisable from what it was when I first got here, and it's not going to stop where it is now, I can promise you that. You'll no doubt sell the pub one day to some big businessman or the government or whatever –' He was about to interject again, but she waved a hand irritably. She was tired now.

Mick remained silent, waiting while she wheezed enough air into her diseased lungs to continue. It was amazing that she'd talked for this long without suffering a coughing fit, but it appeared Ma's sheer determination could achieve miracles.

'You say you and Red are to marry.' Her voice was weaker when she finally spoke.

'That's right, probably within the next month or so.' Mick hoped, and even secretly prayed – a ritual he had not practised for some years – that they would *have* to marry within the next month. They had been taking no precautions and Eileen suspected she might be pregnant. The prospect of both marriage and parenthood pleased him immensely and he had a feeling deep down that it also pleased Eileen, although she refused to admit it.

'Red will want you to sell the Hunter's Rest,' Ma said. 'She's a hard girl, with little feeling for others –'

'No, Ma, you're wrong. She's not –'

Another irritable wave of the hand silenced him.

'I mean no criticism, boy. I know full well what's made Eileen the way she is and I respect her for it, but the fact remains she looks after herself and bugger the rest of the world.' Ma paused, once again taking care to pace herself as the wheeze turned into a rattle. 'I want you to promise me, Mick, that you won't sell up until my girls have retired.'

Retirement was Ma's genteel word for that time when a prostitute was too old to ply her trade and was forced to seek employment in a factory or to offer her services as a washerwoman.

'Maeve and Peg will be seeking alternative employment soon,' she continued, 'but the others have a ways to go yet, and I don't want them working the street – that's a dangerous trade.' With the last ounce of strength she could muster, Ma's voice took a commanding turn. 'You are to give me your word, Mick, that you will look after my girls.'

'I'll look after your girls, Ma. You have my solemn oath on it.'

'That's good.' She smiled wearily. The effort of talking for so long and with such vigour had exhausted her, but she was satisfied with the outcome. She took a final swig of her rum, which she always found soothing and which cleared the pipes. Rum was a great comfort. 'Off you trot now. I'm going to have a bit of a snooze, but pour me another tot before you go.'

Mick was not with Ma when she died two days later. No-one was with her, which was strange for as always throughout the day she'd had many visitors. Len, Billy, Freddie, Tiny and every single one of the girls regularly popped upstairs to see her, either to chat, or simply to sit and keep her company. But there was a half-hour or so late in the day when they usually left her alone to nap after a couple of rums, and that was when she slipped away. Quick and quiet on the dot of five-thirty: it was an unexpectedly merciful exercise. She did not choke from one of the painful coughing fits that racked her body, nor did she fight for the last vital gasps of air in a fearful struggle to stay alive. Instead, she succumbed to a mild heart attack as she slept, and died in her armchair as she had determined she would, with a glass of rum on the table before her.

Mick mourned Ma's passing, as did all who knew her. Ma Tebbutt had been a popular figure in Wapping, offering employment and a helping hand to many. Dozens were gathered together in the Trinity Burial Grounds at the top of Campbell Street wishing to show their respects as she was lowered into her grave.

It would have been hypocritical of Mick not to rejoice in his personal gain, however. Eighteen fifty-six it seemed was a year of windfalls for Mick O'Callaghan. Already he had a modest fortune in the bank, and upon the reading of the will he would become the owner of a highly successful pub with a functioning brothel upstairs.

'Sell it, Mick.' Eileen's reaction was just as Ma had predicted it would be. 'Ma's made a real success of that pub,' she said when he told her the news. 'Sell it while it's running well and you'll make a fortune.'

'I'll make more in the long run if I keep the place working successfully,' he replied with a brisk new business-like edge to his voice. The will had yet to be announced, but Mick couldn't wait to leap into the fray. 'Besides, if I sold the pub whoever bought it might close the brothel and then the girls would be out working the street. I can't have that.'

'Why not? It's what a whore does.' Eileen had worked the streets of Dublin at the age of fifteen; she couldn't understand his concern. 'There are good times and bad and you take what comes – every whore knows that. The younger, prettier ones will find a place in another brothel anyway.'

But Mick refused to be swayed. 'I promised Ma,' he said putting an end to the argument.

'Oh well,' Eileen shrugged carelessly. 'It's up to you. But if you're going to run the pub, you'll have to give up your job with Jefferson Powell.'

'Yes I will. I intend to resign as of next week.'

Mick had come to his decision virtually overnight. He'd been in a quandary for some time, indeed ever since he'd accepted Silas Stanford's payoff. One thousand pounds was a lot of money. He was a man of means, he'd told himself, and a man of means did not slog away for a weekly wage

like those of the common classes. He'd become dissatis-
fied with his existence. But after losing fifty pounds at the
card table in less than a week, he'd quickly realised just
how tenuous his position was. Eileen is right, he thought.
One thousand pounds, a sum which most never saw in the
whole of their lives, would not last forever, and certainly
not if he chose to lead the life of a man of leisure. Jefferson
Powell paid a good wage, and with the barges now fully
operational and Powell Channel Transport forging ahead,
there was room for advancement – Jefferson himself had
said so. Common-sense told Mick that it would be foolish
to throw away such a career opportunity. But the easy
money that had come his way had re-awakened his lust
for the good life. It irked him having to work for another,
even another like Jefferson Powell.

Now, thanks to Ma Tebbutt, everything had changed.
He was no longer merely a man of means, but a man of
property, and a businessman to boot. He recalled the advice
of Dan, the tiger man. '*If you want to move up in this
world, Mick … you'd best follow the path of the tiger man
… Take whatever you can get. And use whatever you've got
to take it … You're living in a tiger town, my friend.*'

Mick was no longer interested in a life of leisure, and he
no longer had need of the career Jefferson Powell offered.
A third and far more exciting option lay ahead. He owned
a part of this town now. He was on his way to becoming a
tiger man.

He decided that his parting of the ways with the Powell
Ferry-Boat Service must be kept as brief and uncomplicated as possible. He would simply hand over his letter of
resignation and walk away. He'd already shifted most
of his belongings from the cottage to Eileen's house, in
any event, and was principally living in Hampden Road
these days, although he hadn't told the Powells that. The
upkeep of the cottage and its property was after all part of
the ferry manager's job.

It was a glorious autumn morning as Mick walked along Colville Street on his way to the Powells'. The air was bracing and the sky a pale, cloudless blue, but conditions were unlikely to remain so for the weather had been typically perverse of late. The distant peak of Mount Wellington was laden with the snow of last night's storm and further blizzard activity was forecast. There might well be snow in the streets the following morning. As people were wryly wont to say, the only predictable thing about the weather of Hobart Town was its unpredictability, and the comment rang continually true.

As he turned into Napoleon Street and approached the house Mick felt for the very first time the faintest of misgivings. He didn't see why he should. If he was letting Jefferson down in any way then it was certainly not his fault. He had fresh responsibilities now. He was leaving due to circumstances beyond his control: he could hardly be held to blame for that. But he nonetheless hoped Jefferson would not be at home – being a weekday it was most unlikely.

He walked up the path, mounted the steps to the front verandah and rapped with the brass door knocker.

'Michael.' It was Doris who opened the door. Her pregnancy having been confirmed in the first weeks of January she was now seven months gone and large with child. 'How lovely to see you – what a pleasant surprise. Do come in.' She opened the door wide and stood to one side, automatically glancing at his boots as she did so, checking for mud. She was pleased to see there was none, although had there been mud Michael would of course have removed his boots and left them on the front verandah as he had always done. The informality of their relationship was a great pleasure to Doris.

'I'm sorry, but no,' he said, 'I can't come in. This is strictly a business call, I'm afraid.'

'Oh.' She seemed surprised. 'Jefferson isn't here of

course –' Mick breathed a sigh of relief '– but is it something I can help you with?'

'Yes, it is actually,' he took the envelope from his pocket, 'I'd be most obliged if you could give him this.'

'Of course,' she said, accepting the envelope and wondering why he was so very serious. 'Please do come in, Michael, if only for a moment. Martha and George will be thrilled to see you.'

'No. No, I can't.' At the mention of the children Mick felt a sudden and unreasonable sense of panic. Dear God, why must the woman make it difficult for him? He couldn't bear the thought of seeing Martha and George. 'I really must go.'

He started to back away, but she reached out and took a hold of his hand.

'My dear,' she said, 'what is it? What's wrong?'

Doris was strong and her grip was firm. Aside from wrenching himself free, he was powerless to leave.

'Nothing is wrong, Doris. It's all there in the letter.'

'What is?'

'My resignation.'

'Oh goodness.' She maintained her grip on his hand, her face now a picture of the deepest concern. 'Something terrible has happened.'

'No, nothing terrible has happened at all.' God, how he wished she'd let go of him. 'On the contrary, in fact – I am to be married.' He had not intended to convey the news of his marriage, but then he had not intended to remain chatting at the doorway. Now, given her grip on his hand and his inability to escape, he was trying desperately to make normal conversation.

Doris was momentarily confused for she'd heard that Michael's courtship of Amy Stanford had proved unsuccessful. She was delighted to discover that she had been wrongly informed.

'That is wonderful news,' she said and her grasp became

even more fervent, 'my sincerest congratulations. You must both be very happy.'

Dear God in Heaven, Mick thought upon registering the confusion, she thinks I'm marrying Amy. 'No, no, you are mistaken,' he found himself stammering in his haste to correct her, 'you are not acquainted with this particular young lady.' He wished now it had been Jefferson who had answered the door: things were becoming altogether too complicated.

'Oh.' What an extraordinarily speedy chain of events, Doris thought, although perhaps the young lady in question was his previous fiancée who had now had second thoughts after breaking off their engagement. In any event, she told herself, it was none of her business. She could not, however, resist the opportunity to offer sound advice. Indeed, as his friend she considered it her duty to do so.

'Forgive me, Michael,' she said, 'but I simply must point out that as you are about to embark upon the commitment of marriage, your employment is of tantamount importance. If you are considering offers from other prospective employers, I do beg that you speak to Jefferson first. I know he has great plans for your advancement.'

'I have received no offers from other prospective employers,' he said stiffly. She had relaxed the firmness of her grip upon his hand and he was finally able to wriggle his fingers free. 'My circumstances have, however, changed considerably. I have come into an inheritance.'

Doris was puzzled. Michael appeared most uncomfortable. In fact he was positively squirming and couldn't wait to get away. Why? 'An inheritance,' she said, 'that is good news, surely.' And why is he unable to look me in the eye? she wondered.

'Yes, it is very good news.' Mick hated Doris Powell at that moment. How dare the woman stand in judgement of him. How dare she make him feel guilty. 'I have new responsibilities now, new obligations. It's all there, in the

letter.' He gestured at the envelope. 'Jefferson will understand, I'm sure.'

'Yes, I'm sure he will.' Doris understood. With a sudden
flash of insight Doris understood everything, and she
wondered how she could have been so blind for so long.
'I take it you will be leaving us?'

'Yes, I shall, that's right, circumstances beyond my
control.'

'Then I wish you well, Michael.' Again he refused to
meet her eye. 'Jefferson and I both wish you well.'

'Thank you, Doris.' He left hastily.

She did not stand on the verandah and watch as he
walked down the path. She stepped inside, closing the
door behind her.

Jefferson returned home in the early evening. Doris
waited until he'd greeted George and Martha, then she
sent the children off to wash for dinner and handed him
the envelope.

'Michael has resigned,' she said.

He sat at the kitchen table and read the letter, which
was brief and to the point. 'He has given no notice,' he
said, passing it back to her, clearly bewildered. 'He says
that due to circumstances beyond his control he now has
fresh obligations.'

'Yes, so he told me, the very same words. He's come into
an inheritance I believe.' Doris sat beside him, skimming
the letter. 'He doesn't mention it here. I wonder what it is.'

'It's a pub in Wapping.' She looked at him in blank
surprise. 'Rumour has it Ma Tebbutt left the Hunter's Rest
to Michael.'

'Where did you hear that? Why didn't you tell me?'

'I didn't know myself until barely an hour ago. It was
the talk of the bar at the Shipwright's Arms.'

The Shipwright's Arms, just a block away on the corner
of Colville and Trumpeter Streets, was a favourite gathering place for the workers from the local ship-building

yards and Jefferson, although not a drinking man, made a weekly habit of calling in for an ale with his friends and workmates.

'It's evidently been the talk of the bar for days now,' he said. 'I didn't really believe it – I thought that surely Michael would have said something.' Jefferson shook his head, confused. 'Why did he not tell me, Doris?'

'There is a lot he did not tell you,' Doris said. 'He did not tell you also that he is shortly to marry.'

'To marry? Really? But I would have rejoiced in the news. Why would he not tell me he was to marry?'

'I believe he was too frightened.' Doris felt the stirring of something close to anger. Jefferson was far more than confused. She could see the disappointment and the hurt in his eyes. How dare Michael, she thought.

'Frightened of what? I would wish him only well, Doris. Surely he must know that.'

'He knows that he is deserting you, Jefferson, that's what he knows.' Doris's temper suddenly flared and she leapt into attack. 'He never intended to remain loyal to you, that's why he's frightened, he knows that he has betrayed your trust. He is a shallow man who believes he no longer has any use for you and so he has moved on.' Doris in anger was formidable. 'Michael is an opportunist, Jefferson, and he always has been. I should have known better than to suggest him for the position. We should have hired a ticket-of-leave couple as you'd always intended. You should never, never have listened to me.'

'My goodness gracious, what brought all this on?' Jefferson found himself wanting to laugh. She looked like a ferocious terrier.

'I'm sorry.' Doris calmed down, aware of his amusement and feeling rather foolish. 'I'm sorry, my dear, please do forgive me.' She smiled sheepishly. 'I'm angry with myself really, not Michael,' she said, gratified to see he no longer looked hurt, and thankful that her ridiculous outburst had at least proved a distraction. 'I believe Michael cannot help who he is. That is probably his cross to bear and in a way I feel sorry for him. But I should have known better than to succumb to his charm.'

'If your assumptions are correct, and it would appear they are, then I am indeed surprised,' Jefferson admitted. 'I am so easily deceived, as we both well know, but you, my dear have always been such an astute judge of character.'

She shook her head wryly. 'Women with children are the most susceptible of all, Jefferson. Mothers are blind to any shortcomings in those whom their children choose to love.'

Jefferson laughed. 'Then I suggest we lay the blame upon Martha and George.'

As if on cue, George swooped into the kitchen closely followed by Martha, both ready for dinner.

'We will need to find a new manager now,' Doris said as she stood, 'and just when you are so busy –' She drew breath and grasped the edge of the table to steady herself as the child in her belly kicked.

'Is it kicking again?' Martha froze, her little currant eyes trained upon her mother's belly.

'Yes,' Doris answered.

'May I listen?'

'Of course you may.'

Martha climbed up onto the bench and placed her ear against her mother's swollen stomach. She solemnly believed she could hear the child in the womb. Even when there was no movement, she swore she could hear it breathing.

Jefferson stood and both he and George placed their hands upon Doris's belly. They all felt the baby as it kicked.

'We will find a new manager tomorrow, my dear,' Jefferson assured her, and Michael O'Callaghan disappeared into yesterday. 'It has to be a boy,' he said. 'Kicking like this it just has to be a boy.'

*

Doris gave birth in June. They named the boy Quincy after John Quincy Adams, the man considered by Jefferson to be one of America's greatest diplomats.

Nearly five months later, in the early days of summer, Eileen O'Callaghan gave birth to the first of her daughters. She and Mick called the little girl Mara.

It was two days after the birth of Mara O'Callaghan that Geoffrey Lyttleton committed suicide. He had been in mental torment for some time, although no-one knew why. As he left no note his family could only grieve and wonder.

OATLANDS, TASMANIA 1884

Mrs Violet Walcott, seamstress, had little time for the Sweeney boys. They were oafs, in her opinion. From her seat in front of the general store, she watched them gallop up High Street to the front of the inn where people were already gathering to watch. They were waving the heads of the wretched animals jammed on the ends of their wooden pikes and whooping and hollering like banshees. Violet detested tigers herself, but she didn't think it proper to display their heads to the whole town as if they were those of murdering bushrangers. They were only dumb animals after all. Killers they may be, but they knew no better.

Arthur Sweeney followed his boys up the street in his dray and halted his weary nag in front of the inn. He was grinning from ear to ear as he pulled back the calico cover and displayed to the gathering throng the decapitated corpses of a dozen or more dead thylacines, several barely half grown.

'I know Squire Jordan'll pay me fine money for this here catch,' he shouted to one and all. 'He put up the reward notice on the front window of the bank, you all seen it, ten shillings for each tiger, and I just know he'll honour that promise, for he's a fine and trustworthy gentleman is the Squire.'

Violet Walcott snorted indignantly. Arthur Sweeney was a low-bred cur of a man who'd steal his mother's funeral savings to satisfy his thirst for liquor. How dare he infer that Squire Jeremy Jordan, a good and Christian man of fine family, might not honour his offer to pay a bounty. And besides, Violet thought, Sweeney would have collected a handsome sum already. He would have sent his boys around to half the farms in the district displaying those heads on sticks. The sheep farmers were so obsessed with wiping tigers from the face of the earth that each and every one of them would have congratulated the lads and given them five shillings a piece.

'He's got a dozen or more of the foul creatures in that dray, Mrs Walcott,' the Reverend Wilberforce said as he sat in the seat beside Violet's. 'The Squire will be most pleased. His flocks have been decimated in recent weeks. Fourteen or more lambs taken, or so I've heard say.'

Young Elspeth Pertwee, standing nearby, recalled how as a small child she'd played with the Latham children, whose family kept a tiger as a watchdog. She'd seen them frolic with the animal and stroke it affectionately and indeed she had patted the thing herself. The tiger had behaved no differently from the domestic house-dogs and Elspeth was not at all sure it was the vicious sheep-killer Mrs Walcott and most of the town's people declared it to be. But she knew better than to say anything. She was apprenticed to Mrs Walcott and was lucky to have such a highly valued position.

'It is indeed an intolerable situation, Reverend,' Violet said. 'The sheep farmers must unite and pressure the people in power to do something about the scourge before there are no sheep left to shear.'

'Well,' the Reverend leant in to murmur confidentially, 'I've heard tell that might be in the wind in the not too distant future.'

'Do tell.' Violet Walcott loved the whispered word.

'Mister John Lyne, a well-known and highly respected politician, is said to be lobbying even as we speak, raising support for a government bounty to be introduced on the cursed animals.'

'He'll be a hero around these parts if he does, Reverend,' Violet nodded sagely, 'for the tiger is the scourge of the farmers. If he brings about the creature's downfall then all good to him, I say, and God bless him.'

'Amen to that, Mrs Walcott, amen to that.'

BOOK TWO

Chapter twelve

Hobart, 1895

The second half of the nineteenth century was a turbulent period in the colonies of Australia. Economic boom and bust was the order of each decade. Men made and lost fortunes overnight, women sought equal opportunity and the right to vote, and immigrants arrived from all four corners seeking gold, freedom and the rights of man.

As a new century beckoned, the nation of Australia loomed large. A proposed constitution and amalgamation of the colonies was discussed at the Corowa Conference of 1893 held by Sir Henry Parkes, premier of New South Wales, and other notable colonists from across Australia. It marked the beginning of the march towards Federation.

The Industrial Revolution did not fail to change the smallest continent, buried though it is in the wilds of the Southern Ocean. The gramophone, ball-point pens, barbed wire, corrugated iron, the typewriter, the telephone and dynamite, the farmer's friend, courtesy of Alfred Nobel, all reached the shores of the Antipodes.

Australians, despite periodic financial and environmental setbacks, lived comfortably on the sheep's back and Tasmania in particular prospered. No more a penal colony Tasmania was now a sophisticated environment, its major cities leading the colonies into modernity. By 1893, Hobart, with a population in excess of fifty thousand, had established a fully electric tram service and, in 1895, Launceston introduced electric street lighting. Both were firsts for the Southern Hemisphere. But Tasmania, now known as 'the Apple Isle', was destined to lead the way on a far broader stage. Outstripping their inter-colonial competitors, a clique of Tasmania's businessmen and entrepreneurs were making their mark upon the international market. The Apple Isle was on its way to becoming the fruit bowl of Europe.

It was early spring, and the Powells were having a birthday party in the grounds of Quincy's house overlooking the orchard. During the warmer months outdoor parties at the orchard were a favourite pastime for the brothers and their families, and had been for years. In the old days when his sons were little, George would row Emma and the boys across the river from his modest home and boat-building yard at Wattle Grove and up the Huon to Castle Forbes Bay, a distance of almost three miles. They would then walk the mile or so to the small cottage on the hill that overlooked the fledgling orchard, and there they would celebrate Christmas or New Year, or whoever's birthday it was, with Quincy and Charlotte and their family, and then George would row back down the river.

Things were different these days. Powell Shipbuilding and Repairs, with a reputation for top-quality workmanship, was a thriving business. George no longer rowed his family up to Castle Forbes Bay. They sailed there in style aboard the *Lady Margaret*, a particularly pretty ketch which was kept for personal use and which Lincoln, the eldest son, had named after his wife. George, keen to father a dynasty, had promised twenty-three-year-old James that upon his marriage a vessel would be named after his wife too, but such an event appeared unlikely. James was very much a bachelor who enjoyed playing the field whenever the opportunity presented itself.

Quincy Powell and his wife Charlotte had also worked hard, their well-earned success born of sheer tenacity, and the family gatherings no longer took place at a small cottage overlooking a fledgling orchard. Charlotte Grove, as they had named their estate, had become one of the top fruit-producing properties in the Huon Valley, and where the cottage had once stood was now an elegant two-storey timber house with broad verandahs. A large upper balcony was complemented by ornate cast iron lacework and from the high, gabled roof of corrugated iron rose four chimneys for the all-important fireplaces that provided heat throughout the home during the bitter-cold winter months.

The circumstances of both families had changed dramatically over the two decades since they'd settled in the region, but one element remained constant – the parties at Quincy's place. The surrounds were a little more spectacular, certainly, and the numbers present were greater, having burgeoned with each new arrival, but the Powell gatherings had always been a celebration of family, and today was no exception. Indeed today was a typical example of Powell solidarity, for with the Hobart contingent in attendance, the entire clan was there, including the matriarch herself, Doris.

Seventy-three-year-old Doris had travelled down from Hobart aboard the *SS Emma Jane* with her daughter, Martha, Martha's husband, Simon Hawtrey, and their two almost-grown children. The journey had been no hardship for the indomitable Doris, who remained in fine physical health. She made the trip down the Derwent to the D'Entrecasteaux Channel and up the Huon River at least once a year – for Quincy's Christmas party or for a special family occasion such as today – and she chose always to travel aboard her husband's favourite vessel, the impressive *SS Emma Jane*, which did the regular run between Hobart and the Huon Valley, transporting both passengers and cargo.

Built of the finest Huon pine, the ninety-foot *Emma Jane* had been the first steamship commissioned by Powell Channel Transport. Jefferson Powell had converted several of his six barges to steam in the late seventies, but upon her completion in 1886, he had instantly declared the *SS Emma Jane* the pride of his fleet. Everyone in the family knew that Jefferson's real pride had been in her creator, for the *Emma Jane* had also been the first steamer built by Powell Shipbuilding and Repairs and as such was a credit to the master shipwright who had designed her, George Brindsley Powell.

Jefferson and George had originally intended to name the vessel after the woman who had been an inspiration to them both. But Doris had flatly refused to accept the honour.

'It is a tribute to you, my dear,' Jefferson had urged.

'The *SS Doris May* is a fine name, Mother,' George had insisted.

'Rubbish,' she'd replied, 'no ship should be called Doris. You must name her after your wife, George. Look to the future, not to the past.' As always, Doris had had the last word, and the pride of the fleet had been named the *SS Emma Jane*. The solidarity of the Powells as a family had only served to strengthen their business alliance. Powell Channel Transport and Powell Shipbuilding and Repairs worked in close association – with, indeed, the orchard of Charlotte Grove as well, for it was Powell vessels that transported the crates of apples and pears to the jam factories of Hobart, and to the city wharves for shipment overseas.

Jefferson Powell had felt an inordinate sense of pride as he'd watched his sons prosper over the passing years. And as he'd watched the sons of his sons become men and take up their fathers' mantle, he'd gained great satisfaction from the knowledge that he had founded a dynasty to be reckoned with.

Including the several infants, there were twenty gathered around the huge weathered table that George had built years before, specifically for Quincy's outdoor parties, and either by blood or marriage seventeen of those gathered were Powells. The non-family members were the Müllers, Gustav and Heidi and their eleven-month-old daughter, Eugenia.

'... Happy birthday David!' Quincy declared.

It was baby David's first birthday and everyone applauded boisterously as Charlotte arrived with the birthday cake, Quincy as always the loudest. Quincy had a robust tenor voice, played the piano accordion with gusto, and always led the troops when it came to a celebration. He was louder than ever today, and with just cause. The first birthday of a man's first grandson was a momentous occasion.

The applause continued as, with great ceremony, Charlotte placed the giant cake on the table. The cake was large enough to amply feed all, with second serves for those of hearty appetite, making the one house candle that flickered in the middle particularly ludicrous, which was the intention.

Olivia Powell leant forward, her infant clutched to her breast, and as she blew out the candle a cheer went up.

Quincy winked at his daughter-in-law and started to sing. *'For he's a jolly good fellow, for he's a jolly good fellow ...'*

They all joined in, singing at the tops of their voices while Quincy pumped away at his piano accordion.

'Hip, hip ...' Then came the three cheers, by which time both babies, David and Eugenia, were crying from the sheer cacophony. Their discomfort did not halt the raucousness, however. Indeed the candle was re-lit and the whole process repeated for Eugenia's sake.

It had been decided that as baby Jeanie would turn one in just four weeks, her first birthday would be celebrated along with David's. The Müllers were like family to the Powells, and any family occasion called for celebration.

Finally, when the 'hip hips' were over and the last rousing cheer had died away, Olivia and Heidi were able to escape with their wailing infants to the grove of birch trees and the bench that overlooked the valley below.

Whether it was the reduction in noise or the distance from the crowd or simply the tranquillity of their surrounds no-one could say, but the babies quickly calmed down and within only minutes the women sat peacefully gazing out over the vast sea of blossom. It seemed the entire landscape was in flower. Below them, the main orchard was a blaze of white, while to the left stood the groves of cherry and plum trees in varying and vibrant shades of pink. Spring in the Huon was a colourful time.

Quincy Powell had only recently re-entered the berry and stone-fruit markets, the principal produce of Charlotte Grove being apples with a healthy sideline in pears. He had discovered in the early days that raspberries, strawberries, plums and cherries intended for jam production did not travel well. If the trip up the Channel proved rough, as it certainly could, the fruit was more often than not badly damaged and useless by the time it reached Hobart. But things had changed since H. Jones & Co. had built its new factory just up the road at Franklin. The fruit could now be processed in the valley and transported as pulp, making berries and stone fruit a viable business.

A half-mile away to the right, beside the orchard and with access to the nearby road, were the outbuildings: the tractor shed and the barn, the stables and harness room, and the sprawling all-important packing shed, which during harvest time was a hive of activity. But most impressive of all, from up on the hill where the house stood, was the view beyond the outbuildings and beyond the road, for there just one mile away lay the broad highway of the Huon River, ambling its way down to the D'Entrecasteaux Channel. The Huon was more than a waterway of great beauty. Given the treacherous road over the hills to Hobart, the Huon was an essential means of transportation for the timber merchants and orchardists, and a lifeline for all those who lived in the region.

The two young women sat gazing out over the vista for a full five minutes before Heidi spoke.

'I love that I sit here,' she said in her quaint way, 'it is such beauty.' Heidi's English pronunciation was excellent, but her syntax dreadful. She'd been twelve years old when her parents had emigrated from Breisach in the Black Forest region of Germany. Her father had pursued his trade as a timberman, and the family had led a remote existence. The Knopfs senior had seen little reason to educate either themselves or their daughter in any more than the basic requirements of communication, which were exercised only when they left their log cabin to visit the timber mill or to buy supplies in the township. Heidi's English had been virtually incomprehensible until she'd met Gustav Müller, who was the foreman at the timber mill in nearby Geeveston. It had improved immeasurably during the several years of their marriage, for Gus had been born in the colony and spoke like a local; indeed, despite his German heritage Gus Müller considered himself a true Tasmanian. His wife's linguistic idiosyncrasies had, however, become so firmly entrenched that there was little Gus could do to change them, and he didn't want to anyway. He liked the way Heidi simply could not put words in the right order.

'Yes,' Olivia agreed, 'it is certainly very beautiful.' She turned her attention from the orchard and the river to her friend. 'You really are remarkable,' she said, shaking her head with admiration. Heidi had admitted that she was once again pregnant, even as she now rocked an eleven-month-old baby in her arms. 'I cannot believe you are going through that whole process all over again, and so *soon*!'

The bond between Olivia and Heidi had been forged during their pregnancies. Both of them young, not yet twenty at the time, each carrying her first child and fearful of what lay ahead, they had been a great strength to each other. As friends they appeared an unlikely pair, the dark-haired, precisely-spoken young Englishwoman and the blonde, square-faced German with the quaint way of talking, but the two were destined to remain a strength to each other throughout their lives.

'So soon, yes, but this I wish.' Heidi smiled. 'Gus says I beg for punishing, but I think is best I get things done and over with soon more than late.'

Olivia did a quick mental translation. Heidi's adaptation of Gus's phrases could be obscure at times, but she'd become quite adept at working them out. 'You're a beggar for punishment all right,' she said. 'I intend to wait at least two years before I go through all that again.' In response to her friend's quizzically raised eyebrow, she hastily added, 'Well, that is, if I can. Thomas wants at least three sons, but he's happy to wait a couple of years between each. And there are *ways* you know.' The women shared a smile. Olivia glanced down at the baby, who was now squirming restlessly in her arms. 'They'll need feeding soon. Shall we go up to the house?'

As they walked back up to the homestead, the party continued behind them.

The younger members of the family, having finished scoffing cake, were playing cricket, and Lincoln's wife was overseeing her wayward son, Gordon. Eighteen-month-old Gordie was trying to ride Falstaff the pig. Falstaff had no objection, he was a most amiable animal, but Gordie kept slithering off his back so, grasping her son firmly by the shirt collar, Margaret held him on board and followed the pig around as it snuffled in the grass seeking the apples that had been especially strewn about for it. There were several pigs that roamed the orchard, eating the rotten apples and generally keeping the place clean, but Falstaff was special. Falstaff was as obedient as any dog and just as loving: he adored the family. The feeling was mutual.

Everyone else was still gathered around the table, George having refilled the women's glasses with the Champagne he'd brought in from Hobart especially for the occasion. None of the men much cared for 'the fancy French stuff', as they called it, and were sticking to their preferred Cascade Ale.

'To Jefferson.' It was Doris who proposed the toast. Doris always proposed the toast at the larger family gatherings. When she was present, as a mark of respect, the others made a rule of waiting until Doris chose the moment before they embarked upon the inevitable round of toasts, which always started with Jefferson.

'To Jefferson,' they said, raising their glasses in a salute.

Doris sipped her champagne. She would not finish the glass: she did not enjoy the taste. The only time alcohol passed her lips was when she toasted her husband and family.

'A second great-grandson,' she gave a nod of satisfaction, 'how very proud he would be.'

Jefferson had not lived to see the first of his great-grandsons. He had died two years before Gordon's birth, succumbing to a heart attack at the age of seventy-one. Doris missed him sorely, but she was never maudlin about his passing. The strength of her faith convinced her that Jefferson was watching over his family anyway, just as the strength of her faith convinced her they would all one day be reunited.

The wheels having been set in motion, a whole series of toasts ensued. Quincy toasted his son and his absentee daughter-in-law, congratulating them on a job well done. 'And so early in life,' he said. 'Childhood sweethearts, just like Charlotte and me.' He beamed at his wife as he raised his glass. 'To Thomas and Olivia.'

'To Thomas and Olivia,' the others chorused obediently.

Quincy downed a swig of ale and turned to his older brother. 'Start breeding them young, George: that's the way to go.' Quincy was eight years George's junior and proud to be a grandfather at forty. 'The younger the better, I say.'

George shared a surreptitious smile with his sister, Martha – they each knew what the other was thinking. Quincy was incorrigible and always had been. Indeed, George thought, Quince might even be considered by some a larrikin, which was a rather derogatory term, but he was such an engaging fellow you couldn't find him offensive. Strangely enough, there were times when George, who was governed by a strong sense of propriety, rather envied his younger brother's lack of inhibition.

It was time for the next toast, which George rightfully took to be his turn. He looked about at all those gathered. 'I propose a toast to the new generation of Powells and Müllers,' he said, 'to Gordon and David and Eugenia.' His eyes met Gus Müller's, and Gus nodded, clearly delighted by the inclusion. George raised his glass. 'To the new generation,' he said.

'To the new generation,' everyone chanted.

'Now there's an excellent idea,' Quincy said after he'd taken a swig of his Cascade. 'David and Jeanie. We'll marry them off before they're twenty, what do you say, Gus? A new generation in less than two decades.' Everyone laughed, although for once Quincy wasn't actually joking.

Several more toasts to family and friends followed, and then the talk turned to business. The Powell gatherings invariably led at some stage to a business discussion, before Quincy would call a halt and demand a sing-along. But as the discussion today revolved around Henry Jones, Quincy was more than happy to delay the sing-along. The jam-manufacturing business played a key role in all of their lives and the burgeoning success of Henry Jones was a source of particular interest to Quincy.

'Jones's new factory premises at Old Wharf will be completed in the next eighteen months or so,' Martha's husband, Simon Hawtrey, said. 'Certainly within two years, I'd say.' Simon, a skilled accountant, managed the affairs of Powell Channel Transport and was an invaluable ally to the family in general, offering sound financial advice on all their ventures. Furthermore, as he and Martha lived in Hobart, Simon could be relied upon to keep the Huon connection up to date with the latest developments in the city.

Doris nodded. 'Jones has acquired half the buildings on Old Wharf now,' she said. Doris was still very much a part of the business and liked to have her say. 'Mostly the burnt-out tenements,' she added, referring to the fire that had swept Wapping five years previously, gutting many of the properties. 'He's been buying them up ever since the fire.'

'How convenient,' Thomas said cheekily. 'I wonder if he started it.' Twenty-one-year-old Thomas was a bit of a larrikin like his father, but unlike Quincy who never meant any offence, Thomas actually enjoyed ruffling feathers.

'What a terrible thing to say.' Martha was truly shocked. 'Ninety people lost their homes in that fire, Thomas. As if Henry Jones would leave his own workers and their families homeless! That is a shocking and libellous statement!'

'He's joking, Martha,' Quincy said.

'Oh.' Martha looked at Thomas who, mission accomplished, grinned back. 'I see,' she said, although she didn't really. Martha had no sense of irony – she always took people at their word and could never understand her nephew's sense of humour. 'I think it is a joke in rather poor taste,' she said, and she didn't in the least care if she sounded stuffy. Martha was not one to back down when she considered a person had been unjustly maligned, be it in jest or otherwise.

'Quite a lot of the workers are moving out of Wapping.' Simon, always the diplomat, came smoothly to the rescue. He was an implacable man, and despite – or perhaps because of – his very blandness, at times impressive in the way he could control a situation. 'The tramway and the new urban train system have made the suburbs accessible to the working classes, as they can now travel to and from the city factories. Jones is actually helping them by buying up their properties.'

Martha flashed a dimpled smile at her husband before giving a stern 'so there' nod at her nephew, but Thomas didn't feel at all chastened. He loved the way he could always get a rise out of his aunt Martha.

'In any event,' Simon continued, steering them back to the subject at hand, 'Jones is set to change the face of the industry. There's been no stopping him ever since he bought out old George Peacock, and when the new factory's fully operational his output will be phenomenal. He already has the British market and Europe will follow.'

'Which can only be to our advantage,' Quincy said. 'He's a good man, Jones; I like doing business with him. He's tough, certainly, but he strikes a fair deal, and I must say his processing plant at Franklin has been a godsend.'

'So long as he doesn't get too big for his boots, Quince,' George sounded a warning. 'You orchardists wouldn't want to see a monopoly come into play. What'd happen to your prices then?'

'No,' Quincy was instantly dismissive, 'with Peacock at the New Wharf I'm not worried about a monopoly. He and Jones might be friends, but they're still rivals. Between the two of them they'll keep the industry competitive.'

The friendly rivalry between William Peacock and Henry Jones was a well-known fact. Jones owed a great deal to the Peacock family, having started out as a lad of twelve pasting labels on tins at George Peacock's jam factory on Old Wharf. So astute was the lad at learning the trade that he'd become factory foreman by the time the old man had retired, and in the early nineties after buying Peacock out he'd taken control of the factory as H. Jones & Co.

in partnership with A.W. Palfreyman and George Peacock's younger son, Ernest. George's older son, William, had set up a rival jam factory on the opposite side of the harbour, fondly known as New Wharf, where the recently constructed Princes Pier was an impressive addition to the dockside reformation. The Jones and W.D. Peacock jam factories of Old Wharf and New Wharf now faced each other across Sullivan's Cove like duellists poised for a fight to the death, but there was no real enmity between the men at the helm. Tasmania had entered the world arena on many levels. The island colony already produced the Huon pine that made the strongest ships and the Merino sheep that provided the purest wool. It was now poised to offer to the world the top quality fruit that created the finest jam. Tasmania was a paradise for any tiger of industry. There was room for two jam barons.

'I tend to agree with Quincy,' Simon said albeit a little warily, 'Jones and Peacock will maintain the competition. It's my personal belief that Jones's sheer ambition will take over at some stage, which could present a problem in the future, but I would say that in the long run he will prove an honourable man ...' He tailed off with a shrug, giving the impression of something left unsaid, which was frustrating for the others.

'So what's the problem then?' Thomas's query was belligerent; he found Simon's diplomacy irritating at times. Martha cast a critical glance at her nephew, but on this occasion, although the family members may have disapproved of his manner, young Thomas was asking the question that was on all their minds. Simon's innuendo demanded explanation.

There was a pause as they all waited.

'If I have any concerns, it is not so much with Jones himself, or not at this stage anyway, but rather with the man who has funded him,' Simon said. He'd been reticent about voicing his feelings, but he decided there was no point in hedging any longer. The family deserved to know about the matter that had been gnawing away at the back of his mind for some time now. 'Does anyone know who financed Jones in buying out Peacock?' He looked about the gathering like a mild-mannered teacher testing his students.

The family shared glances and there was a general shaking of heads.

'Exactly. I've made discreet enquiries, no-one knows.' He again looked about the table before hitting them with the next question. 'Does any know how Jones survived the worst years of the Depression?'

Again the family exchanged glances and again they shook their heads, a little guiltily this time, like schoolchildren who hadn't done their homework. But Simon was not seeking answers, his point being that there were none.

'Our businesses were all firmly established by the early nineties,' he said, addressing the senior family members, George, Quincy, Doris, and his own wife, Martha, 'yet we came close to collapse, all of us. In fact without the family's mutual support we quite possibly would not have survived.'

There were nods all round. Everyone remembered with fearful clarity the hard years of '91 to '93.

'How come Henry Jones avoided financial problems when banks and major businesses across all the colonies of Australia were forced to close down?' This time Simon did not wait for a response. 'The truth is, Jones not only survived during that time, he prospered. He had funds enough for his share in buying out George Peacock, whose business was in decline like everyone else's, and he had funds enough to build that business up. Funds from where?' No longer did Simon appear the mild-mannered teacher, his normally bland expression now replaced by the fierceness of his desire for answers. 'Jones was not born a wealthy man, although he is clearly set on that path, particularly now he has the assistance of the Commercial Bank of Tasmania. But who financed him when the banks had no money? Who has been helping him buy up property over the years for his new factory? Who is behind his rise to power?'

By now it was understood that the questions were rhetorical and no-one made any attempt to reply.

'Someone recognised the potential in Jones and decided to champion him. That someone is rich and powerful, probably with interests in many areas, and he wants to expand his domain without his identity being known. There lies the unseen worry in my opinion, for a man like that would be ruled by greed.'

There was silence around the table. Simon Hawtrey rarely spoke with such force, and his unaccustomed vigour had had an unsettling effect upon the family.

'It's time for the sing-along,' Quincy said finally and he picked up his piano accordion. This was a party after all.

'First rate, Henry,' Reginald Stanford gazed at the open pages of *The Mercury* that Henry Jones had set down on the desk before him, 'a fine piece of advertising, very elegant indeed.' Reginald actually found the new advertising campaign a little gaudy with its overly busy pictures of flowers and fruit dominated by the bold letters IXL. In his opinion it was anything but elegant, although he was certainly not about to argue the point. Jones knew his business, and Reginald never argued with a man who knew his business. He simply put up the money and took his share of the profits. His own astuteness lay primarily in recognising the market and the need, and, on occasions, recognising the right man to back. Jones and his jam factory fitted the bill in all categories.

The two men were seated in Henry's upstairs office at H. Jones & Co. on the Old Wharf. They presented an odd pair. Henry, at thirty three, was short and stocky and looked rather like a generously moustachioed pugilist, while Reginald, two years his senior, was tall and somewhat dapper with the neatest moustache and a trimly cut beard. Despite the fact that both were successful, their appearances, for those who recognised the signs – and most would – denoted their backgrounds. One came from the poorer classes, and one did not.

'Excellent effort all round,' Reginald said. 'In fact you've excelled yourself, Henry, you really have.'

'Why thank you, Reginald.'

They shared a brief laugh, enjoying the joke. It had been only a year or so ago that Reginald had said those very same words.

'You've excelled yourself, Henry,' he'd said. He'd long since forgotten exactly what he'd been congratulating Henry Jones upon, but it was a favourite catchphrase of his when he wished to encourage a business partner's efforts. Men needed compliments. Appealing to a man's ego spurred him on to greater heights. 'You've excelled yourself yet again,' he'd said.

'That's it.' Henry Jones had grabbed at the word. He'd spelt out a phrase, emphasising each syllable with the utmost care. '*I-excel-in-all-I-do.*'

'True, true indeed,' Reginald had agreed. The appeal to the man's ego certainly worked, he'd thought, although it wasn't really surprising – Henry Jones was a cocky little chap at the best of times.

'No, no, we use that as my motto, don't you see? *I excel in all the products I make,*' Henry had said, once again with pedantic emphasis. 'And that motto becomes the company's brand name, the letters *I-X-L*. It's perfect, absolutely perfect.'

Reginald had found the use of the personal pronoun rather egotistical himself. The man did, after all, have two partners. But then Achalen Palfreyman and Ernest Peacock had agreed to the partnership being known as H. Jones & Co., so they would no doubt embrace the suggestion.

Besides, if Henry was stimulated by the brand name then Henry would make it work, for that was the sort of businessman Henry Jones was.

'It's a stroke of genius, Henry,' he'd said expansively, 'a stroke of pure genius.'

Henry Jones had since adopted the brand name for each and every one of his factory products. Every label and every piece of advertising now bore the proud banner 'IXL'. Reginald had congratulated himself on picking another winner in Henry Jones.

'I must be off,' he now said. 'We'll keep in touch about the purchase of the hop estate in the Derwent Valley. It's a project I'm most interested in.'

H. Jones & Co. was broadening its horizons. Henry had been personally approached by his good friend and financier David Barclay of the Commercial Bank of Tasmania, enquiring whether he might be interested in taking over the Shoobridge Brothers Estate at Bushy Park. The bank was concerned about the survival of its investment in the hundred-and-fifty-acre commercial hop-growing property, which had fallen upon hard times.

'I see a great future for you in the hop industry,' Reginald said. 'I believe this purchase will be the first of many.' He smiled conspiratorially. 'Of course the current transaction will be perceived as an arrangement between H. Jones & Co. and the Commercial Bank, but I take it an ongoing "silent partner" would be a welcome ally in the venture?'

'A silent partner is a most valued partner, Reginald.' Henry returned the smile.

Through David Barclay, the Commercial Bank was presumed to be Henry Jones's principal financier in many an enterprise, which was exactly the way Reginald Stanford liked it. Stanford Colonial Enterprises was not seen to support flashy entrepreneurs like Jones. Stanford Colonial, as the firm was fondly known, was primarily associated with the long-established and reputable export industry of Merino wool and also, more recently, of high quality timber. Furthermore, with the elderly Silas Stanford as its titular head, Stanford Colonial retained its reputation as a company that strongly lent its support to philanthropic works. Upon taking over the management of his family's business, Reginald had expanded their interests significantly, but he'd been hampered by his father, who was set in his ways. The company, in Reginald Stanford's opinion, was old-fashioned and outdated, and while he was happy to maintain the public profile demanded of him, indeed very much enjoying the respect his status commanded, he was determined to conquer fresh fields. There were riches ripe for the plucking and if in taking advantage of the opportunities on offer he was occasionally forced to act in a covert fashion, then so be it.

'I'll see myself out,' he now said as he stood.

Henry rose also and accompanied him to the door.

Reginald took his straw boater from the hat stand. He preferred casual dress when attending a clandestine meeting, the image of a straw boater and Norfolk jacket signalling a gentleman simply out for a stroll. Had he been conducting business on behalf of Stanford Colonial, he would have outfitted himself in a bowler hat and a fine dark wool suit with the obligatory watch chain decorating its waistcoat. Clothes sat well on Reginald and he enjoyed dressing as befitted the occasion. Besides, a change of image was all part of the game.

'Cheerio, Henry.'

'Goodbye, Reginald. I shall be in touch soon, I promise.'

The two men shook hands.

Reginald donned his boater, trotted briskly down the stairs and stepped out the front doors into the busyness that was Old Wharf.

He walked along the dockside, past the newly constructed Victoria Dock and past the Alexander and Dunn

Street Piers, heading towards Argyle Street. Up ahead the other five piers pointed out into the water like the fingers of a giant ever-busy hand. Hobart's harbour had changed over the years, just as Ma Tebbutt had said it would.

Reginald turned into Argyle Street, enjoying the crispness of the afternoon: spring was his favourite season. Well, spring and autumn. Summer too hot and winter too cold, he preferred the more temperate months. Although one can hardly rely upon the constancy of the seasons in this part of the world, he thought as he rounded the corner into Macquarie Street. Hobart weather was so capricious that spring could become winter in a matter of minutes.

A tram rattled past, women on its open upper deck clasping their hats to their heads, and Reginald smiled at the ding of its bell. He even gave the driver a wave, as if the bell had been sounded just for him. Reginald very much liked trams.

Reginald Stanford was in a surprisingly good mood today. He had no idea why – nothing of any great magnitude had occurred. But Reginald's moods were rather like the Hobart weather, unpredictable and at times even more contrary. Spring could become winter in only seconds.

He stopped to admire the magnificent stonework of the Town Hall, its grand front portico and its Tuscan columns. Reginald had a great love of fine architecture, of which there was now a great deal to enjoy in Hobart, but the two-storey Town Hall of Italian Renaissance design was, in his opinion, the finest. He walked on past Franklin Square with its grand government buildings, and then a block further past the mighty tower of St David's Cathedral, admiring each architectural delight along the way. And as he walked he nodded good day and smiled and tipped his hat to any passers-by whom he knew. He was so inexplicably ebullient that even the prospect of a meeting with his father could not dampen his spirits.

*

'Good afternoon, Father.'

As he entered the sitting room, Reginald tossed his straw boater on the sofa and joined his father at the table, where Silas was patiently waiting for his tea: Mathilda always delivered it on the dot of four.

'Good afternoon, Reginald.' Silas glanced critically from the boater on the sofa to his son's Norfolk jacket. There were times when he did not at all approve of Reginald's choice of dress. It was far too flamboyant for a thirty-five-year-old businessman, and a married man at that. What, did the boy think he was twenty? 'You'll be taking tea, I presume?' Although he avoided any specific comment, his tone clearly indicated that Reginald couldn't possibly be committed to any business appointment, dressed as he was.

Reginald recognised the inference. He knew every single one of his father's disapproving nuances, but today nothing could ruffle him.

'That would be very jolly, thank you.'

'Good. Your mother will be pleased. She had thought this might be another of your fleeting visits.'

'No, no. I shall stay. I shall stay and I shall devour every single one of the chicken sandwiches she makes for you. What do you say to that?'

Was there the flicker of a smile in the faded blue eyes? Reginald found it impossible to tell, and he didn't care anyway.

Silas was now ninety years old, and looked every day of it: a fragile, shrunken shell of the man he once had been. But his mind was still sharp, and his will as forceful as ever, and therein lay the problem. Reginald, for all of his dapper style, was a hard man, not one to cross, nor one to frighten easily, but memories of the fear his father had instilled in him throughout his childhood remained in the depths of his psyche. Silas had been fifty-five years of age when Mathilda had borne him a son, and Reginald had grown up with an old man as a father. And not just any old man, but a fearsome one. He detested Silas for the tenacious hold he had on life. The man was decrepit, he should be dead or senile, yet here he was, still playing the tyrant.

Reginald looked about at the dour Georgian home of his childhood, which had become even gloomier over recent years. Silas's eyes being affected by glare the drapes these days remained closed for the most part. Nothing about the house had changed in all the years Reginald could remember. The furniture was the furniture from his childhood, as were the rugs and the lamp fittings and the curtains – all was the same. Silas believed in the long-term serviceability of things: new acquisitions were considered an indulgence. Reginald often wondered how his mother could have borne life with such a man, although possessions were probably of little importance to her too. Mathilda, like her husband, was devoted to helping the underprivileged. Reginald couldn't grasp the philosophy himself. Why should one work hard to achieve success and then give away the proceeds? Indeed, why should the successful and privileged work at all for the profit of others? That was the job of the working classes.

'Reggie.' Mathilda appeared with the tea tray, and her face lit up with pleasure at the sight of her son. Well into her sixties, her face was lined and her hair steel-grey, but there was nothing fragile about Mathilda. Mathilda remained a strong and capable woman.

'Hello, Mama.' Reginald jumped to his feet and kissed his mother on the cheek as he took the tray from her. 'I've come to eat all of Father's chicken sandwiches.'

She laughed. 'How lovely,' she said. 'Get started right away and I'll fetch another cup.'

She disappeared into the kitchen and was gone for a good ten minutes, having decided to make an extra sandwich. By the time she returned her husband and son were in the midst of a heated business discussion, as was invariably the case.

'The upkeep of Merinos is so very costly, Father. Our output would be far greater if we diversified –'

'Stanford Wool has a reputation to uphold, Reginald.' Silas cut in coldly. They'd had this conversation before and it always annoyed him. Reginald rarely even visited the property at Pontville, showing no interest in it whatsoever apart from its output. Silas himself was beyond making the trip these days, as travelling by train and then trap jarred every bone in his body. He thanked God daily for his daughter and her husband. The property remained in good hands with Amy and Donald Balfour, and there was even a Stanford ready and waiting to take over. Silas loved Amy with all his heart for having named her son Stanford-Balfour. It pained him to admit the fact, but with his life nearing an end, he needed assurance that a Stanford would protect the property and its reputation against the greed of his own son. And that man would be Edwin Stanford-Balfour.

'Quality not quantity has always been our motto, boy,' he said, making no attempt to mask his disdain. 'Let the mainlanders provide wool for the masses. Stanford wool will remain the purest Merino.'

'I made an extra chicken sandwich, Reggie,' Mathilda said brightly, placing the dish and the fresh cup and saucer on the table, 'just to keep the peace,' she added, her message abundantly clear. She sat, looking meaningfully from one to the other, but her warning was addressed principally to her husband.

'Thank you, Mama.' Reginald smiled; he adored his mother. Her freedom in using the diminutive form of address was proof of the fact. Reginald was Reginald to all who knew him, family or otherwise, and should anyone, in a fit of bonhomie, attempt a 'Reg' or a 'Reggie' they met with very short shrift. 'Reggie' was the special preserve of the woman who had provided the one source of warmth throughout the coldness of his childhood.

'There you are, you see, Father,' Reginald turned his smile upon Silas, 'saved by the woman who loves you.' He picked up a sandwich and took a large bite to prove his good humour. He would not allow his father to annoy him today. He would retain his cheerful mood at all costs.

'Indeed, Reginald, I am a fortunate man.' Silas returned the vestige of a smile. 'Thank you, my dear.' He nodded apologetically to his wife, aware that he had become unnecessarily heated. Why did he allow the boy to rile him so? The fact that he still thought of his thirty-five-year-old son as 'the boy' was perhaps part of the problem, but he simply couldn't help himself. Somewhere along the line Reginald had proved a disappointment. He had not become the man Silas had wished his son to be.

'The lad has no moral fibre,' he'd long ago complained to his wife. 'He's received the best education money can buy, he leads a life of privilege and yet he seems to accept it all as his God-given right. He's a selfish boy who takes and does not give.'

'You're too critical, Silas,' Mathilda had said. 'You expect too much of him. If you set your standards so high this early in his life, he is destined to disappoint you.'

Perhaps she was right, he thought. He'd been so excited by the birth of a son that his expectations had possibly been unreasonable. And Reginald had, after all, fulfilled the most important duty required of a son and heir.

Silas took a sandwich from the dish, signalling a truce. 'How is Evelyn?' he asked, although he already knew. Mathilda visited their daughter-in-law daily at Stanford House, the mansion Reginald called home in nearby Davey Street.

'She is doing splendidly, thank you, Father. Doctor Harvey tends her regularly and is most satisfied with her condition. He sees no cause for concern.'

'That is excellent news.'

Reginald's wife, Evelyn, was due to give birth in less

than a month. The delivery of a healthy baby was eagerly awaited by the couple for in the five years of their marriage Evelyn had had three miscarriages and it had been feared she was unable to carry a child to full term.

'Excellent news indeed,' Silas said, and he bit into his sandwich. Dear God, how he prayed the child would be a boy. He wanted so desperately to die with the knowledge that his direct line would continue.

They drank their tea and the conversation progressed along safer lines, the men taking care not to aggravate one other, although business as always was the topic of the day. Business after all was their only common interest.

Silas enquired after the new steam-driven ketch commissioned by Stanford and Hazeldene Timber.

'She's a fine vessel, Father,' Reginald said. He'd returned only two days previously from his trip to the timber mill at Kermandie in the Huon Valley to take delivery of the *SS Lady Evelyn*. 'George Powell is without a doubt one of the finest master shipwrights the colony has to offer.'

'So I've heard,' Silas said. 'I shall look forward very much to seeing the vessel when she makes her first delivery to the Hobart docks. You must keep me informed, Reginald.'

'I shall, I promise. Evelyn, too, is of course eager to see her namesake.'

Reginald had made a most fortuitous connection when he'd married Evelyn Hazeldene, the only daughter of a wealthy timber merchant. The new business partnership of Stanford and Hazeldene had prospered and Silas Stanford had finally been forced to broaden his horizons, even agreeing to the formation of Stanford Colonial Enterprises. Silas had found the name a little grandiose himself, but he'd been outvoted by the members of the Board.

'When the baby is born we'll make a special family trip to the harbour,' Reginald said. 'All of us,' he added, with a smile to his mother. We will watch the *SS Evelyn* arrive in all her splendour.' Reginald would far rather have named the vessel *Mathilda* in honour of his mother, but he'd decided it politic to keep his wife and old man Hazeldene happy.

'We most certainly shall,' Silas agreed. 'I very much look forward to it.'

Mathilda poured them all a second cup of tea and Reginald decided that, as he and his father were getting along so well, he would test the waters.

'Do you remember when I personally invested in the new electric tram system, Father? You wouldn't have a bar of it. Do you recall how you laughed at me?'

'Yes, yes?' Silas's tone clearly demanded to know where this was leading.

'Well, I currently stand to make a great deal of money, for as you will have witnessed yourself, the people of Hobart have taken the trams to their hearts. Yet at the time you told me electricity was *the tool of the devil*. Those were your words, Father – your very words!'

'And I'm not at all sure I wasn't right,' Silas muttered rebelliously.

'With the greatest respect, sir, a new century beckons. Scientific advances are being made every day.' Reginald took his father's mutterings to be purely defensive. 'What about that William Davidson fellow from New Zealand? In the '80s when wool prices fell by a third, what does he do? He builds a slaughterhouse at Oamaru, refits the *Dunedin* with a compression refrigeration unit and ships frozen lamb to Europe! Refrigerated shipping! What a dashed clever notion. Now there's a man who moves with the times.'

Silas's expression was a baleful glare, but as it usually was and as he'd made no further attempt to halt his son's flow, Reginald decided to follow through with his test.

'I believe our own Henry Jones is cut from the same cloth,' he said. 'Jones is gaining momentum each day with his IXL exports –'

But by now Silas had had quite enough. 'Don't talk to me of Jones. It was men like Jones who brought the colonies to their knees barely three years ago. Have you forgotten the Great Banking Crisis?'

'No, Father, I have not, but –'

'Well I'll tell you here and now it was brought about by the likes of Jones and his IXL. Yes, yes, and your New Zealand fellow and his refrigeration. Rash young entrepreneurial types creating a false economy, encouraging a flood of foreign investment to choke our financial system.' Silas was angry now. 'The banks collapsed! Half the companies in the country suspended trading!'

'You're exaggerating, Father –'

'I most certainly am not! We have only recently recovered from the worst financial depression this country has experienced and impatient young men like your Mr Jones will lead us straight into another one! Let me tell you, boy,' Silas shook his gnarled fist, 'it will be over my dead body!'

How Reginald wished he could arrange that.

'Calm down, Silas.' Mathilda was concerned. 'Please dear, please calm down.' She cast a look of appeal at her son.

'Yes, do calm down, Father,' Reginald responded obediently, 'you mustn't get yourself so worked up.' Perhaps, he thought, there might come a day when one of his father's temper tantrums would lead to a heart attack. God he wished the old man would die: it was positively obscene he should have lived this long. 'I didn't mean to upset you so. Drink your tea, Father, do.'

At least I know where I stand with regard to Henry Jones, Reginald thought. He was not in the least surprised, but good God, if the mention of IXL Jam elicited a response like this, just imagine the reaction he'd get if he suggested investment in the hops industry? The Stanford name associated with the production of liquor? Never! Oh well, he and Nigel would manage. They always did. He and Nigel were masters of subterfuge.

Nigel Lyttleton of Lyttleton Holdings & Investment was

ten years older than Reginald, but their families had had
business connections for years. Nigel had been six years
old and his sister eleven when their father Geoffrey had
committed suicide, but their mother Phyllis had soldiered
bravely on, appointing experts to run the company until
her son was of an age to assume his rightful place at its
head. Nigel, with virtually no memory of his father, had
remained quite dispassionate about the suicide. Indeed he
appeared to rather relish the fact that he worked in the
same office where his father had blown his brains out.
'In that very chair,' he would say, pointing to the Queen
Anne walnut elbow chair. He'd kept the chair when he'd
modernised the office. A damned uncomfortable thing, he
never used it, but being a collector's item it was worth a
fortune – besides which it made such an interesting talking
point. 'And to this day no-one has any idea why he did it,'
he would say with a shrug.

Reginald and Nigel had an excellent business arrangement. They were chairmen of their respective companies
and each sat on the board of the other. Far from being
rivals, they were collaborators who surrounded themselves
with carefully handpicked supporters. Clever lawyers and
accountants ensured that transactions were within the
boundaries of the law, and the board members of both
companies were 'yes men' who were easily manipulated by
minds as astute as Reginald's and Nigel's. Silas's position
as a director of Stanford Colonial was titular only. He
was invited to attend board meetings on a quarterly basis,
more as a measure of respect than anything, and keeping
him unaware of certain company investments was not
particularly difficult.

Reginald watched as his father, still agitated, sipped his
tea in an effort to calm down. Silas Stanford's deception
was a source of great satisfaction to Reginald.

'I shall pay a visit to the property next week, Father,' he
said. He didn't really want to, the countryside bored him,

but it would placate the old man if he did so. 'I've been remiss of late, I know, and I shall enjoy seeing Amy and Donald and Edwin.'

Mathilda flashed a look of gratitude to her son. A visit to Pontville would surely please Silas, who was forever complaining that Reginald showed no interest.

But Silas merely scowled. 'It won't do you any good, you know. They won't listen.'

'I beg your pardon?'

'Amy and Donald and Edwin. They're committed to Merino production: you won't be able to talk them around.'

'Oh good heavens above, Father, that was not my intention.' Reginald gave a laugh of sheer delight. 'As if I would do anything behind your back,' God, how he did enjoy the game. 'I must go now, Mama.' He crossed to the sofa and retrieved his straw boater. 'No, no,' he said as his mother rose from her chair, 'don't see me to the door. I know my way out.' He kissed her on the cheek.

'Take care, Reggie.'

'I shall. Goodbye, Father. I enjoyed our chat as always.'

Silas responded with a grunt. Why did the boy so get on his nerves! Then he caught his wife's glance. 'Good news that Evelyn's in fine health,' he said, trying his best to sound gracious. 'Give her my best wishes when you get home.'

'Of course.'

But Reginald didn't go home to Stanford House. At least not for some time. It hadn't been his intention from the start. He had no desire for Evelyn's company.

Instead of walking the one block down to Davey Street, he turned right along Macquarie, and then right again into Molle Street. He needed nurturing of the kind his heavily pregnant wife could not offer. But then even in the early days of their marriage, Evelyn had never excited him the way Shauna could. In fact Reginald doubted there was a woman on earth able to match the talents of his mistress.

He passed the T-junction of Collins, crossed over Liver-ool Street and stopped at the stone cottage on the corner.

He gave his special knock and the door opened, only a foot or so, just wide enough for the shaft of sunlight to hit the fiery red mane of her hair.

'Hello, Reginald,' she said, fox eyes gleaming.

Four whole years and still just the look of Shauna O'Callaghan excited him.

'Come in,' she whispered.

CHAPTER THIRTEEN

Of the five O'Callaghans, Shauna was the only one to have inherited her mother's colouring. Her two older sisters and her two younger brothers had the dark-haired, olive-skinned gypsy looks of their father. But there was no denying, the O'Callaghans were striking, every single one them. Heads turned when an O'Callaghan walked down the street.

'It's in the blood,' Mara the eldest would say with a toss of her raven black hair. The comment could be taken as arrogant, but it wasn't really. The O'Callaghans had inherited not only their looks from their parents, but also their boldness. They did not shy away from speaking their mind, or in Mara's case, simply making a statement.

Their father, Mick, had weathered time exceptionally well. At least it would appear so: in truth he was plagued by a stomach ulcer that gave him hell. But he was still slim and blessed with a fine head of hair and a bounce in his step – there remained a boyishness about Mick O'Callaghan. The grey at his temples and the crinkles about his eyes, particularly when he smiled, only added to the roguish quality that had always been there and, although now in his sixties, he looked a good twenty years younger. Indeed, Mick O'Callaghan seemed ageless.

Eileen had not fared as well. She was still striking, but

the fire of her beauty had faded and she looked her age. The fierce red of her hair was now a gingery grey and her body had thickened with the birth of five children. But there remained something arresting about Eileen, something that people at times found confronting. It was her demeanour, the way she carried herself with such pride, and the way those animal eyes seemed to see into the minds of others. Eileen O'Callaghan was a strong woman, with a tough streak that could appear ruthless to some.

Mick and Eileen still lived in the cottage in Hampden Road, indeed the very same cottage where they'd brought up their five children. Things had not worked out quite as Mick had intended. He hadn't become the rich man he'd presumed he would, and the Hunter's Rest hadn't proved the automatic road to success he'd imagined he could make it. All of which was his own fault. He'd taken the easy way out right from the start, appointing a manager to do the hard work while he posed as the publican and gambled away much of the profits. The manager he'd chosen had proved slack, the pub had gone downhill, and Eileen, after bearing the situation for a full five years, had issued her ultimatum.

'Your daughters will need an education, Mick,' she'd said, 'and that takes money. If you don't mend your ways I'll leave you, and I'll take the girls with me, I swear I will.'

Whether or not her threat was an empty one, the mere thought of life without Eileen and his three little girls had been incentive enough for Mick. He'd cut his gambling back to a minimum, sacked the manager and worked hard to bring the pub back to the glory days it had known under Ma Tebbutt's reign. He'd also introduced a lucrative sideline that Ma had not been involved in: the sale of contraband liquor. French cognacs, Scottish whiskies and fine Spanish sherries were among the many commodities smuggled into Hobart to avoid import tax. They fetched an excellent price on the black market. The Hunter's Rest had proved an ideal storage venue and sales outlet and Mick had proved the perfect middleman between the smugglers and the wealthy drinkers, who wanted ready access to the best alcohol money could buy at the best price it could be bought. Paying off the police and the customs officers who occasionally visited the premises had been simple. Every official who covered the Wapping area could be bought.

Through Mick's endeavours, the family's fortunes had improved immeasurably, but he and Eileen had not sought to enhance their own lives. They lived comfortably enough anyway and they liked their cottage. Instead, every penny had been put aside to provide the all-important education Eileen demanded for their daughters.

'They will have the opportunities I was denied,' she had insisted. 'Never mind that they're girls, they'll receive a proper education.'

Eileen had actually felt guilty when her first three children had all proved to be girls. First Mara, then Kathleen, then Shauna – couldn't one of them have been a son? she'd thought.

'I'm sorry, Mick,' she'd said as she'd laid back wearily against the pillows, her new baby, also weary from the effort of being born, now sleeping peacefully in her arms.

'What for?' he'd replied with his irrepressible grin. 'Look at her, will you? Just look at that hair.' Shauna had been born with a downy flame-red skull-cap. 'How could you not love a thing like that now?'

'But you wanted a son, I know you did.'

'Rubbish,' he'd said dismissively. Of course he'd wanted a son – Mick had ached for a son – but it would not stop him loving his daughters. 'What good are boys, I ask you? Wastrels every one of them. There's much more money in girls.'

'No, I won't have that,' she'd said firmly. 'Our daughters are not going into the business. I will not allow it.'

'Of course they're not, are you daft?' He'd been surprised and even a little shocked that she'd presumed he meant such a thing, particularly as he'd only been trying to comfort her. But then that was Eileen. There were times when even Mick could not fathom his wife. 'We'll marry them off to wealthy men is what I meant. There's money to be had in marriage.'

'There certainly is,' she'd agreed, 'and if not marriage, a benefactor. Wealthy men abound in Hobart.'

A benefactor, Mick thought. Isn't that rather like going into the business? But then he supposed marrying for money was too, wasn't it? Either way, his girls would make wealthy matches, of that there was no doubt.

'Just look at her, Eileen,' he'd said, running the tip of his little finger over the child's perfect mouth, 'between us we've bred beauties, that's for sure.'

'The next one will be a boy,' she'd promised, and she vowed to herself that if it wasn't, then she'd keep having girls until she produced a son. And not just for Mick. Eileen wanted a beautiful boy of her own.

Two years later, in the winter of 1862, Colin O'Callaghan was born, a perfectly formed baby, as beautiful as his sisters.

Mick was ecstatic, a son and heir. As the child grew, he even proved himself a very replica of his da: audacious and cheeky, with winning ways. Mick recalled his father's proud boast about himself when he was a boy. *He could charm the wings off a butterfly that one*, Patrick Kelly would say, *and the butterfly would walk away flightless and happy. The boy has the true gift, there's no doubt about it*. Mick spoiled his son shamelessly, rarely disciplining young Col even when he knew the child was telling a tissue of lies. 'The gift' after all, if put to good use, could prove a valuable tool in life. By the age of six, Col O'Callaghan had his father under his spell.

Eileen was true to her promise regarding the girls' education. When they were little, she had them privately tutored

by Madame Elodie Beauchesne, widow of a French merchant
and proprietress of the Beauchesne Preparatory School for
Young Ladies in Boothman's Terrace, Battery Point. Then
in 1869, when they were thirteen, eleven and nine, she
transferred them to Mount St Mary's College, the new girls'
school that had been established just the previous year in the
grounds of St Mary's Cathedral in Harrington Street.

Mount St Mary's offered exclusive and expensive education for the daughters of Hobart's wealthier Catholics
and Eileen wasted no time having her girls enrolled. But
she also insisted they keep their regular Saturday morning
attendance at Madame Beauchesne's in order to continue
their French lessons. She knew the value of fluent French
among the upper classes. It was the stamp by which all
young ladies were judged.

Following Colin's birth Eileen had decided there would
be no more children. She had fulfilled her duty in providing a son and four was quite enough. But even her well-
practised methods of contraception were not infallible
and when Colin was eight she gave birth to his younger
brother, Bernard.

Bernard, like his siblings, was a physically beautiful child,
but growing up in the shadow of a brother who was so well-
established as his father's favourite, young Bernie developed
problems at an early age. He desperately competed for his
father's affection and approval, but invariably he failed.
It wasn't because Mick disliked him. Mick simply didn't
notice Bernie very much. Bernie didn't have Col's charisma.
And as Col grew towards manhood his charisma grew with
him. Just like his father, he could charm the wings off a
butterfly, and just like Patrick Kelly, Mick's pride knew no
bounds. Bernie spent his childhood more or less invisible
to his father and, sadly, to a certain extent also his mother.
Eileen was not immune to Col's charm either.

Fortunately for Bernie, he had his sisters. The girls
adored their baby brother, particularly Shauna, who

always came to his defence when Col accused little Bernie of being a sissy. Shauna, who worked as a part-time governess and tutor teaching French to the offspring of the rich, was sensitive to the feelings of children, particularly those of her little brother. 'You're full of shite, Col,' she would say, and the others would take up the chant. The girls weren't fooled by Col for a second, and why would they be? Colin O'Callaghan didn't bother wasting his charms on his sisters.

'If the lad grows up spineless it'll be your fault, Shauna,' he'd say. The battle was always on between Col and Shauna. 'You're turning him into a sissy, the lot of you.'

To give Col his due, he was actually trying to help his little brother. He'd grown up with three older sisters himself and he knew just how overwhelming the experience could be. Teasing Bernie about being a sissy was his way of issuing a warning. Sometimes he even gave the boy a lecture. 'Don't let yourself be mollycoddled, Bernie,' he'd say. 'You mustn't allow yourself to be governed by women.' Then he'd proffer that devilish grin of his. 'At least not women who're your sisters.' Just turned eighteen, Col O'Callaghan's only problem with girls was how to stop those he bedded falling hopelessly in love with him.

Bernie's life was complicated. His sisters' affection had become a double-edged sword. Much as he welcomed their love and much as he loved them in return, he did not want to be perceived as under their influence. He tried to distance himself from them and assert his own personality. He wanted to be like his brother. No, more than that, much more than that. He wanted to *be* his brother. He wanted his mother to laugh at his stories the way she laughed when Col told one of his tales; and above all he wanted his father to admire him the way he admired Col. But try as he might, when Col was around, Bernie remained somehow invisible.

Then, at twenty years of age, Col decided to leave home.

He was not the first of the O'Callaghan offspring to fly the nest. Kathleen had two years previously married a man she'd met at the wedding of one of her old school friends, with whom she'd maintained close ties. Mick and Eileen had been thrilled, for Kevin was a banker and very well-to-do. They had not been thrilled, however, to discover that Kevin was based in Launceston. It wasn't right, Eileen had said – what was the point of having a wealthy daughter who lived more than a hundred miles away? O'Callaghans stuck together.

'I'm going to Sydney,' Col announced to the family as they sat around the dinner table. The kitchen being too small, the living room had long served as both the dining area and the place where they generally gathered. The house, although crowded, was comfortable enough: the girls shared the second bedroom, and the boys the extra room that Mick had built out the back.

'Sydney?' Mick looked up from his lamb and potatoes. 'You're going to Sydney?'

'To start with – after that, who knows?' Col gave an expansive wave of his hand. 'The world, Da. I intend to see the whole, wide world.'

'That's a fairly big place.' Mick felt his heart sink. He knew already there was nothing he could say to dissuade the lad, and why should he? Col was only doing what he'd done himself, except he was doing it four years later in life. Mick had left home to see the world at the age of sixteen.

'When do you intend to leave?' Eileen, practical as always, got straight to the point.

'I haven't made my plans yet. I'll enquire around the docks tomorrow and see what openings there might be. I intend to work my passage.' Upon completing school, Col had not decided on any particular path in life and had become quite an accomplished jack-of-all-trades. 'There'll be no problem getting work,' he said confidently.

'You surely wouldn't dream of leaving before your

sister's wedding?' Eileen's eyes dared him to even think of such a thing.

'Not for a minute, Ma,' Col smiled his reassurance. 'As if I would let Mara down on her big day.'

'Don't go doing me any favours,' Mara said with a shrug of indifference. 'My heart won't break if you're not there.'

'Of course it will.' Col winked cheekily at his sister. 'You know full well it won't be the same without me.'

'You're full of shite, Col,' Shauna said, but the response was automatic. There was no real enmity and, even as twelve-year-old Bernie darted nervous looks from one to another, expecting a fight to ensue, his three older siblings shared a smile. Bernie didn't understand their volatile relationship. Perhaps he was simply too young; perhaps he would develop their strength as he grew. Or perhaps he really was the runt of the litter.

The event of Mara's wedding was without doubt the most important date on the family's calendar. Mara had done her parents proud in scoring as her husband-to-be none other than Archibald Dimbleby. She'd done so simply by shopping at Dimbleby's Emporium in Murray Street, where she'd caught the eye of the eldest son and heir. Archibald had become instantly smitten and the courtship had been swift, for Mara, like all the O'Callaghan girls, was not only strikingly beautiful; she was clever. Well-educated and intelligent, she had acquired skills that had not been available to her mother; in addition she had the skills that only Eileen and *not* education could impart. Mara, like her sisters, knew how to snare a man. She knew how to tease and to fascinate, how to be innocent yet provocative and, although still a virgin, she knew, as Archibald Dimbleby was soon to discover, how to sexually excite beyond all expectations. She had also learnt, as had her sisters, how to avoid pregnancy, although in Mara's case this would not be necessary as Archie was eager to produce an heir of his own in order to secure the next generation's inheritance.

Despite the fact that the couple had not met through the customary social channels, Mara's beauty and education had afforded her acceptance into the Dimbleby family, her fluent command of the French language having apparently sealed the bargain.

Charles Dimbleby had known his son's choice of bride sprang from a shady background, to say the least, but he'd also known his son was besotted and that nothing would turn Archie from his chosen course of action. Anyway, who in this town hadn't emanated from some shady past, Charles had thought philosophically; rattle any family closet in Hobart and there was bound to be the echo of bones. Besides, the girl spoke French like a native.

'They believe I'll be a godsend in Paris,' Mara had told her mother with a laugh. 'Archie normally has to hire a translator when he travels to Europe to deal with the French suppliers.'

Eileen had congratulated herself on her foresight.

The hurdle of religion had been overcome with surprising ease.

'No matter, dear,' she'd said when Mara had brought up the subject of Archibald's Anglican faith,' God will understand; He will not abandon you.'

Eileen O'Callaghan had always been malleable. Her whole life had been led along flexible lines, including her relationship with the Roman Catholic Church, which was just another example of hedging her bets on all sides. Better to be safe, because you never really knew. Eileen had her own relationship with God. Her God would not see a member of His flock starve rather than make a good match, and Mara's match was undoubtedly one of the best.

Charles Dimbleby had recently handed over the reins of Dimbleby's, grown to a chain of emporiums, to his sons Archibald and Vernon. Charles had single-handedly built the family business into the empire it was, his brother Gerald having died of syphilis-induced kidney failure at the age of thirty. There were Dimbleby stores in Melbourne, Sydney and Adelaide, but the grandest Dimbleby's of all was without doubt the original emporium in Hobart. Mara O'Callaghan had certainly done well for herself.

'She's hit the jackpot,' Mick boasted with pride, using a term common amongst his poker-playing friends. 'She's hit the jackpot all right, there's no doubt about that.'

Col stayed for his sister's wedding, which was indeed a splendid affair. Mara and Archie were married in St David's Cathedral, after which the guests were transported in a convoy of fine carriages to Charles Dimbleby's mansion, overlooking Sandy Bay, where a feast awaited them. Musicians were playing, champagne was flowing and the reception continued into the wee hours of the morning.

Three weeks later, Col left Hobart.

The night before his departure, he and his father took their glasses of ale outside and sat on the cottage's single front doorstep. When the nights were mild the front doorstep had always been their favourite spot to escape the chaos of women, and although with Kathleen and Mara gone things were now quieter, they maintained the habit. Bernie would join them occasionally, saying little, knowing it wasn't his place, but enjoying the male company nonetheless.

'Not tonight, Bernie,' Eileen said as she and Shauna collected the dishes from the table. 'Leave them be.'

Bernie remained poised regretfully at the front door. It was his brother's last night and he would like to have joined the men.

'Bernie,' Shauna said, 'would you like to play draughts after we've done the washing up?' Shauna always knew when Bernie felt left out.

'Best of three?'

'Aye. Best of three.'

'All right.' Bernie nodded happily. 'I bags black.'

Outside, Mick was successfully managing to disguise his despondency, although his heart was heavy at the thought of losing his son. Life wouldn't be the same without Col.

'It's a wonderful adventure you're embarking upon, son,' he said, with an enthusiasm he didn't feel. 'I wish I was your age and doing it all over again.'

'That's it exactly, Da,' Col's eyes gleamed with excitement, 'I want to do everything you've done. Sydney's only the start. I want to sail the high seas. I want to know what's out there. I want to see all the parts of the world you've seen.'

His son's face was clearly visible in the light of the gas lamp shining through the sitting-room window. Mick was looking at himself thirty years ago. 'A toast,' he said. 'To the great big world that's out there waiting for you, Col.' He raised his glass. 'To the world.'

'To the world,' Col responded, and they clinked.

Mick took a swig of his ale and looked into the night, trying to appear casual, trying not to sound desperate. 'You'll write home, won't you? Your mother will want to know you're safe.' He turned to his son, with an air of happy camaraderie. 'And I'll want to hear all of your adventures – every single one of them, mind.'

'I'll write regular as clockwork, Da,' Col said, 'and I won't hold back a thing. It'll be like you're with me, I can promise you that.' There were times when Colin O'Callaghan even sounded like his father.

Life was very quiet with Col gone. A year later, when twenty-three-year-old Shauna moved out of the house, things became even quieter.

Eileen welcomed Shauna's move, believing her youngest daughter to have found herself an excellent match, a match furthermore who lived most conveniently nearby. In Eileen's opinion Shauna was extremely lucky, for the foolish girl had come very close to ruining her chances.

Shauna had accepted a position as tutor to two small children shortly after Col's departure. The children's father, a successful shipping agent with offices and a warehouse in Salamanca Place, was a widower in his forties whose wife had died two years previously. Shauna would report to Melvyn Billing's home in Montpellier Retreat (only several blocks away) five times a week, where for three hours she would tutor his six-year-old son and eight-year-old daughter. Eileen O'Callaghan had considered the arrangement perfect and the outcome inevitable, and of course she had proved correct. Melvyn had quickly become enamoured of the flame-haired young beauty and six months later he was eager to marry her. Things couldn't have been better, Eileen had thought, but Shauna had presented a most unexpected problem.

'You don't want to marry him? In God's name, why?'

'Mr Billing is a very nice man, but I don't love him.'

'Oh for goodness sake, Shauna,' Eileen had been most impatient, 'you can't expect everything to happen at once. Marry the man and please him. Love will follow.'

But much to Eileen's chagrin, Shauna had remained resolute. She had continued to refuse Mr Billing, despite his relentless pursuit, for Melvyn, who was besotted, did not intend to give up easily. Then, a further six months later, to her mother's utter astonishment, Shauna announced she was moving to the house in Montpellier Retreat.

'I have accepted Mr Billing's offer of a position as live-in governess to the children,' she said and, as her mother stared at her in open amazement, she added the obvious: 'I have agreed to become his mistress.'

Eileen was astounded. She could not for the life of her understand her youngest daughter's reasoning. If mistress, then why not wife? But she welcomed the arrangement nonetheless. Shauna was bound to give in and marry the man eventually, and in the meantime she had found herself a wealthy benefactor.

Shauna's reasoning was actually simple. She wanted to experience sex. Her sister Mara had told her it was the height of pleasure: 'Not a duty at all. Mother is quite right, one should please the man, but oh Shauna,' she'd said, her face radiant, 'in pleasing the man, how one does so end up pleasing oneself. The sensation is utterly indescribable,' she'd added with a hopeless shake of her head. Then she'd gone on to describe it anyway, recounting each erotic moment and sparing no detail.

For years Eileen O'Callaghan had drummed into her daughters the value of their bodies. They had been warned not to give themselves to some hot-headed young rake, but to keep their virginity as a treasure for one who could afford it. They were bred for wealthy men, she'd told them. She'd told them about sex too, explaining the way they could use their bodies and the tricks they could employ; she'd been quite graphic. Their duty was to please, she'd said. 'Do not seek your own gratification. Focus at all times upon the man. Remember always, the more you pleasure your man, the more he will desire you and the less likely he will stray.'

Mara's version of sex differed considerably from their mother's. Shauna found it arousing and couldn't wait to experience the joys her sister so vividly described. Besides, by giving herself to Mr Billing she was not disobeying instructions. Mr Billing was no hot-headed young rake but a wealthy man who was offering to keep her in style, albeit in secret style to avoid undue gossip, which of course was understandable.

Sex for Shauna proved every bit as enjoyable as Mara had promised it would be. The O'Callaghan girls, all three, did not suffer their mother's inhibition. They practised the tricks she had taught them indeed, but they were sexually abandoned creatures who gave themselves up wholeheartedly to their own pleasure as well as their partner's.

Melvyn Billing's life would never be the same. A conservative man, the radical step of taking a mistress had been

most out of character, but his infatuation with Shauna
O'Callaghan and her refusal to marry him had driven
him to make the offer. He now found himself awakened
to an insatiable lust he hadn't known he possessed. He
wanted to have her morning, noon and night, and be it
morning, noon or night when he visited her quarters, she
was ready for him. More than ready: she was always eager
and waiting. Melvyn lived in continual states of arousal,
ecstasy and exhaustion. Throughout the ten years of his
marriage sex had never been like this.

The governess's quarters were in a separate wing of the
house, but the situation was nonetheless obvious to the
servants. The cook, the housekeeper and the maid knew
exactly what was going on. The cook and the maid, who
both liked Shauna, thought it was lovely that Mr Billing,
a lonely widower for two long years, now had a companion, but Flora, who had kept house for the past ten years,
was of quite a different opinion. Flora had hoped that she
might replace her former mistress in the master's affections
and she found the current arrangement disgraceful. She
strongly disapproved of Shauna, whom she considered no
more than a whore, and she made her disapproval evident,
although never in the presence of the master.

Shauna didn't care in the least. She thought it rather stupid
of Flora to make an enemy of her when she could so easily
have had her dismissed – for Melvyn would do anything
she wished – but she did not exercise her power. A good-
natured, easy-going girl, she chose instead to let the insults
bounce off her and ignored the woman, which was an added
irritant to Flora, who had wished to provoke her.

As the months passed Melvyn was faced with a
dilemma. He remained obsessed with his young mistress's
beauty and sexuality, but he was now captivated also by
the woman herself. Infatuation had become love. Melvyn
loved everything about Shauna: her carefree nature, her
feistiness, her sense of humour. He desperately wanted

her to become his wife, and a mother to his children, who clearly adored her.

But the more Melvyn sought to legalise their relationship, the more Shauna backed away. She wasn't altogether sure why. She liked Melvyn and the lifestyle he provided, and she very much liked his children, but she found herself instinctively balking at the prospect of marriage. Somewhere in the back of her mind was the vaguely romantic notion that marriage involved love and that love meant forever. She preferred to live for the moment, even accepting the fact that it was quite likely she would never experience love and never marry; at least as a mistress she could always walk away.

Melvyn had no option but to accept their relationship on Shauna's terms, and the arrangement continued for a whole two years. Then Shauna moved back into her family home. The move was governed by a certain sense of fair play on her part for she had decided that if Melvyn was so keen to have a wife it was probably not fair of her to remain his mistress. However, her action was not as altruistic as it might have appeared. Melvyn's love had become stifling and the sex not as exciting – and, having left, she quickly found that she missed the children she'd been teaching far more than she missed the man she'd been sleeping with.

'You foolish, foolish girl.' Eileen was dismayed. 'A fine man like that with a respectable position in society – he would have made the perfect husband.'

'I know, Mother,' Shauna replied with a sublime lack of concern, 'but I'm not sure I would have made the perfect wife. I fear marriage would bore me. In fact I've come to the conclusion that I'm designed more to be a mistress than a wife.'

Her words proved prophetic for over the following five years she was to become mistress to two men, each relationship lasting two years. Shauna found relationships tedious after two years and was driven to move on.

Bernie was delighted to have his favourite sister home again. Since Col's departure he hadn't become the focus of his father's affections as he'd hoped he might. Quite the opposite in fact: the harder he'd tried to win favour the more he'd seemed to disappoint.

Mick, to give him his due, had done his best not to let his irritation show. He was aware the lad was trying to emulate his brother, but he wished like hell he wouldn't. Bernie wasn't Col and he never would be – he simply didn't have it in him.

Col's letters were by now few and far between, but whenever one arrived it provided immense excitement, for he would write in great detail with the deliberate intention of entertaining. Col could tell a story as well on paper as he could in real life, and his letters were read out loud over and again whenever one of the girls called in or when there was a family gathering. It was as if Col was right there with them.

Bernie could not compete with his brother's letters. Even in absentia Col was the clear family winner. So Bernie decided he would try winning friends elsewhere. Shortly after his sixteenth birthday he left school and moved out of the cottage; his radical behaviour appeared to his parents an overnight rebellion, but Bernie had long had enough.

He got himself a room in a hostel in George Street, just around the corner from Salamanca Place, and found work as a docker, loading cargo on and off ships and in and out of warehouses.

'So much for an education,' Mick complained to Eileen. 'What on earth does the lad think he's doing with his life – at least Col had the brains to finish school.' Mick couldn't fathom the behaviour of his youngest son.

Bernie grew up quickly on the Hobart docks. With no older sisters to baby him and no older brother to over-whelm him he became his own man. Or at least he thought he did. His body filled out, certainly – the physical work

was demanding – and given his good looks he was popular
with women. Bernie never had to buy sex: it was there for
the taking and he certainly availed himself of the offers. He
drank and he womanised and when he had enough spare
cash he gambled. In fact he did everything his brother
had done, but Bernie's problem was he didn't do it with
style. He couldn't handle his drink the way Col could and,
although women gravitated to him, they didn't stay long.
They didn't fall in love with him as they had with Col.
Perhaps they sensed his weakness.

By the time he was twenty, the drink was starting to get
a grip on Bernie. When he visited the family home, as he
regularly did for a baked lunch on Sundays, his parents
were worried by the way he knocked back the hard liquor
he brought with him.

'You want to watch it, boy: you're turning into a
drunk.' Mick's method of dealing with the problem was to
be harshly critical in an attempt to shock his son.

'Come home, Bernie.' Eileen, not sure Mick's severity
was the right tack to take, chose a motherly and more
caring approach. 'Come home where you belong, love.'

Both tacks were wrong. Bernie was sick and tired of
not meeting his father's expectations, whatever they might
be, and he wanted no more mollycoddling from women.
He was a man now and he lived by his own rules in a
man's world.

The only one who seemed neither to stand in judgement
of him nor to fuss over him was Shauna.

'Would you like a game of draughts, Bernie?' she'd say.

Shauna also visited the family home regularly for the
Sunday baked lunch; in fact it was one of the stipula-
tions she set in place when coming to an agreement with
a benefactor. She was between patrons at the moment,
however, her two-year boredom threshold having recently
run out, and had shifted back in with her parents. Once
again she was teaching, but this time on a voluntary basis

at a school for orphans, a position that had been arranged by her sister.

Mara Dimbleby was deeply committed to the Hobart Orphan School Association, one of the many philanthropic causes of which her husband's business was a major supporter, but she had an ulterior motive in seeking to engage her sister's involvement. Aside from Dimbleby's there were any number of other wealthy businesses that funded the association, and Mara thought it an excellent means through which Shauna might hopefully meet the right husband. Mara, like her mother, considered it high time Shauna embraced the security of marriage.

Mara had certainly selected the right way to introduce her sister to wealthy men, but as it eventuated, Shauna's personal choice proved not to be of the eligible kind. Shauna's choices rarely were these days. She was not attracted to safety.

'Reginald, may I introduce my wife's sister, Shauna O'Callaghan? Shauna, this is Reginald Stanford.'

Archibald Dimbleby made the introductions. Reginald had demanded he do so the moment he'd seen her from across the other side of the ballroom.

'You don't happen to know that glorious creature do you?' he'd muttered. He and Archie had been standing right beside their wives, and a number of other wives whose husbands were currently mingling, but Reginald had been unable to take his eyes off the woman in the green taffeta gown, her flame-red hair swept high, her neck and shoulders flawless. He'd seen her in the street on the odd occasion and admired her beauty, but their paths had never crossed socially. And now here she was: it was a God-given opportunity.

'Of course I know her, old man,' Archie had whispered. 'She's one of the O'Callaghan girls, my sister-in-law what's more.' Archie never strayed himself, why would a chap bother when he had a wife like Mara, but he knew

Reginald did. Reginald Stanford was continually unfaithful to his wife. His affairs were brief and discreet and nothing that would damage his image, but most of his business acquaintances knew that Reginald simply could not resist a challenge.

'Introduce me,' Reginald had demanded under his breath. Then he'd turned to Evelyn and the other wives. 'Will you excuse us, ladies,' he'd said, 'a bit of business to attend to, won't be long,' and he and Archie had left, ostensibly to circulate among their colleagues.

The 1892 Spring Charity Ball, held in the opulent grand ballroom of the Town Hall, was the social event of the season, attracting the who's-who of Hobart. Up on stage, in front of the ornate arch that housed the organ, a band was playing a waltz, and in the glittering light cast by the three chandeliers that hung from the ballroom's massive ceiling, couples glided gracefully about the floor, women glamorous in their gowns, men handsome in their evening dress. Around the perimeters of the ballroom were those watching the dancers: the elderly, who were seated enjoying the spectacle; and those standing nearby, hiding their longing with careless smiles as they waited to be invited onto the floor. Others were paying little attention to the dancers as they mingled, chatting among themselves, some exchanging niceties, some conducting business, and some unmistakeably flirting.

'How do you do, Mr Stanford,' Shauna boldly proffered her gloved hand to be kissed in the French manner of greeting. Reginald Stanford of Stanford Colonial – she knew exactly who he was, and she liked what she saw. He was handsome in an elegant way, with his ramrod-straight back, his formal evening suit stylishly cut and fitted to perfection: a man of obvious position and power. But she sensed something else, something lurking beneath the dapper surface. In the ice-blue eyes she saw danger. Shauna liked danger, it excited her. Danger was an aphrodisiac.

'Miss O'Callaghan.' Reginald took her hand and obediently touched his lips to her glove, surprised but intrigued by the boldness of her gesture. He was surprised and intrigued also by the way she was so blatantly assessing him. The audacity of the woman.

'Shauna has volunteered her services to the cause, Reginald,' Archibald said. 'She teaches our orphans three mornings a week.' Stanford Colonial was a longstanding supporter of the Hobart Orphans School Association.

'Ah,' Reginald said, 'we welcome generosity like yours, Miss O'Callaghan.' Her eyes were focused on his mouth now as if she were devouring him, or rather as if she might wish to. Remarkable, he thought, quite remarkable. Women simply did not look at men in such a manner. Far from being disconcerted, Reginald found her behaviour extremely erotic – which is no doubt her intention, he thought. The woman was a predator. How very exciting. 'On behalf of the Association,' he said, 'I thank you most sincerely for donating your time and your expertise.'

'It is no hardship, I can assure you,' Shauna replied with an easy smile, her eyes now meeting his. 'I very much enjoy teaching children.' It was true she did enjoy teaching at the school, but she was grateful for the secret remuneration she received from her sister. Heavens above, she was between lovers: she couldn't survive on air. Although perhaps, she thought as she saw Reginald Stanford's eyes flicker to her bare shoulders, perhaps her pecuniary difficulties were about to be resolved.

'I think it's time we were moving on, old man,' Archibald said with a signalling glance towards the opposite side of the ballroom, where Evelyn was looking steadfastly in their direction. 'There are several colleagues we need to chat to.'

Reginald did not acknowledge Archie's warning; he didn't give a damn about his wife. Evelyn knew he had dalliances, and why shouldn't he? She was not only unexciting in bed, she was infertile. Reginald was sick of Evelyn.

'It's been delightful to meet you, Miss O'Callaghan. I do trust you'll enjoy the ball.'

'I know I shall, Mr Stanford.' Her smile was intimate, as if they were lovers. 'I am already enjoying myself,' she said, 'very much indeed.'

'Perhaps we will meet on the dance floor. They're bound to play a progressive waltz, wouldn't you say?'

'Yes I would, and perhaps we will. If so I shall look forward to our reunion.'

'And now, Archie, you're quite right,' Reginald dragged his eyes away from her, 'we must mingle; there is business to be done.' He might not give a damn about his wife, but he had a respectable position in society and appearances must be observed. Talking with Shauna O'Callaghan was like making love in public.

Half an hour later, following an energetic polka, the music ceased and the bandmaster stepped forwards.

'Ladies and gentlemen,' he announced, obeying the instruction relayed to him personally by Reginald Stanford, 'take your partners now please and form a circle for "The Parmelia Progressive Waltz".'

'Would you care to dance, my dear?' Reginald offered Evelyn his arm.

'I'd be delighted,' she said and they stepped out onto the dance floor.

Evelyn knew exactly what was going on. She and Reginald had had one obligatory dance early in the evening, after which he'd left her with the other wives while he mingled. It was true many of the husbands spent the evening conferring – a great deal of business was conducted at social functions like this – but other men's business did not include intimate conversations with beautiful, bare-shouldered redheads. And now Reginald was keen to participate in the progressive waltz.

As they took their places in the circle, waiting for the music to commence, Evelyn watched the woman with the flame-coloured hair being partnered onto the dance floor. This woman will be my husband's next conquest, she thought, and there was nothing she could do about it.

Evelyn Stanford's marriage was not a happy one, but like many a barren wife she held herself principally to blame. Reginald desperately wanted a son, and in two years of marriage she had failed to become pregnant. She annoyed him now and she knew it. They coupled regularly in the hope that she might conceive, but there was no joy in the act, so it was little wonder he sought his pleasures elsewhere. Evelyn prayed with all her heart that she would conceive and that God would grant her a son. If He did, then her husband would come back to her.

The band struck up and the dance commenced. In barely half a minute the couples would part, the ladies progressing on to their next partner.

Reginald watched as she came ever closer. He released his current partner from the circular waltz and held his hand out to receive the next woman in line. He enjoyed dancing, but his mind was not on the dance as hand in hand he and his new partner stepped forward three paces and then back three paces. He could no longer see her: she was behind him now. Then twenty seconds later, the circular waltz and there she was again, the green taffeta gown and red hair clearly visible in a sea of twirling bodies. He tried counting how many couples were between them, but the moment was too brief and she was still too far away. More partners arrived and moved on in the never-ending circle of the dance, and closer and closer she came. It was easy to count now: she was only three couples away. Then two couples, then one, and now as he stepped forward with his new partner she was right behind him.

The circular waltz, then the progression and suddenly her hand was in his. They had little time. There was no point in wasting it.

'We must see each other alone,' he said as they took their three paces forward and their three paces back.

'Yes, we must. Where do you suggest?'

'The Orient. Suite number eleven on the second floor.' Stanford Colonial maintained a regular suite at the Orient Hotel for the accommodation of visiting colleagues and as a venue for business meetings. The arrangement proved extremely convenient for Reginald.

'When, and at what time?' Shauna knew Hadley's Orient Hotel in Murray Street. Everyone did. It was the most elegant hotel in Hobart.

'Tomorrow afternoon, three o'clock.'

They were facing each other now in the next sequence of the dance, holding both hands, stepping towards each other and then back.

'Tomorrow is Sunday.' She twirled under his arm and they changed sides to repeat the step.

'So?'

'Sunday is the day I visit my family.'

'Monday then –' the circular waltz was coming up, they were running out of time '– Monday, three o'clock.'

'I shall be there.'

He put his arm around her waist, holding her close as they waltzed the final steps. 'I'm married,' he said. Best to prepare her, in case she had any illusions he was available.

'Of course you are,' she whispered into his ear. As if she didn't know that. Then she smiled and glided on to the next partner.

Reginald was accustomed to making his conquests with relative ease. Money and power could eventually seduce even the most proper of women, he'd found. But this evening, although his assignation had been made with record speed, he did not feel like a conqueror at all. To the contrary, he felt as though *she* had conquered *him*. How tremendously exciting, he thought. This affair was destined to be a torrid one.

The following day, Mara Dimbleby called around to her parents' home in Hampden Road. Mara visited at least once a month, always staying for the Sunday baked luncheon and always with her small son and daughter in attendance. She was rarely accompanied by her husband. Archibald found the O'Callaghan home stifling and unpleasant, particularly when Bernie was there, which he invariably was on a Sunday. Bernie's drinking habits disgusted Archibald. He would have steered his children well clear of the place if he'd had his way, but with a feisty wife like Mara he couldn't. 'You can like it or lump it, Archie,' she would say, 'but the children will grow up knowing their grandparents.' Mara openly acknowledged that she'd married a snob – it was one of the prices one paid for the security of a good marriage, she said to her mother, and Eileen was hardly likely to disagree. Archie was very generous to his wife, and his wife in turn was very generous to her family.

This Sunday, however, Mara had left the children at home with their nanny. She wanted to speak to Shauna alone, she announced with a meaningful look to her mother. Eileen, welcoming any sound advice Mara might offer to her wayward youngest daughter, refused any help in the kitchen and, while the roast was cooking, the two went into Shauna's bedroom.

The same room we shared as girls, Mara thought. It looked even smaller and there'd been three of them then with Kathleen at home. Behind her in the main living room, her father and her young brother were seated at the dining table drinking and chatting. Bernie was knocking back straight rum and Mick was sipping from a glass of rum-spiked milk. He'd given up the ale lately as it irritated his ulcer. Their talk was amicable enough as they played the charade of father-and-son camaraderie, but before the day was out Bernie would become obstreperous and Mick would become irritable. Mara closed the bedroom door.

'What's going on, Shauna?' she demanded as they sat opposite each other on the two small bunks. Like her mother, Mara always got straight to the point. 'I was watching you last night. I saw how you set your hat at Reginald Stanford. Why on earth did you bother?' Mara was justifiably annoyed. She'd gone to a great deal of trouble for her sister. 'The object of the exercise was to find you a husband. I introduced you to at least three eligible men last night, all of them ideal husband material –'

'And they were boring, every one of them,' Shauna said with a shrug, 'Reginald Stanford wasn't.'

'You're thirty-two years old, for God's sake.' Mara felt like hitting her sister. 'You need security in your life. Stanford is hardly going to offer you that.'

'How do you know? He's very wealthy. He may not be "husband material",' Shauna softened her mockery with a smile, 'but he is excellent "benefactor material", wouldn't you agree?' Much as she appreciated her family's care and concern, Shauna was heartily sick of Eileen's and Mara's nagging. When would they realise that 'husband material' did not interest her? When would they simply allow her to lead her own life?

'No, Shauna, you are wrong, Reginald Stanford is not excellent benefactor material at all.' Mara refused to lose her temper. She was determined to issue a serious warning. 'He does not keep mistresses. Archie tells me that to the best of his knowledge Stanford has never once kept a mistress. The man has brief *affaires de coeur* only.'

'Which means, like me, he is easily bored.' Shauna decided to call a halt to the discussion. 'We must therefore make it our mission to excite each other.'

'You have agreed to meet with him already?'

'Tomorrow, the Orient at three o'clock. I must say I'm very much looking forward to it.'

Mara found her sister's flippancy intensely annoying.

'Your last two lovers were married, weren't they?' she

said. The question was clearly rhetorical and Shauna simply nodded. 'Did you ever consider the wrongs that were perpetrated upon the wives of those men?

Her sister stared back uncomprehendingly.

'Those loyal women who wait at home faithfully while their husbands betray them,' Mara said coldly. 'Do you never think of your lovers' wives?'

'Are you worried that Archie might be cheating on you, Mara?' Shauna found the notion absurd – Archibald Dimbleby was besotted with his wife – but she couldn't understand why else her sister would pose such a question.

'Don't be ridiculous,' Mara said dismissively. She was supremely secure in the hold she had over her husband. She made it her mission in life to keep him satisfied. Archie would never stray. But in her heart of hearts, there were times when Mara secretly wished that *she* could. Sex was no longer the delirious, heady experience it had once been and, if the truth were known, there were occasions when she found herself actually envying her sister's freedom.

She curbed her impatience. 'I'm merely saying that I know Evelyn Stanford and she is a good woman.' It isn't fair of me, she thought, to blame Shauna for escaping the tedium of marriage. 'Reginald's multitudinous affairs have caused his wife quite a deal of pain over the past year or so.'

'Then just imagine how much happier her life will be when he has a regular mistress,' Shauna said. 'He will make a far better husband if he is not out seeking fresh conquests.' She was not being in the least facetious: the argument made perfect sense to her. And she *would* become Reginald Stanford's mistress, she decided. Mara's warning had only served to further whet her appetite – indeed she found the prospect of the challenge he presented most exhilarating.

Mara could see the eager light of anticipation in her sister's eyes. 'I worry for you, Shauna,' she said. 'You cannot spend your whole life chasing excitement.'

'Why not? If love isn't present, excitement is surely the next best thing. In fact I am of the opinion excitement may even surpass love.'

'There is a compromise, you know,' Mara drily suggested. 'There is marriage.'

'Not for me.' Shauna jumped to her feet. 'I shall become Reginald Stanford's mistress, thereby doing his wife a great favour. I shall keep him off the streets for a whole two years.' She laughed. 'Who knows, if he doesn't bore me, perhaps even longer.' She grabbed her sister's hand and hauled her to her feet. 'Now come along, Mara, do. The lecture is over. Lunch must be nearly ready, and I'm starving.'

Four years later, Shauna was still keeping Reginald Stanford off the streets. But their relationship was not at all as she had anticipated. Within just one year it had taken a turn she could never have foreseen. Shauna was in love.

CHAPTER FOURTEEN

'How is Evelyn?' she asked.

The late afternoon sun streamed through the heavy lace curtains of the bedroom window as they lay together naked, side by side, holding hands while they talked. Reginald, a private man, had never been comfortable in his nakedness. Even with his wife he had observed the niceties, never appearing unclothed before her, and sex, be it conjugal or adulterous, had always been a furtive affair conducted under the cover of darkness. Things were different with Shauna. In defying convention herself, Shauna had freed him of the inhibitions of a lifetime.

'She is strong,' he said. 'The doctor is most pleased with her progress.'

'I'm glad to hear it.' When their time was limited, as it was today for he was not staying the night, they didn't allow themselves the luxury of drifting off to sleep. Instead, they talked, and she always asked after Evelyn.

'Only several weeks now; God how I pray all goes well,' he said fervently, 'and how I pray it's a boy.'

'All will go well, dearest.' She could see the innate fear in his eyes. 'Evelyn has carried the baby to nearly full term and the doctor says she is strong. I am sure there will be no cause for concern.' She propped on an elbow and smiled down at him, the glare of her hair startling in the sun's rays. 'And if by chance the child is a girl,' she said challengingly, 'do not demean her, for we women are remarkable creatures.'

He laughed. 'Some of you are, my love.' He pulled her to him and kissed her. 'Oh yes, indeed, some of you certainly are,' he said as he felt himself becoming aroused. Again, he thought, and in such a short time. She was remarkable – there was no doubt about that.

During the four years of their relationship, Reginald had not once felt the desire to seek fresh conquests. In his eyes, no woman could match his mistress's beauty, and he doubted there were any who could match her sexual expertise. But there was another service Shauna offered that over the years had proved of inestimable value, more than even he could have realised. Shauna was his confidante, and as such she was possibly his very sanity.

Reginald had shared his feelings with no-one throughout the whole of his life, his anger and resentment remaining bottled inside, fermenting, occasionally exploding in a flash of rage or a black mood that seemed to come from nowhere. Now finally there was someone with whom he could communicate, someone he could trust. He had found an outlet.

It had been just one year into their affair when he had first poured out his rage: the day after his wife's first miscarriage.

'She lost the child!' He paced about the living room of the cottage in Molle Street, fists clenched as if he might smash everything in sight. 'The incompetent bitch couldn't carry it past four months!'

Shauna watched in silence. She'd never known the reason for his mood swings and she'd never enquired, she'd simply soothed away his anger by making love to him. She made no move now, but waited while he vented his anger.

'She's been barren for nearly three years.' he raged. 'Dear God, that should be grounds enough for divorce! I married her to expand the company, the perfect business merger ...'

So it isn't only women who marry for money, Shauna thought, detached and quite unmoved by his tirade. Men, even wealthy ones, sold themselves for a 'business merger', which only proved that everyone had a price.

'... I would build an empire for our sons to inherit, that was the plan. But what happened? She was barren! The bitch was barren!'

Reginald smashed his fist on the wooden mantelpiece above the small stone fireplace. A porcelain vase toppled on its side and crashed to the floor. He appeared not even to notice and Shauna made no move to retrieve the shattered remnants.

'The woman can't produce an heir! What damn use is she, I ask you.' The anger and frustration continued to spew out of him. 'Barren for three whole years, and now a miscarriage – what sort of a wife is that!'

'One who's not barren.'

It was the first time she'd spoken and her words brought him to a halt.

'What?' He looked at her, bemused, perhaps by her comment, or perhaps by the mere fact that she'd had the audacity to respond to his rhetoric.

'Your wife is not barren, Reginald. Evelyn has proved to you that she can conceive. It is a great shame for you both that she has miscarried, I agree, but she will conceive again; you just have to be patient.' In only seconds she had defused his anger. Then she boldly went one step further. 'And I believe also that you must be kind. It is difficult, I am sure, for a woman to conceive if she lives in fear of her husband.'

Their relationship had changed from that day on. Subtly at first, but as the months passed it became obvious they had moved to another plane altogether. They talked now. When he was in one of his moods, she would ask what was troubling him and, if he knew, he would tell her, although more often than not he had no idea what had triggered his ill-temper. Shauna observed that his moods often followed a visit to his father, and when she mentioned the fact he told her of his childhood, openly admitting to fears and resentments he would never have thought to tell a soul. As their discussions took on new depth, Reginald discovered a sense of freedom in Shauna's company. She had a calming effect that remained with him for some time after he'd left her. In fact she was the perfect mistress in every conceivable way. He congratulated himself on having found her.

Shauna may perhaps have outsmarted herself. She may have been subconsciously observing her mother's advice. 'In order to maintain a man's interest you must pretend an interest of your own,' Eileen had long ago instructed her daughters, 'give him your undivided attention and find him fascinating at all times.' Shauna's problem was, in becoming the outlet through which Reginald could channel his anger, she *had* found him interesting and he *had* become fascinating. During the first year of their affair he'd remained attractive to her, his moods and unpredictability merely adding to the sense of danger that had drawn her to him from the outset, but now she was discovering a new dimension, a vulnerability that only she was privy to. No-one else in the world knew Reginald Stanford as she did. But such intimacy came with a price. She found herself in love for the very first time, and this lent her a vulnerability of her own. It was a price she was prepared to pay.

She never told him she loved him. Such an admission might invite complacency, which would court disaster, but she was convinced he loved her too, in his own way. He'd proved it surely when he'd taken her to Europe. It had been over a year before. They'd travelled separately to the mainland, boarding the ocean liner in Melbourne, and the ensuing four months of their travels had drawn them closer than ever, cementing their relationship. He'd never openly admitted his love, it was true, and he probably never would, but he'd recognised his need for her, particularly during the crises of his wife's ongoing miscarriages. She'd been indispensable to him then.

'Be patient, Reginald: she carried the child for a full six months this time, be patient and kind, other chances will follow ...'

And then the third time, when he'd been in despair and revisited by the blackest of rages. 'You must not give up hope, dearest. The doctor has said she is to be confined to her bed throughout the next pregnancy. Every care will be taken; you must not give up hope.'

The doctor had actually voiced his doubts as to whether Evelyn was capable of carrying a child to full term, and by now Shauna thought he was probably quite right, but it was her duty to comfort Reginald, and she did.

Never once had she held any personal expectations, even when after the third miscarriage Reginald had sworn at the height of his fury that he would divorce his wife and find another. She doubted he would carry out such a threat, given his business involvement with Evelyn's father, but were he to do so she had no delusions that she would be his next matrimonial choice. She had nothing of value to bring to a marriage, no family fortune, no business or social connection that would be to his advantage. But marriage was immaterial anyway. The trip to Europe had sealed their bond and she was content to remain his mistress in the knowledge that their relationship was superior to that of husband and wife. Whether Reginald was prepared to admit it or not, he loved her. And that gave her a power no other woman in his life had ever possessed or was ever likely to.

'I've promised Father I'll visit the property at Pontville next week,' he said as he dressed. 'I could tell Evelyn I'm staying there two nights, what do you think?' He made the suggestion hopefully.

A whole night to themselves, how she would welcome the prospect, but she gave a light laugh and shook her head. 'Oh Reginald, you never stay longer than one night at Pontville. Evelyn is fully aware you detest the country.'

Shauna rose from the bed and shrugged on her silk dressing gown. She had never once met Evelyn, but she had spoken so often on her behalf she felt she knew the woman intimately. Indeed, she felt sorry for Evelyn and was quite comfortable, even genuine, in coming to her defence. Admittedly, there was an ulterior motive involved. Reginald had never loved his wife and never would. The preservation of Evelyn's marriage was very much to Shauna's advantage.

'You're right, as always,' he agreed. 'Wishful thinking on my part I'm afraid.'

She'd advised him that during his wife's confinement he should arrange stringently legitimate excuses for a night away from home. 'Be attentive, Reginald,' she'd urged, 'be attentive and loving, give her no cause to doubt you. She must avoid stress at all costs.' Now, with the birth so close and all appearing safe, it seemed to Reginald that, as usual, Shauna had been right.

'What would I do without you, my love?' he said, and he kissed her tenderly.

'What indeed?' she replied. If that wasn't a declaration of love, she didn't know what was. 'Enjoy the country-side,' she said helping him on with his jacket. 'I'll see you when you get back.'

He slipped out into the early dusk of the day and she locked the door behind him. She had wondered whether or not she should tell him her news, but she had decided to leave it for now. Better to wait until after Evelyn had given birth. Besides, she needed another fortnight to be absolutely certain, although in her heart she knew she was pregnant. She hoped that when the time came it would be a boy, for if Evelyn's child proved a girl, then at least Reginald would have a son. Not one he could acknowledge, it was true, not the legitimate son and heir he so craved, but a son nonetheless. She would ask and expect nothing beyond the current support he provided, but the child would be a secret the two of them could share, it would be a further bond between them.

Reginald left Stanford House early on the Monday, bidding Evelyn a fond farewell before he went.

'I shall be gone overnight only, my dear,' he said as he sat on her bed holding her hand, 'and when I return I shall not leave your side until the baby is born, I promise.'

Evelyn smiled gratefully. He'd shown such kindness and consideration during this pregnancy that he seemed like a different man. She'd lived for so long in a state of anxiety, fearing to disappoint him yet again, but of late her tension had eased in his company. She'd gained confidence; she felt strong now. She would bear him a healthy child. She could only pray that it would be a son. 'Have a safe trip, dear, and do give my fondest regards to Amy and the family,' she said.

'I shall.' He leant down and kissed her cheek. 'Take care.'

He caught the train to Brighton, a journey of around thirteen miles or so, crossing the Derwent at the causeway that led from Granton to Bridgewater and, when he arrived, Amy was waiting at the railway station.

She is so unmistakeably a woman of the land, he thought as he stepped off the train and saw her there. The slender young creature he vaguely recalled from his childhood days was long gone. Amy was stout and matronly and her hair, without the restrictions of a bonnet or scarf, was a mass of wild grey curls. She rather reminded him of one of the Merinos she so successfully bred.

Only one other passenger alighted at Brighton. As the train puffed up steam and chugged off on the next leg of its journey to Launceston, Reginald crossed the semi-deserted platform and greeted her.

'Hello, Amy, you're looking well.'

'Hello, Reginald,' she gave him a hearty hug. 'Good to see you at long last.'

He tried to return the hug with equal heartiness for he liked his half-sister, but heartiness did not come naturally to Reginald. 'Most flattering, I must say, to be picked up by the lady of the house,' he said as he followed her out into the street where the horse and trap were waiting. Her husband Donald or her son Edwin collected him as a rule, or else they sent one of the farm labourers.

'It's the lambing season so the men are busy,' she said, hauling herself up into the trap, 'besides which I haven't seen you for so long. I thought it would give us a nice chance for a chat.'

As he tossed his small travelling case in the back and climbed into the passenger seat he wondered whether her mention of how long it had been was intended as a criticism, and he wondered also what exactly she might wish to chat about. Given the recent discussion with his father, Reginald was immediately on the defensive.

'How is Evelyn?' Amy flicked the reins and the sturdy grey gelding set off at an obedient trot.

'She is very well, thank you,' he replied stiffly. 'The child is due in little more than a fortnight and the doctor does not envisage any problems.'

'Oh, what wonderful news.' Amy's homely face broke into a broad smile. 'I am so happy for you, Reginald.'

He relaxed: she was clearly genuine. 'Yes, it is a relief, I must admit.'

'And how is Father?'

His guard was up again in an instant. 'Father is father,' he said with cold indifference. 'Some things never change.'

'I meant his health, Reginald.' Amy, sensing her brother's defensiveness, decided she would have none of it. 'I hardly expect to hear of any change in Father's character – he will remain the cantankerous old man he has chosen to become – but he is ninety after all, and it is only natural I should enquire after his physical well-being.'

Realising he'd overreacted, Reginald gave a wry smile. 'I'm sorry to report that Father is as fit as ever,' he said, 'unfortunately for us all he'll probably live to a hundred.'

She laughed. 'He probably will. I am sure it is his intention.'

They relaxed in each other's company. She asked after Mathilda, noting the change in his face, how it softened when he spoke of his mother. What a strange man he is, she thought. But then the circumstances of his life had been strange from the start, growing up in that gloomy house she'd been so glad to escape from, and under the rule of an old man who'd turned into a tyrant. Their own relationship was bizarre to say the least. Here she was, his half-sister, yet she was only four years younger than his mother and had a son his age. No doubt it all compounded to make Reginald the remote man he has become, she thought, although he seemed that way even as a small boy. She recalled the occasion of their first meeting. He'd been six years old when she'd brought little Edwin to the city to visit his grandfather. Edwin had met his grandfather in the past when Silas had visited the property at Pontville, but it had been her first trip into town since her son's birth and the first meeting for both the boys and herself.

'Edwin, this is Reginald,' she'd said. It had felt odd to be introducing her six-year-old son to her brother of the same age.

'Hello, Reggie,' Edwin had said. He'd heard Reginald's mother call him Reggie and he was trying to be friendly.

'It's Reginald.' The voice had been firm, the ice-blue eyes unwavering, and poor little Edwin had been totally

flummoxed. Then Reginald had shifted his focus to gaze up
at the woman they had told him was his sister. 'My name is
Reginald,' he'd said in a tone that did not belong to a six-
year-old child, and Amy had been as nonplussed as her son.

He is a strange man indeed, she thought, noting that as
they talked he paid no attention at all to the surrounding
countryside. He never did. They were travelling through
the prettiest pastoral lands, where rolling hills and grassy
valleys were vibrant with early spring growth, but he might
as well have been at home in his own sitting room for all it
meant to him. Reginald was a creature of the city.

'Tell me about your latest trip to Europe,' she said. 'Did
you go to the Louvre?'

'Good heavens above, Amy – that was over a year ago.'

'I haven't seen you for eighteen months.'

'That long? Really?'

'That long, really,' she said with a smile to assure him
no criticism was intended. 'Now tell me about Europe.
I'm always so envious when you travel. Did you get to
Florence? Did you visit the Uffizi?'

He wondered what she would say if she knew the truth
behind his last trip. He regularly travelled overseas to
check on the company's business interests in London and
to meet with the French and Italian agents who handled
the sale of Stanford Merino wool to the fashion houses
of Europe, but last year's trip had not been for business
purposes. He had fled in order to escape his wife and the
madness that threatened to engulf him. After the third miscarriage his anger had been so uncontrollable he'd feared
he might kill Evelyn if he was forced to remain in her
company. Thank God for Shauna, he thought, remembering the pride he'd felt as he'd flaunted her beauty around
Europe, aware of the envy of others, the style of the
woman, her easy command of the French language. He'd
come back a different man. His anger gone, he'd been able
to offer sympathy and support to his wife, and now Evelyn

was about to bear his child. Shauna had proved yet again to be his very sanity and he wondered what in the world he would do without her.

'I saw Stefano in Milan and Jean-Pierre in Paris,' he said, about to recount his meetings with the wool agents, but Amy cut him off.

'No, no,' she said, 'we can discuss business later – I want to hear about the Louvre. And the Uffizi Gallery, did you get there? And did you see any theatre in London's West End? Do tell me every detail, Reginald. I rely upon you for my regular dose of culture.'

He obliged happily enough, finding it no hardship for he had a keen interest in the arts. His overseas trips invariably included visits to galleries and a night at the theatre. There had been more outings than ever this time of course, with Shauna as his companion, but that was not a fact he chose to share with his sister.

Amy listened attentively, enjoying the imagery he evoked of another world, but she was enjoying the scenery too. They were approaching Pontville now; up on the rise to their right stood the Catholic church and the cemetery. They travelled over the bridge and past the old military barracks and suddenly there they were in the middle of town with the gathering of stone cottages on the right and, up ahead on the left, the tavern and the general store. Then, just as quickly as they had arrived they were leaving, passing St Mark's Anglican Church at the top of the hill, the township now behind them.

'Blink and you'll miss us,' Amy always said with a laugh, but she liked Pontville and the village life it offered. Pontville was more than a pretty little town: it was a community of people who shared a love of the land and a loyalty to each other as strong as any family's. Probably stronger than some, she thought with a wry glance at her brother.

The Stanford property was barely a mile or so north of the village, and the sturdy grey gelding without a touch to the reins made an automatic turn into the drive that led to the family home. Set back just a quarter of a mile from the road, it was a beautiful two-storey stone farmhouse with a front garden that Amy personally tended and which was currently riotous with spring blossom.

'The garden's looking nice,' Reginald said.

'Thank you.' Amy smiled to herself. It was the first time during the entire trip that he'd appeared to actually notice something.

Donald, as always, took Reginald on a comprehensive tour, describing in detail each new piece of equipment that had been purchased. Reginald, as always, wished that he wouldn't. He had little interest in farm machinery and even less in Donald, who was a nice man, but a farmer with whom he had nothing in common. In fact Reginald could not understand what Amy, a well-educated woman, could see in her husband, but then he couldn't understand what she saw in the countryside either. It was abundantly clear, however, that she loved both. His sister had embraced the life of a farmer's wife in every possible sense.

Amy Stanford-Balfour did indeed love her husband very much, but upon marrying her father's overseer she had become far more than a farmer's wife. She had turned her intellect to the family business, developing a great passion for, and a great knowledge of, Merino breeding. There was no denying Amy had inherited her father's talents as a producer of fine wool. Little wonder Silas Stanford had been happy to leave his cherished property in the hands of his daughter and the highly capable man who had managed it for years.

Upon the men's return to the farmhouse Reginald continued to hide his boredom to the best of his ability, but with little success, which Amy as usual found mildly amusing. Her brother was first and foremost a business-man and his sporadic visits to a property that ran like clockwork without any necessity for intervention were either to appease his father or to irritate him – she was never sure which – and in the process he bored himself for no purpose. The relationship between Stanford father and son borders on ludicrous, she thought.

To Reginald's vast relief, the customary gathering of the clan was not to take place that evening. Edwin, who lived with his family in the comfortable home he'd built on the sub-divided property just a mile or so away, was keen to get back to his wife, who had not long ago given birth to their third child.

'We won't be coming over for dinner,' he said. 'I'll be getting home to Liz. I hope you don't mind, Reginald.'

'Not at all, not at all.' Reginald accepted the big farmer's hand Edwin offered. Like father like son, he thought.

'Wish Evelyn all the best for when her time comes,' Edwin said. He felt sorry for Reginald, who must surely be worried for his wife. It didn't seem fair that Evelyn should have such trouble giving birth while his own Liz popped her babies out like peas from a pod. 'Everything will go well, I'm sure,' he said awkwardly.

'Yes, I'm sure it will,' Reginald replied.

Edwin beat a hasty retreat, grateful for the excuse to leave: he never felt comfortable in Reginald's company. If the truth be known, he didn't actually like the man.

Business discussion cropped up over dinner, which was natural enough, there was little else they had in common, but after recounting to his sister and her husband the reports of his meetings with the European wool agents the previous year, talk turned towards the recent acquisition of two new stud rams and Reginald became bored. His mind started to wander.

There was no denying the Stanford-Balfours were good farmers and top breeders and, despite the needling he gave his father (more to irritate the old man than anything), Reginald believed they were correct in keeping the property exclusive to Merino wool production. But his eye was always on the far broader picture. Regardless of quality, the selling of a commodity was never enough, in his opinion. The path to wealth and power lay in total control. He'd told Henry Jones so just the other day.

'Set your sights on tin mining, Henry,' he'd said. 'There's big money in tin, and you can cut out the middle man in your cannery.' Jones had been very keen on the idea and would no doubt see it through, for he was an extremely crafty businessman. Indeed *The Mercury* had recently referred to Henry Jones as 'a tiger of industry' – a term which had rather annoyed Reginald. Half of Jones's ideas had come from him, after all, and where would the man be without the initial funds he'd provided? Reginald was aware his irritation was unreasonable for it had been his choice to keep their relationship shrouded in secrecy, but he considered himself far more 'a tiger of industry' than Jones. Besides, the term was altogether too grand for Henry. Henry was such a common little man.

Common or not, though, Henry is certainly moving up in the world, Reginald thought as he feigned interest in Donald's talk about the healthy number of spring lambs the ewes were producing this season.

'We need to police the births rigorously though,' Donald was saying, 'we've had a bit of a problem with feral dogs lately …'

Reginald nodded, although he hadn't really heard what was being said at all. Henry understands the importance of control, he thought. Why, Henry Jones's business was well on the way to becoming The House that Jack Built. He has the fruit that gives the pulp that makes the jam … The rhythm of the nonsense poem from his childhood bounced about in Reginald's brain. He has the mine that yields the tin that makes the cans that store the jam … he has the mill that cuts the wood that makes the crates that hold the cans that store the jam … Reginald found himself so amusing he nearly laughed out loud. Good God, he thought, all the man needs now are the ships that carry the crates that hold the cans that store the jam across the seas to England.

And therein of course lay the problem that confronted the Tasmanian export market in general. 'We must turn our attention to shipping,' he announced.

His comment was so abrupt and unexpected that Donald came to an immediate halt. *What does shipping have to do with feral dogs?* he wondered. Amy stared at her brother. *He hasn't heard one single word that's been said,* she thought.

'For some time now the larger shipping lines, particularly P & O and the Clan Line, have been sending fewer and fewer freighters to Hobart.' Reginald, undeterred by his audience's confusion, quickly warmed to his theme. 'With the expansion of the fruit export market, local shipping agents have been competing for growers' produce and booking more freight space than they can fill. It's hardly surprisingly the larger lines are refusing to come here when there's barely sufficient cargo to fill half their vessels' holds. This is an untenable situation for all of us in the export business. Fruit sits rotting on the harbour –'

'Wool bales don't rot,' Amy interrupted coldly. She was cross with her brother. Boredom was one thing, but it was quite another to be so blatantly rude, and particularly to Donald, who was always so good-natured.

Reginald ignored the interjection: her comment was not worthy of response anyway, and she was only on the defensive because he'd interrupted her husband. 'In order to ensure regular freight service with the major lines,' he went on, 'we need to book large amounts of cargo space and offer firm guarantees that we'll fill them.'

'That makes sense,' Donald said with a nod to his wife. Donald needed no-one to spring to his defence. He was an easy-going man, comfortable within himself, rarely threatened and rarely offended. 'How do you suggest going about it?'

'I shall enter into an agreement with several other

like-minded businessmen,' Reginald said – in fact he had already done so with both Henry Jones and W.D. Peacock – 'and between us we shall act as our own agents and offer our own guarantee. I'm sure there will be others queuing up to tender their cargo, which will pay for the exercise.'

'There'll no doubt be a lot of unhappy shipping agents too,' Amy commented drily.

'Quite possibly, yes.'

'Very clever, Reginald.' Donald gave an approving nod. 'Very clever indeed.'

'Thank you, Donald.' Amy's husband really isn't a bad chap at all, Reginald thought. In fact there were times when he quite liked Donald Balfour.

The following morning Amy drove Reginald back to Brighton, dropping him off at the train station.

'I won't wait around for the train,' she said as he was about to step down from the trap, 'I'll head off home if you don't mind. There's a lot to be done.'

'Good heavens above, yes, you get back to work.'

She gave him another hearty hug, which he returned as best he could. 'Don't leave it so long next time, Reginald,' she said.

'I won't,' he replied, but they both knew he would.

He climbed from the trap and stood waving to his sister as the sturdy grey gelding trotted off up the dusty road on its way home to Pontville.

A half an hour later, while the train puffed up steam in preparation for the final leg of its journey to Hobart, he leant back in his seat and breathed a sigh of relief. Thank goodness, another stultifying trip to the country was over and he could return to the stimulation of the city.

Reginald returned to far more than stimulation. He returned to the all-too-familiar signs that spelt chaos and disaster.

The moment he entered the house he knew something was wrong. For a start, Clive wasn't there to take his hat and his coat and his travelling case, and if Clive was engaged in other duties, then where was the maid? Where was the housekeeper? What was going on?

Even as he stood in the front hall wondering, the door that led through to the dining room and beyond that to the kitchen, opened. Young Dot, the maid, appeared carrying a bowl of hot water, fresh towels draped over her shoulder. Reginald dared not ask the question that sprang first and foremost to his mind.

'Where's Clive?' he asked instead.

'Mr Gillespie took the trap to the station hoping to meet you, sir,' Dot said as she started up the main staircase.

He followed her. 'I caught the tram.' He tried to sound normal, tried not to let his panic show. 'Why did he go to the station? What's going on?'

'Oh everything, sir,' Dot was taking the stairs two at a time, trying not spill the water, as this was her second trip to fetch fresh supplies, 'everything's happening all at once, it is.'

On the landing at the top of the stairs they encountered the housekeeper. Iris Watson bustled out of the master bedroom to take the bowl and towels from Dot, and through the open door behind her the muffled sounds could be heard of a woman fighting to stifle cries of pain.

'What's going on?' Reginald demanded. 'Is she miscarrying again?'

'No, sir,' the housekeeper answered, 'she's giving birth. The doctor and the midwife are both with her. Clive fetched them before going to the station in the hope of meeting your train.' Iris Watson was aware of the master's panic and, given past circumstances, she was not in the least surprised. 'Everything is going splendidly, sir. It's a little premature, but a perfectly normal birth the doctor says.' She smiled reassuringly. 'You stay here, and I'll leave the door ajar so you can hear the baby's first cries, it shouldn't be too long now.' She darted a glance at the maid. 'Wait on the landing, Dot, in case you're needed.'

Dot nodded, and the two of them waited, Reginald sinking into one of the two chairs that flanked the pedestal with its massive floral arrangement, and Dot standing rigidly to attention, like a miniature soldier in mob-cap and apron. Neither said a word, but both sets of eyes remained fixed on the four inch gap where the heavy wooden door sat ajar.

Evelyn's stifled cries were intermingled with voices, one of which Reginald recognised as Dr Harvey's. He couldn't actually hear what the man was saying, but he could make out the words of the other voice, a woman's; clearly she was the midwife.

'Push, dear,' she was saying, 'don't forget to breathe, there's a good girl. Nice big deep breaths. That's the way, very good. Now push, dear. Push and breathe, push and breathe …'

On and on she went, a meaningless litany, which Reginald presumed was supposed to be of some assistance to the woman in labour, although it didn't seem to be having a great deal of effect. Evelyn's cries were now more like strangled gasps as if in fighting them back she was suffocating.

Then the doctor spoke again, and this time Reginald could hear the man's words.

'It's all right to cry out loud, Evelyn,' Dr Harvey said, raising his voice to reach her beyond her pain. 'Don't hold back. You're nearly there, the baby's helping you, it wants to be born. Cry out if you wish.'

And Evelyn did.

Reginald jumped to his feet, shocked by the primal scream that sounded more animal than human. But the doctor seemed pleased.

'That's it. Good girl. I can see the head now. You're doing wonderfully, Evelyn, not long to go.'

Reginald stood by the door, staring at the four inch gap that led to the other room, hearing his wife cry out, hearing the doctor's words of assurance, hearing the midwife's litany of instruction, but all the while he was listening for just one sound: the cry of a newborn child.

Then everything changed. Evelyn's cries continued, but the doctor was not offering words of assurance now. The doctor was anxious. Reginald couldn't hear the exact words he muttered to the midwife, but alarmingly it was something about feeling no movement from the child. His instruction to Evelyn, however, was loud and clear.

'Push, Evelyn,' he said. 'Push as hard as you can.'

The midwife joined in, her words no longer a meaningless litany, but a series of distinct orders. 'Take both my hands, dear. Come along now, hang on to me and push with all your might. That's it. And again, push. And again, harder.'

Reginald listened as Evelyn's screams became guttural growls that issued from the very core of her being.

'Push, Evelyn, push,' the doctor urged.

'Hang on and push again, dear,' the midwife ordered. 'Push even harder.'

'It's coming,' the doctor said. Reginald could hear his every word now. 'It's coming, it's coming, well done, Evelyn, you're nearly there.'

Then Evelyn's unmistakeable wail of relief as she delivered her burden into the world.

Reginald waited breathlessly for the child's first cry.

But there was none. He heard no cry at all. Instead, he heard muttered words from the doctor to the midwife, but he couldn't distinguish what was said.

He waited a second longer and then another second, and still no newborn's cry. What was going on? He had to know.

He pushed the door open and stepped inside. No-one noticed him as he stood there watching the doctor free the cord from around the baby's neck.

He watched the doctor hold the child upside down by its ankles and smack its bottom sharply. Still there was no cry. There was no sign of life whatsoever and the child's face had a distinctly bluish tinge. It was a boy, Reginald noticed.

He watched the doctor hand the child to the midwife and turn his attention to the mother, his duty now clearly directed to the living.

'Rest, Evelyn,' he said, 'you've done very well, and now you must rest.' Evelyn was becoming agitated: she too was listening for the cry of a newborn.

Reginald's eyes did not leave the child. He watched as the midwife continued to perform presumably life-offering ministrations, patting its back, even blowing air into its tiny mouth as some midwives did in such situations. What is the point? he thought dully, the child is dead. The son that should have been his was dead.

Iris Watson, who had been positioned to one side waiting to be of assistance, made the sign of the cross and turned away from the sight. It was only then she noticed him standing motionless where he was over by the door.

She quickly came to his side, her movement calling the midwife's attention to the fact that the master of the house was present. The midwife frowned disapprovingly but did not cease her ministrations. She kept patting and puffing as if the child might live.

'What a tragic thing, sir,' Iris whispered, 'how sad you should be witness to such a sight. But rest assured, the mistress has survived. Your wife is quite safe. '

Reginald said nothing. He wished his wife was dead. His eyes remained fixed upon the child's lifeless body. His wife had given birth to a stillborn. He wished she'd died along with this corpse that should have been his son.

'Come away, sir,' Iris whispered. The poor man is in shock, she thought. 'Come away, sir, please. Come outside.'

Reginald did not budge. He continued to stare at the

corpse as though mesmerised. But surely his eyes were deceiving him. He blinked to clear his vision. He could swear he saw movement.

The midwife saw it too. She felt the child stir and saw the quiver of a hand, and she held the infant out before her, waiting expectantly as if she had known this would happen. Then the baby lifted up its head, and the mouth in the little blue face opened wide like a miniature cavern. The chest gave a mighty heave as tiny lungs hauled in air and suddenly the room was filled with the scream of a newborn child who was very much alive.

The midwife would later boast it was her ministrations that had saved the day, although the doctor swore the triumph was the child's. The baby had put up its own fight, he said; the baby had simply wanted to live. Whatever the reason, within only seconds the baby's face became a rosy red and its little arms and legs punched the air as if announcing a personal victory.

'You have a healthy son, Mr Stanford,' the doctor said, joining Reginald at the door. The midwife, who was now placing the baby in its mother's arms, had informed him of the intruder. 'I suggest you wait outside while we prepare the room. You may see your wife and child shortly.' The doctor too considered Reginald's presence to have been most unseemly.

'Of course.'

Reginald did as he was told and meekly retired to the landing where he sat by the flower arrangement and watched as Dot and Iris bustled past on their way down the stairs with armloads of bloodied linen and towels and bowls of murky water. He watched them again as they came back up the stairs with armloads of fresh linen and towels and bowls of clean water; each time they bustled past Iris Watson gave him a special smile.

Finally the servants and the midwife departed and Reginald was summoned to the bedside.

'You may see your wife and son now, Mr Stanford,' the doctor said, stepping out onto the landing. 'Both are in good health, although your wife is weary. She needs to sleep. I shall leave you alone together and call back tomorrow morning. In the meantime, Mrs Watson has my full instructions.'

'Thank you, Doctor. Thank you very much.'

The two men shook hands, the doctor left and Reginald stepped into the bedroom, closing the door behind him.

She was sitting propped up by pillows, the baby asleep in her arms, and crossing to the bed he sat gingerly beside her, wary of any movement that may disturb. He gazed down at his sleeping son, at the curl of the eyelashes, at the curve of the lip, at the little hand that clutched the edge of the blanket with such seeming purpose, the perfect little hand with its perfect little fingers and perfect little finger-nails. Everything is so beautifully formed, he thought, lost in the wonder of it all.

'Meet Rupert Stanford,' Evelyn said with a smile.

He dragged his eyes from the feast of his son and looked at his wife. Her hair, normally held in a tight black bun, hung freely to her shoulders. It was freshly brushed, but still damp with the perspiration of her efforts and there were deep shadows of fatigue under her eyes. Reginald thought she had never looked lovelier.

'My love,' he said, 'my dearest love,' and, leaning forward, he kissed her gently on the lips.

He has not called me his dearest love since the early days of our marriage, she thought. Not since those days when he'd shared his dreams with her, his dreams of the empire he would build for his sons to inherit.

'There will be other sons, Reginald.' Evelyn gave thanks to God. Her prayers had been answered. Her husband had come back to her. 'There will be other sons, I promise.'

Hobart, the sixteenth of September 1887

The Customs House Hotel on the docks was just across the road from Parliament House and therefore a favourite watering hole for parliamentarians. On this pleasant spring evening, a group of ten or more men were gathered at the bar discussing the legislation passed just the previous night when the voice of a stranger politely intruded.

'Excuse me, gentlemen, but may I enquire, have you ever seen one?'

The speaker who addressed them was an Englishman, a tall, lean man with a weathered face, sporting a top hat and cane and wearing a cravat with a large gemstone attached.

'Sorry?' A short chubby man with an iron-grey beard queried.

'Pardon the intrusion,' the stranger said, 'but I couldn't help overhearing your discussion about the new bill placing a government bounty on the head of the thylacine.'

'Ah yes?'

'Well, I've been asking around ever since I arrived in Tasmania and no-one I've yet encountered has seen one. A thylacine that is, a native tiger.'

'I've seen one,' the chubby man replied, 'I've seen several of them actually.'

'Where?'

'In Regents Park Zoo in London.' There was an appreciative titter from his drinking companions. The chubby man was known as a bit of a wag.

'Oh yes, I've seen those,' the Englishman replied, 'there are also specimens in the Paris and Berlin Zoos, but apparently they don't last long in captivity. I meant have you encountered one in its natural habitat.'

'Dear me, no,' the chubby fellow said, 'you wouldn't catch me out there in the wild. Not my cup of tea at all.' He glanced around at his companions, all of whom nodded.

'If one is to believe Mr John Lyne and the other parliamentarians pushing the resolution through so vociferously last night,' the Englishman said, 'these animals are responsible for the deaths of between thirty and forty thousand sheep annually. Surely that is an exaggeration, wouldn't you say?'

'It does seem like an inordinate amount.' The chubby man smiled as if at some private joke. 'Are you sure you heard correctly?'

'Oh, yes.' The Englishman nodded. 'I was in the public gallery. Mr Lyne went on to say that these "dingoes" run whole flocks of sheep down into gullies and maim more than they kill, and that they are the greatest pests the colony has.'

'John Lyne is renowned for his fertile imagination and the sometimes outrageous claims he makes from the floor of the House,' the chubby man said, again with a humorous twinkle in his eye. 'Why only last month he claimed there were seven hundred thousand fewer sheep in the colony than there should be, primarily because of tigers.'

'That is, indeed, a lot of sheep.'

'I'm of a mind to agree with you, sir. Given that the total number of sheep in the entire colony

is just over a million, one might be inclined
to believe Mr Lyne's mathematical skill leaves
a lot to be desired.' The last statement caused
a roar of laughter from the group. 'Forgive me,
stranger,' the chubby man said apologetically, 'a
little "in-House" joke you might say. Please allow
me to introduce my dear friend, the Honourable
member for Glamorgan, Mr John Lyne.'

An old man, eighty or more years of age stepped
forwards. 'John Lyne,' he said, extending his
hand. 'And whom do I have the honour of addressing?'

'Charles Elliot,' the Englishman replied, shaking
Lyne's hand, 'formerly Captain Charles Elliot of
Her Majesty's 3rd Dragoon Guards and now a special
correspondent for *The Times* of London.'

'*The Times*, no less!' Lyne cocked an eyebrow.
'So Captain Elliot, you were in the gallery and
witnessed last night's debate. Will you be reporting the resolution to our home country cousins?'

'Well, the sad plight of a little animal on
the far side of the world is hardly front page
news, Mr Lyne, but I must say there is concern
among some Fellows of the Royal Society in London
regarding the fate of this particular marsupial.
Several are of the opinion that its very existence
is threatened.'

'Nonsense,' John Lyne said dismissively. 'The
Tasmanian dingo is the scourge of the wool
industry. The entire colony is awash with the
things and the parliament has agreed they must be
stamped out once and for all. If you were in the
public gallery last night, you surely heard the
decision. Practically unanimous it was!'

'Twelve ayes and eleven nos is hardly unanimous.'

'I said practically unanimous,' Lyne replied,
and he guffawed at his own wit, bringing another
round of laughter from his cronies.

Charles Elliot had up until now successfully

contained his anger, but in truth he couldn't decide which he found more unforgiveable: the man's ignorance or his arrogance. Lyne had incorrectly referred to the thylacine as a dingo last night too, in parliament of all places, and the barefaced fabrication he and others had used to sway the vote had been nothing short of disgraceful.

'Mr Lyne, I feel bound to tell you that the contempt for the democratic process I witnessed last night compels me to submit a report to *The Times* by telegram at the earliest possible opportunity –'

I beg your pardon!' Lyne blustered.

'Your behaviour, and that of your accomplices, made a mockery of democracy –'

'Damn you, sir!'

'I shall tell my editor that you are not fit to hold public office –'

'Oh will you just? Well let me tell you, sir,' Lyne trumpeted triumphantly, 'the editor of *The Times*, Thomas Chenery, is a very close and dear friend of mine and –'

'If that is the case, sir,' Elliot interrupted, 'you will be deeply saddened to learn that Mr Thomas Chenery died three years ago. My editor is Mr George Buckle.' In the silence that followed Charles took a deep breath. 'Now, please excuse me,' he said to the group in general. 'I suddenly have the desire for fresh air and a ship to carry me far away from this hateful city as quickly as possible.'

CHAPTER FIFTEEN

Reginald did not visit Shauna for a whole fortnight after the baby's birth, which was most unusual: as a rule he called upon her at least twice a week. Far from berating him for his neglect, however, she greeted him with the warmest congratulations.

'A son and heir,' she said as she ushered him into the Molle Street cottage, 'oh my dearest, how wonderful.'

Shauna had heard the news from her sister Mara. In fact she had heard the news only the day after the birth. Mara had called around with the express purpose of telling her.

'Evelyn Stanford gave birth yesterday,' Mara had announced dramatically, 'Archie told me. Reginald has been broadcasting the news to all his business acquaintances.'

'Oh.' Shauna had indeed been surprised. 'A little premature, but I take it all went well?'

'Exceedingly well,' Mara had said with ominous overtones.

'What's that supposed to mean?'

'It was a son.'

'So?'

'So do you still think he'll welcome your bastard child?'

Shauna had told Mara of her pregnancy just the previous week, swearing her to the utmost secrecy, and

Mara had been horrified. Shauna's decision to have a child was, in Mara's opinion, quite insane and now more so than ever.

'He has a legitimate son and heir, Shauna, why would he want a bastard?'

'Because he loves me.'

Mara had given a snort of derision. 'Reginald Stanford is incapable of love,' she'd said.

Shauna had refused to find the remark offensive, taking the lofty stance instead. 'You really shouldn't pass judgement upon a subject that is beyond your comprehension, Mara,' she'd said. 'You have never been in love, so how could you possibly know?'

Mara's misgivings had, however, aroused a vague uncertainty in Shauna. It would perhaps have been preferable if Evelyn's child had been a girl, she thought.

'I am so happy for you, Reginald,' she now said. Despite any doubts her sister may have instilled in her she *was* happy for him. The anger had left him: she could see it in his eyes. 'You are content, I can tell.'

'Yes, my love, I am. And it is all your doing.' Taking her hand in both of his, he turned it over and kissed her palm, a gesture of both affection and gratitude.

She laughed. 'I am hardly the one who just gave birth to your son, dearest.'

'I believe without you it would never have happened,' Reginald replied in all seriousness. 'My anger lived like a poison in that house. Without your influence and the wisdom of your advice, I doubt Evelyn would ever have given birth. She feared me. She has told me so.'

'I am glad she is now able to speak openly with you.'

'So is she,' he said with a smile. 'We are closer than we have ever been, and all because of you, my love.'

Any uncertainty Shauna may have felt disappeared as he kissed her. Reginald's love was palpable.

His desire too was strong and their lovemaking passionate.

'God how I've missed you,' he said when they lay sated, their bodies entwined and still damp with the sweat of their exertion.

She sat and pulled the coverlet over them. It would soon be November, but the afternoon was unseasonably chilly. Then she lay on her side facing him to deliver her news.

'I am carrying your child, Reginald.'

He turned to look at her. He made no comment and his expression was unfathomable; he seemed to be waiting for her to go on.

'I've wanted to tell you for the past fortnight or so, but I thought it wise to wait until after Evelyn had given birth.'

'You have known for some time?' Again his reaction was unreadable. He appeared puzzled more than anything.

'I have suspected, yes, but I am now quite certain.'

'You seem pleased.'

'I am. I long to bear your child, Reginald.' Shauna did not expect him to embrace the idea immediately, at least not until she had given him the full assurance he was owed. 'I will ask nothing of you. I naturally will expect no recognition of the child, and I will need no further financial support – your current generosity will amply provide –'

He interrupted. 'You have very cleverly avoided conception for four years, Shauna. Is this pregnancy a deliberate act on your part?'

She recognised the accusation in his tone, but decided nonetheless to answer honestly. 'It was not a conscious act, I promise you, but perhaps in my heart of hearts I willed it to happen. I only know that when I suspected I was pregnant I welcomed the idea. I am thirty five years old, Reginald, and had thought never to experience motherhood. The prospect of bearing your child fills me with the greatest of joy –'

'You will get rid of it.' He threw back the coverlet, rose from the bed and started dressing.

She sat up, her face a picture of dismay. 'You surely do not mean that.'

'Of course I mean it.' He didn't even deign to look at her as he pulled on his trousers. 'What else did you expect me to say? You will get rid of the child. Those are my instructions.'

'But Reginald, please reconsider, I beg you. I am asking nothing of you that you do not already give –'

He spun about to face her. 'You are asking the *world* of me, you foolish woman!' In one split second his coldness had turned to black rage. 'Did you seriously think I would threaten my reputation and that of my family by agreeing to sire a bastard? Did you seriously think I would do such a thing?'

'But no-one would know, I swear.' She had seen his black rages on many an occasion, although never once directed at her. 'The child would be our secret, our bond. It would be the gift that we shared with each other.

'And why would I share such a *gift* with you, Shauna,' he spat the words out with contempt, 'when the discovery of such a *gift* could bring about my downfall? Why would I do such a thing, tell me that!'

'Because you love me, that's why!' She hurled it at him like an accusation.

The black rage seemed to depart as quickly as it had appeared, and he studied her for a moment or so, openly admiring her naked beauty. 'You're right,' he said, 'I do love you.'

She felt a surge of triumph. She knew it; she had always known it.

'I love the way you look,' he said. 'I love the way you are in bed. I love the way you walk and talk and laugh, I love everything about you.'

If this is a declaration of love, she thought, why is it made so coldly?

'But I hardly love you enough to destroy myself. I will not have my standing in society compromised simply because you have a whim to give birth.' He put on his jacket and crossed to the door. 'You will get rid of this child, Shauna. You will get rid of it, or I will get rid of you. The choice is yours.'

He left, closing the door quietly behind him.

The choice is not mine at all, Shauna thought. He had made it for her in no uncertain terms. She could not bring up a child on her own without support, or if she could she had no desire to do so. But the choice he had made for her was not based upon practicalities in any event: it was far simpler. Him or the child, he'd said.

Four days later, at the appointed hour of seven o'clock on Saturday night, Shauna opened the door to Eliza Godfrey. Eliza Godfrey was a midwife who doubled as an abortionist for those who had the extra cash to pay. She made discreet visits to people's homes upon request and was known to be highly efficient.

Shauna ushered her inside and locked the door.

The gathering at the O'Callaghan house that Sunday was a very low-key affair. It was not one of the weekends Mara had chosen to visit with her children and for some strange reason Shauna was not there. No-one knew why she hadn't turned up, for she never missed the family baked lunch, but with only her parents and brother present she was sorely missed. Shauna was the regular buffer between Mick and Bernie and, without her calming influence, Bernie became more obstreperous, Mick more abrasive, and Eileen lost her temper with them both.

The following morning, Eileen called around to the cottage in Molle Street to check if everything was all right.

She knocked several times on the front door; there was no answer so just by chance she tried the handle, although she did not for one moment expect the door to open. It did. How odd, she thought. Shauna never left the front door unlocked.

She stepped inside. The sitting room was deserted.

'Shauna?' she called. No answer.

She walked through to the kitchen, which was also deserted.

'Shauna?' she called again. Still no answer. Eileen was puzzled. Why would Shauna go out and leave the house unlocked? Then she walked through to the bedroom.

'Oh God,' she breathed, 'oh dear God, no.'

Shauna might have been asleep, lying on the bed in her nightdress as she was, her eyes closed, seemingly at rest. Except that her face was stark white and the bed and the nightgown were all drenched in her blood, as was the rolled-up towel she had placed between her legs to stem the flow.

Eileen had seen such a sight on a number of occasions. Many a whore in the brothels where she'd worked had taken this dangerous path.

She crossed to the bed and looked down at her daughter, reading the tell-tale signs, adding up in her mind the sequence of events. It was quite clear the abortion had not been self-induced. Shauna had hired an abortionist, who had completed the task and left presuming all had gone satisfactorily, which would explain why the door was unlocked. But after the abortionist had left, Shauna had started to bleed. Judging by the rolled up towel between her legs she may even have considered it a normal part of the process to start with. The scenario was a simple and age-old one. And so were the questions such a lonely death raised.

How long had it taken, Eileen wondered. Had Shauna realised she was dying? Had she been terrified, watching her life's blood ebb from her? Or had she lapsed into unconsciousness without knowing she was bleeding to death? Eileen decided upon the latter. Not only because it was of some comfort, but because Shauna did, after all, look at peace.

She removed the towel, now stiff and matted with her daughter's blood, and eased the nightdress down over Shauna's legs. This is the price you pay, my darling, for becoming a rich man's mistress. She wasn't sure whether or not she said the words out loud. So many women had paid the same price, and so many women would continue to pay it. How very sad it all was.

She sat on the blood-drenched bed, ignoring the still-moist congealed pools that rested in the linen's folds, and she smoothed her daughter's hair back from her white, white face.

'Oh, my darling girl,' she said, 'oh my darling, darling girl.' Then she leant down and, gathering her daughter in her arms, she rocked her as she would a baby and wept. Eileen O'Callaghan had wept only once before in her whole life. It had been the day her father had abandoned her and she'd been thrown out of her home. On that day she'd walked through the streets of Dublin swathed in tears. She had thought she would never cry again.

Ten minutes later, she gathered herself together and left the house to inform the family of the news.

'She's a very fine vessel indeed, there's no denying it,' Silas said admiringly and beside him Mathilda nodded agreement.

'She certainly is, Reggie, you've every right to be proud.'

It was Tuesday morning and Reginald had brought his parents down to Constitution Dock to admire the SS *Lady Evelyn*, which had arrived from the Huon just the previous day bearing a full cargo of timber for shipment to the mainland. Evelyn had not accompanied them to view her namesake for it was barely three weeks since the birth of baby Rupert.

As the three of them stood amid the hustle and bustle

of the docklands, their coat collars turned up against the nip in the southerly breeze, they were not the only ones to admire the new steamer. The *SS Lady Evelyn* looked particularly elegant amongst the other working vessels sitting in the dock and many a comment could be heard from passers-by.

'Yes,' Reginald said, 'George Powell is a master craftsman, there's no doubt about that.' He decided to take advantage of the moment and push another expansion idea his father's way. In Reginald's opinion Stanford Colonial should aim to acquire its own fleet for trade with the mainland and perhaps even Britain, thereby eliminating altogether the need to rely upon major shipping lines. He was aware his father would dismiss such a grandiose plan, but he felt there was no harm in planting the seeds that might eventually lead them in the right direction

'The Powell family is rather impressive all round, Father,' he said, 'and I'm thinking we should perhaps join forces with them. They have a whole fleet doing the Huon run, you know.'

'A whole fleet, eh.' Silas was beyond dismissive. He didn't even register the topic as worthy of conversation. 'They'd better watch out is all I can say. A whole fleet can spell disaster. Look what happened to Alexander McGregor.'

Reginald felt a flash of annoyance. Was it the old man's intention to irritate? 'I fail to see the logic in that remark, Father,' he said icily. 'Fifty years ago McGregor's was the largest and most successful individually owned fleet operating south of the equator. Where is the warning in that?'

'Ah, but the death of whaling saw the death of his fleet, didn't it?' Silas pointed a bony and triumphant finger at his son. 'He overextended himself. 'No whales left and too many ships: that's not sound business logic. Keep your parameters realistic, I say.'

Reginald longed to hit his father. How smug, he thought,

how smug and how totally irrelevant. The old man was deliberately baiting him.

Mathilda, sensing her son's annoyance, came smoothly to the rescue. 'I like Alexander McGregor,' she said. 'He is a fine man.'

'Yes, you're right, my dear,' Silas agreed, 'he is a good man. Popular fellow too.' Silas had not been deliberately baiting his son at all. Silas Stanford was in an excellent mood. He felt quite sprightly and was very much enjoying being out and about. 'And the man has excellent taste, I'll give him that much.' He jabbed his walking cane in the direction of Battery Point, where McGregor's stately mansion, Lenna, sat high on the hill overlooking the Derwent and the whole of Sullivan's Cove. 'That's a damned fine piece of architecture.'

They gazed across the harbour at the elegant sandstone building that dominated the skyline, and for once Reginald couldn't disagree with his father. Lenna was in his opinion one of the finest homes in Hobart, far finer than Stanford House, and its position was undoubtedly the grandest. A perfect example of Italianate style architecture, the building was a thing of beauty and its location a symbol of power. Reginald longed to own Lenna. Were he ever successful in purchasing the property he would of course change the name to Stanford Manor to lend it the dignity it deserved. McGregor's choice of an obscure Aboriginal word apparently meaning 'living place' was utterly absurd.

Reginald had already tried to purchase Lenna. Twice he'd approached the old man and made offers, but each time the answer had been a resounding no. The McGregor clan had even looked upon his offers as in rather poor taste, given the fact that old Alexander had been suffering bouts of dementia for several years. But Reginald hadn't cared. Business was business and if, in a moment of demented confusion, McGregor had said yes, Reginald would have held him to it. Allowing sentimentality to play any part in a deal was foolish.

'Let's go for a stroll,' Mathilda suggested, gratified her change of subject had proved successful and that argument had been avoided. 'The fresh air is doing you the world of good, Silas, I can tell.'

'You're right my dear, it is, it is.'

They set off down Morrison Street where, just one block from the wharf, ships' chandlers and providores did a roaring trade alongside the hotels and the alehouses that never seemed to close.

As they reached Elizabeth Street, Reginald was about to make his excuses and leave his parents to themselves: he had no desire to walk with his father and there was little advantage to be found in any business discussion, for the old man was clearly in a mischievous mood. But before he could say anything, Archibald Dimbleby appeared by his side, breathless and in a state of obvious agitation.

'I've been looking for you everywhere, Reginald. I must speak with you immediately.' He tipped his hat to Mathilda and apologised profusely to Silas. 'Please forgive the rudeness of this intrusion, sir, I beg you, but it is a matter of some urgency.' Archibald Dimbleby, like most, held old Silas Stanford in the greatest esteem.

'Yes, yes, I can see that.' Silas waved his cane at them as if they were children. 'Off you go then. Come along, my dear,' he offered his arm to his wife, 'we'll be on our way.' Mathilda smiled a farewell over her shoulder to her son as her husband marched her across Elizabeth Street.

'I went to your offices and they didn't know where you were.' Archibald was more than agitated, he was on the verge of hysteria. 'And then I called around to Stanford House and your man told me you were down at the docks ... I've been looking for you everywhere, Reginald –'

'What the devil is the matter with you, Archie? Get a grip on yourself, do.' Reginald frowned disapprovingly. Archie was making a spectacle of himself. 'Come along now, calm down. Take a couple of deep breaths and pull yourself together, there's a good chap.'

Archibald did as he was told.

'Right,' Reginald said when he could see the man had regained a semblance of control, 'now tell me what's going on. What the deuce has happened to get you in such a state?'

'It's Shauna O'Callaghan.'

Reginald glanced about at the busy intersection. Workers were carrying barrels of ale from a dray into the Franklin Hotel and pedestrians were standing on the corner waiting for a carriage and four-in-hand to pass before crossing Elizabeth Street. Archie had not spoken loudly, no-one could have heard him, but one's mistress was not a topic normally bandied about in public places.

'What about her?' he muttered.

'She's dead.'

Reginald stared uncomprehendingly at Archibald Dimbleby. What had the man just said? Had he just said that Shauna was dead? Was that really what he'd said? Reginald wasn't sure if he'd heard correctly.

'She bled to death in her own home, on her own bed – an abortion. Her mother discovered her yesterday.'

So it's true, Reginald thought, I *did* hear correctly. Shauna is dead. But how could it be? That glorious creature, gone from this world, gone from his life ... Why did he find it so impossible to believe?

'We have to talk, Reginald. This affects us all.' Archie was becoming jittery again. Why in God's name was the man not saying something? 'We can't allow the story to become public: it could ruin us. We need to talk for heaven's sake, we need to make a plan –'

'You need a brandy, that's what you need.'

Grasping Archie firmly by the arm, Reginald steered him into the Franklin Hotel and through the bar where, even at ten o'clock in the morning, there were a number of hardened drinkers. He walked him on into the back parlour, which was fortunately deserted, and seated him in the corner.

'Stay there and pull yourself together,' he said, 'I won't be long,' and, dumping his light felt hat on the table, he returned to the bar.

When he reappeared several minutes later with two glasses of brandy he was relieved to discover Archie in a considerably calmer state. Reginald, having recovered from his initial shock, found the man's show of hysteria intrusive and intensely aggravating. He wanted to be left alone; his mind was jumbled and he needed to think.

'So what exactly is this *plan* you believe we should talk about?' he said coldly. The loss of his mistress was surely none of Archibald Dimbleby's business.

'Mara is utterly distraught,' Archie said after he'd taken a sip of brandy, trying not to cough for he rarely drank hard liquor and certainly not at ten in the morning. 'She was sobbing throughout the night. She didn't sleep a wink, and she was still crying this morning – I've never seen her so distressed.'

Of course, Reginald reminded himself, Mara Dimbleby is Shauna's sister. He supposed that did give the man some justifiable degree of involvement.

'Mara knew that her sister was pregnant,' Archie went on. 'She says they discussed the matter at some length and that Shauna very much wanted to have the child. She blames you, Reginald. She holds you responsible for the abortion and therefore the death of her sister.'

'Does she now?' Reginald said. 'Does she really?' There was an unpleasant edge to his tone. 'And how about you, Archie. What do you think?'

'Me?' Archie was unnerved. 'What do I think about what?'

'Are you also apportioning blame? Can you tell me in all honesty that you would allow a mistress of yours to bear your child?'

'Of course not,' Archie nervously avoided the ice-blue eyes, 'unthinkable, utterly unthinkable.' I wouldn't have had a mistress in the first place, he thought, but he didn't dare say it out loud. He found Reginald's manner most intimidating. 'But you must understand that Mara's reaction is indicative of her family's,' he said with some urgency, 'and this is where our problem lies.'

'I see.' Reginald nodded thoughtfully. He did indeed see that it was to his advantage to pay attention to Archie. Shauna had told him only the barest facts about her family; a hard-nosed businesswoman of a mother and a publican father, he recalled. Two sisters – one in Hobart, one in Launceston; two brothers – one disappeared overseas and one a drunk. So much he'd gleaned, but little more. And they were likely to cause trouble, were they? Archie had married into this motley bunch, so he should know. 'Go on,' he said.

'The family is distraught. They're Irish, you understand, and very prone to drama. They're also common, although I must admit appearances can be deceptive, certainly where the daughters are concerned. They are unconventional and show little regard for the normal standards of social behaviour. In fact they don't seem to care what people think of them, even when it comes down to an event as shameful as this ...'

Archibald Dimbleby detested his involvement in the whole sordid business. This is the price one paid for having married beneath oneself, he thought. Much as he loved his wife, Archie cursed her family. He cursed the O'Callaghans, and he cursed himself for introducing Reginald to Mara's slut of a sister, and above all he cursed Reginald Stanford for his infidelity. Why couldn't the man honour his marital obligations and live as decent men should?

'The O'Callaghans are quite likely to spread this hideous news all over Hobart, Reginald,' he burst out. 'I cannot have it known that my wife's sister died aborting your child. I dread to think what it would do to the Dimbleby name.'

'A great deal less than it would do to the Stanford name, I should imagine,' Reginald said caustically, although the irony of his remark went quite unheeded.

'Exactly,' Archie agreed with fervour. 'Neither of us can risk this story becoming public. The Dimblebys and the Stanfords are among those who made this town, Reginald. Our families' names are synonymous with respectability, with philanthropic works, with the building of churches and schools. We cannot allow ourselves to be dragged through the mud. I will not have my family –'

'Look to your own house, Archie.' Reginald cut him off: he was not about to be lectured to by the likes of Archie Dimbleby.

'I beg your pardon?'

'Your wife. Can she be trusted to keep her mouth shut?'

'Oh dear me, yes. Mara would not allow the name of her children to be besmirched. Much as she grieves, she will take the secret of her sister's death to her grave rather than threaten –'

'Good,' Reginald said abruptly, 'and the rest of the family, do you think they can be bought?'

'I don't know.' Archie started to dither. Reginald's sharpness was unsettling. 'I suppose they might, I really couldn't be sure. They're a strange lot, the O'Callaghans.'

'The parents live in Hampden Road, don't they?'

Archie nodded. 'The white wooden cottage near Runnymede Street,' he said. 'What do you intend –'

'Finish your drink. It'll do you good.' Reginald donned his hat as he stood. 'Have mine too while you're at it,' he said and he left Archie sitting in the parlour like a lonely drunk with two full glasses of brandy.

Reginald visited his bank, where he withdrew quite a sizeable amount in the form of a letter of credit. He collected some papers from his safety deposit box and completed a little further business with the bank manager, and it was close to midday when he knocked upon the front door of the O'Callaghan's house.

Mick had just arrived home for lunch. He always came home for lunch these days, Eileen's potato soup being kinder to his ulcer than the rich stews they served at the Hunter's Rest.

Eileen had left him in the kitchen tending the saucepan on the stove while she set the table. She carved two chunks of bread from the loaf she'd purchased that morning and was about to spread them with a thick layer of butter the way Mick liked them when she heard the knock on the front door.

She recognised him in an instant.

'Mrs O'Callaghan?'

She made no move and said nothing.

'I'm Reginald Stanford.' He took off his hat but didn't offer his hand – it seemed fairly evident she would refuse it.

'I know who you are.'

'May I come in?' Silence. 'Please, Mrs O'Callaghan. There is something I very much wish to say to you.'

She shrugged indifferently, stepped to one side, and he entered.

Mick had heard the front door and he peered through from the kitchen to see who the visitor was. He too instantly recognised Stanford.

'Mr O'Callaghan.' Reginald was surprised to see the Irishman framed in the kitchen doorway. He'd expected him to be at work and had presumed he would be dealing with the woman of the house only. 'How do you do, sir, I'm Reginald Stanford.' He made no move to offer his hand, sensing again that it would be rebuffed.

'What are you doing here?' Mick stepped into the dining room.

Eileen closed the front door and, as husband and wife

joined forces beside the table, Reginald wondered if he should feel threatened.

'I have come to offer my sincerest condolences,' he said. 'I loved your daughter very much. Indeed, had I been a free man I would have wished with all my heart to marry her.' He could tell they didn't believe him. The Irishman's expression was one of loathing and the eyes of the woman, eyes so like Shauna's he realised, were studying him with calculated scepticism, wondering why he'd come.

'I swear to you I have never loved anyone as deeply as I loved Shauna,' he said, marvelling at the fact that it was actually true, 'and I know I will never again experience a love such as we shared. You may believe that or not, choose as you wish, but I am telling you no lie.' It was indeed no lie, for although Reginald had allowed himself little time to dwell upon the personal impact of Shauna's death, he knew he would never again seek another mistress.

He waited for their reply, but they remained silent, their expressions unchanged; and realising his declaration had made no helpful impact Reginald turned to business.

'I naturally wish to pay for Shauna's funeral and for any other expenses that may be incurred throughout this whole sad business,' he said with all the sincerity he could muster, 'and to that end I have with me a letter of credit.'

He took a sheaf of papers from his inner coat pocket and, selecting the letter from among them, he held it out wondering which of the two would take it. He was not surprised when it proved to be the woman.

Eileen unfolded the letter and looked at the sum. Very generous, she thought, enough for any number of funerals.

'I also have here the deeds to the house that was Shauna's home for the past four years,' Reginald said. 'I cannot bring myself to visit the place and I no longer have any wish to own it, given the memories it holds.' He placed the papers on the table. 'The Molle Street property is yours to do with as you will. I have had the deeds signed over and all the arrangements made. You need only complete your details and present them to the bank manager in order to finalise the transaction.'

Again he awaited their response. Would they throw the papers back in his face and tell him to get out? Would the man attack him? He certainly looked as if he wanted to – his loathing was palpable. The woman, on the other hand, was less readable. He sensed no personal hatred from her. She is hard, he thought. She is hard and calculating. He'd put his money on the woman taking the practical path.

The woman did. She picked the papers up from the table and without even looking at them she handed them to her husband. Reginald waited to see what the Irishman would do.

Mick stared down at the deeds. For the past four years he'd found it ironical and even vaguely amusing that his daughter was being kept in style by Silas Stanford's son. And now his daughter was dead and Silas Stanford's son was buying his silence with a house. Mick remembered how all those years ago Geoffrey Lyttleton had bought his silence with the very house they were standing in. History seems to be repeating itself in so many ways, he thought. But this time things were different. This time things weren't right. They weren't right at all. The fingers of his right hand balled into a fist. Stanford will pay for the death of my daughter, he thought murderously. Then he looked at his wife.

'We can't bring her back, Mick.' Eileen's voice was devoid of emotion; she was just stating the facts. 'We can't bring her back.'

The fight suddenly went out of Mick. What's the use, he thought. He shoved the papers in the pocket of his jacket and looked down at the floor.

Transaction completed, Reginald left. He had successfully bought off the O'Callaghans. An implicit understanding had been reached between them and upon the parents' instruction the rest of the family would follow suit.

The rest of the family, as it turned out, did not include Bernie.

Bernie called around to Stanford House the following night. It wasn't even late, barely eight o'clock, but Bernie was already staggering drunk. He'd been drunk for three days, passing out for a few hours and then starting all over again. He hadn't drawn a sober breath since he'd learnt of his sister's death.

'You tell Stanford I want to see him, do you hear me? You tell Stanford I'm here and I want to see him.'

Reginald heard the commotion and opening his upstairs office window he parted the curtains and peered out to see what was going on in the courtyard below. It appeared a drunken oaf had had the audacity to come to the front door and Clive Gillespie, having shepherded the young man from the porch, was now trying to see him off the property.

'You tell Stanford that Bernie O'Callaghan wants to have a word with him,' the young man persisted, stumbling a little, but holding his ground. 'You tell him it's about my sister.'

Reginald quickly stepped away from the window and let the curtains fall back into place. O'Callaghan's ramblings were barely coherent at the moment, but God knew what accusations might be hurled for all to hear if the fool caught sight of him. He watched through the slit of the curtain as the action, clearly visible in the courtyard's lamplight, unfolded below and he listened intently for any giveaway comment that might spew from the mouth of the drunkard. Thankfully the bedrooms and nursery were to the rear of the house and Evelyn was well out of earshot.

'You will leave this property immediately or I shall summon the police.' Clive Gillespie, a burly man, was not easily intimidated and certainly not by a young ne'er-do-well like this. He could have flattened the chap had he the mind, but that would only have presented further complications. It was better to do things by the book and usher the intruder out into the street. 'Off with you now.' He turned Bernie around and with a hefty shove in the back propelled him in the direction of the front gate.

But Bernie refused to go quietly. He whirled about, pointing an accusing finger at the house – even, it seemed, at the very window where Reginald stood watching. 'He thinks he can buy us all off,' he was yelling now, 'well he can't, the bastard. You tell him that.'

'Come along.' Clive decided to apply some force and stepping forward he grabbed Bernie's wrist, twisted his arm behind his back and started marching him to the front gate. 'Leave the premises this minute or I'll have you arrested for trespassing.'

Bernie realised he was overpowered and gave up the struggle, but he didn't give up his drunken ranting. 'You tell Stanford he can't buy *me* off like he bought the others,' he yelled. 'He'll never buy me off, you hear me? *Never!* You tell the bastard that.'

Then he found himself sprawled face down in Davey Street. He picked himself up and, staggering around the corner into Hampden Road, set off for the Prince of Wales where, every night of the week except Sunday, he propped up the bar.

Reginald waited a minute or so before venturing downstairs, and he arrived in the hall just as Clive was closing the front door.

'What was that terrible racket about?' he asked casually. 'I could hear it from my office window.'

'To tell you the truth, sir, I've no idea. It was a young drunken oaf who made no sense at all. He went on about not being "bought off", or words to that effect.'

'Ah.' Reginald nodded. 'A worker disgruntled by a business takeover I suppose.'

'I suppose so, sir. In any event, I thought it best not to disturb you.'

'Very considerate, Clive,' Reginald made his decision in that very instant. He started back up the stairs. 'I shall be locked away in my study for the next hour or so. See to it that I remain undisturbed, will you?'

'Of course, sir.'

Upstairs, Reginald took out the considerable sum of money which he kept in his study safe, together with the pistol that was housed there, and barely five minutes later, he left by the back staircase that led to the tradesmen's entrance. His departure was unobserved.

He walked down to Salamanca Place, a rough, tough dockside street where, amongst the warehouses and factories, bars and brothels thrived and drunkenness and lechery was the nightly order of things. He did not look particularly out of place. In his loose woollen coat with its collar turned up and his dark felt hat, he typified those of the upper classes who visited the brothels or gambled at the card games conducted in the back rooms of disreputable hotels. Many a gentlemen chose to 'slum it' in such a fashion, and Reginald, like the more experienced of them, carried a pistol in his coat pocket to ward off any pickpocket or cutthroat who might see him as fair game.

He walked with purpose, not once questioning the drastic course of action upon which he had decided, for it was clear that he had no option. Bernie O'Callaghan's tirade may have been just so much drunken rambling, but it would not stop at tonight. Bernie would not wake up sober tomorrow, or next week or the week after that. Bernie was a drunk. Left to roam free he would continue to make his accusations and spread his family's story all over Hobart. The man must be silenced.

Arriving at the Esplanade, a hotel with a particularly unsavoury reputation, Reginald stepped through the front doors and into the main bar, where he was assailed by the din and the fug of tobacco smoke. The night was not overly warm, but inside the crowded bar the air was fetid and the smell of stale beer mingled with the stench of urine. The sawdust that was laid out on the floor to soak up the spillage from beer glasses and bladders alike was not changed often enough.

He edged his way through the crowd, past a couple fornicating against the wall, past a man urinating and past two louts about to embark upon a brawl. If a fight did break out, they would be evicted into the street, for fighting was not allowed in the bar. Reaching the door at the far end, Reginald opened it and stepped through to the rooms out the back.

A card game was in progress, but nobody looked up as he walked through the back room to another door that led to another smaller back room. There were several back rooms at the Esplanade, rented out for sundry purposes about which the hotel did not enquire. The larger rooms upstairs also did a lively trade, the working girls paying the barman for the use of the palliasses that were laid out side by side, a number to each room so that several whores could accommodate their clients at the same time.

Reginald tapped on the door to the smaller back room, but there was no answer and, glancing at the card players, he saw that the man he sought was there.

The man had seen him too. Alf had not once looked up from his cards, but Reginald had been in his peripheral vision from the moment he'd entered from the bar: Alf always sat to one side with a clear view of the room. He glanced up now and gave a surreptitious nod that clearly signalled 'go ahead'.

Reginald returned the nod and, opening the unlocked door, he entered the realm of Alf Jordan. He closed the door behind him and sat in the chair beside the small desk as if awaiting a business appointment, which of course he was. Tiny though the room might be, housing no more than the desk, two chairs and a palliasse at the far end, it was more than Alf Jordan's living quarters, it was his office.

Twenty-five-year-old Alf had inherited his father's business. Or rather he'd inherited his father's reputation as a reliable man for hire. Charlie Jordan had worked out of Wapping where the Jordan family had lived for three generations, and he'd risen from the ranks of thuggery to become an expert at his trade. Unfortunately, Charlie had been killed in a pub brawl six years previously, an unexpected end for a man as canny as he was. Meanwhile, his nineteen-year-old son, by then fully trained in his father's skills, had taken up the mantle. Charlie would have been proud, the family agreed. Later in the year of Charlie's death, the great fire had swept Wapping, destroying tenements and shanties alike, and the extended Jordan family, who numbered in their dozens, had left the inner city to settle in the suburbs like so many others. Alf hadn't. Alf had moved across the bay to Salamanca Place and into his little back room at the Esplanade Hotel where it was business as usual.

Reginald didn't have long to wait. Alf Jordan knew better than to keep a valuable client hanging around in a place where he didn't want to be seen. Within only minutes the door opened and he stepped into the room.

He was a strongly-built young man, as his trade required, thick-set and well-muscled, but not clumsily so, and he moved with a certain grace born of the need on occasions for stealth.

He closed the door and crossed to sit behind the desk before he spoke.

'Good evening, sir.' It was a voice of the streets, rough and uneducated, but the tone was respectful. 'How can I be of service?' Alf knew Reginald Stanford of course, he'd done several jobs for the man in the past, but a client's name never passed his lips. To Alf a client was always 'sir', so that it was clear he understood the need for anonymity.

'Do you know a Bernie O'Callaghan?'

Alf nodded. He knew every man who worked the docks. 'Irishman,' he said, 'comes in here for a card game now and then, drinks mostly at the Prince of Wales.' Odd choice of target, Alf thought. The three previous jobs he'd done for Stanford had involved two debt collections and a city councillor who'd been proving troublesome with a building project. Why Bernie? he wondered. Bernie was a drunk. Bernie had nothing.

'I want O'Callaghan to meet with an accident.'

'Right.' Must be a personal grudge, Alf thought. Stanford's jobs had never required violence: intimidation had always sufficed. 'What sort of accident?' he asked.

'A permanent one.'

'I see.' Having expected nothing more than a good walloping, Alf was certainly surprised, but he didn't allow it to show. 'Permanent accidents are expensive,' he said.

'I'm fully aware of that,' Reginald replied tartly and, taking an envelope from his coat pocket, he put it on the desk. 'One hundred pounds up front and another one hundred upon completion.'

'Agreed,' Alf said. More than generous, he thought. He would have taken on the job for a hundred all up. Hell, for an easy mark like Bernie he'd have accepted fifty. 'When do you want it done?'

'Immediately. Tonight if possible.'

'Right you are then.' For two hundred quid anything was possible.

'It is absolutely imperative,' Reginald said, 'that the event appear an accident – you do understand that, don't you, Mr Jordan? There must be no suspicion of foul play, none whatsoever.'

'Oh yes, I understand that, sir. Rest assured I do. You can rely on me.'

A half an hour later, having checked that Bernie O'Callaghan was indeed ensconced in his customary spot at the bar of the Prince of Wales Hotel, Alf set up his vigil outside. Merging into the shadows of Kelly Street, he waited. Alf was accustomed to waiting all night if need be, and as he waited he wondered what a harmless drunk like young Bernie could possibly have done to offend a man like Reginald Stanford. Ah well, hardly his place to question a client's motives. As his father had always said, 'Take the money, do the job and never ask why.'

It was just before ten, and he'd been there less than half an hour when Bernie staggered out from the bar. This'll be an easy job all right, he thought, particularly given the condition of his target.

Bernie had actually come outside to vomit. The barman had suggested he do so in no uncertain terms. 'Don't puke in here, Bernie,' Stan had said, 'get outside for God's sake.' Stan was sick of cleaning up Bernie's spew.

Grasping hold of a window ledge to steady himself, Bernie heaved his guts out onto the pavement. He felt quite a deal better when he'd finished and, wiping his mouth with the back of his sleeve, he was wondering whether he'd return to the bar or head for home when a friendly hand clapped him on the shoulder.

'Hello, Bernie,' a voice said and Bernie peered into a face he knew. Alf Jordan – he'd played cards with Alf a number of times, Alf was a good bloke.

'Want to come down to the Esplanade?' Alf put a comradely arm around Bernie, shepherding him away from the spill of light that came through the hotel's windows. 'There's a poker game on.'

Bernie gave a lopsided grin. 'I reckon I'm a bit far gone for cards, mate.'

'Why don't you join us for a drink then?' Alf kept walking him on down Kelly Street towards the cut and the steps that led to Salamanca Place. 'And maybe a bit of a tickle with one of the girls. What do you say?'

'Yeah, why not?' Bernie said. I could do with some company, he thought, although he wasn't sure if he was up for one of the girls. In fact he might even have another spew coming on.

They reached Kelly's Steps. The cut was narrow and dimly lit and the stone steps were steep. Alf glanced around. There was no-one in sight: the conditions were perfect.

They'd just started down the first of the two flights of steps when Bernie felt himself trip. He didn't know what had tripped him, but suddenly there he was hurtling head first down Kelly's Steps. He ended in a heap on the central landing and sat up, shaking his head groggily and puking all over the place, wondering what the hell had happened.

Alf joined him to kneel at his side. 'You all right, Bernie? That was a nasty fall.' It was the sort of fall that would have knocked most people out, as had been Alf's intention, but Bernie had bounced around like a rag doll, inviolable as drunks so often were. Ah well, Alf thought, no matter.

'Yeah, I'm fine, thanks mate,' Bernie said and, wiping the vomit from his mouth with his shirt sleeve, he started to struggle to his feet.

But he never got there. An arm locked about his head, a hand gripped his jaw, and the crack of Bernie's neck as it broke was audible. There was no-one around to hear it though, no-one except Alf.

Picking Bernie up by the belt of his trousers, Alf hurled his body down the second flight of steps like a sack of wheat, watching as it tumbled to the bottom. Then he briefly surveyed the scene. It was a perfect drunkard's death. The man had stopped on the landing to puke and had fallen down the steps, breaking his neck in the process. No-one could construe it as anything other than an accident.

Alf walked back up the steps to Kelly Street and, circling around via Montpellier Retreat, he returned to Salamanca Place and the Esplanade Hotel. The entire exercise had taken less than an hour.

CHAPTER SIXTEEN

Mick hoped that Col would come home. He'd not heard from his son for over a year, but he hoped with all his heart that Col, upon learning of the deaths of his sister and his young brother would return to Hobart, for Col was perhaps the one person in the world who could have eased the terrible sense of loss.

He'd posted his letter with its dreadful news to the Kalgoorlie post office box number he'd had for the past two years, assuming that if Col had moved on from the goldfields he would have informed the family. And in writing to the son he adored, Mick had poured out his grief. He'd told the lie that Shauna had died of a ruptured appendix certainly – it was the story he and Eileen and Mara had agreed to maintain even within the family circle – but everything else had been honest and heartfelt. Shauna's death had come as the most shocking blow to them all, he'd written, and with Bernie's drunken accident being only days later, the two had of course been inextricably linked.

'*Bernie's been a lost man for a long time, Col, Mick had written, and Shauna's death pushed him over the edge. You know how close they were. He drank himself into a state of oblivion. It was the sort of stupid, meaningless accident that's been waiting to happen for years I have to say, but that doesn't make it any easier to bear. Shauna and*

Bernie, both dead, just like that. Young lives snuffed out like candles. God is so cruel. The whole family is bereft as you can well imagine. I wish you were here, son. I really wish you were here.

Mick had stopped short of begging, but his meaning had been implicit, he was clearly saying 'come home'.

Col didn't come home, but he did the next best thing. He wrote a lengthy letter, as heartfelt as his father's, expressing his shock and sorrow upon hearing the news. Then he went on to explain why he couldn't come back to Hobart, at least not just yet.

I'm truly sorry for being so remiss with my letters, Da, particularly as I have had news of my own to impart for some time, news of the utmost importance. Perhaps now though, with the tragic loss of our darlings, the timing may be right after all. Perhaps it may be of some comfort for you and Ma to know that the O'Callaghan family has acquired a new member. Do you recall I mentioned in my last letter that I was contemplating marriage to a girl named Fiona? Well we didn't get around to it, or we haven't yet – marriage doesn't seem of great importance here on the goldfields – but Fiona gave birth towards the end of last year. I have a son. His name is Oscar.

It is for this reason that I cannot come home, Da, not at the moment anyway, much as I would like to. Oscar is not yet one year old and too young to travel. When he is a little more robust, perhaps in another year or so, I shall bring him home, I promise, and you shall meet your grandson.

In the meantime, I share with you the burden of our family's terrible loss. Tell Ma I shall say a prayer for Shauna and Bernie. Give her my love and hold her tight for me.

I remain forever your loving son, Col.

Although it was not the letter Mick had hoped to receive
– one announcing the imminent arrival of his son – it
provided the fillip that helped him through many a sleepless night. I have a grandson called Oscar O'Callaghan,
he would tell himself as he stared up into the blackness.
He already had three grandsons, one by Mara and two by
Kathleen, but none of them bore the O'Callaghan name.
And Oscar was Col's son. It was certainly something in
which to take comfort. There was now all the more reason
to count the days until Col came home.

Eighteen months later, Col had still not returned, but
something else happened to raise Mick's spirits. In the
autumn of 1897, he sold the Hunter's Rest, and for a very
tidy sum, in fact quite a deal more than the property's
market value. It was just as Ma Tebbutt had predicted
all those years ago. '*You can't halt progress, Mick,*' she'd
said – he could remember her very words: '... *you'll no
doubt sell the pub one day to some big businessman or
the government or whatever ...*' He remembered too how
she'd waved aside his protestations. Ma had known there
would come a day when he'd receive an offer too good to
refuse and as always Ma had been right.

Mick had honoured his promise to Ma. He'd long since
closed the brothel in favour of the contraband liquor trade
that was far more lucrative, but he'd kept the upstairs
rooms in operation until the last of the girls was nearing
'retirement age', after which he'd employed them in the
kitchen. Not one of Ma Tebbutt's girls had ended up in
the streets. And now the Hunter's Rest was about to be
transformed altogether, Mick thought, times are indeed
changing.

The offer of purchase had come from none other than
Henry Jones. Henry Jones had for some time been acquiring properties and expanding his IXL jam factory. Indeed
the massive demolition and reconstruction undertaken by

Jones in the expansion and modernisation of his factory's facilities and warehouses had changed the face of Old Wharf and Wapping forever.

The Hunter's Rest was the last property to be purchased for inclusion in the complex and as such its acquisition became headline news. Henry Jones and the modernisation of IXL were always a newsworthy topic and *The Mercury* wanted a picture of Henry and Mick standing outside the Hunter's Rest for its front page. Henry, who never shunned publicity, was only too happy to oblige, and Mick found that overnight he'd become a celebrity.

'*THE HUNTER'S REST TEAMS UP WITH IXL*', the headline said, and beneath a picture of Henry and Mick shaking hands and smiling at the camera with the hotel in the background was the caption: *Publican Mick O'Callaghan congratulates business mogul Henry Jones on his latest acquisition.*

'You look so handsome, Mick,' Eileen said, 'much more handsome than Henry Jones. Younger too, I might add.'

'Get away with you, he's got at least thirty years on me.'

'Well, it doesn't look that way in the picture.' Eileen thought how good it was to see him smile again: she'd worried about him lately. He was not well. She was glad he'd sold the hotel. Their financial situation was now secure and Mick could retire. With the sale of the house in Molle Street and now the Hunter's Rest, he need never work again. 'I swear you look as handsome as you did the day I first met you,' she said.

Mick cut the picture out and posted it to Col.

There were times when Reginald missed Shauna. His world was a lonelier one without her companionship. Shauna had known him as no other person ever had and there was no longer anyone in whom he could confide. He refused to agonise over her loss, however, castigating himself for his weakness instead. He should never have allowed himself to become so vulnerable. He would eschew personal relationships altogether in the future, he vowed. Keeping a mistress was far too dangerous. He'd behaved like a fool. But much as he'd continued to berate himself, it hadn't stopped him missing Shauna.

He'd turned his mind to the home front, determined to concentrate upon his wife: it was imperative Evelyn remain happy. Indeed he could hear Shauna's voice telling him so. Her advice remained with him, a constant reminder. '*You must be kind, Reginald,*' he could hear her say, '*it is difficult for a woman to conceive, I am sure, if she lives in fear of her husband.*'

Shauna's advice had once again proved sound. Evelyn, content in his love, had not only conceived with ease, she had carried the child without difficulty and now, barely one year after the birth of Rupert, she was just weeks away from delivering a second child.

Again it was Shauna's voice that kept Reginald in line. '*Be attentive and loving,*' he could hear her say. '*Evelyn must avoid stress at all costs.*' He'd continued to follow Shauna's advice throughout the pregnancy, although for the past two months he had found it exceedingly difficult.

'I've been afraid that something like this might come to pass,' Dr Harvey had said.

The doctor called in regularly to check on Evelyn. One visit, after he announced he was satisfied with her condition, she had asked him to examine Rupert. The child did not seem to be making the progress she had expected. He was a very contented baby, she told the doctor, in fact, she added, he was almost too contented. He very rarely cried or wailed to be fed, and he seemed to lack interest in his surroundings. Even her attempts to capture his attention failed. Nothing she did could hold his interest for more than a few seconds. Surely this was unusual for a child of twelve months.

'Since Rupert's birth I've been hoping this moment

would not arrive,' Dr Harvey had said after his examination, 'but now it has and … well …' he coughed uncomfortably. 'I'm afraid Rupert may have suffered damage due to deprivation of oxygen during his birth,' he said.

'What sort of damage?' Reginald hadn't waited for Evelyn's response. He'd leapt straight in demandingly.

'I fear there may be some intellectual impairment, although at this stage –'

'Are you telling me my son is a simpleton?'

Dr Harvey was not the only one startled by the hostility of Reginald's sudden outburst. Evelyn's look to her husband was fearful. This was the Reginald of old.

'I am telling you, Mr Stanford,' the doctor said in carefully measured tones, 'that at this stage it is impossible to predict the degree of impairment. Only time will reveal that. Rupert may well grow up capable of leading a normal life. Meanwhile it would be to everyone's advantage if you were to practise patience.' He glanced meaningfully at Evelyn: he'd seen the look of fear in her eyes. 'As time goes on your son will respond well to affection, and his progression will be speedier if he is in a peaceful environment.'

'Of course, Dr Harvey, I quite understand.' Reginald backed off immediately. 'Just came as a bit of a shock, that's all.' He did not like being talked down to in such a manner, but he'd definitely got the message. He put a comforting arm around his wife. 'We'll keep little Rupert happy between us, won't we, my love?'

'We will indeed.' Evelyn smiled, thankful that the storm had blown over.

'He *is* a happy little boy, my darling,' she said when the doctor had left. 'Whatever happens he is the dearest child, so loving and sweet-natured –'

'Yes, yes, of course he is.' Reginald did not wish to discuss the subject.

'And Dr Harvey said he may well grow up to lead a normal life –'

'He did, my dear, he did. We shall just have to wait and see what happens, shan't we?'

Since that day, Reginald had found it increasingly difficult to be attentive and loving towards his wife. He detested Evelyn for having given him an imperfect son. Whether the boy grew up capable of leading a normal life or not, he was damaged goods and Reginald had no wish for a son who was damaged goods. Sometimes, when he looked at the two of them, the little boy seemingly normal and chortling happily as his mother bounced him on her knee, he would have to leave the room. He hated them both.

He managed to keep up the facade of affection, however, for it was essential Evelyn remain happy and healthy. Now more than ever he needed a second child, and now more than ever he needed that child to be a son.

Hugh Stanford was born at eleven o'clock on a spring morning in early September 1896. Although premature, the birth was uncomplicated and the baby was healthy. Reginald's prayers had been answered.

'Well done, my love.' He kissed his wife with infinite tenderness. Evelyn's place in his affections was fully restored. It was easy to be attentive and loving now. He would be able to ignore the simpleton now. In fact Rupert could cease to exist altogether now that he had his perfect son.

After the sale of the Hunter's Rest Mick's health deteriorated rapidly throughout the following year, and in the early spring of 1898 he took to his bed. At first he'd thought it was simply his ulcer playing up, but Eileen knew better: he'd lost so much weight so quickly, it had to be something more serious. It turned out it was. Apparently he didn't have an ulcer at all. Apparently he'd never had an ulcer. The cancerous tumour that had been eating away at Mick for years was finally claiming him. The doctor said he would not see the year out.

Eileen wrote a note to Col. Or rather, she printed it. Mick

had taught her to read and write many years before, but she had mastered only the basics, and never the art of copper-plate. The note was simple. In her childlike hand it just read: *Come home. Da is dying. He needs you, love Ma.*

She received a brief reply within the fortnight. Col wrote that he was making his arrangements. He would be coming home as soon as possible, he promised, and he would be bringing his family with him.

'He's coming, Mick,' she said. 'Col's coming home.'

'Col's coming home, you say?' The news reached Mick through the laudanum cloud that fogged his brain and he smiled. 'In that case I'd better hang on, hadn't I?'

Several days later, in early November, a stranger appeared on their front doorstep.

'I'm after Mick Kelly,' he said when Eileen answered the knock on the door. He was a burly young man in his thirties, an Irishman judging by his brogue, and his manner was belligerent.

'There's no-one here by that name,' she said coldly, but as she went to close the door he thrust his foot forwards and wedged it open with his boot.

'Mick O'Callaghan then, he'll do. The fellow in this picture,' he thrust a newspaper cutting at her, 'I've been told he lives here.' It was the picture of Mick and Henry Jones that had appeared on the front page of *The Mercury* a whole year ago. It seemed Mick's brush with fame may have backfired on him.

'He's not in.' Eileen refused to be intimidated. 'Now get your filthy great boot away, you're trespassing.' She tried to jam the door closed but was sent reeling as the stranger thrust it open and barged inside.

'Get out,' she screamed, 'get out of my house!'

She followed him as he opened the door to the girls' bedroom and peered inside, and she followed him into the kitchen.

'Get out of my house,' she screamed again.

Then she followed him as he strode off in the direction of the main bedroom, but not before she'd grabbed the carving knife from the kitchen bench.

Eileen stood in the doorway of the bedroom, the knife hidden behind her back, and she watched as the stranger approached the bed.

'Leave him be,' she said, 'he's dying.'

'Yes indeed, I can see he's not well.' The stranger's manner was mocking as he thrust the newspaper cutting in Mick's face. 'You're a bit different from your picture in the paper, aren't you now, Mick Kelly? Not quite such a handsome chappie these days.'

Mick was propped up in bed. He'd been waiting for Eileen to deliver his mid-morning cup of tea and had dozed off only to be aroused by her screaming. Now he looked in confusion at the stranger waving a piece of newspaper at him. What was going on? Had someone called him Mick Kelly? He hadn't been called Mick Kelly for over forty years.

'Some of the old boys from '48, they live in Kalgoorlie now, on the goldfields, wouldn't you know. Well, it seems they seen this picture and recognised you straight off, and being upset like they were, they sent a message home lettin' the Brotherhood know you was alive and well. And you know the Brotherhood, Mick: they never forget.' The voice ceased to mock and became openly threatening. 'You have a debt to pay, Kelly, and I've been sent, all the way from Ireland, to see that you pay it.'

Behind her back, Eileen clenched the fingers of her right hand firmly around the knife, prepared to charge at any moment.

Mick tried desperately to clear the fog from his brain. 'Do I know you?' he asked, peering at the man.

'No, you don't know me, but you know of my family,' the stranger said. 'The name's Jamie and I'm a Meagher if that rings any bells.'

It did. The names and the events of a lifetime ago had been ringing many bells in Mick's mind lately. He'd been living more in the past than he had in the present as he'd drifted between the laudanum and the pain, his childhood and his youth much clearer than recent times that had become little more than a blur.

Meagher, he thought. Thomas Francis Meagher, leader of the Young Irelander Rebellion of 1848. The Battle of Ballingarry, in County Tipperary near the Kilkenny border. How could he ever forget that? Why he remembered the very date: the twenty-ninth of July.

'You know who I'm talking about, don't you?' Jamie Meagher could see the recognition in his eyes.

Mick nodded. 'The Young Irelanders,' he said, his voice husky, but his words quite clear, 'the rebellion at Ballingarry.'

'And you know what you did that day, don't you, Mick Kelly?'

Jamie Meagher sat casually on the bed as if he was making conversation with a sick friend, but his manner remained threatening.

Eileen steeled herself for the attack, watching and waiting for the first show of violence.

'Yes, I know what I did.' Mick met the man's gaze, refusing to show fear, although he remembered how in his youth he had dreaded the thought of a confrontation such as this. 'I ran away. I was sixteen years old and I was scared.'

'You dare to offer youth as a defence?' The remark clearly angered Jamie Meagher. 'A soldier of the Brotherhood is a man at sixteen. We all know that, just as you knew it back then. You were a Young Irelander. You'd accepted a man's job.'

'I had, I had, you're quite right. I was a coward, and that's the truth.'

'You were more than a coward, Kelly. You were a traitor. You betrayed your brothers.'

'No, no, I didn't.' Mick tried to sound forceful, but his strength along with his bravado was starting to fail him. 'I didn't, I swear.'

'You told the police where the leaders could be found, you bastard.'

'I didn't. I swear I didn't.'

'You might as well have led the raid yourself. It was because of you Meagher and O'Brien and the others were taken hostage –'

'It wasn't me, I swear it wasn't.' Mick was becoming agitated as he relived the fear and turmoil of that day. He'd been so young and so scared. He was no soldier like the others. He hadn't cared tuppence for the nationalist movement. He'd joined the Young Irelanders for adventure, so that he could get to carry a gun and boast about his exploits. He'd been terrified when the police had caught him, and only too willing to strike a bargain.

'We all knew where that house was,' he said desperately. 'Every one of the fighters knew where Meagher and the others were holed up.' This was what he'd told himself at the time, he remembered, and he'd persuaded himself it was true. If he didn't tell the police, then someone else would. The rebellion had been doomed from the start. Fighters were being captured all over the place. 'It could have been any one of the others,' he said.

'But it wasn't any one of the others, was it?' Jamie Meagher sneered. 'It was you. '

Mick had exhausted himself. What was the point in protesting any longer? He didn't have the strength anyway.

'Why,' he asked, 'why are you doing this? Why are you pursuing me? The Young Irelander Movement is long dead and gone. Dear Mother of God, it was fifty years ago, you weren't even born then.'

'The Brotherhood never dies, Kelly. The Brotherhood lives on with each new generation. And the Brotherhood never forgets a traitor.' Reaching his hand inside his open shirtsleeve, Jamie Meagher withdrew the stiletto blade from the sheath attached to his wrist. 'I've been sent to teach you a lesson.'

At the sight of the blade, Eileen sprang into action, lunging forwards with the carving knife, bent on attacking the man who threatened her husband.

Jamie had known the woman was hiding a weapon behind her back. He'd been waiting for her to make a move and was on his feet in an instant. Whirling to meet her he grabbed her wrist and wrenched it painfully behind her back; the carving knife clattered to the floor. The woman followed suit, sprawling to the ground as he threw her effortlessly aside. He picked up the knife, tossed it onto the bed, and ignored her as he returned his attention to the man.

'I've not been ordered to kill you, Mick Kelly,' he said. 'The Brotherhood doesn't send one of its valuable soldiers on an assassination assignment for scum like you. You're not worth it. No, I'm here to make an example of you so others may learn that no matter how far, or how long, they run, they'll be hunted down, because the Brotherhood never forgives, or forgets.' He waved the stiletto teasingly. 'And maybe I'll leave a scar or two of shame, for good measure.'

Mick felt the tip of the blade trace a path across his forehead.

'The letter T, what do you say? T for traitor ...'

As the blade's razor-sharp tip continued to play across his eyelids and over his face, Mick remained deathly still, too frightened to move.

'Or maybe a T on each cheek might be better, what do you think? That way it would be clearly visible from either side,' the stiletto was now drawing a pinprick of blood here and there, 'and you'd be able to see it twofold every time you looked in the mirror. But then, with scars like that you probably wouldn't look in a mirror very often, would you?'

From her position on the floor, Eileen watched breath-lessly, waiting for the moment when the blade would cut deep into Mick's face.

'But what's the point?' Jamie said finally, withdrawing the stiletto. 'You're not going to live long enough for the scars to heal and become a badge, are you? And to tell you the truth, Mick Kelly, you're not worth the recognition of being branded a traitor. Why should we let it be known you were once accepted as one of us?' He returned the blade to its sheath and glanced down at Eileen. 'You've got a brave wife, though, I'll give you that much,' he said. Then he turned on his heel and left.

Eileen picked herself up from the floor. She sat on the bed and, with the hem of her apron, dabbed at the spots of blood that bubbled from the nicks in his face. She was about to speak, but Mick got in first.

'So there you have it,' he said, trying for a touch of the old nonchalance, trying to sound as if he didn't care in the least, 'now you know the coward you married.'

'I married a man just like any other,' she replied in her prac-tical fashion. 'Don't be too hard on yourself, Mick. You're no demon – believe me there are far worse in this world. I'll get a damp cloth and I'll bring you your cup of tea.'

She went off to the kitchen and Mick felt at that moment that he could not possibly have loved her more.

Col made it home in the nick of time, or so it seemed to Eileen, for Mick was fading fast. He arrived in the second week of November, and he brought a surprise with him.

'This is your grandson, Oscar,' he said as with one hand he grabbed the arm of his beefy little three-year-old and hauled him up onto the bed like a sack of potatoes, 'and this is your new granddaughter, Caitlin,' he added, refer-ring to the child of barely twelve months who was cradled against his chest.

'Granddaughter?' Mick cast a befuddled glance at Eileen

as she rescued him from Oscar, who'd started leaping about on the bed. Had he missed something?

'No, you've missed nothing,' she said, reading his mind. She put the boy down and he scampered off to explore the rest of the house. 'Col didn't say anything about Caitie in his letter.'

'I wanted to surprise you,' Col said with the familiar grin that gladdened Mick's heart. It had been sixteen years since he'd seen his son, but Col was the same cheeky charmer he'd always been. If anything he's more devilishly handsome than ever, Mick thought with pride. The lad who'd left Hobart had returned a strong and impressively fit-looking man.

He waved a frail hand at the little girl. 'Just look at that for hair, Eileen –' Caitie had a thatch of fiery red hair '– she's Shauna all over again.'

'She is that,' Eileen agreed, marvelling at the change Col's arrival had wrought. For the past several days Mick had been barely lucid, but now his eyes were bright and focused.

'Where's your woman?' Mick peered about as if expecting her to jump out from wherever she was hiding. 'Where's Fiona?'

'Back in Kal,' Col gave a careless shrug, 'she didn't fancy coming to Hobart so I left her behind.'

'You broke up your family to come and see me?' Mick asked incredulously.

'Well, no not exactly,' Col admitted, catching his mother's glance. 'The truth is she left me, Da. The fool of a woman ran off with another man,' he said light-heartedly, 'can you believe that?'

'But the children ...' Mick was confused. 'What about the children?'

'She left them too, apparently,' Eileen said drily. She'd been confused herself when Col had told her. She hadn't believed him at first.

'No mother leaves her children like that,' she'd said.

'Not all women take to motherhood like you did, Ma. Fiona certainly didn't; she was just after a good time.'

'But to run off with another man and desert your children, it's not natural.'

'It is when the other man's struck gold. She'll be living the high life now. If I'd had a strike like Bobbo, she'd still be with me.' Col's bitterness was obvious, but its direction was unclear. He didn't know who he hated most, Fiona for leaving him or Bobbo for striking it lucky. 'That's life on the goldfields for you, Ma.'

'Col's better off without her, Mick,' Eileen now said, taking the little girl from her son, 'and so are the children. They'll have a far better home right here with me.' She cradled Caitie in her arms, the child gurgling happily. As far as Eileen was concerned Fiona had ceased to exist.

Over the next several days, Col's presence seemed to breathe new life into Mick. They all commented on it, Mara and her children who regularly visited and also Kathleen who'd made another trip down from Launceston, this time on her own.

'It's a miracle, Col,' Kathleen said. 'I'd thought I wouldn't see him again after the last trip.' Kathleen had brought her three children down just the previous month in order that they might say goodbye to their grandfather. 'You're certainly doing him the world of good.'

On the eighteenth of November, barely a week after his arrival, Col planned a special treat for his father. A big night was in store for Hobart and, determined that Mick would be a part of it, he went out to Dimbleby's Emporium that very morning and purchased a wicker wheelchair.

It was lunchtime when he returned. Eileen was sitting at the kitchen table feeding Caitie and trying to control an unruly Oscar.

'What are you thinking of?' she said when he wheeled the chair in and announced his plan. 'Are you mad? You can't charge your father around the streets in that thing: you'll kill him.'

'But he has to be a part of it, Ma, he has to see it for himself. You can't deprive him of the experience of a lifetime, that's not fair.'

'Experience of a lifetime,' Eileen gave a humourless laugh, 'the death of him more like.'

'The man surely has the right to decide for himself,' Col said rebelliously. 'You might at least let me ask him.'

'Very well, ask him,' Eileen said, thin-lipped. 'The decision is his, but it's a lunatic idea and I shall tell him so. Put that down, Oscar.' She smacked the little boy's hand as he picked a knife up from the table, then she went back to feeding Caitie.

Col sat on the edge of the bed and held Mick's hand, as he often did when they talked. Mick took unashamed pleasure in the touch of his son.

'How'd you like to see the electric street lights come on, Da?'

'Oh, that'd be something now, wouldn't it? Yes, that'd be something indeed.'

'It's happening tonight, you know.'

'What is?'

'The electric street lights. They're coming on tonight.'

'Are they really?' Mick was hazy about what was happening these days. Someone had said something, but he'd forgotten what it was and who'd said it. He racked his brains trying to remember. Then it came to him. 'Kathleen told me we've had electric street lights for years,' he said, puzzled, 'I didn't know that.'

'No, no, she was talking about Launceston, they're three years ahead of us.'

'Oh, I see.' Mick nodded; he was having trouble keeping up.

'Hobart's turning on its electric street lights tonight, Da. They're turning them on for the very first time.'

'Well, well, that'll be an exciting event, won't it?'

'Yes, it'll be a very exciting event, and it's one you're going to see ...' Col sprinted from the room and Mick was left gazing at the open doorway, bewildered by his son's abrupt departure. '... And you won't be seeing it through a window, what's more,' Col said as he re-appeared with the wheelchair. 'You're going out tonight. You and me and half of Hobart I'll bet. We're going out to watch the electric lights come on.'

Mick looked at the wheelchair with trepidation. He hadn't been outside the house for the past three months. Dear God, he hadn't even been outside the bedroom for weeks. Getting himself to the sitting room, where he'd liked to watch the world through the front window, was too painful an exercise these days.

'Don't be afraid, Da, I'll look after you. This'll be something to remember,' Col urged; he was brimming over with enthusiasm. 'This'll be a once in a lifetime experience.'

How can I possibly refuse? Mick thought. He would do it for Col, he decided. He'd do it for Col even if it killed him, which it very well might.

'In that case I shall need to be suitably dressed,' he said.

Eileen, after voicing her strong disapproval, realised protestation was useless and decided to make it a family outing. They would all go, she said. They would take the children with them and watch the lights together.

She helped Mick to bathe, holding the bowl and wringing out the flannel for him as she always did. She was allowed to bathe his feet, but he insisted upon washing the parts of himself he could reach, which principally meant his genitals. She chided him for it often.

'A little late in the day for modesty,' she'd say, 'I've

bathed you often enough in the past. You're becoming very prudish in your old age, Mick.'

When he was washed and in his underwear she called Col in and they sat him on the edge of the bed and dressed him. They worked as slowly and gently as they could. Any amount of movement was tiring and often painful.

Mick had insisted upon formal wear. His striped trousers, he said, a high starched collar and tie, his dove-grey waistcoat, black frock coat, spats and, of course, his top hat. It took them twenty minutes to dress him and when they'd finished, his emaciated frame swam in the fine clothes. Even the top hat seemed too big.

'You look very grand, Da,' Col said.

Mick had made no complaint throughout the exercise, but Eileen could tell that he was exhausted. 'You don't have to do this, you know,' she said tartly.

'Of course I do. I must.' He tried to sound forceful. 'I want to, Eileen.'

'If you must you must, I suppose,' she said with a shrug, 'but lie down for now.' She took off his top hat. 'We won't be leaving for at least half an hour. I have to get the children ready yet.'

He lay back, allowing her to lift his feet up onto the bed. Within only minutes he'd dozed off.

When they returned with the children, he appeared to be sound asleep.

Col was about to wake him.

'Don't, son,' Eileen said, and she shushed Oscar, whose hand she was holding. 'Don't wake him, leave him be. Even being dressed tired him out, you can see that ...'

But Mick's sleep was no more than a light doze and the sound of her voice awakened him. He opened his eyes. 'Are we ready now?' He smiled at the sight of his family gathered before him. 'Let's be on our way then. I'm raring to go.'

They sat him up and put on his shoes and spats.

Mick doffed his top hat and held his hands out to his son for assistance, but as Col helped him stand his knees gave way and he sank back onto the bed.

'Hold on to your topper, Da,' Col said. Scooping his father up effortlessly in his arms he placed him with great care into the wheelchair.

Eileen winced at the sight. Col had been as gentle as possible, but the suddenness of the action would have caused Mick considerable pain. To his credit he'd bravely hidden it and she admired his stoicism. She took the bottle of laudanum from the top drawer of the dresser and slipped it into the inner pocket of his frock coat.

'You'll need this,' she said.

Mick smiled gratefully. He would try and avoid the laudanum if possible, he wanted to keep his wits about him, but he was comforted by the knowledge that it was there.

The afternoon was starting to fade as they left the house. When dusk set in it would do so quickly, it always did in Hobart, but there was still nearly an hour before the street lights were scheduled to come on.

They set off along Hampden Road, Eileen carrying Caitie, and Oscar perched on Col's shoulders in his customary manner, strong little legs wrapped around his father's neck and fistfuls of thick black hair grasped firmly in his hands. Col always travelled hatless for the express purpose of accommodating Oscar. Ahead of them was Mick in the wheelchair all dressed up to the nines, Col doing his best to steer him clear of the bumps.

'You're leading the way, Da,' Col announced as they headed for the city.

Col had mapped out the route they would take that morning. They would not cut through the back streets and the wharf area as he would normally have done. The wheelchair would travel more smoothly if they stuck to the wider main roads, he'd decided.

They were not the only ones making their way towards

the central city blocks where the lighting would be at its most impressive. By the time they reached Davey Street they met up with dozens heading into the centre of town; and when they turned into Murray Street there were dozens more. Minutes later, upon reaching the corner of Macquarie Street, they looked down the broad avenue to discover the pavements on either side crowded with spectators, all waiting for the magical moment.

Holding Oscar in place on his shoulders, Col leant down to Mick. 'Like I said, Da, you and me and half of Hobart,' he raised his voice above the general hubbub, 'I told you this'd be something to remember.'

'You did indeed, and so it is.' Mick looked about, overwhelmed by the sight of the crowd and the sense of expectation that was palpable. He'd found the journey jarringly painful despite the care Col had taken, and he'd surreptitiously downed a hefty swig of laudanum, which had now taken effect. He'd presumed no-one had noticed him attack the laudanum bottle, but of course someone had.

'Are you all right?' Eileen asked. Having carried Caitie all the while, she was weary herself, and it would be a harder walk back, for much of it was uphill, but her main concern was for Mick.

'I certainly am, girl.' The laudanum had not only dulled the pain, it had heightened in Mick a dreamlike sense of unreality. Was this really happening? Was he really out of his little bedroom and here with these hundreds of people? He found it difficult to believe. He smiled up at his wife, his eyes bright with excitement. 'This is something to remember all right, Eileen – you can feel it in the very air.'

Col decided they might as well stay where they were. The other major streets would no doubt be just as crowded, and they'd walked far enough.

'Make way, make way.' Ignoring the odd disgruntled mutter, he manoeuvred the wheelchair through the onlookers to the edge of the pavement, positioning it where Mick could have a full view down Macquarie Street. He secured the chair's brake. 'Come on, Ma, take a seat,' he said, patting the arm of the wheelchair, 'make yourself comfortable.'

Eileen sat thankfully, bouncing Caitie on her knee. The little girl, far from being sleepy, was taking an avid interest in her surrounds.

Squatting beside his father, Col leant an elbow on the other arm of the wheelchair. Oscar, still perched on his shoulders, was gazing about as spellbound by the crowd as Mick was. Never in his short life had he seen so many people.

'Not long to go now, Da,' Col said.

The family watched and waited in silence.

As the afternoon light faded and the first shadows of dusk started to creep in, the crowd too grew silent. The babble of voices gradually faded and all the way down the street eyes looked up expectantly at the brand new lights overhead. The seconds ticked steadily by. And then ...

'Ten ...'

Three men standing nearby started the countdown. They were three very smartly dressed young businessmen and their eyes were not trained on the street lights, but rather on the fob watches they held in their hands. One of them was a Lyttleton – Nigel's son, Walter. It was a Friday and twenty-two-year-old Walter and his friends had left work early to witness this very moment.

'Nine ... Eight ...'

With no idea whether or not the countdown was correct, others about them took up the chant.

'Seven ... Six ...' Col and Mick and Eileen joined in too, and then the whole crowd was chanting.

'Five ... Four ...'

It seemed all of Macquarie Street was giving voice, and perhaps it was the same in Elizabeth Street and Collins

Street – perhaps the whole of Hobart was counting down the seconds.

'Three ... Two ...'

Then the moment they'd been waiting for. Who could possibly have doubted Walter? He was a Lyttleton after all, and meticulous to the letter. He and his friends' fob watches were perfectly synchronised, both with each other and with Greenwich Mean Time.

'One ...' the crowd chanted. And a second later the lights came on. They came on just like that, a startling sea of light. In an instant, the street was illuminated, and not by the gentle glow of gas lamps, but by lights far fiercer, far brighter, lights that cut through the gloom of approaching dusk with an edge not seen before. The crowd burst into applause.

To Mick, already in a state of drug-induced unreality, it seemed incredible. He gazed about, awestruck.

'Dear Mother of God,' he murmured, shaking his head in wonderment, 'who'd have thought it possible? You wouldn't believe it if you hadn't seen it with your own eyes now, would you?'

'I was right, wasn't I, Da?' Col grinned, thrilled that his plan had proved such a success. 'This is a once in a lifetime experience.'

'It is indeed, son. Oh yes, indeed it is. We're witnessing the birth of a new age, there's no doubt about that.' He turned to his wife. 'And just to think, Eileen, I lived to see it.'

There was such zest for life in his eyes that the years dropped away; for a second Eileen felt she could have been looking at the young Mick O'Callaghan.

'You did, Mick, you did at that.' She cast a quick glance at her son and nodded. Col's lunatic idea had proved a good one after all.

The crowd soon started to disperse, but Mick insisted the family stay until nightfall and, as dusk descended, he remained lost in the world that unfolded before him. Macquarie Street had become a fairyland.

When they finally got home they were exhausted, all of them. The children were fast asleep, Eileen felt she couldn't walk another step and even Col, after carrying Oscar on his hip and pushing the wheelchair with one hand, and uphill for the most part, was feeling weary. As for Mick, well, Mick wasn't feeling much of anything. During the return trip, the pain had attacked with such a vengeance that he'd dosed himself up with more laudanum, and by the time they put him to bed he was in another world altogether. But he seemed happy enough.

'Incredible,' he kept muttering, 'who'd have believed it possible ...?'

He died several days later.

Eileen wasn't sure whether or not Col's lunatic jaunt had hastened Mick's death, but she didn't care anyway, it had been worth it. She didn't shed a tear. She had loved Mick and she would miss him, but she wouldn't waste time grieving. She had two children to raise.

CHAPTER SEVENTEEN

The dawn of the twentieth century loomed, bearing with it the promise of Federation and a bright new future, but the old century, in closing, had one final event to deliver that would have a dramatic impact upon the colonies of Australia. In 1899 the colonial military forces responded to Britain's request for assistance in South Africa.

Following the lead of the other colonies, the Tasmanian government lent its resources to the Boer War. The requirement being for mounted troops with bushcraft and shooting skills, recruits were drawn principally from rural areas and there was no shortage of volunteers eager to sign up.

On the twenty-eight of October, 1899, the 1st Tasmanian Mounted Infantry Contingent, numbering eighty-four men under the command of Captain Cyril St Clair Cameron, departed Hobart aboard the troopship *Medic*, bound for South Africa.

Enthusiasm was not limited to the departing troops. Fifteen thousand people crammed the wharf to farewell the vessel that would carry their brave young men off to serve the Motherland in her hour of need.

Among the well-wishers was a considerable gathering of the Powell family, many of whom had travelled up from the Huon. They were there to farewell George's younger son, James. Twenty-six-year-old James Powell, who could ride like the wind and was a crack marksman, had been eagerly snapped up by the recruiting officers. He was 'off to fight the Boers', he'd proudly announced, much to the envy of his young city cousin.

'Why can't I sign up like James?' William had complained to his parents.

'Because they wouldn't want you,' his mother Martha had said in her customarily blunt fashion, 'you can't ride a horse.' Will had only just turned nineteen and Martha was thankful for the perfect excuse.

With the exception of the matriarch, Doris, who at seventy-seven avoided crowds, the city arm of the Powell family was all there at the wharf: Martha, her husband Simon Hawtrey and their two children, William and twenty-one-year-old Edith. Edith had brought her fiancé, Samuel, along.

The Huon contingent was also well represented, although George and his older son Lincoln had not brought their wives. Father and son planned to stay in town several days on business, so James had said his goodbyes to his mother at home, Emma saying that she preferred it that way. Quincy, however, in delegating his son Thomas to represent their side of the family, had boosted the numbers considerably: Thomas had not only brought his wife, Olivia, and his five-year-old-son with him, he'd brought their best friends, the Müllers, and their two children as well. James was being farewelled in style by three generations of family and friends.

'They look so much handsome,' Heidi yelled in her fractured English, pitching her voice above the sound of the brass band and the noise of the crowd as she and Olivia stood in the forefront with their children waving up at the troops.

'They certainly do,' Olivia agreed. The men do indeed look impressive, she thought, in their plumed slouch hats, bandoliers, khaki and puttees. 'Very handsome,' she yelled back to Heidi, 'and very proud, as well they should be.'

The gangplank was lowered onto the wharf and, as the ship's forward and aft lines were released, the excitement reached fever pitch. The brass band broke into 'Soldiers of the Queen', the stirring march that was currently resounding throughout every British military outpost across the world; people started hurling streamers up to the men who were leaning over the railings and the men hurled them back; girls blew kisses to beaus; men saluted with top hats and cloth caps; and women and children frantically waved.

'Bye, Uncle James! Bye!'

David, who'd just turned five, screamed out his goodbyes at the top of his lungs and beside him, egged on by his excitement, little Eugenia jumped up and down.

'Bye-bye, bye-bye,' she squealed.

The two having been born just one month apart and their mothers being best friends, David Powell and Jeanie Müller were inseparable.

Heidi held three-year-old Max, the latest addition to the Müller family, up in her arms waving his chubby little hand at James, and James waved back.

James waved to them all, his father and brother and cousins and family, and his friends and their family too.

As the ship slowly pulled away from the dock, James Powell and every other member of the 1st Tasmanian Mounted Infantry Contingent waved farewell not only to their families and friends, but also to their homeland, most of them for the very first time in their lives. The great adventure had begun.

'It's the soldiers of the Queen, my lads,
Who've been, my lads, who've seen, my lads ...'

The brass band had reached the chorus of 'Soldiers of the Queen', and all around the wharf people took up the song.

'In the fight for England's glory, lads,

When we've had to show them what we mean.'

Up on the ship's deck and down on the wharf, troops and well-wishers sang as one.

'And when we say we've always won

'And when they ask us how it's done ...'

The voices swelled to a crescendo as thousands gave voice, the docks and the streets of Hobart ringing with the sound.

'... We'll proudly point to every one

Of England's soldiers of the Queen.'

The band finished the march with bravura and, as everyone cheered, they started it up all over again.

Those on the wharf kept singing and waving until the ship was well out into the Derwent and the men on board barely visible. Then voices slowly faded, but it was only when the ship was completely out of sight that the crowd finally dispersed and people went their own ways.

The Powells and the Müllers retired to Martha and Simon's house in Napoleon Street, where Doris had prepared tea and scones. Doris now lived in the refurbished servants' quarters at the rear of the house, which she had insisted upon giving to Martha and Simon. Her generosity served a practical purpose for she rightfully knew her daughter would look after her in her dotage, but she had determined to die before becoming a burden. As yet, however, infirmity seemed to have overlooked Doris Powell, whose health remained strong and whose wits were as sharp as ever.

George and his son Lincoln were staying at the house for the duration of their three-day trip to the city. George always stayed with the Hawtreys when he had business in town. It not only provided a pleasant reunion with his mother and his sister and her family, it was convenient for business. The meetings relating to the joint interests of Powell Shipbuilding and Powell Channel Transport were conducted in Simon's office, the office which had once been Jefferson Powell's study. The old family home held many memories for George.

Thomas Powell and Gus Müller had booked their respective families into Hadley's Orient Hotel in the centre of town. They'd stayed there the previous night following their arrival and would stay tonight, returning to the Huon the following morning. Martha had urged them all to stay at Napoleon Street, but they had insisted that with three children in tow it would be far too crowded; and besides, Thomas had explained to his aunt, Olivia and Heidi were looking forward to the Orient as part of their treat.

The women, whose visits to the city were rare, had indeed planned to tie the trip in with a touch of luxury and a long overdue shopping excursion. New clothes for each member of their respective families was the common objective and with only Friday afternoon to find all they wanted they'd eagerly accepted Martha's offer to babysit.

Upon the mass return to Napoleon Street, everyone gathered in the front sitting room overlooking the garden and, as tea was served and countless scones devoured with jam and cream, they discussed at length the historic events of the morning. They toasted the troops and their success in South Africa and they toasted James and his safe return and they toasted family and friends – no gathering of the Powell clan was ever complete without such a toast – and they finished with a special toast to Edith and Samuel, who had announced their engagement just three months previously.

Finally, it was time to get on with the rest of the day. When the tea things had been cleared, Martha took the children out into the back garden to play while Olivia and Heidi prepared to leave for the city.

Gus Müller had reluctantly agreed to accompany his wife shopping. He would rather have stayed with the men, who were shortly to have their business meeting, but he considered it his duty to go with the women in order to carry their purchases.

'I'm to be a packhorse,' he announced good-naturedly as they were about to take their departure.

'You are to be a new suit,' his wife corrected him. 'You are to be fitting the tailor.'

'I don't know why,' he said with a shrug. 'The man has my measurements.'

'You're more than welcome to stay here, Gus,' Thomas said, openly goading his friend; he considered Gus soft for accompanying his wife shopping. Thomas would never have gone shopping with the women himself. Why bother? Surely they'd be happier on their own, and they could have their purchases delivered to the hotel anyway.

Thomas may have had a point in his reasoning, but he failed to recognise the basic difference between himself and Gus Müller. Gus was not soft at all: Gus was a born gentleman. Thomas, rebellious from childhood, was not. The remarkable fact remained, however, that the friendship shared by Thomas Powell and Gus Müller was as close as that shared by their wives.

'Uncle George and Simon and Lincoln wouldn't mind if you sat in on the meeting, I'm sure,' Thomas said with pretended innocence. It was a presumptuous suggestion on his part as, in a way, he was a guest himself – the business of Charlotte Grove Orchard was not scheduled for discussion.

George and Simon exchanged a glance. Thomas was out to cause trouble as usual, even if it was only in poking fun at his friend.

'Of course you're more than welcome to sit in on the meeting, Gus,' George said, 'you're part of the family after all.'

'No, no, I wouldn't dream of intruding,' Gus insisted with a scowl at Thomas, who grinned cheekily back. 'Besides,' he added, 'I shall enjoy being the envy of every man in town.' He offered an arm each to Heidi and Olivia, who'd been patiently waiting, and the three left the house and set off down the street bound for the tram from Sandy Bay into the city.

The men retired to Simon's office. Powell Channel Transport had a booking agency and offices in town, which were run by senior management and staff, and the company also retained an employee who lived with his family in the cottage on the point, overseeing the vessels' repairs and maintenance at the nearby shipyards, but Simon preferred to conduct most of his business from home.

Young William accompanied the men, but sat to one side ready to take notes as his father had instructed. Will had only recently joined the family firm and was serving his apprenticeship in a secretarial position.

Simon took up his customary post behind the desk – he always chaired the meetings – and George, Lincoln and Thomas sat opposite.

As they took their seats, George Powell looked about the office. It was here that he felt his father's presence most strongly. Simon had long since replaced the old desk and chairs, but the room still seemed the same as it had in Jefferson's time. It still smelt of wood and leather, and the surrounding shelves were still lined with beautifully carved boats of all size and description. Most of them were models of vessels George himself had designed and built for Powell Channel Transport. He and his father had worked very closely here in this room.

George had felt not a shadow of resentment when his mother had gifted the family home to his sister and her husband, nor had his brother Quincy. Doris had discussed her plans with them both and they had all been in agreement. Jefferson Powell had been more than generous in helping his sons set themselves up in their respective businesses. It was only fair the house should go to Martha.

'And besides, it means you boys won't be saddled with me until I die,' Doris had said; and although they'd laughed they'd known she hadn't been joking. Their mother didn't make jokes.

'I've received an expression of interest from Stanford

Colonial,' Simon said, getting straight down to business, 'from Reginald Stanford himself, I might add. He talked a lot about you, George, sang your praises most highly.'

'Yes, we built the *Lady Evelyn* for Stanford and Hazeldene Timber as you know, and he was very pleased with her. In fact we saw him at the timber mill just recently, didn't we, Lincoln? He was hinting at possible further commissions on a much grander scale.'

Lincoln nodded, but looked sceptical. 'He was pretty evasive though, Pap, you have to admit.' Unlike his father, Lincoln was something of a cynic. In fact there were times when he felt quite protective of his father, whom he considered an innocent. 'I mean he was very flattering and all that, but he didn't make any definite offer. I got the feeling he was just trying to butter us up.'

'He was,' Simon said. 'He's trying to butter all of us up.'

'What was the offer he made to you?' George asked.

'Well, it wasn't really an offer at all. As I said, it was an expression of interest. He was sounding me out more than anything.'

'About what?' Thomas demanded impatiently. He didn't care that the current conversation had nothing to do with him, he just wished, as he so often did, that Simon would get to the point.

'About a possible merger between Stanford Colonial and Powell Channel Transport,' Simon replied.

There was a moment's silence. Even Thomas was taken aback. That's certainly getting to the point, he thought.

'Stanford set out to impress upon me the possibilities of such a merger,' Simon continued, unruffled as always, but aware that he'd dropped a bombshell. 'He talked about extending the fleet. That's when he sang your praises, George,' he added in an aside to his brother-in-law. 'He went on about the excellent relationship he'd developed with you during the construction of the *Lady Evelyn*. Obviously he was hinting to me of the advantages to be reaped by the Powell family in general should a merger take place.'

'But he made no offer?' Lincoln queried suspiciously. 'It was just talk, as it was with us at the timber mill?'

'That's right, which leads me to believe he wants us to have a meeting such as this, where we'll talk it over and see the advantages to be had on all sides. Stanford Colonial is a powerful organisation with a lot of money to invest. They could certainly broaden our horizons. He talked also of the possibility of opening up regular freight runs to the mainland, perhaps even to England, thereby doing away with the necessity of relying on the major shipping lines.'

'I for one wouldn't say no to that,' Thomas interjected. 'It'd save us having to book our freight space with Jones and Peacock.'

Simon displayed no annoyance at the interruption; indeed he rarely allowed his irritation to show. 'It's fortuitous that you're here actually, Thomas,' he said. 'The discreet investigations I have made into Stanford Colonial's business transactions will be also relevant to Charlotte Grove, I should imagine.'

He redirected his attention to George and Lincoln. 'However, with regard to the current matter, I have discussed Stanford Colonial's expression of interest with Doris and Martha and the other directors and senior management of Powell Channel Transport and we are all in agreement there will be no merger –'

'Why ever not?' It was Thomas again, and this time Simon ignored him.

'Stanford does not intend a merger at all: he intends a takeover. It's the way he works. I hope, George, that our refusal will not adversely affect any future dealings you may have with Stanford Colonial, though I must say I'm inclined to share Lincoln's mistrust. I believe that the man's hints about commissions on a far higher scale were intended to make you look favourably upon a merger.'

'I've more than enough work without Stanford's commissions,' George stated firmly. 'We run a family business, Simon, and we want to keep it that way.' He looked at Lincoln, who nodded. 'Like you, we don't want to be gobbled up by big investors. Our businesses will be handed down to the sons of our sons –'

'What did you find out about Stanford that relates to Charlotte Grove?' Thomas could be downright rude at times.

Simon appeared to once again ignore him, although he was in fact answering the question. 'Stanford Colonial has financial interests everywhere,' he said to the gathering in general, 'real estate, both here and on the mainland, Merino wool and timber of course, and recently, unknown of by most, sugar refinery in Queensland. Also unknown of by most are their investments in the local hop industry, the fresh fruit market and fruit-based foods, including of course jam produce.'

His audience was suitably impressed and the men exchanged glances. None of the family knew how Simon managed to obtain the information he did. If they asked him he was always evasive. 'Oh, I do my homework,' he would say modestly, 'and I have the odd contact here and there.' It sometimes appeared as if mild-mannered Simon Hawtrey had a network of spies at his beck and call.

Simon's gaze finally came to rest upon Thomas. 'Fears of a monopoly have been raised in your industry, Thomas, and they're perfectly justified. But I'm not sure if Henry Jones, or Peacock for that matter, are the men you should fear. Reginald Stanford wields a great deal of power behind the scenes, and he, unlike Jones and Peacock, is a man who would abuse it. Certainly, with wool, timber, hops, fruit, jam and other fruit products to export, it's little wonder he has secretly set up a cartel to control the booking of freight space. It is even less wonder that he wants his own shipping line.'

Thomas's question had been well and truly answered and he had very little to say after that. Simon promised he would keep them all informed of any direct offer he received from Stanford Colonial, and the meeting concluded not long afterwards.

Tasmanians welcomed in the New Year with all the jubilation a brand new era demanded, and also with a keen sense of expectancy. They were eager to embrace the twentieth century and the promise it offered, particularly that of Federation.

In the referendums of the late nineties, the islanders had voted overwhelmingly in favour of Federation. There had been the grim-faced few, wealthy landowners for the most part, whose desire to cling to the English class system had seen them vote in the negative, but they had been a distinct minority. Most Tasmanians were only too keen to put behind them forever the memory of penal colonialism and the master–servant system their island had suffered throughout the past century.

Along with impending federation, the war in South Africa remained an issue of principal focus. Patriotic fervour abounded in Hobart as reinforcements were sent to join the first contingent, and when, in rapid succession, the second and third contingents were farewelled at the docks. So eager were young men for the privilege of serving with the Tasmanian Imperial Bushmen, as the units were to become known, that the applications were oversubscribed by more than five to one.

But as the year progressed there were some families who did not celebrate the Boer War, some who felt no triumph in its victories, only a tragic sense of loss. The Powells were one such family. In early May 1900, after serving on active duty with the Tasmanian Mounted Infantry for over six months, Private James Powell was killed in a Boer ambush in South Africa's Northern Cape Colony.

George bore his loss bravely. He was proud of his son, he said. James had died in the service of queen and country: no man could do more. His wife did not feel the same way at all. Emma Powell was bitter. Her son was buried in a foreign land – she couldn't even visit his grave. The war had robbed her of her boy and she saw nothing noble in it. But she kept her silence, knowing that speaking her mind in such a manner would be disloyal to James, and knowing also that her husband was dealing with his own grief in his own way, as it seemed so many men did.

Federation became a reality on the first of January 1901. When Alexandrina Victoria died three weeks later, the timing seemed eerily fitting. The Victorian Empire, which had ruled the colonies since 1837, ended with the death of its queen and the ascension of Edward VII at the very time when Australia came of age.

John Adrian Louis Hope, seventh Earl of Hopetoun, was appointed Governor-General and Edmund Barton became the nation's first Prime Minister. Sir Henry Parkes, 'the Father of Federation', had sadly not lived to see the day, having died five years previously, but his dogged persistence had won out and his ultimate goal had been realised. The once fractured colonies had at long last become the Commonwealth of Australia, the youngest nation on earth.

The Boer War now took on an even greater significance for Australians, not least for the island state of Tasmania. Australia was at war as a nation for the very first time and, when the first two Australian-born soldiers ever to be awarded the Victoria Cross proved to be Private John Hutton Bisdee and Lieutenant Guy George Egerton Wylly, both of the 1st Tasmanian Imperial Bushmen, the islanders' pride knew no bounds. Hobart claimed the young VC winners as its own. They were boys from the Hutchins School.

For many the Boer War symbolised victory, for some it brought personal tragedy, and there were those for whom it was a financially profitable enterprise.

'How very thoughtful of the British Army to consider its troops' palates in such a manner,' Reginald had drily commented when Henry Jones had approached him. Henry had wanted to know whether he might wish to help finance the increased jam production required to satisfy the Imperial Defence contracts IXL had undertaken.

'Army rations are monotonous in content,' Henry had told him, 'and jam is a delicacy much sought after by the troops, strawberry and raspberry in particular, I'm told.'

Henry had appeared mystified and even a little offended by Reginald's response. 'I'd hardly put it down to thoughtfulness,' he'd said. 'Jam is a highly nutritious source of energy.'

'Of course it is, Henry, of course it is. So we are to satisfy the troops' sweet tooth, boost their energy and assist the war effort all at the same time. Jolly good, very patriotic, I say.' Reginald had congratulated himself yet again on having backed Henry Jones as a winner. How clever of the man to have gained the defence contracts, and so quickly off the mark.

'Yes, yes,' as usual Reginald's irony had been wasted on Henry, 'but we need to finance the smaller fruit growers in order to increase production if we're to meet the army's demand. I've secured a loan from Barclays Bank for the purpose, but I thought you might like to be in on it, Reginald.'

'I most certainly would, old man. After all one must do one's bit for the cause, mustn't one?'

'One must! Oh yes indeed, one most certainly must!' Henry had thumped his fist on the table with such emphasis that Reginald had wondered whether it was possible the man had actually persuaded himself there was a vestige of altruism in his actions.

The Boer War was not the only event of significance
that was proving financially advantageous to Reginald
Stanford. The birth of Federation brought about the final
dismantling of the tariff barriers that had had a crippling
effect on inter-colonial trade – particularly for Tasmania,
with its limited population and isolated position.

The Colonial Tariff Wars had seen the downfall of
many a business during the latter half of the nineteenth
century. The colonies, each concerned for its own survival,
had introduced customs barriers and tariff restrictions that
were absurdly protectionist in order to stifle importation
and prevent competition. Federation was to be a blessing
for those enterprising men of industry set upon broadening their horizons, and Reginald had been quick to antici-
pate their needs. Such men, in expanding their mainland
interests, would not only require investment: they would
need to purchase or hire offices and factory sites and warehouses. Stanford Colonial had, for some time now, been
acquiring suitable real estate in Victoria and New South
Wales, and sales and rentals were already booming.

Business was going exceedingly well all round for
Reginald, with one major exception: the Powells.

After dangling the carrot in front of Simon Hawtrey
and dropping hints to George Powell, Reginald had bided
his time, leaving the family to contemplate the obvious
benefits of a future merger between Stanford Colonial and
Powell Channel Transport. They were bound to see the
advantages that could be had by all, and they would be
further tantalised if he kept them waiting.

Then, upon hearing of the death of young James, he
had decided to wait even longer, allowing time for the
family to grieve before putting a proposal forward. He'd
sent a letter of condolence to George and flowers to the
boy's mother. It was wiser to leave his approach until after
the New Year anyway, he'd decided. With the new trade
opportunities that would follow Federation, a regular

freight service to the mainland would be invaluable and given the tie-up between the Powells' respective businesses they'd leap at the chance.

It had been the tie-up between the Powells' businesses that had attracted Reginald from the outset. The Powells represented the perfect commercial proposition. They were a ready-made operation: the work was all done for him. It only needed someone with money and a broader vision to step in and take over.

Reginald had waited until February before making an appointment with Simon Hawtrey and, on a bright summer's morning, he had presented himself, together with Nigel Lyttleton, at the house in Napoleon Street. The two of us are bound to have an impact upon the man, he thought, particularly as Hawtrey's office – in his family home no less – was so extraordinarily drab and unimpressive.

They were greeted at the door by Hawtrey's homely wife, who was cordial enough, but seemed incapable of smiling. Reginald had encountered her on his previous visit and had found her a most dour woman. And with such a successful business, surely the Powells could have a servant or two? Did they care nothing for appearances?

He introduced Nigel to Martha Hawtrey, although it appeared the two knew each other on a vague social level, having apparently met at several charity fundraising functions. Which means that I've probably met the woman myself on previous occasions, Reginald thought, but he'd certainly forgotten where or when. Nigel laid on the charm, as indeed he did himself, but there was still not a smile to be had.

She showed them to the study, where Hawtrey welcomed them, and when she left they set out on the desk the full presentation, an imposing folder with pages and pages of data designed to overwhelm.

But it didn't. Astonishingly enough, it had no effect at all.

'I'm so sorry,' Hawtrey said after barely five minutes, 'but had I known you'd gone to such trouble I'd have told you not to bother. I'm afraid the answer is no, gentlemen. I do sincerely apologise, Mr Stanford, if I have unwittingly given you any reason to believe the answer would be in the affirmative, but I have heard nothing from you since your original approach, so I presumed –'

'Have you discussed my proposal with other branches of your family?' Reginald demanded.

'If you're referring to my brother-in-law George Powell, yes, most definitely.' Simon did not mince words; when he wished to be direct, he certainly could be. 'The whole family has discussed the matter. The answer is an unequivocal no,' he said.

And that, it appeared, was that.

Reginald was furious. How dare this nondescript little man have the audacity to turn him down! He said as much to Nigel as they left the house.

'How dare he turn me down like that?' he said as they headed for the horse and trap where his coachman was waiting. 'How dare he?!'

'Steady on, old chap,' Nigel said reasonably, 'you can't win them all, you know.'

But Reginald wasn't listening. The plans he had laid in place for the past year had been thwarted and he was in the blackest of rages. 'Who the hell does he think he is?' he said, climbing into the trap. 'Good God, I offer him and his wretched family the opportunity of a lifetime, a chance to move up in the world! They come from convict stock, for God's sake.' Reginald had looked into the Powells' history, as he always did when he intended to buy up a family concern. 'They should be grateful to be associated with a firm like Stanford Colonial. What in God's name would induce them to refuse such an offer?!'

'Perhaps they don't want to be taken over,' Nigel

suggested mildly as the trap set off up the hill. The remark did not improve Reginald's humour.

So convinced had he been that his takeover of the Powells was a fait accompli that Reginald remained in a rage for weeks after the meeting. He detested the Powells for having shattered his dream of a Stanford Colonial shipping line. There was nothing he could do about their decision, however, and no alternative solution offered itself. He certainly did not intend to set up the business from scratch: it was far too risky. He would now have to forgo his grand plan, and all because of the wretched Powells. It rankled immensely.

Reginald did not plot revenge, much as he would have liked to, simply because he couldn't. He was powerless. The family was too self-sufficient, their businesses were impregnable. One day, however, an opportunity presented itself that he simply couldn't resist. Here is a chance to get back at a branch of the Powells, he thought, and without their knowledge that I am in any way responsible. There would be no repercussions. It was perfect.

He'd arrived at the wharf warehouse late in the day with the intention of checking through the list of freight that was booked aboard the P & O freighter due to depart for the mainland early the following morning. He noticed a large Charlotte Grove shipment sitting on its pallets. Charlotte Grove Orchard belonged to one of the Powells, didn't it? He wondered whether the shipment was awaiting collection for the local market or whether it was booked on the freighter.

There were workers around, but nobody took any notice as he slipped into the deserted foreman's office. He rifled through the paperwork and discovered that the shipment, arrived from the Huon Valley aboard the *SS Emma Jane* that very afternoon, had been booked into the warehouse by Quincy Powell and that space had been reserved aboard the P & O freighter the following morning. Reginald then checked the list drawn up by the foreman, and there it was among the dozens of names, conveniently written in pencil as changes were constantly being made: Charlotte Grove Estate.

Without giving it a second thought he erased the booking. It was doubtful the warehouse foreman would check the paperwork. To facilitate speediness he would no doubt issue orders directly from the list, and the dock workers wouldn't raise a query. They would simply load what they were told to load. All of which meant that, hopefully, the Charlotte Grove shipment would be left to rot in the warehouse. The Powells would have no idea he was involved. The Powells, like everyone else in the fruit market, booked their freight space through Henry Jones and WD Peacock. The unfortunate episode would be interpreted as a mistake by the warehouse foreman or the booking clerk – such things did happen – and no-one would be any the wiser. But it would be a costly mistake for the Powells of Charlotte Grove Estate. The sheer spite of the act gave Reginald immense satisfaction. So much so that in the weeks that followed he was able to put the Powells right out of his mind.

There was a recognisable tap on Reginald's study door.

'Come in, Clive,' he called. 'Yes, what is it?' he said as his manservant appeared.

'A Mr Powell is downstairs, sir. He says he wishes to discuss the proposed merger you put to Mr Hawtrey some time back.' Clive looked dutifully apologetic. It was not his place to know the master's business dealings. 'Forgive me, sir, but he was most specific and most insistent that I state his case –'

'And so you should. It's perfectly all right, show the man up.'

So George Powell has called cap in hand to see me, Reginald thought with smug satisfaction as Clive disappeared, closing the door behind him. There could be only one of two reasons for the man's visit. Perhaps he wished to join forces and was offering his support in the persuasion of his brother-in-law to agree to the merger, in which case they could do business. Or perhaps he was making a plea for the commissions that had been dangled before him prior to Hawtrey's blanket refusal of the offer, in which case he would be shown the door. Either way, the meeting promised to be intriguing.

'Come in,' he called as the familiar tap once again sounded. He did not bother rising from his chair.

The door opened. 'Mr Powell,' Clive announced.

Thomas stepped into the room, and Clive left, once again closing the door behind him.

Reginald was confused. This was not George Powell. This was a young man, still in his twenties by all appearances. He'd hardly come dressed for a business meeting either: hatless and leather-coated he looked like a man of the land and there was a distinct air of aggression about him.

'Who are you?' he asked.

'Thomas Powell of Charlotte Grove Estate.'

'Ah.' Reginald nodded pleasantly: he refused to be unnerved. It had been a whole month since his act of sabotage and he'd all but forgotten about it, although he had heard to his intense satisfaction that it had proved most successful. The entire Charlotte Grove fruit shipment had rotted away in the warehouse, having mystifyingly been left off the freight list, a regrettable incident indeed, but one which could not possibly be linked to him. 'And what can I do for you, Mr Powell?'

Thomas strode to the desk and, resting his hands on it, he leant forward, his face threateningly close to Reginald's.

'You can leave my family alone, Stanford, that's what you can do. None of us wants a bar of you and your *merger*,' he said scathingly, 'and if you intend to make us pay for that, then you'd better think again.'

'What on earth do you mean?' Reginald tried to bluff his way out of the situation, although there appeared little point – they clearly knew he was the culprit. 'I have no idea what you're talking about.' Even as he pretended innocence he wondered how on earth they could possibly have found out.

Thomas could see the puzzlement in the man's eyes. 'Oh, we know a great deal about you, Stanford, believe me,' he said. 'And I'm here to warn you, if you do one more thing that in any way damages any member of the Powell family or his business, you'll regret it.'

Thomas was in fact not speaking on behalf of the family at all. The family didn't even know of his visit. Indeed, they'd advised him against seeking a confrontation.

'We can't prove anything, son,' Quincy had said. 'You can't go around accusing people with no proof.'

'But you weren't at the meeting, Pappy. Everything Simon told us points directly to Reginald Stanford. He wanted the merger and when he didn't get it, he sought revenge. The man would cripple the whole lot of us if he could.'

'I've spoken to Simon and he tends to agree with you,' Quincy had said, 'but Simon himself has advised against taking action with no proof. We'll just have to make sure in the future that one of the family is there at the warehouse to see the shipment on board. You'll have to leave it at that I'm afraid.'

But inaction was not Thomas's way. He'd decided to take matters into his own hands, and a threat involving an army of Powells was far more effective than a one-man confrontation. Besides, if it came to a war he knew he was right. Powells stuck together.

'There's something you need to remember, Stanford,' he now added, his tone laced with menace, 'something that you really should bear in mind. There's only one of you. And there are a whole lot of us. I'd think about that if I was in your shoes.'

Reginald felt outrage rather than fear. 'Are you threatening me with physical violence?' he demanded.

'I most certainly am.'

'We'll see about that.' Reginald rose from his chair and crossed towards the bell-pull, which hung beside the windows looking out over the courtyard. He would summon Clive and have the young blackguard bodily evicted.

But Thomas was too quick for him. Thomas was lean and fit and fifteen years Reginald's junior, and he was suddenly very, very angry. The man's arrogance infuriated him and in an instant he was by Reginald's side, his hands around his throat.

'I mean it, Stanford,' he said. 'You do one thing to damage our family and I'll kill you, I swear I will.'

Reginald struggled to free himself, but he was no match for the younger man. Thomas hurled him aside, sending him crashing into the desk; he fell to the floor among a pile of books, the desk lamp shattering beside him.

Thomas, for all his rebellious nature, was not a violent man and he was a little taken aback by his own reaction. He stood watching as Reginald climbed to his feet and again made resolutely for the bell-pull.

'Don't bother,' he said, 'I'm leaving.'

He strode out the door and, half way down the stairs he encountered Clive Gillespie who, having heard the commotion, was on his way up to investigate.

'Your boss wants you,' Thomas said and he passed on by.

Clive paused for a moment, wondering whether he should apprehend the young man, and if he should, what for, but it was too late, Powell was already striding across the hall towards the front door. Clive continued up the stairs.

Reginald was not accustomed to being threatened, and he didn't like it one bit. He also took offence at being personally assaulted. How dare the young thug manhandle him in such a manner. He longed to seek retribution. If only he could employ Alf Jordan to teach the blackguard a lesson, but of course he didn't dare. If any harm came to Thomas Powell the family would know he was responsible. Just as they would know he was responsible for any acts of sabotage upon their respective businesses. There could be no retaliation.

Reginald's anger and frustration knew no bounds. Once again the Powells had aroused in him the blackest of rages.

It was May 1902 and the Boer War was over. Victory was celebrated throughout the nation, and nowhere with greater pride than in the island state of Tasmania. Approximately 860 Tasmanians had served in South Africa, the vast majority as mounted infantry and, of all the Australian units to take part in the conflict, the 1st Tasmanian Imperial Bushmen was the most highly decorated, winning two of the six Victoria Crosses awarded to Australians. Little wonder Tasmanians held their heads high.

'I see no cause for celebration,' Silas croaked cantankerously. 'Twenty-seven of our young men lost their lives. What is there to celebrate in that?'

Silas Stanford had been against the war from the outset. He was against war in general and extremely outspoken in his views.

'The only people who gain from war are the pariahs who get fat on the misery of it,' he'd say time and again. 'The profiteers and the warmongers, Godless men every one,' he'd rant. 'War brings out the very worst in mankind.'

Now, even as Tasmania celebrated the return of its sons and sang the praises of its heroes, Silas would not leave the subject alone.

'Damn good thing the whole wretched business is over,'

he croaked to his son. His voice these days crackled with age and phlegm, and Reginald found it incredibly nerve-jangling.

Reginald found everything about his father nerve-jangling. At the age of ninety-seven the old man was in a state of decay. Emaciated, skeletal and sunken-eyed, he reeked of death. The only trouble was, he refused to die. And even worse, he refused to shut up.

'My only wish is that this war might have ended before men managed to reap personal gain from it,' Silas continued. 'The whole business is immoral –' He would have gone on further if Reginald hadn't interrupted him.

'Tasmanian industry benefited from the Boer War, Father,' he said. Sometimes he let the old man ramble, trying in vain to close his ears to the crackle of phlegm; on other occasions, dependent upon his own mood, he would goad his father into an argument. Today he was not inclined to sit in silence while his nerves were stretched to screaming point. 'In fact the state of Tasmania is in a far better financial position than it was prior to the conflict in South Africa.'

'Shame,' Silas declared dramatically, 'shame on those profiteers I say!'

'They weren't profiteers at all,' Reginald countered, 'they were honest men who accepted contracts from the Imperial Defence Force. In supplying goods to the army they assisted the cause.'

'And got rich in the process, boy, don't forget that.' Silas's head started to quaver as it always did when he became overheated and argumentative. 'They got rich in the process, my word. Why, just look at that Henry Jones. Tasmanian jam sales were at an all-time low in '99.' He waggled a claw-like finger at his son. 'I keep my eye on the market, boy, I know what's going on. Smaller factories were closing down, but what does Jones do? He gets rich supplying jam to the army. That's profiteering, that is.' By the ring of triumph in his voice Silas was clearly declaring himself the winner.

'I follow the market too, Father,' Reginald said calmly. Nothing was to be gained in allowing his irritation to show, for his father would only see it as a further sign of victory. 'And lucrative though Jones's defence contract may have been, it is also well known that he personally supplied one million pounds of jam to the war effort without taking payment.' Reginald remembered being flabbergasted at the time. It is surely some misguided public relations gesture on Henry's part, he'd thought, unnecessary, wasteful and quite foolish, in his opinion.

'Covering his tracks,' Silas crowed triumphantly. 'Covering his tracks. The man's a profiteer –'

'Don't overexcite him, Reggie, he's not been well lately.'

Reginald was relieved at the arrival of his mother with the tea and chicken sandwiches. It was pointless discussing the war with his father.

Mathilda sat and started to pour. 'I was hoping you'd bring Evelyn and the boys around for morning tea, dear,' she said. He often did these days.

'I wanted to, Mother, but Hugh has the croup and Evelyn decided to stay home with him rather than leave him in Nanny's care.'

'Oh, what a pity.'

Reginald placed his father's chicken sandwich on the table beside him, wishing the old man would choke on it.

'You should have brought Rupert,' Silas said accusingly.

'I would have, Father,' Reginald replied with a tight smile, 'but you know Rupert: he won't go anywhere without Hugh.'

Reginald would never have dreamt of bringing Rupert along on his own. He avoided at all costs being alone in the boy's company; if it had been possible he would have avoided the child altogether.

'It's charming, isn't it,' Mathilda said, handing Reginald

his father's cup of tea, 'the way the boys are so close at such a tender age.'

At seven and six, the brothers were inseparable, a fact which infuriated Reginald. Adorable as everyone appeared to find Rupert, surely the company of a simpleton could not benefit a normal, healthy child. He worried for Hugh.

'Yes, Mother, the boys' affection for each other is a delight to us all.' The greatest dissembling feat of Reginald's life was living the lie that he felt any fondness for his eldest son. His wife sensed his discomfort, certainly, but even Evelyn was not aware of the extent of his loathing.

Reginald handed his father his cup of tea.

'You should have brought Rupert,' the old man said again, and Reginald wanted to kill him.

'I will next time, Father, I promise. I'll bring both the boys next time. They always love to see you.'

Strangely enough, the boys didn't seem to find the old man obscene at all. They'd quite happily climb up onto his lap and play with his beard; they didn't even seem to notice his rancid breath. Indeed, Silas and seven-year-old Rupert had developed a particularly fond relationship. They found each other funny. Silas's galah-like cackle when the child pulled his beard would set Rupert off and he'd give his donkey-like bray in return. Then everyone would join in: Evelyn, Mathilda and young Hugh, they'd all laugh. The women appeared to find it charming and Hugh obviously thought it was hilarious. Reginald didn't. The sight of the cadaverous old man and the vacuous boy with the donkey laugh disgusted him, and he would find a pretext to look away.

It surprised Reginald that many, upon first meeting Rupert, failed to register the child was retarded, for he was a good-looking boy. The laugh gave him away, of course, and very quickly because Rupert laughed a lot, but to Reginald just one glance was enough. The wide-eyed vacancy, the broad dimwitted smile, the constant need to be tactile, running his hands over things and people: this was not a normal child.

Reginald had hoped to ignore Rupert, but as the years passed it became more and more difficult. Everything about the boy rankled.

'Well I'll leave you two to chat,' Mathilda said twenty minutes later when she'd poured the men their second cup of tea. 'I must hang out the washing in order to catch the afternoon sun. If there is to *be* any sun of course,' she added as she stood. 'With winter coming on one is really reliant upon the breeze.'

'Let me help you, Mother.' Reginald rose from his chair. The fact that they didn't employ a washerwoman annoyed him: that would be his father's meanness, of course.

'No, no, Reggie, stay and amuse your father, I insist – he sees all too little of you these days. And Silas, dear, do eat your sandwich,' she instructed, 'you need to keep your strength up.'

'Yes, yes.' Silas reached for his side plate. He'd forgotten the sandwich was there, and he very much enjoyed his chicken sandwiches.

'I shall have to be going soon, Mother,' Reginald said. He hated being left alone with his father when the old man was eating. The sight revolted him.

'Finish your tea first, dear. And don't forget your own chicken sandwich. You haven't touched it.'

'Of course.' Reginald obediently sipped his tea, but he didn't touch the sandwich. He couldn't possibly while his father was eating.

'Come and say goodbye before you go,' his mother called over her shoulder as she left the room.

'Of course,' he called after her. He rose and crossed to the window, peering through the drawn curtains, pretending to check on the weather; anything to avoid the old man and his sandwich. 'It's getting a bit nippy, isn't it?'

'You should have brought Rupert,' Silas muttered petulantly through a mouthful of chicken.

Reginald turned from the window. 'Actually, Father, I'm thinking of having Rupert committed.' He didn't know exactly what made him say it. He'd been thinking of no such thing, but the desire to shock was overwhelming.

Silas stared at his son in slack-jawed amazement, the forgotten mouthful of chicken sandwich unattractively evident. Rupert committed? Surely he had heard incorrectly.

'Yes,' Reginald continued. He found the old man's reaction intensely gratifying. 'I've been giving it quite a bit of thought lately. Rupert will soon be of school age, and he naturally can't be enrolled in any normal educational facility. I really do believe the lunatic asylum might be the place for him.' Bent purely on shock though he was, Reginald suddenly found the idea appealing. Why had it not occurred to him before? But of course his wife and his mother would never allow it. What a pity, he thought.

Silas was outraged beyond belief. A lunatic asylum? Little Rupert? How could Reginald contemplate such a thing? He hastily swallowed his sandwich in order to protest. *Are you mad, boy?* he was about to roar, *he's your son! He's a Stanford! Stanfords do not commit their sons to lunatic asylums!* But he didn't get a word out. A lump of chicken lodged in his windpipe and he gagged instead.

'I haven't made any firm decision as yet,' Reginald said, very much enjoying the apoplectic rage he could see in his father's eyes. The old man was so angry he couldn't even speak. 'It's early days, of course, but I do find the impediment Rupert threatens to Hugh's future development rather worrying at times, and the lunatic asylum would appear to be one solution to the problem.'

Silas couldn't breathe. He pummelled his chest with his fist and gestured for Reginald to thump him on the back as he fought to dislodge the food stuck in his throat.

Good heavens above, Reginald thought as he registered

what was happening. How often had he secretly prayed for this? Every single time he'd given the old man his chicken sandwich he'd wished that he'd choke on it, and now he actually was.

'You're getting a little overexcited, Father,' he said. 'You mustn't, you know. As Mother keeps telling you it's not good for your health.' He smiled benignly. 'Besides, I was only joking, I wouldn't really put Rupert in an asylum, you know that.' Not long to go now, surely, the old man was starting to turn blue.

Silas struggled for breath, his hands clawing at the arm rests. The boy could see he was choking, why didn't he do something? He stared up at his son in disbelief. His son could see he was choking and his son was doing nothing.

His son continued to do nothing.

Reginald watched his father die, and his father, right up until the end, watched him watching.

When it was over, Reginald waited for a further moment or so. Then he went out to the rear of the house where his mother was hanging up the washing on the back verandah.

'I insist you let me help,' he said. 'Father's in a cantankerous mood so I've left him with his chicken sandwich.'

'You two are utterly incorrigible,' Mathilda said, handing him a pillowslip.

Ten minutes later they went back inside, where they discovered to their mutual horror that Silas had choked on his chicken sandwich.

CHAPTER EIGHTEEN

Eileen O'Callaghan knew her son was using her. It had been apparent right from the start that Col had brought his children home for her to look after. But to his credit he hadn't dumped them with her and left; and as the years had passed she wouldn't have minded if he had anyway. Now, a decade on, young Oscar and Caitlin had become her very life. They were rascally and personable, both of them, reminding her strongly of her own brood as children. At eleven Caitie, destined to be a beauty with her flame-red hair and emerald eyes, could have been Shauna all over again, and thirteen-year-old Oscar was a beefier version of Col as a boy, cheeky and fearless. The children gave meaning to Eileen's existence; it was for their sake she must stay healthy, and now well into her seventies she had never felt better.

Col was still something of a child himself, parenthood appearing to have little effect on him. He loved his children, but he was a terrible disciplinarian. No rules were laid down. He'd spoil little Oscar and Caitie with lollies and he'd show off to make them laugh, his idea of fatherhood being to give his children a good time. It certainly endeared him to his children, but not to his mother. 'You can't let them run wild,' Eileen would complain time and again, but it would make no difference. Like his father, Col was a loveable rogue with no sense of responsibility. He was, also like his father, a wastrel with money and Eileen had been compelled to exercise a degree of control over his life, just as she had over her husband's.

'Your children will need a proper education, Colin,' she'd said sharply after having put up with the situation for a whole two years. She never called him Colin unless she really meant business. 'And a proper education takes money.' I might as well be speaking to Mick, she thought. 'You will give me half your salary each week and I shall put it aside for Oscar and Caitie's schooling. The rest you may gamble away or spend on your fancy clothes or do with as you wish, but those are the rules from now on – do you understand me?'

'Yes, Ma.' Col hadn't dared argue back. Even in her advancing years, his mother remained a formidable woman. Besides, he was grateful to Eileen for having taken on the upbringing of his children: they were much better off under her control.

Col had found himself an excellent job. 'You're looking at Col the Cooper,' he'd jokingly announced the day he'd got it, 'Col the Cooper of Cascade Brewery, no less.'

Good coopers were highly valued employees and Cascade Brewery was known to look after its workers well. Col was happy with the job and the perks that it offered, particularly the free ale that was supplied during morning and afternoon tea breaks and also at lunchtime. It made for a convivial workplace, as the bosses well knew.

Each day he would catch the tram to and from the brewery; and at the end of each week he would return home with his pay packet, which he would hand directly to his mother, who would extract half the money. Col would buy toys and lollies for the children, but most of the other half went on the card tables and the brandy and cigars he shared with his like-minded friends or on the purchase of a snappy new item of clothing – he had inherited his father's taste for the good life. Occasionally, when he'd had a win at cards, he would spend up handsomely wining and dining a woman he'd met, but only if he knew there'd be an exchange of favours at the end of the evening. Col, who was still highly popular with women, never needed to buy sex, but he believed in wooing his way into a woman's bed: it was all part of the fun.

'Don't you dare bring one of your fancy tarts back here,' Eileen would warn him when she saw him dressed up to the nines on a Saturday night. 'I won't have any of that hanky-panky going on in my house.' Eileen had become very straitlaced in her old age. 'I will not have the children exposed to women with loose morals,' she'd say primly, although she was secretly glad that Col was playing the field rather than seeking a wife as he should. She didn't want to share the children with another woman.

Col was smart enough to toe the line; he knew better than to abuse his mother's trust. He was living the good life and all because of Eileen. He had two children who adored him and whom he adored in return and yet none of the responsibilities that went with them. Indeed, he was leading the life of a bachelor, and very much enjoying himself.

Eileen had enrolled Oscar and Caitie at St Joseph's College and St Mary's College respectively. They were the same Catholic schools to which she had sent her own children, although both were well-established now, and St Joseph's had relocated since then. Both were now in Harrington Street, both had fine reputations and both were expensive. The cash that had been set aside from Col's wages would not fully cover the ongoing costs, but Eileen had known it wouldn't. She had quite a lot of money sitting in the bank earning interest and was happy to make up the difference herself, although she would not tell Col. Perhaps her son, in presuming that he had taken on the responsibility of his children's education, might finally grow up himself, although she somehow doubted it.

'Did you know that Mount Wellington used to be called *Kunanyi*?' Caitie said.

'By who?' Oscar demanded.

'The Aborigines. It's an Aboriginal word, Sister Brigid says.' Caitie adored school, and particularly Sister Brigid, who was her form mistress. '*Kunanyi* was what the Aborigines called the mountain thousands and thousands of years ago. Sister O'Donaghue says they had other names for it as well, but that one's her favourite.' Caitie nodded decisively. 'It's mine too,' she said.

'That's very interesting, Caitie,' Eileen remarked.

The family was gathered about the dining table for the evening meal. Eileen had just said grace, having re-introduced the ritual for the benefit of the children, who were now receiving religious instruction at school. 'We must be seen to do the right thing, Col,' she had said when he'd ribbed her good-naturedly.

'That's very interesting indeed, dear,' she added as everyone tucked into their stew and potatoes and Brussels sprouts. The family dinner invariably opened with discussion about something learnt at school that day and Eileen strongly encouraged the practice.

Oscar didn't find it in the least bit interesting. 'I kicked four goals this arvo, Da,' he said, 'more than anyone else on our team.'

'Good on you, lad,' Col beamed his approval, 'well done.'

Like father like son, Eileen thought and she wondered wryly whether it was something in the O'Callaghan blood. There seemed to be a recurring pattern that the O'Callaghans produced smart girls with enquiring minds and boys with no academic interest whatsoever. Mick had said as much himself all those years ago. '*What good are boys*', he'd said, '*wastrels every one of them.*' It seemed he was right when it came to the O'Callaghans.

'Did you learn anything of particular value today, Oscar?' she asked, just a little archly.

Thirteen-year-old Oscar, aware he was being put to the test, was not in the least daunted. He had his grandmother's measure and knew exactly how to get around her. 'I learnt that the Duke of Wellington commanded the allied army that defeated Napoleon at the Battle of Waterloo,' he said looking her boldly in the eye, 'and I learnt that that's who Mount Wellington is named after.'

Col gave a hoot of laughter, and Eileen herself could not resist a smile. Oscar might grow up a wastrel like his father and his grandfather, but like his father and his grandfather, Oscar was not stupid. He had a ready wit and cheeky charm that could take him anywhere.

The only one who didn't join in the joke was Caitie who, as bold as her brother, was determined to have the last word.

'*Kunanyi*'s much prettier,' she said.

Eleven-year-old Hugh Stanford was also enjoying school, although he missed the company of his older brother. Rupert was tutored privately at home while, each day, Hugh walked to the Hutchins School, which was barely a block away.

'Rupert can't go with you, darling,' his mother had explained several years previously when he'd first been enrolled. 'Rupert needs a special sort of teacher. But you'll be able to discuss your lessons when you get home,' she'd added brightly. 'That'll be fun, won't it?'

Reginald had fumed as he'd heard Evelyn say that. Fun? It would be disastrous. Indeed it was just as he'd feared. The simpleton would retard Hugh's development.

So far, however, Reginald had been wrong. If anything, the relationship between the boys had strengthened his younger son. Hugh had learnt that his brother was different, that even though Rupert was the older, he was somehow younger in the head. The knowledge brought out a caring instinct in Hugh that lent him a maturity unusual in one of his age.

'You don't do it that way, Rupert,' he would say very patiently when Rupert forgot his table manners and picked up his knife or fork incorrectly. 'You do it like this,' he'd say and he'd demonstrate. Rupert would then imitate his younger brother, and he'd imitate not just the way Hugh held the utensil, but his instruction and the very way he spoke.

'You do it like this, Rupert,' he would say, sounding exactly like Hugh – he was a clever mimic – and Hugh would laugh. Rupert loved making his brother laugh. 'You write a "b" this way, Rupert,' he would say, painstakingly copying the way Hugh had written it down on the notepad for him, 'and a "d" goes this way.'

'That's right, you're always getting them mixed up.'

'That's right, I'm always getting them mixed up.' So eager was Rupert to please his younger brother that he learnt more from Hugh than he did from his tutor and his parents together.

According to medical opinion, Rupert was not expected to make any further progress intellectually. At twelve years of age he could read and write a little, but his skills were unlikely to improve for his powers of concentration were minimal. It was considered worthwhile continuing with a tutor, though, in order to keep him stimulated and mentally active. He could dress himself and take responsibility for his personal hygiene, his ability to communicate was more than adequate and although his vocabulary was limited his speech was coherent, particularly when he imitated others, as he often did. He would never support himself, however, and would require a lifetime of care. His intellectual capacity would remain that of an eight- or nine-year-old, Evelyn was informed, and his emotional responses would continue to be extremely childlike; he would crave and give affection at all times. By now the diagnosis came as no surprise to either Evelyn or Reginald.

Hugh was not only caring of Rupert, he was strongly

protective, and it was at school that his protective instincts came most strongly to the fore.

'What's wrong with your brother?' his classmates would ask when there was a school fete or an intra-school football match that families attended. Evelyn always took Rupert along on such occasions; she considered it good for him to socialise with other children. Reginald never attended, saying he would go to the football matches when Hugh was older and playing on the school team.

'Rupert's just different, that's all,' Hugh would reply. His young classmates happily accepted the explanation, but some of the older boys, particularly those of Rupert's own age, would snigger and point; and when he laughed his donkey laugh they'd openly jeer. That was when Hugh would fix his icy gaze upon them. He would simply stare them down until they felt uncomfortable and looked away. The expression may well have been one he'd learnt from his father, but Hugh had made it his own and it proved very effective.

It wasn't long before Rupert lost his curiosity value. The older boys ignored him and the younger ones found they liked him. They thought his laugh was funny just as Hugh always had and there was no malice when they laughed along with him, which Rupert himself always enjoyed for he liked to see people happy. Strangely enough, Hugh's young school friends even learnt things from Rupert, discovering through him a whole new tactile world. When Rupert focused upon the silky surface of a cricket bat, stroking it with infinite care, or when he slowly and tenderly ran the tips of his fingers over the petals of the roses that grew in the school's front garden, they were compelled to do the same.

Reginald Stanford found his son's obsession with the tactile unbelievably irksome, particularly when it was practised upon him.

'Don't do that,' he'd snapped the first time when, as an

eight-year-old, Rupert had quietly approached him and, standing beside his armchair, had started stroking his face.

He'd slammed down the newspaper he'd been reading, his reaction startling the child, who'd stepped back alarmed, looking from his mother to his brother and back to his father, wondering what he'd done wrong.

'He's only trying to make you happy, dear,' Evelyn had said. Distracted from her petit point, she'd been watching the boy's concern for his father, and she'd been touched by the tenderness of his action.

'I'm perfectly happy, thank you.'

'You didn't look it. You were frowning.'

'I was reading the newspaper. I was distracted.'

'It *looked* as if you were unhappy. Rupert was just trying to make you smile. Isn't that right, darling,' she'd said comfortingly to the child, 'you were trying to make Daddy smile.'

Rupert had nodded, his wary eyes not once leaving his father.

Dear God, Reginald thought, can't a man frown in his own house? But he'd smiled obligingly nonetheless. Evelyn was pregnant again at long last and he daren't upset her.

'There you are, Rupert, a great big smile, see? Daddy's very, very happy.'

The boy had grinned inanely back and rejoined his brother on the sitting room floor where they'd been playing with their toy train.

'He's such a sweet-natured child, Reginald,' Evelyn had said quietly, 'he's always concerned for the feelings of others. And we must remember that the doctor –'

'I know, my dear,' he'd replied, stemming his irritation, aware of the gentle reprimand. 'The doctor says that he will respond well to affection, and we have certainly observed this to be true; he just took me by surprise, that's all. I'm sorry, do please forgive me.'

'Of course, dear.' Evelyn had smiled her wholehearted forgiveness and returned to her petit point.

Five minutes later, Reginald had retired upstairs. 'I must get an hour or so's paperwork in before dinner,' he'd said as he stood.

'On a Sunday?' she'd queried. 'You work altogether too hard, Reginald.'

'I know.' He'd kissed her on the forehead and retreated to the sanctity of his study.

Given the fact that his wife was in her fifth month of pregnancy at the age of thirty-eight, Reginald had determined to do all in his power to maintain a harmonious household, but to his mind having to put up with the caresses of his cretinous son was pushing things altogether too far.

Evelyn had not kept the baby. She had miscarried just a month later. It was her second miscarriage since Hugh's birth, and of all the miscarriages she'd had over the years it was the one that had very nearly killed her. Reginald had been warned by the doctor that any further attempt by his wife to bear a child would most certainly cost her her life.

'Evelyn is in a very weakened state, Mr Stanford,' Doctor Harvey had said rather severely, as if it were somehow Reginald's fault. 'She is nearly thirty-nine years of age, and yet she tells me she wishes to bear you another son. I'm afraid you must both accept the fact that this is not possible. There will be no more children.'

It had been a bitter blow for Reginald and the following year he'd taken himself off to Europe on a business trip to escape the gloom that had enveloped him.

He'd bought a car while he was there, and not just any car. He had planned for some time now to join the motoring era in a grand manner, his intention being to lead the way and show Hobart's men of industry just who had the greatest style. Upon visiting the British

International Motor Show in London he had discovered the perfect vehicle. There it was on display, the brand new Rolls Royce 40/50.

Reginald had never seen such magnificence. An open-topped vehicle with front and rear leather-upholstered seats and graceful lines that featured broad, sweeping mudguards and running boards, the bodywork shone brilliant silver and the fittings were of highly polished brass. The effect was dazzling. This was a car designed for a man with style, flair and money, and Reginald had all three, although the expense, he had discovered, was prohibitive. Eight hundred pounds and a further one hundred in shipping costs had been more than he had reckoned upon paying, but not for one minute had he wavered in his decision. Such a show of wealth was irresistible. Why the Joneses and the Peacocks and the Lyttletons and the Dimblebys and all those other barons of commerce had nothing like this. They'd be green with envy, every one of them.

After placing an order for the vehicle, which was as yet not even on the market, he'd had to wait a whole two years before it had finally been delivered. But on the day when he'd first driven his Rolls Royce through the streets of Hobart, Reginald had considered the wait worth every minute. With Evelyn seated beside him in her pretty straw hat and motoring veil, and the boys perched behind them in the rear seat, he'd felt like a king, and he'd known that he looked like one as every head had turned and people had stopped to stare and point. We are royalty on parade, he'd thought, and he hadn't even minded the donkey brays he could hear coming from the back. Royal families after all were renowned for having their share of demented offspring.

The car had proved a great salve, and having now resigned himself to the fact that there would be no more sons, Reginald's domestic life settled into a comfortably acceptable pattern. Evelyn and Hugh protected him from Rupert's constant desire for physicality, although in doing so they were no doubt protecting Rupert from any adverse reaction.

'Father doesn't like to be cuddled, Rupert,' Hugh would say when Rupert would occasionally forget his instructions and try to snuggle up against his father.

Rupert would back away immediately. 'Father doesn't like to be cuddled, Rupert,' he would remind himself. Then he would look at Reginald with infinite compassion. 'Poor Father,' he would say.

Reginald would smile at the boy, a smile that was not even forced. 'Yes, poor Father,' he would say. With the rules laid down, he found it quite easy these days to be pleasant to the child.

The following year, however, the harmony of Reginald's personal life was shattered by the shock of his mother's death. Mathilda Stanford, always a strong, capable woman, had shown no sign of illness and her death came as a surprise to all those who knew her.

'She had a good innings, Reginald,' Amy said, intending in her practical fashion to offer comfort to her brother. 'Mathilda was four years older than me, which would put her well over the three score years and ten that one hopes for, and she felt no pain. There's little to grieve over, really.'

Amy Stanford-Balfour had come into town for the funeral, her son Edwin accompanying her on the train. Amy had considered it a show of respect to her father's memory that she should attend his wife's service and burial, and so, it appeared, had others. Mathilda's funeral, although hardly the tribute to a life of prominence that Silas's had been seven years previously, was well-attended, and by a number of Hobart's most eminent citizens. Reginald, following the same plan he'd adopted at his father's funeral, had invited everyone back to Stanford House for the wake.

'But it was so unexpected, Amy,' he said as they sat together in a corner sipping at their glasses of fruit punch, while the servants milled among the guests with cups of tea and drinks and trays of sandwiches and cake. 'My mother never had a day's illness in her life.'

'I think she'd simply lost the desire to live,' Amy said. 'Our father had been her entire existence – she really did love him, you know. With no purpose in her life, she just faded away. At least that's my opinion.'

Reginald took umbrage. 'What about me and my family?' he said indignantly. 'Surely we were purpose enough.' He'd nearly said 'me and my son', but he'd managed to stop himself in time.

'That's just it, Reginald,' Amy tempered her reply, realising how deeply affected he'd been by the shock of his mother's death. 'You have a family,' she said gently. 'Much as you loved your mother, you didn't really *need* her, and Mathilda needed to be needed, that's all I'm saying.'

'Yes,' he said thoughtfully, 'yes, I suppose you're right.' Reginald stared down at his glass of fruit punch, remembering with fierce clarity the conversation he'd had with Amy after their father's funeral. They'd been seated right here in this very same corner on these very same chairs

'Fancy Father choking on his chicken sandwich like that,' she'd said, 'what a terrible pity you weren't with him.'

'Yes,' he'd agreed, 'I was out of the room for only ten minutes or so. It must have happened just after I'd left.'

'Oh well,' Amy had shrugged in her no-nonsense way, 'he was a grand age, something had to take him at some stage and it might as well have been a chicken sandwich.'

Now, as Reginald stared unseeingly at his glass, he couldn't help wondering whether, if he hadn't let his father choke to death, his mother might still be alive. If that was the case, then he'd not only killed the man he'd loathed throughout the whole of his life, but also the one person he'd truly loved.

'How's Hugh enjoying school?' Amy, noticing her

brother's pensiveness, decided to change the subject in order to distract him.

'Very much indeed.' Reginald snapped himself out of his mood; there was no point in being maudlin. 'And he's an excellent student.'

'I'm glad to hear it. He'll be joined by his cousins soon. Wesley and Harold will be starting next term.' Edwin Stanford-Balfour had enrolled his sons as boarders at the Hutchins School. 'Harry will no doubt be in Hugh's class as they're near the same age,' Amy said. 'I think eleven is a bit young to be a boarder, but Edwin is not in the least concerned. He says Wesley will look after his little brother, and I must say for a boy who's not yet thirteen Wesley is certainly a responsible child.' Amy's face clouded with concern: she doted on her grandsons. 'I can't help but worry though. Harry is still such a baby.'

'I shall keep a close eye on them for you, Amy,' Reginald promised. 'They shall come around to tea regularly, and any weekends they wish to spend here with us, they are more than welcome.'

'Why Reginald, how very kind of you.' Amy was most surprised by the offer, her brother had never appeared to enjoy the company of children. 'That would relieve me of all my worries – I really would be most grateful.' She hoped he didn't think she'd been hinting.

'What else are families for?' he said with a smile. 'I shall look forward to becoming acquainted with the Stanford-Balfour boys.'

The prospect of the boys' visits very much pleased Reginald, who always encouraged Hugh to bring his schoolfriends home. Indeed, the cook was instructed to keep up a regular supply of pasties and scones and cake for hungry little boys. Reginald was of the opinion that a social life with normal children would rescue Hugh from the damage that might result should he be left too much in the sole company of his brother.

'I feel I should warn you,' Amy said laconically, 'that they'll no longer be *Stanford*-Balfours.'

'I beg your pardon?' Reginald's look was blank.

'Edwin asked me whether I'd mind if Wesley and Harold dropped the hyphen. He said they'd rather not have a double-barrelled name as the other boys at school might think they're trying to be fancy. Darling Edwin,' she said fondly, 'he was so embarrassed when he asked me, I'm sure I've saddled the poor dear all these years with a name he can't stand. I did it purely for Father's sake, of course. It seemed the only way to continue the family name. And then lo and behold you came along,' Amy gave her brother the brightest of smiles, 'and what's more you presented him with another two Stanford males ...'

Another *one*, Reginald thought, only another *one*.

'... so my good intentions proved quite unnecessary.'

'Balfours or Stanford-Balfours, Amy, it doesn't matter either way,' Reginald said, 'I shall look forward to the company of Wesley and Harold. Now let's have a cup of tea, shall we?' He signalled to the maid, who was passing with the tray.

Wes and Harry, as the Balfour brothers quickly became known at the Hutchins School, proved to be pleasant lads, although on their weekend visits to Stanford House, Reginald found them a little rustic. Hardly surprising, he supposed. Like their father and their father's father, they were simple country boys, but they were highly respectful, their manners were acceptable enough, and most important of all they provided valuable company for Hugh.

He was interested to learn that the older boy, Wesley, was an accomplished athlete. Perhaps Hugh will gain inspiration from his cousin, Reginald thought. He certainly hoped so. A record of fine sportsmanship stood high on the agenda he had planned for his son.

'Wes is playing footie above his grade, Father,' Hugh

said, 'and it looks like he'll be selected for the school seniors next year.'

Reginald had popped into the breakfast room next door to the kitchen where a casual lunch was served up to the boys on a Saturday. He made a habit of popping in to have a brief chat when the Balfour brothers were staying. He thought it only proper to show an interest.

'Is that so, Wesley?' He pulled a chair up beside the table, where all four boys were seated scoffing down the warm Cornish pasties cook had just delivered. He avoided looking at Rupert, whose face was covered in chutney.

'Yes, sir.' Wesley's voice was muffled as he fought to reply without showing a mouthful of pasty. He always tried his hardest to observe his manners in front of Hugh's father, whom he'd been told to call 'Uncle Reginald' – though 'sir' seemed to fit much better. At least Wes thought so. Harry, quick to follow his big brother's example as usual, had also opted for 'sir' and, as neither of them had been corrected, Wes had presumed he must have hit upon a safe bet. It was strange really, because they were quite happy to call Hugh's mother 'Aunt Evelyn'. They liked Aunt Evelyn.

The Balfour boys were both a little overwhelmed by Stanford House and all it entailed. The family farmhouse at Pontville was big and spacious, but it was nowhere near as grand, and they didn't have servants who waited on them, they had labourers who worked side by side with their father. They didn't have a whopping great silver Rolls Royce either, much as they'd love to, although their father intended to buy a car soon. It was the way of the future, he said – they'd motor into town instead of catching the train. Things were done differently at Stanford House too. Dinner in the formal dining room on a Saturday night could be a daunting affair, what with wondering which fork or spoon to use. Wes had got it down to a fine art now though. He'd just follow Hugh's lead and nudge Harry if he got it wrong.

'The school seniors?' Reginald queried. 'But you'll be only fourteen next year. That's a very young age to be playing for the senior football team, surely.'

'Yes, sir,' Wes said again, very clearly now that he'd swallowed the mouthful of pasty. 'But I don't know for sure whether I'll be selected,' he added modestly.

'You will be,' Harry piped up: he was dead proud of his brother.

'Wes'll be the youngest footie player on the senior team, Father,' Hugh said with equal pride. 'Nobody gets to play for the firsts until they're at least fifteen. That's how good they reckon Wes is.'

Pleased though Reginald was that Wesley Balfour's sporting prowess had made such an impression upon his son, he did wish Hugh would avoid the use of slang and diminutives. But he supposed he couldn't blame the Balfours for that. Such bad habits were bound to be picked up at school. The young were so slovenly in their speech these days.

'I'm most impressed, Wesley,' he said, 'well done.' Thank goodness they can't make a diminutive out of 'Hugh', he thought.

'Thank you, sir,' Wes replied, 'fingers crossed though, I'm not on the team yet.'

Reginald stood, his duty done – he could play the jovial father for only so long. 'What are you boys up to this afternoon?'

'We're going to the Domain to kick the footie around,' Hugh said.

'Jolly good. Perhaps tomorrow morning after church,' he suggested casually, 'we might all go for a little spin in the car. What do you say?'

Wes and Harry exchanged a look of sheer delight. They were lost in awe of the silver Rolls Royce. Hugh's father had taken them for a ride in it once before and it had been the greatest thrill of their lives.

'Oh yes, please sir,' Wes said and Harry nodded furiously while Rupert bounced up and down in his seat braying.

'Excellent.' Reginald smiled. He enjoyed being popular with the boys. 'We'll set off around eleven o'clock. Wipe your mouth, Rupert, there's a good lad.'

The following year, Wes Balfour *was* selected for the Hutchins School senior football team, and he *was* the youngest member on the side. Training began in earnest for the first inter-school game of the year, the annual grudge match to be played against St Joseph's College in the autumn of 1910.

Also on the team were the Powell cousins, Gordon and David. Like the Balfours, they too were boarders, and had been for several years. Gordie, who had never outlived his childhood nickname, was seventeen now and a giant of a lad. Standing over six feet tall and with a strong physique he was an invaluable full forward. Gordie Powell could mark over the heads of his opponents, and once he'd done so remain steady as a rock. With his hands locked around the football there was no moving Gordie, or the ball for that matter; he just stood there while others who'd gone for the mark careered into him and each other.

Gordie's cousin, fifteen-year-old David Powell, lean and fit and fast, played in the ruck alongside Wes Balfour and the teamwork between the two was excellent. But of all the players, it was without doubt young Wes who was the prettiest to watch. Wes was an all-rounder. He was nimble. He could dodge and weave in spectacular fashion, his marks were dazzling, his goal kicking accurate and he could outrun anyone on the ground. When Wes had the ball none could catch him. The older boys had a great deal of respect for Wes Balfour's skills and they'd very quickly dropped their initial jibes about playing footie with babies.

The big day dawned and the weather was perfect. At least it was perfect in the morning: one could only hope that it would remain so. Given Hobart's unpredictable weather anything could happen.

The match, which was to be played at the Sandy Bay recreation oval, was scheduled for mid-afternoon on a Friday, and classes finished early, allowing time for those senior students wishing to attend the game to catch the tram. Virtually everyone was going. The sportsmaster and the team had departed a good hour or so earlier and were currently limbering up.

Harry Balfour was about to leave with the general exodus of boarders who had been herded into the court-yard by two of the teachers.

'I'll see you there, Harry,' Hugh called as he headed for the main gates.

'I'll save a place for you both,' Harry called back and he waved. Hugh was going home to collect Rupert.

By the time Hugh and Rupert arrived at the oval, the match was just about to start. The two had had a bit of a delay en route.

'Where's my scarf?' Rupert had said, suddenly panic-stricken as they'd arrived at the tram stop. 'Where's my scarf? I haven't got my scarf!' They'd had to go back for it, of course. Rupert always wore Hugh's school scarf at footie games: it made him one of the gang.

Hugh looked about the grassy perimeters of the oval. There was a good turn-out of supporters from both schools. Prominent on one side were the magenta and black of the Hutchins School and, on the other, the blue, white and gold of St Joseph's College. Elsewhere, pockets of people were sprawled on the grass. A number of families had laid out picnic rugs and were set up for afternoon tea with Thermoses and sandwiches, proud parents and siblings of the team members, no doubt. The weather had remained kind and the atmosphere was festive.

Hugh saw Harry wildly beckoning from the sea of magenta and black, indicating that he'd saved them each a space, but out on the field the two teams were assembled and the umpire was about to blow the whistle: any second the ball would be bounced. Hugh didn't want to disrupt the moment by wending his way through to Harry, so he waved back and pointed to the ground indicating they'd stay where they were. They'd join the others at quarter time, he decided.

'We'll sit here, Rupert,' he said and Rupert plonked himself down on the grass, his eyes trained unwaveringly on the ball in the umpire's hands.

The whistle sounded, the ball was bounced and the match was under way.

The centre clearance was carried out with clockwork precision by the Hutchins School team. The ruckman tapped the ball to David Powell who broke two tackles and swiftly passed to Wes Balfour, and then Wes was off like the wind. At the end of the field, big Gordie dodged his defender, and was in a perfect position to mark Wes's kick, planting himself tree-like while other players charged into him. He lined up his kick, which was an easy one as he was right in front of goal, and the ball sailed square through the middle of the sticks.

The Hutchins School supporters went wild. They'd scored within just one minute.

Rupert sprang to his feet. Waving his scarf madly, he jumped up and down cheering at the top of his voice; his fourteen-year-old voice, now broken, carried a lot of power.

The ball returned to the centre.

'Sit down, Rupert,' Hugh instructed, as the teams gathered for the bounce.

Rupert immediately sat. He always obeyed Hugh's instructions, knowing that he sometimes forgot when to be quiet.

The second goal proved just as easy. The centre clearance was again quick and faultless and within seconds

Wes Balfour had the ball. This time, however, with two St Joseph's defenders covering him, big Gordie Powell had trouble getting clear so Wes bounced the ball and kept running and, thirty yards out, he kicked for goal himself. The ball again went straight through the middle, and the Hutchins School supporters again went wild. The score was twelve points to nil within barely three minutes: it looked as if they might have the match sewn up right from the start.

But as it turned out they didn't. The next clearance was not so easily won. The St Joseph's centre man, having read the play between the opposing team's ruck players, seemed to leap out of nowhere and the ball never reached Wes Balfour. The centre man tapped it to a team-mate who deftly hand-passed it back, and before anyone could respond he was sprinting for goal. A quick pass to another player as he was about to be tackled, a dodge and a weave to get clear, and the same centre man had the ball again. None could catch him, and his running kick for goal just ten yards out was an easy one. The score was now twelve points to six.

It was the St Joseph's College supporters' turn to go wild, and they did. They'd been waiting for this to happen. It appeared that, just like the Hutchins School, they had their own football hero.

The game didn't continue as cleanly as it had started – there was fumbling and messy play on both sides – but the principal focus remained on two players, Wes Balfour and the St Joseph's College centre man. Their all-round skills were so superior to those of their fellow team members that it seemed to become a personal contest between them.

Shortly before quarter time, two girls arrived and settled themselves on the sidelines not far from Hugh and Rupert. They spread a rug out on the grass and sat down to watch the game. They were wearing St Mary's College uniforms and clearly barracking for the team from St Joseph's. Hugh barely noticed them, but Rupert did.

Rupert lost all interest in the game once his eyes fixed on the girl to his left, not five feet away. She was seated a little further down the slope, slightly in front of them, and her face was only visible in an occasional profile as she followed the action of the ball, but he wasn't watching her face anyway. He was transfixed by her hair. She was hatless and the thick tresses, which reached below shoulder length and were tied back by a ribbon at the base of her neck, were a fiery chestnut-red. Rupert had never seen hair that colour before.

A huge cheer went up from the Hutchins School supporters as another goal was scored, but Rupert didn't notice. He had eyes only for the hair.

Hugh glanced at his brother: how come Rupert wasn't jumping up and down? But Rupert appeared to have gone off into one of his other worlds, as he often did, although rarely at football matches, so Hugh returned his attention to the game.

Rupert needed to touch the hair. It was so alive where it hung there. The girl's slightest action set it moving with a life of its own, like the wild chestnut mane of an untamed horse. He was compelled to feel its texture. He shuffled sideways until he was right behind the girl. Then edging himself forwards he reached out his hand and with the very tips of his fingers he stroked the gleaming tresses.

His touch was so soft the girl didn't feel it.

Just like a wild horse, he thought, a wild horse that I'm taming through my fingers, the ripples of its mane responding to my magic. Rupert was mesmerised by his own power.

Then, in following the action of the game, the friend of the red-haired girl turned and saw him. She let out a startled scream, and Rupert scuttled away a yard or so on his bottom, people nearby turning to investigate the commotion.

'I'm sorry, I'm sorry, I'm sorry,' he said over and over; he was even more startled than the girls.

Hugh leapt to the rescue. 'What have you been up to, Rupert?' he said, crouching by his brother's side.

'I'm sorry, I'm sorry, I'm sorry.' Rupert flapped his hands and jiggled up and down on the spot as he always did when he was distressed.

'It doesn't matter,' Hugh said and very firmly he took hold of his brother's hands, 'it doesn't matter, calm down now. Calm down.'

Rupert's panic quickly subsided, although he kept muttering 'I'm sorry' to himself.

'He never means any harm,' Hugh said apologetically to the girls. 'What was he doing anyway?'

'He was stroking Caitie's hair,' one of them said.

'That was a bit rude – wasn't it, Rupert?' Hugh scolded in the gentle manner Rupert always responded to.

'Yes, yes.' Rupert nodded furiously. 'Sorry, sorry.'

'That's all right.' The red-haired girl smiled. She's extraordinarily pretty, Hugh thought. More than pretty in fact, she was beautiful. 'You're Hugh Stanford, aren't you?' she said. 'Your father owns the silver Rolls Royce.'

'That's right.' His father's Rolls Royce had made him famous at the Hutchins School, but Hugh hadn't realised how widely his fame had spread.

'I'm Caitie O'Callaghan and this is Mary Reilly. I've seen you driving around in your father's car, very flash. I've seen you too,' she said to Rupert.

She's certainly bold, Hugh thought: he wasn't accustomed to meeting girls as forthright as Caitie O'Callaghan. 'How do you do?' He nodded to both girls. 'This is my brother, Rupert Stanford,' he said. He always introduced Rupert in a formal fashion.

'Hello, Rupert Stanford.' Caitie smiled warmly at the childlike boy, who she'd recognised as simple.

Rupert, realising all was forgiven, gave a quick happy guffaw and his eyes once again fixated upon the hair. Everything else was forgotten. All he could see was the hair.

Then Caitie O'Callaghan did a wonderful thing. At least Hugh thought it was wonderful. Her friend Mary Reilly was clearly appalled.

Caitie O'Callaghan reached behind her head and undid the ribbon at the nape of her neck. She shook her head and tilted it to one side so that her hair hung free like a thick red blanket. 'There you are, Rupert,' she said. 'Go for your life.'

Rupert's eyes widened and his mouth opened into a great silent O. He was utterly speechless. He shuffled over beside her and with his open hand he carefully lifted up the mane of hair, letting it rest there on his palm, examining it closely, admiring its colour. Then very gently with the fingers of his other hand he started to stroke it. Lost in the richness and the texture he could quite happily have gone on stroking it for an hour, as his brother well knew.

'All right, Rupert, that's enough now,' Hugh said.

Rupert immediately obeyed as he always did. 'That's enough now, Rupert,' he told himself, and letting the hair fall gently back into place, he moved a respectful distance away.

'He likes to feel the texture of things,' Hugh explained unnecessarily, aware that Mary Reilly had found the episode embarrassing and was staring out at the match even though the whistle had sounded for quarter time and the players were walking off the field.

'That's fairly obvious.' Caitie laughed as she tied her hair back in place.

'Thank you,' he said, 'it was very nice of you.'

'Don't mention it,' she replied and they shared a smile.

'What's happened to the game?' Rupert asked looking out at the oval. His curiosity satisfied, the hair was now forgotten. 'Oh hello, Harry.' He beamed as Harry Balfour joined them.

'I kept a place for you,' Harry said, squatting beside them, 'why didn't you come and –' Then he noticed the pretty russet-haired girl who'd been chatting to Hugh. 'Oh.'

'The game was just about to start. I didn't want to

disrupt things.' Hugh hastily made the introductions. 'We've only just met,' he added, self-consciously, aware that Harry thought he had a secret girlfriend.

They chatted politely for a moment or so before Harry rose to his feet, impatient to leave.

'Come on, let's get back to the others before the second quarter starts,' he urged.

Hugh stood and they farewelled the girls, Rupert waving madly to Caitie.

'It's a darn good match,' Harry said as they turned to go. 'Who the heck is that centre man for St Joseph's?'

'He's my brother,' Caitie called over her shoulder with an unmistakeable ring of pride, 'my brother, Oscar O'Callaghan.'

Oscar O'Callaghan's name was on everyone's lips at the end of the game, as was Wes Balfour's. The two had been the undisputed stars of the match.

The older, seasoned members of the Hutchins School team knew Oscar O'Callaghan. He'd played for St Joseph's the previous year. Just like Wes, he'd been the youngest player on the field at the time.

'You've got to admit, he's not bad for a Mick,' big Gordie Powell said with a grin as, having shaken hands with their opponents, the victorious Hutchins School players left the field to join their supporters on the sidelines.

Wes Balfour and David Powell exchanged a wry smile. Gordie's comment was something of an understatement. Their team may have won the match, and so it should, they'd been the decidedly stronger side, but they'd won by just seven points. It could have been anybody's game, and purely because of Oscar O'Callaghan.

The players, especially Wes, were greeted enthusiastically by their schoolmates, Harry joining in with the others thumping his brother on the back. They all knew that without Wes they would have lost the match.

'Good on you, Wes.' Hugh shook his cousin's hand enthusiastically while Rupert jumped up and down on the spot, braying and waving his scarf at each and every member of the team. The whole school had by now come to know Rupert, particularly at football matches where he was accepted as their most avid supporter.

In typically perverse fashion, clouds had gathered and the day had turned chill, and it wasn't long before people started to disperse. Families packed up picnic rugs and hampers, and the Hutchins School students headed for home or, in the case of the boarders, back to school.

'We're not going back to school,' Wes Balfour explained to the Powell boys as a group of them prepared to set off for the tram. 'Harry and I are going back to Hugh's place, we're staying there the weekend.'

'Why don't you come home and have some pasties?' Hugh suggested to Gordie and David. 'Our cook makes the best pasties in the world, I can guarantee it.' The Powell boys being older, Hugh didn't know them particularly well, but he was eager to entertain two members of the footie team and they were obviously good mates with Wes.

At the mention of 'our cook' Gordie and David shared a glance. Young Hugh Stanford seemed nice enough, and Wes certainly liked him, but everyone knew his father was as rich as Croesus. Indeed their own fathers considered Reginald Stanford a man who abused his position of wealth and power. The boys didn't know why and they didn't particularly care, but Hugh Stanford was bound to be a spoilt brat.

'Can Max come too?' David asked, indicating their friend Max Müller. Thirteen-year-old Max had arrived from the Huon just the previous year to be enrolled as a boarder at the Hutchins School, and of course the Powell cousins had taken him under their wing. The Powells and the Müllers remained family at all times.

'Of course,' Hugh agreed, 'the more the merrier.'

'Will you give us a look at your father's Rolls Royce?' It was a cheeky request, once again from David. David, like his father Thomas, tended to push boundaries. He'd seen the Rolls Royce in the streets on occasions, they all had, and Wes Balfour had told him that he and Harry had ridden in it. God, how he'd envied them.

'Yep,' Hugh said expansively. 'I'll even let you sit in the driver's seat if you like.' The invitation was a bold one. Much as he was encouraged to bring his school friends home, Hugh wasn't sure whether such an offer would meet with his father's approval, but he very much wanted to impress the older boys. And besides, his father wouldn't be home, his father was off at a business meeting.

'Right you are,' David said and, after reporting their movements to the teachers in charge, they set off, all seven of them, the Stanfords, the Balfours, the Powells and young Max Müller, for the tram that would take them to the city.

Reginald Stanford was deriving a great deal of pleasure from Henry Jones's ongoing predicament. For several years now he'd been enjoying the fact that there was one major element missing from Henry's 'house that Jack built'. The man had the fruit, the processing factories, the tin mines, the timber mills – indeed all that was necessary for the production and packaging of products that sold to a world-wide market – with the exception of one vital ingredient: sugar.

'I'm at a loss, Reginald,' Henry said as he paced his office floor, 'it's been going on for far too long. I've been thwarted in every direction. What in God's name am I to do?'

Apart from fruit, the major constituent of jam and preserves was sugar, which made it an essential commodity to Henry Jones. The Australian production of refined sugar, however, was controlled by the Bundaberg-based Colonial Sugar Refinery Ltd, which, with the apparent approval of the Commonwealth Government, had a monopoly on the industry. The factories of Henry Jones Co-operative Ltd, the public company which had succeeded H. Jones & Co., had long been given discount prices and preferred shipping dates by CSR, but this had not satisfied Henry, who had been continuously frustrated by the fact that he did not have total control. Just two years previously, in an effort to break the monopoly, he'd imported refined sugar from Jamaica, incurring the wrath of CSR, who had made it abundantly clear that should he try such a ruse again, Australian sugar would be withheld from his factories. Furthermore, he'd been told, pressure would be brought to bear on the federal government to reassess the import duty on Jamaican sugar. It had seemed Henry's hands were well and truly tied.

'You could try pushing the government again on the sugar beet issue,' Reginald suggested. He sipped at the cup of tea the secretary had brought him and watched the portly little figure pacing about the office. It amused him that Henry Jones had finally come up against a monopolistic industry that he could not bend to his wishes.

'Yes, sugar beet would certainly solve the issue, you're right,' Henry said. 'If only the wretched government would agree.'

The Tasmanian climate was ideal for the growth of sugar beet crops, which would have provided an alternative source of sugar to that derived from the Queensland-grown cane. Henry had tried several times to establish a sugar beet industry, but he'd been thwarted by the Commonwealth Government's consistent refusal to extend the bounties to sugar beet that it extended to sugar cane. Without the government bounties in place, the planting of sugar beet was an uneconomic proposition. Henry's hands were still tied.

'It might well be worth another try, old chap,' Reginald said encouragingly. 'You really shouldn't give up.' Sugar beet wouldn't be worth another try at all, he thought. No political party would risk antagonising the powerful Queensland growers and refiners. Henry's idea of sugar beet as a viable option, brilliant though it was, had been unrealistic from the outset. The sugar barons of Queensland had their own state government and the Commonwealth government safely in their collective pocket. 'Of course,' he added thoughtfully as if the idea had just occurred, 'there is one other possibility.'

Henry stopped pacing. 'What, Reginald? What?'

'The Jones Co-Operative could become the local agent for CSR.' Reginald could see that Henry was unimpressed. 'I know, I know,' he added with a wave of his hand, 'it's not the ideal solution, but do give it some thought. You could carry massive stocks right here in the Old Wharf warehouses. Imagine what you'd save on delivery costs. And you'd not only have a ready supply for your own factory use, you'd have a healthy business on-selling to retailers.' He noted that Henry was starting to look interested. 'Just a thought, old man. I'll leave it with you.' He downed the last of his tea and placed the cup on the desk. 'Now I really must be off.'

Reginald felt smug as he stepped out of the IXL building into the chaos of Old Wharf. Henry was bound to adopt the agency idea when his sugar beet proposal was again knocked back and, although he might not consider it the ideal solution, to Reginald it represented a small personal triumph. As one of Henry's investors, some benefit would probably evolve from the agency proposition, but far more rewarding for Reginald was the sense of one-upmanship gained in the knowledge that Stanford Colonial had substantial investment in CSR, a fact of which Henry Jones was quite unaware.

He set off along Davey Street. It was late afternoon; dusk would soon be descending and, having left work, people were queued up at tram stops eager to get home to the suburbs. He would walk to Stanford House instead of catching the tram, he decided; it was not far and he would enjoy the constitutional. He had not driven to the meeting: he never did. The Rolls Royce was driven around Hobart purely for show, either by himself or by his chauffeur, after which the vehicle was always returned to the safety of its garage.

He wondered, while he walked, why he felt the need to best Henry Jones as he did. He had championed the man at one stage, congratulating himself on having discovered a winner. But Henry's rapid rise to power now grated. It was probably because he was common, Reginald decided. Success like Henry Jones's was the preserve of loftier men, in his opinion. Having to accept Henry as an equal was irksome. Surely when recognising an ally or competitor of any worth, one would wish him to be a man of some rank, and cut from a cloth finer than that of Henry Jones.

The moment Reginald set foot inside the front door of Stanford House, he heard the sound of boys' voices echoing raucously from the breakfast room.

'Hugh brought some friends home from the football match, I take it,' he said to Clive Gillespie, who met him in the hall.

'Yes, sir,' Clive said, taking his hat and coat. 'Boarders, sir, friends of young Master Wesley's. Several members of the team, and they're celebrating a win I'm glad to say.'

'Excellent, excellent.' Reginald sailed off to the breakfast room.

Clive was thankful the master hadn't arrived home a half an hour earlier when he'd discovered the boys inspecting the Rolls Royce and even climbing in and out of the driver's seat. They'd done no damage, admittedly – indeed, they'd treated the vehicle with great respect – but they would most certainly have been in trouble had the master caught them at it.

Clive had actually stood guard for the boys. 'Five minutes, Master Hugh,' he'd warned. 'Five minutes and no more, then you are to lock the garage doors and return the key.'

'Yes, Clive. Thank you.'

Hugh had known that he could trust Clive. Clive had been his ally in the past when he'd committed the odd misdemeanour. The only one to worry about, he'd thought, was Rupert.

'Not a word to Father, Rupert,' he'd made his brother promise. 'Not one word.'

'Not one word,' Rupert had agreed and he'd clapped his hands over his mouth to show he understood.

Reginald was delighted that Hugh had invited some friends home, and members of the school team no less. Extending weekend hospitality to the Balfour boys had proved an excellent idea; young Wesley was setting a fine example in sportsmanship.

'Well, well,' he said jovially as he entered the breakfast room, where the boys were sitting around the main table scoffing their pasties and chocolate cake. 'A win, I hear – my heartiest congratulations.'

The boys rose respectfully to their feet.

'No, no,' he said, 'sit, sit.' They did, and Reginald pulled a chair up to the end of the table. 'Now who do we have here,' he said beaming around, avoiding Rupert, who'd been into the chocolate cake, although for some strange reason Rupert had suddenly clamped both hands over his mouth.

Hugh made the introductions in descending order of age. 'This is Gordie Powell, father,' he said, 'and David Powell, and this is Max Müller.'

Reginald leant across the table and shook hands with each one. 'How do you do, lads?' he said, the boys chorusing 'How do you do, sir?' back. Reginald's smile was just a little fixed now. The boys are Powells, he thought, and they're boarders. They would surely be members of the Huon Powells, but from which family, he wondered. 'You're brothers, I presume,' he said, looking from Gordie to David.

'No, sir,' Gordie answered, 'we're cousins.'

'I see. And I take it you're from the Huon …' he hesitated briefly, '… Gordon, was it?' He was damned if he was going to call the oafish giant of a lad 'Gordie'.

'Yes, that's right, sir, we're from the Huon.'

'I'm well acquainted with your family, Gordon,' he said pleasantly, 'and which particular branch do you happen to be from?'

'My father is Franklin Powell, sir, of Powell Ship-building.'

'Ah yes, of course, we've met on several occasions. I know your grandfather George well. He designed my favourite ship, the *SS Lady Evelyn*. And you, David?' he said, turning to the younger lad. He knew the answer, of course – the boy was the spitting image of his lout of a father.

'My father's Thomas Powell of Charlotte Estate, sir, we grow apples.'

'Yes, yes, so I've heard, and most successfully.' Reginald didn't bother addressing the nuggetty boy they'd called Max, who had the look of a peasant about him; there wasn't any point. 'Welcome to Stanford House, lads,' he said as he rose, 'I trust Hugh has looked after you well.'

'Oh yes, sir,' David said with a meaningful grin to the others, 'Hugh's been an excellent host.'

Reginald glanced around the table; was there insolence intended in the remark? 'I'm glad to hear it,' he said a little icily.

Gordie cast a warning glance at David. David's cheekiness was always getting them into trouble. 'Thank you for your hospitality, sir,' he said, 'the food was excellent.'

'Yes, we're very fortunate with our cook. It's been pleasant meeting you lads. Feel free to stay as long as you like.' Reginald gave a brisk nod to the group and took his leave.

Gordie, David and Max left only ten minutes later. They'd be in trouble, they said, if they weren't back before curfew.

When they'd gone Hugh was summoned to his father's study, where he stood to attention wondering why he'd been called.

'I would prefer you did not invite those boys home again,' Reginald said, pen in hand and without looking up from his papers.

'Why ever not, Father?' Hugh was bewildered. He'd always been encouraged to ask his friends back to the house. Perhaps he's found out about the Rolls Royce, he thought, but if so surely I am the only one to blame. 'They didn't do anything wrong,' he protested, 'it was my idea —'

'I'm fully aware they did nothing wrong, Hugh.' Reginald put the pen down and looked up from his papers. 'But you have no need to associate with boys like that.'

'Boys like what?'

'They're a little uncouth, don't you think?,' he said pleasantly. He had no wish to alienate his son. 'I certainly found them to be so. It is not surprising of course as they're from the country, but —'

'Wes and Harry are from the country.'

'That's true.' Reginald maintained his patience, although he felt a flash of irritation: he was not accustomed to his son talking back to him in such a manner. 'But Wesley and Harold are related, Hugh; they have Stanford blood in them. Which, I must say,' he added with a smile intended to be humorous, 'does not stop them from being a little rough about the edges. You must surely have noticed that.'

'No.' Hugh shook his head. 'No, I haven't noticed that.'

Reginald refused to lose his temper. Nothing was to be gained from snapping at the boy, who was clearly in need of guidance. 'Sit down, Hugh.'

Hugh sat, and Reginald embarked upon his lecture. He was rather grateful to the Powell boys now for having triggered advice that appeared so timely.

'School can breed a general sense of camaraderie, which is admirable,' he said, 'particularly on the football field and such, but one must never lose one's abilities of discernment, Hugh. You have been born into a life of privilege and, as you get older, you will realise that you have a position in society that must be upheld ...'

Hugh didn't say a word, but he was shocked as he realised what he was hearing. His father was telling him he was better than others.

'The Hutchins School attracts the finest families seeking the best education for their sons,' Reginald continued, 'and as such it presents the perfect opportunity for you to form bonds with those of similarly privileged background, bonds which will be of great advantage in the future. Do you understand me?'

'Yes, Father, I believe I do.'

'Excellent.' Reginald smiled fondly; he was so proud of his son. 'All I'm saying, Hugh, is that you will cultivate a better class of friend if you're a little more selective.'

'Yes, Father, I know *exactly* what you're saying.'

'Good lad. Now go and get dressed for dinner. That is, if you can fit anything in after all those pasties and cake.'

Hugh left his father's office a different boy from the one who had entered it. For the whole of his life he had been brought up to have the utmost respect for his father. Reginald Stanford was known as a man of immense integrity, a pillar of the community, a committed philanthropist. Never once had it crossed Hugh's mind to question the judgement of such a man.

Now, on this day barely two months before his fourteenth birthday, he found himself not only questioning his father's judgement but vehemently disagreeing with it. This was the day Hugh's father fell from his pedestal, the day

Hugh realised that the man whom he'd so respected and admired was a snob and a hypocrite. The realisation came as a shock, but it bred in Hugh a quiet rebellion. No-one would dictate to him his choice of friends: no-one.

NEW YORK CITY, 1909

As young James Flood accompanied his host, Mr Haskel Slabodsky Junior, on a tour of his Fifth Avenue mansion on New York's Upper East Side, he could only stare in awestruck amazement at the 'trophies' Mr Slabodsky Senior had collected throughout the last three psychotically violent decades of his life.

The stuffed animals were everywhere. Mostly they were heads, together with endless sets of horns and antlers, but dotted about in corners and alcoves the occasional complete stuffed beast looked forlornly out at the world from its own glass case. The trophies covered every spare foot of wall space in the absurdly large house where Haskel Slabodsky Junior solemnly stated he lived, 'alone and haunted'.

'My father killed every single one of them himself,' Haskel said, peering about through thick horn-rimmed glasses and stroking the crown of his bald head in what James correctly assumed was a nervous mannerism. 'All fifty-six rooms full, plus every hall, corridor and stairway. Thirty-five thousand dead animals in thirty years, Mr Flood. That's roughly three creatures per day.'

'But your father was a stockbroker, wasn't he?'

James hurried to keep up with the little man. 'Didn't he found Slabodsky, Loewe and Partners?'

'He did indeed found the company, Mr Flood, but I proved to be the financial wizard. It was I who bought and sold and traded and bartered, becoming in the process the eighth-richest person in the world, whilst my father at the age of forty-five suddenly and inexplicably pronounced himself a big-game hunter and took off around the globe killing defenceless animals for sport. He never even had the good grace to offer me, or more importantly my mother, an explanation.' Haskel Slabodsky finally halted in his march through the labyrinthine halls of his house. 'What do you say to that, sir?'

'It does seem a little uncaring.'

'My father was a monster, Mr Flood! A fiendish individual who killed unthinkingly, like a rabid dog!' Haskel, aware of his escalating blood pressure, took a deep breath and held himself in check. 'It is my avowed intention,' he continued calmly, 'to ensure that this monument to death serve some purpose, which is why I have summoned you here today.'

'I don't understand, sir.'

'You are a zoologist. You are assistant to Mr William Temple Hornaday, director of the New York Zoological Park in the Bronx, correct?'

'Yes, sir.'

'I intend to donate this entire building and its sad ghosts to the City of New York as a museum. All profits will go to the American Bison Protection Society, which I recently founded with your Mr Hornaday and President Roosevelt. I intend also to fund other wildlife foundations upon request. As you can see, Mr Flood, I am determined my father's monstrous legacy be put to good use.'

'Most admirable, sir,' James wondered where exactly he fitted into the scheme of things. 'But I'm afraid I still don't quite —'

'Mr Hornaday has strongly recommended that you be appointed the museum's first director.'

'Good heavens above.' Young James Flood was overwhelmed. 'I would be only too delighted to accept such an appointment, Mr Slabodsky,' he said eagerly.

'There is however, one proviso.'

'A proviso?'

'A *Thylacinus cynocephalus*.'

'You mean an Australian marsupial wolf?'

'Exactly, the so-called Tasmanian tiger. My informants tell me it could very well be on its way to extinction.'

'They are very rare, Mr Slabodsky. We actually have two at the Zoological Park.'

'I know.' Haskel waved an imperious finger. 'I want one.'

'But ... er ...' James looked about at the sea of dead animals' eyes. 'They're still alive, sir.'

'I'm fully aware of that. I want one, or better still both, when they die. I shall have them stuffed and put on show in the museum's foyer. They shall be the shining light of the entire display. Who knows, perhaps we may generate enough interest and funds to save the poor creature from its imminent fate.'

'That sounds like a wonderful idea to me.'

'This venture must succeed, Mr Flood. I cannot bear the thought of dying without having attempted to redress, at least in some measure, my father's wrongs.' Haskel Slabodsky Junior's shoulders suddenly slumped and he looked all of his fifty years and more. 'I ask you, what makes human beings capable of such cruelty? Why are we the only species of life on this planet that is capable of killing purely for sport?'

'I'm afraid I cannot answer that question, Mr Slabodsky.'

'No, of course you can't, my friend. Who can?'

Haskel looked up at his young guest and smiled wearily. 'Would you care to join me for lunch while we discuss the project in more detail?'

James Flood returned the smile. He felt a sudden fondness for the strange little man. 'I would be honoured, sir.'

BOOK THREE

CHAPTER NINETEEN

In the European summer of 1914, the assassination of Austrian Archduke Franz Ferdinand resulted in untold chaos. A series of inexplicable political decisions, ineffectual diplomacy and the sabre-rattling of powerful royal houses quickly escalated into war and, within just two months, the deadly dance of empires had begun.

On the fourth of August, Britain declared war on Germany. When she called upon her dominions to take up arms against a common foe, she did not find Australia wanting. Indeed Australia was only too eager to heed the summons.

For the second time in its short history, the nation was to fight under its own flag, as it had in South Africa, but this time the fight was not for the preservation of a remote colonial outpost. This time Australians would be fighting in direct defence of the motherland. Patriotism ran rife throughout the nation and recruitment stations were overrun by adventurous young men eager to sign up and defend Britannia against the scourge of the Hun.

'You're what?'

'I'm going to enlist, Father.'

Reginald leant back in his chair and glared at his son, outraged by the boy's temerity. How dare Hugh stand there and make such a ludicrous announcement.

'Don't talk rubbish,' he snapped, 'you're not even eighteen.'

'But I will be in less than a month.'

'What difference does that make? You're still too young.'

'Exactly. That's why I need your signature.' Hugh placed the registration papers on the desk in front of his father. 'They told me at Anglesea Barracks that as I'm under twenty-one I have to have parental permission.'

Reginald stared down at the papers. His son had reported to the barracks without telling him? And if parental permission had not been required would his son have enlisted without telling him? What the devil was going on? Hugh had always been an obedient boy, obedient and respectful. Such an act of defiance was quite out of character. And his attitude, his composure: it's thoroughly outrageous, Reginald thought. The boy's manner was bordering on impertinent.

'You surely don't think I'll sign that,' he said contemptuously.

'Yes, Father, I think you will.' Hugh had known he would meet with opposition, and he was quite prepared to stand his ground. 'I mean no disrespect, sir, but I *will* go to war, with or without your permission.'

'Really?' Reginald's tone was frigid. 'And how would you propose to go about that, pray?'

'I'm not sure.' Hugh appeared to give the matter some thought. 'I could forge your signature, I suppose, but of course you'd find out and put a stop to it. I'd probably run away, sign up under a false name, lie about my age, I really don't know. But I would find a way, of that I'm certain.'

Reginald felt a sudden stab of fear. The boy's confidence was unsettling. He tried once again to assert his authority. 'You would defy me, Hugh. This is what you are saying?'

'I would prefer not to, Father. I would very much prefer you to sign the papers.'

The confrontation was becoming a clash of wills, and

Reginald had the distinct feeling he was losing. I must buy time, he thought, I must reason with the boy.

'Sit down, Hugh,' he said.

Hugh sat, and Reginald took a moment to compose himself before he spoke.

'You seem so very sure of your convictions, my boy,' he said. 'I trust you have given the matter serious thought.'

'Oh I have, Father, I have, believe me.'

'And yet you have come to such a speedy decision. War was declared only a matter of days ago, why the haste to sign up so soon?'

'*Everyone* is signing up, Father,' Hugh said eagerly, glad now that his father was prepared to be reasonable. 'Have you not been out in the streets? Have you not been caught up in the fever? The call to arms is everywhere.'

It's true, Reginald thought. Australia had gone into a patriotic frenzy the moment war had been declared. It seemed to have happened overnight. Everywhere you looked shopfronts and lamp-posts were strung with red, white and blue bunting. Children ran through the streets waving Australian flags, and young men gathered in parks and town squares where brass bands and bugles and pretty girls urged them to enlist. There were queues at post offices, and already recruitment centres were springing up like mushrooms all over the land.

Reginald supposed it was natural that Hugh should become infected by such hysteria. The whole country it appeared was urging its sons on to war. But not *my* son, he thought. Please, dear God, not *my* son!

'You're so young, Hugh,' he said, trying to quell a rising sense of panic. 'I'd rather you didn't rush into things. Why not wait a while – at least until after Christmas?' The war will be over by then, he thought.

'What would be the point?' Hugh replied. 'The war will probably be over by then. Besides, nearly everyone signing up seems to be young. At least that's what it looked like to Wes and Harry and me. The boys queued up at the barracks all seemed to be around our age.'

'So I take it Wesley and Harold also intend to enlist,' Reginald said coldly. Of course, he told himself, that's it. Hugh would never think to sign up on his own. It wasn't the general patriotic fever that had infected him at all: it was the Balfour brothers. Reginald's anger started to build. Those boys have been guests under this very roof, he thought, and without a word to me they've taken my son up the street to the Anglesea Barracks to enlist, the traitorous young bastards.

'Oh my word, yes. Wes and Harry can't wait.' In his enthusiasm, Hugh hadn't noticed the steely edge that had once again crept into his father's voice. 'We went up to the barracks on Saturday morning before the footie match. We've made a pact. We're going to enlist together so that we'll be in the same unit.'

'I see.' Reginald cursed his own lack of prudence. He should never have allowed Hugh to remain so involved with his cousins following their schooldays. He'd only suffered the connection because of family ties – there was no value in the friendship – and now look at what had happened. It was unforgiveable.

Every weekend for the past two football seasons, Reginald had extended his hospitality to the Balfour brothers. Wesley played for the North Hobart Football Club these days and each Saturday the brothers would come into town for the match, stay overnight and return to Pontville on the Sunday. Sometimes they even came in on a Friday, and Wesley more often than not stayed one night during the week, when he would travel to town for an afternoon's training session. And this, Reginald thought, is how the young ingrates repay me; by inveigling my son to go to war.

'So what does Edwin Balfour think of his sons' plans to enlist?' he enquired. 'Or, like me, was he not told of their intention?'

This time Hugh recognised his father's displeasure. 'He was told, Father,' he replied, looking rather shamefaced. 'I'm sorry. I didn't wish to be hurtful in going behind your back. It's just that I knew you would try and stop me, and I needed to convince you of the seriousness of my intent.'

'Oh I am convinced, Hugh, rest assured I am. So tell me, please do, what was Edwin's reaction to the news?'

'He was proud. He gave Wes and Harry his blessing. Uncle Edwin said that whatever happened he was proud that sons of his should be prepared to offer their lives in the service of their King and country.'

The fool of a man had said *that*! Good God, the stupidity! But then of course Edwin had a third, older son whose wife, Reginald had recently heard, was pregnant. Perhaps the man feels secure in the knowledge that he can safely risk the loss of two sons without at the same time losing his family name, Reginald thought contemptuously. He could have strangled Edwin.

'Leave the papers with me, Hugh.' He stifled his anger. 'You've rather taken me by surprise, I must say. Give me twenty-four hours. I shall let you know tomorrow morning whether or not I'll sign them.'

'Thank you, Father.'

The moment his son left, Reginald telephoned Amy in Pontville. He was thankful he'd insisted upon having the property connected. Amy herself hadn't cared whether they had the telephone or not, but he'd told her it was imperative for business purposes.

'Dear God, Amy,' he ranted, 'isn't there anything you can do? You're the matriarch; Edwin listens to you. Tell him that under no circumstances must he grant his permission. He must forbid his sons to sign up.'

'They would enlist anyway,' Amy replied. 'They are determined, and nothing will stop them.'

The calmness of her voice down the line infuriated Reginald further. 'But Edwin's *encouraging* them, for God's sake. The fool's giving them his *blessing*! He said he's *proud* of them, damn him. I mean what sort of idiocy is that?!'

Amy held the receiver an inch or so from her ear as her brother bellowed his rage. 'He *is* proud of them, Reginald,' she said when the tirade was over. 'There are many who are proud that their sons wish to serve their country. But Edwin is not quite the fool you have always thought him to be,' she added coolly. 'He knows he is powerless to prevent his boys from enlisting. If he withheld his permission they would run off and join up anyway, and he will not have them go to war without his blessing. I suggest you follow his example.'

'You approve?' Reginald would have ranted on a great deal further, but he was halted in his amazement. 'You actually approve?'

'No, Reginald, I do not approve. But then I do not approve of the war. I do not approve of any war. It appears I am out of step with the whole country, for if I had my way there would be no enlistment at all, but as there is I believe that, like Edwin, you have no option but to grant Hugh the permission he seeks and give him your blessing.'

Reginald said nothing. He knew he was defeated. He'd lost the battle a good fifteen minutes earlier, he realised, when he'd seen the resolution in his son's eyes.

Amy put his fear into words. 'You might lose your son to this war, Reginald,' she said. 'Would you have him die without the comfort, at least, of your love and approval? Or would you risk alienating him and losing him forever regardless of what befalls him on the battlefield? The decision is yours.'

He hung up the receiver, and the following morning he signed the registration papers. He even falsified Hugh's date of birth by three weeks.

On the fifteenth of August 1914, Hugh Stanford and Wesley and Harold Balfour, members of 'A' Company of the 12th Battalion, 3rd Brigade, 1st Australian Imperial Force, reported to Brighton Army Camp roughly fifteen miles north of Hobart, along with hordes of other new recruits, for a rigorous two months' training.

The eight companies that would form the 12th Battalion were to comprise four from Tasmania, two from South Australia and two from Western Australia, and with the exception of the companies from WA all were to be trained at Brighton Army Camp. Of the four companies from Tasmania, 'A' Company had been recruited from the Hobart and Huon areas.

'Well, blow me down,' David said with his larrikin grin as the new recruits milled about on the parade ground awaiting instructions, 'looks like the Hutchins School boys are off to war.' David Powell, his cousin Gordon and young Max Müller, as it turned out, were also members of 'A' Company.

'It's Miller now though,' Max explained after they'd clapped each other on the back and shaken hands all round. 'Don't you blokes go giving me away – I've been told it's illegal to change your name on the registration form. "Müller" looked a bit German though, and I was buggered if I was going to risk being knocked back when Gordie and David were all signed up.'

'It's illegal to give a false date of birth too.' Harry Balfour winked and pointed an accusatory finger at Hugh. 'He won't be eighteen for another two weeks.' Harry himself had crept in by barely a month.

'We'll keep each other's secrets, Max, don't you worry,' Hugh said.

As they looked around at the others, they noticed quite a number of familiar faces in 'A' Company, but for Wes Balfour one face was particularly conspicuous.

'If we get up a footie team, I know who I want on my side,' he said and he wended his way through the crowd to renew acquaintance with Oscar O'Callaghan.

The training at Brighton Army Camp proved arduous; to the disappointment of all they weren't even supplied with uniforms. 'You'll stay in civvies until you've earned the right to a uniform,' the sergeant barked, although in truth the uniforms hadn't arrived yet.

The day started with parade drill, then a breakfast that most described as 'pretty rough tucker', then more drill and musketry instruction, then an hour's break to learn the King's Regulations, more drill, more weaponry instruction, then lessons on general soldiering, hygiene, map reading and the like, more drill, more musketry, and on it went, tiring and relentless. Then there was the interminably boring twenty-four-hour sentry duty where men were rostered in turn to stand watch for two hours at the main gates and at various perimeter points around the camp. But worst of all, they agreed, were the night marches, which entailed hikes anywhere between five and fifteen miles in the dark with full battle pack and rifle.

'War's got to be better than this,' David grumbled as he dumped his pack on the ground and lit up a smoke. His mates all heartily agreed: they couldn't wait to get into uniform, get over to England, and get stuck into the real fighting.

The only one among the already tight-knit group who made no complaint was Hugh Stanford. Hugh was too busy working hard to keep up. He'd discovered that he had quite a deal more to learn than his country cousins and friends, all of whom were experienced in bush skills, knew how to handle a rifle and were physically tough young men. It didn't help when his mates borrowed horses and went for a wild ride around the countryside on a Sunday afternoon either. The Powells and the Balfours and Max Miller had palled up with the men of 'C' Squadron 3rd Light Horse, country boys like themselves, who were also in training at the camp. Horse riding was not a skill required of 'A' Company's infantrymen, but for Hugh his mates' proficiency only served to further feed a general sense of his own inadequacy. He wondered if others from the city felt as inferior as he did.

'How do you do it, Oscar?'

He sought advice from Oscar O'Callaghan who, like himself, was a creature of the city. Oscar didn't seem to be having the same trouble keeping up.

'I cheat,' Oscar said with one of his lazy smiles. It was true, he did cheat during any form of written test: he couldn't be bothered studying. He had an uncanny ability too to dodge some of the more tedious duties – no-one knew quite how he did it. But it was also true that, as a natural athlete, the physical aspects of training presented no hardship to Oscar. 'You're too honourable, Hugh, that's your trouble,' he said. 'You have to learn to bend the rules a bit now and then. You'll find it makes life a whole lot easier.'

Hugh decided that Oscar probably wasn't the right person from whom to seek advice, and he just kept ploughing away, doing the best he could, feeling the results pay off as his body toughened up. So determined was he not to be found wanting that Hugh Stanford quite possibly worked harder than any other member in the whole of 'A' Company.

Then, on the twentieth of September, they got their uniforms. Things changed after that. The drill wasn't as tedious, the sentry duty wasn't as boring, and even the night marches didn't seem as tough as they once had.

The uniform and the pride they took in it had a psychological effect on the recruits – no-one would have denied it, but the simple truth of the matter was they were turning into soldiers.

A parade was organised for the fourth of October.

The men of the 12th Battalion and the men of 'C' Squadron 3rd Light Horse were accompanied by a military band as they marched through the jam-packed streets of

Hobart. It was a proud day for all. The troops in their khaki and slouch hats were proud and the thousands who'd gathered to watch them were proud. There was no screaming or raucous cheering, none of the general hysteria that might have been expected, just respectful applause as the men passed by. Thousands were paying tribute to their fellow countrymen, who would shortly be off to fight for the motherland. And the troops themselves couldn't wait for the day. They were ready to do battle now and craving adventure.

A ball was to be held at the Hobart Town Hall the following weekend, organised by the Hobart Ladies' Auxiliary Committee, a group of wealthy men's wives raising funds for the war effort.

With the backing of Hobart's most influential businessmen, the 'Friends of the AIF Fundraising Gala Ball' promised to be quite an event. The military hierarchy would be there, and those troops who wished to apply for Saturday night leave in order to attend were invited to do so. The presence of uniforms was considered essential in order to encourage donations and inspire enlistment.

Gordie and David Powell, together with Max Miller, opted out of the ball with some relief, but also with good reason. The three had applied for and been granted extended weekend leave and were going home to the Huon. Wes and Harry Balfour also opted out, but with no reason other than the fact that they, like many others, thought it would be a boring, official affair with the top brass around and too much hassle catching the late-night train back to camp. Hugh Stanford and Oscar O'Callaghan, however, were more than happy to oblige their superiors. Hugh knew that his attendance would please his father, who was bound to be involved with the ball as he was with every major fundraising event, and Oscar welcomed the chance to mingle with women, even if they were of the stuffy variety: at least he'd be able to dance. Both had been granted twenty-four-hour leave, and would stay with their families in the city.

Leave was now being granted with far greater leniency than it had been in the past. Indeed, company commanders were recommending that men take rostered weekend leave in order to say farewell to their families. Embarkation orders would not be announced publicly owing to the military censorship that had been invoked by the Australian government shortly after the outbreak of war. Even the troops themselves would not be told of their movements until the very last minute. There would be no time then for farewells.

The ballroom of the Hobart Town Hall, grand at the best of times, was particularly spectacular this evening, the Ladies' Auxiliary Committee having done themselves proud. The motif of course was patriotism. A grand portrait of King George V adorned the wall to the left of the arch where the organ stood, while on the wall to the right hung the Union Jack and the Australian flag. Silk streamers of red, white and blue fluttered overhead and the stage was decorated with magnificent floral displays of red roses, white lilies and blue hyacinths, courtesy of the floristry department of Dimbleby's.

'A triumph, my dear,' Archie said to his wife, raising his voice above the sound of the military band that was playing up on the stage. 'You've done a wonderful job, my congratulations.' Mara Dimbleby was one of the leading lights of the Ladies' Auxiliary Committee.

'Yes, things have come together very well, I must say,' Mara agreed, 'and there's an excellent turn-out even this early in the proceedings.' She looked at the dance floor where couples glided past in a military two-step. 'It's good to see so many uniforms – they will certainly assist in the recruitment drive. And people already seem bent on enjoying themselves, which is marvellous.'

'Not exactly surprising though,' Archie said, 'can't be

long before orders come through. In a way it's a bit of a
farewell to the boys.'

'Well yes, I suppose it is, I hadn't thought about that.'
Mara looked once again at the young men in their uniforms.
She believed very strongly in the war effort and the need to
answer Britain's call, but she felt a little hypocritical urging
young men to volunteer when, in her heart, she was glad her
son was not one of them. Malcolm was twenty-eight now
and he had longed to enlist, but with two small children of
his own he had chosen not to do so for his family's sake.

As she gazed across the dance floor, she spied Reginald
Stanford and Nigel Lyttleton, who had just arrived with
their wives. Reginald's son was with them, Mara noted,
looking particularly handsome in his uniform: there's a
young man who knows how to carry himself, she thought.

'Make sure your friends post massive pledges, Archie,'
she said, getting back to business. 'Go and chat to Reginald
and Nigel,' she waved an imperious hand in their direction, 'while I hunt out Henry Jones. Henry's proving one
of our staunchest allies, I must say.'

Archie watched his wife sail off. When Mara decided to
take on a cause she did so with a passion that was typical.
He had no intention of nagging his friends about posting
their pledges in the donation boxes that were placed so
conspicuously around the ballroom. There would be
constant reminders throughout the night from the master
of ceremonies, and Reginald and Nigel ranked among the
most generous of Hobart's benefactors at any fundraising
event without encouragement from him. He wandered off
to join them anyway. His wife was bound to be keeping
her eye on him.

'You really should have asked Mary,' Caitlin said as she
and Oscar walked up the steps of the town hall's grand staircase; on the landing above them stood another spectacular
red, white and blue floral arrangement courtesy of Dimbleby's. They were just one couple of several ascending the

grand staircase, the women resplendent in their ballgowns. 'Mary would have loved all this pomp and ceremony.'

Oscar gave a careless 'so what' shrug and didn't bother to reply. Caitie was only reiterating the conversation they'd had at home.

'Why didn't you invite Mary Reilly?' she'd said that very afternoon when he'd asked her if she wanted to go with him to the ball.

'Why would I invite Mary Reilly?'

'Because ... well, I don't know ... because she's special to you. She is, isn't she?'

'No, she's not special at all. She just thinks she is.'

'Oh Oscar, that's terrible.' Caitie had laughed – she hadn't been able to help herself. She'd always had the feeling that Mary Reilly clung to their old school friendship simply to maintain a ready link with her brother. She'd even felt a bit sorry for Mary, although admittedly Mary Reilly could be pushy at times. 'You're an arrogant pig, you know, you really you are.'

'It's not my fault Mary's got a crush on me.' The insult had bounced off Oscar. He didn't actually mind Mary at all; in fact, he'd always found her rather attractive. But he had made the mistake of kissing her at a party six months previously, and he'd been regretting it ever since. Mary's expectations were of the most serious kind and Oscar was bent on avoiding involvement with girls who wanted anything more than a good time. 'Besides, if I asked Mary to the ball I'd be stuck with her,' he'd said, 'whereas if I ask my sister I can dance with whoever I like. Do you want to come or not? I'm more than happy to go on my own.'

'Of course I want to come! Don't you dare go on your own. You might have given me a bit more notice though,' and Caitie had headed off to seek her grandmother's advice on what she should wear, advice that Eileen was eminently qualified to offer.

Hugh, having detached himself from his parents and

their friends, went off in search of some younger company. He helped himself to a glass of punch from the refreshment table and, after chatting with a couple of the boys he knew from camp, stood on the sidelines watching the dancers. Oscar O'Callaghan had arrived, he noticed. Oscar was dancing with an attractive older woman, a brunette of around forty or so in a bright yellow gown that stood out among the more conservative pastels worn by her contemporaries. He was holding her extremely close, but the woman didn't seem to mind in the least, and Hugh smiled to himself as he remembered Oscar's comment on the train coming into town.

'You know it might not be the stuffy affair the others reckon it'll be at all,' Oscar, the perennial optimist, had said. 'We might even find ourselves a bit of fun. One lives in hope, Hugh,' he'd added with a suggestive smile and a wink, 'one always lives in hope.'

Oscar was a rogue, there was no doubt about that, but somehow you just couldn't help liking him.

The band finished its bracket and the master of ceremonies stepped out on stage to drum up some fundraising enthusiasm.

'Ladies and gentlemen, as we all know we are here to assist the most worthy of causes ...'

While the MC enthused about the posting of pledges, unnecessarily pointing out the locations of the highly conspicuous contribution boxes, Hugh watched Oscar return the brunette in the canary-yellow dress to the company of a man who was obviously her husband. The man, tall, grey-haired and around fifty, clapped Oscar on the shoulder and shook his hand, clearly congratulating the lad on being in uniform. He has no idea, Hugh thought, that if the slightest opportunity were to present itself, that lad would seduce his wife.

'My aunt thinks you have excellent carriage,' a voice said behind him.

He turned, his heart starting to pound ridiculously at the sight of her.

'Caitie,' he said, doing his best to sound casual. God, she was more beautiful than ever. 'Hello.'

He'd bumped into Caitie O'Callaghan in the street on the odd occasion over the past several years, and each time she'd treated him like an old friend. She would ask how Rupert was and they would chat briefly, but after only a minute or so he would make his excuses and go on his way. He wasn't sure why he felt so self-conscious in her presence – perhaps it was her beauty.

'My aunt is of the opinion that excellent carriage is the sign of a true gentleman,' Caitie said.

'And who would your aunt be?' he asked.

'Mara Dimbleby.'

'Ah. Well, a lady of her stature would be bound to know.'

'Exactly.'

They shared a smile, and Hugh felt suddenly relaxed in her company, as if indeed they were old friends. 'I've become good mates with your brother at camp,' he said.

'Yes, so Oscar tells me. I hope you'll be able to teach him a few manners.' Hugh Stanford has grown up, Caitie thought. The shy, tongue-tied boy she'd encountered in the street was gone. But then he'd always been such an intriguing mixture. She remembered the compassion he'd shown towards his brother at the football match and how he'd handled the situation with such maturity. He'd been more like a parent than a younger brother really. He'd impressed her that day. The combination of boy and man had been attractive even then.

Up on stage the MC had finished his spiel and the band had struck up again, this time with a waltz, 'When Irish Eyes Are Smiling'.

'Aren't you going to ask me to dance?' she said.

'Of course I am.' He offered her his arm and they stepped onto the floor.

They remained there for quite some time. After the waltz there was a quick-step, and then a series of foxtrots, which they danced to bouncy ragtime rhythms – 'Oh, You Beautiful Doll', 'It's a Long Way to Tipperary', 'Alexander's Ragtime Band' – Hugh and Caitie were indefatigable.

From the other side of the ballroom, Reginald watched them. He'd been unable to take his eyes off the girl from the moment he'd seen her. She was Shauna all over again, her flame-red hair swept high, her neck and shoulders flawless. Even the satin ballgown she wore, although simpler in line, was a deep emerald green, just as Shauna's had been that night when they'd first met, right here in this ballroom. The evening was taking on an eerie quality for Reginald as he watched the spectre of his dead mistress dancing with his son.

It was the bandmaster who called a halt. The bracket was over, the band was to take a break, and Hugh and Caitie were finally forced from the dance floor.

'I think a glass of punch is in order,' he panted, 'what do you say?'

'Yes.' She didn't have breath enough left to say anything more.

'Come on then.' He took her hand and they made their way to the refreshment table. He loved that her hair was coming down and she didn't seem to care.

They gulped their punch back thirstily and he refilled their glasses. Then they found themselves some space at the far end of the ballroom where they stood and talked.

From afar, Reginald followed the couple's every move. He watched the intimacy of their body language, the way Hugh had taken her hand instead of offering his arm, the way they stood close together as they talked. The haunting image of Shauna had ceased to be of any interest, his only concern now was his son. The girl was clearly an O'Callaghan and not at all the right choice for Hugh.

'Oscar says this will probably be his last trip into town.'

Caitie decided it was foolish to waste their limited time on small talk. 'He says you'll all be leaving soon.'

'Yes, that's what they're telling us. I shall be saying my farewells to my family tomorrow.'

'I'll write to you while you're gone, Hugh. That is if you want me to.'

'I do, very much.'

'To your safe return.' She raised her glass.

'To the safe return of us all.' They clinked and drank.

'Rupert will miss you.'

'Yes, he will. He's missed me hugely these past six weeks. He can't understand why he's not allowed to come to training camp with me.' Hugh smiled. 'He thinks the camp's something to do with footie training.'

'I'll call around and visit him while you're away, if you like.'

'Would you really do that?' He was taken aback by the offer. He didn't quite know why, but it seemed to him extraordinarily caring. 'You don't have to, you know.'

'Of course I don't have to,' Caitie gave a careless shrug that to Hugh was very reminiscent of her brother, 'I'd do it because I want to. I like Rupert.'

The band was back on stage and as the musicians struck up a lively rendition of 'Give My Regards to Broadway' several of the younger set took to the floor.

'Oh my gosh,' Caitie said, 'they're doing the turkey trot. Come on.' Dumping their punch glasses on a nearby side table they headed hand in hand for the dance floor.

The turkey trot was followed by the other ridiculous 'animal dances' that constituted the latest craze, and the older members present stood on the sidelines bemused as the young ones took over the dance floor.

'Where's Oscar?' During a brief hiatus following the kangaroo hop, Caitie looked around for her brother. He usually took centre stage when it came to the modern dances.

Oscar was indeed nowhere to be seen. Hugh gazed

about the ballroom and could see no sign of the woman in the canary-yellow dress either. Her husband was still in evidence though, enjoying a glass of ale with his friends at the refreshment table.

'He's probably popped out for a bit of fresh air,' he said. Then the band segued into 'Bill Bailey, Won't You Please Come Home?' and as the duck waddle took precedence Oscar was forgotten.

He reappeared only several minutes later, dancing the grizzly bear right beside them with a young fair-haired girl of around sixteen, the daughter of one of the Auxiliary Committee ladies.

Hugh glanced over at the refreshment table. The woman in the canary-yellow dress was chatting with her husband and his friends. He had surely been imagining any link – it was better not to think about it.

All too soon the evening was over. For Hugh and Caitie, who had not left each other's side, it seemed to have passed in an instant, and yet that instant somehow signified a lifetime. This was a night that had changed everything. And now the band was nearing the end of its very last waltz. 'After the Ball Is Over' had been the bandmaster's highly appropriate choice.

He held her close as they danced. 'May I escort you home?' he asked: he couldn't bear the thought of saying goodbye.

'I'm afraid not,' she said regretfully. 'Oscar would be in dire trouble if you did. I've been entrusted to his care for the evening, and my grandmother can be a positive virago when it comes to anything she perceives as a threat to my virtue.'

'Of course.' He couldn't disguise his disappointment.

The waltz was over and, as the last strains of the melody hung in the air, the bandmaster turned and bowed, then stretched out his arms in recognition of his musicians. Those on the dance floor clapped and cried 'bravo' and within seconds the entire ballroom had erupted into applause. The evening had been an unqualified success.

'Oscar says you're catching the midday train back to camp tomorrow,' Caitie said as the applause finally died down and the crowd started drifting off the dance floor.

'That's right.'

'I shall be at the station at a half-past eleven.' She offered her hand and they shook. 'Good night, Hugh, it's been a wonderful evening.' The handshake didn't seem quite enough, so she leant up and kissed him on the cheek. 'Truly wonderful,' she said, and then she was gone, leaving him standing in the middle of the semi-deserted dance floor.

He joined his parents, who were once again chatting to the Lyttletons.

'Ah, there you are, dear.' Evelyn smiled. She was looking very fragile these days. 'We've barely seen you all night. Did you have a good time?'

'I had a splendid time, thank you, Mother.'

Of course you had a splendid time, Reginald thought, fuming. 'The car will have arrived, Hugh; we'll be leaving in ten minutes or so,' he said pleasantly, guarding any show of irritation.

'If you don't mind, Father, I'll walk home. I feel like a bit of a stroll.' His father's chauffeur had dropped them off in the Rolls Royce, and Hugh had felt shockingly self-conscious as they'd pulled up outside the town hall. The show of ostentation had seemed so wrong. He didn't wish to hurt his father's feelings, however. The vehicle was Reginald Stanford's pride and joy, he'd worked hard to earn it and he had every right to enjoy it. Hugh did not stand in judgement of his father, but from his own point of view the silver Rolls Royce had lost its charm.

'Of course, my boy,' Reginald clapped an arm around his son's shoulder, 'we'll see you at home then.' The boy chose to walk, did that mean an assignation – was the slut perhaps waiting for him? If so, excellent, he thought. The lad was undoubtedly a virgin, a quick bout between the sheets would do him the world of good. But the situation had looked far more serious than that.

He edged Hugh a little to one side. 'Tell me,' he said quietly, 'the young lady whose company you were enjoying – very beautiful I might add, you show great taste –' he smiled in man-to-man fashion, then added as if it were merely a matter of interest '– she's an O'Callaghan, isn't she?'

'That's right, Caitlin O'Callaghan.'

'Ah yes, I thought so.' Reginald nodded sagely. 'They're a handsome family, all right.'

Hugh knew just what his father was thinking. The O'Callaghans weren't good enough. Is it because they're of the Roman Catholic faith or is it because they're not filthy rich? he wondered. A mixture of both probably. Either way, Hugh was not in the least bothered. For several years now he'd accepted his father for what he was.

'Mara Dimbleby is Caitie's aunt,' he said. That should surely keep the old man happy, he thought. 'See you at home, Father.'

Reginald watched, powerless, as his son walked away. Now was hardly the time to put his foot down, he realised, but he did hope the girl wouldn't prove a problem in the future. Yet again, he cursed Archie Dimbleby for having married so far beneath him: it set such a bad example.

The following morning, the family gathered in the front drawing room and Hugh made his farewells as he'd planned. He'd already said goodbye to each of the servants, who had now tastefully withdrawn to give the family their privacy.

He embraced his mother, holding her close.

'Take care, Hugh,' Evelyn said. 'I shall pray for your safe return. May God go with you.' Evelyn had determined she would not shed a tear. Not until she was alone anyway.

'We're proud of you, my boy.' Reginald shook his son's

hand. He still blamed the Balfour brothers for inciting in Hugh the desire to go to war, but he *was* proud of his son. Already the army had turned the boy into a man. 'I know you'll serve your country well.'

'Thank you, Father.'

For Hugh the delicate part of the exercise was saying goodbye to Rupert. 'I am going away to serve a very important duty, Rupert,' he said to his brother.

'Can I come too?'

'No, you can't, because you have a very important duty of your own to serve right here.'

'What? What?' Rupert was only too eager to serve a duty like his brother.

'You will look after Mother while I am gone.'

'Yes, yes.' Rupert gathered his mother in his arms. 'I will look after Mother,' he said, and he held her to him as if daring anyone to part them.

Rupert's newfound sense of responsibility was proving exactly the distraction Hugh had intended it should, but Reginald found the sight of the hulking nineteen-year-old cuddling his mother undignified and intrusive on the solemnity of the occasion. Surely they had gathered to farewell Hugh upon his imminent departure for the battlefields of Europe, not to cater to a simpleton.

'Let me drive you to the station, son. Please, I insist.'

'No, Father.' Hugh had refused the same offer earlier. 'As I've said, I wish our goodbyes to take place here.'

It was clear no negotiation was to be entered into, and Reginald had no option but to stand on the front porch with Evelyn, who was still locked in Rupert's protective embrace, and watch as his son crossed the courtyard, turning to wave before walking through the main gates and disappearing from their lives, possibly forever.

Hugh arrived at the station at a quarter-past eleven. The platform was not yet crowded with the troops who would be catching the midday train to Brighton and he positioned himself where he would see her the moment she appeared.

Then, on the dot of half-past eleven, there she was. Her hair was pinned up beneath the toque that she wore, but the flash of red caught his eye in an instant. Oscar was by her side.

He waved and they joined him, Oscar immediately voicing complaint. 'I told the family they weren't allowed to come to the station,' he said, 'but Caitie maintains she's here to say goodbye to you, not me ...'

'Hello, Hugh.'

'Hello, Caitie.'

'... She even made me get here twenty minutes earlier than I'd planned.'

'I'm glad she did.' Hugh smiled, his eyes not leaving Caitie's for a second.

'Oh well,' Oscar gave one of his insouciant shrugs, 'I'll just fill in some time over here, shall I?' He didn't bother waiting for a reply, but ambled off and lit up a smoke.

'Thank you for coming,' Hugh said.

'I have something for you.' She took an envelope from her purse and gave it to him.

He opened it. Inside was a photograph.

'It's not a very good one,' she said apologetically, 'but it's the pick of a rather pathetic collection. I don't have many I'm afraid.'

The small black and white picture was a full-length portrait of a pretty girl whose pose was most demure. She was seated very properly on a small hardback chair, her feet not visible beneath her long skirt, her hands placed delicately in her lap. But the girl's expression defied the pose, telling a different story altogether. She seemed on the verge of laughter. The curve of her lip was mischievous and her eyes sparkled with a humour that she appeared barely able to contain. The photograph may not have done her beauty full justice, but it had captured the very essence of Caitie O'Callaghan.

'It's beautiful,' Hugh said.

'I wrote on the back.'

He turned the photograph over. *Come home safely*, she'd written, *with all my love, Caitie.*

'I couldn't think of anything fancy,' she said. 'I tried, but it sounded wrong somehow.'

'I wouldn't have wanted anything fancy. This is exactly right.' He returned the photograph to its envelope and carefully placed it in the breast pocket of his army jacket.

Neither one of them initiated the kiss. It just seemed to happen. They just seemed to drift together in some inevitable fashion. Then, as their lips met, their arms rose to an embrace and they became oblivious to everything around them.

When they finally parted, Caitie looked about at the platform, which was now quite crowded. 'Just as well Oscar didn't let the family come to the station,' she said. She smiled and linked her arm through his. 'Come on, let's go and join him. I feel a bit guilty.'

'Ah, the lovebirds,' Oscar said upon their approach. He frowned. 'I hope your intentions are honourable, Hugh – she is my sister you know.'

Caitie cocked a quizzical eyebrow at Hugh. 'Should we tell him we're engaged?' she asked, and when he stared back at a loss for words she added, 'We are, aren't we? Good heavens, a kiss like that is the act of a fiancé, surely.'

Hugh grinned. She was thoroughly outrageous. 'We're engaged, Oscar,' he said.

'Goodo.' Oscar ground the butt of his cigarette out with the heel of his army boot.

Caitie took a folded piece of paper from her purse and handed it to her brother. 'I've been asked to give you this,' she said. 'I didn't want to do it in front of the family.'

Oscar unfolded the note to discover a photograph of Mary Reilly.

'I saw her at nine o'clock mass this morning,' Caitie said.
'She'd hoped you'd be there so that she could give it to you herself, but I told her you were visiting relatives in Sandy Bay and
had to go straight back to camp afterwards. In other words I
lied,' she added accusingly, 'and in church, what's more.'

'Thank you, I'm very grateful.'

'I do think you might have called on her to say goodbye;
she very much hoped that you would.'

'I have my reasons for avoiding Mary,' Oscar said,
skimming the brief note. *Dearest Oscar, carry this
photograph into battle and know that my heart is yours.
May the strength of my love protect you always, Mary.* 'I
have my reasons, believe me.' He shoved the note and the
photograph into the pocket of his greatcoat. God, how he
wished he hadn't kissed her.

The minutes ticked speedily by and suddenly the guard was
sounding the boarding call. Fervent embraces were shared by
a number of people on the platform. Who knew when they'd
next hold their son or dearest love in their arms again?

Oscar hugged his sister and climbed onto the train,
leaving Hugh and Caitie to say their goodbyes.

'All aboard,' the guard called.

They shared a last kiss.

'I was only joking about being engaged,' Caitie said as
they parted.

'I wasn't,' he replied.

'All aboard,' the guard called again, and the train started
to move off.

Hugh scrambled aboard and stood on the step waving
as the train chugged its way out of the station. He kept
waving until he could no longer see the fiery glimmer of
red beneath her toque.

The Powell cousins and Max Miller returned from the
Huon the next day, and after dinner in the Other Ranks
mess tent the talk was all about David's engagement.

'We haven't got the ring yet,' he said, 'but there was a whopper of a farewell party at Dad's place on Saturday arvo and we announced it to the whole family. It's official all right.'

Big Gordie laughed. 'It's been official since they were a year old,' he said to the others, 'David's grandfather Quincy reckons he had them promised at their first birthday party.'

'We're talking about Jeanie, I take it,' Wes Balfour said. David's girl, Jeanie, had cropped up in conversation a number of times.

'Yep,' David couldn't wipe the grin from his face, 'it sounds a bit soppy I know, but Gordie's quite right, we've been childhood sweethearts for as long as I can remember.' He fished his wallet from his pocket and took out the photograph that he always carried. 'That's her,' he said passing it around proudly. 'Jeanie Müller, she's Max's sister. We all grew up together.'

Oscar turned to Hugh. 'Seems to be a trend,' he commented dryly, 'mates' sisters becoming sweethearts.'

'Just as well she copped the looks in the family,' Harry said, studying the pretty fair-haired girl in the photograph, 'it'd be a right bugger if she'd turned out like you, Max.'

Then the ribbing started in earnest, Max taking it good-naturedly as he always did. Short and bull-like in build, he was not particularly prepossessing, it was true, but he was popular with the men and much respected for his sheer physical strength. Max, although a good eight inches shorter than his mate Gordie, was every bit as strong.

The photograph was passed back to David who kissed it flamboyantly before returning it to his wallet, which was a direct cue for Gordie, who reached for his harmonica. Gordie was the musical one and his harmonica had led to many a sing-along over the past weeks.

I dream of Jeanie with the light brown hair,
Borne like a vapour on the summer air ...

The moment Gordie played the first note David burst into song, and of course he knew every word of the lyrics. He always maintained that Stephen Foster had written them just for him.

I see her tripping where the bright streams play,
Happy as the daisies that dance on her way.

The others joined in with the bits they knew and la-la-ed along to the bits they didn't. Then a bloke at another table produced his guitar and very soon everyone in the ORs mess tent was singing.

The following weekend being the last rostered leave granted, it was the Balfour brothers' turn to make their family farewells. Unlike the others, Wes and Harry didn't need to catch the train home, they just walked the mile or so up to Pontville, then a further mile north and they were at the Stanford-Balfour property.

Just like the Powells' gathering in the Huon, the Balfour boys' farewell party was a huge family affair conducted in true country fashion. They congregated at midday on Saturday, all four generations of them, and the chosen venue was the old farmhouse so that Donald wouldn't need to travel. Donald Balfour, now eighty, suffered shockingly from arthritis and was confined to a wheelchair for much of the time. His wife Amy, however, the matriarch of the clan, remained seemingly indestructible. It was Amy herself who cooked the massive baked luncheon that would feed them all. Three legs of lamb just to be on the safe side, she'd decided: her grandsons alone would eat one leg between them.

The families travelled to the farmhouse from their various homes on the property; Constance, the boys' older sister, with her husband and brood of three; twenty-five-year-old Norman, their elder brother, with his pregnant wife; and of course the boys themselves, who arrived with their mother and father in Edwin's brand new Model T Ford.

The day soon turned boisterous. The brothers, always quick to egg each other on, insisted upon driving the 'Tin Lizzie', as the popular American Model T Fords were nicknamed, and Edwin gave them brief instruction, freely admitting that he'd only just got the hang of the thing himself. Then he stood to one side and watched as his three sons took turns racing the vehicle up and down the quarter-mile drive that led from the house to the main road, seeing who could get it up to the highest speed.

It was Wes's suggestion that they add another component to the exercise and pit the car against Belle. Belle was a coal-black, four-year-old mare, the prettiest and fastest horse on the property. Harry and Norm agreed that it was an excellent idea and Wes went off to bring her in and saddle her up.

A half-hour later, the entire family gathered in the front garden to watch as Harry called the start of the race.

He raised his hand high in the air. 'Ready ...' he yelled. 'Set ... Go!' and he flagged them away with a wave of his arm.

Norm took off in the Tin Lizzie and Belle leapt into action, Wes riding her at full gallop towards the main gates, Connie's three small children squealing with excitement and running after them. But over the quarter-mile distance it proved no contest: Belle was the undisputed winner.

They switched places for the return trip – Wes drove and Norm rode – but Belle once again romped home for the win.

'The car takes too long to build up momentum,' Wes said as he climbed out in a cloud of dust. 'We need a longer course. Why don't we make it a race from the front gates to the bridge at Pontville. It's your turn, Harry – you want to drive or ride?'

That was when Edwin finally put his foot down. 'Harry will do neither,' he said firmly. 'The car's not to be raced in the main road. You'll stay on the property.'

'Oh, rightio. Where do you reckon then, Norm?'

'From here to our place,' Norm suggested, 'that's a good mile.'

'You're on. What's your pick Harry, the car or Belle?'

Harry, however, was destined for disappointment. 'There'll be no more racing,' Amy said. 'Sorry, boys, but I won't have the roast dinner spoiled. Wes, see to Belle, we eat in half an hour.'

Amy's word as always was final, and she disappeared inside with the other women to set the table for a luncheon that was already an hour later than she'd intended.

The boys actually weren't too disheartened. Healthy appetites coupled with the prospect of one of their grandmother's roast dinners formed a powerful distraction, particularly to Wes and Harry, who'd been living on army food.

They ate and drank for a solid three hours. After several plate loads of lamb and roast vegetables smothered in gravy, the men sat back with their glasses of ale while the women cleared the table, then twenty minutes later they hoed into massive bowls of the rice pudding and custard that Connie had brought along.

'Crikey, we haven't eaten like this for a while,' Harry said.

'And it'll be a while before we do again. Make the most of it, I say.' Wes passed his bowl to Connie for a second serve even though his belly felt about to burst.

After pudding, the women once again cleared the table, and then they served tea, although the men, even Donald, decided to stick with ale, at least for the moment. Norm was about to propose a toast, and you didn't drink a toast with a cup of tea.

After refilling their glasses Norm rose to his feet. 'I'd like to propose a toast to my brothers,' he said. 'I wish I was going with you boys, I really do ...' It was true, Norm had ached to enlist, but it wouldn't have been fair. He glanced down at his wife who was eight months pregnant.

Beth smiled sympathetically up at her husband, aware of how he envied his brothers their great adventure. 'Frankly I don't know how you'll manage without me,' Norm continued and everyone laughed, 'but I'm sure you'll find a way.' He dropped the banter. 'In fact I'm sure you'll do this family great honour,' he added seriously. 'We're proud of you, Wes and Harry, very, very proud, and we wish you a safe and speedy return.' He raised his glass. 'To Wes and Harry,' he said.

The others all rose to their feet – at a nod from Connie the children did too.

'To Wes and Harry,' they chanted.

After that the brothers proceeded to get drunk, all three of them, not staggeringly so, but it seemed only right that they should. Men didn't go off to war every day of the week.

Night was falling as the families started to wend their way homewards. Wes, however, didn't accompany Harry and his parents in the Tin Lizzie. Wes didn't go home at all. He borrowed a torch and set off in the dark for Pontville. His parents made no comment. He was clearly going to visit a woman, as presumably many a young man did before departing for battle, although they wondered just who the woman might be.

Harry didn't wonder. Harry knew. Wes had been sleeping with the widow on a regular basis for nearly a year now. The widow worked behind the bar at the tavern and she was thirty-nine, nearly twenty years older than Wes. Harry was dead bloody envious. He couldn't wait to lose his virginity.

The Balfour boys returned to camp late the following afternoon, and just over a week later the big day finally arrived.

On the twentieth of October 1914, a chilly spring Tuesday, the 12th Battalion, along with the 3rd Light

Horse Brigade, assembled at dawn. Bulging kitbags slung over one shoulder and rifles over the other, they marched to the railway station at Brighton and boarded a train bound for Hobart. Then, upon arrival at Hobart Station, they marched the half-mile or so through the streets of Wapping and along Old Wharf to the newly-built Ocean Pier. There the entire battalion and the troops of the 3rd Light Horse were embarked on board the *SS Geelong*, a P&O merchantman of 8,000 tons now designated HMAT, His Majesty's Australian Troopship. The *SS Katuna*, which was docked nearby, took on board the horses of the 3rd Light Horse, artillery pieces and the medical unit. The entire embarkation was completed by ten o'clock in the morning.

Due to military censorship, there had been no announcement that the troops were leaving, but word of mouth spread the news like wildfire and by mid-afternoon, as the hour of departure neared, the docks were packed not only with those from the city and suburbs, but also those who'd travelled from far and wide.

The Balfours had heard the news from their neighbours in Pontville, who had heard it from their neighbours in Brighton, and Edwin and Norm had jumped in the Tin Lizzie and headed for Hobart.

In the Huon, the Powells had heard the news from Simon Hawtrey, who had telephoned the post office in Franklin, and the entire Powell brigade, together with the Müllers, had set off for Hobart aboard the *SS Emma Jane*.

Other families had used whatever means they could to travel to the city and farewell the troops and, as the hours passed, the huge new dock of Ocean Pier became a seething mass of well-wishers.

There was no longer any point keeping the departure a secret so members of the battalion's brass band struck up an impromptu series of rousing songs to match the occasion.

Aboard the *HMAT Geelong*, men leant from the railings

waving to loved ones in the crowd. Those who couldn't find a vantage point at the rails climbed high in the rigging to seek out the faces they knew, while others climbed up into the lifeboats that were hanging from davits. It seemed the entire ship was festooned with uniforms dangling like ornaments from a Christmas tree.

The Powell boys and Max Miller were glad now that they hadn't been able to score a possie by the railing. The *Geelong* was docked facing the city so the men were all leaning from the starboard side. From their vantage point up in one of the lifeboats, Gordie, David and Max had a view from the port side as well. They'd spied the Hawtreys in the crowd on the docks early on, which was good, but they couldn't believe their luck later in the day. They'd heard the honk of a steamer's horn and there she was right beside them, the *Emma Jane*, with the whole damn tribe of Powells and Müllers aboard. The sight had sent the boys into a frenzy of screaming and waving. 'Up here, up here,' they'd yelled, finally catching their families' attention. Then they'd quickly climbed down and raced over to the port side.

Now, at four o'clock in the afternoon as the *HMAT Geelong* cast off, the *Emma Jane* prepared to follow her out into the Derwent, the Powells and the Müllers drinking in this last image of their sons.

David was drinking in *his* last image of Jeanie, her mass of fair curls tossed about by the wind as she blew kisses up to him. My Jeanie with the light brown hair, he thought. It seemed most appropriate that, at that very moment, the musicians should choose to strike up 'The Girl I Left Behind Me'.

From his position beside Oscar at the railings, Hugh was thinking exactly the same thing as he looked out across the sea of people to where Caitie stood.

Oscar, in true form, had scored them both a prime position. 'She's over there,' he'd said when he'd spotted his father and sister, and oh my God, he'd thought, Mary Reilly as well.

But Hugh had needed no prompting in order to find her. He'd already seen the flash of red among the hordes. She had deliberately come hatless in order that he should.

The musicians continued to play 'The Girl I Left Behind Me' as the troopship made its way out into the harbour. Many aboard found it a poignant choice, but not one man had a single regret. The girls would be there when they came home again. In the meantime, they were off to fight a war.

CHAPTER TWENTY

The *HMAT Geelong* docked in Albany for the embarkation of the two Western Australian companies that completed the 12th Battalion, and it was there in the massive bay of King George's Sound that the ship joined up with the rest of the convoy. The fleet included twenty-six Australian and ten New Zealand troopships, escorting battleships and the cruiser *HMAS Sydney*. Stretching three miles in length and carrying thirty thousand troops, the convoy departed Albany bound for Colombo on the first of November.

Several weeks later, letters started to arrive home, although some took a little longer getting there than others. Oscar wrote to Eileen, Col and Caitie:

7 November 1914

Dear All,
I hope this letter finds you well. That is, when I finally post it. The word around the decks is that the convoy will be putting in to Colombo on the island of Ceylon, so with luck, I may be able to send it from there.

We left Western Australia a week ago and, if the truth be known, I've started writing out of sheer boredom. Life aboard ship is monotonous, unless of course you happen to be an officer. They're living the life of Reilly up on their own deck with canvas chairs and by the smell of it wonderful food. We of the rank and file are not so lucky, we live on the troop deck where there is not room to swing a cat and the food is truly terrible. The last of the bread on board is now hard and dry and the meat is as tough as boot leather. The only alternative is British government rations, biscuits hard as river rocks and Fray Bentos corned beef in a tapered tin with a side-key opener, bully beef the Tommies call it. I can soon see us Australian lads getting mighty sick of it.

9 November
There was much excitement aboard ship when the news arrived this evening. And not just aboard our ship either – I could hear men cheering from other boats in the convoy. This morning about daybreak, the Australian battleship HMAS Sydney *took off for all she was worth, full steam ahead, and later in the morning we heard the roar of heavy gunfire away to the west. Apparently there was a fight between the* Sydney *and a German raider called the* Emden *and the* Sydney *done for her right royally as they say, shot her to pieces at a place called the Cocos Islands, which are supposed to be part of Australia, but I've never heard of them.*

16 November
We anchored in Colombo yesterday and first thing we saw was the HMAS Sydney. *She sailed right past us and the lads all lined the decks and gave her three rousing cheers. I went for a walk around the city this morning, a pretty place with pretty women by the dozen, dark eyes, beautiful skin, a man could easily lose his soul if he were so disposed. Fortunately I'm not that way inclined, isn't that right, Da?*

20 November
Oops, I missed the mail boat. I'll have to post this at
the next port of call, wherever that may be. We're on
our way again, heading towards the Suez Canal, or so
the word is, and then through the Mediterranean Sea
and on to our final destination, Britain herself. Who
knows, maybe I'll get over to Ireland and look up the
family. Can Gran remember if there's anyone there
owing her money? Just kidding, Eileen, just kidding.

4 December
Oops again. We're not in Britain at all. We're in
Alexandria. That's Egypt of all places! Can you
believe it? I'm posting this to you right now. There's
a mail boat going out today.
You probably won't hear from me again for a few
weeks, so a very Merry Christmas to you all,
Love Oscar.

Hugh Stanford's first letters home were even slower to
arrive, but not because he'd missed the mail boat.

Mena Camp
Cairo, Egypt
29 January 1915
Dearest Mother and Father,
I am so sorry I have not corresponded until now, but
I have been rather ill. Not long after we arrived in
Egypt I was stricken with measles, as were quite a few
of the battalion. Then an outbreak of influenza ran
through the camp and those weakened by the measles
seemed particularly prone. It took quite a toll on all
who suffered it, but thankfully the epidemic seems to
have run its course.
Who would ever have guessed we would end up
in Egypt? We were all so convinced we were headed

for England. We docked in Alexandria in early December, which seems a lifetime ago now, and after being entrained some one hundred miles to Cairo, we were marched to Mena Camp, a massive tent city for want of a better description. My own tent is not four hundred yards from the Great Pyramid of Cheops and the inscrutable Sphinx, which I remember so clearly from books and lessons in my childhood. Oddly enough, these ancient wonders make me think of home. It seems strange to stare at them now in reality and have memories of Mother, Rupert and me in the library poring over the pictures of the pyramids and Rupert lamenting the Sphinx's missing nose. Remember, Mother, how he would worry that the Sphinx must have trouble breathing?

Heaven alone knows what we are doing in Egypt while the war rages on in Europe, but to paraphrase Tennyson, ours is not to reason why. This place is indeed a land of contrasts, with the countryside lush and verdant in the Nile Delta between Alexandria and Cairo, but quickly giving way to desert, as it is where we are here at Mena. Cairo itself is both repulsive and fascinating. We go by tram from the camp to the city centre and for the entire day we are plagued by scruffy street urchins begging for money and old men attempting to sell us every conceivable artefact, from statues of mummies and 'antique' coins, to jewels they swear have come from a pharaoh's tomb and a funny style of hat called a fez.

I have included a photograph for Rupert. The camel I am on is called Mahmood and, as you can see, the Sphinx is in the background. Rupert would love this place. The Cairo Zoological Gardens would enthral him, I know. I've been twice to date and still not seen all the wonderful creatures on show; they must number in their hundreds.

I trust this letter will find you well, and I promise that I will write again soon now that I am in better health.

Give my love to Rupert, and to you both I remain, Your loving son, Hugh

Hugh wrote also to Caitie, again apologising for the delay and again, as he had done in the letter to his parents, downplaying the severity of his illness. *It laid me pretty low, I have to admit,* he wrote.

I simply didn't have it in me to put pen to paper. And now three letters have arrived from you all at once, I feel very guilty. But I cannot tell you my dearest girl how much comfort I found in your photograph during my illness. I would kiss it before I went to sleep at night. I still do in fact. When I mentioned that to Oscar he called me a sook, but I don't care. I love you, Caitie.

The truth was, Hugh's mates had been desperately worried about him. Several soldiers had died as a result of the influenza outbreak, and Hugh Stanford had very nearly been one of them.

In their letters home Wes and Harry had not written of Hugh's illness. Hugh had made them promise not to, just as he had made Oscar promise. He didn't want his family or Caitie worrying unnecessarily.

'I'll be up and about in no time,' he'd said during his lucid moments, and he'd been convinced that he would be. It was only when he was over the worst of it that he discovered just how close he'd come.

'Those poor lads,' he said when he learnt of the soldiers who'd died, 'fancy going like that, without even getting a chance to fire a single bullet.'

Hugh's illness was not the only subject omitted from the

letters home. The boys didn't write about their riotous, drunken nights in Cairo, and Harry Balfour and Max Miller made no mention of their recent expedition to the red-light district of Haret el Wassa, although both would actually have loved to announce to the entire world that at long last they had lost their virginity. They supposed it was a subject that called for censorship, however, particularly where family was concerned, and common-sense prevailed.

'No man should go into battle a virgin,' Oscar had declared dramatically and Harry and Max had jumped at his suggestion they rectify the situation. The other two sexual innocents of the bunch, despite the urging of their mates, had refused to join them. Hugh hadn't even used his weakened state as an excuse, swearing that he would have no girl but Caitie, and David, for all of his larrikin behaviour, had similarly determined to remain a virgin until the day he married Jeanie Müller.

Caitie couldn't help but experience a sense of relief when Hugh's letter finally arrived. The family had by now received two letters from Oscar, and she had started to feel just a little insecure. Could Hugh's feelings for her possibly have waned? She chastised herself now for such girlish self-doubt, which was indeed out of character. The poor boy had been ill, and who knew, perhaps more severely than he was leading her to believe.

The following Saturday morning, she called around to Stanford House. She had after all promised to visit Rupert, and perhaps, without alarming the family, she might make some discreet enquiries about Hugh's state of health.

The housekeeper showed her into the smaller front drawing room where Evelyn was sitting with her petit point and Rupert was kneeling on the floor, his eyes riveted upon the coffee table where a half-completed jigsaw puzzle was laid out.

The moment she was announced, he jumped to his feet, bobbing up and down on the spot, waiting until he was allowed to say hello.

'Ah, Miss O'Callaghan ...' Evelyn stood. She was not yet fifty, but looked older, her body frail, her once-rich black hair now quite grey. She put down her petit point and extended her hand. 'How lovely to meet you,' she said.

Caitie crossed and shook the woman's hand, surprised by the warmth of her reception. She had presumed Hugh's mother would not know who she was. 'How do you do, Mrs Stanford? I'm a friend of Hugh's –'

'Of course you are, my dear. I saw you at the ball, and Hugh has told me all about you.' Evelyn turned to the housekeeper, who was awaiting instruction. 'We'll have some tea, thank you, Iris.'

'Yes, ma'am.' Iris departed, leaving the door ajar.

'Hugh told me that you might be calling in to see Rupert. How very kind of you.' At the mention of his name, Rupert's bobbing became fiercer. 'Yes, dear,' Evelyn said, 'you may say hello now.'

'Hello.' Rupert dived forward to grab Caitie's hand and pump it up and down enthusiastically.

'Hello, Rupert. You remember me, don't you? I'm Caitie.'

'Caitie, yes. Caitie with the beautiful hair.' He stopped pumping her hand and studied the fiery tresses that framed her face beneath the small straw hat she wore. 'It's shorter,' he said.

'Yes, I had it trimmed recently.'

'Oh.' Rupert appeared critical.

'Sit down, my dear, please.' Evelyn gestured to an armchair and Caitie sat. 'You too, Rupert,' she said, and Rupert pulled a hardback chair up close to Caitie's and plonked himself on it. 'Have you heard from Hugh?'

'Yes, I have, Mrs Stanford. I received a letter just several days ago. He said in it that he had suffered some illness ...' She left the query gently dangling.

'That's right. A nasty bout of the measles, followed by influenza, most unpleasant I should think. He's over it now, I'm glad to report.'

'That is good to hear indeed.'

Rupert interrupted, even though he knew he shouldn't have. 'Hugh sent me a photograph,' he said and he looked pleadingly at his mother. 'May I show her?'

'Yes, you may, dear.'

Rupert took the photograph from his top pocket. It had become his prize possession and was transferred on a regular basis to the pocket of whatever shirt he was wearing. He presented it to Caitie.

'The camel is called Mahmood,' he explained, 'and that's the Sphinx there.' He leant in close and pointed out the Sphinx just in case she should miss it.

'So it is,' she said. 'What a lovely photograph.' Caitie felt rather envious and she resolved there and then that she would demand Hugh send her a photograph of her own. 'You're a very lucky young man, Rupert.'

'Yes.' Rupert smiled happily and returned the photograph to his top pocket.

The women talked about the surprising news that the battalion's destination had proved to be Egypt and, after a brief interruption caused by the arrival of the tea, they went on to discuss the mystery of where the troops might be sent after their desert training.

'The location will no doubt be kept a secret until the very last minute,' Evelyn said. 'In fact we probably shan't learn where they are until they're actually doing battle.'

'Yes, I daresay you're right.'

It was a sobering thought and there was silence but for the tinkle of spoons as the two of them stirred their tea. Rupert, having by now lost interest in the conversation, had taken his biscuit and glass of milk and returned to his jigsaw.

Over the next twenty minutes, they avoided further discussion of the war. They talked about the ball instead, and Caitie helped Rupert with his jigsaw puzzle when he complained about a tricky bit.

'The sky's always hard,' he said, 'all the bits are blue.'

She knelt beside him. 'Those two pieces look as if they might fit,' she suggested, pointing them out – it was a child's jigsaw puzzle and very simple. He tried them and they did. 'Oh, and look, Rupert,' she said, 'there's a bit of a cloud in that one.'

'Yes, yes,' he jiggled about, excited by the breakthrough, 'it's much, much better when you get to the clouds.' He fitted the pieces together and grinned at her admiringly. Caitie wasn't just pretty, Caitie was clever.

'Thank you so much for the tea, Mrs Stanford.' Ten minutes later, Caitie took her leave.

'It was a pleasure to meet you, my dear.' Evelyn stood and started towards the door, Rupert scrambling to his feet and joining her.

'Oh please don't see me out,' Caitie insisted, 'I can find my own way, really.'

'Heavens above, no, we insist,' Evelyn said, 'don't we, Rupert?'

'Yes, we insist.' Rupert skipped on ahead and opened the drawing-room door for the ladies as he'd been taught to do.

They stepped out into the main hall just as Reginald reached the bottom of the stairs.

'Well, well,' he said, stopping dead in his tracks at the sight of Caitlin O'Callaghan, 'I was not aware we had a visitor.'

'This is Miss O'Callaghan, dear,' Evelyn made the introduction. 'Miss O'Callaghan is a friend of Hugh's.'

'Of course, the young lady he met at the ball.'

'How do you do, Mr Stanford?' Hugh's father seems rather stern, Caitie thought, and there was no offer of a handshake, but then many older men did not shake hands with young women, and those of the stature of Reginald

Stanford would probably never dream of doing so. 'I actually knew Hugh prior to the ball, sir.' She made the correction politely and pleasantly. 'Not well indeed, but we had bumped into each other on a number of occasions.'

'Really? I was not aware of that. And to what do we owe the pleasure of your visit, Miss O'Callaghan, Hugh as you would know being overseas?'

He doesn't like me, Caitie thought. In fact he actively *dis*likes me. Why, she wondered, but she was saved from answering his question as Evelyn leapt in, aware of her husband's displeasure although unsure of the reason for it.

'Miss O'Callaghan came to visit Rupert, Reginald. She told Hugh that she would do so. Isn't that kind?'

'Most kind, most kind indeed.' Reginald turned to Rupert. 'Did you thank Miss O'Callaghan for coming to visit you, Rupert?'

Rupert felt nervous. Father was not happy. Rupert was always nervous when Father was not happy, and he wondered if it was because of something he'd done. He bobbed up and down to Caitie. 'Thank you for coming to see me, Caitie.'

'The pleasure was mine, Rupert.'

'Perhaps you would care to see your guest to the door, Rupert?'

'Yes, Father, yes.' He scampered ahead and opened the main door.

'Thank you so much for coming, my dear –' Evelyn said, and she was about to add 'do call again', but Reginald got in first.

'Yes, thank you, Miss O'Callaghan, most kind.'

Caitie crossed to the door. 'Goodbye, Rupert,' she said and she kissed him on the cheek. She could see he was upset by his father's displeasure. I won't call again, she decided.

As Rupert carefully closed the door behind her, Reginald turned to his wife.

'Don't encourage the girl,' he snapped.

'Why ever not?' Evelyn was bewildered. 'She seems most presentable and Hugh's very fond of her.'

'She's from Irish scum. She's not good enough for him.' Reginald strode off to the garage where the chauffeur was waiting. He would be late picking up his colleague from the Orient Hotel now, and all because of that wretched girl.

The patriotic fervour that had swept Tasmania soon developed an element of paranoia. Any name that was Germanic in origin came under suspicion and intense scrutiny. The town of Bismarck was ridiculously rechristened Collinsvale, and across the island those of German descent were persecuted for no other reason than the sound and the spelling of their names.

Thomas Powell was unexpectedly confronted by the situation when he went into Franklin to pick up supplies and post a letter to his son David.

'What's going on?' he asked Millicent Lansbury who worked behind the counter at the post office. Millicent knew everything that went on in the entire district. 'I just saw the Schmidts outside the police station,' he said. 'Karl was carrying a suitcase and his wife and daughter were crying, and then he farewelled them and went inside like a man under sentence.'

'Yes, that'd be right,' Millicent said with a knowing nod.

'But why, what's he done?' Thomas was amazed: Karl Schmidt was the most peaceable man. 'Is he under arrest or something?' Impossible, he thought.

'Sort of, yes.'

'What for?'

'The government's rounding them up,' Millicent explained patiently. 'Lists have been sent out to all the townships. Their names are checked and they're told to report to the local police station, then they're collected and taken to the internment camp at Dennes Point on Bruny Island.'

'Who are "they"?' Thomas remained as confused as ever.

'Enemy aliens.'

'*Enemy aliens*?' he queried as if she had to be mad.

'That's right: Germans. All Germans are enemy aliens.' He obviously hasn't heard the term, Millicent thought, but more importantly he didn't seem to be grasping the general picture. 'It's essential they be locked up, Thomas,' she said firmly, 'you never know, any one of them could be a spy.'

'A spy? Karl Schmidt's an orchardist. He and his family have lived here for twenty years.'

'Doesn't make one bit of difference.' Millicent shook her head decisively, she was a patriot through and through and her views were unshakeable. 'It wouldn't even matter if he was born here: he's still a German. He still has ties with his own country, and you never know where such a man's loyalties might lie, so it's best to be on the safe side. The government's doing the right thing rounding them up. They're to be locked away for the duration of the war, and that's just as it should be.'

Thomas didn't stay to hear any more. He posted his letter, forgot about the supplies he'd intended to pick up, and drove his horse and dray at top speed the ten miles or so to Geeveston, hoping he'd reach the Müllers in time. He wasn't sure of his intention. Perhaps he'd hide Gus away at the orchard, perhaps he'd hide the whole family away, he really didn't know. He had no specific plan, just a desperate desire to get to his friend before the summons arrived, as it surely would.

But Thomas was already too late. Gus Müller had been sent home from the timber mill where he worked that very morning. He'd been told to report to the police station that same afternoon, and was currently packing the one suitcase he was allowed to take with him. Or rather his wife Heidi was. Gus was doing his best to buoy up her spirits, while his daughter Jeanie watched sullenly from the sidelines, angered by the injustice being perpetrated upon her father.

'Don't take things too hard, Heidi, love,' Gus said cheerily, 'it won't be for that long. The war can't last forever.'

'Your heavy coat you will wear,' Heidi said, 'your wool sweater also and your scarf.' She didn't look at him, but focused upon the suitcase, as she tried desperately to stem the tears that threatened. 'There is not such room here.'

'Come on then,' he enfolded her in his arms, 'have a good old bawl if you want to, get it out of your system.' She did, and he stroked her hair comfortingly. 'Right,' he said finally as she dried her eyes, 'now let's have a nice cup of tea – I don't have to report in for a good two hours. Whack the kettle on, Jeanie, there's a good girl, and we'll have some of your mother's cherry cake too.'

An hour or so later, there was a knock on the front door and Jeanie opened it to reveal Thomas Powell.

'Is he still here?' Thomas asked. 'They told me at the timber mill that he'd been sent home to pack.'

'He's still here,' Jeanie said, and she led the way through to the kitchen.

'Thomas,' Gus rose from the table and embraced his friend, 'you're just in time to say goodbye, mate. I'm about to be interned.' He smiled to lighten the moment. 'Apparently I'm a threat to the nation.'

'Do you know what they're calling him?' Jeanie said, her blue eyes ablaze with anger. 'An enemy alien,' she spat.

'I know. That's why I'm here. Don't go, Gus.'

'What?'

'Don't go,' Thomas urged. 'Don't report to the station, don't let them take you. Come with me, you can hide out at the orchard, I'll keep you safe.'

'Yes Pappa, do,' Jeanie joined in excitedly. 'Go with Thomas, that's a wonderful idea.'

'And what would happen to you and your mother? You'd be hounded day and night –'

'Bring the girls with you, that's even better,' Thomas said, 'everyone will think you've left town with your family. They might even think you've left Tasmania.'

'And what would happen to *you*, Thomas?' Gus shook his head at the ridiculousness of the suggestion. 'Everyone knows we're friends, you'd be investigated immediately. They'd find us and you'd be arrested for harbouring an enemy alien –'

'I don't care –'

'I know, I know, you're always the rebel, but *I* care, Thomas, *I* care! Now sit down and let's talk calmly.' Thomas sat. Gus sensed his daughter was about to argue further. 'Fetch some more cake, Jeanie,' he said, 'and would you mind, Heidi love?' He smiled at his wife. 'Could we have another pot of tea?'

While Heidi made the tea and Jeanie cut fresh slices of cake, the two men talked, Thomas curbing his passion as best he could, but with little success.

'Let me come with you to the police station, Gus,' he implored. 'I can vouch for you. I've known you all my life. You were born right here, you're as Australian as I am –'

'They're aware of that, Thomas,' Gus said patiently, 'they know me too. We drink at the same bar on a Friday night, our wives shop at the same butchers and green-grocers. It's going on like this throughout the entire district,' he said with a shrug. 'The police are simply doing their job. Some agree with it, some don't, but it's a job they've been ordered to do.'

'Then I'll appeal to the government. There's no reason for your internment. You were born in this country, your daughter's engaged to an Australian, your son's in the Australian Army, what threat could you possibly represent?'

'My name is Müller. That's the threat. That's all they can see.'

Gus's resignation was getting on Thomas's nerves. 'Good

God, man,' he burst out, frustrated, 'your son is fighting for this bloody country – surely that says something.'

'It should, but apparently it doesn't.' Gus remained unruffled.

'At least let me put your case to the authorities,' Thomas insisted, 'I'll explain your circumstances, I'll tell them your son's in the army and –'

'No, Thomas, I cannot allow you to do that,' Gus interrupted with a force that successfully called a halt to his friend's persistence. 'It might pose a serious threat to Max. They could discover he enlisted under the name of Miller.' His expression was whimsical as he leant back in his chair. 'Ridiculous isn't it,' he mused, 'the difference one little letter makes? Max knew when he filled out the registration form that it was illegal to give false information to the army, but he just thought he was making things easier. I discovered – only today, strangely enough – that it's now against the law for anyone to anglicise a German name. Did you know that? Someone told me at work. I was quite taken aback, I must say.'

The women rejoined them at the table with the fresh tea and cake.

'So there's nothing I can do?' Thomas asked helplessly.

'Yes, there is something,' Gus said. 'You can drink your tea and eat your cake, and then you can drive me to the police station. I have forbidden the girls to come, and it'll save me lugging the suitcase.'

Twenty minutes later, Gus made his farewells to his wife and daughter and climbed up into the passenger seat beside Thomas. The horse took off down the street and Heidi and Jeanie stood at the cottage gate waving until the dray had rounded the corner out of sight.

It was barely a five-minute drive to the police station. Thomas pulled up outside and was about to alight.

'Don't,' Gus said, 'I've had enough goodbyes for one day.' He offered his hand and they shook. 'Thanks for the lift, mate.' He climbed down from the dray and took his suitcase from the back. 'By the way, I don't want Max to hear about this. It'd make him angry, and he doesn't need the distraction.'

'Fair enough, I'll pass word around the family. Take care of yourself, Gus. I'll look after your girls for you.'

'I know you will.'

Thomas watched as Gus Müller, suitcase in hand, walked through the front doors of the police station. It was an image that would remain etched in his mind for years to come.

Mail from the troops continued to arrive home over the following two months, although in early March the men were no longer writing about Egypt. Wes Balfour wrote:

> *3 March 1915*
> *We're on the move, the battalion sailed out of Alexandria yesterday. Hooray, at last we're about to see some action. Life in the desert had become wretchedly tedious, I can tell you. Even the odd shenanigan we got up to in Cairo had lost its appeal. We're raring to get into the real stuff ...*

But the 'real stuff' didn't appear to be immediately on offer.

We're still holed up aboard ship, Max Miller wrote, *and have been for weeks now.* Then he went on to describe a rather dull existence, more to fill in the page than anything as they were not permitted to write about their location or the battalion's activities.

The troopship was only one of many docked alongside all other manner of warships at the island of Lemnos in the Aegean Sea, roughly fifty miles from the Turkish mainland. The troops' mail home was censored, and if a soldier inadvertently let slip a piece of information, a thick black line was drawn through the reference.

All of us are bored rotten, and the food, what little there is of it, is truly awful. Some blokes are getting crook, which doesn't help matters. Max, like all the others, couldn't resist including a complaint about the food, which was not only justifiable, but hugely understated. The British government's rations were so insubstantial in quality and quantity that combined with a shortage of fresh water, it was making the men seriously ill. Some were even hospitalised on Lemnos.

Gosh I sound like a whinger, don't I? Don't really mean to, it's just that we're itching for action and this is getting us all down. Hope everyone's well at home. Keep those letters coming. The arrival of the mail is the only thing stopping us from going barmy, I swear.
Love to you all, Max

In compliance with Gus's instructions, Max had not been informed of his father's internment. Heidi and Jeanie kept the news to themselves and the Powells made no mention of it when they wrote to Gordie and David.

The last of the letters written aboard the troopship left with the mail boat on the twenty-first of April. The letters home after that would never be the same.

It was late in the afternoon, the sun just beginning to set across the Aegean Sea and, from where he lay in the scrub two hundred feet above the beach, Hugh looked at the carnage below. So this is war, he thought, this butchery is war. But surely it hadn't been meant to happen like this. It couldn't have been, he thought as he gazed at the flotsam and jetsam of men dead and dying that littered the beach. There must have been a mistake. Something must have gone dreadfully wrong.

Hugh Stanford had been in the first wave of the 3rd Brigade to reach the beach. A number of men in his landing boat had been killed, but he'd managed to get ashore, discarding his pack in the water when it threatened to drag him down and losing his rifle as he swam the last several yards. Then there'd been the mad dash across the beach for the shelter of the steep cliffs that confronted them. Bullets had whizzed past, thudding into sand, scrub and men alike, and artillery shells had burst overhead spitting shrapnel, but he'd made it, even managing to score a rifle on the way. He'd grabbed it from the hands of a dead man on the beach. He hadn't needed to stop and check, he'd known the man was dead: half his head was missing.

Scaling the cliff heights had been almost impossible. Perhaps a feat only possible for men driven by fear, he now thought, looking down at the bloodbath he'd so miraculously escaped. He'd killed a man on the way up, possibly two – he hadn't checked on the second one he'd shot. He'd taken a look at the first Turk though: a lad younger than himself, no more than sixteen. The entire landing was a fiasco, he thought, companies, platoons, even sections split up, scattered in all directions. No-one had known where their units were. In fact, no-one had known what the hell was going on; in the massacre it had been a race for survival.

Above the beach and out of the immediate danger zone, he'd managed to catch up with his platoon sergeant, who had already gathered a number of men from various units, including David Powell, Oscar O'Callaghan and Max Miller. With some semblance of military command restored, they'd fought and clawed their way higher to their objective rendezvous point at 400 Plateau. The platoon's orders had been to support an Indian artillery unit that was setting up position there. Upon arrival, they'd been ordered to dig in by a British major – who had promptly disappeared.

The Turkish batteries, however, alerted to the presence of the Indian artillery unit, had opened fire, a fresh hell had broken loose, and Hugh couldn't remember anything after that. He had no idea what had happened to the others, but he'd finished up halfway back down the slope, unconscious. That's where the medic had found him some time later.

He'd been hit twice, not fatal wounds, but painful and bloody. A Turkish bullet had opened a rip in the muscle of his upper arm and a piece of shrapnel from an artillery shell had sliced his thigh. The medic from the Field Ambulance Unit had stemmed the bleeding, bandaged him roughly and told him to make his way down to the far side of the cove, where a casualty clearing station had been set up.

'Sorry, mate, can't do any more,' the man had said, 'you're on your own, but you'll live.' Leaving a water bottle, he'd moved off to answer the call of other wounded.

Hugh had watched from the slopes as down on the beach the slaughter had continued. He'd seen the troops of the 7th Battalion, 2nd Brigade literally shot to pieces by Turkish machine-gun fire. Oh dear God, he'd thought as he'd watched the men being systematically mowed down, oh dear God, those poor lads, every one of them's copping it.

Now, with the advent of dusk, things had at last eased. He hauled himself to his feet and using his rifle to assist him started his painful trek down to the cove.

On reaching the foreshore, he wended his way through the carnage towards the clearance station, where a tent had been set up for emergency operations and where, in a nearby triage area, troops were being treated for minor wounds. Out in the open, lined up on stretchers, were dozens upon dozens of men waiting to be ferried to the hospital ship in the transport barges that ran continuously to and fro.

Hugh reported to the triage area where exhausted members of the medical unit were working at a feverish pace.

'Well blow me down, look who's here,' David said with the broadest grin. 'We thought you'd copped it, didn't we, Oscar?' Both were having bayonet cuts stitched; David's wound was in his upper arm and Oscar's in his left side.

'We certainly did,' Oscar agreed, 'one minute you were there and the next you were gone, we thought you'd been blown up. Ouch, that hurt.'

'You'd make it easier on yourself if you stood still,' the doctor said tetchily.

Hugh waited his turn, which didn't take long coming – the medics were moving from one man to the next with amazing efficiency. He gritted his teeth while his thigh and upper arm were tamped and bandaged and fifteen minutes later, like David and Oscar, he was declared fit to fight.

'I suppose we don't get out of it that easily,' he said as he limped from the triage area. The tamping of his open wounds had been extremely painful. 'We're the lucky ones who get to fight another day.'

He'd said it jokingly, but looking down the beach at the dead – who had not yet been collected, for ambulance teams were too busy collecting those who might possibly be saved – and looking over at the row upon row of wounded men awaiting transport to the hospital ship, they knew it was no joke, all three of them. They were indeed the lucky ones, so far anyway.

Hugh drained the water bottle the Field Ambulance man had given him.

'We need to get you another pack,' Oscar said and he walked off down the beach, returning only minutes later with a full kitbag. 'There are plenty around,' he said. He wasn't trying to be funny.

They found a spot up near the cliffs safe from sniper fire and sat on the rocks, Hugh easing out his throbbing leg while David and Oscar lit up cigarettes.

'So what happened to Max,' Hugh asked, 'do you know?'

'No idea,' Oscar said. 'We were too busy running for cover and when we found he wasn't with us, we thought he must have copped it like you.'

'We were going to go back and look for him,' David said, 'but that's when we bumped into Johnny Turk, and I mean literally. We fell right into a dugout where they were holed up. Surprised them even more than us. They were focused on the Indian artillery unit below, so we had the advantage.'

'There were five,' Oscar added, 'it was a pretty good fight.'

'You killed all five?' Hugh was impressed.

'Three,' Oscar said, 'the other two got away. You should have seen David though, God it was funny. He was so shocked when he landed on the Turks that he dropped his rifle. He actually dropped his bloody rifle.' Oscar threw back his head and laughed. 'I tell you, the look on his face! But he didn't pause for a second. He whipped out his bayonet and gutted two of the Turks straight off. I managed to get in a head shot first up, but after that there was no space to move so we took on the other two hand-to-hand – they had their own bayonets out by then.' He grinned at David. 'It was no match though, was it?

'No match at all, that's for sure.' David grinned back. 'They got in a couple of jabs and then took off like frightened rabbits.'

'Well done,' Hugh said.

'How about you,' Oscar asked excitedly, 'did you kill any Turks?'

'I don't know, I shot a couple.'

'But did you *kill* them?'

'I don't know, I just kept running, I didn't stop to look.' He had stopped of course. He had looked. And he'd decided that he would never stop again.

Hugh could see the light of battle in his friends' eyes, the slightly mad, unreal, adrenalin-rush of victory. He understood their exhilaration. He felt it too. Was it the thrill of killing? Had they in some way been blooded? Or was it because they had survived to tell their tales?

'What about the others,' he asked, 'do you know how they fared?'

'Gordie made it safely across the beach,' David said, 'but I haven't seen him since then. We saw the Balfours up on a ridge digging in though, didn't we, Oscar, and they were in good nick.'

'Yeah, we bumped into Wes and Harry just before we came down here to get stitched up. They lead charmed lives those boys – not a scratch on either of them.'

'So maybe there's only Max to worry about,' Hugh said. 'Let's check the wounded.'

He held out his hand, they hauled him to his feet and the three of them wandered over to where the rows of stretchers were laid out on the sand.

They walked along twenty yards or so and there he was. He appeared to be asleep.

'G'day, Max,' David said.

Max's eyes sprang open and he beamed up at them with a slightly crazed expression.

'Well blow me down, what do we have here?' He grinned at David as he employed the commonly used phrase of his lifelong friend. 'Half the gang, if I'm not mistaken. Where are the others?'

They squatted beside him on the beach, Hugh awkwardly with his wounded leg stretched out, and they told him that Wes and Harry were safe, but that they didn't know about Gordie.

'Oh Gordie's determined to become some sort of hero,' Max said. He was quite lucid although clearly full of morphine and tending to gabble a bit. 'I was waiting to be treated in the hospital tent and Gordie came in with a bloke over his shoulder. He'd carried him all the way down those ridges, poor bastard had a foot missing. Anyway, Gordie dumped him down and went back up, presumably to fetch some other poor bastard.' Max gave a slightly demented laugh: the opiates were having a strange effect on him. 'Good old Gordie, true hero material, but he's safe and that's the main thing.' His face cracked into a manic grin. 'Which means we boys made it,' he said triumphantly. 'Given the law of averages, not bad for a day like today, eh? I reckon we're damn lucky to have survived in one piece. Lesson learnt though,' he added in all seriousness, 'we can't let them get the better of us like that again. We'll have to sort them out tomorrow, that's for sure.'

Max was delirious. He didn't seem to know that he was one of many seriously wounded lying on a stretcher waiting to be taken to the hospital ship. He didn't seem to know also that he had a limb missing. Below his right knee was a crisp white bandage binding the stump where, in the emergency tent, they had amputated and cauterised the shredded remnants of his leg to prevent him from bleeding to death.

'Yeah, we boys made it, Max,' Hugh said, 'we survived all right,' but not in one piece, he thought, and we're not boys, not any more.

CHAPTER TWENTY-ONE

It was some time before the devastating statistics of the Gallipoli landings reached home. The British Army refused to make public the details of the disastrous invasion, or to admit to accusations of military ineptitude; and the Australian government, with its need to meet an agreed quota of troops for the British, was wary about frightening off volunteers and adversely affecting the recruitment drive.

The truth could not be denied for long, however. As telegrams arrived informing families that their men had been killed or lost or wounded in action the enormity of the disaster started to sink in.

Heidi and Jeanie Müller received the telegram from the AIF Base Records Office in Melbourne on the second of May. It was addressed to Mr G Miller – when listing his nearest of kin, Max had made the same alteration to his father's name.

REGRET REPORT SON PRIVATE MAX G MILLER WOUNDED WILL ADVISE ANYTHING FURTHER RECEIVED.

The telegram's wording was not only abrupt, it was terrifyingly inconclusive. How severely had he been wounded?

Where had he been taken? Was he expected to survive? Heidi and Jeanie were in turmoil. There were so many questions and no answers forthcoming. Should they send word to Gus at the internment camp? They decided to wait until they found out the truth. Not knowing was torturous.

Eventually they found out through David Powell, although not directly. David wrote to his father, Thomas. He did not, as he had in the past, include his mother and sisters in his letter, which also lacked its normal larrikin tone. Indeed, his writing was uncharacteristically cynical.

Dear Dad,
I don't know how long it'll take for this to reach you. Given the chaos that reigns over here probably some time, but I thought I'd let you know about Max. In all this madness it's doubtful the army will supply much detail and you can pass the news on to Heidi and Jeanie. I reckon it'll be easier if they hear it face to face, and frankly I don't want to be the one to tell Jeanie her brother's coming home with one leg.

Mind you, the fact that he'll be coming home at all will be of huge comfort, I'm sure: there are thousands who won't by the time this bloody campaign's done. But from what I can gather, Max will be all right. He's a strong little bastard as we all know.

We saw him on the beach that first day, not long after Gordie had carried him down from the ridges. He was off his trolley, didn't even know Gordie had brought him in or that his leg had been taken off in the casualty station.

We've made enquiries with the medics since then. They say he's been evacuated to Malta and from there he'll probably be shipped over to England. So that's some cheering news you can pass on.

I have to tell you, Dad, strictly between us (and it's good to be able to write honestly instead of sugaring

*the pill for the girls), Max might well be one of the
lucky ones. For a start he's alive, which has to be a
bonus; and as for wounds, I've seen sights that beggar
description. If some of those poor bastards do manage
to survive, how they'll live with such disfigurement
and debilitation is beyond me.*

*The fact is, this is a filthy, ugly hell on earth and
there are only two things that will see you through
it. The first of course is sheer bloody luck. After
that, you have to be tough. You're undone if you let
yourself go under.*

*I'll write a letter to Jeanie now telling her that
Max will recover and that you have the news about
him. Sorry to land you with that. And I'll write a
letter to Mum and the girls telling them that I'm all
right (which I am) and that the food's bloody terrible
(which it is).*

*Good to let off a bit of steam, I must say. I miss
our talks.*

Lots of love, David

When the first batch of letters arrived home from the
front, Heidi and Jeanie, who had as yet received no further
word from the military, were overwhelmed with relief to
discover that Max was safe. At last they could let Gus
know.

The timing as it turned out was fortuitous. One month
after Gus Müller received word of his son's safety, the
internees of Bruny Island were transferred from Dennes
Point to Holsworthy Camp in New South Wales, a location
far removed from the Huon. Gus was now a world away
from his family.

The horrendous war news continued to seep into the
Australian consciousness. The burgeoning statistics could
no longer be denied; brutal telegrams were delivered to
front doors with relentless regularity; and now the letters

reached home from the troops themselves. The magnitude of the loss was finally revealed and Australians across the country were shocked to the core.

Evelyn Stanford fretted day and night for her son's safety. Her anxiety exacerbated her already frail condition and in early June she fell gravely ill. At first her family thought her bronchitis the lingering result of a severe cold she'd caught in the spring, but her lungs became infected and she developed pneumonia. She died two weeks later.

Reginald was thoroughly disoriented by the loss of his wife. He was in a state of shock and confusion as much as grief, for despite her fragility it had not occurred to him until near the end that she might actually die. Life without Evelyn was something he had never contemplated. And to make matters worse, there was Rupert.

Twenty-year-old Rupert was more than disoriented: he was distraught with grief. He wept incessantly over the loss of the mother, who had been the centre of his existence. Iris Watson, the housekeeper, a kindly woman, did her best to comfort him. She would cuddle his hulking frame to her matronly breast and he would cling to her like a baby, crying 'Mummy, Mummy' over and over again.

'Mummy's in heaven now, dear,' Iris would say as she stroked his head soothingly, 'Mummy's with the angels,' and Rupert would wail all the louder.

The sight and the sound put an unbearable strain on Reginald's already frayed nerves and he did all he could to avoid his son's presence, even having his meals delivered to his study and leaving Rupert to dine in the kitchen with the servants.

Rupert, either through a sense of abandonment or perhaps in an attempt to share his grief with a fellow sufferer made the mistake of appealing to his father. Late one night, dressed in his pyjamas, he visited Reginald's bedroom.

Reginald, who had been fast asleep, was surprised to find himself awakened by someone climbing into his bed.

'Daddy,' Rupert said tearfully, and he started to snuggle up against his father, reaching out his man's arms for a cuddle, 'Daddy, Daddy –'

It was more than Reginald could bear. He sprang from the bed and switched on the light. 'Get up,' he snarled. 'Get up this instant.'

Rupert scrambled out of the bed and stood there, literally shaking with fear, his head quivering and his hands flapping as they always did when he was distressed.

Fighting down the urge to yell, Reginald tried his hardest to reason with his son, to make some form of intelligent connection. 'You must listen to me, Rupert,' he said firmly. 'You're a man now, do you understand? You must pull yourself together and you must act like a man. Do you understand me?'

Rupert looked down at the floor, his head continuing to quiver, his hands continuing to shake. 'Yes, Daddy,' he said.

Reginald's nerves suddenly snapped. 'I am not *Daddy*,' he yelled, 'I have not been *Daddy* since you were eight years old! I am *Father*! Do you understand? I am *Father* at all times. Say it, boy. Say it.'

'You are Father, you are Father.' Face twitching, limbs jerking: the whole of Rupert's body was a quivering mess.

'Get out! Get out – do you hear me?'

'Yes Father, yes Father.' He raced clumsily for the door.

The situation grew even more unbearable for Reginald after that night. Rupert developed facial twitches he'd never had, his hand-flapping became more pronounced than ever, and he would make little whimpering noises that drove Reginald to distraction. Was the boy trying to impose guilt upon him for having yelled as he had? Was he to be held responsible for the fact that his son's condition appeared to have worsened? Reginald refused to accept blame and felt neither guilt nor remorse, but now more than ever he could not bear Rupert's presence. Without the protective buffer of his wife, he could no longer live under the same roof as his son.

Less than a month after Evelyn's death, much to the shock of the household staff, Reginald had his son committed to the Hospital for the Insane in New Norfolk.

'But I'm willing to look after him, sir,' Iris Watson insisted when he announced his intention, 'and Clive also is happy to take on the responsibility. Between the two of us we can manage.'

'A very generous offer, Iris,' Reginald said, 'and most appreciated. But we must be realistic. You and Clive are both nearing retirement age, you cannot look after Rupert forever. And as you will have noticed, his condition has sadly deteriorated since his mother's passing. It is quite apparent that he now requires professional care. There are specialists at the hospital who are trained to cater for needs such as his, and Rupert will be happier there in the long run.'

Obviously no discussion was to be entered into, and Iris Watson found herself feeling as sorry for the father as she was for the retarded son. The poor man had been driven to distraction by the death of his wife, they'd all seen it, and now, without the mistress by his side, he simply could not cope with his son's affliction. It is very sad, Iris thought, very sad indeed.

Reginald drove Rupert the twenty-two miles to New Norfolk in his recently acquired Model T Ford. Even he had realised that the ostentation of the Rolls Royce could be perceived as tasteless in wartime. He chatted pleasantly to his son as he drove and Rupert appeared relaxed, twitching a little as was his custom, but nodding and saying 'Yes, Father' whenever it was expected of him.

Rupert wasn't actually absorbing what his father was saying: it was something about a 'holiday', but he didn't really know what that meant. He was thoroughly enjoying the outing, however. It was a long time since he'd been

taken for a drive and he loved being in a motor car.
The sights and the sounds and the smells of the passing
countryside enthralled him, but he remembered to keep
glancing at his father and nodding now and then. He must
not make Father cross.

Set in the beautiful rural surrounds of the Derwent Valley,
the hospital precinct covered an area of approximately three
hundred acres. The buildings were magnificent models
of colonial Georgian architecture, some in the Palladian
barrack style, with verandahs surrounding a huge central
courtyard. Reginald, always an admirer of fine architecture,
had been most impressed several days earlier when he'd
visited the place to fill out the registration forms.

Now, the two of them stood in the reception hall, the
suitcase Iris had packed for Rupert having been taken
away by an attendant. Rupert's attention was captured
by the flower arrangement on the nearby sideboard. He
turned away to gently stroke the buttery surface of a lily
while Reginald chatted to Sister Cartwright, the pleasant
middle-aged Englishwoman who personally supervised the
hospital wing in which Rupert was to be housed.

Eunice Cartwright was large, strongly-built and obviously capable of managing the more troublesome patients.
No doubt a mandatory prerequisite for a nurse in a lunatic
asylum, Reginald thought.

'You have been informed that he is not violent, I take
it?' Although unswayed from his purpose, Reginald felt
the need to ensure that Rupert would not be housed with
the more dangerous cases.

'Oh yes indeed, Mr Stanford, I have the full history you
submitted to administration when Rupert was registered.'
Eunice tapped the folder tucked under her arm. 'You may
rest assured that your son will receive the particular care
and attention a case such as his demands.'

'Yes, yes, I was informed he would be with others of
similar intellectual impairment rather than ...' Reginald

broke off. He didn't quite know how to finish the sentence and he was beginning to feel most uncomfortable. Images of his mother and his wife had suddenly flashed alarmingly in his brain. What would Mathilda and Evelyn say if they could see him leaving Rupert here? He wanted desperately to get out of the place.

'Of course, Mr Stanford,' Eunice said understandingly, 'have no fear, Rupert will be in a special wing with others like himself.' She could see the man was agitated, but then most people were when committing a family member. 'Would you care for the guided tour? I would be most happy to show you around Rupert's new home.'

'No, no,' Reginald said hastily, 'I had a look about on my visit several days ago,' it was a lie, he hadn't, 'and I have a pressing business engagement in the city.'

'Yes sir, I understand.' He's feeling guilty, she thought, they always do, and he's recently lost his wife, poor fellow. 'Well then,' she turned to Rupert with a hearty mixture of professionalism and motherliness, 'I suppose it's time to say cheerio, Rupert?' But Rupert, engrossed in his lily, made no response as he continued to stroke its softness.

'Sister Cartwright spoke to you, Rupert,' Reginald said sharply.

Rupert's head jerked up and he turned, face twitching, hands starting to flap a little. He looked at his father and then at the nurse, unsure what was expected of him.

'Time to say cheerio, Rupert.' Eunice smiled encouragingly.

Cheerio wasn't a word Rupert was particularly accustomed to, but he obliged anyway; the lady seemed very nice.

'Cheerio,' he said, and he waved goodbye. He was a little surprised when she didn't go anywhere.

'You will be staying here with Sister Cartwright,' Reginald explained brusquely. He had to get out; he couldn't stand it a minute longer. 'And I will come and visit you, do you understand?'

'Yes, Father.' Rupert didn't understand at all, but he would do anything rather than upset his father.

'Goodbye, Rupert.' Reginald extended his hand. He couldn't bring himself to embrace his son for fear the boy would cling to him.

'Goodbye, Father.' Rupert shook his father's hand man-to-man, knowing it was expected of him, and then he waited to see what would happen next.

'Good day to you, Sister Cartwright.' Reginald tipped his hat.

'Good day, Mr Stanford. I look forward to seeing you when you next visit.' She doubted he would visit at all. Eunice was reassessing her sympathy for the man. The son was frightened of the father, and the father couldn't stand the son. She did not pass judgement – she understood the phenomenon, having witnessed it on many an occasion – but she no longer felt sorry for Reginald Stanford. 'Come along, Rupert.'

She reached out her hand and Rupert took it immediately. He enjoyed holding hands. But he was a little bewildered. Come along where? he wondered.

'I'll show you the garden,' she said, 'even though it's winter we have some very pretty flowers.'

Instantly intrigued, Rupert allowed himself to be led off. 'I like flowers,' he said.

Reginald walked out into the bitterly chill winter day exhaling a huge puff of steam with his sigh of relief.

Caitie O'Callaghan was saddened to hear of Evelyn Stanford's death: she'd very much liked the woman upon their one meeting. She wondered if the family had informed Hugh of his mother's passing. Surely not. She made no mention of it in her own letters. There was enough death to contend with at Gallipoli. They all knew it now. Families lived in constant fear of any telegram, or an envelope bearing the military insignia, and when the latest casualty lists were posted up outside the GPO and the *Mercury* offices, there was all too often a cry from amongst the crowd gathered as some unfortunate learned of the news they dreaded.

Not wishing to intrude upon the grieving household, Caitie waited a full month after Evelyn's death before calling in to see Rupert on a Saturday morning. She wasn't sure if she would be welcome, given the cool reception she'd received from Reginald Stanford upon her initial visit, but she felt it only proper she should offer her condolences and she wanted to make sure Rupert was all right. She also considered it essential she find out, for the purposes of her own correspondence, whether or not Hugh was aware of the news.

'Miss O'Callaghan.' Reginald entered the small front drawing room where Caitie stood waiting by the windows. He'd been irritated when Clive had told him Iris had invited the girl to wait in the drawing room rather than the main hall. *At least she has not taken the liberty of seating herself*, he thought. 'What can I do for you?'

The reception she was being offered was as cool as it had been the first time, and again Caitie wondered why.

'I was very saddened to hear the news of your wife's passing, Mr Stanford, and I wished to offer my condolences.'

'Most kind.' *Surely a note would have sufficed*, Reginald thought.

'I also wish to offer my deepest sympathy to Rupert. I know his mother meant the world to him. He must be shockingly stricken by her loss.'

'He is. We all are.'

'Of course.' Caitie refused to be cowed by the brusqueness of the man's manner, which was bordering on rude. 'May I see Rupert, sir? That is of course, if he is receiving visitors.'

'I fear that won't be possible, Miss O'Callaghan. Rupert is no longer here.'

'No longer here?' she echoed dumbly, aware that she sounded a little stupid, but wondering where else he could possibly be.

'Rupert was so deeply traumatised by his mother's death that he suffered a severe relapse,' Reginald explained. 'It has been necessary to have him hospitalised at New Norfolk.'

'New Norfolk? You mean the Hospital for the Insane?'

'Sadly, yes. His condition has deteriorated immeasurably.'

'Oh my goodness,' Caitie was shocked, 'oh my goodness, that is sad news indeed.'

'Yes, it is, isn't it? Very, very sad. I thank you for your obvious concern.' The girl barely knows Rupert, he thought with disdain, how dare she pretend such intimacy with the family.

There was a light tap at the drawing-room door, which was ajar, and he turned to discover that Iris Watson had popped her head in.

'Shall I serve morning tea, sir?'

Reginald was about to say no, but Caitie got in first.

'Thank you so much, Mr Stanford,' she said charmingly, as if the offer had come directly from him, 'but I'm afraid I can't stay.'

The cheek of the girl.

The housekeeper left and Caitie decided there was no point in continuing with any further niceties. The man obviously did not like her, so she might as well get straight to the point.

'Does Hugh know about his mother and his brother, Mr Stanford?'

'What the deuce business is that of yours, girl?' Reginald snapped. The audacity!

'I correspond with Hugh, sir. It would be an advantage to know which topics should be avoided.'

Damnation, he thought, of course they correspond. Why hadn't that simple possibility occurred to him? He'd been thinking out-of-sight-out-of-mind and hoping Hugh would forget the O'Callaghan girl while he was serving overseas.

'My son knows about neither his mother nor his brother, Miss O'Callaghan,' he said stiffly, 'I thought it best not to burden him.'

'On that subject at least we are in agreement, sir. I too have no intention of adding to his burdens. I bid you good day.'

'Good day, Miss O'Callaghan.' He opened the drawing-room door wide for her.

Instead of passing him by, she halted and looked him directly in the eyes. 'Why is it you do not like me, Mr Stanford?'

He had to admit she had guts. But then all the O'Callaghan girls had guts.

'It's nothing personal, my dear. I don't actually dislike you at all. In fact I rather admire you. But I sense you have designs upon my son, and you are simply not good enough. I certainly could not allow you to marry him. I feel it only fair that I should warn you of this in case your inclinations are currently trained in the direction of matrimony.'

'I see. Thank you for your honesty.'

Caitie swept past him and out into the hall, her head held high, but she felt decidedly rattled. Was Reginald Stanford spiteful enough to disinherit his son if Hugh chose a girl who did not meet with his approval? She had the distinct feeling that he was. If such was the case, then she must bow out rather than ruin Hugh's life. But she would not think about that now. His father's stand against her would be another in a burgeoning list of subjects that she would avoid in her letters to Hugh.

In the meantime, she would catch the ferry up the Derwent to New Norfolk at the first opportunity and visit Rupert. Whatever his condition, she would not desert him as his father clearly had.

*

Three months of trench warfare on the hills and ridges of Gallipoli Peninsular had resulted in a daily existence that now seemed hideously normal to the hardened troops. The stench of excrement and blood and their own foul body odour seemed normal. Flies swarming over food, the continual itch from body lice, dysentery and red-raw backsides all seemed normal. Even death seemed normal as they ate their maggoty meals beside rotting corpses.

Gone now were the fresh-faced young men eager for adventure; in their place were soldiers toughened by the horror of war. Some had gone under, succumbing to shell-shock, others had managed to disguise their shattered nerves and fight on, but most ANZACs, as the troops of the Australian and New Zealand Army Corps had become known, had adapted to the fearsome reality of battle, dealing out death with ferocity and accepting their own fate with a sense of the inevitable.

The arrival of the mail, which continued miraculously to find its way through the hellfire, was without doubt the highlight of life in the trenches. Men treasured the link with home. Huddling in the filth, they read the precious words, hearing the voices and seeing the faces of families and sweethearts, and in the days that followed they scribbled feverish replies with stubby pencils.

The mail was also something to be shared. News from home was read out loud, family pictures passed around, wives and sweethearts shown off and dutifully admired. Those who'd missed out on a mail delivery didn't feel altogether excluded, as they shared in the letters of others. The arrival of the mail raised everyone's morale.

'Listen to this,' Hugh said to the Balfour boys. Hugh Stanford had been promoted to lance-corporal by his Company Commander and placed in charge of a section of seven men, including Wes and Harry Balfour. Along with other troops of the 12th Battalion they were holed up in a reserve trench awaiting orders. The stink from the nearby latrines was particularly nauseating, but Wes was still managing to scoff down his bully beef, digging it out of the tin with his knife while flapping a hand ineffectually at the swarm of flies surrounding him. Harry had just read out a letter from their big brother Norm, and it was now Hugh's turn to share some of his news from Caitie. Having read all three of her letters (they had arrived at once, as they so often did), he was naturally selective in his choice. Wes and Harry were both very fond of their cousin Rupert.

'*I called in to see Rupert again on Saturday. As before, and upon his insistence, we spent the entire afternoon playing games. There we were sprawled out on the floor eating biscuits and playing endless draughts and snakes and ladders. I must confess that I have developed a routine. I always let him win at draughts in order to hear that terrible laugh of his …*'

Wes and Harry grinned. They found Rupert's laugh so funny themselves it had been a regular habit of theirs to set him off, which had never been difficult. Wes opened up his mouth to give a donkey bray in imitation of Rupert, but quickly choked on a fly. Hugh waited until he'd swallowed it before continuing.

'*… and I always ensure that I win snakes and ladders simply because a girl has to have some pride. Then last Saturday, as if that wasn't enough, he insisted we start on the jigsaw puzzle I'd bought for him, a bucolic picture of a farmhouse and cows, I know how much he likes jigsaw puzzles. Rupert opted to do the cows, of course, and I had to do the sky, because as I am sure you're well aware he does not like the blue bits.*'

Hugh smiled to himself. Caitie's voice sprang off the page. He could just see her and Rupert sprawled out on the floor of his mother's front drawing room. He was glad his family had so welcomed her into their lives, and also, he had to admit, just a little surprised. He'd suspected on

the night of the ball that his father hadn't considered her
as coming from quite the right stock.

Caitie never lied in her letters, but she allowed Hugh
to assume she visited Rupert at Stanford House, and she
always wrote in a lighthearted vein. Rupert did indeed
respond well to her visits and being gregarious by nature
had made some friends amongst his fellow inmates at New
Norfolk, but according to Eunice Cartwright, with whom
he had become a favourite, his nights were tortured.

Hugh read a little more of Caitie's letter out loud. She
wrote of the latest football results, as she always did,
although they knew them already from Norm's letter to his
brothers, and then she gossiped about her new secretarial
position with the legal firm of Kramer, Fox & Hutchinson,
telling wicked stories about the people who worked there.
Caitie always went out of her way to provide amusement
and was sometimes quite outrageous.

'That's it,' Hugh said, 'the last bit's private,' and Harry
and Wes made foolish kissy noises.

But Caitie did not close solely with expressions of affection. In response to Hugh's previous letter, she had been
compelled this time to end on a serious note.

*Oh my dearest, I cannot leave off without telling you
how deeply I was affected by your account of the truce
that was called in order for the troops of both sides to
bury their comrades. You have never written to me of
such things before and I know this is because you wish
to protect me from worry as much as possible, but
you have also never before written in such a heartfelt
manner. I wept as I read your words. The fact that
you no longer see the Turks as the nameless, faceless
foe, but as lads just like yourselves, is extraordinarily
moving. What a terrible, terrible thing war is.*

*I cannot help but wonder though, why you left it so
long to confide in me. You say the truce was on the*

twenty-fourth of May, and yet your letter was written well into July. Have you been plagued by the need to share your thoughts all this while? I would beg you Hugh not to be over-protective of me. Write to me about anything and everything you feel the need to express. I am strong; I can take it.

I pray God keeps you safe my darling, and know always that I love you with the whole of my being,
Your Caitie

He *had* felt the need to share his thoughts, but he couldn't have written about that day any earlier. Not while the images were still so stark in his mind and the stench of burning flesh still lingered in his nostrils. They hadn't buried all of those who'd been putrefying in the sun for days. They'd doused some in petrol and set fire to them. The smell of burning flesh was as bad as the smell of rotting flesh, he'd decided. But during the weeks that had followed the truce, the lingering memory of that day had been one of mutual respect. This much he had been able to share with Caitie, and he'd needed to share it with someone, the recognition between both sides that they were really no different. They'd seen it in each other's eyes. They'd exchanged cigarettes and communicated in ridiculously charade-like exchanges while they'd disposed of their dead. They'd liked one another. From 0730 to 1630 they'd been friends. Then the killing had started all over again. Caitie's right, Hugh thought, war is a terrible thing; it is also bloody ridiculous.

Further down the trench photographs of sweethearts were being bandied about. Several Western Australian soldiers had started the ball rolling, one of them having received a photograph in a letter. The other two produced the pictures they carried with them always.

David Powell, not to be outdone, took his wallet from his top pocket and passed around the well-worn picture of his fiancée. He'd just received two letters from Jeanie and was glad to show her off to a fresh audience.

'That's my Jeanie,' he said.

Big Gordie looked at Oscar and rolled his eyes comically. David flashed Jeanie's picture at every given opportunity.

David, like Hugh, had been promoted to lance-corporal and placed in charge of a section of seven men, including his cousin Gordon and his friend Oscar O'Callaghan. Following the death of so many platoon members, new NCOs had been needed and the Company Commander had clearly seen leadership qualities in both Hugh Stanford and David Powell.

'I've got a picture too,' Gordie said with a wink at Oscar, and he took out the photograph that he'd just received from his younger sister. Nineteen-year-old Cynthia had a very droll sense of humour.

I worry that as you do not have a regular sweetheart, Gordie, she'd written, *you may long for the image of a female face to carry close to your heart.* Cynthia well knew that her brother treasured his bachelorhood and had no desire at all for a regular sweetheart. *I therefore enclose a photograph of Delilah, which I took during a visit to Charlotte Grove last weekend. Her company I'm sure will help you through many a lonely night.*

Gordie handed over his photograph. 'That's my girl,' he said as it was passed around by the half dozen or so men. One by one they burst out laughing, some covering their mouths to keep away the flies, others catching one or two and hawking them out or swallowing them. The picture was a close-up shot of a huge sow's face, snout glistening, eyes staring lovingly into the camera lens.

'That's Delilah,' David said, recognising the family pet. Delilah had the run of the orchard and household alike as had Falstaff before her.

'It certainly is,' Gordie replied in all apparent seriousness. 'As you know, I have a particularly soft spot for pigs.

I think it's extremely thoughtful of Cynthia to go to such trouble on my behalf.'

The mail had as always distracted the men from the surrounding muck and the stench and the flies, but Oscar had noticed that one of the Western Australians, a young chap from Perth, no more than eighteen, whose name he thought was Ben, hadn't joined in the fun. Ben was hunkered down to one side, chewing on a dry biscuit and appearing to take little interest in the proceedings, but Oscar knew he was following every word. Ben hadn't received any mail and he was trying to pretend it didn't matter. Oscar could also see that Ben was one of those whose nerves were shot to pieces. He could read the signs; they all could. He squatted beside the boy.

'Ben, isn't it?'

'That's right.'

'I'm Oscar.'

'Yeah, I know.'

'Fancy copping a picture of a pig, eh?' He grinned, just trying to cheer the lad up.

'Yeah,' Ben smiled, 'that's real funny,' he said, and something in his response led Oscar to believe that Ben would have given anything for a picture of his own, even a picture of a pig.

'You got a girlfriend, Ben?'

'Nup.' He didn't shrug and he didn't pretend nonchalance. There was both regret and longing in the brevity of his answer. Ben was not only frightened, he was lonely.

Without giving the matter a second thought Oscar dug a hand into his pocket and produced the photograph of Mary Reilly. 'There you go,' he said, handing it to the lad, 'you keep a hold of that.'

'Eh?' Ben stared blankly down at the photograph.

'She'll be good company for you. She's very nice.'

'Are you mad?' Ben looked incredulously from the photograph back to Oscar. 'I can't take this.'

'Why not?'

'Why *not*? She's your girl.'

'Nah,' Oscar waved a hand airily, 'she's not my girl, she's just a friend. Like I said, she's very nice – a really good person, you know what I mean? She'd like to think she was of some comfort, I know she would. That's the sort of girl she is.'

Ben's eyes returned to the photograph. 'She's very pretty.'

'Yes, she is isn't she? Her name's Mary. Mary Reilly.'

'You're sure she wouldn't mind me having her picture?'

'She'd consider it an honour, Ben. I know she would.'

Oscar was really pleased with himself. He'd done his good turn for the day, and if they ever got out of this hellhole alive, which was doubtful, Perth and Hobart were worlds apart. Ben and Mary would never meet. He didn't give a damn if they did anyway.

For the past week or so there had been rumours of a big push to be conducted against the Turk and, on the morning of the sixth of August, the troops of the 12th Battalion were ordered back to their lines to support the 1st Brigade in a charge on the Turkish position known as Lone Pine.

The attack was planned as a diversion. The assault on Lone Pine was aimed to coincide with the assault of the 4th Brigade who, along with New Zealand, Gurkha, Indian and newly arrived British troops, were to take possession of the strategically all-important heights of Chunuk Bair.

Waiting in reserve, the men of the 12th watched as the 1st Brigade made its charge, timed for 1630 when the late afternoon sun would be shining in the eyes of the Turkish defenders. The charge was swift and victorious, and by 1800 the frontline trenches were taken. Then, at 1900, the troops of the 12th Battalion were ordered forward to replace the wounded and the dead.

Hugh Stanford and David Powell led their sections in the one-hundred-yard dash up the hill, trying their hardest to avoid stepping on the bodies of comrades as they ran. Some of the prone figures were still alive; and the ever-present cry of 'stretcher bearers' rang out. The victory, swift though it had been, had come at a cost.

The sight that greeted them at their destination was not pretty. During the initial attack, troops had ripped aside the covering pine logs to leap into the trenches; without room for rifles they'd fought hand to hand with bayonets. The dead and the dying of both sides now lay skewered together in gruesome embraces.

The assault, however, had proved successful. In the rabbit warren that constituted the Turkish entrenchments, the Australians had secured the frontline and connecting communication trenches. The Turks had been forced to retreat to their nearby reserve and supply trenches, where they could call in reinforcements. The Australians, aware that the enemy would launch a counterattack, dug in and prepared to defend their new frontline.

The Turkish reinforcements were not long arriving. Fresh troops and weaponry poured into the reserve trenches and, once the counterattack began, it raged non-stop for two days. Still, the Australians held their position.

Then, on the night of the eighth of August, the enemy changed tactics. Instead of hand-to-hand combat they launched a massive 'bomb assault' from their position only yards away. The Ottoman Army was in possession of an endless supply of German-made hand grenades, a form of weapon the Australians did not have, and the Turks bombarded the trenches, hurling their bombs into the frontline by the dozen.

Harry Balfour dived for cover as a grenade exploded a little further down the line. 'Jesus Christ, what the hell do we do?' he yelled scrambling to his feet.

'We hurl them back,' David Powell shouted from nearby.

David's idea corresponded with that of his superiors; the official order quickly went down the line. The troops were not to take cover, but to pick up the grenades and throw them back into the Turkish trenches, the closest of which was barely five yards away.

As the night progressed the battle turned into a heart-stopping game of Russian roulette. In the dark, a man had only seconds to react, to see the bomb land, to pick it up knowing in that moment he held his death in his hands, and then to throw it back.

Hugh Stanford found inspiration in David Powell. As the grenades continued to land, David went out of his way to pick them up while others stood rigid with fear. He laughed as he flung them back over the parapet. There was no doubt a mixture of adrenalin and bravado in the instant the bomb left his hand, but the sight was inspiring nonetheless. Hugh joined in the game, defying the odds with a vengeance.

Beside them, Gordie Powell did not shirk from the task. Gordie was hurling back the bombs with all the power only big Gordie could, although he was overshooting the target – a lob would have served better. But, strangely, Gordie was also reciting fractured pieces of the twenty-third psalm. Hugh had never known him to do that before.

'The Lord is my shepherd; I shall not want,' he was saying. 'Yea, though I walk through the valley of the shadow of death, I will fear no evil, for thou art with me.' He kept chanting the same phrases over and over again.

Harry Balfour felt a thump on his shoulder. The grenade dropped to the ground and rolled away a yard or so. He stared down at it dumbly; he could hardly see it lying there in the dark.

'Pick it up, Harry! Pick it up!' Hugh yelled from some distance away.

But Harry couldn't move.

Hugh's call had gained Wes Balfour's attention. He saw

the grenade resting near his brother's feet and he knew that Harry had left it too late. In the split second before it went off, he threw himself upon the bomb, dying instantly, his chest ripped to pieces.

The Turks, imagining their enemy weakened by the grenades, entered the trenches. Fighting continued hand to hand with bayonet and rifle, man against man, desperate and bloody.

Oscar O'Callaghan dodged as a Turk lunged. He felt the blade slice through his left arm and lunged forward with his right, driving his own fixed bayonet deep into the man's stomach. Nose to nose, the two of them stood motionless in the mayhem and Oscar watched the expression on the young soldier's face change from shock to the acceptance of death. Then, as he ripped back his rifle, the last light of life left the man's eyes. His wounded arm hanging uselessly by his side, Oscar turned and prepared himself for the next onslaught.

The fighting continued throughout the night and, although the Australians maintained their position, dawn revealed the terrible price paid. The trenches were littered with the dead, those bayoneted and those blown to pieces. Many who'd been unlucky in the Russian roulette stakes had suffered severe facial injuries which, if they survived, would leave them hideously scarred for the rest of their lives.

Hugh Stanford and David Powell had lost four men from their sections, amongst them their close friend Wes Balfour. Harry was discovered at dawn in a traumatised state, his brother clutched in his arms, drenched in Wes's blood. He'd been like that throughout the chaos of the night.

Shortly after dawn, the platoon was drawn out of the line and returned to the reserve trenches while fresh troops were brought in. The wounded, including Oscar O'Callaghan, whose bayonet injury was severe, were evacuated to the casualty clearing station. The men took no further part in the battle, which continued to rage for the whole of the next day.

Back in the reserve trenches, Hugh, David and Gordie worried for Harry's sanity. He had refused to relinquish his hold on Wes's body and his arms had to be prised apart. Now, he sat staring blankly at nothing. They washed his brother's blood from his face and his hands – they couldn't do anything about his uniform, which was drenched – but then they were covered in blood themselves, either their own or someone else's. They spoke to him soothingly, told him it wasn't his fault, but Harry continued to stare at nothing. Then, later in the afternoon, he started to shake uncontrollably. His head quivered, his hands fluttered and his whole body shuddered. It reminded Hugh of Rupert when he was upset and having one of his fits, so he did exactly as he would have done with Rupert. He took Harry in his arms and cuddled him.

'There, there,' he said, stroking his cousin's head and rocking him in his arms, 'there, there.' And Harry started to cry. He continued to cry throughout the night, and Hugh continued to cuddle him as he always had Rupert.

The battle concluded the following morning, the Turks conceding defeat, but it was a pyrrhic victory for the Australians. There was disastrous loss of life on both sides. They would later learn that the four-day assault on Lone Pine, which had been planned purely as a diversionary tactic, had cost the lives of two thousand Australians and seven thousand Turks.

CHAPTER TWENTY-TWO

The Gallipoli campaign came to an end in December 1915, when the British finally admitted defeat.

At seven o'clock on the morning of the twentieth, Turkish troops advanced on the ANZAC trenches to find them deserted. During the two previous nights, forty thousand soldiers had been secretly and silently evacuated from the peninsula. The withdrawal of troops had proved the only truly successful operation in the entire eight-month campaign.

'Well blow me down, look who's here.' Oscar grinned as he greeted his mates with David's catchphrase, which had become their common salute. 'And all in one piece, I see.' They were too: Gordie and David Powell, Hugh Stanford and Harry Balfour. Looking pretty good considering, Oscar thought. Even Harry, who he'd been sure would never see out the campaign, had got through.

They slapped one another on the back, laughing and embracing, grateful to be alive and glad to be reunited.

'In time for Christmas what's more,' David said as they settled themselves on their canvas army stools and lit up their cigarettes.

It was Christmas Eve and, having been evacuated from Gallipoli, the ANZACs had just arrived at the vast tent city of Abbassia Camp in Egypt. Oscar had arrived well before them: he'd been at the camp for the past fortnight.

'What happened to you?' Hugh asked. 'We heard you'd been taken to Malta for treatment, but we were sure they'd send you back.'

'Yeah, you lucky bastard,' Harry said, 'how'd you manage to get out of the rest of the donnybrook?'

'Brains, Harry, that's what it takes,' Oscar tapped a finger to his forehead, 'all a matter of brains. You just have to fool them into thinking you're dying. They don't send dying men back to the front. I decided to wait it out in comfort until the campaign was over,' he said breezily.

They all laughed, although Hugh suspected Oscar's nonchalance was a total sham. The medics were not that easily fooled, even by a trickster as smart as Oscar O'Callaghan.

Hugh was right. Oscar had very nearly died. He'd contracted a serious infection at St Andrew's Hospital on the island of Malta, his survival indeed surprising the medics. Instead of being sent back to Gallipoli, he'd been sent to Egypt to convalesce.

The boys sat around sharing news from home and reading out bits and pieces from their latest letters. They'd been greeted by a new mail delivery upon their arrival, and it had perked everyone up amazingly. In fact, spirits were high throughout the camp. Australian reinforcements had been arriving in Egypt by the thousands since October, and their presence breathed fresh life into the weary troops who were now determined to put Gallipoli and its horrors behind them.

Oscar did touch briefly upon the horror, however: a little later in the day he took Hugh aside to ask him about Harry. Harry seemed perhaps a little too bright-eyed and jumpy, perhaps a little too animated, Oscar thought, but certainly a whole lot better than one could ever have expected.

'How is he, Hugh? I'll never forget seeing him that

morning, hanging on to Wes like he was. I thought he'd lost his mind completely.'

'I think he did.'

'He seems all right now though.'

'He's not really. I doubt he ever will be. He has the most shocking nightmares.' Hugh shrugged. 'But then I suppose everyone does. The biggest worry about Harry is the way he puts himself at risk these days. He should have copped it by now given the chances he takes.' Hugh glanced across at his cousin and shook his head, perplexed. 'I really don't know, Oscar, it's as if he's trying to pay the price for Wes's death with his own.'

'You want to watch yourself, mate.' Oscar sounded a warning. 'If Harry's determined to get himself killed, then you'll just have to let him. No point trying to save him and copping it yourself. That wouldn't be doing either of you a favour.'

Hugh nodded. 'Yes, you're certainly right there.' He was grateful for the advice. 'Anyway, the bullets have dodged him so far. For someone who thumbs his nose at death Harry seems to be leading a charmed life.'

'The luck o' the Irish,' Oscar said, adopting the lilt of his clan, 'must be a drop o' the Celtic in him.'

They shared a smile and rejoined the others.

Christmas Day turned into quite a party. The Australian Comforts Fund had supplied billy tins packed with sweets and cigarettes and biscuits, which were doled out to the men, lending a festive air to the proceedings.

Gordie Powell produced his harmonica and struck up the first in a round of Christmas carols. He was quickly joined by another man on a concertina and soon the sing-along was under way.

Men started to gather in droves, several mouth organs were added to the band and before long the carols gave way to popular songs, requests being yelled out from the crowd.

'"Jeanie with the Light Brown Hair",' a voice called – Gordie didn't need to search the faces to know where that one had come from.

'"Too Ra Loo Ra Loo Ral",' another man yelled.

'"On the Road to Mandalay",' said another. Then 'Oh You Beautiful Doll', 'When Irish Eyes Are Smiling' ... On and on they went, the requests coming in thick and strong, the men belting out the lyrics and the sound ringing loudly through the clear desert air. It wasn't a particularly harmonious sound, it was true, but no-one cared: it was joyful.

We'll make a bonfire of our troubles and we'll watch them blaze away

And when they've all gone up in smoke clouds,

We'll never worry should they come another day ...

Hugh Stanford lent his voice to each song as loudly as the next man, but he couldn't help thinking 'Blaze Away' was the one that most summed up this Christmas Day of 1915.

And as the bonfire keeps on burning,

Happy days will be returning.

While the band keeps playing

We'll let our troubles blaze away.

He also couldn't help wondering what the hell was going to happen next.

The Australian military had decided to divide the old battalions and create new units for the 1916 campaign in Europe. The original 12th Battalion, bolstered with fresh volunteers newly arrived from Australia, was split into two, becoming the 12th and 52nd Battalions. Hugh Stanford and David Powell, both now confirmed in the rank of corporal, remained in charge of seven-man sections consisting primarily of new recruits, with the exception of their old mates Gordon Powell, Oscar O'Callaghan and Harry Balfour. The lads were now part of the 52nd Battalion, and their destination was France.

On the first of June 1916, following months of rigorous training in Egypt, the 52nd Battalion sailed from Alexandria aboard the *SS Transylvania*. They were bound for Marseilles, from where they would be entrained to the area of their encampment in Northern France near the Belgian border.

After three days' train travel in open wagons designed for horses – forty men to a wagon, standing all the way – the troops found it a relief to be on the march to their billets. There were well over a thousand of them, marching along the dusty country road and through the main streets of villages, and as they marched they sang.

It's a long way to Tipperary,
It's a long way to go.
It's a long way to Tipperary,
To the sweetest girl I know ...

The lads were in fine spirits. They were in France after all, and they liked what they saw.

Pack up your troubles in your old kit bag
And smile, smile, smile.
While you've a Lucifer to light your fag,
Smile boys, that's the style ...

The countryside they were passing through was indeed picturesque, a colourful patchwork of little fields growing all manner of crops and vegetables, gentle slopes interspersed with copses and hedgerows. Nestled cosily in valleys were villages, each with its church spire rising importantly above the thatched roofs of tiny cottages. The men were entranced. This was unlike anything they'd seen in Australia.

They were overwhelmed too by the welcome they received. Every township they passed through greeted them effusively. Villagers lined the street or leant from front windows, waving and calling out '*Australie!*' Girls blew them kisses, old men nodded respectfully and women waved the chubby arms of the babies they held up in greeting. The

Australians' reputation as fighters had preceded them via their French comrades-in-arms at Gallipoli, and the citizens of France eagerly embraced their arrival.

The battalion's encampment was on three large rural properties that had been requisitioned by the French government for military purposes. The farm owners were wealthy and the farms impressive, with two-storey houses and extensive outbuildings. The men were billeted in the high-roofed, thatched barns and sheds and stables that abounded, sleeping on straw with issued blankets. They were comfortable enough. The weather was a little cold and rainy despite it being the first month of summer, but the lads didn't care: they'd been fed up with the heat and sand of Egypt.

'I could do without the pong of horse dung though,' Gibbo complained. Brian Gibson was one of the new recruits in Hugh's section, a nice young lad from Launceston who hadn't as yet been involved in any conflict.

The seasoned campaigners exchanged a glance – the pong of horse dung was eminently preferable to the pong of rotting corpses.

'I love the pong of horse dung,' Harry Balfour declared, 'it reminds me of the farm.'

David Powell agreed. 'Crikey, I love the whole set-up,' he said, gazing about the huge stables. They were standing beside the two horse stalls that he and Hugh had snared for their sections' billet and, grand though the farm's stables were, the smell of straw and horses reminded David of the stables at Charlotte Grove. 'All the comforts of home,' he said with a smile.

'Well *I'm* happy,' Gordie chimed in. 'You know they've got a pig pen, don't you?'

Everyone laughed, even the new recruits. Gordie's picture of Delilah had become a running joke.

'Better be careful, Gordie,' Oscar said with a suggestive wink, 'farm residents are strictly off limits. No fraternising, remember?'

The men were worked hard over the next month or so with endless brisk hikes up and down country roads, drill and musketry exercises, then more hikes, then more drill: the training was relentless. But to the Gallipoli veterans it was like being on holiday, and they managed somehow to find holes in the day. Oscar O'Callaghan certainly did.

'I have a present,' Oscar said smugly.

It was approaching dusk. Their platoon had just returned from a ten-mile march and Oscar had mysteriously disappeared, returning to the stables after a half an hour or so, a cloth bag slung over one shoulder and something bulky conspicuously concealed beneath his coat. Beckoning his mates to follow, he ducked into one of the horse stalls.

'*Voila,*' he said with a flourish. There was a moment's silence as they stared down at the billy tin he was holding, and at the five eggs nestled within it.

'You'll have to put them back,' David said.

'Put them back. Why?'

'*Why?!* You'll get court-martialled if they find out you nicked them, that's why. You could land us all in a hell of a lot of trouble. Now I'm not asking you, Oscar, I'm ordering you. Put them back where you found them.'

'I didn't nick them.' Oscar appeared insulted by the suggestion. 'And I'm certainly not giving them back. She'd be offended if I did.'

'Eh?' David stared at him uncomprehendingly; they all did.

'They're a present. Yvette gave them to me.'

Yvette Picot was the youngest daughter of the property's owner. She was a pretty girl of around twenty, and the men lusted after her from afar.

'She *gave* them to you,' David scoffed, 'she *gave* them to you, just like that, right out of the blue.'

'Yep.' Oscar nodded happily. 'We had a bit of a chat yesterday. She wanted to know about Australia – she's a nice girl, very inquisitive. Anyway, she said she'd have

a present for me today and here they are,' he held out the
billy tin, '*oeufs*, for your information,' he added with a
superior smile. 'So who wants one and who doesn't?'

David supposed, as Oscar's corporal, he should issue a
warning about fraternisation, but Gordie jumped in with
the question that was foremost in all their minds.

'How'll we do them, boiled or scrambled?'

'No need. They're boiled already.' Oscar handed the billy
tin to Gordie and took the cloth bag from his shoulder.
'*Voila* again,' he said, producing a loaf of home-baked
bread and a wedge of cheese, '*le pain*,' he announced triumphantly, 'and *le fromage*.'

David's resistance went right out the window.

'What about the others?' Hugh queried. Like David, he
felt that as the leader of his section he should voice some
concern for his men. 'Shouldn't we share it around?'

He was met by a blank stare from his mates.

'There are only five eggs,' Oscar said. The silence that
followed was a statement in itself.

That night, seated outside with their backs against the
wooden walls of the stables, looking up at foreign stars in
a cloudless sky, Oscar, Gordie, David, Hugh and Harry
voted it the best meal they'd ever had in their lives.

The eggs, bread and cheese were only the first in a
number of treats Oscar provided over the following weeks
courtesy of Yvette. Next came a billy tin full of apples.

'They're called *pommes d'Api*,' he announced in his
rapidly improving French as he passed them around.

'Not where I come from,' David said, inspecting his
apple with a professional eye. 'They're Lady apples where
I come from. We used to grow them in the Huon, but
we don't any more. They don't sell as well as Pippins or
Cleopatras.'

'I wonder why,' Harry mumbled juice dribbling down
his chin. 'Apples never tasted this good at home.'

'You can only sell so many varieties,' David explained

with a direct quote from his father, Thomas, 'people get confused otherwise. I'll tell you something for nothing though, Harry,' he said with a mixture of defensiveness and pride, 'I'll bet you half the apples in Europe come from Tassie these days.'

But as David bit into his *pomme d'Api*, he had to agree with Harry: apples didn't come any better than this, not after bully beef and biscuits anyway.

Oscar's next present was even more impressive.

'*Le gateau*,' he said a week later as he unveiled the cake. Wrapped in a blue-and-white striped tea towel, it was large and mouth-wateringly impressive. 'Yvette baked it especially for us.'

That was when David decided to read Oscar the riot act for his own safety's sake, but he waited until after they'd demolished the cake, which they cut up and shared with the others (he would have had his own riot to deal with otherwise).

'You have to stop this, Oscar,' he said, taking him to one side, 'you know that, don't you?'

'Stop what?'

'Orders have been issued about fraternisation and you damn well know it,' he said firmly, finding his friend's pretended innocence just a little irritating. 'Whatever's going on between you and Yvette has to stop right now or you'll find yourself court-martialled.'

'But there isn't anything going on.'

'Oh come off it, Oscar,' David was exasperated, 'a woman doesn't bake a man a cake for nothing.'

'Yvette does. She's that sort of girl. She's really nice, if you know what I mean: a really good-hearted person.' Oscar went on before David could interrupt, arguing his case with vehemence. He was a man misunderstood. 'I ask you seriously, David: what am I supposed to do? If she wants to stop and have a chat am I supposed to ignore her? And if she wants to give me a present to share with my Australian comrades, for whom she has the greatest respect I might add, am I supposed to throw it back at her? You tell me, mate. You tell me, because in all honesty, I don't know. What am I supposed to do?'

David gave up. What was the point? If Oscar was determined to get himself court-martialled, so be it. The situation was out of his hands.

The weather had turned fine and sunny and, with the arrival and disbursement of the ever-welcome mail, the troops enjoyed the luxury of reading their letters sprawled out in a paddock.

The mail brought with it as always several letters from Caitie, and Hugh was able to catch up on the latest reports about Rupert. His father never wrote to him of Rupert, and he relied solely upon Caitie for news of his brother.

Hugh had known of his mother's death for some months now. When, at Christmas, there had still been no direct correspondence from her, he had demanded his father tell him the truth. *You always write only that Mother is ill with a bronchial condition but sends her love, Father, yet this has been going on for so long. Even the bed-ridden can put pen to paper, as I know Mother would. I demand the truth.*

Reginald had responded immediately, informing Hugh his mother had died of pneumonia some time ago. *I am so sorry, my boy, it is the saddest news. I had thought to keep it from you, hoping you would be home in only a matter of months and not wishing to add further to your present burden. Please forgive me if this was wrong.*

Much as he had expected the worst, Hugh had been sorely hit by the news of his mother's death. Camped out there in the Egyptian desert, surrounded by thousands upon thousands of men, he had suddenly felt very much alone. He'd needed to talk to someone. Normally he would have turned to his cousins Wes and Harry, but Wes was dead and Harry was not the same any more. He'd turned instead to David Powell. They'd sat up smoking and talking well into the night, or rather Hugh had. David had simply puffed away and listened. Hugh had sung his mother's praises. He'd talked on and on about all that she'd meant to both him and his brother, and also to their father, who couldn't have been the easiest man to live with. David was a good listener and a good friend, and Hugh had felt a great deal better in the morning.

Paying tribute to the memory of his mother had helped salve his own grief, but Hugh's main concern had then been his brother. How had Rupert fared? Rupert surely would have been distraught, yet his father had made no mention of him. He'd written once again demanding news, but his father had replied in characteristically abrupt fashion, which, although intended to allay any fears, had contained no particular detail. *We were all deeply affected by your mother's death, Hugh, Rupert included. But he is healthy and well looked after I can assure you. You must concentrate upon your task at hand, my boy. I will not have you jeopardise your safety by undue worry about your family at home. I can assure you all is well.*

Hugh was obviously supposed to have been satisfied with that. It's so typical of Father, he'd thought. Thank goodness for Caitie. He'd written to her immediately.

I realise now, my darling, that, like Father, you considered it in my best interests not to burden me with my mother's passing. Thank you for your consideration, but as you can see, I now know the truth, and I need also to know that Rupert is all right. Has he come to terms with his loss? I cannot imagine it somehow. Indeed I cannot imagine him at all without Mother.

Father says that Rupert is healthy and well looked after, but he refuses to write any further on the subject for fear I will worry. I do worry about Rupert though,

Caitie. I worry that even dear Iris, who is so very fond of him, could not substitute for Mother. I worry that he might break under such pressure: he is such a delicate creature.

I bless you for visiting him as you do, my darling, but please be honest with me, I need to know. Is Rupert suffering?

Caitie had written back as truthfully as she'd dared.

I do not know how deeply Rupert is suffering. I am told he cries himself to sleep at night, so he is clearly still grieving. But I can tell you this, Hugh: upon my visits, which as you know are regular, I believe I have become something of a mother figure to him. He loves me dearly, just as I love him. I have written of how we laugh and play games and go for walks together. Well I can tell you now that we also cuddle a great deal and that I sing to him. I believe that Rupert is gaining strength, Hugh. I do not believe he will break under the pressure as you fear. I promise you, I shall make sure he does not.

That was as far as Caitie had dared go. She never lied, but the subterfuge continued. Hugh still believed she visited his brother at Stanford House. She could not allow him to believe otherwise. He would be tormented by the truth.

August found the 52nd Battalion moved south and held in reserve at the rear of the Somme Offensive Line. Rigorous training continued, but the previously boring manoeuvres now had a different meaning. With the constant sound of artillery and gunfire echoing from the front, their drills now had a clear and deadly purpose, and the reports of battle that reached the troops' ears were chilling. The men had learned of the disastrous attack by the AIF's 5th Division several weeks previously upon the town of Fromelle fifty miles from the Somme. Another deployment intended by the British as a 'diversionary tactic', this time to draw German attention from the Somme offensive, the attack had proved an ill-planned fiasco which had served no purpose at all. Two thousand Australians had been killed in twenty-four hours, and for nothing. To the seasoned Gallipoli campaigners it sounded all too familiar.

Now, nearly a month later, Australian forces continued to fight in and around the town of Pozières. Thousands more had been killed or wounded with little or no sign of progress and certainly no hint of victory. To many it seemed that the incompetence displayed by High Command in Turkey was repeating itself on the Western Front, and the old hands whinged to one other. 'Bloody Pommie commanders,' they said, 'ratbags every one – can't they get it right?' But they didn't bellyache in front of the new lads. They didn't want to rattle them.

In late August, the troops of the 52nd Battalion were ordered into the reserve trenches, where they awaited command. The object of their attack would be the trenches surrounding Mouquet Farm just north of Pozières, where the battle had been raging for the past three weeks.

A huge, once fine property with a homestead and outbuildings constructed in a rectangular shape like an old castle or fort, Mouquet Farm, aptly nicknamed 'Mucky Farm' by the Australians, had been reduced to mud and rubble by the artillery barrages that had preceded the initial attack. Despite fierce fighting around the farm a stalemate had been reached. There seemed no particular front line for either side as trenches were won and lost and won again, and fresh connecting trenches dug. The fact that the Germans had built a series of tunnels underground from the farm's original cellars didn't help either. The battlefield had become a veritable labyrinth. Indeed, in the aerial photo-

graphs taken from observation balloons the intricate trench
system of Mouquet Farm looked for all the world like a
spider's web. It was an unnerving way to do battle for both
sides. No-one knew who was going to pop up from where,
or from around which corner the enemy might appear.

The 52nd Battalion was called into the line on the 3rd
of September. The troops were ordered to attack at 0510
and, following their initial assault, the fighting continued
non-stop for nearly thirty-six hours.

It was late afternoon on the second day, and Hugh
Stanford's and David Powell's platoon had been badly
depleted. With barely a dozen men left, they had maintained possession of the section of trench they were in,
but for how long they could keep it was anyone's guess.
Their situation was mirrored down the line and in other
Australian-occupied trenches. The assault of the 52nd Battalion had proved successful, but they had paid in numbers
and their position was tenuous.

A bomb exploded nearby, showering the men with debris
as they crouched together in the filth. The stink of blood and
excrement was overwhelming, but they no longer noticed it.
They'd stacked the dead, their own along with the enemy's,
against the trench walls to make room; amongst the bodies
Hugh could see young Gibbo from Launceston sandwiched
between two Germans. Gibbo had copped it neatly and
quickly, a bullet through the brain, which was the way
they'd all like to go if they had a choice.

At least the old gang's still here, he thought as he
looked about distractedly, for the moment anyway. David,
Gordie, Oscar and Harry were all mad-eyed like himself,
crazed from lack of sleep and, whether or not they'd admit
it, shell-shock.

It was difficult to tell who was injured and who was
not as the recent summer rainfall had turned the trenches
into quagmires and everyone was covered in muck and
mud and blood. But there were moans from the seriously

wounded, poor lads, some of whom wouldn't make it through until nightfall, when the stretcher bearers would come in under the cover of darkness. Perhaps, we might get some fresh supplies then too, Hugh thought. They'd run out of food and water and tobacco.

There was a lull in the shelling, as there quite often was, a sudden hush both merciful and eerie. Even as the brain welcomed the silence, it questioned where the next shell would land.

'Crikey, what I'd give for a smoke,' David said.

'Shh,' Gordie held up a warning finger, 'what's that?'

They listened intently and in the silence they all heard it. Up ahead to the right came the guttural mutter of a language foreign to them and the rattle of military accoutrements. German troops were creeping through the maze of nearby trenches.

Seconds later, from not far away, a German machine gun opened fire. It was a concerted attack. The Germans were closing in, and if the Australians attempted to flee the trenches they would be mowed down.

Hugh remained momentarily frozen. His instinct was to retreat. They should back down the line and try to link up with others from the battalion. Their platoon had been so sorely depleted they were sure to be outnumbered.

In that split second, even as his brain sought a valid reason, Hugh actually just wanted to run away. Then, as in past times, David Powell proved inspirational.

'Come on, mate, let's stick it to them!' David yelled and, as the German troops appeared in the trench system up ahead, he charged at them, screaming like a banshee.

Galvanised into action, Hugh charged along with him and the rest of the troops followed, all of them screaming at the top of their lungs.

Despite their fatigue and shell-shock, or perhaps because of it, they fought like madmen, thrusting with rifles and bayonets in a fearsome frenzy of killing.

Outnumbered though they were, their sheer ferocity was paying off. Several enemy lay dead, others lay wounded and the German troops were starting to fall back along the trench.

Moments later the Australians halted their attack: they had repelled the Germans, who were now in full retreat.

Then, in a rearguard action, an enemy pistol was fired.

Hugh felt the bullet tear through the upper right side of his chest and he staggered under the impact before dropping to his knees. He started to struggle to his feet once again, but five yards away one of the retreating Germans had turned.

'Look out, Hugh!'

David flung himself at the German soldier whose rifle's sights were trained upon Hugh and, as he did so, the weapon went off.

It was a freak shot. David had not intended to throw himself directly into the line of fire, nor had the German purposefully altered his aim, but the cry of warning had proved a distraction. The bullet hit David directly between the eyes, killing him instantly.

Something happened to Hugh then. He went insane. In a mindless rage, he rushed the German soldier, thrusting his bayonet into the man's guts, ripping it upwards, disembowelling him. He picked up the man's Mauser and turned it on the last of the retreating German troops. There were only four of them. He shot the first.

'Kamerad! Kamerad!' the other three yelled, holding up their hands in surrender.

He shot all three. Then he stared wildly about. There was no more enemy, but in his madness he couldn't stop. In his madness he no longer sought just to avenge David's death, he sought to pay for it with his own. He would not stop until he had, and he would take along with him as many enemy as he could.

The German machine gun was still firing from nearby.

There was the yell from an officer for someone to silence it. Hugh needed no more than that. In only seconds he was up and over the parapet, defying them to kill him as he charged the German machine-gun nest.

From the trenches, men watched in amazement, expecting any moment that amongst the hail of bullets he would fall. But miraculously he didn't.

There were three enemy troops manning the Maxim. Come on, kill me, kill me, his mind dared them. He shot the first two and the third man turned to run, but he didn't get far. Five paces and he fell to the ground, shot in the back.

The machine gun was silenced. The tide of battle had changed.

Returning to the trench in full view of the enemy, Hugh automatically started to run, but with no specific target in sight there seemed little purpose so he slowed down to a walk, his mind still saying *kill me, kill me* as he waited for the bullet.

The entire episode had been watched in open-mouthed awe by Oscar and Gordie and Harry and other members of the battalion. Now they continued to watch as Hugh ambled across the open field of fire. He's asking to be killed, they thought, why the hell doesn't he run?

He was barely ten yards away when rifle fire sounded from the German trenches.

'Jesus,' Harry muttered as Hugh fell to the ground and, without giving it a second thought, he too was up and over the parapet. He raced to Hugh, and slung him over his shoulders like a sack of grain. He turned and dodged his way back through the enemy's fire while Oscar and Gordie shot wildly at the German trenches in an effort to cover him.

Harry made it back safely with Hugh still alive.

Later that night when the stretcher bearers arrived, Hugh was evacuated with the wounded. He was conscious, but appeared to have no memory of the events that had taken place.

The exhausted Australians remained fighting in their trenches until the morning of the sixth, when they were relieved by Canadian troops. The 52nd Battalion had captured and held the German trenches; in doing so they would prove to be the only troops to take and hold their initial objective during the entire allied assault in the Pozières Sector of the Somme Offensive.

Australian Prime Minister William Morris Hughes was faced with a serious dilemma. The massive casualties at Fromelle and the ongoing losses at the Somme had led to a severe decline in enlistment. Australia had agreed to the delivery of a regular quota of troops to the British, and something must be done to ensure that the quota was met.

Hughes embarked upon an aggressive recruitment campaign. Businesses were encouraged not to employ single men of recruitment age; those considered 'shirkers' were openly harassed; and in the press eligible young men were urged to do their duty for their country. Finally, the federal government announced that on the twenty-eighth of October a national vote would be held on the issue of conscription.

Hughes's personal and passionate drive to introduce conscription had been dividing the nation for some time. Across the country, supporters and opponents alike vigorously campaigned, each side convinced of its own moral ground. Now, as the referendum drew closer, the arguments grew ever more bitter and divisive.

In Hobart, with only several days to go, the Queens Domain had become a gathering place for campaigners vying to be heard. They were women for the most part.

'Enough is enough,' one woman screamed, while her supporters waved placards emblazoned with the words VOTE NO! 'Do not send any more of our boys to their deaths!' she yelled. 'Vote no to conscription!'

Nearby, an opposing crowd brandished campaign

posters depicting a woman standing behind a soldier. Both were bearing arms, and the butt of the woman's rifle was emblazoned with the word YES. The slogan beneath said STAND BY YOUR OWN!

'Mothers of Australia, do not desert your country,' Marge Henderson of the Women's Protestant League urged, 'Britain needs your sons: do your patriotic duty and vote yes to conscription!'

Norman Balfour was among those at the Domain, watching and listening to the spruikers as they preached from their soap boxes. He'd driven the Tin Lizzie into Hobart to collect some equipment for his father, grateful for the excuse to get away on his own. Norm felt restless these days – restless and useless. He had ever since Wes's death. Jeez, who'd believe it? he thought. That was over a year ago now.

It was a lovely spring morning and he'd decided to take a walk to the Domain, perhaps to watch the kids playing footie or perhaps to look at the view across the bay, but most likely to buy a bit more time on his own. He rather wished he hadn't. He found the women and their ranting unsettling. He hated the war. It hadn't proved the adventure all the lads had thought it would be – 'kill a few Huns and home by Christmas' – it was wholesale slaughter.

'And all you able-bodied men,' Marge Henderson continued, her eyes seeking out eligible volunteers, although there didn't appear to be many, 'enlist today!' Then her gaze alighted upon Norman. 'You, young man,' she yelled, 'why are you not in uniform?! Shame upon you, I say! Sign up and fight alongside your brothers!'

'Shame, shame,' several other members of the Women's Protestant League started to chant, and Norm felt himself flush with the guilt that had been secretly gnawing away at him. The woman could not possibly know how the literal truth of her slogan applied to him. Of course he should be fighting alongside his brothers. As the eldest he should have been leading them into battle. Now Wes was dead, young Harry was fighting on, and he was living a safe and cosy life back at home.

He turned and started to walk away, but one of Marge's supporters followed him, still carrying her placard with the campaign poster. She grabbed him by the arm and he was forced to turn back and face her, a hardened little woman with bitterness in her eyes.

'You should be ashamed of yourself,' she spat the words at him. 'How dare you stand there, a strong, healthy lad like you, while others are dying for their country?' Prudence Farmer did not need the urging of Marge Henderson to ignite her passion. Prudence had lost both her boys at Gallipoli.

Norm could have said he had a son who would turn two the next month. He could have told her his wife was pregnant. He could have pleaded baby Stephen and his unborn child as an excuse, but he didn't. He sensed that would make no difference to the woman – just as it didn't to him. The love and loyalty he felt towards his wife and son did nothing to assuage his sense of guilt.

Dipping a hand into the top pocket of her blouse, Prudence produced a white feather, which she thrust at him and which he automatically took. 'That's what we think of men like you,' she said venomously. Prudence Farmer carried white feathers about her person at all times, not only to rallies but wherever she went, because you just never knew when you might need one. 'Shirkers, the lot of you,' she loudly declaimed, 'shirkers and cowards, every one!'

Norm closed his fingers around the shameful symbol and walked off, cries of 'hear, hear' echoing behind him as Prudence rejoined Marge's group of supporters.

The national outcome of the referendum proved to be a narrow victory for the No vote. The federal government's drive for conscription had failed, this time around anyway:

'Billy' Hughes, a tough aggressive little man, was not one to readily throw in the towel.

The outcome of the vote had little bearing in the case of Norman Balfour, however. Prudence Farmer's action had been enough. The white feather had tipped the balance. Norm had gone straight to the nearest recruitment centre that day. He'd signed up, knowing how deeply it would distress his wife, but knowing also that he had no option.

CHAPTER TWENTY-THREE

Hugh Stanford was hospitalised in England to have his wounds tended. His chest injury healed well – the bullet had passed through the right side of his upper body without causing significant damage – but it took several operations to repair the shattered bone of his upper left arm, which the doctors had at first considered amputating.

In March 1917, after months of convalescence, he was finally declared fit for duty, but before returning to France he attended an investiture ceremony at Buckingham Palace, where he was awarded the Victoria Cross by King George V.

Hugh did not inform his father of the date of his investiture. Indeed, in an uncharacteristic and outright lie, he wrote to his father at Christmas saying that it was unlikely he would be presented with his award for at least another six months. He feared that, even with the difficulty of wartime travel, his father would find a way to attend the ceremony. Reginald Stanford would certainly wish to attend, and when Reginald Stanford wished for something he usually got it. Hugh did not want his father to be there. Hugh did not want anyone to be there.

The entire ceremony registered as something of a blur to Hugh. There were a number of them lined up to receive their medals, two English soldiers also receiving the VC, and to Hugh the military pomp and splendour of the ritual, together with the grandeur of Buckingham Palace and even King George himself seemed somehow unreal. As his citation was read out, all he could think was: 'Did I really do that?' He had no memory of his actions. The death of David Powell remained crystal clear in his mind. Everything after that was a blank.

Following the investiture, Hugh Stanford was promoted to the rank of sergeant and returned directly to the front-line. His left arm did not function particularly well, but this was not considered an overly serious incapacitation: he was right-handed after all, and a VC winner was bound to prove inspirational to the troops.

Hugh's photograph, taken at Buckingham Palace on the day of his investiture and wearing his VC, made the front pages of newspapers throughout Australia, Hobart's *Mercury* in particular. HOBART'S HERO, the headline screamed.

Reginald Stanford was bursting with pride, but he cursed the army. Why the devil hadn't they given Hugh more notice? Come hell or high water he would have found a way to be at his son's investiture. In fact when he'd received Hugh's letter telling him the award would not be presented for a whole six months, he'd contemplated bringing his considerable clout to bear in order to rectify the situation. He'd resisted the urge, however, knowing that his son would be utterly appalled if he interfered. And now the army had changed its mind. They'd sprung the investiture on Hugh with virtually no notice. The fickle-ness of the military, he thought, damn their hide.

It did not for one moment occur to Reginald that his son may have lied. Hugh never lied. He toyed with the idea of lodging a complaint with his connections in military high places, and he most certainly had connections, but again for Hugh's sake he decided against it.

Reginald Stanford had lent his full support to the war
effort. Or rather, he'd been seen to do so. Patriotic duty,
like philanthropy, was essential for a man in his position.
He'd even donated an aeroplane – that is, the two
thousand pounds necessary for the purchase of an aeroplane. During the early days of the war several barons of
Australian industry had led the way in donating aircraft
to Britain's Royal Flying Corps. The Cattle King, Sidney
Kidman, had even donated two, which Reginald had
found unnecessarily excessive, but he'd quickly followed
the trend himself. He would not be left behind in the
patriotic stakes, particularly as Henry Jones had donated
an aeroplane.

Poor dear Henry had rather cruelled his own pitch
though, Reginald thought. Henry's aeroplane had been
delivered to the Royal Flying Corps with the IXL brand
painted on both sides. So crude. They'd refused to accept
it, of course, until the symbols had been removed. Henry
had been quite miffed at the time. Reginald had pretended
sympathy, but he'd found the episode amusingly typical.
Henry was such a vulgar little man.

And now, in the patriotic stakes, no-one can touch me,
Reginald thought as he gazed at Hugh's picture on the
front page of *The Mercury*. His son had been awarded
the highest military honour a soldier could receive. No
donation in the world could compare to that. The benefits
to be reaped from the VC, for Hugh and also for the
family name, were inestimable. All that was needed now
was his safe return.

Reginald prayed daily for Hugh's safety. Hugh was
his bloodline, his one and only precious son, who would
inherit his life's work. If Hugh were to die Reginald's own
life would be meaningless.

Upon his return to France, Hugh found that due to the
depletion of its numbers at Mouquet Farm the 52nd

Battalion had been split up and the troops sent to other battalions as reinforcements. Gordie, Oscar and Harry – and now Hugh himself – had finally been forced to go their separate ways.

The war ground relentlessly on for a further eighteen months. The slaughter continued, fresh recruits were needed, and there was another bid by Australian Prime Minister 'Billy' Hughes to bring in conscription. Again a referendum divided the country, and again the NO vote prevailed, but this time with a slightly larger margin.

Then, finally in November 1918, 'the war to end all wars' was over. The British claimed victory, but the cost to both sides was staggering. A generation of young men had been wiped out.

Per capita, the Australians had suffered the highest casualty rate of any allied country participating in the conflict. With a male population of less than three million, Australia had lost close to sixty thousand men, and tens of thousands more had been wounded.

Gordie, Oscar, Harry and Hugh were among those who survived, but Harry's older brother Norm was not. Norman Balfour had been wounded in action on the twenty-eighth of March 1918 during the German spring offensive at Morlancourt. He'd been taken to a casualty clearing station with gunshot wounds to the hip and stomach and had died the following day. Sergeant Norman Donald Balfour was buried at the Doullens Communal Cemetery, France, one month before his thirtieth birthday. He left behind a wife, and their three-year-old son and one-year-old daughter.

Some of the troops were sent home to Australia in October on what was amusingly called '1914 leave'. '1914 leave' was granted to those surviving members of the AIF who had enlisted at the outbreak of war. The lads found it a bit of a joke that after fighting non-stop for nearly four years without leave, they should get a few weeks off when it was virtually all over. Word had got around that the war would end the next month anyway.

The survivors of the original 12th Battalion came home in dribs and drabs.

Gordie Powell and Harry Balfour arrived together, stepping off the ship from Sydney onto the docks of Hobart. God, but it was good to be back on home soil.

Gordie had quite a pronounced limp. He'd been wounded several times, although never badly enough to earn a respite in England. Considered a fine soldier by his commanding officer, Gordon Powell had been mentioned in despatches three times and had ended the war as a company sergeant major.

Harold Balfour, considered risky as leadership material even for one so experienced, had not achieved rank, but had been awarded the Military Medal for his action at Mouquet Farm in risking his life to rescue a comrade-in-arms while under heavy enemy fire.

The two were met at the docks by Max Müller, who'd driven up from the Huon to collect Gordie. Max had been home for well over a year now, and he'd insisted upon being delegated the job of chauffeur. He wanted to show off the prosthetic leg he'd been fitted with at the Fort Pitt Military Hospital in Chatham.

The boys' reunion was hearty and boisterous as hugs were shared all round.

'Look at that,' Max said, 'you wouldn't even know, would you.' He strutted about like a stocky bantam rooster. 'Your limp's worse than mine, Gordie,' he said, and he was right.

Harry's reunion with his father, Edwin, who'd driven down from Pontville to collect him, was a lot less boisterous, but even more fervent.

'Welcome home, Harry.' Edwin embraced his youngest son, holding him close, trying to keep the tremor from his voice. 'It's good to have you back.' Edwin Balfour had aged.

No longer the ruddy-faced farmer, he was now gaunt and in
his eyes was the sorrow of a man who'd lost two sons.

'It's good to *be* back, Dad.' Neither man needed to say
any more.

Oscar was the next to arrive. Oscar O'Callaghan had been
awarded the Military Medal for bravery under fire at the
Battle of Villers-Bretonneux, and over time had reluctantly
accepted the ranks of corporal and then sergeant upon the
insistence of his commanding officer. That worthy had
indeed been so impressed with Oscar's skills that he'd suggested he remain in the army after the war and take up a
military career. Oscar had given the matter no consideration at all. The army was far too much hard work. And
anyway, he had plans.

'I won't be staying long,' he announced to the family
shortly after his arrival. 'I'll give it six months or so for things
to calm down and then I'll be heading back to France.'

'Why the devil would you want to do that?' his father,
Col, asked.

'I met a girl over there.' Oscar ignored the look shared
between his sister and his grandmother. 'Her father's rich,
landed gentry, you should just see his farm. I'm told he's a
member of the French nobility.'

Eileen gave a contemptuous harrumph. 'And you think
French nobility's going to be interested in the grandson of
a convict, do you?'

She'd successfully halted him mid-stride. 'Really?' Oscar
was surprised. 'I didn't know Grandpa was a convict.'

'He wasn't,' Eileen said shortly, 'I was.'

'Oh.' He appeared to give the matter a moment's
thought. 'How colourful,' he said.

'That's rather cruelled things for you, hasn't it?' Eileen
replied with grim satisfaction. She was well into her
eighties now, and crotchety; she'd decided it was time to
leave this world.

'Not at all, Gran.' Oscar remained supremely confident. 'In fact if I chose to tell Yvette, I'm sure she'd find it most interesting.'

'As would her father, I've no doubt.' In her ill-humour, Eileen found her grandson's arrogance insufferable. 'French nobility indeed,' she scoffed, determined to puncture his ego, 'you don't stand a chance, boy.'

'You never know until you try, Eileen.' Oscar winked and gave her a roguish grin. 'You just never know until you try, now, do you.'

She couldn't help but return a flicker of a smile. He always knew how to win her around. The smile, the way he called her Eileen – dear God, he was Mick all over.

'You're a cheeky bugger, Oscar O'Callaghan,' she said.

'What about Mary Reilly,' Caitie demanded.

'What *about* Mary Reilly?'

'You'll break her heart.'

'There's not much I can do about that, regretfully.'

'She gave you her photograph, Oscar. She's been writing to you the whole time.' Caitie felt the need to show a degree of outrage on behalf of the female sex, although she could see she was making little impression. 'You do at least owe her a visit. Mary's been waiting for you.'

'Yes, she has, and that's sad.' Oscar wondered briefly whether young Ben from Perth might have survived. And he wondered briefly whether, if he had, young Ben might come looking for Mary Reilly from Hobart. That could be a nice happy ending, he thought.

'But I'm in love, Caitie,' he said, putting a hand to his breast. 'You of all people know what that means. I'm in love and I must go where my own heart leads me.'

The autumn of 1919 brought the last of the old gang home. Hugh Stanford, who had been promoted to the rank of captain, had been at the mercy of the army's public relations department, which had arranged for as many recipients of the Victoria Cross as possible to attend a series of official functions and publicity events throughout Britain. Then, upon his arrival back in Australia, the rigmarole had repeated itself all over again. Australian VC winners, as many as possible, had been called together for publicity purposes, first in Sydney and then in Melbourne.

By the time he was free to go home, Hugh was so fed up with the frenzy of photographers and reporters that he determined to arrive in Hobart unannounced. He telephoned his father with the date and details of his arrival. He was taking the overnight boat from Melbourne to Launceston on Friday, he said, and would catch the nine o'clock train to Hobart Saturday morning.

'I shall be at the station to meet you,' Reginald announced.

'You won't bring the Rolls Royce, will you, Father?'

'Why ever not?'

'I don't want the press alerted,' Hugh said. 'You will make sure not to tell anyone, won't you?'

'Of course, Hugh, mum's the word. I quite understand.' Reginald considered it a wasted opportunity. Surely Hugh should arrive home in a blaze of local publicity. It didn't really matter, he supposed. The photographs from the mainland had been plastered all over the front pages of every newspaper throughout Tasmania, and there would be a wealth of local coverage when Hugh's return was duly announced to the press.

He chastised himself. Of course it didn't matter. It didn't matter at all. Hugh was coming home. Nothing else was of any consequence

'Oh, my boy, it is so good to hear your voice at long last.' Reginald could not remember when he had felt such a sense of pure joy.

Hugh rang Caitie at the offices of Kramer, Fox & Hutchinson and informed her also of his arrival, warning her not to tell anyone.

'Not even Oscar,' he said, 'not yet. There's something I must do before I catch up with the old gang.'

He sounds rather mysterious, she thought. She could understand his wish to avoid the press, but keeping his arrival a secret from his closest friends seemed strange.

'I promise I shan't tell a soul,' she said. 'As if I would wish to anyway,' she added in that seductively teasing manner of hers, 'I want you all to myself.'

Hugh rather wished he hadn't called his father now, but of course filial respect had demanded that he should.

Reginald pulled up at the train station in his Prince Henry Vauxhall tourer ten minutes before the train was due to arrive. The Model T Ford he'd purchased in order not to appear overly ostentatious during the war years had been a short-lived affair. He'd detested being 'one of the common herd'. Besides, people must surely realise that, given his position in society, a certain image needed to be maintained. After donating the proceeds of the Ford's sale to the war effort, he'd purchased the Vauxhall, which, although the vehicle of a wealthy man, was less grandiose than the Rolls Royce that was kept mainly for show. He always employed the services of his chauffeur when driving around the city – he had no wish to be seen crank-starting a vehicle in public – but today was different. Today he did not want the chauffeur's presence. I'll have my son all to myself, he thought happily as he climbed out of the car. Besides, Hugh could crank the vehicle.

He took his fob watch from his waistcoat pocket and checked the time. Ten minutes to twelve. Excellent. And he walked through the station and out onto the platform.

She was the first thing he saw. How could one fail to notice the beacon of her hair? She wasn't even wearing a hat. Damn the girl's hide, he thought.

Caitie felt someone's eyes on her and she turned. He was staring at her from barely twenty yards away and made no move to greet her. She crossed to him.

'Good morning, Mr Stanford.'

'Miss O'Callaghan.' He gave a curt nod. 'I take it we are here for the same purpose.'

'Of course.' Refusing to be intimidated, she smiled. 'You must be so happy to have him home.'

'I am,' he said brusquely, 'very happy indeed,' and averting his eyes, he looked down the track.

Caitie saw no purpose in attempting to pursue further conversation and they stood side by side, watching for the train in pointed silence.

Once the train had pulled into the station, Hugh was the first person to alight. He'd seen them through the window from some distance away: his father, straight-backed and austere, but also dapper in his perfectly cut suit; and beside him, Caitie, more beautiful than ever. He wondered why Rupert wasn't with them. Father must have left him at home, he thought, which was probably wise. Rupert would have become overexcited.

'Father.' Dumping his kit on the ground, Hugh embraced Reginald first.

'Welcome home, Hugh.' Reginald was not given to public demonstrations of affection and would normally have shaken hands by way of welcome, but he found himself returning his son's embrace with fervour.

Then Hugh turned to Caitie, taking her by the hand, saying nothing, just drinking in the sight of her.

'Hello,' she said. He looks so much older, she thought. The boy in him had gone.

'Hello, Caitie.'

They stood for a moment gazing into one another's eyes, everything around them disappearing. Then they drifted into each other's arms.

Reginald watched, appalled. They were kissing in public. It was positively obscene. He backed off several paces and turned away, disassociating himself from them.

A minute or so later Hugh and Caitie joined him.

'I'm sorry, Father,' Hugh said as they stood together hand in hand, 'we didn't mean to embarrass you.'

'Yes, Mr Stanford, I do beg your pardon.' Caitie also felt the need to apologise.

'No matter,' Reginald said as graciously as possible, determined not to mar his son's homecoming. 'War does alter the social code of conduct, does it not?'

'Yes sir, I believe it does,' Caitie replied, grateful for his apparent understanding.

'Come along then.' He turned and led the way out of the station. War is no excuse for immoral behaviour, he thought. The girl is wanton. The fact might well prove a blessing, however. She'd be easily bedded. Hugh wouldn't need to marry her: he could keep her as a mistress. Reginald had no objection to that.

'May I give you a lift home, Miss O'Callaghan?' he said as they arrived beside the Vauxhall. Loath though he was to make the offer, he was socially obligated to do so.

'Oh, Caitie must come with us to Stanford House, Father.' Hugh dived in immediately. 'I'm not about to let her out of my sight just yet,' he said with a grin. 'I'll drive her home later. Besides,' he added, 'Rupert will want to see her.'

Caitie and Reginald exchanged the flicker of a glance.

'Very well then.' Reginald climbed into the driver's seat and turned on the ignition. 'I shall need you to crank the vehicle, Hugh,' he said as he adjusted the advance on the steering column.

Hugh opened the rear door for Caitie, who climbed in, and when he'd cranked the car he joined Reginald in the front. He was relieved the station was not busy; the Vauxhall was attracting nearly as much attention as the Rolls Royce. His father's passion for luxury cars clearly had not deserted him, Hugh thought, amused.

Caitie felt nervous as they drove off, wondering what on earth would happen when Hugh discovered the truth about his brother. She was not only worried for Hugh, she was suddenly also nervous on her own behalf. Perhaps he would hate her for her duplicity.

'I'm so proud of you, Hugh, so very, very proud.' Reginald was surprisingly talkative during the drive to Stanford House, perhaps in order to allay any queries about Rupert. He too was feeling a degree of trepidation. Hugh must be informed about his brother in precisely the right manner. He must be told, calmly and quietly, that for Rupert's own sake there had been no alternative but hospitalisation. In order to do that, Reginald needed complete privacy. The girl was an annoying intrusion.

'I only wish with all my heart that I could have been at your investiture,' he said. 'What a damn shame, the army changing its mind and springing the ceremony on you like that.'

'Yes, it was a shame.' Hugh looked guiltily out the window. He'd hated lying to his father.

'You do realise, don't you, that as a Victoria Cross winner, there is now nothing you cannot achieve. The VC will open every door of international business you care to knock on.' Reginald flashed a triumphant smile at his son. 'The world is yours, Hugh. The world is yours.'

'I hadn't really anticipated using the VC for business purposes, Father.'

'Oh, my dear boy, you won't be able to help it. There's no going back now. You've immortalised the Stanford name.'

Hugh didn't answer, but continued to look out the window. How typical of his father. Of course Reginald Stanford would view the Victoria Cross with an eye to material gain. The man simply couldn't help himself.

When they arrived at Stanford House, Reginald left the car parked in the front courtyard in order for Hugh to drive Caitie home. He hoped she would have the grace not to stay too long.

They entered the house and found the servants gathered in the main hall to welcome the young master home.

Hugh was introduced to the new chauffeur and maid and warmly greeted by the cook and others he knew, particularly Clive Gillespie and Iris Watson, who had been with the household for as long as he could remember. But by now, he was feeling bewildered.

'Where's Rupert?' he asked as the servants left.

Reginald steeled himself for the moment of truth. 'I need to talk to you privately, Hugh. Come upstairs to my office.' He turned to Caitie. 'Would you mind waiting in the drawing room, Miss O'Callaghan?' he said, indicating the door that led to the smaller of the front rooms, the one that had always been Evelyn's domain.

'No, Father.' Hugh took Caitie's hand as she started to move off. Something was terribly wrong, he realised. 'Anything you have to say about Rupert can be said in front of Caitie. We shall all go into the drawing room.'

He led the way and his father had no option but to follow.

As Reginald Stanford closed the door behind them, Caitie stepped to one side, leaving father and son to confront each other.

'What is it you're keeping from me,' Hugh demanded. 'Is Rupert ill?'

'I'm afraid so, yes,' Reginald replied gravely. 'As I'm sure you'll understand, I had no wish to burden you with the news while you were away, it would only have added to –'

'What has happened?' Hugh was alarmed. Had there been an accident? 'What has happened, Father? Tell me!'

'Rupert had a mental breakdown, I'm sorry to say. He went completely to pieces. It was so sad to see.'

'When?' Hugh glanced at Caitie. The news was upsetting, but also confusing. He'd received letters from Caitie in London, she'd said nothing about a breakdown – it must have been very recent. 'Why did he have a breakdown? When did this happen?'

Reginald presumed that would have been obvious. 'Following your mother's death, of course,' he said.

'But that was three years ago!'

'Yes indeed. He was driven insane with grief, poor boy. He lost his mind altogether and there was no coming back, I fear, no chance of recovery. For Rupert's own sake, it was necessary to provide specialist care ...'

Hugh was now in a state of utter confusion. He turned to Caitie. 'But you visit Rupert here every Saturday. You didn't tell me he'd gone insane.'

'He hasn't. And I don't visit him here.'

Reginald glanced at the girl. She'd been visiting Rupert?

'Oh my God,' Hugh turned back to his father, 'what have you done?'

'I had no option,' Reginald said firmly, 'you must understand that.' Damn the O'Callaghan girl, he thought. Things were not going as planned, and it was all her fault. 'Rupert had to be hospitalised for his own safety's sake, he could have damaged himself –'

'Hospitalised? Where?'

'New Norfolk. They have specialists there who –'

'The lunatic asylum!' Hugh burst out, appalled.

'The Hospital for the Insane,' Reginald stiffly corrected him.

'The bloody lunatic asylum! Jesus Christ, you had him committed!'

'I most certainly did, in the boy's own interests.' Reginald took the high moral ground in an attempt to stamp his authority. 'And I would ask you not to use that tone of voice with me. I will not have bad language and blasphemy uttered in this house.'

Hugh gazed at his father, horror-struck. 'Rupert was grieving for his mother and you had him committed! Your own son! Dear God, man, where's your compassion? Where's your humanity?'

'You have no right to judge me, Hugh.' Reginald tried to remain authoritative but he was getting desperate. 'You didn't see Rupert. You were not witness to his demented state. He was insane, irreparably insane –'

But Hugh wasn't listening. He'd grabbed Caitie's hand and was heading for the door.

'Get back here, boy,' Reginald called after him. 'Where in Hell do you think you're going?'

'I'm going to get my brother.'

Reginald didn't follow. He knew it was useless. A minute or so later, he heard the car being crank-started, and he watched through the drawing-room window as the Vauxhall drove out through the main gates.

During the hour's drive to New Norfolk, they talked. Caitie reassured Hugh about his brother's condition. Rupert had been well cared for, she said. He had recovered from his initial distress and was strong. Lonely though he still was for his mother, the strain of his grief had not broken him, nor, fortunately, had the strain of institutionalisation.

'You should have told me, Caitie.'

'Why? What could you have done?'

'Nothing,' he admitted, 'but I should have known.'

'You would have worried yourself sick, Hugh. You would have been utterly powerless and tormented by the truth. I thought it kinder to keep you in ignorance.'

Hugh fell silent, his eyes trained on the road. She is right, he thought, she is actually right. And she'd never once lied: she'd just allowed him to believe she visited Rupert at home, all the time sending caring accounts of his brother. Indeed, had he ever learnt the truth, Caitie's reports would have assured him that Rupert was not the dire case his father would surely have purported him to be. Everything she'd done was right, Hugh realised. Caitie's deception had been an act of love.

His silence worried her. 'I'm sorry I deceived you.' She

sounded forlorn. She had believed so strongly that she was doing the right thing. 'I hope you will forgive me.'

'There's no call for apology, Caitie. I owe you a profound debt of thanks. I thank you for loving me as you do. And I thank you for looking after my brother.'

They arrived at the hospital, which now boasted a change of name. No longer the Hospital for the Insane, it had officially become the Mental Diseases Hospital.

'A sign of the times,' Caitie explained as they walked into reception. 'Eunice Cartwright says the intention is to change community attitudes towards mental illness. I must say, having learned quite a deal during my visits here, I consider it an excellent idea.'

She introduced Hugh to Eunice. The two women had established a friendship over the years.

'Sister Cartwright is in charge of Rupert's wing,' Caitie said. 'Eunice, this is Rupert's brother, Hugh Stanford.'

'Mr Stanford, of course,' Eunice said as they shook, 'I recognise you from your photograph.' Hugh assumed she meant the newspaper photographs, which Eunice had indeed seen, but Eunice was not referring to those at all. 'Rupert shows his picture of you and the Sphinx to everyone he sees. We all feel that we know you. Do please come this way.'

Caitie followed them, but kept her distance, remaining in the background as they entered the lounge. A number of inmates were playing games or simply doing what they always did. Caitie knew every one of them. Betty, a woman of around thirty, was sitting in the particular corner that she'd made her own for the past decade, cradling the same rag doll in her arms and singing the same song to it. Walter was conducting the orchestra that lived in his head, rocking backwards and forwards on his heels and jabbing the air with his invisible baton. Ivy, still in her teens, was wandering around having an agitated conversation with herself. Ivy was restless: she never sat down. Two other inmates were arguing about a game of draughts as they always did, and seated at a table all on his own was Rupert, a jigsaw puzzle laid out before him.

Eunice and Caitie, after exchanging glances, remained by the door as Hugh approached his brother.

So focused was Rupert upon his jigsaw puzzle that he paid no attention to the figure that arrived to stand beside him. Even when the figure cast a shadow across the table he took no notice. He just bent closer to the puzzle, waving his hand over the top of it, his eyes seeking the spot where the piece he held in his fingers might fit, his tongue sticking out, his concentration total.

'Hello, Rupert.'

Rupert's hand stopped waving. He froze at the sound of the voice, hand poised above the board, eyes staring now unseeingly at the puzzle. This was the voice he heard in his head daily. This was the voice he talked to. But it sounded so close and so real. He didn't dare move.

'Aren't you going to say hello?'

Still Rupert didn't move. This is a trick, he thought. Someone was playing a game with him, trying to make him look stupid, but he wasn't going to fall for it.

'Stop pretending I'm not here, Rupert. It's rude. You don't want to hurt my feelings, do you?'

Rupert shifted the direction of his gaze to the floor and saw the army boots. Then very slowly he looked up, taking in the uniform piece by piece, and finally the face of his brother. His jaw dropped and he stared at Hugh in open-mouthed amazement.

'Better shut your mouth before the flies get in,' Hugh said.

It was a phrase commonly bandied about in their child-hood, and Rupert laughed his silly laugh. He stood and threw out his arms for a cuddle, and Hugh gathered him in. If anything Rupert was the bigger of the two, but the cuddle as always was that of a child, Rupert's arms around his brother's waist, his head tucked into Hugh's shoulder.

Hugh held him close, but Rupert sensed something a little different about this cuddle.

'What's the matter with your arm?' he said as they parted.

'I hurt it.' Hugh could lift his left arm only halfway to shoulder height. 'It doesn't work as well as it used to.'

'Oh, poor arm,' Rupert said, gently stroking the injured limb, 'poor, poor arm.' He concentrated upon the healing process for a full ten seconds or so and then he stopped. 'Hugh?'

'Yes, Rupert?'

'Can we go home now?'

'Yes, mate. We can go home now.'

Caitie and Rupert waited in reception while Hugh talked with Eunice Cartwright in her office.

'My father will be more than happy to sign all the necessary paperwork for Rupert's discharge, Sister Cartwright,' he said, 'and I can assure you that the paperwork will be posted directly back to the hospital, but I must warn you that I intend to take my brother with me right now. Is there some way you can arrange to have him signed into my care?'

Hugh didn't actually need to sound as forceful as he did. He had an ally in Eunice Cartwright.

'I shall sign him into your care myself, Mr Stanford,' she said.

Caitie insisted upon sitting in the back for the trip home so that Rupert could have the front passenger seat beside his brother. But as it turned out Rupert took little notice of his brother. He spent the entire time with his head out the open window, his hair blowing wildly, hooting a laugh at every sight that caught his fancy. It was cold with the window open, but the others didn't have the heart to make him close it.

Hugh dropped Caitie home before going on to Stanford House. At her suggestion they pulled up a good block before the cottage in Hampden Road.

"Don't drop me at the front door,' she'd said, 'not if you wish to remain incognito, anyway. My grandmother's bound to be watching. She spends most of her days at the bay window studying what's going on in the street.'

Hugh drew the car into the kerb. 'I shall be motoring down to the Huon tomorrow,' he said, 'just a quick trip there and back. I've some business to attend to.' He hauled on the hand brake, but kept the engine running as he turned around to face her. 'Would you like to come for the drive?'

'Of course I would.'

'Me too, me too.' Beside him, Rupert bounced up and down.

'Would you mind?' Hugh murmured to Caitie.

'I positively insist that Rupert come with us,' she said.

'All right, Rupert, you can come on two conditions,' he said sternly. 'You sit in the back, and we don't have the window down.'

'Yes, yes. In the back, no window. Yes, yes.'

Hugh climbed out and opened the rear door for Caitie. 'I'll pick you up at nine o'clock. Oh no, that's probably too early, isn't it?' he said realising that tomorrow was Sunday and that she probably went to church. 'Would you prefer to make it later?'

'No, no, nine o'clock is perfect.' She'd be harangued by her grandmother for skipping Sunday morning mass, but she didn't care.

'Excellent, we'll get to Franklin in time for morning tea. See you tomorrow then.'

'I'll be waiting right here on the corner,' she said.

They shook hands. There were several people in the street, and another kiss in public would be more than her reputation could stand.

Reginald had been keeping a keen eye out for the Vauxhall's return. He had decided there was only one course of action open to him. For appearances' sake he must welcome Rupert home, and although he had no intention of humbling himself he must do all in his power to placate Hugh. Nothing must endanger their relationship. He had informed Iris and Clive that he had arranged for Rupert to be discharged from hospital. Both had been overjoyed by the news. He had further instructed them to keep the staff at bay while he personally welcomed his son home.

'We must bear in mind Rupert's delicate condition,' he'd said caringly, although it was Hugh he was really worried about. Would there be a confrontation? If so, Reginald did not want the servants present.

Now, as the Vauxhall pulled up in the front drive, he stepped outside to greet it. The brothers alighted from the vehicle, Hugh with a folder of papers under his arm, and Reginald was deeply relieved to see that the girl wasn't with them. He stood on the front porch, the benign lord of the manor, watching while Hugh lifted Rupert's suitcase from the boot. Then painting a smile on his face he held his arms out in greeting.

'Welcome home, Rupert,' he said.

Rupert stopped right where he was. Father was smiling. That meant Father wasn't cross, which was good. But open arms normally meant a cuddle and cuddles made Father very, very angry. Rupert was confused. What should he do? His face started to twitch, and his hands started to flap a little.

Hugh noticed the reaction. 'Go on, Rupert,' he gently urged, 'say hello to Father.'

His brother's voice had an immediate calming effect and, instead of giving in to panic as he'd been about to, Rupert suddenly came up with the right answer. Man-to-man, that was it. Father liked to say hello man-to-man.

He walked towards the porch and then up the several steps with his arm outstretched.

'Hello, Father,' he said.

They shook, Reginald taking Rupert's hand in both of

his, an unusually effusive gesture for a man like Reginald
Stanford.

'Goodness me, Rupert, don't you look well? A great
deal better than the last time I saw you, I must say. Your
stay at the hospital has wrought wonders indeed.'

Hugh was not in the least impressed by the performance, which he knew was solely for his benefit. He could
have confronted his father. *The last time you saw him,
Father,* he could have said, *and when precisely was that?
One month after Mother's death, I believe.* He'd been
appalled when Eunice Cartwright had told him Reginald
Stanford had not once visited his son. Hugh, however,
had no desire to confront his father. He did not wish to
exchange one word upon the matter. What would be the
point? His father's actions had been unforgiveable.

He joined them on the porch.

'These are Rupert's discharge papers for your signature,'
he said handing the folder to his father. 'I have told the
hospital authorities they will be in this afternoon's mail.'

'Of course.' Reginald took the folder. 'Thank you for
bringing him home, Hugh. You were quite right to do
so. I am glad to see that he has made such a remarkable
recovery, I had not thought it possible –'

'I should like to borrow the car again tomorrow, Father,
if you don't mind.'

'Yes, yes, my boy, feel free, most certainly. Would you
care to avail yourself of Nelson's services? He's an excellent chauffeur and I'd be more than happy –'

'No, thank you. I intend to take Rupert and Caitie for a
drive in the country. I'll be leaving shortly before nine.'

'Oh. But surely you'll be attending church with me in
the morning?'

'No, I'm afraid I shall not.'

'Very well, as you wish.' Reginald was thankful there
was to be no confrontation, but he found his son's distant
manner extremely daunting.

They went inside and the moment they entered Rupert headed without a word straight for his mother's drawing room.

Hugh put down the suitcase and was about to follow, but his father stopped him.

'No, Hugh, please, give me just one moment.' Hugh dutifully waited. 'I sense you are standing in judgement upon me without knowing the true circumstances,' Reginald went on. 'Rupert was not the only one devastated by your mother's death. I was under a great deal of strain, in fact I believe I had my own form of breakdown. I simply could not handle Rupert's as well, can't you understand that?'

'No.'

'I could no longer *care* for him, Hugh. Without your mother I could no longer be responsible for Rupert's welfare. I didn't know what to do. I was too distraught ...' In the face of his son's coldness Reginald fought to justify himself, but he was making no headway at all.

'You're a wealthy man, Father, you have servants. You can employ others to take on the burden of care.'

Realising he was running out of options, Reginald decided after all to humble himself. 'I do recognise now that I was wrong, Hugh. I was so distressed at the time that I wasn't thinking like a sane person, but I acknowledge now that I made a terrible mistake.' Dear God, he thought, why is the boy looking at me in that way. Am I supposed to beg? Very well then, he would if he must. 'I am sorry, Hugh, believe me. I am deeply, deeply sorry. What can I possibly do to make amends?'

'You can't.'

Hugh walked off into the drawing room and Reginald was left in a state of emotional turmoil. He was angry. What right did the boy have to stand in judgement upon him? He was also frightened. Had he alienated his son forever?

Rupert was curled up ball-like in the armchair where Evelyn had always sat doing her petit point. Tears were running down his cheeks, but strangely enough he did not appear distressed.

Hugh knelt beside him. 'Are you all right, Rupert?'

He nodded. 'Mummy's in Heaven with the angels.'

'Yes, I know she is.'

'God's looking after her, isn't He, Hugh?'

There had been some whose faith had helped them through the horrors of war. Hugh's hadn't. Hugh's faith had died on the battlefield. He didn't have time for God any more.

'That's right, God's looking after her.' He lied for Rupert's sake.

They picked Caitie up on the dot of nine o'clock. She was waiting on the corner as she'd promised.

'My, my,' she said, looking him up and down as he opened the passenger door for her, 'very handsome.' Hugh was out of uniform and in a light sweater and blazer. She climbed into the car. 'Hello, Rupert,' she said, 'you're looking very handsome too.'

Rupert gave a happy guffaw. 'Hello, Caitie,' he said.

The day was clear and sunny and they drove with the rear window down after all; it kept Rupert happy.

'I presume this means you're not in the army any more,' she said indicating the blazer.

'That's right. I am now officially a civilian,' he announced. 'As of today the army no longer owns me.'

'I bet they wish they did.' He looked a query. 'Captain Hugh Stanford, recipient of the Victoria Cross?' Caitie smiled. 'I should imagine they were most reluctant to let you go.'

'Yes, you're right. In fact they did everything humanly possible to persuade me I was destined for a brilliant military career.'

He sounds cynical, she thought, which is unlike him. 'And I take it you weren't tempted?'

'Not for one minute. I'm not a natural soldier, Caitie.' His eyes remained fixed on the road. 'There are others far braver than I could ever be. There are those born to lead. I am not one of them.'

She could have disagreed. She could have said that the army didn't award VCs for nothing. But she didn't. She didn't say a word, because she knew that although he appeared to be speaking to her his mind was somewhere else entirely.

The road to the Huon was hilly and treacherous, winding its way along the side of Mount Wellington, but the country-side was dramatic and the native forest with its giant timber majestic. Then once in the valley and on the flat, the scenery changed radically. They were now in the lush orchard area where gentle slopes were lined with rows upon rows of trees, the majority of which were laden with fruit: apples for the most part, and pears, here and there cherries and plums.

They reached Huonville, situated on the eastern bank of the Huon River and, crossing the bridge there, they continued southwards along the main road that now ran beside the mighty Huon. Here in the heart of the valley and its townships, they were surrounded by colour. The early settlers had planted deciduous trees as reminders of home, so the landscape was a kaleidoscope of rich reds, deep purples and flashy yellows. Caitie was entranced. She'd never been to the Huon before.

'Autumn is the best time of the year to be here,' Hugh said, 'at least in my opinion.' He'd accompanied his father on a number of business trips to the Huon. 'I find it even more impressive than the spring, when the fruit trees are in blossom. That too is a sight. I must bring you back in the spring.'

They'd enjoyed the drive, all three of them, although Caitie had sensed from time to time that Hugh was pre-occupied. He seems a little worried, she thought, somehow distracted, or perhaps I'm imagining things.

It was late morning when they arrived in Franklin, and Hugh suggested they stop for tea at the Lady Franklin Hotel, a very popular and very grand two-storey hotel with balconies that looked out over the river. The licensed premises were closed, it being Sunday, but the tea rooms were open.

The streets of Franklin, like the streets of the other towns they'd passed through, were busy even though it was the sabbath. This was the fruit-picking season, and the valley was teeming with itinerant labourers.

They sat on the balcony, and Hugh ordered a pot of tea and scones with jam and cream. It was only when the morning tea had been delivered to their table that he sprang his surprise.

'Caitie, I have a favour to ask,' he said quietly, casting a glance at Rupert. His brother was paying no attention anyway, focusing instead on the scone that he was smothering with a thick layer of jam. 'Would you mind if I left you both here for a while? There's something I have to do.'

'Of course I don't mind, my darling. I shall look after Rupert.' This was why he'd been distracted during the drive. This was the mysterious duty he'd alluded to on the telephone when he'd asked her not to tell anyone of his arrival. 'Not even Oscar,' he'd said, 'not yet. There's something I must do before I catch up with the old gang.' She wondered what it could be.

'I shouldn't be too long,' he said apologetically, 'a half an hour, perhaps three quarters at the very most ...'

'We'll be perfectly happy here, Hugh.' She smiled and indicated Rupert, whose face was covered with jam. 'Take your time.'

'Thank you, my darling.' He kissed her on the cheek. Then he stood. 'I'm leaving you with Caitie for a little while, Rupert. You behave yourself, won't you?' Rupert nodded vigorously. 'And don't forget to use your napkin.'

*

Hugh's destination lay less than two miles south.

Charlotte Grove Estate was difficult to miss with its huge packing shed and outbuildings near the main road and its elegant two-storey timber house perched on the hill overlooking the orchard. Hugh turned into the driveway and drove directly up to the main house.

He knocked on the front door. There was no answer and he was about to knock again when it opened. A man whom he judged to be in his early sixties stood there, a man who looked vaguely familiar.

'Mr Powell?' he asked.

'Yes, that's right.'

'My name is Hugh Stanford, sir. I fought in France with your son.'

'Oh yes, I know who you are, Mr Stanford. I read the newspapers.'

'I wanted to tell you, sir, that I was with David at the end. I wanted to let you know that he died instantly. He would have felt no pain.'

'Thank you, my boy, thank you. It will be a great relief for the family to know –'

The man seemed about to go on, but Hugh had more to say. He'd rehearsed his speech over and over in his head. 'I also wanted to tell you that –'

Surprisingly enough, he was interrupted.

'However, I'm afraid you've come to the wrong place.'

Quincy Powell was glad that Hugh Stanford had come to the wrong place, he wouldn't have missed this moment for quids. 'It's not me you're after, it's my son Thomas,' he said and, stepping out onto the verandah, he pointed to the house that was clearly visible in the valley a mile or so away. 'That's Thomas's place,' he said, 'the road there leads around past the cherry orchard.' He offered his hand and they shook. 'I thank you for coming, Mr Stanford. Your visit will mean the world to my son.'

Quincy stood on the verandah and watched the car as it drove down the road by the cherry orchard.

This time a young girl answered the door. She was dressed in her Sunday best. The family had recently returned from church.

'Dad's around the back chopping wood,' she said when Hugh asked after Thomas Powell. 'Shall I fetch him or do you want to come through?' She opened the door wide.

'No, no, please don't bother. I'll find him myself.'

Hugh walked along the side path that led to the rear of the house. A pig was snuffling about under the nearby apple trees. He wondered at first whether it might be Delilah, but no, he thought, it's too small. Perhaps it was one of Delilah's offspring.

Beside a trellis of vines, a man was wielding an axe at a chopping block: a wiry, fit man. Hugh waited until he'd split the log before speaking.

'Mr Powell?' he said.

The man turned, the sun catching his face, and Hugh might have been looking at David twenty years down the track. Except that David would never grow to be a man in his forties.

'That's me,' Thomas said, shielding his eyes from the sun's glare. 'What can I do for you, young man?' He couldn't see the lad properly, but from the cut of his clothes and the sound of his voice he certainly wasn't a labourer. Thomas presumed he was after work nonetheless – a university student probably. All types turned up for the apple-picking season.

"My name is Hugh Stanford, sir. I fought in France with your son.' Hugh embarked upon his speech and this time he delivered it in its entirety. 'I was with David at the end, and I wanted to tell you that he died instantly. He would have felt no pain. I also wanted to tell you that he was the bravest man I ever knew, and that I owe my life to him.'

Thomas, who had remained motionless throughout, put

down the axe and stepped out of the glare into the shade of the house. He recognised the face that he'd seen in the newspapers, but Hugh Stanford's name meant far more to him than that of the war hero they'd all read about.

'David wrote of you often, Hugh. He told me you were his dearest friend. It's good to meet you at long last.' They shook hands. 'Bless you for coming. My wife and I will be able to rest easier now. We all agonise over how our boys died,' Thomas said. 'It keeps us awake at night, every single one of us. You bring the news a grieving parent longs to hear and I thank you from the bottom of my heart.'

'I'm glad to be able to offer some comfort, sir.'

'You certainly have that. Will you come inside and meet my wife? I know Olivia would wish to offer her thanks.'

'If you don't mind, Mr Powell, I'd rather leave you to relay the news.'

'Yes of course.' Thomas could see that, having fulfilled his duty, the lad felt awkward and was keen to leave. He probably had no wish to talk further about his war experiences, which was understandable. 'Thank you once again.'

But Hugh had a further task to perform.

'I have something which I believe rightfully belongs to David, sir, and I urge you please to accept it on his behalf.' He took a small container from his blazer pocket and handed it to Thomas.

Thomas opened the lid of the velvet-lined presentation case. Inside was the Victoria Cross. He looked at Hugh in dumbfounded amazement. The boy surely did not intend to give away his VC.

Hugh registered Thomas Powell's disbelief, but he continued with the speech he'd prepared in his head during the drive down to the Huon. 'David was a born leader, Mr Powell. His bravery was inspirational to all of us, particularly to me. I believe he saved the lives of many through his example, and I know for a certain fact that he saved mine. Please believe me that the medal would be going to its rightful owner.'

'I'm overwhelmed by your offer, Hugh,' Thomas said gently. He had no wish to be hurtful. 'And I thank you for your recognition of my son. But under no circumstances could I possibly accept your VC.' He closed the presentation case and handed it back, but Hugh refused to take it.

'No, no, sir, you don't understand.' Hugh had not wished to spell out the truth, but he now found himself bound to. 'In saving my life, David forfeited his own. You would not only be accepting the VC on his behalf, you would be relieving me of the burden it symbolises.'

Thomas's heart went out to young Hugh Stanford. He could see that the lad was in anguish. 'You were at war, Hugh,' he said. 'Men's lives were sacrificed every minute of every day. You cannot feel guilty because you lived and David died.'

'I know, sir, I know, I must learn to live with that and I shall. But please accept the medal. Please, I beg you.'

Thomas made a split-second decision. 'I shall be honoured to accept the medal on David's behalf,' he said, 'and I shall donate it to the Hobart Museum in both of your names. How would that suit?'

'That would suit very well, sir. Thank you.'

Soon afterwards, Hugh was back at the Lady Franklin Hotel. He'd been gone exactly thirty-five minutes.

'Let's take a little drive along the river,' he suggested as he joined Caitie and Rupert.

'Shouldn't we order some more tea and scones for you?' Caitie asked. 'You haven't eaten anything.'

'I'm not hungry. Come on.' He paid the bill and they left.

He drove only a mile or so out of town to a quiet spot by the river away from prying eyes, where he parked the car and climbed out to open the passenger door for Caitie.

'You wait here, Rupert,' he said, 'I want to talk to Caitie.'

'Can I sit in the driver's seat?'

'*May* I sit in the driver's seat.'

'May I sit in the driver's seat?'

'Yes, you may.'

They walked twenty yards or so from the car to a large golden ash tree, the brilliance of its leaves reflected in the river's gently flowing waters.

He kissed her. 'How soon can we be married?' he asked.

'As soon as you wish,' she said, 'but your father won't like it.'

'Who cares about Father?' He kissed her again.

During the drive home, Caitie sensed a difference in Hugh. He was no longer preoccupied, the worry had left him; she was glad.

Hugh sensed the difference himself. Perhaps he had put some demons to rest – who could tell? The war would never leave him: it would be there always, a part of who he was. But he was ready now to get on with the rest of his life.

Chapter twenty-four

Hugh let the boys know he was back in town and the following week they arranged a reunion in the bar of the Customs House Hotel. Harry drove down from Pontville, and Max and Gordie drove up from the Huon. Hugh and Oscar, of course, just walked down the hill to the dockside.

The boys got drunk that night. It was their intention, indeed – as Max declared – their bounden duty to do so and the Customs House Hotel was only the starting point. They went on a pub crawl after that, ending up in Salamanca Place at one of the illicit back-room bars that stayed open until all hours, singing raucous songs and, in Gordie's hungover words the next day, making one hell of a night of it.

'Mademoiselle from Armentières, parlez-vous,' they yelled at the tops of their voices. They sang the parody version of course, the bawdy one. As the night wore on the songs grew even bawdier.

We're trying to pretend we're those same boys who got drunk in Cairo, Hugh thought, looking about at the old gang. But they weren't and they all knew it: they'd never be the same. Harry in particular was damaged goods.

At the outset of the evening, when they'd raised their glasses in a toast to David and Wes and Norm, Hugh had seen the look in Harry's eyes, a look that spoke more than sorrow over the loss of his brothers. Harry was still haunted by guilt. Hugh wanted to say 'You saved my life, mate, surely that balances things out.' But he didn't, because it would make no difference. Hugh knew exactly how Harry felt. His own guilt had been greatly relieved by the absolution he'd received from Thomas Powell, but it didn't rid him of the image of David copping the bullet that was meant for him.

They were all haunted in their own way, he supposed. You could see it in them, even Oscar, who pretended to have come out of the war unscathed. Hugh looked at him now, flirting with the barmaid. Oscar carries his scars just like the rest of us, he thought, only Oscar's better at hiding them.

In that very second, as if to prove him right, Oscar turned and their eyes met. He had been watching Hugh in the mirror behind the bar and he knew exactly what Hugh was thinking. They shared a moment of recognition. Then Oscar added an impudent wink by way of sheer bravado, and Hugh laughed out loud.

One thing's certain, he thought. Scarred as they were, the bond between them was unbreakable and would remain so for the rest of their lives. They were more than mates: they were brothers. He stopped thinking at that point and threw himself into the raucousness of the evening.

Gordie, Max and Harry ended up spending the night at Stanford House. All three were far too drunk to drive. They parted company with Oscar in Salamanca Place, Oscar weaving his way up Kelly steps towards Hampden Road, the others staggering off in the direction of Davey Street.

They were noisy upon their arrival at Stanford House, and Clive Gillespie appeared in his pyjamas and dressing gown. He caught them raiding the larder.

'Shall I rouse cook, sir?' he asked. 'She'd be happy to make you a late supper, I'm sure.'

'Heavens no, Clive,' Hugh said, 'we can look after ourselves. You go back to bed.'

'Very good, sir.' Clive retired. He had been almost sure the racket was the arrival of the young master rather than a clumsy burglar, but he had nonetheless arrived on the scene with a revolver concealed beneath the folds of his dressing gown.

The boys devoured a loaf of home-baked bread, a large block of cheese and half a jar of cook's tomato and onion chutney. Then they wended their way up to the bedrooms, where they passed out.

From his own bedroom, Reginald heard them clumping up the stairs like a herd of buffalo. He was intensely annoyed. They were waking the whole household with their din.

But the following morning when they appeared in the breakfast room a little the worse for wear he didn't reprimand them. He offered a warm welcome instead.

'Hello, Harry,' he said, rising from the table to shake his nephew's hand; he hadn't seen the boy since his return from the front. He had of course conveyed his condolences to the family upon the loss of Wesley and Norman. Thank God at least one of them had survived, he thought.

'Welcome home, lad,' he said, 'indeed welcome home to you all.' He shook hands with the other two as well. He didn't know their names, but he remembered having met them when they were boys. The bigger of the two was a Powell, he recalled. 'It must be good to be back.'

'It is sir, yes,' Gordie said.

'It seems you lads had quite a night.'

'I'm sorry if we disturbed you, Father,' Hugh said apologetically. 'I gather we were rather loud – we woke poor old Clive. He caught us raiding the larder.'

'No matter, my boy, no matter.' Reginald waved a dismissive hand. 'I'm delighted to be given this opportunity to say hello to our brave lads here.' He beamed jovially from one to the other. 'Now let's get some breakfast into you, shall we?'

Reginald was leading a tightrope existence. In the short week or so since Hugh's arrival home his life had changed radically and in a way he had not for one moment envisaged. His son's triumphant homecoming was supposed to have bonded them. Together they were to have been an unconquerable team, he and his war hero son. Instead, they were distanced and he was forced to play a continuous role in a bid to forge the gap. Forever on guard, wary of any reaction on his part that might further alienate his son, he was unable to be himself and felt like a stranger in his own home. The situation was hideous.

The most irksome of the roles forced upon him was undoubtedly the charade of enjoying Rupert's company. Mealtimes had become a particular nightmare. 'Close your mouth when you chew, Rupert, there's a good lad,' he would say pleasantly, fighting back the urge to scream. Rupert would do as he was told, but a little while later something would distract him and he'd forget, and there would be the food again. The sight of Rupert eating reminded Reginald of Silas and his chicken sandwiches. Both were disgusting, his decrepit father and his cretinous firstborn, both equally repulsive. But still he played the game, determined to repair the rift that had come between him and his precious younger son. Reginald would do anything and everything to win Hugh back.

Hugh and Caitie decided to follow through with their plan to marry as soon as possible, Hugh amazing Caitie with his offer to convert to Roman Catholicism. If the church demanded it and if it was what she wished, he told her, then he would willingly oblige. Knowing Hugh to be a non-believer, Caitie found the offer extraordinary, and she told him so.

'Just because I've lost my own faith doesn't mean you should lose yours, Caitie,' he replied.

But she adamantly refused his offer. To Caitie the dilemma was not a particularly confronting one anyway. Despite her Catholic schooling, she had inherited her father's lackadaisical attitude to the Church. Her brother Oscar was the same. It appeared that over the years Col O'Callaghan had made an indelible impression upon his children, just as his own father Mick had upon him. The only member of the family who had always insisted upon following a traditional path was Eileen.

Caitie's one concern in marrying outside the faith was the hurt it might do her grandmother. But as it turned out Eileen raised no objections. In fact, Eileen was surprisingly supportive.

'God will understand, Caitie,' she said. 'You're a good girl, and you have your own relationship with Him. God does not stand in the path of true love.'

The girl will never want for money, Eileen thought, delighted that Caitie had made such a match. No matter that the boy wasn't a Catholic. No matter that the boy was a Stanford either: the sins of the father should not be visited upon the son. Hugh Stanford was a fine young man. God would not condemn such a union. As with the marriage of her daughter, Mara, Eileen's views remained flexible to the end.

Hugh bluntly informed his father of the news.

'Caitie and I have decided to get married next month, Father,' he said, and he waited for the tirade that was sure to follow. He was aware his father did not consider Caitie an appropriate choice.

'I see,' Reginald replied after a moment's pause. The boy had the audacity to announce it just like that! The boy was not seeking his approval or opening the subject for discussion as a dutiful son should: he was making a blanket statement, damn his hide. This typifies the rift between us, Reginald thought, this complete lack of respect.

'Miss O'Callaghan is of Irish background, Hugh,' he

replied carefully, aware that here was yet another occasion when he must walk the tightrope of diplomacy. 'I presume that means she follows the Roman Catholic faith?'

'Yes, Father, she does.'

'Surely that will present some problems?'

'I had thought so myself, it's true,' Hugh agreed, 'but when I offered to convert she wouldn't have a bar of it –'

'You did what?' Reginald wondered whether perhaps his ears had deceived him.

'I offered to convert to Catholicism,' Hugh said. 'I had the rather cavalier notion that as a non-believer it wouldn't matter, but Caitie was very much against the idea. She said it would be the height of hypocrisy and of course she's quite right.'

Reginald was struck speechless in his outrage. Did the boy not realise that the Stanford family had been one of the greatest stalwarts of Hobart's Anglican Church for well over seventy years? Why, Silas Stanford had devoted half his fortune to the Church and its good works. Bad enough the boy should deny his own faith, that at least could be kept quiet, but conversion to Catholicism? Unthinkable!

'We've decided to get married at the Registry Office,' Hugh said with an air of defiance. He knew his father was shocked, and that his own manner was hurtful in its curtness, but he didn't care. He wanted it made quite clear that no discussion was to be entered into. 'It'll save a lot of fuss in the long run.'

Reginald was appalled by everything he was hearing. Hugh Stanford should be marrying the daughter of one of Hobart's elite. The nuptials should be taking place at St David's Cathedral. The marriage should be the wedding of the year. Instead, he was to wed the offspring of Irish Catholic scum at the Registry Office? Reginald felt the stirring of an anger that should it escape might prove uncontrollable. He had not experienced one of his black rages for some years now. He certainly could not afford to succumb to an outburst in the presence of his son.

'The Registry Office,' he said tightly, 'is not the customary venue for a Stanford wedding. I must admit to a degree of disappointment.'

Hugh could see that his father was extremely upset, indeed that he was fighting back emotion. Having expected to be met with a litany of disapproval and endless objections he was thankful that Reginald had resigned himself to the situation. He could not help but feel guilty, however, for causing his father such distress.

'I'm sorry, Father. I don't mean to be hurtful, really I don't. Caitie and I have no wish to offend, I promise you, but we want the minimum of fuss, and this is the easiest solution.'

'Yes, I can see that.' Recognising his son's apology to be sincere and heartfelt, the black rage which had threatened now started to subside. Surely this is the breakthrough I've been waiting for, Reginald thought. 'You have my blessing, Hugh,' he said. If in order to win his son back he must accept the O'Callaghan girl then so be it. 'All I wish for, my boy, all I have *ever* wished for is your happiness.'

'Thank you, Father.'

Over the next several days, Reginald persuaded himself that things were perhaps not as bad as he'd first assumed them to be. The O'Callaghan girl was good-looking and healthy: she'd give Hugh strong, handsome children. Furthermore, she was intelligent and comported herself well enough to be socially acceptable. Society tends to forget the background of men's wives anyway, he thought, just look at Archie Dimbleby. Archie had married an O'Callaghan girl and his wife had become quite the doyenne in social circles.

Just when he'd managed to talk himself around, however, something else happened that stretched Reginald's already frayed nerves to breaking point.

'Impossible, I'm afraid, Mr Fothergill. As I've told you

before, Mr Stanford is not meeting with members of the press. I'm sorry to disappoint you, gentlemen.'

Reginald was coming down the stairs when he heard Clive Gillespie at the front door.

'Good day to you both,' Clive said to the invisible callers.

'What the devil's going on?' he demanded, fronting up just as Clive shut the door. 'What do you mean Mr Stanford's not meeting with the press?'

'Master Hugh has left strict instructions, sir,' Clive explained. 'The press has been rather hounding him since his return. Mrs Watson has fielded a number of telephone calls, and this is the third time Mr Henry Fothergill has called around to the house – he's a most persistent journalist. Today he actually arrived with a photographer –'

'Thank you, Clive,' Reginald interrupted tersely. 'Is Master Hugh about at the moment?'

'No sir, he went into town a half an hour ago. I believe he's meeting Miss O'Callaghan for lunch.'

'Very well. Would you ask him to be kind enough to come and see me in my study upon his return?'

'Yes, sir, of course.'

'And tell Nelson not to bring the car around. I've changed my mind. I'm not going out.'

'Very good, sir.'

Reginald was fuming as he walked back upstairs. How dare Hugh refuse to give interviews? What would the press make of it? Word would get around that he was arrogant. The publicity could be damagingly negative. People didn't want their war heroes locked away, damn it: they wanted to claim them as their own! They wanted to share in their fame, to bask in their glory! Hugh has a debt to his public, Reginald thought angrily. He also has a debt to Stanford Colonial Enterprises.

He arrived at the top of the stairs to find Rupert standing there. He hadn't noticed Rupert, but Rupert had noticed him. Rupert had come to a halt the moment he'd seen his father approaching. Father was angry, Rupert could tell.

'Stop that,' Reginald growled. The boy was flapping his hands. It annoyed him intensely.

Rupert clasped his hands tightly together in front of his chest in order to stop them flapping, but his distress now reflected itself in his face, which started to twitch alarmingly.

'Oh for God's sake get out of my sight,' Reginald said.

Rupert scuttled downstairs to the safety of the small front drawing room, where his jigsaw was waiting and where cook would deliver his cheese and tomato sandwich and his glass of milk.

Reginald waited impatiently for Hugh's return. He tried to work but his jangled nerves were getting the better of him and he was unable to concentrate. He poured himself a tot of brandy from the decanter that sat in the corner cabinet. He rarely drank anything stronger than the occasional glass of wine with dinner, but he kept the finest quality scotch and cognac in his study to offer business colleagues. He felt quite a deal better after the brandy, which was just as well for he could not afford to lose his temper. The situation must be handled with care.

By the time Hugh knocked on the study door an hour later, Reginald had planned his approach and was in a much calmer state.

'You wanted to see me, Father?'

'Yes, Hugh, sit down, please.' Hugh sat. 'I trust you had a pleasant luncheon with Miss O'Callaghan?'

'I did thank you, yes. A brief one of course – she had to return to work.' Hugh smiled. 'I do think that as Caitie is shortly to become your daughter-in-law, Father, you might consider using her first name.'

Oh dear, Reginald thought, must I? 'Very well,' he said, returning the smile, 'but I detest diminutives, as you know. I shall call your fiancée Caitlin if you don't mind.'

'I don't mind in the least. It's a very pretty name.'

'Right then, getting down to business.' Reginald had decided a direct common-sense approach was the wisest. 'You've been home only three weeks, and I'm sure you've not as yet considered when you might take up your position within Stanford Colonial. However, I do think –'

'Oh, I intend to assume my full responsibility, Father,' Hugh said, 'I shan't let the business down, I promise. However, I thought I would wait until after Caitie and I are married before –'

'There's no rush, my boy,' Reginald said expansively, 'no rush at all. Good heavens above, you've just come back from a war. I could hardly expect you to dive straight from the battlefield into the boardroom now, could I?'

'No, I suppose not.' Hugh smiled dutifully.

'However, I'm a little concerned by your decision to close yourself off so completely from the world as you have.'

'In what way?'

'Your refusal to meet with the members of the press.'

'Oh, that.'

'Yes, Hugh, *that,*' Reginald said firmly. 'While I do not expect you to set to work immediately, I do expect you to maintain your public profile. I understood your desire for a quiet homecoming after the hectic publicity in Sydney and Melbourne ...' No, he hadn't. '... however, to refuse the members of the press altogether is not a wise move – it could generate a very negative response. People might think you feel you're above yourself.'

'With all due respect, Father, I don't really care what people think.'

'Well, you should,' Reginald snapped: the remark irritated him. 'You have the Stanford name to consider.'

Hugh said nothing, and Reginald took a moment to compose himself. Getting snappy with the boy would serve no purpose.

'Now Hugh,' he said reasonably, 'I understand your reluctance to capitalise on your VC for business purposes …' No, he didn't. '… but you can't go to the other extreme and hide away from the fact that you're a war hero – that's foolish. You have a debt to the public, my boy, can't you see that? They want their champion, Hugh. They're proud of you, just as I am. You mustn't deprive the people of their home-grown hero.'

Hugh had had enough by now. He stood, signalling a halt to the meeting. 'I have made up my mind, Father. I will do no further interviews. I wish to put the war behind me.'

Reginald was angered that his son should behave in so peremptory a fashion and he rose to his feet. 'For God's sake, boy, what's wrong with you?' he snapped. 'You could at least offer the press one simple interview. It'd take you all of ten minutes. Is that too much to ask? A photograph of you and your VC on the front page of *The Mercury* and everyone'd be happy.'

'I couldn't do that, I'm afraid.'

'Why the devil not?!'

'I don't have the VC any more.'

'What do you mean you don't have it?'

'I gave it away.'

'You gave away your VC.' Reginald didn't believe him for a minute. 'You gave it away, just like that,' he said with a click of his fingers, 'a Victoria Cross.'

'Yes I did.'

He's serious, Reginald thought. The boy was looking him straight in the eyes and he was deadly serious.

'What's going on, Hugh? What are you talking about? You gave it to whom? The army? Why would you give your VC back? I don't understand.'

'I gave it to Thomas Powell.'

'Thomas Powell,' Reginald repeated parrot-like. He recalled Thomas Powell, the lout from Charlotte Grove Estate who'd threatened to beat him up all those years before. 'Why would you give your Victoria Cross to Thomas Powell?'

'Because it rightfully belongs to his son David.'

'What in God's name are you talking about?' Reginald was becoming flustered. It was all too ridiculous; this couldn't be happening. 'The medal belongs to you. The deeds of valour that earned the VC were yours. You performed those actions.'

'I don't remember performing them.'

'That's beside the point,' Reginald yelled in his frustration. 'Battle fatigue is common! Men have been known to lose their memory! Your acts were witnessed, for God's sake! I've read the citation! You performed those deeds!'

'I could not have performed them if I'd been dead though, could I, Father?' Hugh calmly replied. 'David Powell saved my life by forfeiting his own. The VC has gone to its rightful owner.'

It was his son's composure that pushed Reginald over the edge. How could Hugh stand there so coolly and throw this insult in his face? Suddenly, and without warning, Reginald was consumed by the blackest rage.

'You've done this to spite me, haven't you, boy? You've done this to get back at me for Rupert.'

'No Father, I have not –'

But Reginald was too far gone. His pent-up anger was unleashed, and there was no holding him back. 'It's all been to spite me! The O'Callaghan girl, the VC, everything! You dare to marry an Irish Catholic whore! You drag our family name through the mud! And now you give away the Victoria Cross! Dear God, how much more am I expected to take?!' He stormed out from behind his desk, his right hand raised, his finger pointing accusingly. 'You're my only son, damn you! I've worked my whole life on your account. I've built an empire for you to inherit, and this is the thanks I get. I give you the world and this is how I'm rewarded!'

The finger was now jabbing the air barely inches from Hugh's face, but Hugh made no move.

'Ingrate!' Reginald screamed. 'Ingrate!'

Hugh wondered whether perhaps he should fetch help. His father's eyes were the eyes of a madman – was he having some sort of fit? Then even as he watched he saw the eyes become confused and lose focus and he saw the trickle of blood coming from his father's nose.

Reginald knew something was wrong. He felt a tingling in his right hand, but when he lowered it and made to grasp it with his other hand he discovered his left arm would not respond. He opened his mouth to scream further invective at his ingrate of a son, but the words that came out were no more than a drunken slur, and for some strange reason he seemed to be losing his balance.

Hugh caught his father as he fell.

The massive stroke Reginald Stanford had suffered had not killed him. It had, however, left him totally incapacitated, with no expectation of recovery. Following his treatment at the hospital, the doctor recommended he be transferred to a hospice where he could receive the constant attention a case like his required until the event of his death, but Hugh would not have it. Hugh insisted his father be brought home to Stanford House. He would employ a full-time male carer and a live-in nurse, he told the doctor.

'Who knows, perhaps there is a vestige of consciousness remaining. Perhaps he may recognise he is in his own home, which would be of some comfort,' Hugh said, looking down at the motionless form of his father.

'I very much doubt that would be the case,' the doctor replied. 'He's showing no such signs, and the stroke was extremely severe. Indeed, it's amazing he survived at all. But he appears to have a very strong cardiovascular system. In fact I must warn you, Mr Stanford, providing your father does not suffer another stroke, he might well live on for years in this semi-vegetative state. At fifty-nine he's still a comparatively young man and, according to his medical history, longevity runs in your family.'

'Yes, indeed it does. My grandfather lived well into his nineties.'

'Well, there you are then, certainly something to bear in mind if you're contemplating home care.'

Reginald heard every single word they uttered.

Reginald Stanford's mind was intact. He knew precisely what was going on. He also knew what he looked like. He saw himself in the mirror every humiliating time they carried him into the bathroom and placed him on the toilet, and then afterwards when they lifted him off and washed his backside. He was abhorrent, his body gnarled, his arms bent, his hands claw-like. His eyes stared vacantly at nothing, his mouth hung open slackly and when they fed him food dribbled down his chin. He drooled even when he wasn't being fed. He was far more grotesque than his father had ever been.

They took him back to Stanford House several days later.

The male carer, a giant of a man called Simon, made a daily habit of carrying him downstairs and seating him by the bay windows of the larger drawing room where the sun flooded in.

It was here that Hugh, having been granted power of attorney, conducted his initial meeting with the chief executives of Stanford Colonial. Hugh considered it only right that the meeting should be conducted in the presence of his father.

Reginald listened as they talked about him, Nigel Lyttleton and his son Walter and the others, saying what a terrible thing his stroke was, glancing occasionally in his direction then quickly averting their eyes. They talked about other things too, and he learnt it was rumoured that Henry Jones was to be knighted for his services to the British war effort.

Henry Jones was to be knighted? Reginald's mind screamed at the idea. *Sir Henry Jones? That vulgar little man? What about me? I donated an aeroplane too!* And he heard them say also that Henry intended to build a fleet of ships.

'They're already referring to it as "the jam fleet",' Nigel said, and the others laughed.

Henry Jones was to have his own fleet of ships? *But that was my dream,* the voice in Reginald's brain screamed, *my dream, mine!*

As they left, they once again looked in his direction pretending sympathy. 'Poor old Reginald,' Nigel said, but it was clear they found the sight of him repulsive.

The only one who was not repelled by his appearance was Rupert. Rupert often sat beside him, wiping away the drool with the bib that the nurse had placed around his neck.

'Poor Father,' he would say, stroking Reginald's withered hand, 'poor, poor Father.'

EPILOGUE

PONTVILLE, 1926

'There you go, Evy, tiger food.' Caitie handed her daughter the parcel of meat scraps. 'There're some nice juicy bits in there – she'll like that.'

'Thank you.' Six-year-old Evelyn took the parcel from her mother then turned and raced full bore out of the kitchen, only to collide with her father, who'd just come in the back door.

'Hello, Evy.' Hugh picked his daughter up in his arms and kissed her. 'Where are you off to in such a hurry?'

'To feed my tiger,' the little girl said, waving the parcel under his nose.

'Yes, of course you are, silly me.' Hugh exchanged a smile with Caitie as he set the child down. 'Off you go then.' Evy, coppery curls bouncing, headed purposefully out the back door.

They'd been humouring her for over a month now, ever since the announcement that had followed their visit to the museum where Evie had seen a stuffed thylacine. Her mother had explained that the animal was known as a Tasmanian tiger. 'They're very, very rare,' Caitie had said. 'No-one sees tigers any more.'

The announcement had come less than one week later.

'I have made friends with a tiger,' Evy had said. It had

been a very solemn announcement, which her parents knew must be taken seriously.

'Really,' Caitie said, 'a tiger – goodness me.'

'Yes. She lives in a little cave among the rocks up on the hill, and she has babies. I talk to her and she understands me. She's my friend.'

'A tiger for a friend,' Hugh said, impressed. 'You're a very lucky girl.'

'Yes, I am.' Evy nodded. 'That's why we have to keep her a secret. You mustn't tell anyone about her, particularly Uncle Rupert, because he gets too excited. Uncle Rupert would scare her and she would run away.'

'We won't tell Uncle Rupert,' Hugh promised. 'We'll keep it our secret.'

Evy reflected for a moment. 'You can tell Uncle Harry, though.'

'Really,' Caitie asked. 'Do you think that's wise?'

'Yes, I do. Uncle Harry will protect her.' Evy trusted her Uncle Harry implicitly. 'If Uncle Harry knows my tiger is there, then he'll keep people from going near her cave. She's very frightened; she told me so. I'm her only friend. And even I don't go too close. She's warned me not to, or she'll run away.'

'Very well,' Caitie said. 'I promise we'll tell no-one except Uncle Harry about your tiger. It will be our very special secret. And we'll keep away from the rocks up on the hill.'

Evy had nodded, she'd been happy with that.

Following his Aunt Amy's death at the ripe age of eighty-six, Hugh had moved his wife and newborn daughter, together with his brother, Rupert, out of the city and into the old farmhouse at Pontville, driving into town every second week for several days of business meetings on behalf of Stanford Colonial. His cousin Harry, who worked the property and chose to live alone in the nearby foreman's cottage, had quickly become a part of the family, he and Evy developing a special relationship over the years.

Hugh and Caitie had presumed the tiger fantasy that had been born of Evy's visit to the zoo would soon fade, but it didn't. As time passed, Evy's newfound friend began to play a more and more dominant part in her life.

'I told my tiger I would bring her some food,' she said one day. 'I told her I would leave it outside her cave, and it was a promise, Mummy, so I can't let her down. She said she would like that very much and she was very grateful, but I forgot to ask her what she eats.'

'I'll get you some meat scraps, darling,' Caitie had said, and that had been the start of the tiger-feeding ritual.

Evy would visit the cave in the late afternoon. She would sit and chat for a while before leaving the meat.

'My tiger loves her dinner,' she told her parents. 'She eats it at night. I know, because it's always gone the next morning.'

'There are lots of animals who might eat the meat during the night, Evy,' Hugh said with care. He was starting to wonder whether things were perhaps getting a little out of hand.

'No, no,' Evy protested, 'my tiger eats her dinner. She tells me so, and she thanks me for bringing it. She's very polite.'

Hugh voiced his concern to Caitie. 'Do you think we're wrong to indulge her like this? It's not altogether normal, surely.'

'Of course it is, darling. Lots of children invent imaginary friends. Evy's been an only child for quite some time now; she's probably been lonely. She'll forget all about her tiger when David's bigger and they can play together.'

After five years, Hugh and Caitie's long-awaited second child had finally arrived. Baby David was just eight months old.

Hugh stopped worrying. 'Of course,' he said. 'You're right.' Caitie knew best. Caitie was a born mother.

The animal senses no threat from the child who visits her daily. But where there is a child there are men, and at dusk when she hunts she can see the house in the valley below. She is forever wary. As soon as her cubs are old enough she will leave this place.

She watches from her small rocky lair as the child places the meat on the ground and sits some distance away. The child talks and the sound of her voice signals no danger, for the animal has become accustomed to it.

The child leaves, and the animal waits, her sharp, black eyes trained on the meat. The meat will provide a tasty morsel for her cubs before she sets off on her hunt. But she will not leave her lair until dusk settles in.

AUTHOR'S NOTE

Henry Fothergill finally completed his novel *A Tiger's Tale* in 1936, closing with the death of the world's last captive thylacine at Beaumaris Zoo, Hobart, on September 7 of that year. He made the wry comment that the Tasmanian government introduced official protection of the species on 10 July, just fifty-nine days before the death of this last known specimen. His work was never published.

Since 1936, numerous sightings of thylacines have been claimed, although none irrefutably confirmed. Wealthy businessmen and magazines have offered massive rewards for proof of the animal's existence, extensive searches have been mounted, and government-funded investigation undertaken, but as yet no conclusive evidence has come to hand. The sightings, however, continue – fleeting, mysterious and elusive as they are.

There are some who believe that in the wild, untamed north-west of Tasmania the tiger exists to this day, safe from its one predator: man. We can only live in hope they may be right.

ACKNOWLEDGEMENTS

First and foremost, my thanks and love to my highly talented husband, Bruce Venables. My thanks also to the family and friends who are always on hand to lend support: brother Rob Nunn, Susan Mackie-Hookway, Michael Roberts, Colin Julin and my agent, James Laurie. Further thanks, too, to those other nearest and dearest who contributed so much by way of research and inspiration: Nathan Venables, Sue Greaves and Patricia O'Brien.

Special thanks to my publisher, Beverley Cousins; my editors, Brandon VanOver and Kate O'Donnell; and the hard-working team at Random House.

For further assistance in the research of this book, I would like to thank Dr Christopher Bradbury; Helen Edwards of the Theatre Royal, Hobart; Warren Glover, Hobart historian; and Jackie Wilson of the Huon Valley Apple and Heritage Museum. A big thanks also to the 'Hobart connection': Lloyd and Jan Clark, owners of the beautiful Lenna of Hobart, Lee Renshaw and the irrepressible Dave Johnson.

Among my research sources, I would like to recognise the following:

A Short History of Tasmania, Lloyd Robson and Michael Roe, Oxford University Press, 1997.

Thylacine, David Owen, Allen & Unwin, 2003.

Down Wapping, A. Hudspeth, M. Luck, K. Pearce, R. Radford, L. Scripps, M. Sprod, B. Stubbs, Blubber Head Press, 1988.

I Excell!, Bruce Brown, Libra Books, 1991.

A Walk in Old Hobart, Charles Wooley, Michael Tatlow, Walk Guides Australia, 2007.

The Huon Valley Yesterday and Today, David Hammond, Southern Holdings, 1995.

Full and Plenty, Catherine Watson, Twelvetrees Publishing Company, 1987.

Heroes of the Huon, Edited by David Hammond and Peter Boyer, Huon Eldercare Foundation Tasmania, 2004.

Crack Hardy, Stephen Dando-Collins, Random House Australia, Pty Ltd, 2011.

Gallipoli, Les Carlyon, Pan Macmillan Australia, 2001.

The Great War, Les Carlyon, Pan Macmillan Australia, 2006.

Other titles by Judy Nunn

Araluen

On a blistering hot day in 1850, brothers George and Richard Ross take their first steps on Australian soil after three long months at sea. All they have is each other.

A decade on, and they are the owners of a successful vineyard, Araluen, nestled in a beautiful valley near Adelaide. Now a successful businessman, George has laid down the roots of a Ross dynasty, born of the New World. But building a family empire – whatever the cost – can have a shattering effect on the generations to come . . .

Beneath the Southern Cross

In 1783, Thomas Kendall, a naïve nineteen-year-old sentenced to transportation for burglary, finds himself in Sydney Town and a new life in the wild and lawless land. *Beneath the Southern Cross* is as much a story of a city as it is a family chronicle. With her uncanny ability to bring history to life in technicolour, Judy Nunn traces the fortunes of Kendall's descendants through good times and bad to the present day . . .

Kal

Kalgoorlie. It grew out of the red dust of the desert over the world's richest vein of gold . . . From the heady early days of the gold rush, to the horrors of the First World War in Gallipoli and France, to the shame and confrontation of the post-war riots, *Kal* tells the story of Australia itself and the people who forged a nation out of a harsh and unforgiving land.

Heritage

In the 1940s refugees from more than seventy nations gathered in Australia to forge a new identity – and to help realise one man's dream: the mighty Snowy Mountains Hydro-Electric Scheme. From the ruins of Berlin to the birth of Israel, from the Italian Alps to the Australian high country, *Heritage* is a passionate tale of rebirth, struggle, sacrifice and redemption.

Other titles by Judy Nunn

Territory

Territory is the story of the Top End and the people who dare to dwell there. Of Spitfire pilot Terence Galloway and his English bride, Henrietta, home from the war, only to be faced with the desperate defence of Darwin against the Imperial Japanese Air Force. From the blazing inferno that was Darwin on 19 February 1942 to the devastation of Cyclone Tracy, from the red desert to the tropical shore, *Territory* is a mile-a-minute read.

Pacific

Australian actress Samantha Lindsay is thrilled when she scores her first Hollywood movie role, playing a character loosely based on World War II heroine Mamma Tack. But on location in Vanuatu, uncanny parallels between history and fiction emerge and Sam begins a quest for the truth. Just who was the real Mamma Tack?

Maralinga

Maralinga, 1956. A British airbase in the middle of nowhere, a top-secret atomic testing ground . . . *Maralinga* is the story of Lieutenant Daniel Gardiner, who accepts a posting to the wilds of South Australia on a promise of rapid promotion, and of adventurous young English journalist Elizabeth Hoffmann, who travels halfway around the world in search of the truth.

Floodtide

Floodtide traces the fortunes of four men and four families over four memorable decades in the mighty 'Iron Ore State' of Western Australia. The prosperous 1950s when childhood is idyllic in the small city of Perth . . . The turbulent 60s when youth is caught up in the Vietnam War . . . The avaricious 70s when WA's mineral boom sees a new breed of entrepreneurs . . . The corrupt 80s, when greedy politicians and powerful businessmen bring the state to its knees . . .